BARBARA CARTLAND

*Five Complete Novels of
Dukes and Their Ladies*

BARBARA CARTLAND

Five Complete Novels of Dukes and Their Ladies

A FUGITIVE FROM LOVE

LUCIFER AND THE ANGEL

THE WINGS OF ECSTASY

THE RIVER OF LOVE

A SHAFT OF SUNLIGHT

WINGS BOOKS

New York • Avenel, New Jersey

This 1995 edition is published by Wings Books,
distributed by Random House Value Publishing, Inc.,
40 Engelhard Avenue, Avenel, New Jersey 07001,
by arrangement with the author.

Random House
New York • Toronto • London • Sydney • Auckland

Printed and bound in the United States of America

Library of Congress Cataloging-in-Publication Data

Cartland, Barbara, 1902–
    Five complete novels of dukes and their ladies / Barbara Cartland.
        p.   cm.
    Contents: A fugitive from love—Lucifer and the angel—The
wings of ecstasy—The river of love—A shaft of sunlight.
    ISBN 0-517-14679-7 (hardcover)
    1 Man-woman relationships—Great Britain—Fiction.   2. Nobility—
Great Britain—Fiction.   3. Love stories, English.   I. Title.
PR6005.A765A6   1995
823'.912—dc20   95-12609
                                                                          CIP

8   7   6   5   4   3   2   1

Contents

The History of
Barbara Cartland
and
"How I Want to be Remembered"

My father, Captain Bertram Cartland of the Worcestershire Yeomanry Militia, married my mother, Mary Hamilton Scobell, in 1900.

The Cartlands are reported in ancient Chronicles as being in Lanarkshire, Scotland before 1200 A.D. There was a village called after them and there are the *Cartland Crags,* which are still a beauty spot.

The name could possibly be of Norman origin and belongs to the 11th Century or even earlier.

One of the first references to it in literature occurs in the Minstrel poem of "Blind Harry" who lived between 1470 and 1495. His poems cover eleven books and contain some eleven thousand lines. In Book VI, Harry writes of how Wallace—one of Scotland's heroes—fought against the English.

Harry recounts that as a young man, after an affray with the English Garrison in Lanark, Wallace fled to the *Cartland Crags.*

His wife delayed the English pursuers by a trick, and when they discovered that Wallace had escaped, they killed her. Later, in the 19th Century, there was a town called Cartland in Lanarkshire.

Some of the Cartlands moved South from Scotland and my Great Grandfather had an Estate in Worcestershire.

When the Industrial Revolution began in about 1840, he moved into Warwickshire. He built a large house in the open countryside which later was to be Kings Norton.

He started a Brass factory in Birmingham which made him very rich. He had a big family and his second son, James Cartland, my Grandfather, became a great Financiér. He helped build up the City of

Birmingham, and was twice offered a Baronetcy and Knighthood, all of which he refused. He fell in love with a Scottish girl who was on the verge of marrying a Peer.

Flora Falkner was beautiful and a direct descendant of Robert The Bruce, the first King of Scotland to be acknowledged by the English. She was swept off her feet by James Cartland.

Their only son, James Bertram Falkner Cartland—my father—was handsome, tall and intelligent. He fell in love when he was twenty-three with Mary Hamilton Scobell—my mother—when he walked into a Ball-Room and saw her dancing.

"That is the woman I am going to marry!" he said.

He had some difficulty as Mary, who was always called Polly, was pursued by a large number of young men.

I had always been told that my Mother's family was an old Saxon family from Devonshire starting with the name Scoberhull which eventually changed to Scobell.

However, there seemed to be little written about them until my Great-Uncle Captain Treweeke Scobell proposed the idea of the Victoria Cross for Valour, to be made from the guns which had been used in the Battle of the Crimea.

This was received with great enthusiasm.

So much so that Captain Scobell was asked to withdraw his motion so that it might be put forward by Queen Victoria herself. My Great-Uncle agreed to this and stepped aside.

My Grandfather Colonel George Treweeke Scobell was a very unusual character. He was one of the first men to climb Mont Blanc, for which he received a Diploma. He was at the opening of the Suez Canal.

He went round the world in a sailing ship three times and boasted of having made love to a woman of every Nationality and thought the Japanese were best.

He and my Grandmother were among the first passengers on the Trans-Siberian Railway.

My grandparents had five children, three girls besides my Mother. The eldest, my Aunt Emily, married Richard Palairet. He and his brother Lionel, at the beginning of the Century, were acknowledged the best cricketers in England.

Another daughter, my Aunt Edith, married The Honourable Alfred Maitland, son of The Earl of Lauderdale. His son, my uncle Sir John

Scobell, was G.O.C. Bombay, commended for his defense of Malta. He later became Governor of the Tower of London.

When my Grandfather married he settled down in a large attractive Victorian house in Redmarley in Gloucestershire.

I remember as a child being impressed by the butler and three footmen who looked after us at meal-times. Also the large number of servants who came in for the Morning Prayers which took place before breakfast every day.

I was the daughter of my Grandfather's third daughter who was christened Mary but called Polly because she talked so much. She was very small, very attractive with deep brown eyes to match her hair.

After my Father and Mother were married, they moved into a large, attractive house in Worcestershire where they hunted. My mother was exceptionally good on a horse—and my father was a first-class game-shot.

Just after I was born in 1901 my Grandfather financed the Fishguard Railway which later was a huge success.

But in 1902 there was a recession and the banks called in their loans, as there was no limited liability in those days. The banks told my Grandfather he would have to live on his Dividends of £6,000 a year, with Income Tax at eleven pence in the pound. But because he was not well at the time, he felt he could not be poor, and therefore shot himself.

Everything he possessed was sold, including a fine collection of Sporting pictures, and my Father was left with only the furniture, which had been a Wedding present.

My Father and Mother had to give up their large and very comfortable house in Worcestershire and move to a smaller house called Amerie Court, at Pershore. It was offered to them by my Father's great friend, the Earl of Coventry, for £40 a year. It was actually quite large with eight bedrooms, a large flower garden, and acres of Pershore Plums. It also had a very large stable.

Although my Father had to give up his horses, he kept one called "Sir Galahad." My Mother, who was an outstanding rider, was always provided with a mount by the Master of Foxhounds Lord Charles Cavendish Bentinck, brother of the Duke of Portland.

He had two little daughters who were the same age as I, and I did lessons with them and their Governess as they lived only two miles away.

ix

I was born in 1901 and christened Mary Barbara Hamilton after Mary Ann Hamilton, my Mother's Grandmother and my Great Grandmother, who came from Philadelphia and was an heiress.

The Hamiltons go back to the first Earl in 1358, and the 6th Earl married the Princess Margaret of England and Queen Dowager of H.M. King James IV of Scotland. His descendant, H.M. King James VI, became King James I of England. The Dukedom of Hamilton was created in 1648 and the present Duke is the 15th.

My Mother's Great Great Grandfather, Andrew Hamilton—a close relative of the 4th Duke of Hamilton—left Scotland under a cloud after he had killed someone of importance in a duel.

He was an exceedingly clever and astute Lawyer. He became Governor of the Jerseys and Defender of Peter Zenger in Pennsylvania. He showed the State of Pennsylvania how to secede from the Crown of England.

He had two sons, one who became Governor General of Pennsylvania in 1783, the other who was the Great Great Grandfather of Mary Ann Hamilton.

She came to England after her father's death and married Captain Septimus Palairet, member of an ancient and distinguished Huguenot family who had settled in England after the troubles in France. Mary Ann was tiny, with feet smaller than Queen Victoria and she had six children—the sixth being my Grandmother Edith. Mary Ann died giving birth to her seventh child when she was twenty-seven.

In 1910, there was a General Election and my Father, as a Knight of the Primrose League for five Counties, organized the Parliamentary Seat of South Worcestershire for Mr. Eyres Monsell—later Viscount Monsell, First Lord of the Admiralty.

They became great friends and my Father worked with him politically. He himself intended to stand later on as a Member of Parliament.

I remember the first motor-car I ever sat in came to the house with Lord Mount Temple, when he married for the second time—the bride was Mrs. Mary Forbes-Sempill—and they came to see us on their Honeymoon.

My Father and Mother became great friends with Lord Mount Temple who gave them his house, Broadlands, for my Father's last leave.

They slept in what was later to be called "The Queen's Room" because Queen Elizabeth II had slept in it on her Honeymoon, and later Prince Charles and Princess Diana did on their Honeymoon.

In 1914, Civil War was expected in Ireland and, at the request of the Duchess of Abercorn, my father was organizing the evacuation of all the women and children from Ulster.

On August 14, War was declared and my father was "called up," having been in the Militia. He joined his Regiment, the Worcestershire Yeomanry, and very shortly he left for France. After four terrible years in the trenches, he was killed in action in the Germans' last push toward Paris before they were defeated.

My Mother was heartbroken. She was left with me, aged seventeen, and my two younger brothers, Ronald and Anthony, who were at school at Charterhouse where my Father had also been educated.

As we had very little money, my Mother asked me where I would like to live. I said, "London," and we moved there. I found it a thrilling and exciting experience, as I wrote in my book *We Danced All Night*.

I published my first novel in 1923. It was a huge success, going into six editions and later published in five languages. After that, I began to write seriously to make money.

I was presented to King George and Queen Mary by my mother in 1925 at a Drawing Room at Buckingham Palace.

I had forty-nine proposals of marriage before, in 1927, I accepted Alexander McCorquodale, a former Officer of the Argyll and Sutherland Highlanders. He had served in the First Army in France, which was commanded by his uncle, Lord Horne of Stirkoke. His Father owned a large Estate and an historically beautiful Queen Anne house in Shropshire.

We had a large wedding at St. Margaret's, Westminster, with Pipers escorting us from the Church.

I was presented again to the King and Queen on my marriage by my Husband's Aunt, Lady Horne of Stirkoke.

In August 1927, we went to Scotland to stay at Saluscraggie in the Strath of Kildonan, with my husband's Uncle and Aunt, Mr. and Mrs. Harold McCorquodale.

I had been to Scotland several times before, but it was the first time I had been so far North. I was entranced by the Beauty of the

Strath and, when I was taken out fishing the first day after I had arrived, I caught my first Salmon in the Surfaceman's Pool. That Salmon weighed fourteen pounds, and I also caught three other fish the same day. Naturally, as I had never fished before, I lost quite a number.

The total bag was twenty-three Salmon and I thought at the time that Salmon Fishing was very easy. I did not know then how many hours I would spend fishing myself, or watching others fish—and catching nothing.

The McCorquodales were a Fief to the Campbells whose Chieftain is the Duke of Argyll. One of their Ancestors, Duncan McCorquodale, recorded Ensigns Armorial in the Public Register of Arms on or about the year 1672. The Chief of the Clan was known as Baron of the Phantilands but the Clan diminished somewhat following an invasion near Loch Awe by the McClouds during which a great many were killed.

For some reason, they did not wear their own Tartan and after I had been married for some years, with the help of the Lord Lyon, I took it out of "retirement." It was a very attractive tartan that had not been woven for over a hundred years.

Alexander and I had one daughter, Raine. She was a debutante in 1946 and was presented to The King and Queen at a Royal Garden Party at Buckingham Palace by The Hon. Mrs. Michael Bowes-Lyon—sister-in-law of The Duchess of York, now H. M. Queen Elizabeth, The Queen Mother.

Raine was acknowledged as the most beautiful debutante of the year. She had three Balls given for her.

1. By me and her Step-Father at our house in Mayfair.
2. By her Godfather The Duke of Sutherland at Sutton Place.
3. By our Member of Parliament for Bedfordshire, Alan Lennox Boyd, M.P.—later Viscount Boyd—at his home near Belgrave Square.

Raine was married in 1947 to Gerald Legge. He became Viscount Lewisham and later the 9th Earl of Dartmouth. They had four children: William Viscount Lewisham, The Hon. Rupert Legge, The Hon. Henry Legge, and Lady Charlotte Legge, now the Ducasa di Carcaci.

In 1976, Raine's marriage broke up, and she married the 8th Earl Spencer whose daughter Diana later became the Princess of Wales.

Earl Spencer died on the 29th of March 1992. Raine married The Comte Jean Francois de Chambrun on the 10th of July 1993.

~

In 1935, my brother, Ronald, who was working at the Conservative Central Office, learned that an Election was to be held in the Labour-held Kings Norton Division of Birmingham.

He was very anxious to be a candidate but he was earning only £4 a week in the Conservative Office.

In those days, a Member of Parliament had to pay his Election expenses, which were about £1,000.

My marriage had come to an end two years earlier and I had divorced my husband. After the divorce case, he went into a Nursing Home for two years because of heart trouble.

I was the innocent party, but Alexander's parents confiscated his money while he was unconscious and refused to give me any. I was, therefore, left with Raine who was four years old and only the Marriage Settlement of £500 a year. I was writing for a weekly magazine and several newspapers, but always under an assumed name so that no one knew who the author was.

When Ronald told me about Kings Norton, I was determined he should stand, and wrote 10,000 words a day to pay his Election Expenses. When the Election came, the Labour Party put forward a well-known and distinguished politician.

Kings Norton had altered very considerably since my Great Grandfather had built his house, which was still there. Now there were the big factories of Austens, Triplex, Cadburys, and the first New Town ever built in Great Britain, filled with the people from one of the "slums."

As the Election day approached, my Mother and I spoke and canvassed to help my Brother. He won with a majority of nearly 6,000 because of his brilliant organization and speeches, and also his high principles and belief in God.

Ronald made his mark as soon as he entered The House of Commons and was befriended by Winston Churchill whom I had met first in 1923.

In the next five years, Ronald made some outstanding speeches in The House. When War came in 1939, he joined the Worcestershire Yeomanry and went to France.

Sir Winston Churchill, then the Prime Minister, said that if Ronald returned from Dunkirk he intended, although Ronald was only 33, to make him a Minister.

He did not return, and after Ronald's death I wrote his biography. This had a Preface by the Prime Minister, Sir Winston Churchill, and the Rt. Hon. L. S. Amery, Secretary of State for India, read and corrected it factually.

Churchill also wrote, "The House of Commons and the Country have also lost in Ronald Cartland a spirit of high endeavour, generous outlook and rare courage."

My biography about Ronald still helps and inspires people even after all these years. I compiled his best speeches into a Compendium with the help of The Rt. Hon. Earl of Selbourne, P.C. It was called *The Common Problem* and was sold for Mrs. Churchill's "Fund for Russia."

The Rt. Hon. Anthony Eden, M.P. Secretary of State for Foreign Affairs wrote, "We were all so sure that he had a great part to play in the world after the War, for he had the true qualities of leadership, vision, courage and faith."

Ronald's Coat of Arms is on the window in The Great Hall of The Palace of Westminster.

At the entrance to Tewkesbury Abbey in Gloucestershire, there is a Calvary erected to the memory of my Father, my Mother and my two Brothers. With Major Ronald Cartland's name is "Killed in Action, 30th May 1940," and beneath it, "I will not cease from mental fight."

My brother Anthony was left to hold back the German advance while the rest of his Regiment escaped to Dunkirk. The German Commander asked him three times to surrender, but he replied, "I will surrender only unto God." These words are written under his name on the Calvary.

When I die, that will be the end of my Great Uncle's branch of the Family. Our motto on our crest is "Loyal Devoir"—Loyal to Duty—and I think that is what we have been.

There are Cartlands in other parts of the world. Sir George Cartland in Tasmania has produced a very large and complete history of the Family.

There are Cartlands in Ireland and America but, as far as I know, there are no more left in Britain, only the Cartland Crags and Cartland Road in Kings Norton.

However there are four Barbara Cartland Rooms:

1. At the Heritage in Helmsdale, Sutherland, Scotland, where there is a model of me, pictures of my Grandparents, my first fish, and a large number of my books. They also play my Cassette, which features me singing with the Royal Philharmonic Orchestra.

2. At Welle Manor Hall, Upwell, Norfolk. It is a very large pink room, and is situated in the home of "Ye Olde Norfolk Punch."

3. The Barbara Cartland Rest Room at Brooklands Race Track, Weybridge, Surrey.

4. A whole Estate and garden, which are entirely pink, called Camfield Estate, Bedforddale, Perth, Australia, is dedicated to me.

~

In 1936, I married Hugh McCorquodale who had been in the Queen's Own Cameron Highlanders and who was very badly wounded at the Battle of Passchendaele for which he received the Military Cross for Gallantry.

My Mother-in-Law had been a Granville, one of the oldest, most romantic and famous families in the country. It started with Rollo, the first Duke of Normandy, who died in 932 and who was a Norseman and a pagan. He invaded Normandy where he became a Christian. He had a large family and his grandsons and their sons were three of the English Kings—Ethelred the Unready, King Canute and Edward the Confessor.

His great-great-grandson was William the Conqueror, who defeated the English at Hastings in 1066. Rollo's granddaughter, Geraldine, married the 3rd Earl of Corbeil and their son became the 4th Earl of Corbeil and also Earl Granville. He was the founder of the Granville family who, over the years, became related to many of the most famous families in England, including the Earls of Devon, Bath, Edgemont and Rochester, the Marquess of Worcester, and The Dukes of Rutland and Sutherland.

Lady Georgiana Caroline Granville married the Honourable John Spencer in 1734 and their son became the 1st Earl of Spencer. This means that my sons, Ian and Glen, are connected to the daughter of the 8th Earl of Spencer, Lady Diana Spencer, now The Princess of Wales.

Late in World War II, we made the somewhat arduous journey to Scotland on holiday. It was safe for my two small sons as there were no bombs on Helmsdale.

My sons, Ian and Glen, adored Scotland and became as attached to it as their father had always been. When my Father-in-Law died, he left the Estate divided among his four sons. Now they are dead and their sons have inherited it so that Ian and Glen have a third part divided between them.

It is a great joy for them to come to Scotland and I never miss my yearly visit. Inevitably, I write a novel with a Scottish background after I have left.

I knew George Granville, the 5th Duke of Sutherland, in the 1920s, and he was Godfather to Raine and a close friend of mine for the rest of his life.

One of the best-looking men I have ever seen, he becomes the hero in many of my Scottish novels. Just as Dunrobin Castle, Dunbeth, Stirkoke or the Castle of May creep into the story, so does the Loch at the top of the river and the people of Helmsdale.

I travel all over the world. I am thrilled by the exotic beauty of the East and the vital virility of the West. But as I turn for home, "My Heart's in the Highlands."

I love my home, Camfield Place, Hatfield, Hertfordshire. A Knight settled on the estate in 1275, and later there was a beautiful Tudor Manor House built there.

This, unfortunately, was pulled down by Beatrix Potter's Grandfather, and the house was rebuilt in 1867. Beatrix Potter wrote that Camfield was the place she loved best and wrote "The Tale of Peter Rabbit" there. I have Mr. McGregor's Garden, but it is surrounded by high Tudor brick walls.

I also have the Oak Tree planted by H. M. Queen Elizabeth in 1550 when she was in prison in Hatfield House. It is believed that the acorns and the leaves bring "Good Luck" to everyone who wears them.

"How I Want to be Remembered"

I was asked recently by the Americans to write how, when I die, I want to be remembered.

After ninety-three years of life, this was quite an undertaking because so many things have happened during those years.

I have been ecstatically happy, very miserable and deeply saddened, especially when I lost first my Father in the 1914-18 War, then both my Brothers at Dunkirk.

Ronald had been a great influence on my life. When War was declared he insisted on joining the Worcestershire Yeomanry but, if he had been examined medically, the Army would not have taken him. As a boy, he had been shot in the leg, and it still gave him trouble.

Since then, I have lost my wonderful Mother, and my Husband with whom I had 28 blissful years, and who died of the wounds he received when he was 18 at Passchaendale. Many of my closest friends who have meant a great deal to me, like The Earl Mountbatten of Burma, whom I knew for sixty years, have also died.

I have been shown great kindness, and I have endured a certain amount of teasing, and sometimes ridicule, by the Press. At the same time, they have helped and supported wholeheartedly my often very controversial "crusades."

For example, at the moment I am fighting so that Mothers who stay at home to look after their small children should receive a National wage. M. Jacques Chirac, the French Prime Minister, brought this up in March 1988. He gave me the Gold Medal of Paris for selling over 25 million books in France and giving a great deal of employment.

~

Before going to Camfield Place, in 1930, I designed and produced the first Pageant seen since the War, in aid of the British Legion.

H.R.H. The Prince of Wales was present and, when I danced with him, he congratulated me warmly on my achievement.

Most of the great Industries were represented by Society Beauties wearing the dresses I had designed.

The Marchioness of Kedlestone was in a huge crinoline of wool. Lady Ashley represented Coal. The Countess of Bective was Machinery. Paper looked lovely on Viscountess Castlerosse and the Baroness Furnival.

I and two of my friends wore an enormous steamship of *The White Star Line*. The famous Lily Elsie, still exquisitely beautiful, was Britannia.

Some of us were also later in the finale of the first Midnight Revue at the London Pavilion arranged by Lady Louis Mountbatten for C.B. Cochran. The sum of £12,000 was collected there for charity.

~

In 1931, I and two young Air Force Officers thought of the idea of an Aeroplane-towed Glider.

It was then a commercial action owing to the Financial Recession, and we thought that an aeroplane could set off with a number of gliders towed behind it, using only one tankful of petrol.

Gliders were, at the time, very cheap, so to prove our point, I started to build my own Glider. Before it was finished, *The Daily Mail* heard that something was afoot and said it would give £1,000 to the first person who could "Glider" the Channel.

They had no idea how it was to be done, but the man who was making my Glider wanted to enter the Competition and we had only one tow-rope.

He, therefore, set off first and when he had gone to the starting-point, I said to the Air Force men, "It is no use our trying to win the contest. We will take the first Aeroplane-towed Air Mail Glider to Reading."

This we did and were met by the Mayor.

Everybody was very impressed by what had been achieved, but a German had crossed the Channel before dawn. Soon afterwards, the Air Ministry banned Aeroplane-towed Gliders because they said they were too dangerous.

The Germans, however, went on with the experiment and used them in large quantities for their invasion of Crete.

We, as a country, did not use Aeroplane-towed Gliders again until D-Day.

No one recognized our idea until in 1984 the Americans realized what had been achieved and I went to Kennedy Airport to receive the Bishop Wright Air Industry Award for my "Contribution to Aviation."

This is a very important Award in America because Bishop Wright was the father of the Wright Brothers who made the first chronicled powered flight in 1903.

~

In 1932, I was asked by the Hon. Wilfred Edgerton to do something extraordinary. That was to reinstate and make a success of the famous Embassy Club.

This was the best-known Dance Club in the whole of London. On Thursday nights, everyone of any Social importance went to the Embassy. It was extremely difficult to become a member. Yet it had suddenly lost its important patrons.

It was a challenge which I could not resist and I had the whole place, which had just been decorated in a modern fashion, altered to the pink and blue which are my own special colors.

I employed Ambrose's Band which was the favorite Band of the period and I had Anna May Wong singing as a Cabaret turn. She was a screen actress who had never sung in a Dance Club before.

I arranged that all the people I personally invited to dine, who were well-known socially, should pay for their drinks, but not the food.

In a few months, it was a huge success with people being turned away at the door and, after that, it ran for several years as the most important and the most glamorous Dance Club in London.

~

In 1939 the War started. We had moved to Bedfordshire with the children to a 400 year old house, which my husband and I used instead of going to his relations.

I started by being with the W.V.S. (Women's Voluntary Service) in Bedfordshire, then I became the only Lady Welfare Officer in Bedfordshire.

I was gazetted an Honorary (unpaid) Captain (Junior Commander) in the A.T.S. (Auxiliary Territory Service), and looked after 20,000 troops, a great many in secret Air Force Stations.

The women in the Services in Bedfordshire were often depressed and miserable because they were allowed only twelve coupons a year for ordinary clothing, which was taken up mainly in stockings and handkerchiefs.

Then I discovered a loophole in the rules regarding Handicrafts and that I could buy any amount of pretty materials for about two shillings a yard from the store called Peter Jones without coupons.

The girls measured it up on the floor of the Welfare Office and made themselves underwear. Every Senior Officer agreed that I had raised morale.

Next, the women came to me in tears saying that they could not be married in their uniforms.

I, therefore, went to the War Office to ask if they could be allowed some extra coupons for their Bridal gowns.

The answer was, "Don't you know there's a war on?"

However, I said to the rather fierce-looking women Generals:

"I think perhaps I could get the gowns without coupons."

"You must have," one remarked sarcastically, "a touching faith in human nature."

To prove my point, I advertized in *The Lady* and was delighted when I was able to buy two beautiful wedding-gowns complete with veils and wreaths, one costing seven pounds, the other eight.

I sent them to the War Office with my compliments.

They replied that they would create a pool of Wedding-Gowns for Service brides—if I would provide them.

By the end of the war, I had bought over a thousand white wedding-gowns which could be borrowed for a pound for the day, not only for the ATS but also for the WAAFS (Women's Auxiliary Air Force Service) and the WRENS (Women's Royal Naval Service).

I can still remember the delight on the women's faces when they knew they could be married in white and feel they were "real brides."

When, in 1989, I was the first person ever to be twice the subject of the TV show, "This Is Your Life," a bride appeared who had been married in one of my Bridal Gowns. She has been very happy with her husband for 40 years.

~

1955. After Ronald's death I was offered three safe Conservative seats but I had a husband and young children so I refused them. Instead, when we had moved to Hertfordshire, I won for the Conservatives the Socialist-held seat of Hatfield for the County Council.

I felt in a small way I could carry on Ronald's fight for the future, the greatness of Britain and for his belief that anything which concerned the people must be just and to their advantage.

I became a County Councillor for nine years.

The first thing I discovered as Councillor was that the Homes for the old people were mostly in a very bad state and very little money was spent on them.

In fact, in some places, a great many repairs to the kitchens, apart from anything else, needed doing.

I was very shocked at what I found and visited every Home in the County. My daughter, then Viscountess Lewisham, visited two hundred and fifty Homes over the whole of England.

When we sent our reports to the Home Secretary, then Mr. Duncan Sandys, he ordered a Government Enquiry into the "Housing and Conditions of Old People," with the result that a great deal more money was spent, visitors were encouraged, and the picture changed over the whole of England.

~

I am delighted that I managed to change the Law of England in 1964, so that Gypsy children could go to School.

I discovered in 1961 that, since the time of Henry VIII when the Gypsies first came to England, nothing had been done for them legally. There was, however, a Police Rule that they should be forced to move on every twenty-four hours.

For me, it was unjust and horrifying that every child in a Democracy could be educated with the exception of the Gypsies!

I found a Gypsy Romany Family who had been born in Hertfordshire, lived in Hertfordshire, and wanted to stay in the County, but they had been told they had to move off the Common where they had always been.

I rang the Chief Constable to ask him where they could go.

"Nowhere!" he said.

"But that is ridiculous!" I replied. "They are human beings. How can they go nowhere?"

"That is the Law," he said.

"In that case," I retorted, "I will get it changed."

It was the most unpopular cause I have ever attempted but after three years of bitter battle because nobody wanted the Gypsies near them, I managed to get the Home Secretary, Sir Keith Joseph, to rule that Local Authorities must provide camps for their own Gypsies.

As an example, I had my own Camp and I put into it the family of Romany Gypsies who had approached me in the first place. They christened it "BARBARAVILLE" after me.

We now have fourteen County Council Camps in Hertfordshire and all the other Counties are following suit so that thousands upon thousands of Gypsy children can go to school.

I checked after a year with a number of Schoolmasters and they all said that the children came to school looking "tidy, clean and looked upon education as a *privilege.*"

In 1964, I thought of and founded the National Association for Health.

My brother Ronald had been the first M.P. to visit the distressed areas in 1935. I helped Lady Rhys William to give vitamins to women suffering from malnutrition and habitual abortion.

I was so impressed that I took a course on Herbal Medicine at Culpepper with the famous Mrs. Leyel.

I was also in consultation with several doctors who were becoming interested in Alternative Medicine.

Dr. Dengler of Baden-Baden allowed me to study some of his cases. He was the first Doctor ever to give unsaturated fat in the form of Olive Oil for cirrhosis and afflictions of the intestines.

In 1955, I wrote my first Health Book, *Vitamins for Vitality*. The same year non-synthetic vitamins first came to England from America.

In 1978, before his assassination in 1979, Earl Mountbatten of Burma opened our Health Conference. He became a very enthusiastic advocate of vitamins after those I had given him helped him so much. Now, we in the Association for Health, are very grateful to H.R.H. The Prince of Wales for his encouragement and championship of Alternative Medicine.

We try to make the public realize that while £2,000 million a year is spent by the National Health Service on drugs, which are often dangerous, *our* products have no side effects.

I answer 40,000 letters a year—30,000 are questions on health. I try everything new which comes onto the Health Market on myself, my family and my household, and I write about them (unpaid) in three Health publications and in any other magazine or newspaper that asks me to do so.

Today, the health movement has a £650 million turnover, a third of which goes in Export. At the Health Trade Exhibition in Birmingham, in March 1988, thirty-eight countries were represented.

If we have good health, we have happiness for ourselves and our children.

∼

In 1974, I was made a Dame of Grace of The Order of St. John of Jerusalem.

I was very proud when I was one of the first ten women for a thousand years to become a member of the St. John Chapter General.

I joined the St. John Ambulance Brigade as Chief Lady Welfare Officer for Bedfordshire in 1943. I had invited Lady Louis Mountbatten, who was one of my oldest friends, to stay with me and talk to the ATS girls at Cardington who were making barrage balloons and were bored because they were seeing very little of the War.

Before she left, I found myself with a St. John Uniform as County Cadet Officer for Bedfordshire, as well as my ATS uniform.

I was asked to raise the social standing of the Brigade in the County.

First, I recruited 2,500 cadets. Then, I produced a St. John Exhibition which was opened by The Queen at St. James's Palace and then toured the country making £35,000 for local funds.

I tried to do the same when I came to Hertfordshire in 1950 and I became Deputy President of the County and Chairman of the St. John Council.

Over the years I have become more and more impressed that the St. John Ambulance Brigade is the only large organization in the world whose members give their services free.

Few people realize that you cannot hold a Football Match, a Racehorse Meeting, a Gymkhana, or in fact anything where there is a large number of people, without the St. John Ambulance Brigade being represented.

They work at their normal jobs all day, then give their services free, and in many cases they themselves raise money in their own Divisions to pay for bandages and other requirements.

It is an amazing organization with 350,000 members, many of them in India, Sri Lanka, Hong Kong and dozens of other countries all over the world.

In 1978, the Royal Philharmonic Orchestra approached me because they said it was the beginning of the Romantic era and asked me to choose Romantic Songs of my period for the orchestra to play.

I was so interested in doing it that I decided that I would sing twelve of the songs myself and EMI made a record with me singing with the Royal Philharmonic Orchestra, which sold both in England and America. I was then seventy-seven and the oldest woman ever to make her first Album of Love Songs.

~

In 1981, I was chosen "Achiever of the Year" by the National Home Furnishing Association of Colorado Springs, Colorado.

I was honored in this way because I designed wallpapers and fabrics with the largest Company of Designers in America—Kirk-Brummel. I opened a display of my designs at Macy's in New York and then my son Ian and I went to Colorado Springs, Colorado, to receive the Award. All the women present wore pink.

~

In 1983, in the U.S.A., Bill Blass voted me the Best-Dressed Woman in the world because he said I wear what suits and becomes me.

In 1927, I visited Egypt and found Howard Carter sitting on Tutankhamen's Tomb which he had recently discovered with the Earl of Carnarvon.

I was so thrilled with the wonderful colors of the Temples and Tombs in the Valley of the Kings that I decided that their vivid pink and scarab blue inspired me more than any other colors and I have used them ever since in my house and for my clothes.

I have taken a great deal of ribbing one way or another because I wear so much pink, but it has only just been realized in America that pink affects the character and personality of a person.

I have heard there is, in Colorado now, a whole prison being painted pink because it has such a good effect on the inmates.

~

In January 1988, I went to the Mairie de Paris to receive "Lá Medaille de la Ville de Paris" (the Gold Medal of the City of Paris).

I would like to be remembered for the honor bestowed on me by the City of Paris. This Award, presented by M. Jacques Chirac, Prime Minister as well as Mayor of Paris at that time, was for Achievement.

Twenty-five million copies of my books, translated into French, had been sold in France, creating a great deal of employment. It is something I will always cherish, and what touched me so deeply was that, when I went to France to receive my medal, my Publishers bought an hour of Television time at a cost of a million francs. I had a charming interviewer and Charles Aznavour sang his romantic songs. The Studio was a mass of pink roses, and rose-petals floated down on me from the ceiling.

After the interview, I was taken outside and sat in an open Rolls-Royce in the Park where, by permission of the Prime Minister, pink fireworks were exploded above my head. The initials *BC* were entwined with a heart and there were great bursts of pink roses!

I believe it was the first time such a tribute had been paid to an Author. I have now sold over 60 million books in France.

My French Publishers also gave me the Duke and Duchess of Windsor Suite at the Hotel Ritz, which is £1,000 a night.

~

In March 1988, I was invited by Prime Minister Rajiv Gandhi and the Government of India to open their Health Resort, one of the largest in the world, outside Delhi.

Because I have always loved India so much, it was not only a great honor, but also a delight, to be able to accept the invitation to open "Body and Soul," which is what this Resort is called.

This, I believe, is the real secret of the great success of Alternative Medicine.

The Resort contains all the latest equipment for Health and Beauty, but there is also a section for Meditation and Yoga. We in the Health Movement believe that this is another secret for health, because you must not only work at it with your body, but also with your mind and soul.

I am delighted to say that I was received with enormous enthusiasm by my Indian "Fans" who feted me with a Reception in the City.

I also received a most attractive embossed plate from the Prime Minister and his Government.

~

The third occasion on which I had the Law of England changed was when I succeeded in 1988 in bringing back prayers to the State Schools.

It is horrifying that the Nation was divided in that for eight years. Only children who went to Private Schools were allowed to learn of God, and the necessity and wonder of prayer.

I was supported in this only by the newspaper, *The Daily Star.* No Bishop or Clergyman had anything to say on the subject. Finally, after I had written to every Member of the House of Commons, both Houses of Parliament brought back Prayers and Religious education.

~

In 1990, the Government of Poland sent their Ambassador to ask me if they could publish my books, because of the morality expressed in my writings. I have since then signed a Contract with the Polish Government.

During the Gulf War, the Arabs printed ten of my novels because they want morality for their women. At the moment, Hungary, Rumania, Czechoslovakia and Russia are negotiating with my son, who is my Manager as well as Chairman of *Debrett's Peerage*. My books are already a great success in Japan and China.

~

Paris has always meant something special to me. When I married my second husband on 23rd April 1936, we went to Paris for our Honeymoon, and it was the most exciting and wonderful time of my life.

We stayed at The Ritz which is undoubtedly the most romantic Hotel in the world and we got to know each other so that our love increased more and more, all of the twenty-eight years that we were together.

My husband, as I have said, had been very badly wounded at Passchendaele in the First World War and I was told that I would be lucky if we had five years together.

Our marriage lasted twenty-eight perfect years due to, I believe, my special Vitamins and Honey.

What I have always advocated to every young couple is that they do what I did. Every year we were married we went back to Paris to have a Honeymoon, where we had our first. It does not matter if they have no money, whether they stay in a tent or go to a Hotel. The great thing is for them to be ALONE together and to make love.

During the years I was with my husband, he did not agree with my belief that there is no death, and that we come back on the Wheel of Rebirth with our talents and our debts.

"I have been nearer death," he said, "than most people and I believe that when you die, you die, and there is no after-life."

I did not argue with him, as that was his point of view, but I am sure he was wrong.

In 1963, when the scar-tissue of his wound touched his heart, he just fell dead. It was a ghastly shock, yet it is the way I would like to die myself without lingering on.

After my husband had been dead for a few days, my Maid said to me, "Did you smell that delicious scent of carnations outside your bedroom?"

By this time it was the beginning of January, and I was surprised as there were few flowers in the house. None of the wreaths had been brought in at the time of the Funeral.

The next morning I got up at eight o'clock to give my son, who had come to stay with me after his Father's death, his breakfast before leaving for London.

For the first time, I noticed in the "entresalle" outside my bedroom, an extraordinary fragrance which was the almost overpowering scent of carnations.

It was not like any carnations I had ever smelled in England. It was, in fact, the exotic fragrance of Malmaisons. I was astonished. Sometimes it was strong and sometimes fainter. I knew exactly what it was.

When we went to Paris, we always went to the Madeleine to say a Prayer for our marriage. Although we were not Catholics, it is the only Church I know which has a Chapel to St. Joseph, who is the Patron Saint of Marriage.

When we came out, sitting on the steps outside the Madeleine, were always a number of women with huge baskets of carnations for sale.

My husband always bought a bunch for me. We took it back, put it on the mantelpiece in our bedroom, and he used to put one in his buttonhole every night when we went out for dinner.

I knew why the smell of carnations was now outside the door. My husband was telling me he was wrong. There was a life after death, and he had come back to tell me so.

The carnations remained there with us for three months and since then I have had many other proofs if I needed them, that there is no such thing as death.

~

*In the 1991 New Year's Honours List, I received from Her Majesty
The Queen, the Award of Dame of the Order of the British Empire,
for my contribution to Literature and for my work for Humanitarian
and charitable causes.*

~

*At the Parliamentary Election in April 1992, I decidedly increased
the Conservative vote.*

According to the polls the Conservatives were likely to lose or, at the
very best, to have a "Hung Parliament" so I sent a letter to 962 newspapers and magazines.

I pointed out that the Church should have made some reference to
the fact that the Labour Party leader, Mr. Kinnock, was an Atheist and
his wife had said publicly, "I do not believe in God, and when I get to
No. 10 I am going to go on teaching children!"

I received an enormous number of letters from people, particularly
men, saying, "I have always voted Labour in the past, but I shall never
do so again!"

~

*I would like to be remembered for my books, especially for my novels,
through which I have tried to give Morality, Beauty and Love to the
world.*

I have written at the moment, 620 books all together and have sold
approximately 650 million. The Guinness Book of Records says that I
am the "Best Selling Author in the World," and it delights me to think
that I am now published in every country.

I have now written the greatest number of books by a British Author,
passing 564 written by John Creasey.

I am in several countries which do not pay, simply because they like
my books, so they have committed piracy and translated them into
their own language.

When I was in Indonesia some years ago to see the Buddhist Temples, I found that every Publisher was bringing out my latest books without paying a penny, using my covers, but with the text going sideways, as it does in Japan.

What really matters, however, is that I do bring happiness to people, for the simple reason that my heroines are the sweet, loving, genuine women who were first portrayed by Shakespeare in *Romeo and Juliet* and whose example has been copied by all Classical Authors. In my opinion, it is they who evoke in a man the real love that is both spiritual and physical, and it is the woman in a marriage who stands for Morality, Compassion, Sympathy and Love.

This is the message I have tried to impart to the world, and when people tell me or write to say that I have made them happy, that is the greatest compliment I can have.

I would add that I have written every other sort of book besides three Autobiographies of myself, the Biographies of my Mother and my Brother, and sixteen Historical works.

I have had books published on Health, Sociology, Cookery, Philosophy, Cartoons, Poems and a Children's Pop-Up Book, as well as a book of Prayers.

I have had two stage plays performed and one on the radio. In 1987, my book, *A Hazard of Hearts*, was made into a film and shown on Television in the U.S.A. receiving a "No. 1 Rating." It has been followed by three more, and they are:

"The Lady and the Highwayman"
"A Ghost in Monte Carlo"
"A Duel of Hearts."

The TV films have been sold to a number of other countries including Britain, Australia, New Zealand, Germany, etc.

I am very thrilled by what I have achieved in my life and if nothing else, I would like to say a prayer of gratitude because I have helped a great number of people, both physically and spiritually, to find love.

To sum up my own philosophy I wrote this poem.

A Prayer

One thing I know, life can never die,
    Translucent, splendid flaming like the sun.
Only our bodies wither and deny
    The Life Force when our strength is done.

We all transmit this wonderful fire,
    Its force and power from God above
And know eternally it is His
    In every act of love.

We each give to the world as much of the Life Force as can flow uninhibited through our confining bodies. This is our task, the reason we exist, to transmit the Godhead through us. How poorly we succeed, and how much more successful we could be!

Awards

1945.   Received Certificate of Merit, Eastern Command, for being Welfare Officer to 5,000 troops in Bedfordshire.

1953.   Made a Commander of the Order of St. John of Jerusalem. Invested by H.R.H. The Duke of Gloucester at Buckingham Palace.

1972.   Invested as Dame of Grace of the Order of St. John in London by The Lord Prior, Lord Cacia.

1981.   Received "Achiever of the Year" from the National Home Furnishing Association in Colorado Springs, U.S.A. for her designs for wallpaper and fabrics.

1984.   Received Bishop Wright Air Industry Award at Kennedy Airport, for inventing the aeroplane-towed Glider.

1988.   Received from M. Chirac, The Prime Minister, The Gold Medal of the City of Paris, at the Hotel de la Ville, Paris, for selling 25 million books and giving a lot of employment.

1991.   Invested as Dame of the Order of The British Empire, by H.M. The Queen at Buckingham Palace for her contribution to Literature.

A Fugitive from Love

AUTHOR'S NOTE

Tangier at the beginning of the century was very different from the attractive place it is now—the streets were filthy, noisy and crowded with camels, donkeys, beggars and lepers.

The prison, which was usually filled with criminals, brigands and murderers, provided no food and the prisoners had to rely on the charity of their friends. This resulted in most inmates being in a state of semi-starvation.

Moslem girls were married at the age of ten or twelve years old. The policy of the Government was oppression, bribery, injustice and plunder.

Nevertheless due to the marvellous, healthy climate more and more English people as well as some Americans built villas in the vicinity of Tangier.

CHAPTER ONE

1903

*T*HE TRAIN DREW INTO MONTE CARLO station and Salena stepping onto the platform looked around her wide-eyed.

It appeared quite ordinary and was neither exotic nor as menacing as she had been led to expect.

When the Mother Superior had learnt that she was to join her father at Monte Carlo she had been undisguisedly shocked.

She had in fact been so disapproving that Salena had been rather surprised, knowing that as a rule the Mother Superior was both tolerant and broad-minded.

The School, which was incorporated in a Convent, to which she had been sent two years ago was not exclusively Catholic.

They admitted girls of all religions, but Salena was well aware that it was due to her Step-grandmother's influence that she had been able to obtain a place.

"The Convent of St. Marie is extremely exclusive and will only take a limited number of pupils," the Dowager Lady Cardenham had told Salena, "but I believe the education is of a very high standard and what is more important is that you should speak foreign languages."

She paused to say positively:

"If there is one thing that is essential for any girl to-day in the Social

3

World, it is that she should be fluent in French and if possible also in Italian and German.''

Salena had the idea that her Step-grandmother had also chosen a Convent for her because she disapproved of the way her father was behaving after her mother's death.

It was no secret that the Dowager Lady Cardenham did not get on with her stepson and that it was only a sense of duty rather than affection which made her assume the responsibility of Salena's education.

"It is the only thing she does pay for,'' her father had said bitterly, "so do not pull your punches when it comes to having expensive books and extra classes—if there are such things.''

There had been quite a number of the latter and Salena had felt embarrassed in knowing that at the end of the term her Step-grandmother would receive a very large bill.

The Dowager Lady Cardenham could well afford it because she was a very rich woman which made it all the more unfortunate that she should have died six months ago, before Salena was to make her début.

The other girls at the School talked incessantly about what they would do once they were grown up, the Balls that would be given for them, the social gaieties in which they would be included.

In consequence Salena had looked forward to the day when she would make her curtsey at Buckingham Palace and become one of the débutantes in what was always described as "a brilliant London scene.''

She was fortunate in that the Dowager Lady Cardenham had paid her school fees a year ahead, but she had wondered apprehensively what she would do when the term came to an end and there was no provision made for her in the holidays.

She had never gone home to England from France after her mother's death.

Instead the Mother Superior had arranged that with several other pupils whose parents were overseas she should go with two of the nuns to a farm in the country and spend a few weeks in quiet, if somewhat primitive surroundings.

Salena had loved every moment of it, but this last year she had found it sometimes frustrating to have so little to relate to her friends when she returned to school.

Nevertheless she had been happy and it had come like a bomb-shell when she first learnt of her Step-grandmother's death and then received a letter from her father telling her she was not to join him in London as she had expected but in Monte Carlo.

Monte Carlo!

The very name was synonymous with all that was raffish and wicked, despite the fact that the newspapers reported that all the Crowned Heads of Europe were gathered there at some time or another, including King Edward and his beautiful Danish-born wife, Queen Alexandra!

But the nuns regarded it as the nearest thing to hell on earth, and Salena half-expected to find the porters looking like devils and the engine of the train itself changed into a fire-breathing dragon.

Instead of which, as she stood looking round her, a smart footman came hurrying towards her to raise his tall, cockaded hat politely.

"*M'mselle* Cardenham?"

"*Oui, je suis Mademoiselle Cardenham,*" Salena replied.

"*Monsieur* M'Lord is waiting for you in the carriage, *M'mselle.*"

Salena turned eagerly to hurry from the station while the footman waited to collect her trunks.

Outside in an open Victoria, leaning back and smoking a cigar, was her father.

"Papa!"

She gave a cry of delight and ran towards him, climbing into the carriage to sit beside him and lift her face to his.

She thought he looked at her scrutinisingly before he kissed her. Then he said in his usual jovial, good-humored fashion:

"How are you, my poppet? I expected to say you have grown, but you are still the little midget you used to be."

"Actually, I am four inches taller than when you saw me last," Salena answered.

Lord Cardenham threw his cigar out of the side of the carriage and putting both his hands on Salena's shoulders held her away from him.

"Let me look at you," he said. "Yes—I was right!"

"Right about what, Papa?"

"I had a bet with myself that you would grow into a beauty."

Salena blushed.

"I was hoping, Papa . . . that you would think I was . . . pretty."

"You are more than pretty," Lord Cardenham replied. "In fact you

5

are beautiful, as beautiful as your mother was, but in a different way.''

"I would love to look like Mama.''

"I like to think you have a bit of me in you," Lord Cardenham said heartily. "Is the luggage coming?"

His last remark was made to the footman who had met Salena on the platform and was now standing beside the carriage.

"A porter is just bringing it, *Monsieur*."

"Is there much of it?"

"No, *Monsieur*."

"Then we will take it with us," Lord Cardenham said.

"Yes, *Monsieur*."

The porter appeared carrying Salena's trunk without any difficulty and a small valise which contained little except books.

"Is that all you possess?" Lord Cardenham enquired.

"I am afraid I have very few clothes, Papa. I have grown out of the gowns I wore before I went into mourning for Step-grandmama, and there seemed no point in buying new ones, when I felt they would be no use once I had left School."

"No, of course not," Lord Cardenham replied.

He pulled an expensive gold-cornered leather cigar-case from his pocket and opened it slowly in a manner which made Salena think that he was considering what he would say rather than concentrating on choosing a fresh cigar.

The luggage was by this time stowed away at the back of the Victoria and the footman climbed up on the box of the carriage as it moved off.

"I think you have something to say to me, Papa," Salena remarked quietly.

"I have a great deal to say to you, my dear," her father replied, "but first let me explain where we are staying."

"Are we staying with friends," Salena asked, a note of disappointment in her voice. "I do so hope to be alone with you, Papa,"

"That is what I would like myself," her father answered, "but quite frankly I have to rely on the generosity of my friends."

"Does that mean you are hard-up, Papa?"

"Not hard-up, Salena. Broke! I have not a penny to my name!"

"Oh, no!"

It was a cry of distress, for Salena knew of old how hopeless her father always was about money, and how ever since she could remember she and her mother had had to skimp and save to make ends meets.

"I suppose," she said tentatively, "Step-grandmama did not leave you anything in her will?"

"Leave me anything?" Lord Cardenham ejaculated. "She would rather leave it to the Devil himself! But what did surprise me was that she excluded you from her list of beneficiaries."

Salena did not speak and he went on:

"I know the reason. She loathed me and she thought that if you had any money I would spend it. It was in just the same way, blast him, that your mother's father behaved."

He paused, then he said puffing angrily at his cigar:

"That means, my poppet, that you and I are down on our uppers. We have to think about what we shall do about it and think fast."

Salena made a little helpless gesture with her hand.

"What can we do, Papa?"

"I have been turning several things over in my mind," Lord Cardenham said evasively, "but I will talk to you about that later. In the meantime make yourself pleasant to our host."

"You have not yet told me who he is, Papa."

"His name is Prince Serge Petrovsky," her father replied.

"A Russian!" Salena exclaimed.

"Yes, a Russian and a damned wealthy one at that! Monte Carlo is full of them, all as rich as Croesus, and, I am glad to say, generous with their money."

"But the Prince is your friend," Salena said. "I hope he does not mind including me as a guest."

"I explained to him frankly that I had nowhere to take you," Lord Cardenham answered, "and immediately he said you must come to the Villa. That was what I expected, but you and I need a great deal more from him than that."

Salena turned her face to look at her father in astonishment.

"More . . . Papa?"

"Even the most beautiful woman needs a frame."

"Papa, you are not suggesting . . . ?"

"I am not suggesting, I am telling you," her father said positively, "that unless the Prince is prepared to provide you with some new gowns you will wear what you have with you or go naked!"

"B—but . . . Papa . . . !"

It was a cry of dismay and as if he felt embarrassed by it Lord Cardenham said almost roughly:

"Now listen to me, Salena, and listen carefully. When I say I am broke, I mean it. I am also in debt. So, to put it bluntly, you and I have to live on our wits."

"You are so clever and amusing, Papa, I am sure people are only too willing to offer you their hospitality, but it is a very different thing where I am concerned! To expect the Prince to pay for my clothes as well seems to me horrifying!"

"There is no alternative," Lord Cardenham said heavily.

"Are you . . . sure, Papa?"

"Do not suppose I have not thought of everything! But even living with other people is expensive one way or another: recently I had bad luck with the cards and have even had to borrow money with which to tip the servants."

There was a note in her father's voice which told Salena exactly how much he was upset by this state of affairs, and although she thought that in the circumstances it was very risky to gamble she was too wise to say so.

Instead for the first time since they had left the station she took her eyes from her father's face and looked to where they were going.

They had moved out of the town and were now on a road with the sea on one side and high cliffs soaring above them on the other.

There was purple bougainvillaea climbing over bare rocks, a profusion of pink geraniums and trees of golden mimosa which seemed to Salena to hold the sunshine.

"It is lovely! Oh, Papa, it is lovely!"

She looked out to sea and exclaimed:

"What a wonderful yacht! Do look at it, Papa."

A white steam yacht with the masts silhouetted against the sky was moving over the azure-blue water leaving a silver wake.

With the white ensign flying from the stern it had such a fairy-like quality it was hard to guess why Lord Cardenham frowned as he remarked:

"That is the *Aphrodite*. It belongs to the Duke of Templecombe, curse him!"

"Why do you curse him, Papa?"

"Pure jealousy, my poppet—Templecombe is, next to Royalty, one of the most important men in England. He has houses, horses, and the best shoots! All things I want and cannot have!"

"Poor Papa!"

"Not exactly," Lord Cardenham said. "I have one thing he doesn't possess."

"What is that?" Salena asked.

"A very lovely and sweet daughter!"

Salena gave a little laugh of happiness and laid her cheek against her father's shoulder.

"I am so very, very happy to be with you," she said softly.

"You will like the Prince's Villa," her father said. "It is very magnificent, although he did not build it himself. He bought it from some poor devil who lost everything at the tables and shot himself rather than face penury."

Salena gave a little shiver.

It was the sort of story she had heard about Monte Carlo.

It flashed through her mind that she would hate to live in a house whose previous owner had deliberately taken his own life.

"It is a way out which I have even considered myself," her father said heavily.

"Oh, no, Papa. You must not say such . . . things! It is . . . wrong. It is . . . wicked!" Salena cried. "Life is very . . . precious and a gift from . . . God."

"It is a pity that God is not more generous in other ways," Lord Cardenham retorted.

Then he looked at Salena and said slowly:

"Yet I think perhaps He has been. He has certainly given me a very beautiful daughter."

Salena moved a little nearer to him and slipped her hand into his.

"It is so wonderful for me to hear you say that, Papa. The other girls at school used to laugh at me and say I looked such a baby that no-one would ever believe I was grown up."

"You certainly look very young," Lord Cardenham said.

Once again he inspected his daughter and with a surprisingly poetical fancy thought she looked like a flower.

Her small face with its pointed chin was dominated completely by her huge eyes. They should have been blue to complement the fairness of her hair, but instead they were grey with faint touches of green in some lights.

Set far apart they had the trusting innocence of a child who has seen nothing of the world.

For the first time since he had thought of his daughter joining him, Lord Cardenham wondered if he was committing a sin against nature in bringing someone so transparently inexperienced to Monte Carlo.

Then he told himself there was no alternative, and perhaps the fact that she was so innocent would prevent her from understanding much that was said or happened.

Aloud he remarked:

"You will find a mixed collection of people staying with us at the Villa, but they all have one thing in common, they live to gamble."

"It is so beautiful," Salena said looking out to sea, "there must be other things to do."

"You will learn that they are not of importance," her father replied dryly.

"They will be important to me," Salena said, "because one thing is very obvious, Papa, I cannot afford to risk even one *centime* in case I lose it!"

"That is an indisputable fact," Lord Cardenham smiled.

The horses were turning off the road.

"Here we are," he said, "and let me tell you I think this is one of the most attractive Villas in the whole of the Côte d'Azur."

They descended slowly down a twisting drive of pine-trees and walls covered with climbing geraniums.

Many feet below the road on which they had travelled a Villa had been built on a small promontory jutting out into the sea.

Gleaming white in the sunshine it was very impressive and as they walked into the cool hall Salena felt she was stepping into fairy-land.

It was certainly very different from the high narrow house off Eaton Square where she had lived when her mother was alive and which had always seemed to be too small for them.

Here was space, luxury, while the mirrors on the walls reflected the sunshine outside the windows so that everything seemed dazzling.

Her father walked ahead of her through a long exquisitely decorated Salon and out onto a terrace where there were blue awnings to protect the occupants from the sun.

There were only two people sitting in low comfortable chairs. One of them was a lady who struck Salena as being outstandingly beautiful, the other a man who rose to his feet to walk towards them.

"Well, here you are, Bertie," he said to Lord Cardenham. "I thought the train must be late."

"It was, but it arrived," Lord Cardenham replied. "Your Highness, may I present my daughter, Salena?"

Salena curtsied and looked at the Prince with interest.

He was a man of about forty who might, she thought, when he was young, have been good-looking. Now he was heavy, both in his features and in his body.

He had dark, rather protruding eyes which inspected her in a manner which made her feel embarrassed.

His hair streaked with grey at the temples was brushed back from a square forehead and he had the look of a man who had lived too well for too long.

"I welcome you, Salena," he said in English, with a distinct accent. "As I expect your father has told you I am delighted that you should be my guest."

"It is very kind of Your Highness," Salena murmured.

Her father was kissing the hand of the lady lounging back in the chair under the blue awning.

"*Madame* Versonne, I want you to meet my little Salena," Lord Cardenham said.

"But of course—I am delighted!" the Frenchwoman answered.

She did not however seem very delighted and Salena felt that she looked her up and down disparagingly.

Salena curtsied and waited to be told what she should do next.

Madame Versonne rose from her chair.

"Now that you have arrived," she said to Lord Cardenham, "I am going to rest. It is too hot for me here, but I was keeping Serge amused, at least I hope so."

She looked at the Prince provocatively and he responded with the compliment she obviously expected.

Then with her silken skirts moving sensuously and leaving behind an exotic fragrance on the air *Madame* Versonne walked along the terrace to enter the Salon through the open window.

"Please sit down," the Prince said. "I am sure, Bertie, you need a

11

drink after having to wait for your daughter's train in this unprecedented heat. I have never known it to be so hot in April."

Salena wanted to say that she thought it was delightful, but she was
occupied in looking around her without appearing to be too inquisitive.

There was a long flight of white marble steps leading down from the
terrace to the garden below and she realised the Villa was on three
different levels.

The garden which had been built on the promontory of rock which
stuck out into the sea was only a little above sea-level.

There was a stone fountain playing in the centre of it, there were
large shady trees around a green lawn and flowerbeds filled with exotic
flowers of which she could only recognise a few.

Beyond the garden, through the trees she could see the sweep of the
coast towards Monte Carlo and on the other side towards, she thought,
if she remembered rightly, the cliffs of Eze.

"How wonderful to be here," she told herself, "and it is even more
beautiful than I expected."

The sea was vividly blue except for where towards the horizon it
merged into an emerald green.

She had often heard the girls talk about the Côte d'Azur, but they
had always stayed with their friends at Nice or Cannes.

Although they had talked with bated breath of Monte Carlo none of
them had ever visited the Principality.

"But I am here," Salena said to herself.

She wished for a moment she could go back to school next term so
that she would have more adventures to relate than any of the others.

"What are you thinking?" a deep voice asked and she turned to the
Prince with her eyes alight.

"It is so lovely!" she said. "I have read about the South of France
and even studied some of its history, but I did not know it would be so
enchanting."

The Prince smiled.

"It is what I felt myself when I first came here," he said. "But my
country also is very beautiful."

"So I have always heard," Salena said.

She had also heard of the cruelties perpetrated in Russia and the
suffering of the great majority of the population, but she did not think
that was the sort of remark she should make.

She thought instead she should ask the Prince about the Russian Court and the magnificence of the Palaces in St. Petersburg.

But before she could formulate her question her father, who was sitting on the other side of the Prince, said surprisingly:

"Take off that unattractive hat, Salena. I want His Highness to see your hair."

Salena looked at him in surprise, but because she was used to obeying orders she immediately took off her hat, feeling a little anxious that her hair might be untidy.

She had arranged it very simply in a knot at the back of her head, but released from the confines of the hat it rose above her oval forehead in a natural wave which held the sunshine.

"There is no-one more experienced than you, Serge," her father said, "when it comes to the female sex. So tell me, how should Salena dress and in what colours?"

"There is only one person in Monte Carlo who could do her justice," the Prince replied, "and that is Yvette. She is an artist in her own way and never makes the mistake of ruining a woman's personality by over-ostentatiousness as so many other dressmakers do."

"Go on, Serge, I am listening," Lord Cardenham said. "I suspect that you too are an artist in your own way, or else it has something to do with the Russian temperament."

"The clothes of a beautiful woman must always be part of herself and her character," the Prince said, "and never, remember this, Bertie, never must she become a 'clothes-horse'."

"I will remember it," Lord Cardenham said, "but as far as I am concerned I can no more pay Yvette's prices than walk on the sea!"

He spoke without any trace of self-consciousness but Salena felt the colour rising in her cheeks.

She was well aware why her father was drawing attention to her and she wished that she could run away and hide rather than hear him leading the conversation in a quite obvious manner round to what he required.

She was aware that the Prince too understood what her father intended, and with only a faint note of cynicism in his voice he replied:

"In my opinion, for anyone as lovely as your daughter, Bertie, only the best is good enough!"

"You mean that?" Lord Cardenham asked without any prevarication.

"Of course," the Prince answered. "Send a groom into Monte Carlo and tell Yvette to call as soon as possible. I imagine she knows her way here blind-fold."

"I am very grateful," Lord Cardenham said, "and I know Salena is grateful too. You must thank the Prince, my dear, for such a generous gift."

"Thank you . . . thank you very . . . much," Salena said obediently.

At the same time she felt so embarrassed that she could not meet the Prince's eyes and a blush still burned in her cheeks.

It was degrading, she thought, that her father should have to ask openly for someone to pay for her clothes.

The Prince of course could well afford it, but she knew it would have shocked her mother and certainly horrified the Mother Superior.

There was a diversion when the servants arrived with a silver ice-bucket in which reposed a bottle of champagne.

Three glasses were laid on the table, but when they would have filled Salena's glass she put out her hand.

"No, thank you."

"You do not like champagne?" the Prince asked.

"I have not drunk it often," Salena answered, "only at Christmas and on Papa's birthday."

"You would prefer some lemonade?"

"Yes, please."

The Prince gave the order to the servants, then he said reflectively:

"You are to be envied, Salena, in that you are starting out in life and everything is new and interesting. I wonder how we would feel, Bertie, if we went back to when we were eighteen?"

"It is a long time ago," Lord Cardenham said. "But I remember being wildly excited when I won a point-to-point."

"I recall most vividly a love-affair at that age," the Prince said reflectively, "by no means my first, but I was infatuated to the point of madness. I saw the same ballet night after night and still found it entertaining."

Both men laughed and Salena thought that in the years to come when she looked back she would always remember her first glimpse of the South of France, the white yacht riding the blue of the Mediterranean.

When she had drunk her lemonade the Prince suggested she might like to see her bed-room.

"Yvette will be here soon," he said, "then we must choose the gown that you will need to-night and others that you can wear until she has time to provide you with everything that is necessary."

"I am sure I shall not . . . need too . . . much," Salena said quickly because she felt shy.

As she spoke she saw her father frown and knew he intended to take everything he could from the Prince.

Again she felt ashamed and when she went up to her bed-room to find her clothes had been unpacked she looked at the picture of her mother which now stood on a dressing-table and wondered what she would have thought.

It was only a sketch done by an amateur artist because Lady Cardenham had never had the chance of being professionally painted, but the artist had caught the likeness and now Salena felt that her mother looked at her reproachfully.

"How can I help it?" she asked. "It is wrong of Papa, but I can hardly stay here with him in this grand Villa unless I have something respectable to wear."

Respectable was certainly not the right word to describe the gowns that Yvette brought with her from Monte Carlo.

She had not arrived as quickly as the Prince had anticipated and because Salena had the idea that her father expected her to wait upstairs she had lain on her bed to look through the window at the view outside.

It aroused her imagination and she had been so deep in her thoughts that she had not realised the passing of time and felt when there was a knock on the door as if it brought her back to earth with a jerk.

The dressmaker was there with a vast number of cases and an assistant to unpack them.

Madame Yvette was a dark, vivacious Frenchwoman, ugly but extremely *chic*.

"I have seen *Monsieur* your father," she informed Salena, "and His Highness, and they have told me that I am to dress you, *Mademoiselle*, in my special creations, then send you down to the Salon where they are waiting to inspect them."

"That will . . . make me feel . . . very shy," Salena replied.

"You will not need to be shy when I have finished dressing you, *Mademoiselle*," *Madame* Yvette said. "But, oh la! la! how any lady can bear to be garbed as you are now is beyond my comprehension!"

Salena explained that she had just come from School and *Madame* accepted the explanation, but threw the plain, badly cut dress in which she had travelled to the floor in disgust.

When finally Salena was dressed in an evening-gown she looked at herself in the long mirror and thought she saw a stranger.

Madame Yvette had in fact started from the very beginning by producing a close-fitting corset, laced so as to reveal the tininess of Salena's waist.

"It is too tight, *Madame!*" Salena exclaimed, but the Frenchwoman paid no heed.

"Your figure is exquisite, *Mademoiselle!* It would be a sin to hide it!"

"But I find it hard to breathe."

"That is because you have allowed your body to become slack. That is wrong, very wrong. The body should always be contained and controlled."

A gown of white tulle, which revealed not only Salena's tiny waist but also the curves of her breast and the whiteness of her skin, seemed very daring.

Yet at the same time there was an ethereal look about it which accentuated Salena's youth and flower-like face.

Madame Yvette surveyed her critically.

"*C'est bien,*" she said. "It needs a little jewellery perhaps, but . . ."

"No, no! Please do not . . . mention such a thing," Salena interrupted.

She had an idea that her father would not hesitate to demand that from the Prince as well as everything else if he thought it necessary.

"Go to the Salon and show yourself," *Madame* Yvette said, "and afterwards I will find you a gown to wear to-morrow."

Salena did as she was told, at the same time when she entered the Salon she felt very shy.

Her father and the Prince were sitting smoking and drinking on a sofa.

The sun-blinds made the room cool and took away the brilliance of the light outside.

But Salena felt it was very revealing as she stood just inside the door, her eyes very wide in her small face, her fair hair seeming still to hold the sunlight.

"Let me look at you," the Prince said insistently.

"You are right, Serge," Lord Cardenham exclaimed, "that woman is a genius! I could not imagine a more appropriate gown to suit a young girl."

Salena moved slowly towards them.

She knew it was stupid but she wished that the gown was not so tight or so revealing.

She felt almost as if the Prince's dark eyes were staring at her naked, and she longed to be wearing the shapeless, rather ugly gown in which she had arrived.

"You look very beautiful!" the Prince remarked, "and doubtless a great number of other men will tell you so before the evening is over."

"I . . . hope not," Salena said quickly.

The Prince raised his eye-brows and she explained hesitatingly:

"I feel . . . shy if people . . . notice me . . . but perhaps you are . . . just being . . . kind."

"Of course I am being kind," the Prince answered, "and I am ready to be very much kinder."

"Y—yes . . . I know . . . and I am very . . . grateful," Salena said stumbling over her words, feeling as if she was not expressing herself at all coherently.

She had a longing to be back at School where she did not say the wrong thing and where no-one looked at her in a manner which made her feel uncomfortable.

When she felt she could bear it no longer she turned towards the door.

"*Madame* has another gown for me to show you," she said and ran from the Salon.

～

Some hours later when Salena was putting on the white evening-gown, having had her hair arranged by a hairdresser from Monte Carlo, she told herself she must behave as if she were grown up and not like a frightened school-girl.

Four times she had gone to the Salon to show her father and the

Prince the clothes that *Madame* Yvette had brought with her and each time she had become more and more self-conscious.

It was undoubtedly because of the way in which the Prince looked at her and the things he said.

His words always seemed to have a double meaning and they often made her father laugh although she did not find them in the least funny.

"I must not make a fool of myself and shame Papa," Salena whispered as she looked in her mirror.

The maid who had helped her into her gown had been most complimentary.

"M'mselle est ravissante! like the lilies we grow for the market at Nice."

"The flower-market?" Salena asked. "I have heard of it and I would like to see it. The flowers must be beautiful."

"The carnations come from all along the coast to be sold there," the maid answered, "and lilies too—lilies for the Churches."

She smiled and made a gesture with her hand that was very French.

"Looking like that *M'mselle* should be in a shrine in one of our Churches not in the gaming rooms in Monte Carlo."

"Are we going to Monte Carlo to-night?" Salena asked.

"Mais oui, M'mselle," the maid replied. "Every night, every afternoon, sometimes in the morning—everyone goes to the Casino. Me—I think it a waste of money."

"And so do I," Salena agreed.

At the same time, because she had heard so much about it she could not help thinking it would be rather exciting to see the Casino, even if she did not gamble.

There was a knock on the door and she knew it was her father who had promised he would take her downstairs with him.

Lord Cardenham was looking very rich and opulent with a pearl stud gleaming in the snowy expanse of his stiff shirt-front and a red carnation in his buttonhole.

He had always been a good-looking man and Salena thought it would be impossible for anyone to imagine that he was as penniless as he said he was.

"Ready, my dear?"

"Do I look all right, Papa?"

"I think the Prince has paid you enough compliments for it to be unnecessary for me to add to them," Lord Cardenham replied.

There was a note of satisfaction in his voice that Salena did not miss.

"How can we tell the Prince how grateful we are for his generosity?" Salena asked.

The maid had left the room and it was a question she had wanted to ask her father as soon as she had him alone.

"I am leaving that to you," he replied.

"To me, Papa? But I do not . . . know what more . . . to say."

"Then make yourself as pleasant as possible," Lord Cardenham advised. "Not many rich men would be so generous to someone they had never seen before and about whom they knew very little."

"I suspect, Papa . . . that you have told him . . . about me."

"I certainly described the circumstances in which you found yourself," her father agreed. "Russians are very sentimental, and as a child without a mother to advise her and a father with a hole in his pocket you are certainly pathetic, to say the least of it."

Salena gave a little sigh.

"The Prince has been very kind . . . but I wish you had not had to . . . ask him."

"He offered," Lord Cardenham said defensively.

Salena wanted to say that he had made it difficult for the Prince to do anything else, but she knew that any protestation she might make was just a waste of time.

Her father always had an eye to the main chance and it was difficult to blame him when they had invariably been on the point of bankruptcy.

"One thing is quite obvious," he went on, "and that is you pay with dressing, most especially when the gown is gilt-edged so to speak."

He put his arm around Salena, drew her to him and kissed her cheek.

"Now just express your gratitude to the Prince," he said, "and for God's sake do not be tongue-tied. The trouble with Englishwomen is that they are never half as effusive as any other race."

"I will . . . try to say the . . . right thing," Salena murmured.

"That's a good girl," her father admonished. "Now let us go downstairs. I want to see *Madame* Versonne's face when she sees you. Be careful with that one—she is a regular tiger-cat."

"In what way?" Salena enquired. "I do not understand."

Lord Cardenham seemed about to explain, then he changed his mind.

19

"You will learn about these things soon enough," he said. "Just be yourself and keep your fingers crossed."

"For good luck, Papa?" Salena questioned.

"For good luck," Lord Cardenham repeated solemnly. "That is what I thought you had brought me when I saw you at the station, my poppet."

He took Salena down the broad stairs to the Salon.

As they entered it seemed to be filled with people.

There was the sound of laughter and the chatter of voices. Then Salena saw the Prince detach himself from a group to whom he was talking, among them *Madame* Versonne.

Salena had thought her beautiful when she saw her on the terrace but in evening dress she was sensational!

Ostrich feathers swirled round the hem of her gown and over her shoulders and made her appear as if she was rising from the waves of the sea.

Everything she wore was the colour of emeralds, complemented by an enormous necklace of the same precious stones.

Her dark hair was elaborately arranged on top of her head and in it she wore an osprey feather held by an enormous diamond and emerald brooch.

Salena was staring at her with so much admiration that she hardly realised the Prince was at her side, then hastily she curtsied.

"You look just as I expected you to," he said.

"Thank you," she answered. "I do not know how to begin to tell you how grateful I am to Your Highness."

"Shall we keep what we have to say until later when we are alone?" the Prince asked.

"Yes . . . of course," she answered, feeling that he did not wish the other people in the room to be aware of his generosity.

"Now I must introduce you to my friends."

He slipped his hand under Salena's elbow and moved her round the room.

There were so many new faces, so many almost unpronounceable names, so many titles, that at the end Salena knew no more about the guests than she had at the beginning.

The Prince turned away when someone else was announced and thankfully Salena moved to her father's side.

He was talking to *Madame* Versonne and she thought as she joined them that the older woman's eyes hardened.

"Your daughter, My Lord," she said to Lord Cardenham, "should be attending a débutantes' Ball rather than making her début at the green baize tables."

"Salena will not be doing that," Lord Cardenham replied. "At the same time I fear that débutantes are in somewhat short supply in Monte Carlo."

Madame Versonne laughed unpleasantly.

"They do not last long in any climate," she replied, "and inevitably they are more short-lived where there are Imperial eagles who peck at them."

There appeared to be a *double entendre* in what she said which again Salena did not understand, but when *Madame* Versonne moved away from them in the direction of the Prince Lord Cardenham said:

"I have warned you about that woman. You keep clear of her claws!"

"She did not seem to like me," Salena said. "I cannot think why, as she has never met me until now."

Lord Cardenham smiled.

"You do not have to search far for the reason."

"Tell me . . ." Salena began, but someone came up to speak to her father at that moment and he was unable to answer her.

She found herself at dinner seated between an elderly Russian who wanted only to talk of the different systems he had tried at the tables, and a Frenchman who paid her such elaborate and extravagant compliments that she found them almost ludicrous.

The food was delicious, the table laden not only with gold ornaments but also decorated with orchids.

Salena looked at it with awe.

She knew they were the most expensive flowers obtainable and it seemed incredible for them to be displayed in such profusion just on a dinner-table.

But then everything about the Prince seemed to be ornate and overwhelmingly extravagant; the food, the wine, the jewels of the ladies, the opulent splendour of the men.

It was a world in which Salena had imagined her father moving but which she had never seen before.

Even the cigars smoked by the gentlemen seemed longer and fatter than those she had noticed in the past.

She could not help feeling that it was incongruous for her and her father to be here when they themselves were so poor and had no idea where their next penny was coming from.

I suppose it would be possible for Papa to work in order to earn money, Salena thought to herself, *but what could I do?*

She had often thought that she had no particular talent that was marketable.

She could draw and paint in an amateurish way, she could play the piano but she was certainly no virtuoso, and she was well aware that the only career open to ladies was that of a Governess or a companion.

She gave a little sigh.

I should hate to be either of those, she told herself, and wondered anxiously what the future held.

She could not help thinking that when they left the Villa they would have nowhere to go.

It would be less of a problem for her father.

There were always people who were prepared to invite him to stay with them and would offer him what he would call "a bed to sleep on and a roof over his head" because he was so charming and such an asset to any party.

Salena remembered her mother saying once when her father had many invitations in which she was not included:

"You see, dearest, everyone wants an unattached man, especially one like your father; but a couple is much more trouble, particularly when they have nothing to offer in return."

"What could you offer in return?" Salena had asked.

"Hospitality," her mother replied. "If we had a house in the country or could give a Ball in London, or even large and amusing dinner-parties, it would be what your father calls a 'pay back'. But we can afford to do none of those things."

Salena had been very young at the time, but as she grew older she saw there were many occasions when even her mother and father's closest friends did not invite them to their parties.

Her mother took it as a matter of course, but it made her father swear and she knew he was frustrated at being left out.

It was all a question of "pay back", Salena thought now, *and how could I ever "pay back" for what anyone does for me?*

She looked down the long table to where the Prince was sitting at the far end with *Madame* Versonne on one side of him and another very attractive lady on the other.

They were making him laugh.

There was something in the attention they were giving him, the manner in which they bent towards him and the expression in their eyes, which told Salena that this was the way they were showing their gratitude and perhaps their affection for him.

That is what he . . . expects, she thought to herself.

The idea that he might expect it from her made her shiver.

CHAPTER TWO

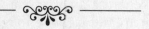

"*N*o . . . Papa . . . I cannot do it . . . I cannot!"

Lord Cardenham walked to the window of Salena's bed-room and looked out at the sea.

He did not speak and after a moment Salena said nervously:

"I want to . . . please you, Papa, but I . . . hate the Prince. I cannot explain . . . but he makes me feel . . . frightened . . . there is something in the way he . . . looks at me."

It was not only the way he looked at her. It was when he touched her that she felt a revulsion run through her as if there was a snake moving over her skin.

He seemed always to be near her, so that his hand touched hers or their shoulders brushed against each other's.

She had had the feeling for the last week that he was encroaching nearer and nearer and at night she fell asleep to wake with a start because he haunted her dreams.

She was well aware that *Madame* Versonne looked at her with hatred

23

and she addressed her in a more and more aggressive manner which made Salena shrink within herself and try to be as inconspicuous as possible.

But now incredibly, unbelievably, her father had said that the Prince wished to marry her.

"He is . . . old, Papa," she protested piteously as still her father did not answer her. "Of course I would like to be married . . . some day . . . but I want to fall in . . . love and with a . . . young man."

"Young men have no money!"

The words came harshly to Lord Cardenham's lips, then he turned round and there was an expression in his eyes that Salena had never seen before.

"Do not imagine I have not thought about this," he said. "I have lain awake at night trying to find another way out, but quite frankly my dear, there is nothing else we can do."

Salena looked at him, her eyes dark and frightened in her pale face.

"You mean, Papa, that I must . . . marry the Prince because he is . . . rich?"

"He has to-day settled £2,000 a year on you," Lord Cardenham answered, "and you are intelligent enough to realise what that means to both of us."

Salena made a little sound, but she did not say anything and her father went on:

"£2,000 a year is a considerable amount of money, besides which . . ."

He paused, looked embarrassed, and Salena said softly:

"He is giving you . . . something . . . too, Papa."

"He is giving me enough to pay my debts and prevent me from feeling as desperate as I have for a long time about the future."

There was silence for a moment. Then he went on:

"It is a question really of asking you to do this, Salena, or I might as well shoot myself and get it over."

"What do you . . . mean, Papa?"

"I mean that if I cannot pay up what I owe, it will result in my being sued, and the inevitable publicity in one particular instance would compel me to resign from my Clubs."

Salena was well aware what this penalty would mean.

Her father's life, when he was not staying with his friends, centered around the two exclusive and smart London Clubs to which he belonged.

"Have you . . . done something . . . wrong, Papa?"

"You, and doubtless your mother, would have considered it wrong," her father replied harshly. "Shall I say I took a gamble which sailed pretty near the wind and I lost!"

"You really . . . mean that if I do not . . . marry the Prince you would be in . . . serious trouble?"

"Very serious!" Lord Cardenham said gravely.

Salena gave a deep sigh which seemed to come from the very depths of her heart.

She might have guessed, she thought, when her father first told her that the Prince wished to marry her that there would be no escape.

Because the idea horrified her and made her feel that she could not contemplate what lay ahead, she rose to run to her father like a small frightened child.

He put his arms round her and held her close against him. Then he said in a voice that seemed to be strangled in his throat:

"I am a rotten father to you, my poppet, but at least you will be safe whatever happens in the future."

Salena's impulse was to reply that nothing worse or more terrifying could happen to her than having to be the Prince's wife.

But she knew that her father was suffering and because she loved him she managed to say with a courage she was far from feeling:

"I will try . . . Papa, to behave as you would . . . wish me to."

Her father put his hand under her chin and turned her face up to his.

He looked down at her for a long moment, then said almost as if he was speaking to himself:

"If only there had been more time, if only we could have waited. There might have been someone else."

Salena said nothing because she did not think an answer was expected of her, but she could not help recalling how many men had paid her compliments since she came to Monte Carlo.

Every night when they went to the Casino and she had kept close to her father's side while they watched the gambling, there had always been men he knew who came up to him quite obviously with the desire to be introduced to her.

Although this had made her feel shy and she had not always known how to reply, what they said did not make her shrink away in disgust and revulsion as did the flowery sentences which fell from the Prince's lips.

One reason why Salena enjoyed going to the Casino was that as soon as they arrived the Prince would be hurried away to the Baccarat tables by *Madame* Versonne.

She would sit beside him and play with his money, and the Prince would concentrate like the other immensely rich men at the table at trying to beat the bank.

Her father had explained to Salena who many of the other players were. When she asked innocently why such wealthy men should have nothing better to do than want to win more money, he answered:

"There is very little sense in gambling, but it gives those who are satiated with luxury a thrill which is irresistible."

Salena knew that he himself was longing to play but could not afford it.

Instead he would stake a few francs on the roulette table or occasionally try his luck at trente-et-quarante.

It made her feel so anxious and so frightened in case he should lose that it was almost an agony to watch the turn of the card or the fall of the little white ball in the roulette wheel.

Then inevitably would come the moment when the Prince would join them, his eyes on her face, his hand reaching out to touch her.

She would long to run away and hide, only to remember almost despairingly that he had paid for the gown she was wearing and therefore she must express her gratitude by being polite to him.

Because everyone staying at the Villa was a foreigner Salena would long for an English face and to talk to someone of the same nationality as herself.

One evening a man who was obviously English nodded to her father as he passed through the rooms.

He was tall, broad-shouldered and fair-skinned although his hair was a dark brown.

He was as smartly dressed as every other man in the Casino yet he gave the impression of wearing his clothes casually as if they were a part of him.

"Good-evening, Cardenham," the Englishman said.

"I hope it will be," her father joked. "But it is too soon yet to tell."

The Englishman knew he spoke of his gambling and laughed.

"Who was that?" Salena enquired.

She watched the tall man with the broad shoulders as he moved through the throng of glittering women and men who seemed somehow stuffed into their evening-clothes.

"That is the Duke of Templecombe," her father replied.

"It was his yacht we saw when I arrived," Salena said, also a little lilt in her voice.

"Yes—the *Aphrodite*," her father answered. "I would like to look over it if I had the chance. I hear it is the most up-to-date vessel of its kind in the whole of Europe."

"I would like to see it too," Salena said.

But although she looked for the Duke hoping her father would get into conversation with him he was not at the Casino the next night or the night after.

"There is something I have to tell you . . ." her father was saying.

She knew by the stiffness of the way he was holding himself, or perhaps it was the tone of his voice, that he was embarrassed.

"What is it, Papa?"

"The Prince wishes you to marry him at once!"

"At once? Oh, no, Papa. That is . . . impossible!"

"He insists," Lord Cardenham said, "and frankly, Salena, I need the money he has promised me."

"How is it . . . possible? How can we be married so . . . quickly?"

She asked the question pathetically and added:

"What will . . . *Madame* Versonne . . . say?"

It had been very obvious even to someone who was as inexperienced as Salena that *Madame* Versonne looked on the Prince as her special property.

She moved everywhere beside him, while her proprietary manner and the way she constituted herself as the hostess in the Villa had made Salena feel, despite the way the Prince looked at her, that it was *Madame* Versonne whom he intended to marry.

She had heard no-one discuss such an idea, but many of the guests spoke to each other in Russian, which she did not understand. Anyway it had never crossed her mind that the Prince was an eligible bachelor.

For the moment she felt stunned by the suggestion that she should marry him and it was even more incredible that it should take place at once.

27

"But . . . how . . . how is it . . . possible?" she asked again.

"The Prince has thought of everything," Lord Cardenham replied, "and he is at this moment informing those who are staying in the house that his personal servant has a virulent form of scarlet fever."

He paused before he continued:

"His Highness is therefore arranging for everyone to move to the Hotel de Paris. He has taken over two floors and I am to play host until you are married and have left on your honeymoon."

"B—but . . . Papa . . ." Salena began to expostulate.

Then she realised that there was nothing she could say and her voice died away.

"The Prince is pretending that as he has been in close contact with his servant, he must be isolated for several weeks."

Lord Cardenham went on:

"The Villa is supposed to be fumigated and in a few days the party will return but by that time you will both have left."

He walked again to the window as he added:

"God knows how I am to break the news that he has left to *Madame* Versonne. She will be furious! At the same time the Prince will undoubtedly placate her extremely generously."

"But . . . what am I . . . going to do? And where will the . . . P—Prince be taking me?" Salena asked.

"You will be married secretly here this evening in the Villa so that no-one will be aware of it," Lord Cardenham said. "You must understand, Salena, that the Prince is supposed to ask permission of the Tsar but he says it would take too long for him to journey to Russia and back again."

"S—surely it would be . . . better for him to do that?" Salena said quickly.

"It would not be better for me!" Lord Cardenham retorted.

"No . . . no, of course not, Papa. I had forgotten about that," Salena said hastily.

"You do understand the need for secrecy?" her father asked. "Besides, it would be extremely uncomfortable for you to face *Madame* Versonne and all the comments his other friends will make."

"Yes . . . of course . . . I have no wish to . . . listen to them."

She told herself that she was in fact frightened of *Madame* Versonne, and everything that was sensitive in her shrank from seeing the anger and envy in the other women's eyes.

All those in the house-party were, she thought, the sort of ladies with whom her mother would have put on a cold air and been very quiet and frigid in their company.

Her mother had never criticised her father's friends, but sometimes when they had come to the house Salena had known that there was an atmosphere of hostility that was unmistakable.

It was then her mother became stiff and quiet, very unlike her smiling, fascinating self.

All the women here seemed to Salena when she compared them with her mother somehow vulgar, or perhaps the right word was fast.

"Men may like her," she had heard her mother say once of some lady of whom she disapproved, "but she is fast in her ways, and as far as I am concerned I hope I never see her again."

Salena was well aware that her mother would have said that of everyone with whom she had been acquainted since arriving at Monte Carlo, and most especially of *Madame* Versonne.

At the same time she tried not to criticize because she knew it would only upset her father and they had nowhere else to go.

But now she thought that perhaps for the rest of her life she would be forced to associate with such women and how unpleasant it would be.

It was not that they were all so vitriolic or disdainful as *Madame* Versonne.

It was, she sensed, their insincerity and the manner in which they gushed over the Prince and every other man, including her father.

It was as if they were acting a part, but underneath all the pretence Salena somehow fancied they were just grasping and grabbing at everything they could get and had no real affection for anyone.

"No, Papa," she said aloud, "I would hate . . . anyone here in the Villa to know about my . . . wedding."

Then she added:

"Must it . . . really be as soon as . . . to-night?"

"What is the point of waiting?" her father asked. "The Prince has arranged everything so that there will be no time for people to question his arrangements."

"But you will . . . stay with me, Papa?"

"I am afraid that is impossible," her father replied. "The Prince is alleging that everyone who has not come in contact with the afflicted servant is safe so long as they leave at once."

"B—but . . . Papa . . . I c—cannot be left . . . alone!"

"I will stay with you for as long as I can," her father replied. "We shall obviously travel in several carriages and I will be the last to leave."

"Surely . . . everyone will . . . expect me to be with . . . you?"

"The Prince has thought of that too," Lord Cardenham replied. "You have been asked by some school-friends to stay at another Villa and I thought it would be nice for you to be with young people."

Salena thought that this was what she would really like—to be with her friends rather than left alone with the repulsive elderly man who was to be her husband.

"I am sorry, my dear," her father was saying, "sorry this has been such a shock. But believe me, if the Prince had not offered for you, I have not the slightest idea what I should have done to save us both from sleeping in the gutter!"

Lord Cardenham looked towards the wardrobe.

It was open and he could see the dozens of gowns that *Madame Yvette* had supplied for Salena to hang inside.

New ones arrived day after day, and with them came boxes filled with lace-trimmed nightgowns, with petticoats and silk stockings, with slippers dyed to match the gowns and wraps edged with fur.

At first Salena had tried to protest that it was too much, she did not need so many things.

But her father had been quite cross with her and so she tried to accept gracefully what she was given and express in stumbling words her gratitude.

As if her father knew what she was thinking he put his hand now into his pocket and drew out a jewel-box.

"His Highness asked me to give you this," he said. "He thought it would please you and mitigate the shock of everything happening so quickly."

He held out the small leather case to Salena and it was with an effort that she forced herself to take it.

She guessed what it contained and thought it was a chain binding her to a man she hated.

Slowly with fingers that trembled she opened the box. Inside was a huge ruby ring surrounded by diamonds.

It had an antique setting and her father explained:

"It belongs, I think, to the Prince's family collection, and I can tell you one thing, Salena, he will load you with jewels because he is completely and absolutely infatuated with you."

Salena did not answer. She was looking at the ruby thinking that it seemed to glow with an evil fire and she hated it.

"In fact the Prince said to me," Lord Cardenham continued, "that he had never in his life been so captivated or enraptured by any woman."

As if he was speaking to himself he added:

"I think he would have paid any price for you."

Salena looked at him and said quietly:

"He is . . . buying me, Papa, and it makes me feel . . . ashamed that he has paid so much . . . already."

"There is no reason for you to feel ashamed," her father replied angrily. "You are beautiful, Salena—beautiful, young, untouched. Any man would be proud to own you."

He looked at her and sighed.

"If only we had more time!"

Salena put the ruby ring down on the dressing-table and closed the box.

"When am I to be . . . ready?" she asked.

"Because the Prince is anxious to be quite certain that everyone has left the Villa you will . . . not be married until after dinner. It will take time for the ladies to pack and of course he had other arrangements to make."

"What are . . . they?" Salena asked nervously.

"I think he intends to take you away to-morrow in his yacht," Lord Cardenham replied. "I suggested you might like to see the Greek Islands. They are very beautiful at this time of the year."

Salena's eyes lit up for a moment. She had always longed to see the Greek Islands. Now she remembered who would be with her and her vision of them suddenly seemed to be covered in darkness.

"The Prince will explain everything to you himself," Lord Cardenham said, "but I think you would be wise to stay here in your bed-room until dinnertime. Everyone is bound to have gone by then."

"Do not . . . go until you . . . have to, Papa. Please!" Salena begged.

"No, of course not," he answered, "but I would like a drink and I suggest that we sit on the balcony of the next room. I know it is unoccupied."

31

He opened the door to look outside in an almost conspiratorial manner, then beckoned to Salena to follow him.

They went into the next room which looked over the garden towards the sea.

It was rather larger than the one occupied by Salena, and outside the window was a large balcony with the awnings down to keep the room cool.

Lord Cardenham rang the bell and when a servant appeared ordered champagne. Then he walked out onto the balcony and Salena followed him.

"A drink will do you good," he said. "I know this has been a shock, and there is nothing like champagne to make one feel that things are not as bad as they appear."

Salena did not answer.

She was fighting an impulse to plead once more with her father; to beg him to save her, to let her run away alone so that she could hide.

But she knew she could not ruin him through sheer selfishness.

Her mother had said to her so often:

"Men are like children, Salena, and we have to look after them, even though they think they are looking after us."

"Do you really look after Papa?" Salena had asked curiously.

"In a thousand different ways of which he has no idea," her mother replied. "In fact, darling, I do not mind telling you he would get into a lot of trouble if I was not there."

That, Salena thought, was exactly what had happened. Her mother was dead and her father on his own had not been able to look after himself.

I have to save him, she thought, *however hard it may be. I must save him for Mama's sake.*

Because she knew perceptively that he was feeling uncomfortable and perhaps miserable, she put out her hand and slipped it into his.

"I am sure it will be . . . all right, Papa," she said as if she was consoling him.

"I am praying that it will be all right for you," Lord Cardenham answered. "Remember dearest, that you will have money of your own and jewels. That is what every woman wants, what every woman should have."

"Where will I . . . live?" Salena asked.

She had a sudden fear that the Prince might take her away to Russia and she would not see her father again.

"I do not know what the Prince's plans are," Lord Cardenham replied, "but I imagine when your honeymoon is over you will go to Paris. He has a magnificent house there, but I am quite sure he will be only too glad to take you anywhere."

"I want to be near . . . you."

"I expect that can be arranged," her father replied. "I have always got on well with Serge, in fact he counts me as one of his closest friends."

"Then will you ask him, Papa, if you can join us as soon as possible?"

"I shall have to be tactful about it," Lord Cardenham replied. "I have a feeling that the Prince will want to have you to himself."

Salena shuddered, but aloud she said:

"How long do . . . honeymoons usually . . . last, Papa?"

"It depends," Lord Cardenham answered evasively.

She had the feeling it would depend on whether she amused the Prince or not. If he found her boring, he would want to return to the chattering laughing people who entertained him.

"Perhaps it will be only a week or so before I see you again, Papa," she said.

"I hope so," her father replied, "but naturally you will not be able to come here."

Salena thought that was because *Madame* Versonne would still be the Prince's guest.

It seemed strange that she should want to stay on if he was married, but she thought it best not to ask too many questions and she was well aware that her father was embarrassed by them.

"We have had so . . . little time together, Papa," she said. "I had hoped that I could live with you and look . . . after you as Mama used to do."

"That is what I wanted too," her father replied, "and if I had not been a damned fool it might have been possible for a little while. But being without money is hell! It is no use pretending, Salena, that one can manage without it, because one cannot!"

"No, Papa."

"And that is why the Prince has solved our immediate problems and we have to settle the future, in a different way from what I anticipated."

"What did you anticipate, Papa?"

BARBARA CARTLAND

"There is no point in talking about it now," her father said quickly. "You will be secure, Salena, and as I have said that is the only thing that matters."

"She could not help feeling that she would be very insecure with the Prince, whatever her position financially. Yet she knew it was no use saying such things.

It had all been arranged and because she loved her father there was nothing she could do but acquiesce and try not to feel almost sick with fear knowing that in a few hours' time she would be married to the Prince.

Then, she supposed, he would touch her and kiss her!

She looked out at the blue of the Mediterranean and wished she could swim away towards the misty horizon.

It was as if all her ideals and all the fantasies she had had about love and marriage were disappearing to where the sea joined the sky.

She had dreamt that one day she might meet a man who would be as good-looking as her father had been when he was young, and he would fall in love with her and she with him.

It would all be very wonderful and she would live happily ever afterwards like the end of the fairy-stories.

But instead . . .

She felt a pain inside her breast which had been there ever since her father had told her she was to be married to the Prince, stabbing her with a physical agony that seemed to intensify with every moment that passed.

The champagne arrived and her father made her drink a little of it, but instead of sweeping away her fears it seemed to multiply them.

Everywhere she looked she seemed to see the Prince's eyes with an expression in them which was terrifying.

Finally she went back to her bed-room and looked again at the ruby ring he had given her and she thought it too held the same expression.

Her father was almost casual in his leave-taking, and she knew it was because he was afraid she would make a scene and also because he too was upset at saying good-bye.

"Take care of yourself, my poppet," he said almost cheerfully. "Remember it is uncomfortable and degrading living without money, and pretty gowns and glittering jewels make up for a great many other things."

34

She knew he was referring to her feelings for the Prince.

When he had left her bed-room, shutting the door behind him, she had to bite her lips not to cry out after him.

It took an iron control to prevent herself from pulling open the door and telling him that after all it was impossible; that she would do anything, go anywhere he liked, but she could not and would not marry the Prince.

Instead she ran to her bed and flung herself face downwards on it.

With a superhuman effort she refrained from crying, even though the tears pricked her eyes. Then she lay listening for the sound of the last carriage carrying her father away from the Villa.

She had a feeling that he would be telling himself all the way to Monte Carlo that nothing mattered except that she had £2,000 a year for the rest of her life.

How could it matter so much when the Prince was so wealthy and she would be his wife?

It was understandable, she supposed, that her father was safe-guarding her against the day when the Prince became bored with her and might then not be so generous.

It was difficult not to hope and even pray that the day in question would come quickly.

"Perhaps after all he will not want me, and decide he would rather marry someone like *Madame* Versonne," Salena said aloud.

Then she knew she was only day-dreaming, telling herself stories as she had done ever since a child when she imagined she was taking part in strange and exciting adventures.

Always the Good Fairy, the White Knight or Prince Charming rescued her at the last moment from the gnomes, the dragon or the wicked Giant.

But this time there would be no rescue and the Prince was certainly not the man she had seen in her dreams.

A maid came to inform her that dinner was at nine o'clock and to prepare her bath.

While it was being got ready a gown-box arrived from *Madame* Yvette and contained, as Salena thought she might have expected, a wedding-gown.

It was even more beautiful than all the beautiful gowns *Madame* had made for her, but she felt as if it was a shroud.

The box also contained a lace veil and a wreath of artificial orange-blossom.

Salena remembered that in her dream-stories she had always worn a wreath of real flowers.

But then my marriage was one of love, she thought. *This is wrong and false!*

As false as the orange-blossom buds which looked somehow coarse and garish when she compared them to the flowers outside in the garden.

She however did not speak but let the maid dress her almost as if she was a doll without any feelings.

"Am I to wear the veil now?" Salena asked and thought her voice sounded strange even to herself.

"I think His Highness expects it, *M'mselle,*" the maid replied.

She was excited at the idea of dressing a bride and chattered away although it seemed to Salena that her voice came from a far distance.

"Earlier this year, before I came to work for His Highness," she was saying, "my sister was married. It was not a grand ceremony, but such a happy one! Everyone in the neighborhood came to the Church and because we could not afford to entertain so many they all contributed a little towards the wedding-feast. We laughed, we sang, we danced. It was the happiest day I have ever known."

And this is my unhappiest, Salena wanted to say.

Instead she watched her reflection in the mirror as the maid arranged the veil over her fair hair and fixed it in place with the wreath of orange-blossom.

"*M'mselle est très belle!*" she exclaimed in almost awe-struck tones.

Salena rose to her feet.

"It must be nearly nine o'clock, I will go downstairs."

She would have left the room but the maid cried:

"One moment, *M'mselle,* you have forgotten your engagement ring! His Highness will be disappointed if you do not wear it for dinner!"

"Y—yes . . . of course . . ." Salena said dully.

She led the maid slip the ring on the third finger of her left hand.

Against the whiteness of her gown she thought it looked like a drop of blood. Hastily she walked downstairs.

The Prince was waiting for her in the Salon and she realised as she entered that the whole room had been filled with white flowers.

He was in evening-dress and two huge diamond studs glittered on his shirt-front.

For a moment when she entered he stood looking at her. Then as her eyes fell before his he walked forward to take her hand.

"This is the moment I have been looking forward to," he said.

He kissed the back of her hand, turned it over and she felt his lips in her palm.

There was something hard and greedy about them, something which made her want to snatch her hand away from him.

I must behave properly. I must behave as Papa would wish, Salena told herself.

The Prince must have known she was afraid for she was trembling, and taking her hand in his he drew her from the Salon into the small room next door.

They were not dining, Salena realised, in the large Dining-Room they had used ever since she had come to the Villa, but in a small room.

It had sometimes been used at breakfastime, but now it had been converted into a veritable bower of white flowers.

There were white orchids on the table and the fragrance of lilies was almost overpowering.

"Our first meal alone together," the Prince said as they sat down. "I cannot tell you, my adorable little Salena, how boring I have found the people who have kept us apart."

If he had been bored he had certainly not shown it, she thought, remembering the loud laughter that had seemed to surround him on every occasion this past week.

"I asked your father to arrange that our marriage should be kept a close secret," the Prince went on, "because I thought we had no desire to listen to the gushing congratulations of others when we would much rather be alone."

He paused to say impressively:

"I cannot begin to tell you how much I have wanted to talk to you."

"What . . . about?" Salena questioned, feeling she was expected to answer him.

"There could be only one subject," the Prince replied with a smile, "and that, of course, is love!"

The way he said the word made Salena hastily take a little sip of champagne that stood beside her, as if she felt it would fortify her.

He was speaking in English and as the servants were French she hoped they did not understand. But there could be no misunderstanding the passionate note in the Prince's voice or the expression in his eyes.

"I fell in love with you as soon as I saw you," he answered, "and I told myself you would be mine."

His eyes were on her face as he went on:

"You are so young, so innocent and so very desirable, but I swore that no-one and nothing should stand between us, and let me tell you, Salena, I always get what I want."

Now there was a fire in his eyes and his voice deepened until it seemed to Salena to be almost like the snarl of an animal.

"I have never ... known anyone ... Russian before," she said quickly, "I hope you will tell me about ... Russia and your ... home there."

"Russia is far away," the Prince answered, "and we are close to each other. That is more important at the moment."

"But naturally I am ... interested in your ... country and ... of course your ... people."

Salena hesitated a moment before she went on:

"I have heard there is much ... suffering in Russia and ... poverty."

"That is the sort of ridiculous story spread about by people who do not know our great land," the Prince replied. "Perhaps one day you will see it for yourself. In the meantime, we have other things to talk about."

Salena was relieved when he said "perhaps." That meant that he did not intend to take her to Russia, not at any rate for the moment.

It meant that she would not lose contact with her father and it was a consolation in itself to know he was only a few miles away.

She had seen the Hotel de Paris when she visited the Casino, and she knew he would enjoy the opportunity of playing host when he did not have to foot the bill.

"What are you thinking about?" the Prince asked.

"I was thinking of Papa."

"You need not worry about your father. As I expect he told you, I have looked after him."

"You have been ... very kind."

"Do you really think so? And do you think also that I have been kind to you?"

"Very kind . . . I am very . . . grateful," Salena said. "I have not . . . thanked you yet for . . . the ring."

She put out her hand as she spoke and the ruby glinted at her.

In the candlelight it seemed, she thought absurdly, to be like the "evil eye" that she had read of in books written about the East.

"I have other jewels to give you," the Prince said. "Necklaces which I will clasp around your throat and brooches I will pin between your soft breasts."

A little shiver of horror seemed to run down Salena's spine.

"Y—you are . . . very . . . kind," she murmured again.

"It is difficult for me to be anything else to you," he said, "but you must also be kind to me."

"Yes . . . of course . . ."

"It will be very exciting to teach you about love," the Prince said, "in fact it will be the most exciting thing I have done for a long time."

It seemed to Salena as if the meal was interminable, but at last it was over. Then the Prince asked a question sharply of one of the servants.

"He is waiting, Your Highness," was the reply.

The Prince turned to Salena and offered her his arm.

She put her hand on it, feeling as if he was taking her to the guillotine.

It flashed through her mind that it was exactly how the aristocrats who met their deaths in the Place de la Révolution had felt when there had been no way of escape.

If they had to die they did so proudly.

Salena put up her chin, and now the Prince was taking her through the hall and along a passage which she knew led to his private apartments.

Unlike his guests, the Prince slept on the same floor as the Salon and Salena knew from something her father had said that his rooms opened onto the terrace.

The passage ended with a door that was opened for them by a servant and now the Prince led her through another door.

Salena found she was in a room that had been arranged as a Chapel.

There were the seven silver sanctuary lamps which she knew were a part of the Russian Orthodox faith, and standing in front of an altar was a Priest with a long beard and a huge crucifix on his black robes.

The Chapel was lit only by candles. The air was thick with incense and there was a profusion of white flowers.

There were two white satin cushions on the floor and Salena and the Prince knelt on them.

The Priest began what sounded like a long prayer but as he spoke in Russian Salena had no idea what he said. When he finished the Prince took her hand in his and drew off the ruby ring to replace it with a gold band.

Then the Priest put his hand over theirs and blessed them and the Prince rose to his feet.

"Now we are married, Salena," he said and drew her with what seemed impatience from the Chapel.

Outside in the corridor he opened another door and now Salena found herself in a large, beautiful Sitting-Room.

"You are my wife," the Prince said, "and at last I can tell you of my love and we shall not be interrupted."

"Can I . . . first look at your room?" Salena asked. "I have never . . . been here . . . before."

As if the Prince knew she was evading him there was a smile on his lips as he said:

"Let me show you your bed-room. That room at the moment is more important to us than any other."

Because there was nothing she could say Salena followed him through another door and found herself in a large room with long French windows opening onto the terrace.

Below in the garden she could see the fountain glowing iridescent through lights skilfully concealed amongst the flowers.

The stars were shining brightly in the dark sky, but it was difficult to look at anything but the large bed which seemed to Salena's imagination almost to fill the room.

There were silk curtains draping it, the sheets were drawn back and she dare not think to herself what was implied.

"Why do we wait?" she heard the Prince ask. "I will ring for your maid. Then when you are in bed I will come back and we can be alone."

He rang the bell as he spoke and as if she had been waiting for the summons the maid who had looked after Salena since she first came to the Villa appeared.

The Prince kissed Salena's hand and said:

"Do not keep me waiting long, my beautiful one."

He walked back into the Sitting-Room, the diamond studs in his shirt glittering as he went.

"His Highness is an impatient bridegroom," the maid said with relish, savouring the drama of the moment.

She took off Salena's wreath and veil and undid her wedding-gown at the back.

Feeling as if she was in a dream Salena hardly noticed what was happening until she was wearing a night-gown so elaborate it might have been a ball-dress.

Of the finest handkerchief lawn, it was inset with real Valenciennes lace and the same lace, only deeper, bordered the hem and the sleeves.

"Let me brush Your Highness's hair," the maid suggested.

Salena turned towards the dressing-table as if she could no longer think but must do what was expected of her automatically.

Then as she sat down she saw there was a letter propped against her hair brushes and realised from the hand-writing that it was from her father.

She tore it open. Her father had written:

My Dearest,

This is just a line to tell you how much I love you, and how much I want your happiness. Send me a note when you can tell me you forgive me, and that you still care for your very affectionate and penitent father.
Cardenham.

Salena felt a surge of warmth rise within her as she read the note through twice.

She felt she understood what her father was trying to say and how it really worried him that to save them both she must do what she hated doing.

She rose from the dressing-table.

"Wait one moment," she said to her maid. "I will just write to my father and perhaps if it is not too late someone could take it to him in Monte Carlo."

"Yes, of course, Your Highness," the maid replied. "It will be quite easy for one of the grooms to carry it."

Standing in the corner of the room was a *Secrétaire*. It was an attractive piece of inlaid furniture, but it was closed.

Salena tried to open it.

"It is locked," she said to the maid, "and I want some writing paper."

"I expect the key is in a drawer, Your Highness," the maid replied. "If not, I'll go and ask the Housekeeper."

"Let me look first," Salena said.

She opened one of the small drawers and discovered the key in a corner of it.

Pulling out the two struts of wood which supported the flap Salena unlocked the desk and found as she expected that inside there was a blotter, writing-paper and envelopes.

She put the blotter down on the flap and as she did so she saw there were two framed photographs pushed against the ink-pot.

She picked one up to look at it.

It was a picture of an attractive woman in an evening-gown, wearing the most magnificent jewels.

Salena wondered vaguely who she was, then saw an inscription on the photograph in French:

To Serge—from his loving wife—Olga.

Salena stared at it in astonishment.

No-one had ever told her, she thought, that the Prince was a widower. It seemed strange that her father had never mentioned it.

There was another photograph and without really thinking she picked it up.

It was the same woman, but this time there were four children forming a group with her, the oldest looking about sixteen.

The writing was in the same hand.

To Darling Serge—from Olga and his loving family—Christmas, 1902.

For what seemed a long time Salena stared at the picture.

Then slowly, as if she was groping her way through a fog, the explanation of what she held in her hand came to her like a far away voice.

The secrecy over the wedding—her father's insistence that she would be safe whatever happened in the future, the way she had been kept from speaking to anyone who might have revealed the truth.

Vaguely at the back of her mind she remembered hearing that the Russian aristocrats who came to Monte Carlo left their wives at home so that they could enjoy themselves *en garçon.*

Now she recalled again as if it came from a long way away, that in the Russian solemnisation of marriage the bride and bridegroom had crowns held over their heads.

This had not happened at their ceremony and she suspected that the Priest had not been a real one, or else the service he had performed over them had not been one of marriage.

She could not move—she just sat staring at the photograph of the four children and the woman with the attractive face.

Behind her the maid said in a frightened tone:

"What is the matter, Your Highness? Has something upset you?"

"I am . . . all right," Salena said after a moment. "Leave me."

"But, Your Highness, your hair!"

"Please leave me!"

"I will be waiting for a summons, Your Highness."

Salena did not answer. She heard the maid close the door, then she rose to stand looking at the photograph she held in her hand.

It might have been a long time, it might have been a few seconds, she had no idea, before the door opened and the Prince came into the room.

He had changed from his evening-clothes and was wearing a thin, Oriental-looking cotton robe which was fashionable in the South of France when it was hot.

Because he had nothing round his neck it made him look different, and at the same time older.

His elegance had gone. He was just a heavy, middle-aged man. Only his eyes remained unchanged and the passion flared into them as he saw Salena's body thinly veiled by her diaphanous night-gown.

"You are ready for me, my beautiful bride?"

"Yes, I am . . . ready for you," Salena answered. "Will you please . . . explain this?"

She held out the photograph as she spoke and saw him start. Then a frown replaced the look of excitement on his face.

"Where did you get that?" he asked. "Who gave it to you?"

"No-one gave it to me," Salena answered. "I found it in the *Secrétaire.*"

"The fools! The imbeciles!" the Prince cried angrily.

43

He snatched the photograph out of her hand and threw it with a crash into the corner of the room.

"This does not concern us!"

"It concerns me," Salena replied. "I am not . . . married to you. You know I am . . . not."

"What does that matter?" the Prince asked. "I love you and I will teach you to love me."

"Do you really think I would let you . . . touch me now that I know you were only . . . pretending to make me your . . . wife?"

"I have told you that is of no consequence.," the Prince answered. "I will look after you—you will have all the money you want—more jewels than you can . . ."

"No!" Salena interrupted. "You have a wife. You have children. It is wicked and wrong to say such things to . . . me when you . . . belong to them."

"I belong to you and you belong to me," the Prince said.

He came towards her and Salena screamed.

"You are not to . . . touch me! I am . . . leaving now! I am going to . . . find Papa."

"Do you think your father wants you?" the Prince asked. "He is very satisfied with what I have paid him for you, and you will soon be satisfied too, my pretty little dove."

"No . . . no!" Salena screamed.

She would have run from the room but the Prince caught her in his arms and pulled her against him.

She fought him frantically, fought with her hands, her arms and her feet.

She was small and delicate, and yet it was impossible for him to hold her still when she struggled against him so ferociously.

She hurt him and wincing he loosened his arms.

"I see you must be treated like a Russian peasant," he said. "Then you shall learn who is the master."

He turned as he spoke and went back into the Sitting-Room.

For a moment Salena was so breathless and had been so intent on fighting desperately to be free of him that she could not realise he had left her.

She stared incredulously across the room, but as she turned towards the door which led into the passage he returned.

There was a cruel smile on his lips and an expression on his face that seemed to her so menacing, so terrifying that for the moment it was impossible to move.

Then she saw that he held in his hand a long, thin riding-whip.

She stared at it in silence as he came towards her and only as he put out his arm did she scream and try to move.

But she was too late!

He flung her forward onto the bed and the next moment she felt the whip strike her across the shoulders.

She screamed and when he had only struck her three times she managed to struggle to her feet and evade him.

He caught at the back of her night-gown and it tore in his hands as she ran across the room to try to reach the door into the Sitting-Room.

She stumbled and only saved herself from falling by holding onto the *Secrétaire*. She clutched at it and felt something hard beneath the fingers of her right hand.

She felt it could be a weapon of some sort with which she could strike at her pursuer.

But before she could realise what it was the Prince picked her up from behind and carrying her back to the bed threw her face downwards on it.

Her nose was buried in the sheets and as she gasped for breath, the whip came down on her back.

Now as she screamed the Prince used the whip relentlessly, each blow biting into her bare flesh like a tongue of fire searing its way into her consciousness.

Everything seemed to go hazy and although someone was screaming she did not even know it was herself.

Then as her voice died into silence the Prince breathing heavily, yet making a grunt of satisfaction, turned her over.

She was helpless in his hands, lying almost unconscious on the bed, her eyes closed.

She was holding in her right hand hidden in the folds of her night-gown the paper-knife she had inadvertently picked up from the *Secrétaire*. In her agony, she had gripped it tightly, and when the Prince turned her over, it pointed upwards.

He did not see it.

With a sound of triumph he flung himself on top of her and the stiletto-like point pierced him in the stomach.

He gave a cry that was hoarse and broken as he rolled off her clutching at the knife.

"You have—killed me! I am—dead! Fetch the Doctor! Save me—God, save me!"

Salena sat up and saw the Prince lying half-naked beside her, his fingers round the jewelled handle of the paper-knife, the blood pouring from the wound it had inflicted onto the white cover of the bed.

"You have killed me! You have—killed me!" he said accusingly in French. "Help—help!"

The last sound seemed lost in the thickness of his throat and to Salena's frightened eyes he was dying.

Slowly, almost as if she could not realise she was free to do so, she moved from the bed and onto the floor."

"I—am—dying!" the Prince gasped and his eyes closed.

His fingers were stained with blood and there was a crimson pool beside him.

With a sound of sheer terror Salena ran through the open window onto the terrace.

She saw the fountain glittering beneath her, and hardly aware of what she was doing she sped towards the steps that led down into the garden.

Her bare feet hardly made a sound on the white marble. Then she was on the green lawn passing the fountain and running through the trees until she reached the end of the promontory.

Just for a moment she hesitated, looking down at the waves swirling below her against the grey rocks.

She threw herself forward, felt the shock of the cold water spray in her eyes.

Then she started to swim frantically, wildly, out to sea . . .

CHAPTER THREE

*T*HE DUKE OF TEMPLECOMBE WAS WINNING, and the pile of gold louis in front of him multiplied with every turn of the cards.

Many of the women who had been watching the players at the other tables came to stand behind him and give little screams of delight every time he won.

There were only about fifty guests of the Grand Duke Boris present, but four gambling tables were laid out in the elegant Salon which opened onto the garden of the Villa.

Standing high above the town it afforded a magnificent view over the harbour, the rock on which stood the Palace and the sea itself.

No-one however was concerned with anything but the play of the cards, and as the Duke won again a murmur of excitement ran through the spectators and even those who were playing against him.

The man who was sitting next to the Duke and who had lost consistently all the evening leaned back in his chair with an air of exasperation and the Duke heard a soft voice say:

"Unlucky at cards—lucky in love!"

It made him remember Imogen and he looked round to see if she was standing as she usually did at his side.

There was however no sign of her and somewhere at the back of his mind he remembered seeing her move some time ago through one of the long French windows into the garden.

He thought, although he was not sure, that the Grand Duke was with her, and for a moment as he waited to play there was a frown between his eyes.

The Grand Duke was noted for his fascination for women. It was not only because he was immensely rich and as generous as he could well afford to be, but also because he was in fact a very attractive man who had a charm which most women found irresistible.

The Duke remembered that Imogen had remarked as they drove up to the Villa how much she was looking forward to seeing their host and how delightful she found him.

The Duke was slightly piqued because he wished Imogen Moreton to think of no other man but himself and particularly to-night.

As they steamed in his yacht from Marseilles to Monte Carlo he had decided that his bachelorhood was at an end and that he would marry Lady Moreton as everyone had been anticipating he would.

Her husband had been killed in the Boer war, but as she had married very young she was now only twenty-five and at the height of her beauty.

The Duke had been pressed by his relations to find a wife, and it was in fact a miracle that he had reached the age of twenty-seven without being propelled up the aisle by some scheming Mama.

He had eluded all the bait that had been held out to him, all the tricks that might have ensnared him, and had determined at an early age that he would not be pressured into marrying anyone if he did not wish to do so.

He had inherited at the age of twenty-one and it had been impossible for him not to be conscious of his importance as one of the premier Dukes of Great Britain.

Women fawned on him and because his name was an old and respected one his company was sought out not only by those of his own generation but also by Statesmen, Politicians and men of distinction who were older than himself.

He had been a friend of the Prince of Wales before he became King and he was always a welcome guest now at Buckingham Palace, as he had been at Marlborough House.

The Duke had considered for a long time whether Imogen, who had been his mistress for over a year, was the type of wife he wanted.

He admired her beauty, they had the same interests and were both *persona grata* in the same society.

It was very important, the Duke told himself, that they should agree on the ordinary things which filled their days, besides which he found Imogen very desirable.

There had been a large party of his friends aboard the *Aphrodite* who had sailed with them from London to Monte Carlo, but they had left to-day and another party was arriving to-morrow.

This meant that to-night when they returned to the yacht the Duke would have Imogen to himself, and he had decided that was when he would tell her that she was to be his wife.

It was something, he was well aware, that she wanted beyond all else, and he did not doubt for a moment that she loved him as a man.

All the same something cynical told him she would not be so keen on marriage if his position was a less eminent one.

But then, he asked himself, how could anyone, man or woman be considered in isolation from their background and their environment?

It was impossible to ask: "Would you love me if I was not a Duke?" or for a woman: "Would you love me if I was not beautiful?"

What was important was they were both well-bred, both came from families which appeared in the history books.

The Cinderella story was only for housemaids and school-girls who read novelettes and consequently imagined that a Prince Charming was waiting to fall down the chimney to make them his bride.

"We will deal well together," the Duke told himself, "and my mother and everyone else will be delighted."

He planned that one of the first people to be told when they returned home should be the King.

His Majesty liked Imogen because she was beautiful and had intimated on two or three occasions to the Duke what a suitable wife she would make him.

I will speak to her to-night, the Duke told himself as they drove towards the Grand Duke's Villa.

But now Imogen was missing and it struck the Duke as strange that she had not returned from the garden.

Impatiently he rose from the table.

"Surely you are not giving up?" the man next to him exclaimed. "Not in the middle of a winning streak?"

The Duke did not answer but leaving his money on the table walked across the Salon and out into the garden.

He was not in the least concerned that his behavior might seem odd or that people would discuss it. They always discussed anything he did anyway, and if he wished to stop gambling that was his business and no-one else's.

The garden of the Grand Duke's Villa was filled with flowers and was extremely beautiful. It was actually one of the famous gardens of the Côte d'Azur.

This was due not so much to the money which the Grand Duke had spent on it, as to the care and love given it by an old lady who had created it during the last seven years of her life.

There was the fragrance of flowers, the soft tinkle of a cascade in the water-garden, the petals from the blossom on the flowering trees dropping silently onto the velvet grass. But the Duke noticed none of this.

He was looking for the scarlet gown that Imogen was wearing, which matched the necklace of rubies and diamonds he had given her before they left England.

The garden was a complication of arbours, twisting paths, flowering bushes and comfortable seats on which one could sit and look at the breath-taking view.

The Duke strode on. The place seemed to be deserted—then suddenly he saw her.

There was no mistaking the colour of her gown silhouetted against the white pillars of a small Grecian temple situated at the end of a grass walk bordered by flowers.

She was standing in a manner which the Duke knew so well which drew attention to the sensuous lines of her figure and the beauty of her long, swan-like neck.

At the sight of her the Duke paused, and now as he watched her he saw the Grand Duke put his arms round her waist and pull her close to him.

She did not resist, in fact she lifted her mouth eagerly to his, and as he kissed her lips her bare arm went round his neck to draw him even closer.

It was the classical symbolic stance of a man and woman in love, and the scowl on the Duke's face deepened. Then after he had stared at the pair passionately entwined he walked away.

He did not return to the Villa but moved through the garden until he came to a gate which led to the road in front of it.

Drawn up in a long line were the carriages and horses of the guests, and it only took him a few seconds to locate his own carriage.

His servants looked surprised to see him. It was early and they had resigned themselves to a long wait, perhaps, as was usual in Monte Carlo, until dawn broke.

The footman opened the door and the Duke stepped into his carriage.

"The yacht!" he ordered.

The horses started off down the twisting road which descended sharply towards the harbor.

Inside the carriage the Duke sat back still frowning, and looking, although there was no-one to notice, extremely formidable.

Those who had heard him speak in the House of Lords knew that he was not only intelligent but he could, when aroused on a subject, be both aggressive and determined.

It was in fact entirely due to him that several Bills that the Lords had meant to throw out had been passed, and the Prime Minister had thanked him gratefully for his assistance.

Those who served the Duke found him a just and generous master, but if he thought he was being cheated or that anyone in his employment was negligent or disloyal he could be completely ruthless.

As the carriage reached the yacht which was tied up to the quay along with a number of others the Duke stepped out.

"I shall not require you again to-night," he said to the footman and walked off.

There was a Petty Officer on deck and like the coachman he also looked surprised to see the Duke returning so early.

"Good-evening, Your Gr—" he began only to be interrupted as the Duke said curtly:

"Tell Captain Barnett to put to sea immediately!"

"Immediately, Your Grace?"

"That is what I said!"

"I will inform the Captain, Your Grace."

The Duke walked to the bow to watch still with a scowl on his face and an almost uninterested air as the sailors came hurrying on deck.

He imagined some of them might have been asleep, but his crew was quite used to his making decisions which changed their course or arriving on board without any warning.

It was the Duke's most explicit instruction that his yacht should always be ready to leave without any previous notification.

51

He knew now that Captain Barnett would not be surprised at being told to leave Monte Carlo and would be only waiting orders as to where they were to head.

The Duke did not expect any questions, but they came nevertheless from his valet, a man called Dalton, who had been with him ever since a boy.

He had been chosen for the promotion by his father because he was a sensible man in whom he had every confidence.

"Excuse me, Your Grace," Dalton said at the Duke's elbow. "I wondered if Your Grace knows that her Ladyship's not aboard?"

"I am aware of that."

The reply was uncompromising, but the valet persisted:

"Her Ladyship's clothes are still here, Your Grace."

"I am aware of that too!"

The valet bowed and departed. The Duke's lips were set in a grim line as he looked up over the town in the direction of the Grand Duke's Villa.

It would come as a shock to Imogen, he was well aware, that he had left the party without informing her of his intentions.

It would be an even greater shock when she found that he had sailed taking with him not only her clothes but also her jewellery by which she set so much store.

The Grand Duke can provide her with more, the Duke thought savagely.

Then he told himself that he had had a lucky escape.

It was bad enough that the woman who professed to love him "as she had never loved a man before" should philander with such a notorious "lady-killer" as the Grand Duke, but it would have been far worse had she already become his wife.

He thought now that he would have been a fool to think that anyone who had been acclaimed and fêted as Imogen had been would ever want to settle down and be faithful to one man.

It was of course a blow to his pride and his self-conceit, and he acknowledged it as such.

He had grown monotonously accustomed to having any woman in whom he was even faintly interested and a great many that he was not, falling ecstatically into his arms.

It was therefore quite a shock to realise that, as his Nanny would have put it, he was "not the only pebble on the beach."

There was a cynical smile on his lips as he felt the yacht moving slowly across the harbour and out into the Mediterranean.

Now there was a faint breeze which he welcomed and as he was deciding where he would tell his Captain to take him, he suddenly thought it was rather exhilarating to be alone.

It was a long time since he had been surrounded by laughing, chattering people.

Templecombe House in London was always filled not only with his friends but also with large numbers of relations who thought it their right to stay there whenever they came to London from the country.

And Combe in Buckinghamshire was far too large for it not to seem imperative to fill the innumerable bed-rooms with innumerable guests and to augment the house-party with his neighbors all of whom expected to be invited whenever he was in residence.

Now he was alone and he thought that it was a desirable condition that he would enjoy to the full.

There were books to read and he would have a chance to think about himself and his future.

The yacht was far enough away from Monte Carlo for the Duke to look back at the glittering lights which were concentrated on the Casino and climbed the hill behind it.

It was very beautiful but he knew that those who visited the Principality seldom raised their eyes from the tables and many in fact never rose from their beds until the glory of the day had passed and they could spend another night in the gambling rooms.

It has a false allure—as false as Imogen's, the Duke thought.

Even as he recalled her, he told himself the sooner he erased her completely from his mind the better.

He did not want to remember his disgust or anger at her behaviour; he just wished to forget.

From the time he was a small boy he would never acknowledge when he was beaten, and would force himself to forget any humiliation he had suffered at school.

It was a sense of pride ingrained in him by a long line of illustrious ancestors which told him that he should not allow other people to encroach upon him unless they were of importance to his happiness.

It was an idea put into his head by his father who had once told him how Mr. Gladstone had written down the names of his enemies and shut the list in a locked drawer.

Years later he had taken it out and found that in nearly every instance he could not remember what that person had said or done, or why he had thought of them as an enemy.

The story had impressed the Duke and it was something that he had tried to do all his life.

"Never give your enemies the importance of thinking of them," was one of his favourite sayings, and he told himself now that he had no intention, if he could help it, of ever giving Imogen another thought.

He would tell Dalton to pack up her clothes and her jewels and have them put in the hold. When they reached London his secretary would see that they were delivered to her house and that would be the end.

It had been an enjoyable association he thought. There was no denying that, and he had in fact begun to believe that Imogen was different from other women.

He thought love meant something in her life that did not resemble the shallow flattery that was so much a part of the social life which centered round the King.

When Edward was Prince of Wales the beauties he had fancied had been gossiped about from one end of England to the other.

There was not a man in the street who did not know of his infatuation for Lily Langtry, for the Countess of Warwick, for half-a-dozen other lovely women.

The Duke had always admired the impeccable way the Danish-born Queen Alexandra behaved.

She never veered in her loyalty and devotion to her husband or in public showed any sign that she was upset or irritated by his constant infidelity.

The Duke supposed that in a way he had always fancied that his wife would behave in the same manner, but now he knew that where Imogen was concerned it was impossible.

She was too conscious of her beauty, too anxious to be admired, too weak to ignore the admiration of another man, even if his reputation was as infamous as that of the Grand Duke.

The Duke had a vision of himself moving down the years towards old age, wondering if his wife was unfaithful to him, always having his suspicions aroused and always being afraid to trust her.

If that is what lies ahead, he told himself, *then damn all women! I shall never marry!*

His thoughts were not happy ones and he decided to go to the Saloon and have a drink.

He knew there would be an open bottle of champagne waiting for him and beside it some wafer-thin sandwiches of pâté de fois gras prepared just in case anyone should feel hungry when they returned on board.

Then as he turned to walk along the deck he heard someone speaking loudly on the bridge in a tone that told him something was amiss.

Curious, it took him only a moment to stand beside the Captain, who had a telescope to his eye.

"What is it?" he asked.

"I am not sure, Your Grace. The look-out spotted what seems to be a body. It is something white—by jove it, it *is* a body!"

"Let me look."

The Captain handed the Duke the telescope and he steadied it in the experienced manner of a man who is used to stalking his own stags.

There was no doubt that there was something in the water and as the Captain had said it was white. Then he was certain he could distinguish a face.

"You had better lower a boat, and see if the person is alive," he said.

As he spoke he thought it would be a suicide who had lost all his money at the tables.

It was the sort of tale that was always being repeated and re-repeated about Monte Carlo, although he had been told that in fact the majority of such stories were untrue.

The yacht hove-to and the sailors let down one of the boats.

At the last moment the Duke decided he would go with those who were manning it.

He thought it would be wise for him to be there in case the body had been in the water for a long time, in which case it would not only be unnecessary but also extremely unpleasant to bring it on board.

He had seen men who had been drowned and their swollen faces and decomposing bodies were enough to turn the stomach of the strongest and toughest old salt.

The Captain had brought the yacht to about a hundred yards from where the body was floating and as they rowed towards it the Duke bent forward to peer into the darkness.

There was no moon that night, but the stars were glowing brilliantly overhead. Nevertheless it was hard to see clearly until they were right beside whatever it was on the surface of the water.

Then to his astonishment the Duke saw that the body was that of a child or a very young woman wearing a white gown and floating on the surface of the sea.

Her arms were outstretched on either side of her, her head thrown back, her hair in the water, and the Duke knew that she was not only alive, but also a very experienced swimmer to be able to float so effortlessly.

The boat drew nearer and still nearer, then the men nearest to the body lifted their oars and looked to the Duke for instructions.

"Catch hold of her hand," he said to the man in the bow.

As he spoke the sound of his voice must have aroused the woman for her eyes opened and she gave a scream.

Then as she saw the boat and the men in it peering down at her she turned and tried to swim away.

She was however too late, for the sailor on the Duke's instructions had caught hold of her hand.

"Let . . . me . . . go! Let . . . me . . . go! I want . . . to . . . die!"

She struggled desperately and taking the man who held her by surprise she was free of him.

There was a struggle, or perhaps because she was so weak she sank, slipping down beneath the water, and for a moment the Duke thought they had lost her.

But she came up again and this time the boat had swung so that the Duke was nearest to her. He reached out and seized hold of her arm, managing to get his hand on her shoulders.

She spluttered and would have protested, then suddenly she collapsed and it was only because the Duke was so strong that he was able to hold her.

Slight though she was, as a dead weight in the water it was quite hard to pull her into the boat.

When the Duke had managed it, with the help of the sailor closest to him he realised that her legs were bare and she was clad only in a night-gown.

It clung tightly to her body and because she was so small and slight the Duke realised that while at a distance it had been easy to mistake her for a child, she was undoubtedly a young woman.

56

They reached the yacht and as the stairway had been let down at the side it was easy for the Duke to carry her in his arms up onto the deck.

The whole crew, including the Captain and Dalton, seemed to be waiting for them and without wasting time in talking the Duke went below followed hurriedly by Dalton.

The woman was entirely unconscious and the Duke even wondered if she was dead as he carried her into one of the empty cabins.

Hastily Dalton laid a number of thick Turkish towels down on the floor and he laid her down on them aware that his shirt front and trousers were wet.

"I'll manage, Your Grace," Dalton said.

"Get some brandy!" the Duke ordered, "and more towels."

"Very good, Your Grace."

The Duke looked down at the woman he had rescued and in the bright lights of the cabin realised he had been right in thinking that what she was wearing was a night-gown.

But it was in fact, an elaborate and very expensive one.

The lace that trimmed it was real and he saw that on her finger she wore a wedding-ring.

He wondered if she had been thrown from a yacht by some murderously inclined husband, but it seemed more likely, because of her cry that she wished to die, that she had tried to commit suicide.

It seemed inconceivable that she had swum so far from the shore. Very few women of the Duke's acquaintance could swim at all.

But wherever she had come from she was certainly a mystery and he noticed too that she was not only very young but very pretty also, even with her hair wet and lank against her white cheeks.

Divesting himself of his evening-coat which was too close-fitting for such athletic exertions the Duke picked up a towel, then decided the first thing he must do was to remove the soaked night-gown of the woman he had saved.

It fastened at the front and he undid several pearl-shaped buttons, then modestly covering the lower half of her body with a towel, he pulled it up.

There was no doubt, he thought, that she was beautifully made. Her body was exquisite and she might have been the young Aphrodite rising from the waves.

I am being poetical, the Duke told himself almost angrily.

57

He had been hating all women until this happened. Now he could not help feeling a rising curiosity about this woman who had come into his life so unexpectedly.

He pulled the wet night-gown up to Salena's head and with an arm under her shoulders raised her a little so that he could remove it altogether. As he did so he found that it was torn from the yoke. Then he saw her back.

He stared incredulously, finding it hard to believe that his eyes were not deceiving him. This was certainly an explanation of her jumping overboard.

The Prince's whip had seared Salena's body in a criss-cross pattern of weals breaking the flesh in several places so that they were bleeding.

The Duke pulled away the wet night-gown, then as he heard Dalton returning he laid Salena down and hurriedly covered her with another towel.

"Here's the brandy, Your Grace," Dalton said handing him a glass, "and two more towels. I'll fetch some others right away."

"Do that."

Very gently the Duke rubbed Salena's hair with one of the towels which Dalton had brought him.

He found it was not loose as he had first thought but there were hair-pins caught in it as if it had been arranged and not free when she had entered the water.

This was another thing to puzzle him and as her hair became drier under his ministrations he saw she was very fair and wondered what colour her eyes were.

Blue, I suppose, he told himself.

She was still unconscious when Dalton returned and the Duke said:

"I think it would be wise to get this young woman into bed before we try to bring her round."

"A good idea, Your Grace."

"I suggest you spread one of the large bath-towels on the bed and fetch some hot-water bottles. She is very cold."

"I'll do that, Your Grace."

The valet pulled back the bed-clothes and spread a Turkish towel on the bottom sheet and a smaller towel over the pillow.

"There's another one handy with which you can cover her, Your Grace. I'll not be long with the hot-water bottles."

He hurried busily away from the cabin and the Duke waited until he was gone before he lifted Salena in his arms.

He had the idea that her nakedness should not be exposed to anyone but himself and as he carried her towards the bed he found how light she was.

"How could any man beat anything so exquisite?" he asked.

Then he wondered if in fact her husband had caught her out in an act of infidelity.

Even so, to have punished her so cruelly and so brutally was something no decent man would have done.

The Duke laid Salena down on the bed, covered her with the extra towel, then pulled on top of it the sheets and blankets.

Her cheeks were almost as pale as the linen and he wondered if she would be happier if he left her. Then he knew it would be a mistake to let her drift into what might prove to be a coma.

He slipped his arm under her head and lifting her said firmly:

"Wake up! Wake up and drink this!"

He had the feeling, although he could not be sure, that she was fighting to remain oblivious of everything that was happening.

He was sure he was right in his supposition when her eyelids flickered. Then as she felt the glass against her lips she tried to turn her head to one side.

"Drink!" the Duke said commandingly.

As if she was too weak to disobey him she swallowed the drops of brandy he tipped between her lips.

She held her breath and he thought she was defying him. Then he forced a little more of the brandy into her mouth, but she struggled to move her arms.

"Lie still and drink!" the Duke said.

"N—no . . . !"

It was a very weak sound but somehow she managed to say it.

He still held the glass to her mouth and finally, when she had taken a few more sips of brandy and swallowed them almost despite herself, her eyes opened.

She stared at the Duke with an expression of horror and because his arm was round her he felt her whole body go tense and knew it was with fear.

"It is all right," he said soothingly. "You are quite safe."

59

"N—no," she managed to say again. "No . . . no . . . let me . . . die!"

"It is too late for that," he said quietly.

Gently he put her head back on the pillow.

She was still staring at him with an expression of abject terror in her eyes. Yet he was not certain whether she was seeing him or something which had frightened her before she entered the water.

"You are quite safe," he repeated, "and now you must tell me where you have come from and where you would like me to take you."

He thought she did not understand what he was saying and when she did not speak he asked:

"Suppose we start by your telling me who you are? What is your name?"

"S—Sal . . . en . . . a."

She spoke the word very slowly with a pause between each syllable.

"And your other name?"

She gave a little scream that was so small and so weak that it was like the cry of a new-born kitten.

She shut her eyes and lay back holding her breath as if she tried to force herself back into unconsciousness and the Duke saw that she was trembling.

He wondered how he should deal with someone in such a state.

He had not realised that it was possible for a woman to look so frightened, so abjectly terrified.

It was not surprising considering the way she had been treated, and yet he thought perhaps, unless he was being over-imaginative, it was not only the beating that had scared her but something else.

He had not spoken or moved, and as if she was curious to see whether he had left, Salena opened her eyes.

She saw him and once again she appeared to shrink away from him, to sink into the bed and try to disappear.

"No-one will hurt you," the Duke said quietly. "There is nothing here to make you afraid."

He was not certain whether she understood. There was only the expression of horror on her face and the pupils of her eyes seemed dilated until they were black.

Dalton appeared with two hot-water bottles.

"I'll slip one in by the young lady's feet, Your Grace," he said, handing the other one to the Duke.

Very gently the Duke raised the sheets to put the bottle beside Salena but on top of the towel which covered her.

"You will feel warmer with this," he said. "It must have been very cold in the sea."

He had noticed that she winced and shrank away from him when he placed the bottle beside her.

Whatever happened to her, he thought to himself, *it has certainly given her a fear of men.*

It was an interesting thought and he looked at her contemplatively noting the flower-like childish face, the huge eyes set far apart, the perfect curve of her trembling little mouth.

Whoever the man was who beat her, the Duke thought, *he is a swine! It would be a pleasure to give him a taste of his own medicine!*

Dalton was picking up the wet towels that had been left on the floor and the sodden night-gown.

He walked to the door before he stopped to say:

"Do you think, Your Grace, I might get the young lady one of Her Ladyship's night-gowns? It'll be too big, but I'm sure she'd feel more comfortable in it."

"That is a good idea, Dalton," the Duke replied, "but I will not put it on at the moment but merely leave it here on the bed. Also bring a dressing-gown and a pair of slippers."

He felt somewhat cynically that he had no compunction about using Imogen's wardrobe seeing that he had paid for most of it.

Salena half shut her eyes but the Duke was sure she was watching him.

It was as if he was a ferocious animal who might attack her and she was too afraid not to keep her eyes on him in case she was taken by surprise.

He walked across the cabin to be as far from her as possible. Then he said quietly:

"You must tell me what you want to do. My yacht hove-to to rescue you, but I must now instruct my Captain where to go."

He spoke slowly, as if to a child, but her eyes were on his face and he had the feeling that she understood exactly what he was saying.

After a moment he asked:

"Do you wish to return to Monte Carlo?"

"No! No!"

There was no doubt of the terror in her voice.

"Then where shall we go?"

"A . . . way."

He could hardly hear the word.

"Very well then," the Duke said. "We will go away from Monte Carlo and as you apparently have no preference I will take you with me to Tangier where I have a villa. It will take us a few days to get there and perhaps by then you will be able to tell me a little more about yourself."

Salena did not reply and he walked towards the door.

"Try to sleep," he said. "Everything will seem better in the morning."

She did not answer but she was watching him and as he went from the room he turned out the lights in the cabin with the exception of the one by the bed.

He was moving into his own cabin next door to take off his damp clothes when an idea struck him.

Once she recovered her senses this girl who had been so anxious to die might easily attempt to drown herself again.

In her present state of weakness it would not be difficult.

The Duke stepped backwards and very softly he shot home the bolt which was on the outside of all the doors on his yacht.

They had been fitted as a precaution against thieves and had a special mechanism which made them impossible to open by those who were not aware of it.

When they were in harbour, although there was always someone on watch, the Duke had learnt with his other yachts that it was easy for an experienced thief to climb aboard and help himself to anything that was available.

These bolts which he had invented himself made this almost impossible.

There were all sorts of new gadgets he had incorporated in his new yacht which had been manufactured to his own specifications.

He had enjoyed building the *Aphrodite* and he had been pleased at the appreciation of his friends when on reaching Marseilles they had first seen her.

He remembered now that he had another party coming from London who would arrive in Monte Carlo to-morrow. They would certainly think it extraordinary that he was not there to greet them.

He decided the only recompense he could make was to send a wireless message first thing in the morning telling them in his unavoidable absence to be his guests at the Hotel de Paris.

They were all people, he thought, who knew the ways of the world and it would not be long before they discovered the reason why he had left and why Imogen had not accompanied him.

"Let them gossip!" he exclaimed savagely.

It suddenly occurred to him that if they knew what was happening at this moment aboard the *Aphrodite* it would give them an even tastier tit-bit of scandal to chatter about.

The idea of his rescuing a half-naked, brutally beaten young woman from the sea would appeal to their imagination and undoubtedly keep them speculating until they discovered the identity of his unexpected passenger.

I am sure I have never seen her before, the Duke thought to himself.

If he had seen anything so young and so lovely in Monte Carlo he would have been bound to notice her.

Later when the Duke returned to bed he found it impossible not to keep going over in his mind the few clues that he had about the young woman sleeping in the next cabin.

She was obviously not poverty-stricken; he could tell that by the expensive night-gown she had been wearing. She wore a wedding-ring, but because she was so young she could not have been married very long.

She was beautiful, and yet, and perhaps because of it, some man had frightened her until she was terror-stricken by the whole male sex.

We certainly have one thing in common, the Duke told himself. *I am hating women at the moment, and she is hating men. Her conversation, if I can persuade her to speak, should certainly be informative.*

It was Dalton who gave the Duke his information the next day that his unknown passenger was awake.

"I took the young lady a cup of tea, Your Grace," Dalton said, "and asked her what she'd like for breakfast. But she seemed almost as frightened, Your Grace, as she were last night."

"Did she say anything to you?" the Duke enquired.

He was having his own breakfast in the Dining Saloon and finding after the drama of the night before that he was in fact surprisingly hungry.

"She said: 'Anything!' Your Grace. Just like that—'Anything,' and sort of shivered when she spoke. I suppose it must be the shock of falling in the water."

"Yes, I expect that is what it was," the Duke said casually. "Take the lady some breakfast, Dalton; then come back. I want to speak to you."

"Very good, Your Grace."

When Dalton returned the Duke was finishing his second cup of coffee, and as the Valet stood waiting by the table he said:

"We will have to use our ingenuity, Dalton, in finding the young lady something to wear."

"I've thought of that, Your Grace."

"You have?"

"Well, thinking how small the lady is, Your Grace, I realised it would be impossible, unless they was altered for her to wear anything belonging to Her Ladyship."

"Exactly," the Duke agreed, "that is what I thought myself!"

"But I remembers, Your Grace," Dalton went on, "the Captain's got a daughter aged fourteen and I knows that he bought her two dresses when we was in Marseilles, pretty and French they are, and just about the right size, I should say."

"That is very helpful of you, Dalton," the Duke approved. "Suggest to the young lady that when she is well enough to use them, she tries them on. Any other garments she may require you may give her from Lady Moreton's cabin."

"Thank you, Your Grace."

"And tell the Captain that of course I will reimburse him, and I am certain he can find something equally suitable for his daughter in Tangier or when we return to Marseilles."

"I'll tell the Captain, Your Grace."

The Duke also remembered to thank the Captain himself when he went up to the bridge.

"I was thinking, Your Grace," Captain Barnett said, "that we were fortunate in finding the young lady. I was moving away from the shore and another second or so and we'd not have seen her."

"She was obviously not meant to die, Captain," the Duke replied.

"Seems strange that she should want to," Captain Barnett remarked.

The Duke, remembering the weals on Salena's back, thought he knew of one good reason why she had no wish to cling to life, but he had no intention of imparting to the Captain or anyone else what he had seen.

When he went to the Saloon before luncheon he found to his surprise that Salena was there waiting for him.

He did not miss the fact that as he entered the room she started and made a movement as if she would run away.

But as he was standing in the doorway and there was no other way out, she seemed to shrink and become even smaller than she was already.

As if her legs would no longer carry her she sat down on the corner of one of the sofas.

"Good-morning, Salena," the Duke said. "I hope you are feeling better. May I say that is a very becoming gown you are wearing?"

It was in fact a very attractive dress for a teenage girl.

Of white, trimmed with broderie anglaise, it was very simple and not expensive, but it had a French style about it that was unmistakable.

"Th—thank you . . . for . . . all your . . . kindness," Salena said in a hesitating little voice, "b—but I . . . wanted to . . . die . . . it was . . . only . . . ."

She stopped and after a moment the Duke prompted:

"Only what?"

"As I can . . . swim . . . I found it . . . difficult to . . . make myself . . . sink."

Salena had learnt to swim first at Bath in the famous Roman Baths where she had gone with her mother one winter after Lady Cardenham had been ill with a touch of pneumonia.

Salena had been very young at the time and her father had laughed at the manner in which she had taken to the water: "Like a small tadpole!" he said.

After that she had always bathed with her cousins when she stayed in her grandfather's house in the country.

Lady Cardenham's father lived in a large mansion with a lake in the park.

His grandchildren, who with the exception of Salena were all boys, had during the summer raced each other across the lake, upset their canoes on purpose and practised life-saving in case they should ever be in a wreck at sea.

Salena had adored every moment of it, and although it had been impossible to swim these last two years when she had been at school, in France she had always managed in the precious summers to swim even when, as she grew older, her mother disapproved of what was called "mixed bathing."

When she had swum away from the Prince's Villa last night she had intended to swim on and on until she was too tired to go any further.

Then she would just drop like a stone to the bottom of the ocean.

That would be the end. No-one would ever find her again and there would be no accusations about the crime she had committed, nor would she have to face trial, imprisonment or perhaps death.

She could not bear to think of the Prince crying out that she had killed him as the blood seeped from the knife-wound in his stomach onto the bed.

She did not want to remember; she did not want to think of it; but she knew that her whole body was tense with fear.

Even to look at the Duke, because he was a man, made her feel a terror rising inside her as it had done when the Prince whipped her.

The Duke sat down in a chair some way from Salena.

"Last night," he said, "you told me your name—at least half of it—but I think now we should introduce ourselves formally. I am the Duke of Templecombe!"

There was a sudden look in Salena's eyes which told him she knew the name.

"You have heard of me?" he asked.

"Then . . . this is . . . the *Aphrodite?*"

"Yes, that is the name of my yacht."

"It is . . . very beautiful."

She was thinking how lovely it had looked and how excited she had been driving along the road with her father.

She had not known then, had not realised what was waiting for her, and she felt herself tremble again as she thought of the Prince.

The Duke was watching the expressions that changed and altered her face.

He had never known a woman who had such expressive eyes, or who seemed so small and pathetic.

He was perceptive enough to realise that she was tortured by her thoughts and he knew that if he was to gain her confidence he must not say anything to upset her.

"I hope you like my yacht," he said in a casual manner. "It is a new acquisition. I designed it myself, and I am very proud of it. It has a lot of features that no other vessel of its kind has ever had. When you are feeling better I will show them to you."

The terror seemed to slip away from Salena's eyes and after a moment she asked:

"W—we are not going back to . . . Monte Carlo?"

"You said you had no wish to go there," the Duke replied, "and so I am taking you with me to Tangier. I told you last night, but I expect you were too upset to understand."

"I—I thought you . . . said that . . . but I was afraid I had . . . misunderstood you."

"We are going to Tangier," the Duke affirmed. "I have a Villa there which as it happens I have not visited for some time. I hope you will find it as beautiful as the *Aphrodite.*"

"I . . . have no . . . money," Salena said.

"As you are my guest that is of no particular importance," the Duke answered. "If when we reach Tangier you wish to go anywhere else, I can always lend you any money you need."

He paused before he added quietly:

"Perhaps you would wish to get in touch with your family?"

"No! No!"

The cry he had heard before was on Salena's lips and once again she seemed to shake with fear.

She thought wildly to herself that her father would never forgive her for her behavior to the Prince and he must believe her dead.

She only hoped he would be able to keep the money which the Prince had already given him. Then she remembered that there could be no argument about that, as the Prince being dead could not claim it back.

Papa will be all right, she told herself, *but he must never know that I am alive.*

It suddenly struck her that it would be impossible to live if she had no money and nowhere to go.

Without meaning to she looked piteously at the Duke and clasped her hands together as if she was a child begging his assistance.

67

"I see you are still feeling upset," he said, "so suppose I ask no more questions and you just try to enjoy yourself? After all, it's a lovely day and we are alone in the Mediterranean and no-one knows we are here."

He thought he saw a light in her eyes and went on:

"I have often thought myself what fun it would be to disappear and start life again. It would be like beginning a new book about one's self."

He saw he was on the right track and he went on:

"If anyone is aware that you fell into the sea and is looking for you, he will be disappointed. And let me tell you that no-one in Monte Carlo has any idea where I have gone, so they are not likely to connect us with each other."

He smiled before he added:

"You are free, free of everything, even the things which are alarming you. Nobody knows where you are or what you have done!"

"C—can that . . . really be . . . true?" Salena asked.

"I am sure of it," the Duke replied.

"But . . . God . . . knows . . . !"

The words were spoken almost beneath her breath, but the Duke heard them.

"Yes, God knows," he answered, "but we have always been told He is merciful and very understanding, and so I assure you Salena, you need not be frightened of Him."

Even as he spoke he thought to himself it was a most extraordinary and unusual way for him to be talking.

But he knew as he saw the tension leave Salena and the calmer manner in which she looked at him that he had said the right thing.

Now what can this child possibly have done, he asked himself, *to make her afraid of the retribution of God as well as of man?*

CHAPTER FOUR

THE STEWARD CAME IN to announce that luncheon was ready, and the Duke saw Salena start as he entered the Saloon and stare at him wildly as if for a moment she had expected someone else.

Pretending not to notice he rose saying:

"As it is such a warm day I thought we would have our meal on deck."

He led the way and Salena followed him to where there were two large wicker chairs filled with soft cushions.

They had foot-rests, and because she realised it was expected of her she lowered herself carefully onto the cushions.

The Duke saw her wince and knew it was from the pain in her back. He was quite suite that by now it was extremely painful as the weals would have stiffened and scabs would be forming over the places that had bled.

When she was in the chair Salena looked at him almost piteously as if she was afraid of what would happen next.

He covered her with a warm rug, then the steward fitted what appeared to be a table top with iron supports into the sides of the chair.

She looked down at it wonderingly and as the Duke sat down in a similar chair beside her he said:

"This is an invention of my own. I thought it would be nice to be outside if I was alone or only had one person to eat with me."

He smiled as he added:

"You are in fact christening my idea; for this is the first time I have seen it in action."

"It is very . . . clever of . . . you," Salena said.

The steward placed another tray already laid with a white cloth, glasses and knives and forks on top of the improvised table.

Other stewards brought out a number of delicious dishes and it was, Salena thought, an original and comfortable way of eating.

There was an awning over their heads, the sea was very blue but calm, and there was only the soft throb of the engines and the cry of the seagulls.

It was very different, she thought, from the noisy luncheon parties which had taken place in the Villa with the Prince's guests talking either in French or Russian.

Their voices had seemed to grow louder as their crystal glasses were filled and re-filled with different wines.

"I am going to persuade you to have a small glass of champagne," the Duke said at her side. "I feel it will bring the colour back to your cheeks and help you to feel happy again."

Salena wanted to say that would be impossible, but she thought it would sound rude and so when the champagne was poured out she took a little sip.

The Duke however was looking out to sea.

"I think there are some porpoises over there," he said. "I hope they come nearer to the yacht. I always find their antics amusing to watch."

"Porpoises?" Salena exclaimed. "I have heard about them, but I have never seen one."

"They are quite frequently to be found in the Mediterranean," the Duke replied.

"One . . . of the . . . Nuns at the . . . Convent," she said in a hesitating little voice, "said that where she . . . came from in the South of Italy the peasants . . . believed that when a sailor was . . . d—drowned at . . . sea his soul became a . . . porpoise . . ."

Her voice died away and the Duke was sure that she was thinking that this was what might have happened to her soul if she had been drowned as she had intended.

Aloud he said:

"Many primitive people who live by the sea have that belief. In the Orkneys and Shetland Isles, for instance, the inhabitants think that the souls of fishermen become seals, that is why they will never kill one."

To himself he thought he had another clue to the puzzle of Salena. She had been at a Convent.

He felt as if he was an archaeologist discovering traces of a bygone civilisation or an ornithologist in pursuit of some unknown species of bird.

He had never in the whole of his life been alone with a woman who was not interested in him as a man, or was so afraid that she winced and shrank away from him when he approached her.

It was a new experience which interested him, and he found himself growing increasingly curious about Salena.

He told himself that sooner or later he would discover what had upset her and find out who she was.

Meanwhile he talked quietly of impersonal things while they ate. Then as he finished the last course he turned to say something else to Salena and saw that she had fallen asleep.

He realised it was a sleep of complete exhaustion and knew that what she had suffered yesterday would have taken its toll of a man, let alone a weak woman.

The steward approached and he put his finger to his lips to ensure silence. The man lifted the tray from in front of Salena and walked silently away with it.

Another steward removed the Duke's tray and offered him brandy which he refused. Then there was nothing to disturb Salena and the Duke looked at her at his leisure.

Her face was turned towards him and her cheek was buried against a soft blue cushion which accentuated her pallor and also the fairness of her hair.

With her eyes closed she looked very young and very vulnerable. Then as she stirred and moved her hand the Duke saw that she no longer wore a wedding-ring.

He had noticed it last night and there was no doubt that it had been on her finger.

He wondered if she had torn it off in disgust for what she had suffered and thrown it through the port-hole, or whether she hoped to deceive him by pretending that she was not married.

Then looking at her he told himself it would be impossible for her to deceive anyone.

There was something so obviously and transparently pure and good about her that it was unthinkable to believe that she was not as innocent as she appeared.

71

And yet, he asked himself, who was he to judge?

He had been deceived by women before, and however innocent Salena might seem it was obvious a man had beaten her, and doubtless it was the man who had paid for the expensive night-gown she wore.

It was an extraordinary situation, he thought, in which to find himself. It gave him a great deal of thought to decide how best he could allay Salena's fears and what he should do with her in the future.

She was like a wild animal, he thought, who had been trapped and ill-treated to the point where it was impossible for her to know who was a friend and who was foe.

He knew that somehow he must gain her trust before he could really help her.

She was sleeping so deeply that he knew for the moment at any rate her fears were forgotten.

He smiled as he thought that none of the people who were certainly gossiping about his precipitate departure from Monte Carlo would, in their wildest imaginings, guess what he was actually doing.

If Imogen, or any other woman on whom he had bestowed his favours in the past, was in Salena's place she would be flirting with him, demanding his attention and striving with every provocative wile to excite him.

He had the idea that if he showed even a semblance of interest in Salena it would terrify her even more than she was already.

Perhaps, he told himself mockingly, *I have been overrating my attractions in the past and this will prove a very salutary lesson to me.*

It was an hour later before Salena awoke with a little jerk.

She looked towards the duke and gave a gasp.

"I—I am sorry . . . I fell . . . asleep," she said. "It was . . . rude of me."

"But understandable that you should be tired," the Duke replied. "I expected you to stay in bed to-day."

"Your valet . . . suggested it," Salena answered, "but I—I wanted to get up."

The Duke guessed that she was afraid of staying alone with only her thoughts but aloud he said:

"On the *Aphrodite* you can do exactly what you wish to do."

She did not answer but looked out on the sunlit water and he thought one of the unusual things about her was that she was so unselfconscious.

Any other woman of his acquaintance, having been asleep in his presence, would now have been tidying her hair, fussing about her complexion, and even daringly, if one of the more sophisticated beauties, applying powder to repair the ravages of the wind and the sea-air.

But Salena just lay still with her hands in her lap and after a moment the Duke said:

"You have only told me your christian name. It is a little difficult to know how the servants should address you. Should they say Miss or Madam?"

He saw the fingers of her hand lying on the rug tremble, then she said:

"I—I . . . am not . . . married."

The Duke raised his eyebrows.

So that, he thought, was why she had thrown away her wedding-ring. But why had she needed it in the first place?

Surely she had not pretended to be some man's wife so that she could spend an illicit week-end or a holiday with him?

Such an idea was so alien to her appearance that he could not entertain it.

Aloud he said in an indifferent voice:

"Then I will tell the stewards that you are Miss Salena, unless you wish to tell me your surname?"

"I—I have . . . forgotten it."

Her eye-lashes flickered as she spoke and the Duke knew that this was not true.

It was so transparently false that he was quite sure that Salena not only found it difficult to lie, but the thought of it was wrong, if not a sin.

That would obviously be part of her Convent upbringing.

"Have you been to Tangier before?" he asked.

"No . . . never . . ."

"I find it very attractive and the climate is perfect at this time of the year."

There was silence, then suddenly in a frightened little voice Salena asked:

"It . . . it does not . . . belong to the . . . French?"

There was no doubt that this idea terrified her and he said soothingly:

"No, not at the moment, although the French are always wanting to occupy certain parts of Morocco."

"But not . . . Tangier?"

"No, and it is very unlikely they will be allowed by Germany or England to encroach further in Northern Africa."

He spoke to allay her fears, but his brain was puzzling out why the idea of the French should be so terrifying.

Then he thought that perhaps either the man who had beaten her was French, or else she had broken a French law which might involve the Police.

It seemed impossible that this child, for it was difficult to think of her otherwise, could do anything that would involve her with the French authorities, but undoubtedly the fear was there.

After a moment the Duke said:

"I do not want to sound conceited, but I have a certain amount of influence both in my own country and abroad, and I think I can assure you confidently that while you are with me you will be safe from anything or anybody who might perturb you."

He thought he saw some light of hope in her eyes. Then she shook her head.

"You must . . . not be . . . involved in any way . . . that might . . . harm your reputation."

The Duke looked at her in astonishment.

"My reputation?" he repeated.

"Pap . . ."

She bit back the word and said hastily as if she thought he would not have noticed:

"S—someone told me how . . . important you were."

So she has a father, the Duke thought to himself, and wondered if in fact it was her father who had beaten her. But if so, why the wedding-ring?

And what man, however bestial, would throw his own child into the sea having maltreated her as Salena had been?

"If I am as important as you say I am," he said aloud, "it gives me the power to help other people when they are in trouble, and that is why I wish to help you, Salena."

"You are . . . very kind . . . but it would have been . . . better if you had let me . . . d—die."

"Better for you or better for me?" the Duke asked lightly.

"I . . . th—think for both of us," Salena answered seriously.

"Well, as far as I am concerned, I am very glad that I rescued you," the Duke said, "and I cannot help thinking it was fate that the *Aphrodite* was passing by at just that particular moment."

He knew Salena was listening and went on:

"My Captain said that a few seconds more and you would have been out of our sight. So you see, Salena, it really was fate—or perhaps, as you might say, the hand of God."

"It is . . . very wicked to try to take one's own . . . l—life," Salena said in a hesitating little voice, "b—but it . . . seemed to me there was . . . nothing else I could . . . do."

"That is what *you* thought, but obviously your Guardian Angel had other ideas," the Duke said.

Salena gave a little sigh.

"I ought to be very . . . grateful, but I do not . . . know what to do now."

"That is quite easy," the Duke answered. "You just enjoy a voyage on the *Aphrodite*. I can assure you that a number of people would be quite eager to be in your place."

"I know that," Salena said quickly, "and I am ashamed of . . . forcing myself . . . upon you."

"I think it was I who forced you to accept my hospitality," the Duke replied, "in fact you were extremely reluctant to be my guest."

He thought there was a faint smile on her lips and he went on:

"I have always imagined, again conceitedly, that people are eager to accept my invitations. It is quite a change however literally to kidnap someone so that I can enjoy their company."

"You are . . . being very kind," Salena said, "and I know I ought to . . . try to amuse you . . . and make you . . . laugh . . . but that is something I can never . . . never do . . . again."

She spoke almost passionately as she thought of the Prince and how her father had told her to be nice to him. She had tried and the result was that he had wanted her in a way which made her feel physically sick to remember.

Her face was very expressive and the Duke rose from his chair to walk to the railing.

"I am looking for porpoises," he said. "Do not move. I will tell you when I see them."

He has been so kind to me, Salena thought to herself, *and he must . . . find me a dismal . . . boring companion.*

75

She remembered the envy in her father's voice after the Duke had spoken to him in the Casino and he had told her who he was.

He had appeared to be alone, but she was quite certain that there had been many lovely ladies glittering with jewels with him or willing to talk to him.

When Dalton had brought her a number of exquisite lace under-clothes such as *Madame* Yvette had provided for her at the Villa, she had looked at them in surprise.

"His Grace says you can borrow anything that you require," the valet explained hastily, "from one of his guests who has stayed behind in Monte Carlo."

"Will she not mind?" Salena had asked, knowing it was a relief to find that she had not to continue to be naked.

At the same time she felt it was somehow wrong to use such beautiful garments which belonged to another woman.

"Her Ladyship won't know, and if she does it isn't likely to trouble her," Dalton replied.

It was obvious to him that Lady Moreton had done something to make the Duke so angry that he had come aboard in a rage and left her behind in Monte Carlo.

The crew were not unnaturally speculating about what had happened.

They had all been betting that the Duke would soon announce his engagement to Her Ladyship and in fact the only person who had been skeptical about it was Dalton.

He had seen so many of the Duke's favourites come and go.

While undoubtedly Lady Moreton had lasted longer than the rest, there was something about her which made Dalton feel that she was not suitable for the master he admired wholeheartedly.

No-one knew better than Dalton that His Grace had never really been deeply and completely in love.

He had been infatuated by and at times even besotted with some alluring Socialite who had pursued him relentlessly and who had captured him with an enthusiastic air.

But somehow, even when the pursuer was certain of the prey, the Duke had always wriggled out of the trap at the last moment.

Certainly he had been extremely attached to Lady Moreton, and watching them together Dalton had at times thought that there would be a mistress at last in the Duke's magnificent houses.

But little things that Lady Moreton had said and done had made the valet think that she was too fond of herself to be whole-heartedly in love with the Duke, however fascinating he was to the majority of her sex.

Nevertheless, by the time they reached Monte Carlo Lady Moreton had been very sure of how their association would end.

She had once said to Dalton in an unguarded moment when speaking of Combe House:

"I shall change that."

He had known that she was referring to when she became the Duchess, and with difficulty he had prevented himself from replying:

"Never count your chickens, M'Lady, until they're hatched!"

I must have sensed this would happen, Dalton had told himself the previous night when the Duke came on board with a scowl on his face and the *Aphrodite* had sailed leaving Lady Moreton behind.

He was an inquisitive little man and he found it exasperating to know he would never learn exactly what had happened.

One thing however was quite certain; Lady Moreton would not become the Duchess of Templecombe, and as far as he was concerned that was a good thing.

He therefore pressed Imogen's most exotic and expensive garments on Salena.

He thought with regret that because she was so small and slight it would be impossible for her to wear any of the elaborate Ball-gowns or the extremely expensive day-dresses which were hanging in Lady Moreton's wardrobe.

Her shoes were too big too, and only by stuffing a little cotton-wool into the toes of her bed-room slippers was Salena able to wear them under the cotton dress which had been bought by the Captain for his daughter.

This unfortunately was a little too long, so that the slippers were hidden, and Dalton decided that when they reached Gibraltar he would ask the Duke if he could go ashore and find some things that would fit her.

He too was intrigued and wondered what had made her so terrified and why she had been floating so far out to sea.

That she had tried to drown herself of course had been repeated by the sailors in the boat and lost nothing in the telling.

She's too young to have suffered so much, Dalton thought savagely.

He tried to show her his sympathy by providing Salena with everything she wanted.

There was no sign of any porpoises, but a fresh wind sprang up and the Duke said to Salena:

"I think you should go below. After all you have been through it would be very easy to catch a chill, and although Dalton would doubtless enjoy nursing you, I would have no-one to talk to at mealtimes."

"But you must have . . . wanted to be . . . alone," Salena said.

"I wanted to be free of noisy parties and people gossiping about each other," the Duke replied. "As you come into neither of those categories, may I say I am delighted to have you with me."

It was a very mild compliment and he was afraid she might be frightened by it, but she did not appear to be listening to him.

Although he did not know it, she was thinking once again of the parties in the Villa and how strange and incomprehensible the conversations had been to her.

The Prince must have banked on nobody speaking of his wife, and that was, she thought, because *Madame* Versonne apparently had such a proprietary hold over him.

It suddenly struck her for the first time that *Madame* Versonne had been the Prince's mistress.

Although she had realised the Frenchwoman was very jealous of anyone else to whom he spoke and especially herself, she had never queried that her position was anything other than that of an ordinary guest.

His mistress!

It seemed horrifying that while having a mistress and a wife in Russia, the Prince had also wanted her and actually paid her father a large sum to possess her.

Salena wanted to cry out with the pain such thoughts aroused in her.

She loved her father; she had always loved him and it seemed incredible and degrading that he would stoop to selling her to obtain money.

Now she understood what he had meant when he kept saying: "If only there was time . . ." Time perhaps to find her a real husband, not a man who would just put on an act for her benefit.

Snatches of conversation, her father's insistence that he was a bad father and yet loved her, and the way everything had been done so quickly and secretly confronted her with the truth.

The knowledge that her father had connived with the Prince to deceive her, simply because they dare not tell her the truth was shaming.

The Duke had turned his back on the sea and was leaning against the railing facing her.

He had wondered why Salena had not replied to what he had said to her and now he saw the expression on her face.

It was as if she expressed her suffering without words, and he knew that whatever had happened had disgusted her to the point where she felt both degraded and humiliated.

Whatever I can say will only make it worse, he decided.

At the same time his curiosity deepened and he had to exert all his self-control not to question her, not almost to beg her to confide in him.

They went to the Saloon and Salena was looking so pale that the Duke suggested she should rest on her bed.

He thought she might protest, but she agreed and he rang for Dalton to fill her hot-water bottles.

Alone in the Saloon the Duke picked up a book that he had been looking forward to reading but found it almost impossible to concentrate on the pages.

All he could see was a flower-like face, filled with two huge eyes that expressed an agony of suffering in a manner he had never seen before.

What the devil can have happened? he asked himself and thought that Salena was more intriguing than a mystery he could find in any book.

He knew he would never rest until he had discovered the whole story of her adventures.

There was no sign of her before dinner and while the Duke changed into his evening-clothes, as he did whether he had company or whether he was alone, he looked forward to talking to her.

It was therefore something of a disappointment when Dalton came into the Saloon to say:

"The young lady is asleep, Your Grace, and I thought it would be a mistake to waken her."

"Of course it would, Dalton. The best thing that could happen is for her to sleep as long as possible."

"It's better than any tonic a physician could prescribe, Your Grace."

"Then let her sleep, Dalton. She will feel all the better for it in the morning."

"I'm sure of that, Your Grace."

The Duke therefore had a lonely dinner, and when it was over he walked about on deck until he too began to feel sleepy.

As he undressed and got into bed he told himself that he had enjoyed the day. It had in fact been quite different from any day he had ever spent.

Dalton was collecting his evening-clothes and he asked:

"There is no sound from Miss Salena. She has not woken?"

"I don't think she's moved, Your Grace. I peeped in a little while ago and she was sound asleep. I just slipped a hot-water bottle into her bed but didn't disturb her."

"Quite right, Dalton. I can always rely on you when anybody is unwell."

"It's easier to treat the body than the mind, Your Grace," Dalton replied.

This was indisputable, and the Duke got into bed determined to read. But he soon put aside his book and turned out the light to lie thinking about Salena.

He must have been asleep for an hour or more when something woke him.

He was suddenly alert, but could hear nothing but the sound of the engines. Then it came again.

It was undoubtedly a scream.

The Duke switched on the light by his bed and hearing Salena scream again and yet again he jumped out of bed and ran to the next door cabin.

As he opened the door he realised that Dalton had foolishly left her in darkness, but by the light streaming from his own cabin he saw her run towards him.

She was wearing one of Imogen Moreton's night-gowns and as it was too long she tripped. As he put out his arms to steady her she screamed again:

"They are . . . after . . . me! They are . . . going to . . . catch me! Save . . . me! Save . . . me!"

She held onto him frantically, her fingers clutching at the folds of his nightshirt and he held her against him.

"It is all right," he said gently, "you are dreaming. There is no-one to catch you. You are safe."

"They . . . are . . . there! I saw . . . them!"

She gave another little scream that seemed to be strangled in her throat and trembling violently she hid her face against the Duke's shoulder.

"You are quite safe here on the *Aphrodite,* Salena."

He felt the name of the yacht penetrated her senses. Then suddenly like a child who has reached the end of its tether she burst into tears.

She cried tempestuously, the sobs wracking the whole of her body, her face still hidden in the Duke's shoulder.

Realising she was past knowing where she was or what had happened to her, he picked her up in his arms.

For a moment he thought he would put her down on the bed, then he knew she was holding onto him convulsively as if he was a life-line from which she could not be separated.

Carrying her he turned from her cabin into his own.

It was very large, stretching across the whole stern of the ship with port-holes on either side of it. Against one wall was a comfortable sofa covered in velvet to match the head-board of the bed.

The Duke sat down holding Salena in his arms and across his knees almost as if she was a baby.

She went on crying against his shoulder and he could feel her tears as they soaked through the thin silk of his nightshirt onto his skin.

She was so slight and small that he felt in fact she was only a child who needed his protection and his voice was very gentle as he said:

"There is no need to cry. Just trust me to help you and no-one will hurt you while you are here with me."

"They . . . will . . . guillotine m—me."

The words were whispered through her sobs and the Duke thought incredulously that he must have misunderstood what she had said:

"I . . . k—killed him!" Salena went on, still in a low whisper. "I did not . . . mean to . . . but I picked up the . . . paper-knife when I was trying to get away from him and he . . . he fell on . . . it . . ."

As if the picture of what had happened came back to her she gave a little stifled scream.

"There was . . . blood all over the . . . bed . . . and he said I had k—killed him as he . . . d—died."

The last words were almost incoherent and now she was sobbing with an intensity that shook her whole body.

The Duke stroked her hair which fell over her shoulders and he realised that Imogen's night-gown which was very daring and revealing had left her arms bare and barely covered her breasts.

"Listen, Salena," he said. "I know whatever you did was an accident, and I promise that even if they discover where you are, which is unlikely, you will not be guillotined."

"B—but . . . I—k—killed . . . him."

"If it was the man who beat you, then he deserved it."

It seemed as if the positive note in the Duke's voice arrested her tears. Then she said:

"H—he . . . beat me . . . b—because I was . . . tr—trying to run . . . away."

"Why?" the Duke asked.

He was almost afraid to ask questions or do anything but try to console her. This was the revelation he wanted to hear and he was cautious lest he might frighten her into silence again.

There was a moment's pause. Then Salena answered the question:

"H—he had a . . . wife and . . . ch—children."

"But you thought you loved him?" the Duke asked.

She raised her face from his shoulder and looked at him incredulously.

In the light from his bed-side lamp the Duke could see the tears on her cheeks and standing on the ends of her long eye-lashes.

Despite everything she looked lovely, and yet at the same time utterly pathetic, a lost waif, driven almost to the point of madness by fear.

"He was . . . wicked . . . evil . . . old . . . and h—horrible!" she said, "but he paid . . . P—Papa for me . . . and there was . . . nothing . . . I could . . . do."

The tears flowed again but now she was crying more quietly and the Duke felt that in a way they were washing away some of the terror.

He was beginning to have a picture of what had happened, and although there were still a hundred questions he longed to ask he knew it would be unwise.

He just held her close against him.

It flashed through his mind that this was the first time in his life he had had a woman in his arms who did not think of him as a man, but just as an impersonal refuge against the terror that possessed her.

"You have been through so much," the Duke said quietly when he thought Salena's tears had abated. "What I suggest you do is go back to bed and try to sleep."

He felt her give a little shiver.

"I shall . . . dream . . . that they are trying to . . . c—catch me . . . I know they will be . . . looking for me."

"You cannot be sure of that," the Duke replied. "And anyway even if they are they will not find you. It was a million to one chance that I picked you up in the sea, and who could possibly suspect that happened?"

"They . . . will think I have . . . drowned?" Salena asked, as if she formulated the idea to herself.

"I am sure of it," the Duke answered.

"And you will . . . not let . . . anyone know I am . . . with you?"

"No-one shall know it."

She did not speak and after a moment he said tentatively:

"When you feel like telling me the whole story, I shall be in the position to make discreet enquiries. After all, you are a very small person and it would be very difficult for you really to kill a man. He may not be dead."

"H—he . . . said: 'You have . . . killed me. I am . . . dying!' He . . . shut his . . . eyes."

The words came jerkily from between Salena's lips.

"It must have been very frightening," the Duke said. "But trust me one day to find out the truth. I think you do trust me, Salena."

"It is . . . wrong for . . . you to be . . . involved," she whispered.

"I will not be," the Duke replied and hoped his confidence was justified.

He realised that Salena was exhausted by her tears and now that she was no longer crying she seemed to be on the point of collapse.

"I am going to take you to bed," he said, "and I think perhaps it would be a good idea if I rang for Dalton to bring you some warm milk."

"No . . . no!" Salena whispered and he felt her pressing herself against him. "I do not . . . want him to . . . see me . . . I just . . . want to be with . . . you."

He was well aware that she did not know what her words implied but was just clinging to him for safety.

With some agility without taking his arms from her he managed to rise to his feet.

"I am going to put you in your bed," he said, "and leave a light burning so that if you wake again it will not seem so dark or frightening. You know that I am only next door, and will hear if you call me."

He thought for a moment she was going to say that she could not bear to be alone. Then she said in a child-like voice:

"Will you . . . leave the door . . . open?"

"I will leave your door open and mine," the Duke answered, "and let me tell you I am a very light sleeper. I shall hear you even if you whisper."

He carried her into her cabin and set her down on the bed. He thought she trembled in the dark and hastily he reached out to switch on the light.

He saw her look round and said:

"You see, there is no-one here and actually nowhere anyone could hide. You are safe, Salena. Just keep saying to yourself: 'I am safe!' and remember, I am next door."

She put her head on the pillow and he pulled the blankets over her.

She looked up at him and he had an almost irresistible impulse to bend down and kiss her. Then he knew it would not only frighten her, but would destroy her confidence in him.

Instead he smiled.

"Go to sleep, Salena. Remember you have only to whisper and I will come to you."

"You are . . . quite . . . sure?"

She disengaged one of her hands from the sheet he had pulled right up to her chin and slipped it into his.

"You will . . . not go . . . away?" she asked a little incoherently.

"We are in the middle of the Mediterranean," he replied, "and it would be a very long swim before I could reach Spain!"

He smiled and added:

"Make no mistake about it, I shall be here in the morning."

He felt her fingers tighten for a moment on his, then as if she was too exhausted to even continue to hold onto him she relaxed and her eyes closed.

The Duke stood looking at her for a long moment. Then he turned very quietly and went from the cabin, leaving the door open.

As he got into bed he thought that never in his life had anything so strange happened to him.

He lay awake thinking over what Salena had revealed and trying to pull all the pieces into place.

He thought now that it was incredible that she could have swum so far, for he was sure she had not been on a yacht and she must therefore have come from one of the Villas outside Monte Carlo which bordered on the sea.

The *Aphrodite* had passed the great rock on which stood the Palace of Prince Charles, then there were the Villas below and above the road which went from Monte Carlo to Nice.

It was, the Duke reckoned, somewhere between Monte Carlo and Eze they had found Salena, and he tried to remember the names of some of the people who owned Villas along that stretch of the Coast.

He had been visiting Monte Carlo for some years, but he had nearly always slept aboard his yacht in the harbour.

Although he had driven along the road he was not as familiar with it as he might have been had he actually owned or stayed in one of the Villas.

The Marquess of Salisbury had built a huge Villa in the neighbour-hood but, the Duke remembered, it was not on sea-level.

It was impossible to imagine that Salena wearing only a night-gown could have climbed any distance down to the road, crossed it, then descended once again to the sea.

He was therefore certain that the Villa from which she came must have been on the sea-side of both the road and the railway.

That, he thought, reduced his research considerably. At the same time he was no wiser than he had been before.

She is beginning to confide in me, he told himself. *Sooner or later she will tell me everything—even her name.*

It seemed extraordinary that he should have held her so intimately in his arms, that he had actually seen her naked, that she had clung to him in desperation to save her from her dreams and her fears, but he still had no idea who she was.

There was no doubt she was a lady, and he thought there was some-thing very aristocratic in her small, perfect features, just as there was something exceedingly beautiful in every line of her body.

She is unique, the Duke said to himself, *and if I were not a practical man I should be inclined to believe that she was in fact a reincarnation of Aphrodite come back to earth with all the complications of love and treachery characteristic of Greek mythology.*

He knew he ought to go to sleep, but as he turned over on his pillow he found he was listening just in case Salena should call him.

He thought that no-one, least of all Imogen Moreton, would believe that a lovely woman had asked him to stay with her and that he had carried her back to bed and left her alone.

She is far too innocent to realise what she asked, the Duke told himself.

At the same time he remembered how he had wanted to kiss her.

He wondered if the man who had beaten her and betrayed her had kissed her passionately, and it made him feel angry to imagine such a thing.

If she had killed him it was exactly what he deserved.

"Blast the swine!" the Duke muttered. "If he is not dead already I would like the chance to kill him myself!"

CHAPTER FIVE

"*C*HECKMATE!"

It was a cry of triumph and Salena clapped her hands with delight as she exclaimed:

"I have won! I have won for the first time!"

The Duke looked at the chessboard with a puzzled expression on his face.

"I must have been asleep or thinking about something else," he said, "to let you get past my guard."

"I really won?" Salena asked. "You were not being . . . generous?"

"Certainly not!" the Duke replied. "I like showing my superiority by invariably being the winner."

"But not this time!"

"No, you have won well and truly," he agreed.

She laughed again with sheer delight and as she rose from the chess-table to walk to the window and look out into the garden he thought it was unbelievable what a change there was in her appearance.

As if she was thinking almost the same thing she said:

"It is so lovely here. Every time I look out at the flowers and the blue of the sea I think how lucky I am."

Then before the Duke could speak she said in a different tone:

"Do you realise we have been here nearly three weeks?"

The Duke found it hard to credit that so much time had passed since they arrived in the harbour.

He and Salena had been on deck to watch the *Aphrodite* steam in amongst the Moroccan dhows sailing lazily up and down and trailing their nets as similar boats had done for two thousand years.

Salena's eyes had been on the great amphitheatre of hills glittering in the sunshine and the minarets rising high above the Sultan's Palace.

The Duke however pointed to where some way from the town there were groves of orange and olive trees.

"My Villa is over there," he said, "and I think you will find it far more beautiful and certainly more comfortable than the Sultan's Palace."

In consequence Salena had expected something exceptional, perhaps on the same pattern as the Prince's Villa in Monte Carlo.

In fact she found what appeared to be a Palace in itself, built in the Moorish style with court-yards, cool verandahs and innumerable rooms occupying a great acreage of ground.

It was surrounded by a garden that was so breathtakingly lovely that she had no words in which to extol it.

The Duke explained that his father had spent the last years of his life in Tangier and had bought the Villa standing on the present site to extend and enlarge it.

The garden was already exceptional, but he had devoted a great deal of time to it and had made it one of the most beautiful places in the whole of Morocco.

The Duke had in fact not visited the Villa for two years, but he had no need to worry as to whether or not it was well looked after.

Soon after he inherited the title, the Curator at Combe, who was getting on in years, was told by his doctor that if he wished to live he must move to a warmer climate.

The Duke had therefore sent Mr. Warren and his wife out to Tangier with nothing more arduous to do than to keep the Villa ready in case at any time he wished to go there.

If he had not had Salena with him, he would in his usual fashion have taken the Warrens by surprise.

But because he wished there to be no difficulties or discomforts where she was concerned he had, in fact, cabled them when the ship reached Gibraltar.

One glance at the Villa was enough to tell him that it had been unnecessary to announce his arrival.

The walls had been newly painted, the rooms were aired and well looked after, and the garden was even more exotic than he remembered it.

He thought that after even a few days the beauty of her surroundings was sweeping away Salena's fears and she was beginning to change back to what he guessed she must been like before her terrible experience in Monte Carlo.

After she had told him so much the night she had cried in his arms, it was easy for him to extract from her almost without her being aware of it the rest of the story.

What she did not tell him was very obvious to the Duke.

He could understand that having no experience of men or indeed of the social world at Monte Carlo, she had found it at first bewildering then terrifying.

She was affected all the more since she had previously been so cloistered and sheltered.

Yet any girl of eighteen, even if more sophisticated, would have been disgusted and mentally upset by the treatment which had been meted out to her.

And the Duke realised that Salena's extraordinary endurance in swimming as far as she had was the direct result of being activated by a violent and unnatural emotion.

It was much the same he told himself as happened to a man who was angry. He was able to fight with a greater strength than was deemed possible simply because he was so emotionally aroused.

After such an experience some degree of mental and physical collapse was inevitable.

The Duke was wise enough to realise it would be a long time before Salena was completely healed and the horrors that had been inflicted upon her were forgotten.

Nothing could be more conducive to this than to be at the Villa with no-one but himself and the soft-footed Moroccan servants who under the tutorage of Mr. Warren were able to make themselves almost invisible.

It was like being alone on an enchanted island, the Duke thought, but what was romantic in theory could often prove in practice extremely boring.

He found however not only that boredom was impossible for him when he was with Salena, but that every day he grew more interested and more entranced by her.

She had described eventually more or less everything that had happened after her arrival in Monte Carlo with the warnings of the Nuns ringing in her ears.

She told him how she had expected to find the station itself looking strange and sinister.

Two of the things, however, she still kept secret—her own identity and that of the man who had deceived her into a false marriage.

It puzzled the Duke why she would not trust him completely, but he did not understand that Salena was in fact protecting her father.

She had taken herself to task the following morning after she had been rescued by the Duke, for having said so much and revealing a great deal that she had intended to keep hidden forever.

But she was certain it would be disloyal and extremely wrong if she revealed to the Duke that her father had been involved in doing anything so shameful as to sell her to the Prince.

They were acquaintances, if not friends, and she knew that the Duke could in fact do her father inestimable harm socially if he wished to.

He must never know who I am, Salena told herself.

Moreover to let him know that it was the Prince who had treated her so brutally might also involve her father.

Mama told me to look after Papa, she thought, *and he must never learn that I am . . . alive and never, never . . . be aware that it was the Duke who befriended me.*

She did not ask herself how she could disappear when the Duke was no longer willing to protect her.

He was beginning to assume a position of more and more importance in her life, so that it was hard for her to visualise even existing if he was not there.

Besides her fear of the Prince and of all men like him, there was also an anxiety about her future which she tried to hide away at the back of her mind.

She told herself that it should not spoil her present happiness or the joy of being in such a wonderful place.

Every night when she said her prayers she thanked God for saving her and for letting it be the Duke and the *Aphrodite* who had come to her rescue.

Yet the thought of other men could still be terrifying, and because of it she had no wish to wander through the Medina where she knew there were booths selling the fascinating Moroccan crafts she had read about in books.

She wanted to see things, but not people, and something very sensitive within her shrank for the moment from contact with anyone except the Duke.

He understood what she was feeling and was in fact extremely relieved that he did not have to trail, as another woman might have expected, through the narrow, airless streets.

He disliked being pestered to buy cheap jewellery, pottery, spices and carpets for which he had no use.

The last time he had come to the Villa he had brought with him a beautiful Socialite who had been one of Imogen's predecessors.

She had wanted everything she saw and while it amused him to pander to her greed he had no desire to repeat the performance.

Instead he took Salena driving away from the city into the fertile plains occupied by the Moorish tribes.

She was thrilled with her first sight of pomegranate trees, with the date-palms, walnuts, figs and olives and the colourful appearance of the people they passed on the road.

The Duke had pointed out to her the water-sellers, clad in bright red and carrying on their backs a goatskin on which the hair still hung, swollen with water.

The women veiled and anonymous in their *djellabas*, the men with red fez hats, baggy green pantaloons and yellow slippers, made her feel as if they were all part of a fairy-story.

The Duke who was extremely well-informed told her about the Berbers who were a magnificent age-old mysterious race who had lived in North Africa, especially amongst its mountains, since the dawn of time.

Salena listened attentively as he explained that a Berber was tall, courageous, often a brilliant linguist and a great agriculturist.

"It should interest you to know," he ended with a smile, "that St. Augustine, amongst other notable men, was a Berber."

It was something very new to the Duke to find that a woman wished to talk to him intellectually, and most unusual of all wanted him to impart knowledge that did not concern her personally.

He found it a revealing experience and an extremely fascinating one to talk while Salena listened to him, her eyes on his face, her mind absorbing everything he said.

Sometimes he tested her a day or so later to see if she had really listened and understood what he told her.

He invariably found that not only did she remember what he had said but had thought about it, adding her own ideas so that they could discuss together what she had learnt.

We have been here three weeks, the Duke repeated to himself.

He was sitting back in his chair and looking at Salena silhouetted against the sunshine outside.

If anyone had told him a few months ago that he would be alone with a woman for three weeks and they could pass so quickly that it might have been three days, he would not have believed it.

Even in his most ardent affairs, when he was not actually making love with the object of his affections, he found that time had seemed heavy on his hands and he had wanted to employ himself in other ways.

Here, surprisingly, every moment seemed a delight and indeed different from the moment before.

He had been with Salena all the time and had not left her even to go riding as he would have done had anyone else been with him.

He told himself it was because he knew she would be afraid in his absence.

From the moment he had begun to see the difference in her, he was determined she should not relapse into the state she had been in when he had first found her.

But he was honest enough to admit now that it was more than that.

He was concerned not only with Salena's health or her mental attitude to life but with his own feelings about her.

He shied away from admitting that he was in love.

But ever since the night when he had wanted to kiss her because she had been so pathetic, the desire not only to kiss her but to hold her in his arms and make love to her had been a constant and ever-increasing temptation.

Having been very spoilt where women were concerned, and having always been the hunted rather than the hunter, the Duke had never had to control his desires or deny his passions.

But with Salena he knew that one unwary word, one action that was not restrained, would shatter her faith and confidence in him and bring back the terror which was not far beneath the surface.

He therefore forced an iron control upon himself and a discipline that was something so new and so unusual that sometimes he laughed mockingly at his own efforts.

And yet he knew that to hurt Salena after she had been frightened so terribly by her father and the unknown man who had pretended to marry her would be an act of betrayal for which he would never be able to forgive himself.

I love her! he thought now. *I love her in a way that I have never loved a woman before.*

He was in fact surprised at his own capability of feeling so intensely and so deeply.

It was almost as if he said, as other lovers had said since the beginning of time: *This is different. I had not realised love could be like this.*

But it was in fact the truth. It was different!

Never before had the Duke wanted to protect a woman, to look after her; never had he been concerned not with his own feelings, but with hers.

Never had love seemed more spiritual than physical, and yet he knew that his need for Salena was like a fire burning inside himself, always growing in intensity.

She turned from the garden to come back towards the Duke.

The huge room in which they were sitting was very cool and decorated with the most exquisite mosaics.

There were rugs that were so precious that they should have been hung like tapestry on the walls and comfortable low sofas piled with colourful cushions.

It was a room made for relaxation besides containing some unique treasures which Salena had handled with awe and admiration.

"When it grows cooler," she said to the Duke, "could we climb down to the beach? It is so lovely by the sea."

There was a twisting, rather dangerous path by which they could descend the cliffs and the Duke would take his exercise by climbing down it with Salena, then walking for miles along the golden sands when the sun had lost its heat.

"I believe that the only reason why you want to look at the sea," he replied, "is because you are longing to swim in it."

"It would be lovely to swim with you," she answered.

"I have been thinking that I might build a swimming bath," the Duke said, "and in fact I have already discussed it with Mr. Warren."

"A swimming bath!" Salena exclaimed. "That would be wonderful! I have not swum in one since I was at Bath. There the water is naturally warm."

"The water is warm here from the heat of the sun," the Duke said. "In fact the difficulty will be to keep it cool."

"When could the bath be ready?" Salena asked.

He laughed.

"It will take time. Nothing is done quickly in Arab countries."

He saw the excitement fade from her face and knew that she would not be here to see it completed.

He did not speak and after a moment Salena said:

"I was . . . thinking last night that . . . soon you will want . . . to leave."

"Why should you think that?" the Duke enquired.

"Dalton was saying that he had never known you to stay here or at any other place for so long. He was not . . . complaining. He . . . likes being here."

"I am glad it pleases him," the Duke replied, "but what about you?"

"You know I love it, it is the most wonderful place I could imagine! It is like stepping into Paradise."

She glanced out of the window, then back at him.

"But I would be . . . happy anywhere in the world . . . if I was with . . . you."

She spoke quite spontaneously as a child might have done, and the Duke realised once again how difficult it was to gauge exactly what she felt about him as a man.

He supposed because she had been in a Convent for the last two years and had had no experience of men that she had no sense of coquetry.

It never seemed to strike her that she should try to attract him as a man.

There was too the natural reaction from being assaulted by a brute whose only thought of her had been one of lust, so that she shrank from anything which might involve her in considering herself as a woman.

Does she love me? the Duke asked himself, as he had asked the same question a thousand times every day and every night.

There was no mistaking the joy that Salena showed in his company.

He had learnt from the very first that it was impossible for her to hide her feelings and when he came into the room her face lit up as though there were a thousand candles inside her.

Then she would run towards him spontaneously and slip her hand into his.

She talked with him easily, unaffectedly and without a sign of self-consciousness.

He came into her bed-room to say good-night to her, and it never occurred to her that it was in any way reprehensible or even unconventional.

The Duke was quite convinced that it was because she turned to him for protection and he was now a symbol of the only thing which was stable in her life.

But it never crossed her mind for one moment that he might be a potential lover.

She came nearer to him and, as she so often did, sat down on the ground at his feet.

"There are so many things I would like to do with you," she said as if she was thinking aloud. "You said I was to wait until I was well enough, and I am well now, really well, I promise you."

"Then what would you like to do?" the Duke asked.

She raised her flower-like face to his and he thought she grew more lovely every day.

There was an ethereal look about her, and she had no awareness of how alluring and enticing she was.

In a way, the Duke thought, he could understand the man who had bought her from her father, desiring her to the point where he lost all control of himself.

Because she was near to him now he could feel his heart thumping against his breast and a throbbing at his temples.

It was with the greatest difficulty that he prevented himself from putting out his arms and lifting her close against him as she had been when she cried despairingly against his shoulder.

He was afraid that if he did so he would see the happy expression in her eyes turn to one of horror and she would run away from him like a hunted animal, perhaps to fling herself into the sea as she had done before.

"What do you want to do?" he asked again, controlling his voice.

She held up her ringless left hand to count on her fingers:

"One . . . I would like to swim with you," she said. "Two . . . I would like to ride as you promised we would. Three . . . I want to explore with you the mountains that lie beyond the plain and where you tell me I shall see a part of the real Morocco where the tourists never penetrate."

"That is quite a programme," the Duke said in an amused voice. "Anything else?"

Salena threw wide her arms.

"Dozens and dozens of things," she replied. "I will write them all down if you like. There are things I want you to tell me, to teach me; and the world is very big."

"By that remark I imagine you are insinuating that the *Aphrodite* is in the harbour waiting to carry us to other lands."

Salena drew in her breath.

"I know that is only an . . . impossible . . . dream," she said, "but sometimes before I go to sleep I pretend that we are . . . steaming away into the unknown to find an . . . ancient land that has never been . . . discovered before."

"There are not many of them," the Duke replied, "and perhaps we are already in a land which is less developed than any other."

"Why is that?" Salena enquired.

"One reason is that the desert plateaux are occupied by fierce tribes of bandits and murderers are rife," the Duke replied.

"Then we will not go there," Salena said quickly. "Supposing you were held captive or . . . murdered . . . I could not bear it!"

There was a throb in her voice which the Duke found very moving.

"I wonder if you would really mind . . ." he began to say.

Then before he could complete the sentence the curtain which covered one of the entrances to the room was swept aside and a native servant bowed someone in.

For a moment the Duke stared incredulously at the newcomer.

Too late he realised that he should have given instructions that he was not at home to visitors and had no intention of receiving any.

He had never imagined that any of his friends would know where he was and now it was too late.

It was Imogen who was moving towards him—Imogen with a smile on her beautiful face.

She was looking extremely elegant and sophisticated in a gown that cried "Paris," and a hat which must have astounded the Moroccans as they saw her driving to the Villa.

"Are you surprised to see me, Hugo?" she asked.

There was a note in her voice which told him she did not expect him to be surprised so much as delighted.

Slowly the Duke rose to his feet and as he did so Salena sprang to hers.

For a moment she looked at the elegant woman advancing towards them, then swiftly and silently she turned and ran out through another entrance.

Imogen Moreton looked after her with a question in her eyes.

"Who was that?" she enquired.

There was a sharp note in her voice which the Duke did not miss.

"Why are you here?" he parried.

"I guessed this was where you would come," Imogen answered.

She reached the Duke and threw back her head in her characteristic manner to look up at him.

"How could you have been so cruel, so unkind, as to leave me in such a way?" she asked softly. "It was so unlike you, Hugo, that I knew I had to come here to tell you so."

"Who brought you?" the Duke asked.

Imogen gave a low laugh.

"There is no need to be jealous, dearest. It was not the Grand Duke."

She gave him a glance from under her long eye-lashes and added:

"They told me in the Villa that you had gone into the garden to look for me and had not returned, so I guessed what had happened."

She made an expressive gesture with her hands.

"Surely, knowing all we have meant to each other for so long, you could not really be angry at something so trivial, so completely unimportant as a kiss?"

The Duke did not answer.

He was in fact wondering how he had ever thought Imogen so attractive.

There was, he decided, something so artificial, so insincere about her that it was astounding that he had not noticed it before.

Aloud he said:

"I am sorry you have come all this way to explain something which really does not need any explanation."

"What do you mean by that?"

"I mean," the Duke said slowly, "that we are both sophisticated people. I am very grateful, Imogen, for the happiness you gave me and for the delightful times we had together, but they are over."

He saw by the astonishment on her face that she had not imagined for a moment that their liaison was really at an end.

She was too conceited for one thing to think that any man would tire of her before she tired of him.

The Duke was certain she had convinced herself that he had gone away in a fit of jealousy and she had only to appear to make him realise that life was intolerable without her.

"You cannot mean that, Hugo!" she said in a shocked tone.

"We had much better be frank about these things," the Duke replied.

With an effort Imogen forced a coaxing note in her voice as she said:

"You are still angry with me, and that is very foolish of you because you know I love you, and there is no other man in my life."

She saw he was unconvinced and added quickly:

"No-one could take the Grand Duke seriously, and you cannot allow him to spoil the happiness that we have found this last year."

The Duke did not reply and after a moment she said:

"If I had a tiny flirtation with Boris it was only because you did not

97

appear to want me with you forever. You did not ask me, dearest Hugo, to be your wife.''

She moved a little closer to him expecting him to put his arms around her and her lips were ready for his.

The Duke turned abruptly away to go to a desk which stood on one wall of the room.

"I will give you a cheque, Imogen," he said, "to compensate you for any inconvenience I may have caused by my precipitate departure. You will also find your clothes and jewels waiting for you on the *Aphrodite*. You doubtless saw her when you came into the harbour."

"I not only saw your yacht, but I have already been aboard her," Imogen replied. "I could not believe that you meant to deprive me of the jewels you have given me and which I value because they expressed your love."

The Duke had sat down and opened a cheque-book.

As if she suddenly realised the softness of her voice and the blandishments she was using were having no effect, she stamped her foot.

"I do not want your money, Hugo, I want you! Stop pretending! You can send for my luggage, and we will be happy together as we have always been."

"I am not pretending," the Duke said harshly. "Nor am I inviting you to stay here as my guest."

"Hugo!" the word seemed to ring around the room.

"I am sorry if I am upsetting you," the Duke said still with his back to her, "but I meant it when I said that anything we have felt for each other in the past is now over and finished."

"I do not believe you!" Imogen cried. "You are merely behaving like this because you want me to go down on my knees and apologise for letting Boris kiss me. It meant nothing! Boris is Boris, and you were amusing yourself at the gambling-tables. Why should I not have a little fun?"

"I am not reproaching you," the Duke said wearily.

He rose from the desk holding the cheque in his hand and came towards her.

"Take this, Imogen," he said, "and let me once again thank you for the past, and do your best to forget me in the future."

"Forget you?" she screamed.

At the same time her hand went out and took the cheque from the Duke.

She looked at it and he knew that she intended to tear it up until she saw the very considerable sum inscribed on it.

"Do you really think you can live without me?" she asked in a different tone.

"I am as sure of that as I am sure that you can live without me," the Duke replied.

Imogen raised her eyes from the cheque to say:

"I always thought, Hugo, that eventually we would marry each other. We are so suited in every way."

"I would not be the right husband for you," the Duke said firmly.

Imogen sighed.

"I suppose you are not the marrying sort, although there will always be women in your life. What does that girl, for she looked little more than a child, mean to you?"

"She is my concern and not yours."

"I have seen her somewhere before," Imogen said, wrinkling her white brow with an effort at trying to remember.

"You have?" the Duke questioned.

He wanted to ask Imogen where she had seen Salena and if she knew her name.

Then he told himself he would not spy on someone he loved and certainly not involve Imogen of all people in Salena's secret.

"I am sure you have a carriage waiting for you," he said. "Or would you wish me to provide one?"

"Are you really sending me away, Hugo? I just cannot believe it!"

Her tone sounded incredulous. At the same time the Duke noticed cynically that she slipped his cheque into the little silk purse which hung by ribbons from her wrist.

"I think it would be uncomfortable for both of us to rake over the past and perhaps spoil the things we wish to remember," the Duke said. "I am sure in the year to come everything will sink into its right perspective and we can be friends."

"I have no wish to be friends with you, Hugo," Imogen retorted. "I love you and you said over and over again how much you love me."

The Duke did not answer, and as if she realised it was hopeless she said:

"Very well, but I cannot help feeling that you will be sorry, that you have dispensed with me quite unnecessarily. You were jealous, absurdly and quite ridiculously jealous!"

99

She paused and when he did not contradict her she went on:

"Because you will not admit that it was wrong and extremely un-chivalrous of you to leave Monte Carlo as you did, you are now cutting me out of your life."

It was an explanation, the Duke thought, she would give herself to put him in the wrong and avoid taking herself any of the blame for what had occurred.

"It may seem ridiculous to you, Imogen," he said, "but it is a fact that you have always been very courageous in facing the truth in the past."

This was not so, but he told himself that it would be a sop to her pride that he thought so.

"If you do not want me, Hugo," Imogen said tossing her head, "there are plenty of other men who do."

She half-turned away from him, then said:

"Shall we kiss each other good-bye for old times' sake?"

It was a last effort, the Duke knew, to arouse him as she had always been able to do before and re-capture him despite himself.

"I think it would be far more natural," he said with a note of amusement in his voice, "for me to escort you to your carriage and for us to part in a friendly fashion."

"Very well, if that is what you want."

Affronted and piqued, Imogen flounced across the room waiting only for the Duke to draw the curtain aside.

She did not speak again until after they had traversed the long corridors and reached the front door.

There were a number of servants in attendance, but before she stepped into the carriage which had a white linen awning to protect her from the sun she held out her gloved hand with an imperious gesture.

"Good-bye Hugo," she said. "If you regret your decision before I leave the harbour it need only be 'au revoir'."

The Duke took her hand, raised it perfunctorily to his lips, but did not reply.

He was aware that she was really pleading with him for another chance, but he knew as she drove away that he had no wish ever to see her again.

It was Salena who had shown him how false and superficial Imogen was and that the feelings he had had for her were not worthy to be called love.

As he walked slowly back to the Sitting-Room he thought that if he had changed Salena's life, she had certainly changed him.

He saw now how he had accepted false values, the spurious and second rate and, what was so reprehensible, had not realised he was doing so.

It was Salena's purity and innocence and her deep, ingrained faith in God which had pointed the way to a very different sense of values that the Duke had in fact not contemplated since he was very young.

Once, he supposed, he had been extremely idealistic and thought of himself as the champion of everything that was fine and noble.

He remembered when he was at Oxford thinking that when he inherited he would use his position to alter so many things in Imperialist Britain that needed reforming.

He had a small circle of friends and they had sat up at night after their studies were over re-planning the world.

They discussed the injustices of the law, the neglect, privation and starvation which still existed in Britain despite the fact it was the richest country in Europe.

They had been, the Duke thought, like Crusaders, dedicating themselves to a Holy War against not the Infidel, but everything that demanded the challenge of fresh minds.

They were prepared to fight for what was right, ready to challenge what was wrong.

Looking back he could see how easily he was diverted from the course he had set himself.

He had come into the Dukedom and there were so many people willing to show him how to be amused and entertained and to help him spend his huge fortune.

There were his race-horses, vast covert shoots at which the Prince was eager to be a guest, entertainments which seemed almost compulsory in London, and in the country innumerable problems that appertained to his estates.

Gradually he lost touch with his Oxford friends, or else like him they had taken the easy course of swimming with the social tide and not against it.

It was Salena, the Duke thought now, who had shown him the way back.

He wondered what she would think of Imogen and was afraid her unexpected appearance might have upset her.

She was not in the Sitting-Room and he went in search of her, being sure she would be in her bed-room. It was a large room next to his own because Salena was still afraid of her dreams.

She was sitting in the window and as the Duke entered she turned her face to him and he saw that he was right in thinking that Imogen had upset her.

"She has gone," he announced as if Salena had asked him the question, "and she will not come back."

He joined Salena on the window-seat as he spoke and sat down on the soft cushions which covered it.

Then as he looked at her expression he asked:

"What is worrying you?"

"I . . . did not . . . think there were . . . women in your life like . . . that."

It was an answer he had not expected, and because he had to think how to reply to it he said evasively:

"I am not certain I understand what you are implying."

"When I first . . . saw you in the . . . Casino . . ."

"You saw me in the Casino?" the Duke interrupted. "You never told me that."

"I saw you walking through the crowd alone," Salena said quickly, "but I supposed there would be lovely women covered in jewels . . . waiting for you."

"Why did you think that?"

"I do not . . . know. I just thought it. Then when you were alone on the yacht and were so kind to me . . . I imagined you were different from the . . . the men I have met who only . . . laugh, drink and . . . gossip about each other."

"I am different!" the Duke said firmly. "And Lady Moreton, for that is who has just called here, means nothing now in my life."

"She is . . . very beautiful," Salena said.

The Duke realised she was comparing herself with Imogen and that it was the first time she had ever been self-conscious, that she had ever thought of herself as competing in his eyes with another member of her sex.

It was then he thought that Imogen had brought a harsh wind of reality into their enchanted island and cursed himself for not having taken precautions against unwanted visitors.

Because he loved Salena and because he was afraid of the expression in her eyes he said:

"I am a man, Salena, and I think it would insult your intelligence if I told you there had not been women in my life since I grew up."

There was silence and the Duke hardly dared to look to see how Salena had taken this. Then she said in a lost little voice:

"I . . . I suppose I should have . . . known that! I know it is what other . . . men are like . . . even . . . P—"

She stopped.

She had been about to say: "even Papa" but instead, after a perceptible pause she went on:

"It is just that you . . . seemed so different. I had not . . . thought of you in . . . that way. It was very . . . stupid of me."

"Not stupid," the Duke said. "I think in these past few weeks, Salena, we have both discovered new things about each other and about ourselves."

He chose his words with care as he went on saying:

"If I never saw you again after to-day, I know that what you have meant to me would still remain and alter my life as I intend it to do."

He smiled as he went on:

"I feel in some way as if until you were with me I was just floundering about trying to make up my mind what course I should take, and finding it difficult to decide which would be the best one."

"You mean . . . a way of . . . living?" Salena asked.

"Exactly!" the Duke agreed. "Now after all our discussions—and we have talked of many serious things together, Salena—I intend to live in a very different manner from the way I have before."

As he spoke he was surprised at his own decision.

He had known that he wanted things to be different, as he wanted Salena herself, but he had not actually formulated his decision in words.

"There are a great many things to do in England," he said, "which I should have attended to a long time ago. When I return I shall look into them very closely and spend a great deal more time than I have done hitherto in the political world."

"I am sure that is . . . right for you," Salena said. "You are not only so ... important ... you are so ... clever ... you have such a ... brilliant mind."

The Duke smiled.

"I hope you are right. Not everybody shares your belief in me."

"They will," Salena said. "I am sure of that."

He wanted to tell her there and then that he needed her help and inspiration, but he felt as if the shadow of Imogen still stood between them. After a moment he said:

"I think it would be a good idea if to-night we discussed the things that we feel should be done and we can perhaps make a list of them."

"You mean things like the ... reformation of the Children's Employment Act?" Salena asked.

"Exactly!" the Duke replied.

"I learnt at the Convent how terribly badly paid the seamstresses are in France," Salena said reflectively. "The Mother Superior who used to lecture to us on these things, said that in England there were women who sew buttons on shirts and have to complete thousands a week even to make a few pence to save themselves from starvation."

"Those are the sort of things we must look into and see what can be done about them," the Duke said with a note of determination in his voice.

He looked out of the window.

"It is growing cooler," he said. "Shall we go into the garden?"

He rose to his feet and put his hand out towards Salena.

He thought that she hesitated for a second, before taking it eagerly as she would have done an hour or so ago.

Because he loved her, because he was unusually perceptive where she was concerned, he knew that since Imogene had intruded on them things had changed.

Salena was for the first time thinking of him as having the passions and desires of a man.

CHAPTER SIX

SALENA WALKED ACROSS THE SITTING-ROOM touching first one thing, then another.

The Duke watched her with a speculative look in his eyes.

He knew that two days ago she would have been sitting at his feet talking to him eagerly and unaffectedly like a child.

But since Imogen had come to the Villa he had known there was now a constriction in her attitude which had not been there before.

She still listened to him intently and he still saw her eyes light up whenever he came into the room; at the same time he was aware that she was tense as she had not been before Imogen's intrusion.

"You are very restless," he said aloud. "Perhaps it is time we left Tangier for 'pastures new'."

He had meant his words to startle her and he certainly succeeded.

She turned round, her eyes wide and questioning, then moved swiftly across the room to stand beside him.

"Do you . . . want to go . . . away?" she asked.

"I was thinking of you," he said. "You seem somehow bored, which you have never seemed to be before."

"Of course I am not bored!" she said passionately. "How could I be bored when I am with you? It is just . . ."

Her voice died away and after a moment the Duke asked:

"It is just—what?"

Salena sat down on the floor beside him. She did not look at him but was staring ahead as if she was choosing her words with care.

"It is just," she said in a low voice, "that I cannot help . . . feeling you might want to be with your . . . friends and are only staying . . . here to be . . . kind to me."

"In the past," the Duke replied, "I have often been accused of being selfish, and thinking about my own interests rather than those of other people."

He smiled as he went on:

"Will it reassure you to know that I am very happy here and that when I am prepared to move I shall say so without any reservation or, should I say, consideration for you or anyone else."

Salena raised her head to look at him.

"Is that . . . really true?" she questioned.

"I assure you that when possible I always speak the truth," the Duke replied loftily. "Lying involves one in so much unnecessary trouble."

"I am sure that is true," Salena agreed, "and I am happy, so very happy to be here. But the . . . time must come when you will . . . have to go . . . back."

He knew she was wondering what would become of her when that happened, and he replied:

"Let us leave that moment until it confronts us. I cannot imagine a more beautiful or more desirable place to be in at this time of the year than Morocco."

He saw that he had reassured her, at any rate for the moment.

As she smiled at him he saw the shadow had gone from her eyes and there was almost a radiance about her.

"Then if we are staying," Salena said, "may I please ride with you this afternoon or to-morrow morning?"

The Duke was just about to reply when a servant came into the room.

"What is it?" the Duke asked impatiently as the man bowed politely.

"There is a lady to see you, Master. She says it is of the utmost importance."

"A lady?" the Duke queried.

"The lady who called the day before yesterday. She seems very agitated."

The Duke frowned.

He had given instructions that whoever called he was not to be disturbed, and never again under any pretext was a visitor to be shown unannounced into the Sitting-Room.

He was well aware, however, that if Imogen wished to see him she would be so insistent that the servants would be over-powered by her.

He was certain too that if Imogen was so intent on talking to him she would not leave until she had done so.

Before he rose to his feet he put out his hand and laid it on Salena's shoulder.

"This will not take long," he said, "and I will order the horses so that we can ride to-day as soon as the sun has lost its strength."

"That will be wonderful!" she cried.

But he knew that as she watched him cross the room the shadow was back in her eyes.

As soon as she was alone Salena rose to her feet.

She felt perturbed and there was a pain in her breast that had not been there before.

Why had the beautiful Lady Moreton who had called to see the Duke the day before yesterday come again? What did she want with him? And why if she was so intent on seeing him had she not asked him to call on her?

There were questions she could not answer and she moved through the open window onto the verandah outside.

The garden was very lovely in the sunlight, but for the first time it failed to evoke a response in Salena.

She could only think of a beautiful face turned appealingly towards the Duke and knew that in contrast to the sophistication and *chic* of his visitor she felt drab and inconspicuous.

Because it was impossible to sit still she walked to the far end of the verandah to look out not at the sea but at the mountains rising blue and purple against the sky.

They were wonderfully impressive, but again it did nothing to erase the pain Salena was feeling or the agitation that seemed to increase within her every moment.

Suddenly she heard in the garden a sound. It was not loud, but it seemed like the cry of a small animal in pain.

She listened and wondered vaguely what it could be. Then it came again and again.

She located it in some flowering shrubs which grew in exotic profusion only a few yards from the verandah.

There must be an animal caught in a trap, she thought.

She looked about for a gardener to whom she could call for assistance but, seeing no sign of anyone, she ran down the steps of the verandah across the lawn towards the shrubs.

The animal was still crying. Then as she parted the branches with their heavy scented blossom she herself gave a shrill scream.

A black cloth was thrown over her head, covering her completely, before she was picked up in strong arms and carried away.

After the first scream Salena was stunned into silence, besides being stifled by the heaviness of the cloth which covered her.

She tried to struggle but it seemed as if she was encompassed about by innumerable iron bands. Only after a few seconds did she realise that they were the arms of the men who carried her.

With an effort, feeling as if it was almost impossible to breathe, she tried again to scream, but it was impossible.

She found too that she could not move her arms and her ankles were held by strong fingers that bit into her flesh.

She was carried some distance while she tried frantically to guess what had happened and also to keep breathing.

She felt as if she must faint or become unconscious not only because it was so difficult to breathe, but also because the grip of the arms holding her was extremely painful.

Then suddenly there was a chatter of voices in Arabic and she was put down on the ground, but before she could make an effort to move a rope was wound round her, keeping her hands to her sides while another rope tied her legs together.

She was picked up once again, and now surprisingly she found herself seated in what seemed to be a chair.

She was being lashed to it with more ropes; someone was giving orders; and as she rocked backwards and forwards she realised incredibly that she was on the back of a camel.

There was no mistaking the uncomfortable angle at which the howdah in which she was sitting moved as the camel rose to its feet.

A howdah was, she knew, a kind of sedan chair made of coloured wicker with a curtained awning above her head.

The camel walked forward at first slowly, then quicker, and she guessed from the sound that there were other camels moving beside her.

She could hardly believe that only a moment ago she was in the safety and security of the Villa with the Duke beside her, and because she was with him she was happy.

Now she was being carried away and she thought despairingly that he would never know where she had gone.

It made her feel panic-stricken and she tried again to scream, but the sound was lost in the folds of the black cloth through which she could not see and in the sound of the camels' hooves on stones and gravel.

They are taking me away! Save me! Save me! Salena cried out in her heart and knew there was no possibility of the Duke hearing such an ineffectual cry for help.

Then it struck her that she was being abducted for ransom.

She remembered one evening when they were having dinner that the Duke had been talking of Europeans who had attractive houses on the higher altitudes in the vicinity of Tangier.

"One of them, a rich man," he had said, "was kidnapped a year or so ago by Moorish Berbers."

"How frightening!" Salena had exclaimed. "Did he escape?"

"He was released when the brigands obtained some concessions from the Moorish Government."

"They did not hurt him?"

"No, apparently they treated him quite well, but because they got what they wanted it has made other residents nervous and feel obliged to worry over their own security."

"You are . . . safe?" Salena had asked breathlessly.

The Duke smiled to himself because her thoughts were for him and not, as any other guest might have re-acted, for herself.

"I assure you," he replied, "that Mr. Warren has not only chosen the servants who work here with great care, but when my yacht is in the harbour several of my crew are also in attendance on me."

Salena knew this was true.

The Duke's valet looked after him, and the delicious food they ate was a predominantly French cuisine due to the capable hands of the Chef on the yacht.

As he picked up his glass of wine the Duke thought there was still a slight look of worry in Salena's expressive eyes.

"You are not to perturb yourself about me or be afraid," he commanded. "I would not have told you the story had I thought it would make you anxious."

"I am not anxious about myself," Salena answered. "No-one would wish to kidnap me and expect a ransom. But . . . you are different."

Now incredibly it was she who had been kidnapped, not the Duke, and she thought how much she would resent his having to pay a large sum for her release.

Why . . . Oh why . . . do such terrible things . . . happen to me? she asked herself.

She wondered how long it would be before the Duke found that she was missing? Then her captors would demand ransom money.

He would be angry, she knew, not because of the price asked, whatever it might be, but because it would infuriate him to give in to brigands and robbers and provide them with an incentive to abduct other victims.

Suddenly she asked herself in a panic if perhaps he would decide to teach the brigands a lesson by refusing to accede to their demands.

Horrified by this idea, she struggled violently against the ropes that bound her arms to the sides of her body and to the howdah.

She was far too weak and the ropes were too thick and strong for the effort to make her feel anything but helpless and more breathless than she had before.

The camel which carried her was not moving as quickly as it had a few minutes before and she knew it was because they were climbing uphill.

They must be leaving the valley of the city, and Salena felt that if once they got amongst the thick trees which covered the lower part of the mountains it would be impossible for the Duke, even if he wished to, ever to find her again.

There was nothing she could do but pray, and her prayers seemed muddled into an appeal both to God and the Duke himself.

Save . . . me! Save . . . me!

She repeated and re-repeated the words over and over again in her mind, her whole being yearning towards him.

She thought that somehow, by some supernatural method she must reach him simply because she needed him so desperately.

I want you . . . I want . . . you . . .

She repeated the words to herself and remembered how he had held her in his arms as she cried against his shoulder in the yacht.

He had been so strong and there had been something so secure and reliable about him that it had swept away all fear and these last weeks had been golden days of sheer, undiluted happiness.

Suppose I . . . never know them . . . again?

She almost felt the question being asked out loud, and as she wanted to cry out at the agony of thinking she might have lost him for ever she knew that she loved him!

She loved him in a manner that she had never envisaged it possible to care for anyone.

It was not just the giving of her heart but of her whole and complete self.

She loved him, she realised, with every thought she had, with every breath she drew, and yet she had not been aware of it.

How stupid . . . how foolish I have been! she told herself.

She might have known it was love when she had found herself happy only when she was with him and it had been hard to go to bed because she must leave him and so many hours must pass before she would see him again.

She might have known it was love when she awoke with a feeling in the morning that something wonderful and perfect was going to happen.

But she had never analyzed to herself why she was looking forward so eagerly and excitedly to seeing the Duke.

I love him! I love him! she said now.

She knew now the pain in her breast when he had left her to go to the beautiful Lady Moreton had been jealousy.

Jealousy because she was afraid of losing him; jealousy too because this other woman was so much more lovely than she could ever hope to be.

Oh, God, let him love me a . . . little, she prayed, *just for a little while.*

She knew that if ever she had to leave him she would want to die.

She thought now of how much time she had wasted in not being aware of her love, of not showing him how much she cared, how much it meant to her to be beside him.

Then she told herself that it would have made no difference and what he felt for her was kindness . . . the kindness of a man who had befriended someone in trouble.

But he obviously had no other feelings for her.

For the first time she wondered how she could have stayed alone in the Villa with the Duke without thinking it wrong or at least shockingly unconventional.

It had seemed so unquestionably right that it was only now that she realised what interpretation the outside world might put upon it.

Perhaps, she thought in sudden horror, Lady Moreton had said scathing things about her after finding her in the Sitting-Room; perhaps she had repeated to her friends, and would certainly repeat to other people in England or Monte Carlo, that the Duke had not been alone.

They will assume that I am his mistress, Salena thought, remembering that was what the Prince had intended to make her.

Yet instead of being shocked or in the least horrified, it struck her that to be with the Duke and to be loved by him would be the most perfectly wonderful thing that could possibly happen to her.

What did it matter what names she was called or what the world said?

If he wanted her, even for a very short time, she would die happy knowing that she had tasted the fruits of Paradise and nothing else in life could ever be the same.

Love me . . . love me just a . . . little, she called to him.

She wished that she could have told him how much he meant to her and how, in the language of the country they were in, she was "at his feet."

That is where I am and where I want to be, she said.

Once again she cried out to him desperately to come to her so that she could tell him of her love.

The camel was traveling fast again and as she was rocked backwards and forwards in the howdah Salena wondered if she would feel sick with the movement.

She thought in fact she was more likely to be suffocated, for she was very hot and the dark cloth which had been pulled tightly round her seemed to press against her face almost as if it was a mask.

They seemed now to be moving almost silently and she was sure that now the camels were walking in sand.

The idea of being carried away to one of the desert plateaux was frightening because these were the places occupied by the fierce Berbers.

She remembered the Duke had described them with a laugh, quoting from some poem she did not recognise as:

"A fair and whited sepulchre full of dead men's bones."

The memory made Salena shiver.

Perhaps that was what would happen to her: her bones would be left in the sand and the sun would whiten them until no-one would ever be able to tell to whom they had once belonged.

By now they must have travelled for well over an hour, perhaps longer.

Suddenly when she felt almost mesmerized by the rocking motion of the howdah there was a word of command and the animal on which she was riding came to a standstill.

With grunts and groaning the camel went down on its front knees, then as Salena fell forward he lowered his back legs and the howdah righted itself again.

She felt hands undoing the ropes which tied her to the seat on which she had been sitting, before being picked up bodily by two men who carried her away from the grunting animal.

Now she knew for sure that they were in the desert, for there was no sound of footsteps and the men seemed to move smoothly, almost as if their bare feet slid deep into a stoneless surface.

They walked for a little distance. Then a man spoke to them and Salena had the idea because they lowered her a little in their arms that they bowed their heads at an entrance.

Her feet were now on the ground and the rope was being untwined from her body.

She drew in her breath and knew that now the moment had come when she would see her captors.

She was afraid of the faces she might see—evil, menacing and cruel. They would be the faces of men who were prepared to risk the death penalty to obtain the money they needed.

The ropes that had tied her ankles and her body fell to the ground, then the cloth that had covered her was lifted.

It was swept back from her head and for a moment it was impossible for Salena to see where she was, because her eyes were dazed by the darkness of the confining cloth and the place to which they had brought her seemed dim.

Then she realised she was in a tent, a large tent draped with rugs and furnished with low cushioned seats, Eastern fashion.

She was standing in the centre of it and because her hair had been pushed over her face by the cloth she put up her hands to sweep it back, aware as she did so how hot she was from being confined.

Only then did her sight seem to clear and she saw that at the far end of the tent, lounging on a low couch and watching her, was the Prince!

For a moment she thought she was dreaming. Slowly he raised himself to a sitting position.

As she stared at him incredulously, too astounded to utter a sound, he smiled and it was not a pleasant sight.

"You are . . . not dead!"

The words seemed to burst from her.

"No, I am not dead," he answered, "and I might have said the same words to you, if I had not learnt two days ago that you were alive and enjoying the society of a nobleman!"

There was something very unpleasant in the way he spoke, but Salena could think of nothing but the fact that he was there and she had not killed him as she had thought! Terrifyingly she was once again in his power.

Instinctively she looked for the two men who had carried her but they had vanished and she was alone with the Prince.

As if he knew what she was thinking he said:

"I made sure this time there should be no weapons by which you can attack me and no method by which you can escape."

"I did not . . . mean to . . . kill you," Salena said in a low voice, "but when I thought it had . . . happened and you were . . . dead, I tried to . . . drown myself."

"That is what I believed had occurred," the Prince replied. "A servant saw you running across the garden and when you did not return everybody assumed that you had drowned."

"I was . . . picked up by . . . a . . . yacht."

"So I have learnt. How very convenient that it was such a luxurious one and your rescuer was the noble and of course attractive Duke of Templecombe!"

"How did you know that?" Salena asked in surprise.

"My informant was a lovely lady to whom the Duke belongs."

Now Salena understood.

Lady Moreton had come to Tangier in the Prince's yacht. Having called on the Duke and seen Salena, she had told the Prince she was with him.

It was not difficult for him to guess how it had come about.

"Lady Moreton described you very accurately," the Prince said, "and

I knew that it was only right that I should claim what I had paid for and what belongs to me."

There was something in the way he spoke which made Salena acutely aware of the manner in which he threatened her, and she looked round once again for a means of escape.

"Before you bother to try the exit," the Prince said, "let me inform you that my servants have instructions to stop you leaving the tent and also to bring you back immediately should you escape and run away into the desert."

"I will not . . . stay here with . . . you," Salena cried.

"You have no choice," the Prince answered, "and besides I assure you we shall be quite comfortable. The Sultan has lent or rather hired me this very luxurious tent and the servants to man it and even provided me with a woman to wait on you."

"I will not . . . stay!" Salena repeated. "You . . . deceived me with a fake marriage and I owe you nothing . . . not even . . . gratitude!"

"I bought and paid for you," the Prince answered, "and I do not allow myself to be tricked, least of all by a woman who is as attractive as you."

His eyes flickered over her and once again she felt as if he was undressing her and she was standing naked before him.

Because she felt despairingly he was speaking the truth when he said there was no way of escape she moved a little towards him, then flung herself down on her knees.

"Please let me . . . go," she pleaded. "You must realise that I hate you and have no wish to be your . . . mistress. There must be many . . . women who would be . . . grateful for what you can . . . give them and who would . . . love you in return."

The Prince smiled again and it made his face seem even more evil than before.

"I like to see you on your knees, Salena," he said, "and that is where you should be after the manner in which you treated me. You have not enquired yet after my health."

"I told you that I did not . . . mean to hurt you—certainly not to . . . kill you. It . . . it just . . . happened."

"Most unfortunately," the Prince said. "But there are skilled doctors in Monte Carlo who patched me up so that I am still capable of making you mine, as I intend to do."

115

"No!"

Salena rose again to her feet.

There had been something so menacing in the way the Prince spoke that it was no longer possible for her to think clearly. She ran across the tent in the direction from which she knew she had entered it.

She pulled aside the curtain which covered the opening.

Outside were standing two turbaned servants wearing huge loose white pantaloons and red sleeveless boleros.

They were tall, dark-skinned men with clear-cut features which told her they were Berbers, and she thought there was something ferocious and threatening in the manner in which they regarded her.

With a sound that was almost a cry she let the curtain fall and as she did so she heard the Prince laugh.

"You see, my little dove, there is no escape," he said, "so let us enjoy ourselves. What can be more conducive to romance than the vast emptiness of the desert and a man who will teach you about love?"

"What you are offering me is not love," Salena said passionately. "It is wrong and wicked. Let me go and I promise that somehow I will pay you back the money you have given my father."

She saw by the Prince's expression that he was only amused by her pleas, and her voice strengthened as she said:

"If you keep me here, then I swear I will try to kill you."

"With what?" the Prince asked.

He made a gesture with his hands that indicated the room empty of everything but the soft-cushioned seats, the low brass coffee-table and the beautiful rugs which covered the floor.

Salena clenched her hands together knowing he was mocking her, knowing he enjoyed in some perverted way of his own the fact she was afraid and was trying to escape.

"You see, my little dove," the Prince said in the silky tones she had always disliked, "the cage is well contrived. Now, as I know you must be hot and perhaps tired after your journey, I will allow you to bathe and change. Then we will talk again. I have a great deal to say to you."

He clapped his hands and from the other side of the tent behind where he was sitting the curtain was raised and Salena saw a native woman.

Because to escape from the Prince's presence even for a few mo-

116

ments was in itself a relief she walked towards the woman, but before she reached her the Prince said with an amused note in his voice:

"Just in case you should contemplate trying to bribe her she is a deaf-mute. Very useful, the Sultan assures me, in certain circumstances."

"A deaf-mute!"

Salena repeated the words to herself and felt as if they made the prison to which she had been brought more frightening and more unpleasant than it was already.

Because there was nothing else she could do she passed through the curtain which the woman held open for her.

She found herself in what appeared to be a small tent which was attached to the huge one in which the Prince was sitting.

It was, she was sure, the type of tent used by the Sultan and important Arab leaders when they travelled with a huge caravan about the country. It would be carried on the backs of animals and erected in an oasis or anywhere they wished to stay.

The larger the tent and the more luxurious from the Moroccan point of view its furnishings, the more impressive was its occupant.

The tent in which she found herself had the floor covered with exquisitely woven carpets and there was a couch piled with silk cushions and what to Salena seemed for the moment a joy she had not expected, a tin bath filled with jasmine-scented water.

She was so hot from being covered and bound and rocked about on the camel's back that she allowed the deaf and dumb women to undress her, noting that she was obviously experienced at her job.

In the cool water Salena tried to think desperately of how she could escape.

She was sure that the Prince would have a number of servants with him, either of his own or borrowed from the Sultan, and he would not be speaking idly when he said they had been told not to let her get away.

Besides, having been unable to see the way they had travelled, she had no idea in which direction Tangier lay, or indeed if there was anywhere she could hide if she could escape from the tent itself.

I have to plan! I have to find some way! she thought.

Once again her mind went to the Duke and she was praying that he would come to her. But how he could possibly do so she had no idea.

117

The woman brought her a towel on which to dry herself, but when she looked for her clothes she could not see them.

In sign language she told the woman what she wanted, in answer the woman picked up from the couch what had appeared to Salena to be a number of gauze scarves.

As she looked at them she saw in horror that it was in fact a native costume.

For a moment she could hardly credit that this was what the Prince had intended.

Then she knew it would be just like him to provide her with something sensuous and exotic and deliberately prevent her from putting on her own clothes.

That indeed was what he had done, and although she tried to explain in every way she could that she wanted the gown in which she had arrived the native woman merely pointed with quiet obstinacy to the garment on the bed.

Salena told herself that she was faced with the alternative of going in to the Prince clad only in a towel or of putting on the dress he had provided.

Gritting her teeth and knowing there was no other course open, she allowed the native woman to drape her in the soft diaphanous veils, for they were little more, in which the Moslem women dressed in a Harem.

They veiled her body and yet there was something so seductive about the effect of the light and soft coloured *mansouriah* that she knew with a shudder it was what the Prince intended.

There were embroidered *babouches*—soft slippers—for her feet and two elaborate necklaces, ear-rings, bracelets and a head-band with hanging pearls.

When she was dressed the woman brought from a corner of the tent a mirror so that she could admire herself, but all Salena could see was her eyes, dark with fright, and her mouth which was trembling.

"What can I do?" she asked her reflection. "What can I do?"

There was no reply.

With a courage she was far from feeling and an agony of fear that seemed to run through her from her head to her toes she passed through the curtain which the woman held to one side for her and into the tent where she knew the Prince was waiting.

He was reclining on the couch on which she had first seen him, dressed in Moroccan fashion in a *serwal*—trousers very loose around his hips and with tapering legs that hugged his calves.

He wore an open-ended shirt which made him look as old and heavy as he had seemed in Monte Carlo.

In front of him was a low table covered with sweetmeats with which Moroccans invariably began or ended a meal.

She saw that he was sipping wine which she knew was against the Moslem religion and thought contemptuously that he made his own rules and would certainly pay no attention to the beliefs of his friend the Sultan.

"Come along, my pretty dove," the Prince said to Salena. "I have been waiting for you with ever-growing impatience. Now let me see how you look in the very delectable clothes I have chosen for you."

"You had no right to take away my gown!" Salena replied.

She thought that instead of conveying her anger her voice appeared weak and helpless, and she felt already she was becoming the submissive woman the Prince wanted her to be.

"Let me give you a glass of wine," he said.

He made a gesture with his hand and a servant who was standing at his side filled Salena's glass as she sat down on a cushion facing the Prince with the table between them.

"Now I can admire you," the Prince said. "You are still the most beautiful and desirable women I have ever seen! How could you imagine for one moment that I would forget you?"

Salena did not answer.

Because she felt weak and limp she drank a little of the wine and accepted the food that was offered to her.

"This is what I have planned and what I have looked forward to," the Prince said.

"Do you imagine that the Duke will let me disappear in this mysterious way without making enquiries?" Salena asked.

She felt the wine giving her a little courage and she spoke loudly and positively because it was a contrast to the soft, insidious and caressing tone used by the Prince.

"I think you over-rate your attractions," the Prince replied. "As I have already told you he belongs to Imogen Moreton and in her arms he will soon forget the waif he fished out of the sea."

119

If he had struck her with a dagger he could not have hurt Salena more.

She was sure that Lady Moreton would have contrived all too willingly to keep the Duke amused while she was abducted from the Villa.

Now she would tell him not only who her father was but how much the Prince wanted her, and he need no longer feel it incumbent upon himself to rescue her.

For a moment the agonising thought of the Duke and Lady Moreton together made her oblivious to her own peril.

Then she remembered that she had hold the Duke very positively how much she hated the man who had tricked her into a fake marriage and how terrified she had been of him.

He knew I was speaking the . . . truth, she told herself. *He will know how . . . frightened I must be now.*

Once again her whole being was crying out to him to save her.

As if the Prince read in the expression on her face what she was thinking, he said.

"I shall not allow you to be unfaithful to me even in your thoughts. You belong to me, Salena, and the sooner you accept that the better! You are mine and after to-night there will be no escape. I doubt if even the Duke will be interested in you once your body belongs to me."

"I will . . . die first!" Salena said.

"Do I have to beat you into submission as I did before?" the Prince asked.

Now there was a cruel, sadistic look in his face which made Salena shrink back as if, although he had not moved, he put out his arms towards her.

He saw how afraid she was and laughed.

"You must learn to do as you are told, my fluttering bird," he said. "You must learn to be submissive. You must learn above all things to be a woman as God intended you to be."

His words seemed to sear her as if he was already wielding the whip she feared.

There was no point in arguing, no point in defying him, she told herself. All she had to do was to find some way to die before he did what was intended. There would be no other way of stopping him.

The servants brought them food. The *harera* was a soup of mutton, chicken's livers, chick peas and a dozen other ingredients. It was,

Salena knew, believed to restore strength and it frightened her to guess why the Prince had chosen it.

After this came *bstila* the zenith of Moroccan gastronomy, containing the meat of pigeons with eggs, spices, cinnamon, and one hundred and four layers of pastry.

There were other dishes, which the Prince and Salena ate in Eastern fashion, with their fingers, and she was well aware why he had so arranged it.

It was quite a long meal. However badly she had wounded him, Salena saw it had not inhibited the Prince's appetite.

He also drank a great deal of the wine and the more he drank the more his eyes seemed to flare with the passion she knew he felt for her.

It made her feel that he was a wild animal waiting to spring on her and devour her.

She ate only a few mouthfuls of each dish, forcing herself to swallow simply because she felt it might give her the strength to resist the Prince, although she had no idea how she could do so.

The meal was finished and the servants carried away not only the plates and glasses, but also the table at which they had eaten.

Now there was nothing between Salena and the Prince but a few feet of carpet.

"Come here!"

It was a command and she knew now that this was the moment when she could no longer fight him and instead must take her own life.

She had no idea how she could do so. Since she could swim, she had been unable to drown herself and she was certain it would be very hard, if not impossible, to prevent herself from breathing.

She felt the trap into which she had fallen was closing in, the walls of the tent were growing closer and the Prince's eyes seemed to grow larger.

He was hypnotising her, she thought wildly, and with an effort which seemed to jerk her whole body Salena looked away from him.

She wanted to speak, wanted once again to plead with him, but her lips were dry and the words would not come.

"I gave you an order," he said softly and insidiously. "Come here, Salena!"

It was impossible for her to move, she felt as if she was nailed to the couch on which she sat.

The Prince raised himself.

"Do I have to make you obey me?" he asked.

Now there was a note in his voice which told Salena that he was excited by her defiance.

She stood up. As she did so she saw that he held a whip in his hand and she screamed . . .

~

The Duke walked through the corridors which led to a small Sitting-Room by the front door where he had told the servants that anyone who called in the future was to be kept waiting.

He entered the room to find Imogen, as he had expected, looking extremely beautiful and bedecked in an alluring gown that he suspected had been chosen deliberately for his benefit.

"You wanted to see me?" he asked, and his tone was uncompromising.

"Yes, Hugo. I had to see you. It is most important."

"What is?" the Duke enquired.

"When I collected my jewels from the *Aphrodite* I found that some were missing."

"That is impossible!" the Duke replied. "They were in Dalton's keeping and you know that not only would he not touch anything himself, but would certainly prevent anyone else from doing so."

"Well, I cannot find the emerald ring you gave me, and you know, dearest Hugo, how much I treasured it."

"You had better look again."

"You gave it to me," Imogen went on it a reminiscent voice, "the night after we first made love together. Darling Hugo, how wonderful it was and how happy we both were!"

"I have already thanked you for the happiness you gave me," the Duke said coldly, "and I really think, Imogen, it is slightly embarrassing and quite unnecessary for us to discuss the intimate details of the past."

"But I want to do so," Imogen replied. "I want to remember everything you said to me and everything we did."

She gave a deep sigh.

"You taught me to love you so desperately, and there will never, I repeat, never be another man in my life."

The Duke smiled cynically.

"You can hardly expect me to believe it, Imogen. I have asked no questions, but I cannot believe that you have journeyed to Tangier alone in a steamer with a number of tourists."

"No. I came with Prince Serge Petrovsky," Imogen replied.

She saw the expression on the Duke's face and said quickly:

"There is nothing like that about it. He was ill. Some woman had stabbed him and even if he had wished to be my lover it would have been impossible."

The Duke was suddenly ill.

"You say some woman stabbed him?" he asked.

"Some girl with whom he was infatuated," Lady Moreton said quickly, as if she thought she had said too much. "But I am not here to talk about him, but about us."

"All the same I am interested," the Duke replied. "Who was this girl and what was her name?"

"I cannot remember," Lady Moreton answered evasively. "What I want to talk to you about, Hugo, is my emerald ring. Please—you must help me find it. Let us go to your yacht now and see how it could have been left behind."

"If it is there, Dalton will find it," the Duke answered, "but I cannot help the feeling, Imogen, even if it is lost, it is not the real reason for your coming to see me."

Imogen Moreton opened her blue eyes very wide.

"Why should you imagine . . ." she began. Then she changed what she had been about to say.

"Of course I wanted to see you," she continued. "I would have made any excuse if only we could be happy together as we were before you left Monte Carlo."

The Duke did not reply and she went on:

"Surely you are not still angry with me because Boris kissed me? Oh, my dearest Hugo, you must grow up and realise that you and I are sophisticated people."

"I have no wish to discuss it, Imogen," the Duke said wearily. "Go back to your Prince and tell him . . ."

He was interrupted as the door opened and Mr. Warren came hurrying into the room.

"Forgive me, Your Grace," he said, "but I have something of the utmost urgency to convey to you."

The Duke looked at Imogen, but she sat down in a chair.

"I will wait," she said sweetly. "I am really in no hurry."

The Duke hesitated as if he would command her to go. Then he went from the room followed by Mr. Warren.

"What is it?" he asked.

"It is Miss Salena, Your Grace."

"What about her?"

"I am afraid, Your Grace, that she has been abducted!"

The Duke stared at the elderly man incredulously.

"One of the gardeners tells me he saw her being carried away by four men. They threw a cloth over her and carried her from the garden. He was too frightened to try to stop them, but came at once in search of me."

"How long ago did this happen?"

The Duke's voice was sharp.

"Perhaps ten minutes or a quarter-of-an-hour, Your Grace. I was not in my house but in the stables, and it took the man some time to find me."

The Duke did not speak and after a moment Mr. Warren said:

"I am afraid it may be a question of a ransom, Your Grace."

"I think not, Mr. Warren."

The Duke stood for a moment thinking while Mr. Warren waited, then he said:

"Send a carriage to the yacht with all possible speed and bring back the Captain and every man who can ride. Tell Captain Barnett they are to bring rifles with them."

Mr. Warren looked surprised but he had been too long in the Duke's service to question any order he was given.

"Have every horse in the stables saddled," the Duke continued.

Without waiting for Mr. Warren's reply he turned and went back to the room where he had left Imogen.

She was smiling as he shut the door behind him and as he walked towards her she asked:

"What has happened? Why are you looking like that, Hugo?"

"I want the truth and I want it quickly!" he said. "You told Petrovsky about the girl who is staying here?"

"What if I did?" Imogen countered. "There is nothing wrong in that."

"He told you then that she was the girl who had stabbed him and who he thought had drowned."

The Duke snapped the words at her and he thought for a moment she was going to deny it, then with a shrug of her shoulders she said:

"What if he did? I do not concern myself with your flirtations any more than you need concern yourself with mine."

"Where has Petrovsky taken her?"

The Duke's question was almost like a pistol-shot.

"I have no idea what you are talking about," Imogen replied.

But he knew by the way her eyes flickered that she lied.

CHAPTER SEVEN

As the Prince came nearer and nearer Salena knew that he was stalking her as if she were an animal he was hunting down.

She felt as if she could no longer move or think, but only cringe away from him against the folds of the tent.

She wanted to die. She wanted to collapse into unconsciousness so that she would not feel the agony of what was inevitable.

Then as the Prince reached her she saw the triumph and excitement on his face and when he raised his arm she screamed again.

It was a very feeble scream, the cry of someone with no more strength to fight, who was utterly and completely defeated.

As she heard her voice, weak and ineffectual, there came suddenly the sound of other voices and as a command rang out the Prince turned his head, surprised by the interruption.

The folds of the curtain parted and the Duke strode into the tent followed by Captain Barnett and several English sailors with rifles in their hands.

For a moment neither Salena nor the Prince could move. He was still standing with his arm raised, a ludicrous expression of astonishment on his face.

But when Salena realised that the Duke really was there, she gave another cry—one of relief and inexpressible joy—as she ran towards him.

She flung herself against him, her arms went round his neck and her lips were on his cheek kissing him with an abandonment that was purely instinctive, and lacked all volition.

He put his arms round her and said quietly:

"It is all right, my darling. You are safe!"

Without looking at the Prince he lifted her in his arms and started to carry her from the tent.

As he passed Captain Barnett he said:

"This gentleman is yours, Captain."

They passed two sailors who were holding the turbaned servants at gun-point and Salena hid her face against the Duke's shoulder. She was trying to make herself realise that she need no longer be afraid.

She was safe, and he was holding her against his heart.

She felt him walking over sand and the air was cool on her cheeks, but she did not open her eyes until a minute or so later he came to a stand-still.

Then she looked up at him and saw waving over his head there were the branches of palm-trees.

"You are safe, my darling," the Duke said again. "He did not hurt you?"

It was a question, but Salena could only stammer incoherently.

"I . . . p—prayed . . . I prayed that you would . . . come and s—save me."

"I thought that was what you were doing," the Duke said in a deep voice.

He put her feet down on the ground but only so that he could clasp his other arm round her, and as she looked up at him wonderingly his lips came down on hers.

Even as she felt the touch of him she knew it was what she had longed for, what she had prayed for, and what she had known would be a bliss and a rapture beyond words.

She pressed herself against him feeling that she must become a part of him, so that she would be safe forever.

Then as his mouth held her captive she felt as though something wonderful and beautiful and quite unlike anything she had ever felt before rose within her, moving through her body, into her breasts and up into her throat.

It was so perfect, so rapturous, that she felt she must in fact have died and reached Heaven itself.

At first her lips were very soft, sweet and innocent, but as the Duke felt her quiver against him and knew that she responded to the insistence of his kiss he held her closer still.

Salena forgot everything she had felt and feared. It had all vanished, while in its place the Duke gave her everything that was beautiful and perfect.

It was as if music enveloped them and there was the fragrance of flowers, and they were no longer human but part of the Divine.

Only when at last the Duke raised his head to look down at Salena's face did he know that he had never seen a woman look so radiant or so happy before.

"I love . . . you!" she murmured. "I love . . . you!"

"That is what I have for a long time, wanted you to say," the Duke answered. "But my precious, I was desperately afraid that I would not be in time to save you from suffering at the hands of that unspeakable swine."

"He was . . . going to . . . beat me," Salena murmured.

Even as she spoke the words she felt they no longer had the power to terrify her. Because she was in the Duke's arms and he had kissed her in some magical way her fears had disappeared.

"Let us go home, my sweet," the Duke said.

His lips found hers and once again he kissed her. He felt her tremble, but it was not with fear.

He took one arm from her and turned her head round. She realised they were in an oasis standing under tall palm-trees, alone except for some camels a little way from them lying down in the shade.

She looked back the way they had come and saw the tent, large and black, and outside it were a number of horses held by sailors wearing a white uniform.

She looked up again at the Duke.

It was impossible for her to think of anyone but him, and he saw with relief he could not express that there was not the stricken terror in her eyes which he had feared.

Instead her eyes seemed to have the light of the sun in them, and as if it reminded him that the day was drawing to a close he glanced a little anxiously towards the West.

"We must hurry back," he said. "Are you strong enough, my darling, to ride? It would be quicker that way."

He smiled and before she could answer he added:

"I promised we would ride together in the cool of the evening."

She gave a little laugh and put her cheek against his shoulder.

He picked her up again and carried her over the soft sand because it would have filled her light embroidered slippers.

As they reached the horses she saw that on one of them there was a side-saddle.

She waited for the Duke to lift her onto it, but he seemed to delay. She looked at him questioningly and saw that his eyes were on the diaphanous gown she wore which revealed the curves of her breasts.

For the first time Salena thought of her appearance and felt shy.

The Duke gave an order to a sailor who had come from the tent, and the man turned and ran back.

"You look very lovely," the Duke said softly, "but I have no wish for anyone but myself to see your beauty."

Salena blushed as the sailor came hurrying back with something in his hands.

"Will this do, Your Grace?"

The Duke took from him what he held and Salena saw that it was an exquisitely embroidered cloth such as in the East was thrown over couches or when ancient and valuable hung on the walls.

The Duke put it round her shoulders, crossed it in front and tied the ends at the back of her waist.

"Now you look a little more respectable," he said with a smile, and picking her up in his arms sat her on the horse's back.

She thought she must look very strange in her diaphanous Moorish dress with a band of hanging pearls round her forehead and glittering bracelets on her wrists.

But nothing seemed to be of any importance except that she was with the Duke and he had kissed her.

Captain Barnett came from the tent followed by the sailors.

The Duke looked at him questioningly and the Captain said:

"His Highness will find it more comfortable, Your Grace, to lie on his face for the next few days!"

Salena had not listened or tried to understand what was being said. She had eyes only for the Duke, thinking how attractive he was and how much she loved him.

He came to me when I called, she thought. *He saved me. He loves me as I prayed he would.*

The Duke swung himself into the saddle and they started off.

Salena knew that at first he set a slow pace until when he realised how proficient a rider she was, they moved more quickly.

They soon left the desert behind since, as Salena saw, the Prince had camped on the edge of it. Now they were moving through the foothills of the mountains until she saw the sea in the distance and knew it was only a downhill ride to the Villa.

By the time they reached the outskirts of Tangier the sun had sunk and darkness was coming swiftly.

We are home! Salena thought.

But to her surprise the Duke did not go in the direction in which she knew the Villa lay but towards the town.

They were riding too fast for her to ask any questions until they were making their way through the narrow, dirty streets crowded with camels, donkeys and beggars towards the harbour.

It was then that Salena realised they were making for the harbour and the *Aphrodite.*

With a sudden lilt in her heart she thought that they would not only be leaving the Prince behind but also Lady Moreton and she would be alone with the Duke.

She knew she wanted more than anything else to be in his arms and for him to kiss her again.

Although it would be perfect wherever they were, it would be a wonder of wonders to know they were at sea and there could be no possibility of interruption.

The horses' hoofs clattered on the stone quay and they rode down the jetty to where the *Aphrodite* was gleaming white and elegant at the far end of it. In the lights from her portholes golden in welcome Salena saw that Mr. Warren was waiting for them at the gang-plank.

The Duke dismounted and lifted Salena from the saddle of her horse.

She felt herself thrill because he was touching her. Her eyes met his and almost reluctantly he put her down on the ground. She walked towards the gang-plank.

"Everything is on board, Your Grace," Mr. Warren said.

"Thank you, Warren," the Duke replied. Holding out his hand he added:

"Take care of everything until we come back."

"You may be sure of that, Your Grace."

With his arm round her the Duke guided Salena on deck and into the Saloon.

He shut the door behind him and without thinking of anything but her need for him she turned to throw herself against him, her lips raised like a child's to his.

He looked down at her for a long moment before he said:

"I have something to ask you, my precious."

Because she wanted him to kiss her she found it hard to listen to what he was saying.

"You are safe and you need not be afraid of ever seeing the Prince again," the Duke said, "but you will be safer still if you belong to me."

Now Salena looked at him questioningly. He smiled as he realised she did not understand and explained:

"I am asking you to marry me, my lovely one, now—at once!"

He thought the expression of wonder that illuminated her face was like the dawn creeping up the sky, before she made a little murmur and hid her face against him.

"I want ... more than ... anything else in the ... world to be your ... wife," she whispered, "but I ... I am not ... grand enough ... and I am afraid too ... that you would find me ... boring."

The Duke held her very close and she felt him kiss her hair.

Then he said:

"You are the most important person in the whole world to me, and I love you! I love you, my adorable one, as I have never loved anyone before."

Salena raised her head and he added:

"That is true, and I shall prove it when you are my wife."

"Are you ... certain ... really certain ..."

"Completely and absolutely certain!" the Duke interrupted. "And now, my darling, if you will wait here for just two or three minutes I will make all the arrangements."

He kissed her gently, then before she could find anything to say he left the Saloon shutting the door behind him.

Only when she was alone did Salena wonder what she looked like and if he could really think her lovely.

There was a mirror hanging on one wall of the Saloon and she moved quickly towards it to see her eyes glowing with happiness and her lips red from the Duke's kisses.

Her hair, thanks to the band which confined it, was not very untidy, but she pulled off the band because it reminded her of the Prince.

She pushed her hair into place, thinking that despite the place from which it came the embroidered silk shawl which framed her shoulders was very attractive.

The necklaces glittered as she removed them, feeling that the Duke would not wish to see her wearing jewellery, however tawdry, that had been given to her by another man.

She flung the necklaces down on one of the chairs, unclasped the bracelets from her wrists. Then as the engines hummed beneath her feet and the ship began to move she knew they were going out of the harbor.

She had escaped! The Duke had saved her at the very last minute and he had said that he loved her! The knowledge seemed to fill the whole world and everything else faded into insignificance.

He loved her!

She had not imagined such a thing was possible, and yet her wildest dreams and yearnings had come true.

The door opened and the Duke stood there, and behind him was the Captain. The Duke crossed the Saloon to Salena's side and took her hand in his.

"It is entirely legal, my darling," he said, "for the Captain of a ship to marry his passengers at sea."

Salena gave him a radiant smile.

She knew why he was explaining to her that it was legal and that this would be no fake marriage such as the one with which the Prince had tried to trick her.

She had no words to say, her fingers could only tighten on the Duke's.

He understood and for a moment as they looked into each other's eyes they were both very still.

Salena felt as if he was not only kissing her, but that she was a part of him and never again would she be alone or afraid.

~

The *Aphrodite* was still moving very slowly and Salena knew because the Duke had told her so that to-night she would barely make headway against the sea so that there would be as little movement as possible.

She turned her head against the Duke's shoulder and although it was dark in the cabin she knew he was awake.

"I . . . have been . . . asleep," she said a little drowsily.

"You must have been very tired, my precious," he said. "You went through so much yesterday, and perhaps I was selfish to make you even more so."

She moved a little closer to him and put her lips against his bare skin.

"It was wonderful!" she whispered. "I did not know that . . . love could be so . . . marvellous . . . so divine!"

"Did I make you happy?" the Duke asked.

"There are no words to . . . express how I felt," Salena answered. "I love you and I want to keep saying over and over again that I love and adore you."

There was an unaccustomed little note of passion in her voice which moved the Duke deeply. Then he said quietly:

"That is what I prayed you would feel, my precious little love."

"I prayed that you would . . . love me just a . . . little," Salena said, "but you are so . . . magnificent . . . so clever . . . so brave . . . so everything a man should be that I never thought my prayers would be heard."

"I do not love you a little," the Duke answered. "My love is boundless, as boundless as the sea and sky."

Salena drew in her breath.

"Will you . . . teach me so that I can . . . keep your . . . love?" she asked.

"I do not think you need be afraid of losing it," the Duke answered. "It is different, Salena, from anything I have ever known or felt before. When I first loved you, which was very soon after as a fugitive you came aboard the *Aphrodite*, I was afraid that you would always be fearful of men and of love."

"It was so foolish of me not to know that you were . . . different or to . . . realise that when I was . . . worshipping you at your feet it was . . . love."

She paused, then said in a hesitating little voice:

"It was . . . only when . . . L—Lady . . ."

The Duke put his fingers on her lips.

"Forget it," he said. "Forget everything that happened. Those people are of no importance to us and we are only concerned with the future."

Salena gave a little sigh and tried to move even closer to him as she said:

"You are . . . right. We will not talk of . . . them again, but there is . . . one thing I must know because I am . . . curious."

"What is that?" the Duke asked.

"How did you know where to find me when I was carried away on the camel? I was afraid that once I was in the mountains it would be impossible for you to have any idea where I had been taken."

"That might have happened," the Duke admitted, "if I had not forced the information from someone who knew where you had been carried."

For a moment there was a grim note in his voice as he remembered how he had half-throttled Imogen to make her tell him where the Prince had gone.

He had also been fortunate that among his servants employed at the Villa was a man who at one time had been in the Sultan's service.

Because he no longer felt any loyalty towards an unjust master he was prepared to guide the Duke and his party of sailors to where he knew the Sultan's tent was always erected on the first stop of any journey leaving Tangier.

Without such help, which seemed providential, the Duke knew that it would have been hard, if not impossible, to find Salena among the oases and date-palms.

Because her happiness in being with him had swept away the terror she had experienced in finding herself once again in the Prince's clutches, he was determined that the past should be a closed book and they should concern themselves only with their future.

Aloud he said:

"Warren had all our clothes packed and brought on board and, my darling, we will stop at various ports and buy you the things I have longed to give you, but which you were always so reluctant to accept."

"I did not . . . want you to be . . . extravagant and . . . spend money on me when I could never . . . repay my debts."

The Duke laughed softly, remembering how she had protested at his buying her anything but the bare necessities when they had stopped at Gibraltar.

In Tangier she had insisted on purchasing only the cheapest materials to be made up by native tailors.

He had understood that it was something to do with the Prince which made her afraid of being under an obligation and he had not pressed her, but because she was so beautiful he wanted to frame her loveliness as it deserved.

"Now I can not only give you clothes," he said aloud, "but jewels. We shall be able to buy some very magnificent pearls and every other jewel when we reach Constantinople."

"Is that where we are going?" Salena asked.

"It is known as 'The Pearl of the East'," the Duke replied, "and I want to show it another 'pearl'—The Pearl of the West—who is so precious and so beautiful that she really needs no adornment other than my kisses."

As he spoke he kissed Salena's forehead, then his lips moved over her little arched eye-brows.

It gave her a strange sensation which seemed to flood like sunlight from her heart into her throat.

Then as the Duke kissed her eyes, one by one, then the tip of her small nose, her lips were ready for his, but instead he kissed her chin, her cheeks and the corners of her mouth.

She felt the sunlight within her intensify until it was burning like the heat of the sun itself.

Her whole body seemed to quiver against his and she yearned for him in a way that she could not express.

Her need seemed to grow and grow until before he could kiss her again, before his lips reached hers she was kissing him.

She kissed him wildly and she knew as she felt his fiery response that this was what he had intended and it thrilled her because she could excite him.

"I want you," the Duke said passionately. "I want you, my beautiful, adorable little fugitive from love."

His voice seemed to come from a long way away and Salena felt as if everything was flooded with a celestial light.

It was a wonder which she knew was love but was so much greater, more glorious and more translucent than she had ever imagined it could be.

"I ... want you ... too," she tried to say. "I want ... you and ... need you. I am yours ... completely and ... absolutely."

But she was unable to speak because the Duke held her lips captive and his hands were touching her body.

Then it was impossible to think as there was only his lips, his hands, the beating of his heart, and him in the whole Universe.

Lucifer
and
the Angel

Author's Note

"One would think the English were ducks; they are for ever waddling in the waters," said Horace Walpole in 1750.

The origins of British Spas date back to Roman times, when the thermal waters at Bath were used for bathing.

In the early Eighteenth Century there were 228 Spas in England and Wales. Today there are few which still have a medical reputation for healing. The most important is Harrogate, which averages annually 120,000 treatments.

The usual crosses of the martyrdom at a Spa had to be borne at Harrogate according to reports published in 1822. When new arrivals met the famous sulphur-waters for the first time—hot, stinking, and fizzing—they surreptitiously hid in corners to spit it out.

Later, one of *Punch*'s anonymous rhymsters, 'Arry at 'Arrygate, reported:

> Reg'lar doctor shop 'Arrygate is; see their
>   photos all over the town;
> Mine is doing me dollops of good, I'm quite
>   peckish and just a bit brown.
> I'm making the most of my time, and laying in
>   all I can carry,
> So'ere ends the budget of brimstone and baths,
>   from your Sulphur soaked 'Arry.

I stayed in Harrogate some years ago when I visited Harewood House, the home of the Princess Royal who married the Earl of Harewood. Built in 1759, Harewood House is a treasure-store of works of art and is now open to the public.

CHAPTER ONE

1860

*A*NITA STOOD AGAINST THE GATE and looked across the field to the little wood where she so often sat when she wanted to be alone to think.

She had actually put her hand out towards the latch when, looking up, she saw the clouds which had been grey and heavy all day suddenly part and a brilliant shaft of sunlight shine down towards the earth.

Instantly there came to her mind the text she had heard yesterday from the pulpit.

It was a somewhat unusual one for the Reverend Adolphus Jameson to have chosen, and it had attracted Anita's attention when, anticipating one of his long, erudite, and incredibly boring discourses, she was already slipping away into her dream-world.

" *'How are thou fallen from Heaven, O Lucifer, son of the morning!'* " the Reverend Adolphus had boomed out.

Instantly Anita had a picture of the handsome Archangel falling and being deprived of *"everlasting bliss."*

His expulsion from Heaven had always fascinated her, and now staring at the sunlight she wondered what Lucifer had looked like before he had sinned.

She had a vision of his face, handsome, smiling, and yet with perhaps even in the celestial regions a somewhat raffish glint in his eyes, as if his fate was already decided for him before the final act which sent him hurtling down to perdition.

Then abruptly, breaking in on her reverie so that she started, a voice asked:

"Well, young woman, are you going to open the gate for me or continue daydreaming?"

She turned round and gave a gasp, for there behind her, seated on a magnificent black stallion, was Lucifer himself, just as she had always envisaged him.

She was looking at his face, which was handsome but undoubtedly cynical and disillusioned, his dark eyes mockingly accentuated by his raised eye-brows, and even the high silk hat set on the side of his dark head seemed appropriate in place of the halo of light which had once been his.

If she was bemused by the gentleman's appearance he was also surprised by hers.

He had thought, seeing a woman or a girl alone, standing beside the five-barred gate which led to the pasture on which he wished to ride, that presumably she came from a nearby farm.

But the small, heart-shaped face with its large blue eyes and the soft, very pale hair which curled round an oval forehead belonged to no milk-maid, and he thought too that the girl was very young, perhaps still in her teens.

Because she was staring at him in a bemused fashion, a faint smile curved the corners of his rather hard mouth and he asked:

"Of whom were you dreaming in such an absorbed fashion?"

Almost as if she was compelled to answer him, Anita replied:

"Of Lucifer!"

The gentleman laughed.

"And now you think you see the Prince of Darkness in person?"

Since this was the truth she was not surprised, but she had no reply and after a moment he said:

"If you knew your poets you would be aware that *The stars move still, time runs, the clock will strike, the devil will come.*'"

He recited the lines as if they were familiar, and as he finished Anita said softly:

"Christopher Marlowe."

"So you do know your poets!" the gentleman remarked. "Well, beware of Lucifer wherever you may find him! That is the best advice I can give you."

He glanced away from her as he spoke, and, as if she suddenly remembered why he was there, she undid the latch on the gate and at her touch it swung open.

"Thank you," the gentleman said, "and remember what I have told you."

He smiled as he spoke, as if he thought it unlikely that she would do so.

Then he cantered away, moving swiftly towards the end of the field, and she thought as she saw him go that he *"went into the darkness of the damned."*

Slowly, still watching him far in the distance, Anita shut the gate, knowing that she had now no wish to visit her secret wood. She would rather go home and think of the stranger she had met, who undoubtedly resembled Lucifer.

She longed to tell somebody of her strange encounter, but she knew only too well that her sisters, Sarah and Daphne, would laugh at her.

They always mocked her over-active imagination and the dreams which made her oblivious to everything that was going on round her.

But this dream was real! Anita told herself. *He was really there, Lucifer, Son of the Morning!*

It was strange that he looked exactly as she had envisaged him: the lines running from his classical nose to the corners of his mouth, the faint shadows underneath his eyes, his lips that she felt could speak bitter and cruel words although he had merely sounded cynical.

"When he falls, he falls like Lucifer, never to hope again."

She had learnt the words from Shakespeare's *Henry VIII* with her Governess, but she thought they were not appropriate for the Lucifer on the black stallion who was obviously not repentant of his fall and not without hope.

Then, remembering Christopher Marlowe, whom he had quoted, she thought of two lines that described him exactly.

It was Mephistopheles who said:

O by aspiring pride and insolence,
For which God threw him from the face of heaven.

141

Pride and insolence—that was what she felt her Lucifer, the one who had spoken to her, had.

Walking back to the Manor, she thought of a dozen things she wanted to say to him, a hundred questions she would have liked to ask.

Then she told herself that he would have thought her crazy. He was in fact only a gentleman, undoubtedly a guest of the Earl of Spearmont, whose parties were the talk of the village and of everyone in the County.

I shall never see him again, Anita thought as she reached the Manor, *but I shall always remember what he looked like.*

"Good-bye, Mama!"

"Have a lovely time, we will be thinking of you!"

"Please write as often as you can."

"Good-bye . . . Good-bye!"

The girls were still repeating the same words as the rather old-fashioned but comfortable carriage carrying their mother and the Squire's wife, Lady Benson, started down the drive.

They watched till it was out of sight, then went back into the shabby hall which somehow seemed empty after being filled only a moment earlier with loving farewells and last-minute instructions.

"Now that Mama has gone," Sarah said, "I want to speak to you, so come into the School-Room."

Daphne and Anita followed her into the room which, even now when they were all grown up, was still called the School-Room, although Mrs. Lavenham had done her best to make it a cosy Sitting-Room where they could keep their own particular belongings.

There was the easel which Daphne used for sketching and a miscellaneous collection of paints and brushes.

There was Sarah's sewing-basket, which was very like her mother's, and Anita's books which filled a whole bookcase and, despite innumerable protests, were piled untidily on the floor.

The sofas and chairs were covered in slightly faded but pretty chintz that matched the curtains.

There were flowers on the table and the sunshine coming through the window made it a very happy room.

Sarah stood on the hearth-rug and waited until Daphne and Anita had seated themselves before she said:

"I have been thinking about this for a long-time."

"About what?" Daphne asked. "And what do you want to speak to us about?"

"That is what I am trying to tell you," Sarah said impatiently.

She was the most spectacular of the three sisters, and her pink-and-white skin, her golden hair with red lights, and her hyacinth-blue eyes had proclaimed her a beauty before she had left the School-Room.

"You must have a Season in London and somehow you must be presented at Court," Mrs. Lavenham had said over and over again, and Sarah had looked forward to it and had been as sure as her family were that she would be a success.

Then disaster had come. Her father, the Honourable Harold Lavenham, had a fall out hunting.

His horse had rolled on him and he had been badly injured.

There had been two long years of pain before finally he died, and now when the year of mourning was over, the Doctors had discovered that the strain of it had affected his wife to the point where they suspected she had a patch on her lung.

"Six months in Switzerland could save your mother's life," the Doctors had said firmly.

They had all thought that such expense was impossible, until the Squire's wife, Lady Benson, who had always admired their mother, had offered not only to take her to Switzerland but to stay with her for at least three months of her time there.

She had been unwell too, but for a different reason, and it seemed not only an excellent arrangement from Mrs. Lavenham's point of view but also a God-send in that they would only have to find one fare and pay for one person in the Hotel where she was to stay for her treatment.

But they were aware that almost all the money that was available would be spent on their mother and there would be little left for those who stayed behind.

Both Daphne and Anita guessed that this was what Sarah meant to talk about now, and they looked at her a little apprehensively.

Sarah was very much the head of the household even when their mother was there.

She was a born organiser, and since her father's death she had undertaken to handle their small finances and prevent the over-spending he had never been able to avoid when he was alive.

"As you are both aware," Sarah began, "I thought that I might be obliged to accompany Mama to Switzerland and I was in fact dreading that I should have to do so."

"It might have been interesting to see a foreign country," Daphne remarked.

"Interesting!" Sarah exclaimed derisively. "The place where Mama has gone is full of elderly invalids, and in the brochure it says the Doctors insist there are no diversions or amusements that might tempt their patients from following diligently the strict routine of the cure."

"Oh, poor Mama!" Anita said sympathetically.

"Mama will not mind," Sarah replied. "She is determined to get well, and besides, she will have Lady Benson to gossip with. But there would have been no-one of my age."

The sharpness of her tone made her sisters look at her in surprise, and Sarah went on:

"Do you two realise that I am nearly twenty-one? And I have never been to a Ball except for the local ones, which do not count. I have never had my Season in London. I have never done anything but wait on Papa and Mama and look after you!"

Before Anita could speak, Daphne gave a little cry.

"Oh, Sarah, I never thought of that! How selfish we have been! But Papa was so ill, and when he died Mama was so unhappy."

"I know," Sarah said dully, "and I have done my best—I really have done my best."

"Of course you have, dearest," Anita agreed.

Daphne jumped out of her chair to put her arms round Sarah and say:

"You have been an absolute brick and we all know it!"

"I do not want your praise," Sarah said. "Sit down, Daphne, I want to tell you what we are going to do."

She paused as if she was feeling for words. Then she said:

"I have already written to Papa's sister, the Countess of Charmouth, asking her if she will have me to stay."

"To Aunt Elizabeth?" Daphne exclaimed. "But she has never paid any attention to us and never even came to the Funeral when Papa died.''

"I am aware of that,'' Sarah replied, "and we know that Papa's family did not approve of his marrying Mama, but there is no reason why they should disapprove of us.''

"The Countess has never invited us to anything,'' Daphne persisted.

"Never, but she will find it very hard to refuse what I have suggested in the letter I have written to her.''

"What have you suggested?'' Anita enquired.

"I have asked her if I can come and stay with her for the last two months of the Season. I explained that Mama has had to go to Switzerland and that as we are left alone here, we are appealing to her, as one of our few remaining relatives, to show some compassion to Papa's eldest daughter because, if he were alive, he would have been so grateful.''

Sarah made what she was saying sound very appealing, and Daphne gave a little laugh as she said:

"You are right, Sarah, I feel she cannot refuse to do what you ask.''

"That is what I am hoping,'' Sarah said, "and that your Godmother, Lady de Vere, will have you.''

Daphne gave a little gasp.

"My—Godmother? But she has not written to me or sent me a present since I was confirmed.''

"I know that,'' Sarah replied, "but she is very rich, and although she is getting old she entertains a lot in what Papa said was a magnificent house in Surrey.''

"I remember his telling us about it,'' Daphne said.

"I wrote her very much the same letter as I wrote to Aunt Elizabeth, and because I am sure she always had a tenderness for Papa, I feel she will agree to have you.''

Daphne clasped her hands together.

"I do hope so!''

"So do I,'' her sister replied.

Sarah's eyes now rested on Anita.

As she did so, she was thinking how very young she looked.

Anita was in fact just eighteen, but as she was so small and had a face like a flower and the look of a small cherub, she seemed little more than a child.

"What about me?" Anita asked as Sarah did not speak. "Am I to stay here alone with Deborah?"

"I have not forgotten you, Anita," Sarah said in a softer tone than she had used hitherto, "but we have run out of relations, except for one."

"Who is that?"

"Great-Aunt Matilda."

For a moment Anita looked puzzled, then she said:

"We have not heard from her for so long! Are you sure she is still alive?"

"I think so. She certainly was when Papa died, because she sent a wreath to the Funeral."

"I had no idea of that!" Daphne exclaimed. "But then, there were so many."

"If you remember, I made lists of who sent them and wrote and thanked everybody."

"Where does Great-Aunt Matilda live?" Anita asked.

"The wreath was sent from Harrogate," Sarah replied. "It came by post and was made of leaves, which I thought very sensible, for flowers would have died on the journey."

"Do you think Great-Aunt Matilda will want me?" Anita asked in a small voice.

"I daresay she will not want you any more than Aunt Elizabeth or Lady de Vere will want Daphne and me," Sarah answered, "but I intend that they shall take us. You do realise, girls, that this is our great chance and, as far as I am concerned, the last."

She saw that Anita at any rate had not understood, and she explained:

"To find ourselves husbands! Surely you are aware that if we stay here, living as we have done for the last three years, we shall all die old maids?"

As her voice seemed almost to ring out in the School-Room, both Daphne and Anita were aware that Sarah was speaking the truth.

In the little village of Fenchurch, where they lived, there were no young people of their own age, and after their father's death it appeared that they had been forgotten by the County families, of which there were not many.

It was Sarah who realised only too clearly that nobody wanted three girls without a man to escort them and, what was more, three girls who were outstandingly attractive.

The Squire, Sir Robert Benson, and his wife invited them frequently to luncheon and dinner, but Sir Robert was over sixty. His son, already married, was serving with his Regiment in India, and his daughter had chosen a life of seclusion as a Nun.

The most spectacular and talked-of house in the County belonged to the Earl of Spearmont, but he and his wife belonged to the smart set that circled round the Prince and Princess of Wales at Marlborough House and they said openly that they "never entertained the locals."

The people who lived near them had to be content with the gossip that was repeated by the servants, or to catch an occasional glimpse of beautiful women and handsome men as they rode or drove in smart carriages through the village.

Sarah was right.

In their way of life since their father's illness and death there had been no opportunities of meeting eligible bachelors, and where Sarah herself was concerned the position was growing desperate.

She was in fact so pretty that it was not surprising that she yearned for a wider and more appreciative audience than her mother and sisters and the Squire and his wife.

"What we have to decide now," she was saying, "is how much we can afford to spend on new clothes, which are very necessary unless we are to appear like creatures out of Noah's Ark."

"Clothes!" Daphne ejaculated almost ecstatically.

"I do not suppose I shall need anything at all smart in Harrogate," Anita said. "From what I remember Papa saying about Great-Aunt Matilda, she is given to 'good works,' and I am therefore not likely to meet a prospective husband with her, unless he is in Holy Orders!"

Sarah laughed. Anita had a funny way of saying things which they all found amusing.

"Do not worry, dearest," she said. "If I can marry someone of importance or at least wealthy, both you and Daphne can come and stay with me, and I will scour London and the countryside, or wherever I may be living, for every eligible bachelor."

"Of course, that is the solution!" Daphne exclaimed. "So you must have the beautiful clothes, Sarah, and Anita and I will manage somehow."

She sounded a little wistful because she had often imagined how exciting it would be to have gowns that had not been passed down to her after Sarah had grown out of them.

"What I am hoping," Sarah said, "is that your Godmother, who I believe is very wealthy, will not only have you to stay but will provide you with the type of clothes you will need as her guest."

"I can hardly ask her to do so!" Daphne exclaimed.

"No, of course, not," Sarah answered, "but I did point out in my letter how poor we are and how we had been very fortunate in being able to send Mama to Switzerland, and then only with the help of her friend Lady Benson."

Anita moved a little uncomfortably.

"It does sound, Sarah, as if we were begging."

"Of course it does!" Sarah said sharply. "And so we are! Make no mistake about it, we are beggars, and I am not ashamed to say so. After all, the Lavenham family owes us something."

"Owes us?" Daphne asked.

"But of course!" Sarah replied. "They behaved abominably when Papa married Mama, simply because Grandpapa, being an Earl, was puffed up with pride in his own consequence. He thought even his younger son should marry someone with a title or money, and Mama had neither. But she was exceedingly beautiful and Papa fell in love with her."

"The moment he saw her," Anita said dreamily, "it was like a story in a book. And Mama said that as soon as she looked at Papa she knew he was the man she had always seen in her dreams."

"It was certainly very idyllic," Sarah said, "but we each want to find the man of our dreams too, and we are certainly not going to meet him or any other sort of man here."

Anita wanted to reply that, strangely enough, she had met a man only that morning, and he was Lucifer.

Then she knew that Sarah would be annoyed at anything which interrupted her recital of her plans.

When Sarah was concentrating on something she expected everybody else to do the same, so Anita went on listening as Sarah told them what money was available for them to spend and what arrangements she had made for the house to be taken care of while they were away.

"You are very sure the relatives you have written to will have us?" Daphne asked at length in a low voice.

"They have to! They have to do what I have asked them to do," Sarah said, and now her voice was desperate. "Otherwise, I feel we are all doomed!"

~

The Duchess of Ollerton, sitting in the window of the large house she had rented in Prospect Gardens, felt that the sulphur-baths and the chalybeate waters she was drinking every morning were doing her some good.

She had come to Harrogate because, after listening to what her Doctor had to say on the subject of her health, her son had insisted that she should do so.

She found it impossible to protest that she had no wish to leave the comfort and beauty of her own house to travel North.

She had learnt since she became a widow that it was useless to oppose her son once he had made up his mind, especially where it concerned her.

He had certainly arranged everything to make her as comfortable as possible.

The house, which had been chosen by his Secretary and Comptroller, was large and extremely well furnished and belonged to an aristocrat who had gone abroad for the summer.

It contained practically everything that a Lady of Quality would need, but when the Dowager Duchess of Ollerton travelled, she moved, as someone had once said laughingly, "like a snail with her house on her back!"

She had therefore travelled from the South with her own linen, her own silver, and of course her own servants. Besides this, there were also what Her Grace was pleased to describe as "knick-knacks."

These alone filled a large number of trunks and required several carriages to transport them from the Duke's private train to the house in Prospect Gardens.

Among the many things without which the Duchess never travelled was a portrait of her son, Kerne, now the fifth Duke of Ollerton.

It stood on a large easel, which had been made especially for it, not

149

far from where the Duchess was sitting, and her eyes softened as she looked at the Duke's handsome face and thought how well the artist had portrayed his dark eyes and firm chin.

Almost as if her very thoughts of him had conjured him up, the door opened and he came into the room.

The Duchess held out her hands with a little cry.

"You have arrived, dearest! I was hoping it would be today, but Mr. Brigstock thought it was more likely to be tomorrow."

"As you see, it is today," the Duke said. "How are you, Mama?"

He reached her side as he spoke and bent down to kiss the softness of her cheek, holding one of her hands in both of his as he did so.

"I am better, I really am better," the Duchess said, "and looking forward to going home."

"You have not been happy here?"

There was a faint frown between the Duke's eyes as he spoke.

"It has been an interesting experience," the Duchess answered, "but quite frankly not one I wish to repeat. You know as well as I do that I hate to be away from Ollerton and from you."

"I too have missed you, Mama."

"It is so very sweet and kind of you to come and see me," the Duchess said.

The Duke released her hand to sit down in a chair opposite her.

"I will be honest, Mama, as I know you would wish me to be, and tell you that although I was eager to see you again, my journey North was not solely a filial duty."

"You had another reason?" the Duchess asked, smiling. "Let me guess—I feel it has something to do with the Earl of Harewood and his superlative horses."

The Duke laughed.

"You are always intuitive where I am concerned, Mama. Yes, it is true. When I leave you I will be staying at Harewood House before I go on to Doncaster for the races."

"Have you a horse running?" the Duchess enquired.

"Three, as it happens," the Duke replied, "and I think one of them will definitely win the best race."

The Duchess sighed.

"How I wish I could be there."

"Perhaps next year, Mama. But if you are well enough, perhaps you could manage one day at Ascot."

"It is something I would most enjoy," the Duchess smiled, "and I am sure Her Majesty would be gracious enough to have me to stay at Windsor."

"You know she would," the Duke replied, "but you must be well enough. All that standing in the Royal Presence might be too much for you."

"It might indeed," the Duchess agreed. "But tell me more about your visit to the Marquis of Doncaster. I have always found him a very charming man."

"So have I," the Duke said, "and that is why you will understand, Mama, that I am interested in meeting his daughter."

There was a moment's silence and the Duchess was very still. Then she said:

"Do you mean—can you be—thinking—?"

"Of marriage," the Duke said, finishing the sentence for her. "Yes, Mama. I have come to the conclusion that it is time I was married."

"Oh, Kerne, it is what I have prayed for!" the Duchess exclaimed. But is it Marmion who has made you decide so suddenly that it is something you should do?"

"It is Marmion," the Duke agreed, "but more directly the Queen."

"The Queen?"

"Her Majesty spoke to me last week."

"About Marmion?"

"That is right."

The Duchess made a little sound that might have been one of horror, but she did not interrupt.

"Her Majesty asked me to speak with her in her private Sitting-Room. I knew at once that what she had to say was serious."

"It was also likely to be only one subject," the Duchess said quickly.

"Exactly! She told me she had heard that Marmion and his wife were in a Box at Covent Garden the night the Prince of Wales was there and they were both behaving in what the Queen described as an 'outrageous manner.' "

"I presume Her Majesty meant that they had both had too much to drink," the Duchess said in a low voice.

151

"I heard from another source that they were disgracefully, revoltingly drunk!"

"Oh, Kerne, what can we do about it?"

"There is nothing we can do," the Duke replied, "except to make sure that Marmion does not inherit the Dukedom after me."

"And is that what Her Majesty said?"

"She pointed out to me," the Duke answered, "that the Duchess of Ollerton is traditionally a Lady of the Bedchamber."

"And of course Her Majesty could not countenance that vulgar creature whom your cousin has taken as a wife in that capacity," the Duchess added.

"That is exactly what Her Majesty implied," the Duke said, "and so, Mama, the time has come, regrettable though it may be, that I must be married."

"Of course, dearest, but must it be regrettable?"

The Duke waited a moment before he said:

"I have no wish to be married, Mama, as I have told you when we have discussed the subject many times before. I am entirely content as I am, but I am well aware that it is my duty to provide an heir to the Dukedom. I therefore need your help."

"My help?" the Duchess echoed in surprise.

The Duke smiled.

"With the exception of the Marquis's daughter who happens to be the right age—and the last time I visited Doncaster she was still in the School-Room—I am not in the habit of meeting young girls, and in none of the houses in which I stay do they feature among the guests."

"No, of course not!" the Duchess exclaimed. "I understand that."

"So, what I am asking you to do, Mama," the Duke went on, "is to make a short list of the girls you think are eligible, and I will look at them before deciding on the one I think most suitable."

The Duchess said nothing, and, looking at her, the Duke asked:

"What is wrong, Mama? I thought that you, of all people, after all you have said about my being married and producing a son, would be delighted that the moment has come when that is exactly what I mean to do."

"Of course I am delighted that you should be married, Kerne dear," the Duchess replied, "but I had hoped, perhaps foolishly, that you would fall in love."

The Duke's lips twisted wryly.

"That is what the servants would call 'a very different kettle of fish.' "

"But your way seems such a very cold-blooded manner in which to get married."

"What is the alternative? You have met most of the charmers—and I am not pretending there are not a number of them—who have engaged my heart for a short period, but none of them is eligible to become my wife."

The Duchess, who knew a great deal more about her son's love-affairs than he imagined, admitted to herself that this was true.

His *affaires de coeur*, though conducted very discreetly, were nevertheless common knowledge amongst the society in which he moved, and the Duchess had friends who were only too willing to tell her the latest gossip.

She was therefore aware that for the last six months the Duke had been constantly in the company of an acclaimed beauty whose husband was quite prepared to ride His Grace's horses, sail in his yacht, drink his wine, and turn a "blind eye" to his host's preoccupation with his wife.

This, the Duchess thought, was very civilized behaviour, an example which had been set by the Prince of Wales.

But there was no doubt that the Duke was correct in saying that at the house-parties at which he was either a guest or a host there was no likelihood of a young, unmarried girl being present.

As if he knew what his mother was thinking, he bent forward to say:

"Do not look so worried, Mama. When I am married I promise you I will behave with great propriety towards my wife. But she must be exactly the right person to take your place, although no-one could ever look as beautiful as you."

He spoke with such sincerity that the Duchess put out her hand to him as she said:

"Dearest Kerne, you have been a wonderful son to me, and I hope that your wife, whoever she may be, will appreciate you. At the same time, a marriage needs love, and that is what I would wish you to find."

As if embarrassed by the turn of the conversation, the Duke rose to his feet.

"Love is one thing and marriage is another, Mama. Let us concentrate on marriage. Find me the right sort of wife, one who must of course grace the Ollerton diamonds."

153

The Duchess smiled.

"That means, as the tiaras are higher and more magnificent than anyone else's, that she must be tall."

"Of course," the Duke agreed. "At least five-foot-nine or -ten, and because the sapphires always look their best on fair women, she should have hair the colour of ripe corn."

The Duchess said nothing, but her eyes twinkled a little as she remembered that the last three women with whom the Duke's name had been associated were all brunettes.

"Then, of course, there are the pearls," the Duke continued, following his own train of thought. "Five rows of them, Mama, need someone with, shall we say, a full figure, to show them off."

" 'Junoesque,' is the right word, dearest," the Duchess said. "It is a description I have always enjoyed myself, and you will remember that until I was afflicted by this terrible rheumatism, I managed to keep a very small waist."

"I am not likely to forget it," the Duke said. "Somebody was saying only the other evening that their idea of beauty was you blazing with diamonds and wearing a long train standing at the top of the staircase at Ollerton House."

"You are always very complimentary, dearest," the Duchess said, "and I love it! I know exactly what your wife should look like, but it will not be easy to find her."

The Duke walked across the room and back again.

"God knows, Mama," he said after a moment, "it is going to be difficult not only to find the type of wife that I require, but also to endure her once I have done so. What does one talk about to an unfledged girl?"

"There is no woman born who is not interested in love," the Duchess said softly.

The Duke made a derisive sound, but before he could speak she went on:

"You should remember, dearest, that the beauties you now find so desirable were once unfledged girls straight from the School-Room. They all start out that way—gauche, shy, ignorant, and uneducated."

"God knows it is a dismal prospect!" the Duke exclaimed.

The Duchess laughed.

"It is not going to be as bad as that! I admit I was shy when I married

154

your father, and I suppose in many ways I was very ignorant. But, although we were brought together by our parents because it was considered a suitable marriage, I made your father very happy."

"You know as well as I do, Mama, that Papa fell head-over-heels in love with you from the moment he saw you. He told me once you were the most beautiful thing out of a stained-glass window he had ever seen in his whole life."

The Duchess smiled complacently while her son went on:

"But Papa added: 'They do not make them like that these days, Kerne,' and he was right!"

"I made your father happy and that was all that mattered," the Duchess said. "There is no reason why we should not find a woman just like me to do the same for you."

The Duke sat down again next to his mother.

"Papa loved you whole-heartedly, Mama, until he died. What about you?"

For a moment the Duchess looked at him with startled eyes, then she asked:

"What do you mean by that?"

"Exactly what I say. Papa was much older than you, and although it was an arranged marriage it turned out, as far as he was concerned, to be a perfect one. But did you fall in love as whole-heartedly as he did?"

Again there was silence, and the Duchess looked away from her son.

"Love, when one finds it," she said after a moment, "is so wonderful, so perfect, that one would never regret it."

"I think you have answered my question," the Duke said. "But it is not really an answer to my problem. You see, Mama, I have never known the kind of love which Papa felt for you and which you have obviously found in your life, if not with him."

The astonishment in the Duchess's eyes was very obvious, and without her having to ask the question the Duke said:

"I know, I know! There have been women in my life ever since I was at Eton, and it seems a strange thing to say, but always sooner or later, generally sooner, they have been disappointing."

"Kerne, dearest, I am so sorry!"

"There is no need to be," the Duke said. "They have given me a great deal of pleasure and amusement, but I have often asked myself,

155

Mama, when I remember what Papa felt about you, if I am missing something.''

"Oh, dearest, I thought you had everything!" the Duchess cried.

"That is what I have wanted to believe," the Duke answered, "but when I am being honest, as I am now with you, I know it is not quite true. Then I tell myself I am asking too much."

The Duchess looked at him with great tenderness in her eyes.

She had always known he had a desire for perfection above that of any man she had ever known.

In everything he did, everything he possessed, the Duke had to excel.

His houses had to be better than anybody else's, his servants more efficient, his horses had to win all the classic races, his shoots had to achieve the highest bag of the Season.

The women he squired were undoubtedly the outstanding beauties of the moment, and now it was understandable, she thought, that there could be one thing which he might find was not perfect.

Just as she was about to say something, the Duke gave a little laugh as if he mocked himself.

"I am becoming maudlin, Mama. You know as well as I do that I am reaching for the moon, and no-one as yet has touched it."

"Perhaps one day . . ." the Duchess said softly.

"No, no, do not let us delude ourselves," the Duke answered. "Let us be practical and go back to the moment when I asked your help. I want a wife, Mama, and I am asking—no, indeed, I am commanding you to find me one who will answer all my requirements, but let me make one thing clear."

"What is that?" the Duchess asked.

The Duke paused for a moment as if he was choosing his words.

"I do not want a woman who is over-demonstrative. Her character must match her appearance. She must be conventional, dignified, and emotionally controlled. That is what I will expect from my wife and the Duchess of Ollerton."

"But, Kerne . . ."

"No 'buts,' Mama. As we have already agreed, marriage and love are two different things and I have no wish to try to combine them in a way which I know would undoubtedly prove a failure."

CHAPTER TWO

———— ❧ ————

As she walked towards the Pump Room Anita looked round her with delight.

She had not expected Harrogate to be so pretty, and she had in fact been extremely apprehensive as she and Deborah had journeyed North in the train which carried them to a terminus in West Park.

The letters that Sarah had written so diligently had all received prompt replies.

The Countess of Charmouth wrote that she would de delighted to entertain her niece for the rest of the Season and would send a carriage to collect her, complete with an elderly maid to chaperone her on the journey.

What was even more practical, she sent Sarah some money to buy a new gown and bonnet in which to travel, and she wrote:

Everything else, my dear niece, can wait until you arrive, and I am quite certain from what you have told me in your letter that you will require a whole new wardrobe with which to appear in Society. I am looking forward to seeing you and I so often think of your dear father and the happy times we had when we were children.

"Nothing could be kinder than that!" Sarah exclaimed in triumph.

"No, indeed," Daphne agreed, "and my Godmother's letter is very pleasant too, although she apparently expects me to find my own way to London, and from there she says a Courier will escort me to her house in Surrey."

"That means," Sarah replied, "that Deborah will have first to take you to London, then travel with Anita to Harrogate."

157

The letter written by Great-Aunt Matilda was not only very much less effusive than those which Sarah and Daphne had received, but enclosed with it was only the fare for two Second Class tickets to Harrogate.''

"Second Class, indeed!'' Deborah snorted indignantly when she was told how they had to journey. "And her as rich as one of them Indian nabobs they're always talking about in the papers!''

"How do you know that?'' Anita enquired.

"I remember your father telling your mother about his Aunt Matilda, and saying she was a miser, while any money she did spend was to ensure herself a good place in Heaven, if she ever reached it!''

Anita laughed. She was used to Deborah's sharp remarks and her familiarity.

She had nursed them all as children and was now getting old, but she still managed in an amazing way to keep the house clean and to bully them into doing all the things their mother would have expected them to do.

"It will be an exciting adventure to go by train to Harrogate,'' Anita said, as if she was anxious to appease the elderly woman.

"You should be travelling First Class, Miss Anita, and I've a good mind to tell Miss Lavenham so when I sees her.''

"Oh, please, Deborah, do not do anything of the sort!'' Anita begged. "She might be so angry that she will send me back right away, and then I should have to stay here alone, and Sarah would be extremely annoyed.''

"Miss Sarah's all right, God bless her. She's picked herself the juiciest plum in the pudding, and let's hope something comes of it.''

Deborah spoke in the voice of one who would be surprised if it did, but Anita knew she was afraid that their desperate adventure would come to nothing and that when the winter arrived they would all be back in the Manor House, skimping and saving and having no-one to talk to but themselves.

Not that Anita would mind.

She could always escape into her daydreams, especially now that she had a very special one to dream about, and that was Lucifer.

The more she thought about him sitting astride the black stallion, the more she was beginning to be convinced that he was entirely a figment of her imagination.

How could any real man look so exactly like the fallen Archangel that the most skilful artist in the world could not have drawn him more accurately?

I dreamt him! I know I dreamt him! Anita said to herself.

Then she remembered the dry, sarcastic note in his voice as he said: "Beware of Lucifer, wherever you may find him!"

If he was really Lucifer, Anita thought, he would not be warning her against himself.

She had spent many hours wondering what wickedness the Devil actually did when he was behaving as was expected of him.

There must be other vices besides pride and insolence, but she had no idea what they could be.

The books she had read in her father's Library, while they certainly improved her mind and added to her knowledge, were not very explicit as to what constituted "sin."

Although the Reverend Adolphus spoke of it frequently, he never added any informative details which Anita often thought might have been interesting.

The gentleman had, however, given her many new ideas to think about and many more dreams to dream.

It was true that the girls were very limited with regard to relatives. Their grandfather, the Earl of Lambourn and Beckive, had three sons but they had all died without producing an heir for the Earldom.

The present and ninth Earl was therefore a very distant cousin, who lived in South Africa and had sold the family Estates.

Anita had often wished that he would invite them to visit him, but even if he did so, she knew they could not afford the expensive fare.

But now she was travelling, if only to Harrogate, and all the way in the train, having been fortunate enough to obtain a corner-seat, she stared out at the countryside, trying to decide which County she was in.

She thought they should really be divided by fences in brilliant colours which would make it easy to distinguish between them!

There was flat land, meadow land, forests, valleys, and dales before finally the train steamed into Harrogate and they were there.

"This is thrilling, Deborah!" she exclaimed when they took an open hackney-carriage to carry them through the town to Great-Aunt Matilda's house.

"Don't go expecting too much. Miss Anita," Deborah replied.

"You'll only be disappointed, and you've got to remember that Miss Lavenham is very old and I don't suppose she's much idea of what young people like."

She snorted and added:

"I'd have thought Miss Sarah could have found you a better place to go."

Anita had heard all this before, but she said gently:

"I am afraid we have very few relations left alive, and as I am the youngest it is only right that I should wait my turn."

To her surprise, Deborah gave her one of her rare smiles.

"You never knows what mightn't turn up, Miss Anita, even in a place like Harrogate, where you'll find most people have one foot in the grave!"

Anita laughed. Then as the carriage began to slow down she said in a low voice:

"I do wish you were staying with me, Deborah. It would be fun if we could be together."

"I'd like that, too," Deborah replied, "but I'm afraid Miss Lavenham will be thinking that I'm one more mouth to feed."

That, Anita found later, was exactly what she did think.

She had already formed a picture of what Great-Aunt Matilda would look like and she had not been far away from the truth.

Miss Lavenham was old, and yet able to sit stiffly upright in her chair, despite the rheumatism which prevented her from walking.

She wore on her grey hair a white muslin cap which was exactly like the pictures of the one worn by Queen Victoria.

She did in fact look very like Her Majesty, except that her face was thinner and more lined and had, Anita thought apprehensively, an undoubtedly grim appearance.

"So you are my youngest niece!" she said in a deep, gruff voice when Anita was announced. "You are very small, and not in the least like your father!"

She made it sound a very regrettable failing, but Anita smiled at her bravely and made the speech she had already rehearsed.

"How do you do, Great-Aunt Matilda, and thank you very much for having me to stay with you. It is very kind."

"Your sister left me very little choice," Miss Lavenham remarked accusingly, "but now that you are here, I daresay you can make yourself useful."

"I hope so," Anita answered, "but in what way?"

"You will soon learn. What about this servant you have brought with you? She can stay tonight, but she will leave tomorrow on the morning train."

Anita hesitated a moment, then she said:

"It would be kind if she could stay just a little longer. It was a tiring journey, and Deborah is not as young as she was."

"She can rest in the train," Miss Lavenham replied in a voice which told Anita that the subject was closed.

So Deborah went back and Anita quickly found that there were a lot of things for her to do.

Miss Lavenham was indeed given to good works, as her father had said, and there were dresses to be made which were straight plain shifts called "Mother Hubbards." They were sent out to the Missionaries in Africa to clothe those who were ignorant enough to walk almost naked.

There were tracts to be addressed and delivered to hundreds of people who lived in Harrogate or in the vicinity, either by Anita or one of the servants in order to save the postage.

There were also collections that were made for all sorts of strange charities which Anita had never heard of before.

She soon learnt that the only people who came to the house regularly were those connected with the religious organisations that Great-Aunt Matilda patronised.

Her own personal Minister, the Reverend Joshua Hislip, was a frequent visitor because, as Anita soon surmised, he never left empty-handed.

Fortunately, Anita learnt the very day after her arrival that Great-Aunt Matilda's health compelled her to drink the waters.

This meant that early every morning they went to the Cheltenham Pump Room.

Miss Lavenham was pushed there in a bath-chair by an elderly footman, and Anita walked beside her, her eyes delighted with everything she saw, especially the people who were journeying in the same direction.

Some were very smart and made her conscious of how out-of-date her own clothes were.

Sarah had looked lovely setting off for London in a new travelling-gown with a large crinoline and a cloak which swung out over it.

Daphne had a new bonnet, but there had been nothing left to spend on Anita. She had, however, bought some yards of blue ribbon to trim the bonnet she had worn for two years.

Although she had not realised it, her blue gown, made by Deborah, with its gleaming white muslin collar and cuffs, made her look very young, very innocent, and more than usually like a small angel.

She was wearing it now and her blue eyes were alight with interest as she followed Great-Aunt Matilda's bath-chair in through the gate.

The Cheltenham Pump Room was the largest public building in Harrogate and had a most impressive Doric-columned portico which reminded Anita of Roman Architecture.

Inside was a large Salon where the invalids congregated to gossip, a Pump Room, and a Library to which fortunately Miss Lavenham subscribed.

Having lived in Harrogate all her long life, she knew practically everybody in the town and looked on it as if it were her own personal property and Estate.

Anita found that Great-Aunt Matilda regarded newcomers with a jaundiced eye and was on the defensive in case any of them, through ignorance, encroached on the privileges which she thought were her right.

Like all old people, she disliked change and wanted everything that happened today to be exactly the same as it was yesterday, the day before that, and back through the years.

She therefore expected her bath-chair to come to rest regularly at the same point inside the Pump Room.

Almost every morning there was a battle because some unwary person who had just arrived in Harrogate had encroached on the actual spot that Miss Lavenham considered to be hers and hers alone.

Anita found that Great-Aunt Matilda had a very scathing tongue, and she felt herself blushing at the rude things the old lady would say, even though the newcomers would quickly make their apologies and withdraw from the sacred unmarked patch on which they had unwittingly trespassed.

When Anita had been there two or three days, she realised that the men who pushed the bath-chairs that were for hire often deliberately took up their position on Miss Lavenham's piece of floor, just for the fun of it.

When they had been forced to retreat she would see them laughing and winking at one another, and she wondered how it could matter so much to Great-Aunt Matilda that she was prepared to make what her father would have called "an exhibition of herself."

However, Anita was clever enough to realise that her Great-Aunt was an eccentric, and, as such, the town in its own way was rather proud of her.

As soon as her bath-chair, which was a very comfortable one with a thickly padded seat, was in the correct position, Anita would be sent to the well.

There she obtained a glass of mineral-water, which had special properties in it, especially iron, and which had brought invalids to Harrogate since 1571 when the waters were first discovered.

Anita had already found a book which described the chalybeate Tewit Well, whose waters *"did excel the tart fountains beyond the seas as being more quick and lively and fuller of mineral salts."*

She thought personally that the waters tasted rather nasty and felt fortunate that, being so well, she did not need it.

This morning, looking round at the many invalids crowded into the Pump Room, she decided to say a little prayer that they might all recover after they had drunk from the well.

The idea made her imagine what a commotion there would be if suddenly all those who were sipping from the glasses their attendants had brought them were suddenly to jump up from their bath-chairs and cry out in amazement that they were cured.

Then she told herself that in that case they would undoubtedly sing a hymn of joy and gratitude, and she could almost hear the Hallelujahs that would rise in a paeon of triumph towards the high ceiling of the Pump Room.

She was thinking how exciting this would be, when a glass of mineral-water intended for Miss Lavenham was held out to her by the attendant at the well.

She took it in both hands, and, still thinking that it might constitute a miraculous cure, she turned round rather swiftly.

As she did so, she stumbled over the foot of the bath-chair that was just behind her and with a little cry half-fell across it, spilling the contents of the glass she held in her hand.

She picked herself up and looked in consternation at the lady in the bath-chair.

"I am sorry . . . I am very . . . very . . . sorry," she apologised. "It was clumsy of me. I do hope I have not hurt you, Ma'am?"

"No, I am all right," a sweet voice replied, "and perhaps we were too near to the well."

"I do hope the water has not spoilt your rug," Anita said, looking down to where there was undoubtedly a wet patch on the pretty paisley rug which covered the lady's legs.

She found her handkerchief and was bending down to wipe it dry when a voice she remembered only too well remarked:

"I think once again you must have been dreaming, but I cannot believe this time it was of Lucifer."

Startled, she looked up and there, standing behind the bath-chair, was in fact Lucifer.

He looked exactly the same as he had when they had met before and as she had visualised him almost every day since.

The only difference was that he was standing instead of riding, while his tall hat was still at a rakish angle on his dark head and his coat fitted as elegantly across his broad shoulders.

She stared at him wide-eyed. Then the lady in the bath-chair said:

"You appear, Kerne, to have an acquaintance with this young lady already. Perhaps you would introduce me?"

"We met by chance, Mama, and as she told me, she was at that moment thinking of Lucifer, I think perhaps I am connected in her mind with that particular gentleman."

The Duchess looked at her son in surprise, then said to Anita:

"Will you tell me who you are?"

A little late, Anita remembered to courtsey.

"I am Anita Lavenham, Ma'am," she answered, "and I am staying in Harrogate with my Great-Aunt Miss Matilda Lavenham."

"Matilda!" the Duchess exclaimed. "Good gracious, is she here?"

"She is over there on your right," Anita replied, "and please, if you will excuse me, I must fetch her another glass of water."

She curtseyed again, hesitatingly and hurried back to the well while the Duchess said to her son:

"I should have thought Matilda Lavenham was dead years ago, but let us go and speak to her. I remember her when I was a girl, and I suspect that your young friend is the daughter of that very handsome nephew of hers, Harold Lavenham."

Back at the well, Anita had waited her turn for another glass of the mineral-water, and when finally she received it, she carried it very much more carefully to her Great-Aunt, to find that the lady in the bath-chair over whom she had fallen was talking to her.

Standing a little apart from them both and looking rather cynical and bored was Lucifer.

"You have been a long time, Anita!" Miss Lavenham said sharply as she took the water from her hand.

"I am sorry, but I had to wait,"Anita replied.

As she spoke she gave the Duchess a glance to see if she would betray her, but she received an encouraging smile. Then Miss Lavenham said in a manner which seemed almost reluctant:

"This, Clarice, is my great-niece, Anita. You may remember her father?"

"Of course I remember Harry Lavenham," the Duchess replied. "He was the most handsome man I ever danced with, and I used to follow him out hunting, knowing he would always be in at the kill."

"Those were the days when he could afford to hunt with a decent pack," Miss Lavenham replied.

Anita knew that once again she was referring to the fact that everything that was luxurious in her father's life had come to an end when he married not a rich bride, as was expected of him, but her mother.

Ever since Anita had arrived in Harrogate, Great-Aunt Matilda had made it very clear that the circumstances in which her great-nieces found themselves at this particular moment were due entirely to their father's profligate life.

Anita knew it would have been quite useless for her to point out that her father had been so happy with her mother that he had never missed any of the advantages he had enjoyed when he had lived at home.

She knew only too well that Great-Aunt Matilda would not understand that love was a compensation for everything else that her father could no longer afford.

She was wise enough to suspect that because Great-Aunt Matilda had obviously never been in love she was inclined not only to disparage that emotion but also to consider it an unnecessary luxury for everybody else.

Now for the moment it was difficult to concentrate on what Great-Aunt Matilda was saying or indeed of whom she was speaking.

Instead Anita found herself vividly conscious that Lucifer's dark eyes were on her face, and she wondered what he would say if she asked him how long he intended to stay away in the Hell he had recently chosen instead of Heaven.

With a faint smile to herself she thought that not only he would be astonished if she said such a thing, but doubtless Great-Aunt Matilda would send her home on the next train for being impertinent.

"I wish I had known you were here before, Matilda," the Duchess was saying. "I have been in Harrogate for five weeks and it would have been pleasant to talk of old times."

"I am too busy to entertain," Miss Lavenham answered sharply, "but if you would care to visit me for a dish of tea next Sunday you will be very welcome."

"Thank you," the Duchess replied. "If I am able, I shall be delighted, and I hope you and your niece will come to me before I leave. I have rented Lord Arrington's house on Prospect Gardens and find it extremely comfortable."

"A ridiculous man who worries far too much about his health!" Miss Lavenham sniffed. "When he told me he was visiting the Spas in France and Switzerland I informed him it was a waste of money."

As she spoke, she signalled the footman who was pushing her chair to take her away, and at the same time handed her empty glass to Anita.

Quickly Anita returned it to the side of the well where a great number of other used glasses had been deposited.

Then as she turned to hurry after her Great-Aunt, who by now had left the Pump Room, she found that she had to pass by Lucifer.

He blocked her passage and she was forced to stop.

"Are you taking my advice, Miss Lavenham?" he enquired.

She knew to what he was referring, and that, knowing what she thought of him, he was mocking her.

"I remember what you said, Sir," Anita replied, "but you forget you also told me that 'the Devil would come.' I am therefore apprehensive as to how I can stop him."

She saw the amusement in his eyes at her reply. Then, without waiting for him to speak, she ran from the Spa, catching up with Great-Aunt Matilda, whose bath-chair was already moving swiftly out through the gates onto the road.

They proceeded for quite some way before Miss Lavenham said:

"I presume you know who those people are?"

"No," Anita replied, "you introduced me to them but you did not tell me their names."

"That was the Dowager Duchess of Ollerton," Miss Lavenham said, "and her son. A frivolous man, from all I have heard, but that might be said of any young man today."

Anita did not reply.

She had already heard, a number of times, her great-aunt's opinion of modern youth and their lack of responsibility.

What did interest her was that Lucifer was the Duke of Ollerton.

Anita had always thought that Dukes were old, pompous, and over-powering. The Duke of Ollerton was certainly the latter, but he was not pompous.

He had a lithe grace about him which had made her imagine he could easily have glided down from Heaven with his wings out-stretched, landing with an athletic ability which prevented him from hurting himself.

The Duke of Ollerton!

It sounded a very formidable title, and now she could no longer think of him just as Lucifer but as a nobleman, and she was quite certain that somewhere she had heard his name before.

It took her a long time to remember where, until she recalled that her father had liked her to read the newspapers to him when he was ill, and that included the reports of race-meetings.

Of course, the Duke was amongst those who owned winners of great races including the Derby and the Gold Cup at Ascot.

Papa would have liked to meet him, Anita told herself.

Then she wondered if he would come to tea with his mother on Sunday when her Great-Aunt had invited the Duchess, but she thought that if he did he would be considerably bored.

She had learnt that usually the only guest was the Reverend Joshua Hislip, and last week there had been two ladies who had devoted their lives to teaching sign-language to children who were born deaf and dumb.

It was all very worthy, Anita knew, but she was quite certain that the Duke of Ollerton would not find it particularly entertaining.

"No, he will not come," she told herself, and wondered if she would ever see him again.

~

In the large Drawing-Room of the house in Prospect Gardens, the Duchess, when she had been seated comfortably in her favourite place in the window, said to her son:

"That was a pretty child with Matilda Lavenham, but I cannot imagine she has much of a life. Matilda is obsessed with the needs of the poor and the needy in every country but her own."

"I could see she was an old battle-axe!" the Duke remarked. "But I imagine the girl is only with her on a visit. When I saw her before it was in Cambridgeshire."

"Was Anita staying with the Earl of Spearmont?" the Duchess asked.

"Good Lord, no!" the Duke replied. "I was riding and asked her to open a gate for me, thinking she was a milk-maid, but she was day-dreaming and she told me she was thinking about Lucifer."

"So that accounts for your extraordinary conversation with her," his mother remarked.

The Duke seated himself in a comfortable chair, and after a moment the Duchess said:

"As you asked me, Kerne dearest, I have made a list for you. It is not a very long one."

She drew out from a silk bag beside her a piece of paper, but as she held it out to him the Duke said:

"There is no need for me to read it. Invite the girls, if you think they are any good, to stay at Ollerton in three weeks from now. I will give a party at which, Mama, you will preside, and although it will be a crashing bore, I suppose I must do my duty."

"We shall have to ask their fathers and mothers," the Duchess commented.

"Of course," the Duke agreed, "and I will include a few friends of my own to cheer up what will undoubtedly be a laborious few days of utter boredom."

The Duchess drew in her breath.

"I hate you to talk like that, Kerne," she said after a moment. "You must remember, dearest, it is your future we are planning, and once you are married there will be nothing anyone can do."

The Duchess spoke a little hesitatingly, and the Duke said:

"I am well aware of that, Mama, but as we have agreed that Marmion and his appalling wife must not on my death inherit Ollerton and all the responsibilities that go with my position, however unpleasant it may be, I must make the best of a bad job."

"I have chosen girls whose parents are an example of propriety," the Duchess said, "and what is more, I know Her Majesty will approve of them."

"Then I can only say thank you, Mama, and beg you to stop worrying about me, as you are doing at this moment."

"Of course I worry. What mother would do anything else in the circumstances?"

"Perhaps it will not be as bad as we both anticipate," the Duke said, "and I am sure, Mama, that, if nothing else, you will think it is very good for my soul. You have accused me often enough of being spoilt and selfish."

"Not where I am concerned," the Duchess said quickly. "You have never been anything but kind and very unselfish to me, and however much you may deny it, that is why you are here at this moment, boring yourself in Harrogate of all places."

"As a matter of fact I am finding it quite amusing," the Duke replied. "Apart from being with you, the Earl of Harewood has told me I can use the excellent horses he has at Harewood House as if they were my own, and I am trying out a team this afternoon. I only wish you were well enough to come with me."

"I wish I were too, dearest," the Duchess replied. "When you return, tell the Earl I hope he and his wife will call on me before I leave. I have not been well enough to drive over to Harewood to leave my cards with them."

"I am sure they will wish to come and see you."

The Duke rose as he spoke and bent down to kiss his mother's cheek.

"You are looking much better, Mama," he said, "and I think we can thank Harrogate for that."

He would have moved away but the Duchess held on to his hand.

"Before I send out the invitations, dearest," she said, "you are quite, quite certain that this is what you wish me to do?"

"Quite certain," the Duke said firmly, "but because it bores me I do not wish to discuss it any further."

"No, of course not," the Duchess said, releasing his hand.

There was, however, a deep sadness in her eyes as she watched him walk from the room and close the door quietly behind him.

~

Three days later, the Duke, driving a team of four perfectly matched chestnuts, turned a corner of the road and saw a small figure running swiftly ahead of him along the pavement.

He thought he recognised the blue ribbons of the bonnet he had last seen in the Pump Room, and it surprised him first of all to see Anita was alone and unaccompanied, and secondly that she should be running away from the town in the same direction as the one in which he was driving.

He was aware that Cornwall Road, once it had passed Knaresborough Forest, would take him out to the open countryside and it was there that he intended to test the speed of the horses which he was driving so that he could report on their progress to their owner.

He pulled his horses in until they were level with the small figure moving surprisingly quickly, then brought them to a standstill.

Anita must have been aware that he was trying to attract her attention, for she turned her face towards him and he saw that her eyes were filled with tears and they had spilled over onto her cheeks.

"You appear to be in a great hurry, Miss Lavenham," the Duke remarked drily. "Perhaps you would find it easier to travel more swiftly, wherever you are going, in my chaise."

"I . . . I am . . . going to the . . . country," she replied after a moment, a little incoherently.

"As that is also my destination," the Duke said, "it is obvious that we should journey together."

He put out his left hand as he spoke, and, almost as if he commanded her to do so, she took it and stepped into the chaise to sit down beside him.

She made no effort to wipe away her tears, and after he had started his horses again the Duke asked:

"What has upset you?"

"I . . . I want . . . to go . . . h—home . . . I want to . . . g—go away," Anita said. "B—but I have . . . no money . . . and I am not sure that I can . . . do so."

"What has occurred to make you feel like this?"

For a moment he thought she was not going to answer him. Then, because he was waiting, and she felt she must reply, she said in a voice that broke:

"Great-Aunt Matilda has told me that I am to m—marry the . . . Reverend . . . Joshua . . . H—Hislip."

"And the idea upsets you?"

"He is . . . old . . . and he is . . . always preaching about . . . the punishments that await those who . . . sin . . . and when he looks at me . . . I think there is . . . f—fire in his eyes."

The Duke thought somewhat drily that perhaps the Reverend Joshua had fire in his eyes for a very different reason than Anita's sins, but aloud he said:

"Surely if you do not wish to marry him it is quite easy to say 'No'?"

"Great-Aunt Matilda tells me that it is my . . . duty because his wife has died and he needs . . . somebody to look after him," Anita replied. "Sarah said we were all to find husbands . . . but I cannot marry him . . . I think I would rather . . . die!"

There was no doubt of the despair in Anita's voice, but the Duke merely asked:

"Who is Sarah?"

"My sister. When Mama went to Switzerland, Sarah wrote to our relations, who had paid no attention to us before, asking them to have us to stay. She thought it was our last chance to find. . . ourselves husbands. There are no . . . young men where you first saw me in . . . Fenchurch."

"So you are husband-hunting?" the Duke said and he made it sound a very unpleasant pursuit.

"Sarah is nearly . . . twenty-one," Anita explained, "and she cannot wait. But I have plenty of time, and anyway . . . I have no wish to . . . marry anyone . . . unless I . . . love him!"

Her voice broke on a little sob.

Then, as if for the first time she realised that her face was streaked with tears, she put up her fingers to her cheeks before beginning to search for a handkerchief.

As she seemed regrettably to have omitted to bring one with her, the Duke took the square of fine linen from his breast-pocket and handed it to her.

As she turned her face to thank him, he thought she cried like a child.

BARBARA CARTLAND

The tears were running down her cheeks whilst her eyes were still wide open and swimming with them, and he knew that he had never known a woman who could cry so prettily without contorting her face.

"Thank . . . you," Anita faltered. "You will think I am very . . . foolish . . . but somehow I know that Great-Aunt Matilda will . . . force me to . . . marry the Reverend Joshua because she thinks him such an . . . admirable man."

"Your father is dead," the Duke said, "but I cannot believe you do not have some nearer relative who could be constituted as your Guardian and to whom you could appeal for help?"

"There is only the Countess of Charmouth, my Aunt Elizabeth, who is Papa's sister," Anita said. "Sarah is staying with her and it would not be . . . fair for me . . . to interfere."

The Duke, being concerned with his horses, did not speak, and she went on:

"I . . . I must run away . . . if I can go home . . . perhaps I could hide so that Great-Aunt Matilda could not make me return to her . . . and the Reverend Joshua could not . . . find me."

She twisted her fingers together for a moment before she said in a very small voice:

"B—but I have . . . no m—money."

"So you are asking me to lend you some," the Duke said.

"C—could you? Please . . . could you do that?" Anita asked. "I promise you I will return it . . . every penny. It might take a long time . . . but you shall have it back."

"If I give you money," the Duke said, "what exactly would you do with it?"

"I will find out what time the train leaves for the South," Anita replied, "then I will creep out of the house and be gone before anyone realises it."

"Do you really think you can travel alone? All the way back to Fenchurch, if that is the name of your village?"

"Yes . . . that is right," Anita said, "and I do not think the . . . Second Class fare is very expensive, or if you prefer . . . I will go Third."

"I would prefer you to do none of those things. We have to think of some alternative."

"There is none," Anita said quickly. "When Great-Aunt Matilda told me after luncheon before she went to lie down that I was to . . . marry

172

the Reverend Joshua, she said he was . . . coming to see me . . . tomorrow. That means I must go . . . tonight."

"But where were you running to now?" the Duke asked.

"I have always found it easier to think when I am in the country," Anita replied simply. "Somehow it is much more difficult in the town where there are houses and people moving about. I thought I would find a wood, like the . . . secret wood I go to at home, where I could sort . . . things out in my . . . mind."

"Is that where you went after we first met?"

Anita shook her head.

"No. I went . . . home."

"Why?"

"I was . . . thinking about you . . . because I thought you were . . . Lucifer. It was so interesting and exciting that it was unnecessary to think in my wood."

The Duke smiled before he said:

"Because it looks as if it may rain later on this afternoon, I suggest I do not leave you in Knaresborough Forest, which I see we are approaching, but we think out your plans while you are with me."

"I have told you . . . I must go . . . home," Anita said.

"If your sisters are away, will there be anybody there?"

"There is Deborah, our old maid. She is taking care of the house until Mama is well enough to come back from . . . Switzerland."

"It does not seem a very satisfactory arrangement," the Duke remarked. "There is also, of course, the chance that you may not get away."

Anita gave a little cry.

"But I have to . . . I have to! If the Reverend Joshua comes to see me tomorrow, I know that however much I may . . . insist that I will not . . . marry him, Great-Aunt Matilda will . . . make me do so. Why should he want me? There must be many other women—the Church was full of them on Sunday—who would wish to be his wife. It is ridiculous for him to want me!"

The Duke looked sideways at her small cherublike face and her large worried eyes.

He thought of quite a number of reasons why the Reverend Joshua should wish to marry her apart from the fact that it obviously had the approval of his most influential patron.

173

Because he had no wish to make Anita more frightened than she was already, he merely said:

"You are quite certain it will not be in your best interests to be married? After all, if, as you say, Fenchurch is so dull, you might find life in Harrogate considerably more entertaining."

"Not with ... that man as my ... h—husband," Anita said in a whisper. "When he ... shakes my hand it makes me ... creep and I feel as if he were a ... snake. How could I let him ... touch me?"

There was such a note of horror in her voice that the Duke almost instinctively tightened his hands on the reins. Then he said:

"I am now going to drive very fast, and when I have tried out these horses perhaps we shall find a solution to your problem."

He did not wait for her answer but cracked his whip and the horses sprang forward, moving quicker, Anita thought, then she had ever travelled before.

The dust from the road billowed out behind them and she thought that she was not travelling with Lucifer but with Apollo as he drove his chariot across the sky, carrying the light from one side of the world to the other.

It made her thrill at the sheer excitement of it, then when they were approaching the end of the straight part of the road the Duke slowed his team down and a few minutes later turned them round.

"That was exciting!" Anita said. "And the horses are superb! Where did you find them?"

"They are not mine, as it happens," the Duke said, "but I have horses of my own which can travel as fast as these, if not faster, although I admit it would be hard to fault them."

"Then please do not try to do so," Anita begged.

"Why not?" the Duke enquired curiously.

"Because it is always so disappointing to find that something we thought was perfect falls short of our expectations."

"You are too young to have found that out already," the Duke remarked, and there was a distinctly cynical note in his voice.

"So we must never expect too much," Anita said, as if she was talking to herself, "but try to be grateful that it is as good as it is."

"The way you are speaking," the Duke remarked, "I feel you would make an excellent Parson's wife."

She gave a cry of horror.

"That is unkind, and cruel of you! You are only saying that to . . . hurt me! I was not sermonising, but I am really trying to work out in my own mind why you should be cynical when as a Duke you must have everything you want in the world . . . and a great deal more . . . besides."

The Duke laughed.

"Who has been telling you tales about me?"

"Not you in particular," Anita replied, "but Dukes are very important people . . . I know that . . . and because they are next in line to Royalty one wants to believe they are happy."

The Duke laughed again.

"You are making me the Duke in a fairy-story, one of those tales you tell yourself when you are looking at the sky or collecting waters from the Spa."

"How do you know I do that?" Anita asked.

"It is obvious."

"I try not to do it . . . all the time."

"I think it would be a mistake to change yourself," the Duke remarked. "Small angels obviously believe that everything is perfect."

He smiled again before he quoted:

" *'Now walk the angels on the walls of Heaven, as sentinels to warn th' immortal souls.'* "

He saw Anita look at him with a sudden light in her eyes and asked:

"Is that what you are doing?"

"Is that what . . . you are . . . telling me I . . . do?" she enquired. "Do I really look like an angel?"

"Exactly!"

"It is a lovely idea," Anita said almost to herself.

"So what could be more appropriate than to be warning his immortal soul when you are driving with Lucifer?"

"I suppose it was . . . impertinent of me to think you . . . looked like him," Anita said. "It is just that when you appeared I was thinking how handsome he must have been before he fell from Heaven."

The Duke thought he had been paid many compliments in his life, but this was the most ingenuous.

"Thank you," he said, and saw a quick blush come into Anita's cheeks.

"Perhaps I should not have . . . said that," she murmured. "The things I think sometimes pop out without my really considering them, so you must forgive me.''

"There is nothing to forgive,'' the Duke said, "and now as we are turning homeward I think I have a solution to your problem.''

"You have?''

Now there was a very different note in Anita's voice as she clasped her hands together.

She turned sideways, looking up at him, her eyes beseeching him.

"Do you really mean, Your Grace, that you will help me? Please . . . please . . . if you will do so I will be . . . grateful all my life!''

"I will certainly try to do so,'' the Duke said. "And I think that you will not be disappointed.''

"Promise that I will not have to . . . marry the . . . Reverend Joshua!''

"Not unless you wish to do so.''

"You know that can never be . . . never . . . never!'' Anita cried. "But how can you . . . prevent it?''

"I think we shall have to have somebody else's help,'' the Duke said.

Then, as he saw the expression of concern on Anita's face, he added:

"Do not look so worried. The person to whom I am referring is my mother!''

CHAPTER THREE

THE DUCHESS was sitting in her favourite seat in the window when to her surprise she saw her son driving back towards the house.

As he had left her well over an hour ago to return to Harewood House, she could not imagine what had made him return.

She waited, and when she heard his footsteps outside the room she looked up expectantly.

He came in, but before he could speak she cried:

"What has happened, Kerne? I did not expect to see you again so quickly!"

"It is nothing to upset you, Mama," the Duke replied as he walked over to her side.

"Then what is it?" the Duchess enquired.

The Duke sat down in a chair next to her before he answered:

"While I was driving I saw Miss Lavenham's great-niece and found her in great distress."

"What can have upset her?"

"Apparently," the Duke said, "your old friend, who you tell me is given to good works, has decided that the child should marry her pet Minister."

The Duchess looked astonished.

"You cannot mean the Reverend Joshua Hislip?"

"I believe that is his name."

"But he is old, and a most unpleasant man as far as I am concerned. When I listened to him last Sunday he was literally mouthing over the punishments the wicked would suffer for their sins, and I had the feeling it was something he would enjoy inflicting personally if he had the chance."

"Then you will understand, Mama," the Duke said, "that it would be criminal to let that young girl be forced to marry someone who is old enough to be her father."

"I believe somebody told me that the Reverend Joshua's wife died fairly recently," the Duchess said. "But of course he is much too old for Matilda's great-niece—what did she say her name was?"

"Anita."

"At the same time," the Duchess went on, "there is nothing I can do about it, and I am quite certain Matilda Lavenham would greatly resent my interfering in any way."

There was silence for a moment, then the Duke said:

"I thought, Mama, that you needed a Reader."

The Duchess started indignantly.

There was nothing on which she prided herself more than that her eyes, unlike those of most of her contemporaries, were exceedingly good. She could see for a long distance, and, what was more, she needed to use a magnifying glass only for the very smallest print.

She was just about to say that a Reader was the last thing she needed,

177

when, as the words came to her lips, she bit them back and instead, after a distinct hesitation said tentatively:

"If you really—think that is that I—require, Kerne, then I am sure you are—right."

"I thought you would agree with me, Mama," the Duke said, "and as you are leaving for home tomorrow, I think you would find it agreeable to have someone to read the newspapers to you on the long journey."

"Are you suggesting that Anita Lavenham should come with me?" the Duchess enquired.

"It would be best if she came here tonight," the Duke replied, "for I understand the amorous Parson will press his suit tomorrow at mid-day."

"Then of course that must be prevented," the Duchess agreed. "What do you suggest I do?"

"I have already ordered the carriage for you, Mama. I think if you drive to Miss Lavenham's house and ask her, as a favour, to lend you her niece, she will be unable to refuse."

"Yes, of course, dearest," the Duchess said. "Perhaps you will ring for Eleanor to bring me my bonnet and shawl."

The Duke rose to his feet to pull the bell, and the Duchess watched him with an astonishment that he did not perceive.

It was true that she had often accused him of being selfish and there had been many people who said he was spoilt because he had been a much-cosseted only child.

The Duchess thought that in the years since he had grown up he had never shown the slightest interest in other people's problems.

"Now I will set off once again for Harewood House," the Duke was saying, "and I hope to have no more adventures on the way. Tomorrow I repair to Doncaster, and I shall be at Ollerton in about two-weeks' time."

"I have invited your guests to stay with us from the twenty-fifth," the Duchess said.

"Thank you, Mama. And of course Brigstock will go back in the train to look after you during the journey and see that you have everything you require."

"I am sure Mr. Brigstock will do that admirably," the Duchess replied. She held out her hands.

"Good-bye, dearest boy. Enjoy yourself at the races, and I hope your horses win."

"I shall be extremely annoyed if they fail."

The Duke kissed his mother and hurried away as if he was anxious to be once again driving the chestnut horses that were waiting for him outside.

As she saw his broad shoulders disappearing through the door the Duchess murmured beneath her breath:

"A Reader indeed! But I suppose it is as good an excuse as any other!"

Anita, having hurried back on the Duke's instructions to her Great-Aunt's house, found that she was in for a scolding for having been away so long.

"There is plenty for you to do here, Anita," Miss Lavenham said severely, "without gallivanting off on your own, which is something of which I do not approve."

"I am sorry," Anita answered humbly. "It was a nice day and I walked farther than I intended."

"This craze for exercise amongst young people is quite unnecessary," Miss Lavenham snapped, "especially, when they are neglecting their duties. Hurry up and finish those letters so that you can give them to the Vicar when he calls tomorrow."

She did not notice that Anita gave a little shiver when she thought of the real reason why the Reverend Joshua was calling the following day.

Already she was beginning to wonder frantically whether the Duke would keep his word and save her from what she thought would be a fate too horrible to contemplate.

It was all very well for Sarah to talk of their finding husbands, but Anita's vivid imagination had already made her realise that having a husband entailed more than just bearing a man's name and looking after his house.

What exactly it was, she had no real knowledge. She knew only that the idea of the Reverend Joshua touching her or kissing her was horrible and unnatural.

When she had seen him in the pulpit the first Sunday after she had arrived, she had though him an ugly, boring man.

Accordingly, she had drifted away into one of her daydreams, which strangely enough concerned Lucifer, although the Reverend Joshua's sermon in no way resembled the one give by the Reverend Adolphus:

"How are thou fallen from Heaven, O Lucifer, son of the morning!"

Anita repeated the words to herself and thought with a little smile that her Lucifer had fallen very comfortably into the position of a Duke.

When the Reverend Joshua had called later that afternoon for tea with her Great-Aunt Matilda, she had thought him even more unpleasant at close quarters than when he was officiating in the Church.

There was something smarmy and certainly slimy in the way he talked to her Great-Aunt, and Anita did not miss the glint of what she was sure was greed in his eyes when, as he was leaving, Miss Lavenham had handed him a sealed envelope.

"Just a little donation to your favourite charity, my dear Vicar," she had said in a surprisingly soft voice.

Anita thought that perhaps she was being unjust, but she had a suspicion that the Reverend Joshua's favourite charity would be himself.

He called very frequently, and it struck Anita the following Sunday that he held her hand in his wet and clammy one rather longer than was necessary.

She also heard him saying complimentary things about her to her Great-Aunt Matilda.

"If he knew what I thought about him," she had told herself, "he would sing a very different tune!"

However, she had not thought of him more than she could help, and this morning she had been preoccupied and excited by the first letter she had received from Sarah, who had written:

I cannot tell you how wonderful it is being in London with Aunt Elizabeth, and she has been kinder to me than I thought possible. The clothes she is giving me are lovely, so lovely that every time I put them on, I feel I am Cinderella and my Fairy Godmother has waved her magic wand over me.

Fancy I have an enormous crinoline and already there are four ball-

gowns hanging in my wardrobe besides a number of absolutely ravishing other dresses!

I want to tell you, darling Anita, about the Balls I have attended and the Reception at which Aunt Elizabeth actually presented me to Princess Alexandra, but I have no time now as I have to get ready for a large luncheon-party.

I hope you are not too unhappy at Harrogate and I will write again as soon as it is possible. This is really just to tell you that I love you and wish you were here with me.

Anita read the letter over and over again. She told herself that Sarah was so lovely that everybody would admire her and she was sure she would find exactly the husband she desired.

She spent the morning daydreaming about Sarah and it was therefore a shock when, as luncheon ended, a plain, rather dull meal, Miss Lavenham said:

"I wish to speak to you, Anita, before I go for my rest."

Anita looked surprised, but she followed her Great-Aunt into the Morning-Room which was adjacent to the Dining-Room.

When they shut the door her Great-Aunt said:

"Sit down Anita. I have something to tell you which I am sure will make you realise what a very fortunate girl you are."

It flashed through Anita's mind that her aunt might be going to give her a new gown, but Miss Lavenham went on:

"You have met the Reverend Joshua Hislip here a number of times and listened to him in Church. You must realise he is a man of out-standing ability and character."

She paused, and because it was obviously expected that Anita should reply, she said:

"Yes, indeed, I am sure he is."

"You will therefore appreciate," Miss Lavenham continued, "what a very great honour it would be to become his companion and wife."

It struck Anita with a sense of some surprise that if her Great-Aunt wanted to marry, it was certainly strange that she should take such a step when she was over seventy.

But when she considered it, she was sure the Reverend Joshua would find it very much to his advantage to have such a wealthy wife.

Also, there was no doubt that Great-Aunt Matilda was extremely fond of him.

Aloud she said:

"So you are to be married, Great-Aunt Matilda! How very exciting! Will I be able to be your bridesmaid?"

There was a moment's stony silence when Anita realised she had said something wrong.

Then, enunciating every word so that there would be no mistake, Miss Lavenham said:

"The Vicar has asked for *your* hand in marriage, Anita!"

Despite the way she spoke, Anita felt she could not have heard her aright. Then with a little cry she exclaimed:

"No—no . . . but he cannot have! How . . . could he? He is much too old!"

"Age is of no consequence," Miss Lavenham replied sharply, "and as the Vicar has said himself, you will bring him the spring when he has existed for so long in the cold and snows of December."

Because for a moment Anita was incapable of speech, Miss Lavenham continued:

"He was referring to the fact that his wife was ill for a number of years before she died. Personally, I always found her a tiresome woman, possessive and querulous, and she failed to give him children, although that might have been an act of God."

"Child . . . ren!"

Anita whispered the words beneath her breath. Then bravely, because her heart was thumping in her breast, she said:

"I am sorry . . . Aunt Matilda . . . but I could not . . . marry any man who is . . . so much older than I am . . . and someone I did not . . . love."

Miss Lavenham brushed her words aside as if they were no more important than the buzzing of a mosquito.

"Nonsense! Nonsense!" she said. "Of course you will marry the Reverend Joshua, and think yourself extremely lucky to do so. You will not have a big wedding. That would be quite unnecessary. I will give a small Reception here, and I presume I shall have to supply your trousseau."

Anita rose to her feet.

"No! . . . No! . . . I cannot . . . and I will not . . . marry the Reverend . . . gentleman!"

"You will do as you are told!" Miss Lavenham retorted. "I have no wish for him to be disappointed and the marriage has my full approval. I presume, as your father is dead and your mother is abroad, that I, as the eldest of the Lavenham family, am in the position of being your Guardian, and as your Guardian, Anita, I will have no opposition to my plans. When the Vicar calls tomorrow you will accept him and I shall make arrangements for you to be married in a month's time."

The way Miss Lavenham spoke was so positive, so overpowering, that Anita felt as if the walls were closing in on her and there was no escape.

With a little cry like that of an animal caught in a trap, she hurried from the room and ran upstairs to her bed-room.

She had locked herself in, and when she heard her Great-Aunt come upstairs to lie down, she had put on her bonnet and slipped out of the house, feeling that only outside the town, in the country, could she breathe and think.

Then the Duke had providentially met her and promised he would rescue her, but how he could do so she had no idea.

She was just now thinking despairingly that she would have to run away tonight and somehow find her way home to Fenchurch when the Butler opened the door to announce:

"The Duchess of Ollerton, Ma'am!"

Miss Lavenham looked surprised but Anita felt her heart leap.

The Duchess walked very slowly and obviously with some difficulty towards Miss Lavenham, who rose to her feet.

"What a surprise, Clarice! I was not expecting you."

She helped the Duchess into a chair, who did not reply until she was comfortable. Then she said:

"I feel very remiss in not calling before, Matilda, and as I am leaving tomorrow this is my last opportunity of paying my respects. Moreover, I want to ask you a great favour.

"I had no idea you were leaving so soon," Miss Lavenham interposed.

"It has been quite a long visit," the Duchess replied. "I am sure the sulphur-baths have done me good, and I certainly feel better for having taken the waters."

"I am very glad to hear that."

Listening, Anita thought her Great-Aunt always behaved as if a compliment to Harrogate was also a compliment to herself.

She had risen from the desk at which she had been writing and now the Duchess smiled at her.

"You appear to be very industrious, my child."

Anita curtseyed.

"Yes, Your Grace. I am writing letters for an appeal which Great-Aunt Matilda is sending out on behalf of the Missionaries in West Africa."

"How kind you are," the Duchess said to Miss Lavenham, "and of course you must let me contribute."

"There is no need," Miss Lavenham replied, but added quickly: "Although, of course, every penny counts."

The Duchess opened her reticule, which hung from her wrist.

"Here are five sovereigns," she said, "and I hope my contribution does all the good you expect it to."

"The natives in West Africa have been sadly neglected," Miss Lavenham said, taking the golden sovereigns which the Duchess held out to her. "The Reverend Joshua Hislip whom you heard preach on Sunday, hopes we shall be able to send our own Missionary from Harrogate to save their souls by converting them to Christianity."

As Miss Lavenham spoke the Reverend Joshua's name, the Duchess was aware that Anita was looking at her with a desperate plea in her blue eyes.

"I actually came to ask you, Matilda," the Duchess said, "as a very great favour, if you would lend me your niece."

"Lend you my niece!" Miss Lavenham exclaimed with an incredulous note in her voice.

"I am travelling home tomorrow in my son's private train—a new acquisition of which he is very proud," the Duchess explained. "But it is still a long journey, even if it will be in comparative comfort—and, my eyes not being what they were, I would so much appreciate having somebody to read to me."

Anita drew in her breath and she thought for one moment from the expression on her Great-Aunt's face that she was intending to refuse.

Then Miss Lavenham said with obvious reluctance:

"It would be difficult for me not to lend you Anita in the circumstances. At the same time, I would wish you to send her back here as soon as you have no urgent need for her."

"But of course!" the Duchess replied. "I realise how much she means to you, Matilda, and it is exceedingly kind of you to let me have her, as my son is unavoidably prevented from taking me home himself.''

"At what time do you wish Anita to be with you?" Miss Lavenham asked.

"I think it would be most convenient if she came with me now," the Duchess replied. "I am sure that while you and I have a cup of tea together, Matilda, and talk over old times, she will be able to get her things packed, and my carriage is waiting outside.''

There was a distinct pause before Miss Lavenham agreed to this suggestion, and Anita thought frantically that she was considering sending for the Reverend Joshua to talk to her before she left.

"If that is what you want, I suppose I must agree," Miss Lavenham said abruptly.

Then, as if she was determined that someone should suffer for her plans being changed, she said:

"What are you waiting for, Anita? Surely you have the sense to realise that you should have asked Bates to bring up the tea! And hurry with your packing! You cannot wish to keep Her Grace waiting.''

"No . . . no, of course not!" Anita replied.

She hurried from the room, feeling as if she had wings on her heels.

The Duke had saved her. He had really saved her! She knew that once she had escaped from Harrogate she would never return.

Driving away with the Duchess half-an-hour later, Anita found it difficult to express her gratitude in words.

"I cannot . . . begin to tell Your Grace how . . . wonderful it is of you to take me away from . . . Great-Aunt Matilda."

"I understood from my son that there was a very special reason why you should wish to leave."

"You have seen the Reverend Joshua," Anita replied. "How could I marry an . . . old man like that?"

"I think, at your age, you would naturally think any man over forty is old," the Duchess agreed.

"There is something horrible about him too," Anita said. "I do not think he is in the least worried about the natives of West Africa!"

She checked herself and looked at the Duchess apprehensively.

"I am sorry if that . . . sounds . . . un-Christian."

The Duchess gave a little laugh.

"I think perhaps you are prejudiced against him," she said. "And I am sure it would be easy to find you a far younger and more pleasant husband."

Anita drew in her breath.

"Please, Ma'am, I do not . . . want a . . . husband!" she cried in an intense little voice.

She knew the Duchess was surprised, and she explained:

"Sarah and Daphne wish to be married, but I would rather remain as I am. At least until I find . . . somebody I really . . . love and who . . . loves me."

"I have always heard that your father and mother were very happy together," the Duchess said, "and I expect that with them as an example, that is what you are looking for in your life."

Anita looked at the Duchess in a manner she found very touching.

"At last I have found someone who understands!" she cried. "Everyone I talk to, even Sarah and His Grace, seems to think that the only thing that matters is that I should be married. I want very much more in life than just a . . . wedding-ring."

The Duchess looked amused.

She did not know, as Anita's sisters did, that she had a funny way of saying things.

"And what else is it you want?" she enquired.

"Love first, of course," Anita answered seriously, "and then someone to talk intelligently to, who would understand what I was trying to say without thinking I was imagining things which did not even exist."

"I think I understand," the Duchess said. "And you will find that when you do fall in love, it is easy to talk with someone who loves you, not only with words but with your heart."

Anita gave a little cry of joy.

"You really do understand what I am saying, just as Mama does. Oh, I am so glad that I met you! It was the luckiest thing that ever happened when I fell over your bath-chair and upset the water on your rug."

"Although I hope I can be all the things you think I am," the

Duchess said, "you have to thank my son. It was he who told me I needed a Reader and suggested that I should ask your Great-Aunt to lend you to me."

"You make me sound rather as if I were a library-book!" Anita said with a smile. "But please, will you thank the Duke when you see him and tell him how very, very grateful I am?"

"You can thank him yourself, when he comes to Ollerton."

There was a little silence. Then Anita said incredulously:

"Are you saying, Your Grace, that you are taking me to Ollerton with you? That I can . . . stay there?"

"That was my idea," the Duchess replied, "unless of course you wish to do something else."

"It would be a marvellous, glorious thing to do!" Anita cried. "It is only that I thought that when you had . . . rescued me and taken me South you would . . . want me to go . . . home."

"And who is there at home?" the Duchess enquired.

After that Anita had to tell her the whole story about her mother going to Switzerland, and Sarah staying with her Aunt Elizabeth and Daphne with her Godmother.

"So there was no-one left for you," the Duchess said at the end, "but Matilda Lavenham!"

"I think she meant to be kind to me," Anita replied, "but because she admires the Reverend Joshua so much, she could never begin to understand why I do not feel the same. In fact, when she first told me he was coming to call tomorrow, I thought that he was intending to marry her."

She said this just as they reached Prospect Gardens and the Duchess was laughing as the horses came to a standstill and the footman opened the door.

~

"The Duke of Ollerton, M'Lady!" the Butler announced.

Lady Blankley, who was posed beside a huge vase of tiger-lilies, turned with affected grace towards the man standing in the doorway.

There was no mistaking her delight as she saw the Duke, looking extremely elegant, put his top-hat and stick on a chair just inside the door before he advanced towards her, a faint smile lighting his eyes.

187

"You are back!" she exclaimed. "I have been counting the hours, I really have! I have been so miserable without you!"

Her voice was musical in a somewhat contrived manner, but, as the Duke had often thought, everything about Lady Blankley was a polished perfection like an article fashioned by a master-craftsman.

The Duke took the hand she held out to him, kissed it, and turned it over to kiss her shell-pink palm.

Then as he straightened himself he said:

"You are even more beautiful than I remember!"

"Thank you, Kerne!"

Her eyes glittered like the emeralds she wore round her neck and he thought that her dark hair, with the blue lights in it, was very alluring.

"As I have been away for so long," the Duke said, "we have a great deal to say to each other. Shall we sit down?"

Lady Blankley moved a little closer to him.

"Why should we waste time with words?" she asked. "George is playing polo at Hurlingham and will not be back for at least another two hours."

As she spoke her arms went round the Duke's neck, pulling his head down to hers, and her lips, fiercely demanding, were on his. . . .

A long time later the Duke was tidying his hair in the mirror over the mantelpiece when a soft voice from the sofa asked:

"When shall I see you again?"

"I am going to Ollerton first thing tomorrow morning," the Duke replied. "I have a party arriving on Friday."

"A party?" Lady Blankley echoed. "And you have not invited me?"

The Duke shook his head.

"It is not your sort of party, Elaine, and my mother is acting as hostess."

"That would not prevent us from being together, if I were one of your guests."

The Duke told himself he had made a mistake in mentioning the fact that he was having a party, and he knew that the last person he wanted at this particular party, at which he was to choose his future wife, would be Elaine.

She was beautiful, there was no denying that. At the same time, he always left her feeling that she wanted more from him than he was willing to give.

He told himself now that although their fiery love-making was in some ways very satisfactory, he invariably had after it a feeling of disappointment which was unaccountable.

"What more do I want?" he had asked himself. "What am I looking for?"

He had thought when he first pursued Elaine Blankley, or rather she pursued him, that she was everything that any man could possibly desire.

She was beautiful, witty, and she had the polished perfection which the Duke had always sought.

She was acknowledged even by her rivals as being the best-dressed woman in London, and it was always said that when the Prince of Wales was in an irritable mood she could charm him out of it quicker than anybody else.

The Duke had found that when he made love to Elaine Blankley there was a raging, primitive fire beneath the controlled, civilised face which she showed to the world, and it inflamed him, giving them both a passionate excitement he had never known before.

And yet now the Duke told himself that there was something missing.

What it was he had no idea. He only knew that for some reason to which he could not put a name, he was glad that he was going to Ollerton tomorrow and would not be seeing Elaine again for at least ten days.

He turned from the contemplation of his reflection in the mirror to look at her.

She had a feline grace that he appreciated, and he knew that the manner in which she was lying on the sofa was deliberately provocative.

"You have made me very happy, Kerne," she said in a soft voice.

"That is what I intended to say to you, Elaine."

She held out her hand and as he took it her fingers tightened on his.

"Come again very, very soon," she said. "You know how much I miss you."

"As I shall miss you," he replied, because it was expected of him, but as he spoke he knew it was not true.

189

He walked to the door, picked up his hat and stick and, without saying any more, left the room.

But as he went down the broad stairs towards the Hall where a number of footmen in the Blankley livery were on duty, he asked himself whether he would ever visit this house again.

~

The next morning, driving his horses because the journey to Ollerton was too short to warrant using his private train, and also because he preferred to be in the open air, the Duke of Ollerton was thinking not of Lady Blankley but of his house-party.

He had received a letter from his mother, telling him, not surprisingly, that all the people she had asked to stay had accepted her invitation.

The young girls who were coming were Lady Millicent Clyde, daughter of the Earl and Countess of Clydeshire, the Honourable Alice Down, daughter of Lord and Lady Downham, and Lady Rosemary, whom he had already met, daughter of the Marquis and Marchioness of Doncaster.

The Duchess wrote:

Having met Lady Rosemary, perhaps you have already made up your mind and the party is now unnecessary.

What was unnecessary, the Duke thought when he read his mother's letter, was that Lady Rosemary should be included in the party.

He had thought last year, although he had paid her little attention as she was still in the School-Room, that she was rather an attractive girl who might easily blossom into a beauty.

But he had been over-optimistic, and when he had arrived at the Marquis's large house which was not far from the Race-Course, he had found that Lady Rosemary was not half as interesting or as attractive as her father's horses.

There was in fact rather a horsy look about her which the Duke did not appreciate in a woman, and he thought the hearty manner in which she spoke was reminiscent of the stables where she obviously spent too much of her time.

When he rode with her and was some time in her company at the races, he realised that she was not in the least the type of woman he would invite to become his Duchess.

Let us hope the other two are better, he thought now as he left the outskirts of London and was in the open countryside.

Then he told himself that the whole idea of being married was so unpleasant that he had a good mind to go straight back to London to seek the familiar amusements that he found entertaining.

But he had a vision of his cousin Marmion with his bloated red face and paunchy figure, and he knew that even if it were not his urgent desire to prevent him from succeeding to the Dukedom, he still had to obey what was to all intents and purposes a command from the Queen.

Yet, every instinct in his body rebelled against it.

He had no wish to be married and he knew only too well that even if he had some sort of interest or even an ordinary natural desire for his wife as a woman, it would very quickly fade.

Elaine Blankley was a case in point.

He had known when he went to bed last night that he was through with her, and although she would doubtless protest and perhaps make a scene if she could get him alone, her name was crossed off his list, and that excluded her from being a guest at Ollerton.

"I wonder who will interest me next," the Duke asked himself, and he thought that the inevitable end of a chase which never took very long was becoming tedious.

"Why are all women so exactly alike?" he asked.

When he met a new beauty for the first time he found himself intrigued like a man exploring new territory or finding a strange, hitherto uncatalogued flower on the side of a mountain.

Then all too quickly he found he knew every move of the game before he made it.

It was like playing chess with an opponent who was so bad that there was never a chance of it being anything but a walkover.

Sometimes he would think that a woman was mysterious and elusive, only to find quite soon that there was nothing Sphinx-like about her and all she wanted was to be in his arms as quickly as possible.

"Dammit all," the Duke said to himself, "I think I shall go big-game shooting."

Then he knew he had done that already, and, what was more, his future was waiting for him at Ollerton—three fair-haired, blue-eyed young women who were tall enough to look resplendent in the Ollerton tiaras, with Junoesque figures to do credit to the ropes of Ollerton pearls.

~

The Duchess had said very much the same thing to Anita when they were traveling down in the train from Harrogate.

Anita had been thrilled and excited by the Duke's train as a child might have been.

"I thought only the Queen had a private train," she had said, "but of course a Duke is very nearly the same as a King, is he not?"

"Not exactly!" the Duchess had said, smiling, "although I am sure Kerne would like to think he was."

"He looks so magnificent and it is only right that he should have everything to enhance his position," Anita said ingenuously. "I am sure when he was a little boy he had a toy train and planned that when he was grown up he would have a real one."

"That certainly never struck me," the Duchess said, "but we will ask him sometime if that was true."

She smiled at Anita, who sat first on one seat of the Drawing-Room compartment, then on another, determined to try out everything.

As servants wearing the Duke's livery brought them luncheon, her eyes were shining and the Duchess thought she looked as if she were watching her first Pantomime.

"I ought to have read to you," Anita said when they had been travelling for a long time and the Duchess said she would go to her sleeping-compartment to lie down.

"I have enjoyed our conversation, dear," the Duchess replied, "and actually I do not really require a Reader."

She saw the disappointment in Anita's eyes and guessed she was thinking that in that case she would dispense with her services very quickly.

"At the same time, I like having you with me," she said, "and because my private secretary is away on holiday, you shall help me, when we get to Ollerton, to arrange the special party that my son is giving."

"A special party?" Anita questioned.

"Yes," the Duchess answered, "and that is why you and I are going to stay in the big house and not in the Dower House where I live when I am alone."

"Tell me, please, tell me exactly what you do!" Anita begged.

She listened with rapt attention while the Duchess explained how sometimes the Duke had parties at Ollerton at which he wanted his mother to be the Chaperone, but otherwise she lived in her own house, which was smaller and very beautiful and where she had all her special things round her.

"Which do you like the best?" Anita asked.

"It is difficult to say," the Duchess replied. "When I first left Ollerton, where I had lived all the years since I became a bride, I am afraid I shed a few tears as I felt I was saying good-bye to my youth. Then I came to love my own house, and it is rather nice to be able to do exactly what I want without worrying too much about appearances."

"I can understand that," Anita said. "But now we are to go to Ollerton?"

"Yes, because this party is a very special one."

"Why is it so special?" Anita enquired.

The Duchess told her the truth.

She was almost certain that Anita was not having romantic dreams about the Duke, but one could never be sure with young girls, and the Duchess wished not only to save her son from any embarrassment but to prevent this engaging child from having her heart broken.

She began to tell Anita exactly what the Duke required of his wife, and she thought, from the manner in which she listened and the enthusiasm with which she asked questions, that she had been quite needlessly apprehensive in thinking that Anita had any foolish aspirations in his direction.

"You must find him somebody very, very beautiful," Anita said.

"That is what I am trying to do," the Duchess answered. "But it is not easy. You see, my son is used to associating with much older women who are sophisticated, witty, elegant, and amusing. This is something impossible to find in a girl who is just out of the School-Room."

Anita nodded her head.

"I can understand that," she said, "and I expect most of them find it very frightening to be launched into the world like a ship which has never been in the water before."

"That is true," the Duchess smiled, "and sometimes it seems like a rough sea."

Anita laughed.

"No-one ever looks her best when she is seasick!"

"I am trying," the Duchess continued, "to find three girls from whom my son will be able to choose a wife who will fulfill all his requirements."

"You will be able to help her," Anita said, "but she will find it difficult, Your Grace, to be as charming or as beautiful as you!"

The Duchess thought she was almost echoing what the Duke had said, and she smiled before she answered:

"It is very sweet of you to speak like that, but I am growing old, and I know that my tiresome rheumatism has put lines on my face, besides making me walk in a grotesque fashion."

Anita thought for a moment. Then she said:

"Would Your Grace think it very impertinent of me if I made a suggestion?"

"Of course not," the Duchess replied.

"Well, we had a Doctor in Fenchurch who was rather a friend of Papa and Mama, and he treated people in the village suffering from rheumatism and he always made them better."

"How did he do that?"

"First, he insisted that they should always walk quite a long distance every day. He said it was fatal for them to become chair-bound because sooner or later they became bed-bound, and then there was no hope for them."

The Duchess looked at Anita in a startled fashion.

"I never thought of that," she said. "I wonder if you are right!"

"I am sure Dr. Emerson was right," Anita said, "and also he used to give his patients a herbal drink which he sometimes asked Mama to make for him, and I can make some for you, if you wish."

"I would try anything to take away the pain and make me mobile again," the Duchess replied.

Anita was silent for a moment. Then she said:

"That day at the well when I fell over your chair, I was thinking how wonderful it would be if the water really worked for those who drank

194

it and they all jumped out of their bath-chairs and shouted that they were cured.''

She paused before adding:

''I said a little prayer that that might happen, but instead I met you and it was the most wonderful thing that ever happened to me! Perhaps if you drink the herbs and I pray very hard while I am mixing them, they may work like a miracle and you will be well, completely well, and your rheumatism will go away.''

''That is a lovely idea,'' the Duchess said, ''and of course we will try it. I too believe prayer can do amazing and unexpected things.''

''Mama always said that God helps those who help themselves,'' Anita replied, ''so we must do our part too.''

''That is exactly what we will do,'' the Duchess agreed.

When they left the train at the Halt which was used only by visitors to Ollerton Park, Anita saw there was waiting an open carriage with a white piqué awning to shade them from the sun.

They drove for a little way through pretty country, wooded and with meadowland brilliant with wild flowers.

Then suddenly ahead of them was Ollerton Park and it was even more magnificent and impressive than Anita had expected.

''It is beautiful, magnificent!'' she cried. ''It is exactly the sort of house the Duke should have! Do you not feel that too, Your Grace?''

''I do indeed,'' the Duchess replied. ''And I felt just like you do the first time I came here after I was engaged.''

''You must have felt that you were stepping into fairy-land,'' Anita said, ''and I am sure you looked exactly like the Princess who married Prince Charming.''

The Duchess smiled.

She was beginning to realise that everything Anita said or thought had a dream-like quality that had little to do with reality.

She thought it was very unusual to find a girl who was so completely unselfconscious and had about her a vivid joy in life which made her different from any young woman the Duchess had ever met before.

Because she had only just thought of it, she said:

''Yes, Ollerton is a fairy-tale building, and I think, Anita, because I hope you will stay with me for some time, that I should give you some gowns which will be complementary to the house in which you will be staying.''

Anita turned to look at her and the Duchess thought that her blue eyes were shining like stars.

"New gowns!" she cried. "Oh, Ma'am, do you mean it? If you do, it will be the most wonderful, exciting thing that could possibly happen."

She paused. Then before the Duchess could speak she said quickly:

"I am sure I should not . . . accept such a generous present from you when you have been so kind already in helping me . . . escape from the . . . Reverend Joshua."

"There are a great many more exciting things to do," the Duchess said quietly, "and I do mean that you shall have some new gowns. You will enjoy Ollerton all the more if you feel you are dressed for the part."

"But of course," Anita said, "and please. . . do you think I could have a new crinoline . . . a really big one?"

She saw the smile on the Duchess's face and added quickly:

"Perhaps not an enormous one . . . because I should look strange as I am so small . . . but just one that is fashionable."

"I will get you one that is exactly right," the Duchess promised.

Anita clasped her hands together.

"I am dreaming . . . I know I am dreaming!" she said. "But I do hope I shall not wake up until I have worn it!"

Once again the Duchess was laughing as the horses came to a standstill.

CHAPTER FOUR

*T*HE DUKE WALKED UP THE STEPS and into the magnificent marble Hall.

The statues were all of goddesses, and he thought, as he had often thought before, that there was no Hall to rival his in any other of the large houses he had visited.

"Welcome back, Your Grace," the Butler said respectfully. "Her Grace is in the Music-Room."

The Duke handed the Butler his hat and gloves, and was feeling satisfied that the six footmen in the Ollerton livery were up to standard.

He had always insisted that they must be over six feet tall and their smartness and bearing was something on which he was particularly insistent.

Leaving the Hall, he walked down a wide corridor hung with portraits of his ancestors which led to the Music-Room, which was in the West Wing.

It was a room that had been redecorated by the Duchess shortly before his father's death and it was in consequence artistic and combined the classical and the modern with great success.

As the Duke drew nearer to it, he expected to hear the music of Chopin or Bach, knowing that they were his mother's favourite Composers.

To his surprise, he heard the unexpected sound of a gay waltz which had been popular in London the previous winter and to which he had partnered many fascinating beauties.

Now that he thought of it, he remembered that it was during the waltz at a Ball given at Marlborough House that he had first been aware of Elaine Blankley's attractions.

She had used every known artifice to make him aware of her as a woman, glancing up at him with her green eyes veiled by her mascaraed eye-lashes and making her hand on his shoulder feel like a caress.

That he should recall Elaine at this moment when he had returned home annoyed him, and there was a slight frown between the Duke's eyes as he opened the door into the Music-Room.

Then he stood still in utter astonishment.

In the centre of the room was his mother and he could hardly believe his eyes when he saw that she was dancing.

She was moving slowly, it was true, but very gracefully, and from the manner in which she held her arms there was no doubt that she was pretending to be waltzing with a partner to a melody played on the huge Broadwood piano at which Anita was sitting.

As the Duchess turned she saw her son and came to a standstill, then a second or two later Anita realised who had come into the room and raised her hands from the key-board.

The Duke spoke and there was no mistaking the amazement in his voice.

"You are dancing, Mama! How is it possible?"

The Duchess would have replied, but before she could do so Anita came running to her across the floor to exclaim:

"You have done it! You have done it! Is it not wonderful? And you told me you would never dance again!"

"But, as you see, I can waltz," the Duchess said.

"Is this what Harrogate has done for you?" the Duke asked.

The Duchess shook her head.

"It helped a little, but that I have been walking and can dance is due entirely to Anita."

"To Anita?" the Duke echoed.

As he spoke he looked at the small figure standing beside him, but her eyes, filled with delight, were on the Duchess's face.

"Anita made me walk and gave me a herbal concoction to drink which I really do believe has performed miracles!"

"It certainly has!" the Duke agreed. "I never expected to see you dance again, Mama, nor for that matter to walk so easily."

"But now I can do both," the Duchess said, "and it is due entirely to this dear child."

She put out her hand to Anita as she spoke.

"You must not forget one important thing, Ma'am," Anita said, "that we both prayed very hard for a miracle."

"Yes, of course," the Duchess agreed. "That is something we must not forget."

Anita looked at the Duke.

"I was praying for a miracle," she said, "when I fell over Her Grace's bath-chair in the Pump Room at Harrogate."

"But instead you 'fell from grace,'" the Duke said with a smile.

"No," Anita replied, "it was the miracle I was asking for, but it came in a most mysterious manner."

She gave a little skip of joy as she went on:

"It was a miracle that you saved me from having to marry the Reverend Joshua; a miracle that brought me here; and a very, very big miracle that the herbs and our prayers have made your mother so much better that she can dance!"

The Duke smiled.

"Do you agree with that, Mama?"

"But of course!" the Duchess answered. "But now, miracle, or no miracle, I would like to sit down for a moment."

The Duke led her to a comfortable sofa and as the Duchess sat down on it Anita said, with a note of anxiety in her voice:

"It has not all been too much for you? Shall I call the footmen to bring your chair so that you can be carried upstairs to lie down?"

"No, I am perfectly all right," the Duchess replied. "It is just that I need a moment to 'catch my breath,' so that I can talk to my son."

"Then I will leave you to talk to His Grace," Anita said tactfully.

"I think first you should show him your new gown," the Duchess suggested.

The Duke looked at Anita and realised why she seemed different.

Now, instead of the plain little dress he had seen on her in Harrogate with its white collar and cuffs, she was wearing an extremely attractive and obviously expensive white gown with a wide skirt that was unmistakably supported by a crinoline.

Above it her tiny waist was encircled by a blue sash, and her pale hair was dressed in a new fashion which made her look, he thought, even more like a small angel than she had before.

After what she had accomplished for his mother, he almost expected to see wings sprouting from her shoulders, especially when she twirled round to show him her gown from the back, saying:

"Her Grace has been so kind, and I never, never in my whole life expected to have such lovely gowns as she has given me. They are definitely part of my miracle."

"And a very becoming one," the Duke said.

There was a slightly mocking note in his voice and Anita was not certain whether he was pleased or thought it presumptuous of her to accept such expensive presents from his mother.

"I want to talk with you, Kerne," the Duchess said, "but before we do so, I would like you to see the way Anita and I have arranged the Ball-Room."

The Duke raised his eye-brows.

"The Ball-Room?"

"Yes, dearest, we are giving a Ball on Saturday night. I thought it would make the party go with a swing and melt away any embarrassment there might be among our younger guests."

She thought there was a slightly ominous look in her son's eyes, and she added quickly:

199

"It will only be a very small Ball, just the house-party and our friends in the immediate neighbourhood. I do hope the idea pleases you."

"Of course, I am delighted with whatever arrangements you have made," the Duke said hastily.

"Then go and look at the Ball-Room," the Duchess suggested, "and if it is not to your liking, then of course we can—change things."

The way his mother spoke told the Duke that it would be a difficult thing to do.

Because he wished to please her, he rose to his feet and Anita ran ahead of him towards the door.

Only as they walked together down the passage which led to the Ball-Room in another part of the great house did she say, a little nervously:

"I do hope you do not . . . mind my . . . staying here as your mother . . . asked me to do. She has also . . . invited me to be . . . present at your . . . Ball."

There was no mistaking the anxiety in her voice, as if she was afraid he might disapprove, but the Duke replied:

"As you are so small, I daresay we can squeeze you in!"

She knew he was teasing her, and once again she gave a little skip as she walked beside him and said:

"It is so very, very exciting! I have never been to a Ball before, and my gown is so beautiful!"

She paused, then she said in a different tone:

"I have been waiting ever since I came to Ollerton for you to arrive so that I could thank you. I have never been so happy as I am here with your mother. We have had such fun arranging the Ball-Room, which I hope will be to your liking."

It struck the Duke that most girls of Anita's age might have found it rather dull even at Ollerton to be alone with an older woman and with no other distractions for nearly two weeks.

But there was no doubt that Anita's eyes were shining and there was an excitement as well as a sincerity in what she said which made it impossible not to believe that she spoke the truth.

They reached the Ball-Room and the Duke standing in the doorway stared about him in surprise.

He had always thought that the long Ball-Room, which had been added at the beginning of Queen Victoria's reign, was not a particularly interesting addition to the house, which was otherwise a fine example of Adam architecture.

Now it was transformed and he wondered how much the transformation owed to Anita's imagination.

Instead of the cream-coloured walls with somewhat pretentious pillars and uninspired decorations, the whole room had been converted into a picture of Venice.

At the far end there was a mural which made him think he was looking onto the canal by moonlight with San Marco in the distance. In the foreground there were lighted gondolas being propelled along the smooth water.

From the ceiling were hung curtains of crimson satin which made the room appear like a tent, and it was lit by the traditional gold lanterns of Venice.

Round the floor in place of the conventional chairs were benches covered with silk cushions and with a high prow at one end such as was to be found on every gondola.

The Duke was aware that Anita was watching his face with a worried expression in her eyes, and after a pause he said:

"Very effective, and something we have not seen at Ollerton before!"

"You really like it?"

"I can certainly recognise it for the place it is supposed to be," the Duke replied.

Anita gave a little cry of delight.

"That is what I hoped you would say. Her Grace has never visited Venice, so we had to rely on the pictures we could find in books in the Library."

"I have a feeling," the Duke said, "this was your idea and you tempted my mother into such extravagance."

"Her Grace did say she thought the room was rather ugly and that perhaps if we had garlands of flowers or something like that, it would be an improvement."

"But instead, prompted by one of your daydreams, you thought up this idea of Venice."

"You are pleased ... you really are ... pleased?" Anita asked anxiously.

"I think you would be very disappointed if I said anything different," the Duke replied.

"I wanted you not to see it until Saturday night," Anita said, "but Her Grace was just a little afraid that you would think it too fanciful."

"I cannot imagine our guests will be able to say such complimentary things as an Italian gallant would manage to do," the Duke said, "but at least I hope they do their best to produce the right amount of romance that you are expecting."

Again he was teasing Anita, and he saw a little flush come into her face and knew without her saying so that because of her experience at Harrogate, she would resist the idea of any man approaching her amorously.

It was an attitude he had not expected.

At the same time, he thought it was inevitable, after she had been so frightened by the idea of being forced to marry her Great-Aunt's pet Parson, that she would be afraid of all men.

She is very young, he thought to himself, *and of course, to her, being brought up in a small village, men are an unknown quantity. It would be a pity if she avoids them too strenuously and misses a lot of fun.*

Then he thought that if in fact she did begin to enjoy being pursued by men, the compliments they would pay her and the flirtations they would expect, it would undoubtedly spoil the child-like atmosphere she created which made her resemble a small angel.

He saw now that she had moved nearer to the mural at the end of the room and was staring at the gondolas on the canal as if she could really see them and the exquisite piazzas behind them.

"Are you praying that one day a miracle will carry you to the most glamorous city in the world?" the Duke asked.

"I was thinking of its history," Anita replied. "When I was looking for pictures of it, I read how the Venetians wasted their lives in pleasure-seeking and so lost their power and even their trade. It seems such a pity."

"Are you really saying that pleasure-seeking is a waste of time?" the Duke enquired.

"I think everyone wants pleasure," Anita replied seriously. "At the same time, it should be earned, like a holiday."

The Duke did not speak, and after a moment she said:

"Your mother has told me how regularly you speak in the House of Lords and how you work at bringing your houses and your Estate to perfection. That is why I so wanted this party to be an enjoyable one for you, especially as there is a particular reason for its being given."

The Duke frowned again.

If there was one thing he disliked, it was having his private affairs talked about, even by his mother.

Then somehow, because Anita had spoken so naturally, it did not annoy him as much as it might have done had she been somebody else.

As if she knew that she had spoken too seriously, she said lightly:

"The scene is set, everything is ready, and it only remains for you to play the part of Paris."

There was a lilt in her voice, as if she found the idea extremely romantic, and the Duke with a wry twist of his lips replied:

"So you are suggesting it is the Golden Apple I am to present?"

Anita gave a little chuckle.

"I think, Your Grace, it is really a coronet, but I expect whoever receives it will feel it is one and the same thing!"

The Duke thought this was really going too far and he felt that it was a definite impertinence.

Then, before he could remonstrate with her, she said:

"I must not stay here talking. Her Grace will be longing to know what you feel about the room. She was so afraid it might not please you. But I will tell her that everything is all right."

She spoke the last words over her shoulder as she began to run along the dance-floor, and before the Duke could think of anything to say, she had disappeared through the door by which they had entered the room.

It was certainly unusual, he thought, for a woman, when she could be alone with him, to hurry away to talk to somebody else!

As he walked slowly back to the front of the house he thought he had been extremely clever to rescue Anita from a disastrous marriage and at the same time to find somebody to amuse and help his mother.

At dinner that evening there were only the three of them and the Duke put himself out to entertain not only the Duchess but Anita, who looked at him with wide eyes and listened with rapt attention to everything he had to say.

At the same time, she was not in the least shy and she made occasional quaint little remarks which made him laugh.

Because he realised that it was no use standing on his dignity when Anita obviously had the full confidence of his mother, they talked quite naturally and without reserve about the three girls who had been invited to Ollerton to meet him.

"I do not mind telling you, Mama," the Duke said, "that Rosemary Castor, on second acquaintance, was extremely disappointing."

"I am sorry to hear that," the Duchess said. "I thought you said last year that she seemed an attractive young woman."

"She is now over-hearty, and she gave me the impression of looking like a well-bred horse!" the Duke remarked.

The Duchess smiled a little ruefully and Anita said:

"When I went down to your stables and saw your horses, I knew I would much rather marry one of them than the Reverend Joshua."

"I was just wondering," the Duke replied teasingly, "if your pedigree is good enough for you to be a suitable bride for Thunderer or Hercules!"

Anita knew he was referring to his two finest stallions, which she had already been told were the pride of his stable.

"I certainly would not aspire as high as either!" she flashed. "But yesterday Thunderer did allow me, with great condescension, to pat his neck and hand him a carrot!"

The Duke frowned.

"You must be careful," he said. "Thunderer is not always to be trusted. I hope you did not go into his stall?"

"I am not answering that question," Anita replied, "in case you are angry with me or your Head-Groom!"

"I suppose you are trying to tell me that through some Divine protection even my horses will not hurt you."

"If I say 'yes' it will sound conceited," Anita replied. "If I say 'no' it might be unlucky!"

The Duke laughed.

"You are not the angel you pretend to be," he said. "I think that in fact you are so devious in your ways, Anita, that you belong to another hemisphere altogether."

"If you recognise me," Anita answered quickly, "there is nothing I can say to defend myself!"

The Duke was amused by the sharpness of her mind and they sparred and argued with each other until the meal ended.

He rather expected, because it would be the usual procedure among his guests, that when his mother retired to bed immediately after dinner, Anita would make some excuse to continue their conversation and remain with him.

Instead she went upstairs with the Duchess and he did not see her again that night.

The following morning after breakfast he went to the stables as he usually did, to look at his horses, and found that Anita was already there.

She was in fact standing inside Thunderer's stall giving him a carrot with one hand and patting his neck with the other.

The Duke watched her for some minutes before she was aware of his presence. Then she looked round and saw him, and there was a faint flush on her cheeks as she said:

"Your Grace is early! I understood that you did not come to the stables before nine-thirty."

"So you were stealing a march on me!"

"I thought I should not come today, as you are here." Anita replied, "but then I thought that Thunderer might miss the carrot I always give him."

"Then I presume, having ingratiated yourself with my horses," the Duke commented, "that you will expect me to take you riding."

He saw by the expression in Anita's eyes that she had never thought such a thing.

She looked into his face to see if he was serious before she said:

"Would you . . . do you mean that? Could I . . . go with you? I have ridden once since I have been here, but I did not like to leave Her Grace alone."

"What is my mother doing at the moment?" the Duke enquired.

"She is having her hair washed," Anita answered, "so that she will look beautiful, as she always does, when your guests arrive this afternoon."

"In which case I presume you are off-duty?"

He paused, knowing that Anita was tense as she waited, almost like one of his dogs who sensed he was about to be taken for a walk.

The Duke drew his watch from his waist-coat pocket and said:

"I will give you exactly five minutes in which to change. I will wait for you at the front door, and if you are any longer I shall leave without you!"

Anita gave a cry of delight.

Then she was running from the stables, holding up her crinoline with both hands as she did so.

The Duke watched her go, then began to talk to his Head-Groom about the horses he had not seen for some weeks.

A little later, riding across the Park, he thought Anita, on a horse that seemed too big for her, looked extremely attractive in a tight-waisted habit of blue piqué and a high hat trimmed with a gauze veil.

The Duke had chosen too many gowns for a succession of lovely ladies over the years not to be a connoisseur of a woman's appearance, and he was aware that his mother, with unerring good taste, had chosen for Anita clothes that were perfect for both her height and her youth.

But no dressmaker could improve her flower-like face, the shining innocence and excitement in her blue eyes, or the mischievous little smile which often twisted her cupid's-bow mouth.

She was certainly an engaging little creature, the Duke thought to himself, and knew he had been right in thinking that she had a way with horses which was something which could not be taught.

Riding beside him, Anita knew that no man could look more handsome, appearing to be an indivisible part of the horse on which he was mounted.

Her imagination made her wonder if in fact there were any animals to be found in Hades.

Then she told herself that animals were born without sin, and if they became bad-tempered or savage it was due entirely to the treatment they received from mankind.

No, Heaven would be filled with animals, for it would not be Heaven without them, while in Hell it would be one of the things one longed for and could not have.

The Duke's voice broke in on her thoughts:

"What are you thinking about?"

Because she did not wish to say that indirectly she was thinking of him, she replied:

"I was thinking of animals and of how much they mean in our lives."

"Have you owned many?" he enquired.

"Papa had a number of horses until his accident, and of course we had dogs, and when I was small I had a cat who used to sleep curled up on my bed."

"And that taught you how to handle a horse like Thunderer?"

"I think the answer to that is that I love him and he knows it," Anita answered. "It is much easier for a horse, and I suppose any animal, to be aware of what we are thinking and feeling than it is for us nowadays to feel the same about a human being."

"Why 'nowadays'?" the Duke asked curiously.

"Because we do not use our sixth sense."

"Do you think that is what you were doing when you recognised me the first time we met?"

"No," Anita replied, "I was seeing with my eyes. It was not until later, when you were so kind to me and helped me to escape, that I realised you had not fallen from Heaven as I imagined but in fact were living in it here at Ollerton."

"I wish that were true."

"But it is true!" Anita said positively. "How can you be so ungrateful?"

"Ungrateful?"

"Not to recognise that there is no place which could be more beautiful or more perfect than the house and Estate that belong to you. Besides which, you have a mother who loves you more than anyone else in the world."

Anita's voice was soft as she spoke of the Duchess.

For a little while they rode on in silence, and it was inevitable that the Duke's mind was on the young women who were arriving to stay that afternoon; one of whom, as his wife, would share with him the perfection of Ollerton.

Strangely, as if she could read his thoughts without his saying them aloud, Anita asked very quietly:

"Must you do this?"

It did not strike the Duke that he should resent her familiarity with his private affairs. Instead he replied:

"I have no alternative. If this party is a failure, there must be another, and yet another. But the end will be the same. I cannot escape!"

Almost as if he could not bear to think of it, he touched Thunderer with his whip and the stallion responded by breaking into a gallop, and there was no chance of continuing the conversation.

Only when they reached home and Anita went up to her bed-room to change did she stand at the window looking out over the Park in which she had just been riding.

The sunshine was glinting on the huge oak trees and on the lake, on which white swans moved with exquisite grace.

"Please, God, let him find someone who will make him happy," she prayed in her heart.

Then quickly, because she thought the Duchess would be waiting for her, she began to change into one of her beautiful new gowns.

As she expected, because they had travelled in the Duke's train and had driven in his comfortable carriages from the Halt, the majority of the party arrived exactly on time.

The Duchess was waiting for them in the Silver Salon, which was on the ground floor, and Anita had put on one of her prettiest gowns.

"Do you want me to be there, Ma'am?" she asked. "Perhaps you and His Grace would prefer to receive your guests alone?"

"No, of course not, dear child," the Duchess replied, "and I think you will be a great help, since this house-party is very unlike Kerne's usual ones."

"You mean because the girls you have invited are so young?"

"Exactly!" the Duchess agreed.

"There is no reason why they should be difficult to talk to, or not enjoy themselves," Anita said. "I am sure Sarah is the life and soul of every party she goes to in London. Mama used to say that Sarah always made a party go."

"I hope you will do the same," the Duchess said with a smile.

Anita knew that Her Grace was apprehensive but she could not understand why.

The Marquis and Marchioness of Doncaster came into the Salon first and the Duke was obviously delighted to see them.

Their daughter, Lady Rosemary, was presented to the Duchess, and immediately Anita knew why she was not in the least suitable to be the wife of the Duke.

There was something "horsy" about her, there was no grace in the way she walked, and she shook hands almost as a man might have done.

The Earl and Countess of Clydeshire's daughter was, however, very different.

She was tall, golden-haired and blue-eyed, and was in fact, Anita thought, extremely pretty.

She had a quiet, rather repressed manner of talking, but that, Anita guessed, was because she was shy.

She moved to her side to ask her if she had had a good journey.

"It was the first time I have been in a private train, and I thought it very luxurious," Lady Millicent answered.

"I thought it was fascinating," Anita said, "and I could hardly believe it was real."

"It was real enough to me!" Lady Millicent replied in a voice Anita did not understand.

There were other friends of the Duke's who had been on the train, one a married couple who were extremely keen on racing, and the other a slightly older man called Lord Greshame.

"Glad to be here, Ollerton!" he said now to the Duke. "I have always said that you have the best horses and the most comfortable houses in the whole country."

"That is exactly the sort of compliment I like to receive, George," the Duke replied. "I think you know everybody except Miss Lavenham."

Lord Greshame shook hands with Anita, but before he could speak to her, Lord and Lady Downham and their daughter Alice were announced.

They had driven down from London and had managed, as Lord Downham averred in a loud voice, to beat his previous record by ten minutes fifty seconds.

Lady Alice was, Anita thought, looking at her, a disappointment.

She was of course tall, fair, and blue-eyed, but she had a somewhat sulky expression, was too fat to be attractive, and there were undoubtedly spots on her chin.

Lady Millicent will certainly have it all her own way! Anita thought, and wondered what the Duchess would think of her prospective daughter-in-law.

There were a number of other guests who arrived in the next hour, making the number staying in the house up to twenty.

"You must be very busy downstairs," Anita said to the maid who looked after her when she was getting her bath ready.

"Not as busy as we are sometimes, Miss," the maid replied. "His Grace has had as many as forty guests staying in the house, and that means, as most of them brings a lady's-maid or a valet, nearly forty extra in the Servant's Hall and Housekeeper's room."

"Then it is a party for you too," Anita said with a smile.

"That's what I feels, Miss," the maid said, "although the older ones grumble."

"I expect they enjoy it really."

She remembered how Deborah often grumbled when there were extra people to meals at home.

But during the time when there had been very few visitors she had complained because, she said, there was no life about the place.

There is certainly plenty of life at Ollerton! Anita thought.

When she was ready and looked at herself in the mirror she could hardly believe that the attractive, fashionable reflection she saw was really that of Anita Lavenham.

She had written long letters to both her sisters to tell them what was happening to her, and Sarah had replied saying how delighted she was and how she had to make the very best of her opportunity of meeting important people at Ollerton.

She had written:

Perhaps, dearest, one of the Duke's friends may take a fancy to you, and if he does, please be practical. You may never have such an opportunity again! Although I agree that it was ridiculous of Great-Aunt Matilda to expect you to marry an aged Parson, I am sure you will realise that the alternative, when the Duchess is tired of you, is to go back to Fenchurch and become an Old Maid.

I am saying nothing yet, because it might be unlucky, but I am keeping my fingers crossed that I might, I just might, have very special news for you in a few weeks. Oh, Anita, please pray that what I am wishing for will come true, because it is what I want more than I have ever wanted anything before.

Sarah is in love, Anita thought as she read the letter, and because she loved her sister she prayed very hard that Sarah might have her wish.

Later that evening, when they were all sitting talking in the Drawing-Room, which was one of the most beautiful rooms in the house, at the Duchess's suggestion Anita moved to the piano.

The Duchess had already told her when they had been talking about the party that she thought music always made people relax and took away some of the stiffness between those who had just met one another for the first time.

Anita therefore chose soft, rather romantic music, knowing that in fact she played it better than the more classical studies which were really Her Grace's favourites.

"Mama taught me to play," she had told the Duchess. "She was really good. I only strum to amuse myself."

"I think you play very prettily," the Duchess said. "It is a talent more women should have, and a very attractive one."

Anita therefore played what she thought would make a happy background for the Duke's guests, but her thoughts swept away towards her own family.

Please, God, help Sarah find a husband, she prayed in her heart, *and let Daphne find one too, but prevent me from having to be in a hurry to choose anyone.*

She was praying so intensely that her eyes were closed, and she started as she heard the Duke say:

"What are you thinking about in the darkness of your mind?"

She opened her eyes to find that he was leaning on the piano, looking at her.

"I . . . was thinking."

"About whom?"

"My sister Sarah."

"I heard when I was in London that she was a great success. In fact, I forgot to tell you, I actually saw her at one party I attended."

"Did you think she looked pretty?"

"Very, but you are not in the least like her."

"I know," Anita admitted. "Sarah is the beauty of the family."

Her eyes lit up as she added:

"If you have heard she is a success, perhaps what she is wishing for has come true. Actually, I was praying that it would."

"For what is she wishing?"

"I think, although she has not exactly said so, that she is in love," Anita confided.

"Then let us hope she catches the man on whom she has set her heart," the Duke remarked.

Anita felt that the way he had said this grated on her, but she knew it was impossible to find fault with him.

Sarah was in fact trying to catch a husband and Daphne was doing the same thing.

It is something I will never . . . never . . . do! Anita silently swore to herself.

Then she realised that the Duke was still looking at her, and although it seemed impossible and she could not explain how, she felt that he knew exactly what she was thinking.

"Later you will change your mind," he said, almost as if she had spoken aloud. "Then you will be like every woman, chasing some wretched man when nature intended that he should chase you."

The way he spoke was so harsh, so unpleasant, that Anita stared at him wide-eyed and the music died beneath her fingers.

Then before she could reply, before she could even deny the charge he had levelled at her, he walked back to his guests.

CHAPTER FIVE

THE DUKE, HAVING PERFORMED FOUR DUTY-DANCES with the most distinguished of his guests, thought the moment had come when he must dance with the girls who had been invited for his inspection.

He had already decided, as Anita had done, that the only one who was even possibly acceptable was Lady Millicent Clyde.

Although her father, the Earl, was somewhat of a bore in the House of Lords, he certainly appreciated good horse-flesh and his house in Huntingdonshire was extremely comfortable.

The Duke had realised the moment the Ball started that his mother—or perhaps, if he was fair, Anita—had been right in decorating the Ball-Room and making it, if nothing else, a good talking-point.

The guests who had come from the County were both surprised and delighted by the decorative effect of Venice, and the Orchestra which had come down from London provided exactly the right type of music.

This was sometimes soft and romantic and at other times gay and spirited, and even if the Duke had wished to find fault, he would have found it impossible not to be aware that the party was going with "a swing."

He knew too that it was a delight he had not expected that his mother was so well and had actually danced with the Lord Lieutenant.

She was looking exceedingly beautiful and was wearing a satin gown of dove-grey, which had been made fashionable by Princess Alexandra, against which the unique Ollerton sapphires looked magnificent.

The Duke thought, as he had so many times before, that it would be impossible for him to find a wife who looked as lovely as his mother or had a character like hers.

He was well aware that the compliments she was paid by everybody present came not only because they admired her but because they loved her.

She had been instrumental in so many reforms that were vitally needed in the County, and she had never been too busy to listen to the troubles of other people whether they were high or low in rank.

It seemed to the Duke as if his father's words kept echoing incessantly in his ears when he had said: "They do not make women like that these days!"

However, duty was duty, and as he walked across the room to where Lady Millicent was standing beside her mother, the Countess, he knew exactly where his duty lay.

Lady Millicent was in fact looking very attractive.

Anita had thought so when they had all congregated before dinner in the Silver Salon.

Her gown of white lace billowing out from a small waist was in a fashion which had been set by the Empress Eugénie and which was particularly becoming for young girls.

Her eyes were blue and her hair was exactly the right burnished gold that the Duke had insisted he required in his wife.

"May I have the pleasure of this dance?" he asked.

As he spoke he expected Lady Millicent's blue eyes to light up with the glint of excitement which he had always seen in any woman's eyes when he invited her to partner him on the dance-floor.

But Lady Millicent merely inclined her head, and it was the Countess who said eagerly:

"That would be delightful, my dear Duke, and you will find that Milly is a very good dancer."

"I am sure I shall," the Duke replied briefly.

Then as the Orchestra began to play a waltz by Offenbach, he led her onto the dance-floor.

As he did so, he was aware that she was also the right height that he had stipulated as being important in someone who would do justice to the Ollerton diamonds and the five strings of Oriental pearls which had once belonged to a Maharajah of India.

One of the Duke's ancestors, who had been one of the first Governor-Generals, had bought them for what now seemed a "song," and every subsequent Duchess had found them extremely becoming.

"Pearls must be worn against the skin," they had been told, and they had not needed this encouragement to drape themselves in what had often been valued at "a king's ransom."

"I hope you are enjoying yourself at Ollerton, Lady Millicent," the Duke said as they moved sedately over the polished floor.

"Yes, thank you."

Her reply was conventional and her voice undoubtedly flat.

"I am sure you find the decorations of the Ball-Room unusual, and I must admit they surprised me when I first saw them."

"It looks very pretty!"

"You have never been to Venice?"

"No."

The Duke thought with a rising feeling of irritation that this was hard going.

Persevering, he said:

"It is a city I find very beautiful, and of course, as I expect you have been told, it is the perfect place for honeymooners."

To his surprise, Lady Millicent stiffened and missed a step. Then she said:

"I believe the canals make it very unhealthy."

"I think it depends in what part of Venice you stay," the Duke replied. "Near the lagoon you have the advantage of the tides."

"All the same, I would not like to visit Venice."

He decided from the way in which Lady Millicent spoke, that this was definitely the end of that subject, and he told himself that if she had no wish to talk he was quite prepared to remain silent.

Then across the room he saw his mother watching him and knew he must make a further effort.

"Your father has some excellent horses," he said. "Are you fond of riding?"

"Not particularly."

"Then what do you enjoy?"

There was a definite hesitation before Lady Millicent replied:

"Quite a—number of things."

The Duke knew that if they had actually been married at this moment he would have wanted to shake her. Instead, he said with an undoubtedly cynical note in his voice:

"That is certainly very enlightening!"

"I cannot think why you should be—interested."

The words came almost inaudibly, and yet he heard them, and he told himself that it was impossible for the Clydeshires not to have been aware why they had been invited to Ollerton.

The Earl and the Countess had stayed there on several previous occasions and they would have seen that the parties the Duke usually gave never included young unmarried girls.

But the rule had been altered, and it had in fact been his mother who had written the letters of invitation, which would have told anyone with the social consciousness of the Countess exactly why the party was being given.

The Duke thought too that the Countess, having seen her daughter's rivals, would have come to the same conclusion as he had: that she was definitely the "favourite" in the race.

Would they, in the circumstances, really have said nothing to Lady Millicent? he wondered to himself.

If they had not done so, that could account for the fact that she was obviously making no effort at all to make herself pleasant.

But perhaps she was so unintelligent that she actually had nothing to contribute to the conversation.

At least when he had spoken to Rosemary Castor and Alice Down during the day they had responded in a manner which left him in no doubt that they were anxious to find favour in his eyes.

The Duke was still puzzling over Lady Millicent's behaviour when the dance came to an end.

Without even smiling at him, she immediately moved to her mother's side, as was conventional, and there was nothing the Duke could do but follow her.

"I was thinking what a charming couple you made on the dance-floor," the Countess said.

"Thank you for a most enjoyable waltz," the Duke said politely.

He would have turned away, but his mother, who had been sitting next to the Countess, put out her hand towards him.

He moved quickly to her side.

"You feel all right, Mama? You must not dance if it is too much for you."

"I am enjoying myself immensely!" the Duchess replied. "I never expected to be here this evening except in a wheel-chair!"

The Duke was about to pay her a compliment when she said in a low voice:

"Can you see if Anita is all right? I have not seen her for some time."

"Yes, of course," the Duke replied. "With whom was she dancing when you last saw her?"

"With Lord Greshame."

The Duke frowned.

He had noticed that at dinner Anita was sitting next to George Greshame.

He had been invited to this particular party because he was a very good mixer, besides being an excellent bridge-player.

The Duke had thought that he would undoubtedly flirt with the two pretty, married women who had been invited.

But he had noticed that during dinner George was paying Anita too much attention, and he had thought it was a mistake.

Lord Greshame was smooth, sophisticated, and a philanderer whom most Society women did not take seriously.

He was invited to all the best parties, first because he was an unattached man, and secondly because he made himself so charming.

The Duke was aware that the women to whom he declared himself devoted laughed at his protestations and often behind his back would say:

"Poor George! He is always seeking the *grande passion,* but after so many false starts, how can he ever hope to be first past the winning-post?''

At the same time, the Duke liked him and had thought that George Greshame would make the party, as far as he was concerned, at least tolerable.

He walked from the Ball-Room into two or three of the Ante-Rooms where a number of couples were sitting and talking, some more intimately than others.

There was no sign of Anita or of George Greshame, and he wondered if she could have been so foolish as to go with him into the Conservatory.

The girls who could be led into the Conservatory during a Ball were always something of a bad joke, but the Duke thought that Anita would not be aware of this.

The Conservatory at Ollerton, which had been erected only thirty years ago, was exceptional. Not only was it larger and better designed than most of the Conservatories attached to other houses, but it contained plants and flowers which had been brought from all over the world to make it a Botanist's delight.

There were azaleas from the Himalayas, lilies from Malaysia, and a number of plants from South America which had never been seen in England before.

The orchids were exceptional, and at Ollerton it had become customary for corsages of them to be sent to the rooms of the lady guests before dinner and buttonholes to the rooms of the gentlemen.

The Duke had noticed that Anita was wearing some small star-shaped orchids that he had thought were very appropriate on her gown, which, he was aware, was a perfect example of the type of gown a débutante should wear.

It was of white tulle which framed her shoulders like a soft cloud, and there were tiny diamantés like dew-drops scattered on it and over the full skirt.

They made Anita shimmer as she moved, and the Duke had felt, as he had noticed her dancing in the Ball-Room, that her gown made her seem as if she were illuminated with a special light.

He thought it was not her gown that people would notice, however, but the excitement in her eyes, and he thought somewhat cynically that there was at least one person who was finding the evening a joy, which was the exact opposite of his own feelings about it.

He opened the door of the Conservatory and felt the warm fragrance of the flowers hit him with the force of a wave.

Then as he moved inside he heard a little voice say:

"N—no . . . please . . . I want to go . . . back to the Duchess!"

"I want to kiss you first," a man replied.

"I have told you . . . I do not want to be kissed. Leave me . . . alone!"

"You say you do not want to be kissed, but I will make you realise it can be very enjoyable, and quite frankly I want to be the first man to touch your lips."

"No . . . no! . . . Let me . . . go!"

There was a note of panic in Anita's voice, which the Duke recognised, and he moved quickly through the foliage of a large eucalyptus plant to see Anita struggling desperately against Lord Greshame, who was pulling her into his arms.

The latter saw the Duke first, and as his hold relaxed, Anita fought herself free of him.

Then as she saw who stood there, she ran instinctively towards the Duke, to hold on to him as if he were a life-line and she were drowning.

He could feel her trembling against him, but he did not put his arms around her; he merely looked over her head at Lord Greshame, who appeared to be somewhat abashed.

Then the Duke said quietly:

"My mother is asking for you, Anita."

She did not answer, she merely moved away from him without looking up and he could hear her footsteps running over the marble floor towards the door.

There was an uncomfortable silence until the Duke remarked:

"Cradle-snatching, George?"

Lord Greshame pulled the lapels of his evening-coat into place.

"A pretty little thing," he replied, "but very unsophisticated."

"Very!" the Duke agreed drily. "I therefore suggest that you leave her alone!"

Lord Greshame smiled.

"Do not sound so pompous, Kerne. Someone will teach her the facts of life sooner or later, and after all, she is only a Reader for your mother."

The Duke understood exactly what his friend implied, and it annoyed him not only for Anita's sake but because he thoroughly disliked the type of man who pursued defenceless Governesses and even servants in other people's houses.

He had not thought before that George Greshame might be one of them, but now he decided that their friendship, if that was what it had been, was at an end, and in the future he would certainly not invite him to any party he gave at Ollerton.

Aloud he said:

"I think you have the wrong impression. Anita Lavenham is here as my mother's guest. Her grandfather was the Earl of Lavenham and Bective and her aunt is the Countess of Charmouth."

"Good God, I did not know that!" Lord Greshame ejaculated. "I thought she had been invited to eat in the Dining-Room only to make the numbers right."

"That is where you were mistaken," the Duke replied.

As he spoke he walked from the Conservatory, not waiting to see whether Lord Greshame followed him or not.

As he walked back to the Ball-Room he realised that it was Anita's frankness that had put her into a position that she would never have envisaged.

He wondered how many other people in the house-party had thought, as evidently Lord Greshame had, that she was little more than a paid attendant on the Duchess.

As he reached the Ball-Room the Duke was wondering how he could set right what had been initiated by himself when he had saved Anita from the elderly Parson in Harrogate.

Then as the Orchestra began another of their romantic waltzes, he knew how he could make her position clear without having to put it into words.

He saw that she was already at his mother's side and he wondered if the Duchess was aware that Anita was upset.

He walked through the dancers to join them, and he knew, as he saw the expression on his mother's face, that she was.

The Duke, however, looked at Anita.

"May I have the pleasure of this dance?" he enquired.

He saw what had undoubtedly been a terrified look in her eyes lighten, and without waiting for her to answer him he put an arm round her waist and drew her onto the dance-floor.

219

She was very much smaller than his other partners, but as he had somehow expected, she was as light as a piece of thistledown, and he found that she had a natural sense of rhythm.

In fact, as they moved round the floor he had the idea that they were floating rather than dancing, and he also knew that she was still trembling a little from the fear that George Greshame had evoked in her.

"Forget what happened," he said quietly. "But let it be a lesson to you never to go into a Conservatory alone with a man unless you want him to make love to you."

Anita gave a little shiver.

"He asked me to . . . do so and I did not like to . . . refuse. When I found there was nobody else there, I knew it was . . . wrong."

"Not exactly wrong, but somewhat indiscreet."

Anita gave a little sigh.

"If Mama were here, she would have told me about . . . these things. But as you see, I am very . . . ignorant."

"You will learn by trial and error as we all have to do," the Duke said.

"I know," Anita said in a low voice, "but he . . . frightened me."

"I told you to forget him."

"I was so happy, and it has been such a wonderful experience to go to my first Ball," she murmured, "but I never expected men to be . . . like that."

"Like what?" the Duke asked, because he was curious.

"Like the Reverend Joshua, wanting to . . . marry me when he had only seen me . . . two or three times, and like . . . Lord Greshame trying to . . . kiss me when he had never . . . spoken to me until we met each other at . . . dinner."

Looking down, the Duke could see the perplexity in her small, flower-like face, and he thought that he could understand the feelings both of the Reverend Joshua and of George Greshame.

Lightly, because he felt he must stop her from becoming introspective about herself, he said:

"I think my mother would be able to tell you better than anyone else of the penalties of being a beautiful woman."

Anita was silent for a moment, then she said in an incredulous little voice:

"Are you saying . . . that you really . . . truly think I am . . . pretty?"

The Duke could not help smiling.

He was quite certain that no other man in the room to whom Anita might have asked the question would realise that she did not desire to be complimented but was genuinely and completely unaware that she was not merely pretty but lovely.

But he knew that her lack of self-consciousness, which he had noticed so often before, sprang from the fact that she was very humble about her appearance.

And when he saw her sister Sarah he had known why.

Sarah was spectacular and colourful. She was the type of English Rose who was admired as the ideal of beauty by artists of every type.

When the Duke had learnt who she was, he had thought her golden hair, her blue eyes, and her pink-and-white complexion would draw the eyes and evoke the admiration of every man in the room.

Anita was different.

She was like a small white violet for which one had to search amongst the green leaves before it was found, or perhaps a better simile was that she resembled the tiny star-shaped orchids which were pinned to her gown.

They were very rare and the Duke was exceedingly proud that he had managed to grow them in the Conservatory at Ollerton.

But he knew that the majority of people when they inspected his orchids were far more impressed by the purple Cattleya and the crimson Sophronitis and barely noticed that one which he preferred.

The answer to Anita's question was easy and he wanted her to believe him.

"I think you are very pretty," he said, "and you will appreciate that I am stating a fact, not paying you a compliment."

For the first time since they had been dancing together, the stars were back in her eyes and he knew she was no longer trembling.

"Now I am happy again!" she exclaimed. "And I promise I will never be so foolish as to go into the Conservatory again, unless there are lots of other people with me."

"And perhaps it would be wiser not to go to Church!" the Duke teased.

"I shall enquire first if the Vicar is married," Anita replied, and he laughed.

He noticed that for the rest of the evening, as he danced with his other guests, including Lady Rosemary and Alice Down, Anita was careful to return to the Duchess's side as soon as each dance was over.

She was never short of partners, and more than once as she danced past him on the floor he could hear her lilting voice talking animatedly to the man with whom she was dancing.

Sometimes too she would be laughing the gay, joyous little laugh that came spontaneously to her lips as it might have come from a child's.

In the early hours of the morning, when the guests who were not staying in the house finally departed, the Duke said to the Duchess:

"I think, Mama, you should go to bed. I am sure your Doctors would disapprove of your keeping such late hours."

"I have enjoyed every moment," the Duchess said simply. "But Anita has already told me that I shall be very stiff tomorrow, so I will obey you."

As the Duchess spoke, Anita came running to her side, followed by two stalwart young footmen carrying a chair in which, when the Duchess had been incapacitated with rheumatism, they had taken her up and down the stairs.

The Duchess looked at it doubtfully.

"I am able to walk!" she protested.

"Not tonight," Anita said. "Please, Ma'am, be sensible, otherwise I shall have to spend all tomorrow brewing herbs."

The Duchess laughed and capitulated.

"You and Kerne both bully me unmercifully," she said, "but I suppose there is nothing I can do about it."

"Except to say good-night quickly," Anita replied. "And you know, Ma'am, you have been the undisputed and unrivalled Belle of the Ball!"

"That is true," the Duke agreed, "and I wish I had said it first!"

"It is not like you to be pipped at the post, Ollerton!" one of the guests remarked.

"I must be growing old," the Duke replied.

"That is not true," Anita said, "but just occasionally an outsider creeps in when you least expect it."

The Duke and those who were standing near were laughing as she followed the Duchess being carried from the Ball-Room.

"That is the most attractive child I have met in years!" an elderly General remarked.

The Duke thought he might say the same, but, before he could speak, the Countess of Clydeshire was gushing at him, telling him what a wonderful dance it had been.

While her mother was speaking, Lady Millicent stood at her side, and the Duke thought she was deliberately not looking in his direction, nor in fact was she making any effort to say a word of appreciation.

The girl is a bore! the Duke thought to himself.

At the same time, when he looked at Lady Rosemary Castor and Alice Down he knew that he could not contemplate seeing either of them at the end of his dinner-table or being obliged to present them to the Queen at Buckingham Palace.

Perhaps Lady Millicent will improve on further acquaintance, he thought *If not, I am done with her, and I will not ask her to marry me.*

Then he knew that if he did not, it would mean, as he had told Anita, more house-parties like this one; more mothers like the Countess, fawning over him in anticipation that he might become her son-in-law.

There would be more days wasted in entertaining people whom he considered bores when he might be amusing himself on the race-course, playing polo, or associating with the social crowd who circled round the Prince of Wales.

He knew that once he was married, these things would never be the same even in the case of the Prince of Wales.

At the moment the Prince never gave a party at Marlborough House to which he was not invited, and the same applied to all his married friends.

"How could we have a party without you?" Lady de Grey had said to the Duke only a few weeks ago. "You keep all the beauties on their toes in anticipation that they may be the next to catch your roving eye, and their husbands tolerate you, however audaciously you behave, for the simple reason that they know you are very well aware of your own importance and will never cause a scandal."

This was the kind of plain speaking for which the beautiful Lady de Grey was famous, and the Duke had not been offended. He merely thought as he was thinking now, that when he was married things would be different.

Of course there would be occasions when he would entertain and be entertained without his wife, but because he had a sense of propriety he knew that they would be few and far between and that as a general rule they must be seen together whenever they were in public.

He felt a wave of resentment sweep over him and decided once and for all that he would not go through with this farce to please the Queen or anybody else.

Then once again he envisaged his cousin's red and bloated face and his vulgar wife, garishly gowned and heavily over-jewelled, swaying as she walked because she had had too much to drink.

How could he allow them to live at Ollerton, to entertain at the family house in London, to inherit his other possessions all over the country?

With an effort the Duke forced a smile to his lips.

"I hope," he said to Lady Millicent, "as you do not particularly care for riding, that you will let me take you driving tomorrow afternoon? There is an attractive Folly not far from here, built by one of my ancestors, which is well worth a visit."

"Oh, what a wonderful idea, my dear Duke!" the Countess exclaimed almost before he had finished speaking. "Of course Milly would love to see the Folly."

"Then that is agreed," the Duke said, aware that Lady Millicent apparently thought her mother had said quite enough and therefore was making no effort to speak.

"Now we must all go to bed if we are to be at Church tomorrow morning," the Countess said. "I hear, Duke, that you always read the lesson."

"When I am in residence."

"Then we shall look forward to hearing you," the Countess gushed. "I am certain that you read as well as you do everything else, which, of course, is perfectly!"

The Duke inclined his head at the compliment, and then turned to say good-night to his other guests, some of whom were already beginning to yawn.

"A most enjoyable evening," they all said.

They walked towards the Hall, where there were footmen waiting for them with lighted candles in silver candlesticks which every guest at Ollerton traditionally carried upstairs to bed, even though the new gas-lighting had been installed in the bed-rooms.

The Duke, who was having a word with his Butler, climbed the stairs last.

"Will you be riding as usual, Your Grace?" the man enquired as the Duke put his foot on the first step.

"Of course," the Duke replied, "and as it is Sunday it had better be eight-thirty instead of nine o'clock."

"Very good, Your Grace."

As the Duke walked up the stairs he wondered who would be riding with him, but he suspected that no-one would be energetic enough to get up early.

Then he had the conviction that that would not apply to Anita, and he was sure that his horses would be a greater draw than the comfort of her pillow.

Thinking of her reminded him that George Greshame had not said good-night but had gone upstairs before the rest of the party.

Perhaps he is ashamed of his behaviour, the Duke thought, *and a good thing, too. Whoever he thought she was, George had no right to behave like that at Ollerton.*

It suddenly struck him that this was the first time in his life he had ever worried about his friends' morals, even though some of them, if he considered it dispassionately, behaved in what seemed an outrageous manner.

Because all the beauties with whom he had enjoyed his usually very ardent but brief *affaires de coeur* had been, like Elaine Blankley, promiscuous and passionate, the Duke realised that he had never thought of women in any other way.

These thoughts continued while he was undressing in silence, and when his valet left him, he got into bed and turned out the light, and found himself remembering how years ago when he had been a young man his thoughts had been chivalrous and, for want of a better word, respectful.

He recalled imagining himself as a Knight when he had sought the favour of the woman he had first loved with a reverence that was almost spiritual.

He had wanted to worship her, thinking of her as if she had the aura of a Saint and the purity of a lily.

Then, because he was so handsome and attractive, she had shown him that she was very human and desired him in a very different way.

So, naturally, he had responded. At the same time, something deep within him had told him that he was disappointed—or was it perhaps disillusioned?

He remembered how his feelings of reverence had changed to simple physical desire.

I expected the impossible, he thought bitterly.

Yet, strangely enough, he could remember exactly what he had felt and how the mere thought of Pauline, for that had been her name, had made him feel as if his spirit was lifted upwards, and he had wanted, because he loved her, to take the stars from the sky and lay them at her feet.

He wanted too to be finer, better, and more noble in himself; to be worthy of her.

He wanted to do great and glorious deeds so that she would be proud of him, and he thought he was ready to die in her defence and would be glad to do so.

I was just being a fool! the Duke told himself.

But he knew that the ideals he had sought then were still there now, beneath the surface, overlaid with cynicism and yet, strangely enough, not entirely extinct.

It struck him that if he had never met Pauline, his life might have been very different.

Then he laughed because it had all happened a long time ago, and he told himself that he was still too young to hanker after the past and what should really concern him was the future.

And his future, much as he disliked the idea, must be linked with Lady Millicent or a girl like her.

"Dammit all—there must be an alternative!" the Duke said aloud in the darkness.

But there was no answer. Only an ominous silence.

CHAPTER SIX

$\mathcal{A}$s the Morning Service proceeded in the little grey stone Church in Ollerton Park, Anita was aware that Lady Millicent was praying with an intensity that she had not expected of her.

They were sitting next to each other and Anita could feel her exuding tension almost like an aura.

Anita had always been sensitive to other people's feelings and she wanted, if she could, to help Lady Millicent.

At the same time, she had no wish to intrude upon her private feelings.

The Duke read the lessons in his deep voice and Anita thought that he not only made the Old Testament and the New sound poetical but also gave the words a meaning which Parsons often failed to do.

The Service ended, and because they were in the Ollerton pew the congregation waited for them to leave first. Then as Anita reached the porch, Lady Millicent, who was beside her said:

"Shall we walk back?"

"What a good idea!" Anita replied. "I would much rather walk than drive."

Lady Millicent told the Countess what they were going to do and the two girls set off to walk across the Park rather than down the oak-edged drive which was the route taken by the carriages.

In the distance Ollerton looked very magnificent with the Duke's standard moving gently in the breeze and the house reflected in the smooth silver surface of the lake.

"It it so beautiful!" Anita said aloud, as she had said so many times before.

Then she looked at Lady Millicent, and there was no mistaking that her pretty but usually expressionless face was filled with a look of suffering.

"What is the matter?" Anita asked. "Can I help you?"

"Nobody can ... do that," Lady Millicent replied with a deep sigh.

There was silence. Then suddenly, in a very different voice from the one in which she had spoken before, Lady Millicent exclaimed:

"I am so— miserable! I only wish I could—die!"

Anita saw that she was about to burst into tears, and, taking her arm, she drew her to where there was a tree fallen on the ground which would constitute a seat on which they could sit and talk.

By the time they had sat down Lady Millicent had her handkerchief to her eyes, although Anita was aware that she was making every effort to control her tears.

"Please let me help you," she pleaded.

"It is no—use," Lady Millicent answered in a broken voice, "Mama—says the Duke will—propose to me this—afternoon when he takes me driving—and I have to accept him."

Anita looked at her in surprise.

"You do not wish to marry the Duke?"

"No—of course not!" Lady Millicent replied. "I hate him—and I want to m—marry S—Stephen!"

Her voice broke on the name and now she sobbed uncontrollably.

"Tell me who Stephen is," Anita asked after a moment, "and why you cannot marry him."

"He is the most wonderful—marvellous man in the whole world!" Lady Millicent replied almost incoherently. "I love him—and he loves me!"

A burst of tears made the words almost unintelligible.

"Why can you not marry him?" Anita persisted.

"I think Papa would have agreed, in fact I am sure he would have, until the letter came from the Duchess asking us to—stay. After that he—forbade me to see Stephen, any more."

"But why?" Anita asked. "I do not understand."

Lady Millicent raised her head to look at her in surprise.

"Do you suppose Papa would miss the—opportunity of having a Duke as a son-in-law—especially one as—rich as this—one?"

"But surely," Anita said, "if your father and mother know you love someone else . . ."

"Stephen is a second son. His father, Lord Ludlow, is an old friend of Papa's, but that I love him is of no—consequence when I—might be a—Duchess."

Lady Millicent was crying once again, crying helplessly, and Anita felt deeply moved by her unhappiness."

"Listen," she said, "you must tell the Duke of this and I am quite sure he will not ask you to marry him."

"It will be too late," Lady Millicent replied. "Mama and Papa would kill me if they—thought he had asked me to—marry him and I had—refused."

"Then he must not ask you."

"How can I stop him?" Lady Millicent asked brokenly.

Anita thought for a moment, then she said:

"Shall I tell him that you are in love with somebody else?"

Lady Millicent took her handkerchief from her eyes to look at Anita in surprise before she said:

"Could you do—that? Would he—understand?"

"Of course!" Anita answered. "The Duke was very kind to me when a horrible, elderly Parson wanted to marry me, and my great-aunt, who has appointed herself my Guardian while my mother is abroad, insisted I should do so. Actually that is why I am staying here."

"And you really think he would—understand that I want to—marry Stephen—rather than—him?"

"Of course he would!" Anita replied.

She knew as she spoke that the Duke had no personal interest at all in Lady Millicent except that she was a means by which he could please the Queen and prevent his cousin from inheriting his title.

Lady Millicent clasped her hands together.

"Oh, Anita, if you can save me from—having to marry the—Duke it would be the kindest and most wonderful thing you could—possibly do for—me."

"Then I will do it," Anita said.

"It will have to be before we go driving. After all, for me to be alone with him is tantamount to a proposal before he actually asks me to be his wife."

Anita nodded.

"I understand that, and somehow I will prevent him from taking you."

"You have saved me when I thought everything was lost and I was doomed never to see Stephen again!"

"I am sure everything will be all right," Anita said.

"Mama told me before we came to Church that the Duke had said we would go driving at three o'clock. She has already decided what gown and bonnet I shall wear."

"Do not say anything to your Mama." Anita replied, "and behave quite normally during luncheon. I will speak to the Duke either just before or just after, depending on when I can get hold of him."

"You—promise you—will do—so?" Lady Millicent asked, the fear back in her voice."

"I promise," Anita answered, "and I am quite certain he will understand. He is a very understanding person."

As she spoke, she thought of how kind the Duke had been not only about the Reverend Joshua but also in saving her from Lord Greshame.

She supposed that as Lady Millicent was so young, it had never entered his mind that she might already have lost her heart to somebody else.

In fact, thinking back over what had been said, she felt that neither the Duke nor the Duchess had thought of the three girls who came to the house on approval as people, but merely as puppets to be manipulated into marriage just to suit him.

The whole idea is wrong! Anita thought to herself.

Aloud she said:

"Wipe your eyes, Milly, and you had better wash your face before your mother sees you. It would be a mistake for her to know you have been crying."

"I am not crying any more," Lady Millicent replied. "Thank you, oh, thank you, Anita, for being so kind to me! Perhaps if the Duke does not marry me, he will now marry Rosemary or Alice instead. I knew last night they were both hating me because he danced twice with me and only once with each of them."

Anita thought privately that neither Lady Rosemary nor Alice Down had any chance of becoming the Duchess of Ollerton, but she thought it would be a mistake to say so.

What was important was that she should save Lady Millicent, and because she was interested she asked her about the man she loved.

Because her feelings had been bottled up ever since she had come to Ollerton, they now seemed to explode and for the first time since she had arrived Lady Millicent talked animatedly and excitedly, and as she did so she looked very much prettier than she had before.

"We have loved each other for over a year," she said to Anita. "At first Papa said it was a ridiculous match and he had no intention of letting me throw myself away on someone who had no chance of coming into the title."

She paused before she continued:

"Then, because Stephen was so charming to him, he had begun to weaken and we were quite certain we would be able to be married before Christmas."

"That is what will happen," Anita said with a smile.

"And you must promise me you will come to the wedding! You must be there!"

"I would love to be invited," Anita replied.

When they arrived back at the house, it was to find that it was too near luncheon-time for Anita to have a chance of speaking to the Duke before they went into the Dining-Room.

She found to her relief that she was sitting a long way from Lord Greshame but was next to a middle-aged Peer who had some excellent race-horses and they talked about his stable and the Duke's all through the meal.

When they left the Dining-Room, Anita saw Lady Millicent give her a frantic look and knew that it was imperative that she should speak to the Duke quickly, because it was already nearly half-past-two.

Therefore, she managed with some dexterity to be the last lady to leave the room, and, slipping past a number of male guests, she reached his side.

"Could I speak to you for a moment? It is very urgent," she said quickly.

He looked surprised, but he answered immediately:

"Of course, Anita. Come to my Study in ten minutes."

She smiled at him and walked after the Duchess, who was going upstairs to lie down as she always did after luncheon.

Seeing that the Duchess's maid Eleanor was there to help her onto

231

a *chaise-longue* near the window so that she would enjoy the sunshine and the fresh air, Anita hurried down a side staircase which she knew would bring her to the Duke's Study without her having to go through the main Hall.

She had learnt that it was a room he kept for his personal use, where no-one intruded unless they were specially invited.

She opened the door and found him waiting for her, standing in front of the fireplace and looking exceedingly elegant, wearing one of his orchids in his buttonhole.

"Come in, Anita!" he said. "What is this momentous thing you have to discuss with me? I hope it will not take long as I have arranged to take Millicent Clyde out driving at three o'clock."

Anita, having shut the door carefully, moved towards him.

"That is what I want to speak to you about."

The Duke looked surprised and Anita went on:

"Milly is desperately unhappy. She is in love with somebody else and she knows if you propose to her she will be forced by her parents to marry you."

The Duke did not speak and after a little pause Anita said:

"I told her not to be upset, that you would understand and make an excuse not to take her driving this afternoon. Then her father and mother will give up hoping that they can have a Duke for a son-in-law and she will be able to marry the man she loves."

When she had finished speaking Anita looked up at the Duke with a little smile on her lips.

"I knew that you . . ." she began.

She stopped suddenly because she had seen the expression on the Duke's face.

Then as she realised something was very wrong, he said:

"How dare you! How dare you interfere in my private affairs and discuss me with my guests!"

"I . . . I am . . . sorry. . . ."

"I have never heard of such impertinence, that you should, in my own house, interfere with my plans and my arrangements. And it is utterly inconceivable that you should take it upon yourself to say what I would or would not do! Dammit all, who do you think you are!"

His voice seemed to ring out in the big room.

Perhaps because he seemed so tall and so overpowering in his rage, Anita gave a little cry of sheer fear and ran towards the door.

As she reached it, she looked back and he saw that her face was very pale.

Then she was gone, leaving the door open behind her as she ran down the passage.

~

The Duchess was nearly asleep when the door opened and Anita burst into the room.

"Oh, it is you dear," the Duchess murmured.

"If you please, Ma'am, I have to leave immediately!" Anita said.

The Duchess was so astounded that she felt she could not have heard right.

"Go—where?"

"Anywhere . . . home," Anita replied.

"What has happened? What has upset you?"

Now the Duchess was fully awake and could see that Anita was very pale and her eyes had a stricken look in them, although she was not crying.

"What has upset you?" the Duchess asked again.

"I cannot explain," Anita answered, "but please, Your Grace, let me go home. I am afraid I have no . . . money to pay the fare . . . but if you will lend it to me I will pay . . . you back."

"Yes, of course," the Duchess said. "But as it is Sunday there will be no trains so late in the afternoon. If you really wish to leave, you will have to wait until tomorrow morning."

"I would . . . rather go now . . . at once."

"I am sure that is not possible," the Duchess replied.

Anita gave a little sob and without saying any more turned and went from the room.

When she had gone, the Duchess rang the bell for her maid, and as the elderly woman who had served her for many years came into the room, she said:

"Something has upset Miss Anita, Eleanor. See if you can find out what it is. I am very worried about her."

"I'll see what I can do, Your Grace."

The Duchess lay back against the pillows.

There was little that went on in the house that Eleanor did not know about sooner or later, and it would be only a question of waiting before she would be informed of what had occurred.

She was not mistaken, for only a quarter-of-an-hour later Eleanor came back into the room and the Duchess looked at her expectantly.

"It appears, Your Grace, Miss Lavenham went to His Grace's Study after luncheon. She was there only a few minutes before she comes out and runs across the Hall and up the stairs to Your Grace's room."

"Have you any idea what upset her?" the Duchess asked.

"No, Your Grace, but I have a suspicion that what Miss Lavenham said to His Grace caused him to send a message to Lady Millicent saying he was unavoidably prevented from taking her driving at three o'clock as had been arranged."

"Then His Grace has not gone driving," the Duchess said quietly, as if speaking to herself.

"No, Your Grace," Eleanor said, "and if you ask me, Lady Millicent must have been confiding in Miss Lavenham that she was hoping not to have to marry His Grace, being head-over-heels in love with a young man she has known ever since she was a child."

"So Lady Millicent is in love with somebody else?" the Duchess murmured.

"Yes, Your Grace. The lady's-maid to Her Ladyship's mother has been telling me, ever since they came here, how surprised they were to get the invitation, seeing as they thought Lady Millicent was to marry Mr. Stephen."

"I am beginning to understand now why Lady Millicent did not seem to be enjoying herself."

"Her Ladyship's maid tells me she cried herself sick at the idea of coming here. Believe it or not, Your Grace, it's not every young lady as wants to marry a Duke, even one as handsome as His Grace."

"So it appears!" the Duchess replied.

She had no wish to talk any more and Eleanor left her, telling her to rest and not to worry.

"Worrying never helps anyone," the old maid said, "except that it hurries one into the grave, and that's a long way off for you, Your Grace, seeing how well you've been since we returns home."

As she left the room there was, however, a very worried expression in the Duchess's eyes.

She shut her eyes and prayed, as she prayed every day and every night, that her beloved son would find happiness.

She knew he had never really been in love, and how could she explain to him how wonderful it was and that if necessary it was worth waiting indefinitely for such rapture?

Suddenly she heard the Duke speaking to somebody outside the door, and she quickly bent to pick up a newspaper which was lying on a low table beside the *chaise-longue*.

When her son came into the room she had the paper in her hand.

"Oh, Kerne!" she exclaimed before he could speak. "I am so glad you are here! Do read me this speech made by the Prime Minister yesterday. It is so badly printed that I cannot see it very clearly."

"Where is Anita?" the Duke asked abruptly with what his mother thought was a harsh note in his voice.

"I expect she is packing."

"Packing!"

The exclamation came from the Duke's lips almost like a pistol-shot.

"She came in a little while ago and informed me that she was leaving," the Duchess said. "She wanted to go today, but I thought it was unlikely, as it is Sunday, that there would be a train so late in the afternoon. Perhaps you would arrange for Mr. Brigstock to take her to London tomorrow. She can hardly travel alone."

Without replying, the Duke turned and left the room.

The Duchess did not seem surprised. She only watched him go, and as the door closed behind him there was a twinkle in her eyes and a faint smile on her lips.

The Duke went downstairs.

As he reached the Hall he said to the Butler:

"Send a message to Miss Lavenham to say I would like to speak to her for a moment."

"Very good, Your Grace."

The Duke walked back to his Study.

He was obviously impatient, for he walked up and down until, after what seemed a long time, the Butler opened the door.

"I have learnt, Your Grace," he said, "that Miss Lavenham's not in the house."

"Then where is she?" the Duke enquired.

"No-one's quite certain, Your Grace, but one of the housemaids thought, although she's not sure, that she saw Miss Lavenham running across the Park towards the Home Wood."

The Duke did not reply and after a moment the Butler said:

"I'm hoping, Your Grace, such information's incorrect, because it looks as though we're in for a thunder-storm."

The Duke glanced out the window.

There was no doubt that the sky was overcast.

He walked towards the door and as he passed the Butler the latter said:

"Does Your Grace require a chaise?"

"I will go to the stables myself," the Duke replied.

Five minutes later, riding Thunderer, he set off down the drive and, having crossed the bridge over the lake, turned towards the wood which covered a large acreage of ground to the west of the house.

It was a wood where, the Duke knew, the trees were thick, though it was just possible to move between them on a horse.

He guessed that Anita, being upset, would, as she invariably did, seek a wood where she could sit and think undisturbed.

He had not forgotten that it was a wood to which she was going the first time they had met, when she had been thinking of Lucifer, and a wood she was running to for solace when she had been told that she was to marry the Reverend Joshua.

The Home Wood was close to the house, so he was certain that that was where she would hide herself when she learnt that it was not possible to leave immediately as she wished to do.

Thunderer was unusually restless and the Duke was wondering why, seeing that he had already ridden him that morning, when a distant clap of thunder told him the reason.

Despite his name, Thunderer disliked thunder-storms, and looking up at the sky the Duke was sure that the Butler had been right and there was undoubtedly going to be one, and very shortly.

He left the Park for the wood, riding Thunderer through the trees along narrow, twisting paths covered with moss.

The Duke knew the wood well and he thought it unlikely that Anita would push her way through the thick undergrowth but would keep to the paths.

As he rode he was aware that except for the distant rumble of thunder, there was that quiet and stillness which came before the storm, and he hoped that he would find Anita before she got wet.

There was, however, no sign of her and he rode on and on, thinking she must have run very quickly to have gone so far in so short a time.

He calculated that it must be nearly three-quarters-of-an-hour since he had raged at her, and by moving swiftly she could have covered a great deal of ground before he could catch up.

However, there was still no sign of Anita. Then, as he was wondering if perhaps he had been mistaken and she had not come to the wood after all, he saw her.

She was in a small clearing made by the wood-cutters and was seated on a recently felled tree, her head bent, her hands covering her face.

Because he had found her, the Duke instinctively checked Thunderer. Then an even nearer, louder clap of thunder made the horse start and rear up on his hind legs.

Anita looked up and when she saw the Duke she rose to her feet.

She was very pale, and her eyes, with a stricken look in them which the Duke had expected, seemed to fill her whole face.

He rode up to her.

"I came to find you, Anita," he said, "and as Thunderer hates the sound of his own name, I think we ought to get home as soon as possible."

"Yes . . . of course," Anita agreed.

The Duke reached down his hand.

She took it in both of hers and he pulled her up so that she was sitting at the front of his saddle.

She was so light that he felt as if she flew from the ground up onto the horse's back.

Then as he made to turn Thunderer there was a streak of lightning across the sky and another clap of thunder which had the horse prancing about so that the Duke found it difficult to hold him.

"Shall I walk?" Anita asked, speaking softly.

"No," the Duke replied. "There is a barn not far from here and I think we should shelter there until the worst of the storm is over."

Another clap of thunder told him that it was in fact getting very much nearer, and now the Duke forced Thunderer quickly down the path which led to the side of the wood.

With Anita in his arms it was not easy, but by a superb piece of horsemanship the Duke managed to guide the frightened animal between the trees and out into the field which was just ahead of them where they could see a hay-barn.

Even as they saw it there were the first heavy drops of rain, followed by the lightning streaking its way across the sky.

Then, before Thunderer could protest, the Duke had ridden into the barn through a half-open door and a great clap of thunder sounded almost directly over their heads.

He and Anita jumped to the ground, both of them concerned with Thunderer, who was protesting violently against the storm in the only way he knew.

It was difficult to hold him but Anita was talking to him in the soft voice she had used in the stables.

"It is all right," she was saying. "It will not hurt you. It is only a horrible noise, and you cannot see the lightning in here."

It was as if the horse was mesmerised by what she was saying.

He was trembling and moving restlessly but he was no longer rearing, and the Duke patted his neck as he held his bridle while Anita went on talking.

Then there was a noise almost like an explosion which seemed to rock the barn, and a gust of wind made the door through which they had entered slam backwards and forwards.

Thunderer was still in sheer terror and Anita gave a gasp, then said in a quivering little voice:

"Oh, Thunderer . . . I am frightened . . . too."

It seemed almost as if the horse understood, for he turned his head to nuzzle against her, and as he did so the Duke, on the other side, realised, as if a thunderbolt had hit him, that he was in love!

He could hardly believe that the feeling which swept over him was real, and yet he knew he wanted almost uncontrollably to put his arms round Anita and hold her close so that she need no longer be frightened.

He knew too, unmistakably, irrefutably, that he wanted to comfort her and protect her not only from the thunder-storm but from anything else that might frighten or perturb her for the rest of her life.

He was astonished by his own feelings, and yet at the same time he knew that if he was honest he should have been aware of them for some time.

It was only his obstinacy and his belief that his organisation was sacrosanct which, even after he had known Anita, had made him go ahead with his plans for choosing a wife.

Now as he felt his whole body throbbing with the sudden awareness of emotions he had not known himself capable of feeling, he knew that he had loved her since the first moment she had turned her little flower-like face towards him and told him that she had been thinking of Lucifer.

He had found himself thinking of her all the time he was journeying to Harrogate, and when he saw her there it had seemed inevitable that he should find her again.

Then when he had rescued her first from the Parson and then from George Greshame, he had told himself that his motives were entirely disinterested and unselfish.

Now he acknowledged that he loved her and she filled his whole life in a way no woman had ever done before.

There was another clap of thunder but now it was farther away, although the rain was teeming down in a torrential storm in the East and the noise on the roof made it almost impossible to hear anything else.

Anita was talking to Thunderer again and the Duke heard her say:

"It is going away. Now we need no longer feel . . . afraid . . . you and I, and anyway it was very . . . silly of us. We are safe . . . quite . . . quite safe . . . and we will not even get wet."

"That is true," the Duke remarked.

Anita looked at him quickly, then away again, and he knew she was shy and apprehensive that he was still angry.

They were still both holding on to Thunderer, and the Duke said:

"It is lucky that I was so anxious to apologise; otherwise you would have been soaked to the skin!"

He saw Anita's eyes flicker but she did not look at him, and he watched her face as he said very quietly:

"I am sorry, Anita. Are you going to forgive me?"

"I—it was . . . wrong of me . . ." she began.

"No, no!" the Duke said quickly. "You were right, absolutely right to tell me, and I will explain to you why I behaved as I did, but not at this moment."

There was silence for a moment, then Anita said:

"I . . . think the rain is . . . stopping."

"Hold Thunderer and I will go and look."

The Duke walked across the barn to stand at the door.

The ground was wet from the rain but the storm was dying away.

He could hear the thunder but now it was only a rumble in the distance, and as he stood there thinking that there was a throbbing in his temples and a very strange feeling in his heart, the sun broke through the clouds and the storm was over.

The Duke drew in his breath, feeling it was a sign that meant something to him personally. Then he turned and walked back to Anita.

The great stallion was eating the hay that was lying loose on the ground, and Anita in her white gown and without a bonnet looked more than ever, the Duke thought, like a small angel.

He resisted an impulse to put his arms round her and tell her how much he loved her.

He knew that she was still upset about the way he had behaved, but his love told him that he must think of her and not of himself and that this was neither the time nor the place to discuss it.

"We can go home now," he said with a smile which most women found irresistible.

"It has . . . stopped raining?"

There was a little quiver in her voice which told him that she really wanted to ask something different.

"It has stopped raining," he said, "the sun is coming out, and it tells me you have forgiven me."

She did not answer and he picked her up in his arms and put her on the saddle.

Only many years of imposing a strict control over himself prevented the Duke from holding her close against his heart and kissing her. Instead he arranged her skirt and as she picked up the reins he mounted the horse behind her.

Now that the noise he disliked was over, Thunderer was behaving with the well-behaved dignity which usually was characteristic of him.

As Anita had nothing to say, the Duke was content to feel her close against his chest.

He could smell the scent she used in her hair, which reminded him of violets, and he thought that everything about her was like Spring and he knew that that was what she had brought him.

Just as last night he had recalled all the feelings of chivalry that had been his when he was young, so now he knew that Anita had revived everything that was fine and noble in his character, and he swore to himself that he would never lose her again.

Only when the house was in sight, glittering in the sunshine, did the Duke feel Anita press herself a little closer to him as if she was afraid of going back.

"Tomorrow," he said quietly, "the party will leave and you and I and Mama will be alone as we have been before."

"I . . . intended to . . . leave."

"But you will not do so because you know I want you to stay," the Duke replied. "Please, Anita!"

He could not see her face because she had her back to him, but he had a feeling that the worry had gone from her eyes.

"I . . . I will stay."

Her voice was very low, but there was an unmistakable lilt in the words and the Duke let his lips touch her hair, although she was unaware of it.

You are mine, he said in his heart, *and I will never lose you, my precious little angel!*

CHAPTER SEVEN

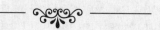

THE HOUSE-PARTY STARTED LEAVING early the following morning, but the Clydeshires and the Downhams were to depart at two o'clock for the station where the Duke's private train was waiting to take them to London.

During dinner the previous evening it was obvious to Anita, and she thought it must be to the Duke too, that there was an expression of disappointment on the Earl's face and a querulous note in the Countess's voice, as if they could not understand what had happened.

But Lady Millicent looked happy and was more animated than she had been at any time since she had arrived at Ollerton.

In fact, she appeared so attractive that Anita wondered if after all the Duke, despite his anger, would not regret having cancelled the drive with her and having made no effort during the evening to seek her out.

The Duchess, with considerable tact, as if she realised the conversation might be uncomfortable, had arranged for a display of magic lantern slides.

Anita had found it entrancing and it was her laughter that had made the others laugh too, and the evening had therefore been an unqualified success except for the two disappointed pairs of parents.

When they had gone up to bed Lady Millicent had flung her arms round Anita and cried:

"You saved me! You saved me! How can I ever thank you?"

"There is no need," Anita said with a smile.

"The Duke obviously does not mind losing me," Lady Millicent remarked. "What did he say when you told him I was in love with Stephen?"

She did not notice that Anita evaded having to answer the question, nor did she know that when she went back to her own room Anita told herself it was something she never wished to think about again.

The horror of the Duke's anger still lay at the back of her mind, and the agony she had felt as she ran away into the wood was now something she wanted only to forget.

The Duke had said he was sorry when he had rescued her from the storm and had taken her back to the house on Thunderer's back, which had been an unexpectedly exciting way to travel.

But Anita still could not understand why he had been so angry.

"It is because I am merely an outsider and have really no right here in the first place," she told herself humbly. "I forced myself upon him and the Duchess, and of course it was impertinent of me to interfere in his private life."

At the same time, she felt as if her heart was singing because he had been glad that the house-party was to leave and, as he had said, they could be alone as they had been before, just the three of them.

"But how long will he stay?" Anita asked herself.

She found herself saying a little prayer that he would not be in a hurry to go back to London.

~

"Good-bye, Ollerton! Thank you for a very pleasant visit," the Earl said, with commendable effort.

"It has been a pleasure to have you here," the Duke replied, and to the Downhams he said much the same thing.

Lady Millicent kissed Anita.

"Do not forget you are coming to my wedding," she whispered as she did so.

"I shall be awaiting your invitation."

The two girls smiled at each other in a conspiratorial fashion.

Then the guests were driving away in the Duke's comfortable open carriage, while the Duchess, the Duke, and Anita waved to them from the steps.

The Duke gave a sigh that was obviously one of relief before he said:

"I expect you will want to rest, Mama."

"I am looking forward to it," the Duchess replied. "If there is one person who makes me tired it is Edith Clydeshire."

"We need not ask them again," the Duke replied, and the Duchess gave a little laugh.

She started to climb the stairs, and when Anita would have followed her the Duke said:

"I thought you would like to see a new orchid which has just arrived for me as a present from Singapore."

"A new one!" Anita exclaimed. "How exciting! What colour is it?"

"Come and see for yourself."

Anita looked at the Duchess for permission.

"Go and look at it, child," she said, "then you can tell me about it when I come downstairs for tea."

Anita smiled at her, and, with one of her little skips that showed she was excited, she walked beside the Duke along the corridor which led towards the Conservatory.

He opened the door and now there was not only the warm wave of fragrance to greet them but the whole place seemed to shimmer with a golden light because of the sun that was shining on the glass.

They walked in silence until they reached the orchids.

They all appeared to Anita to be even more beautiful and more exciting than they had the first time she had seen them.

Almost instinctively she looked for the small star-shaped one which the Duke had sent to her room the first night after she arrived at Ollerton.

243

"They are all so lovely!" she said, putting out her hand to touch a petal very gently. "But this one will always mean something very special to me."

"Just as you mean something very special to me," the Duke said softly.

She felt she could not have heard him right.

Then as she looked up at him enquiringly and saw the expression in his eyes, it was impossible to look away.

"I think you must have forgotten, Anita," the Duke said, "that I told you never to come to a Conservatory alone with a man unless you wanted him to make love to you."

"I . . . I never . . . thought . . ."

"That it applied to me?" the Duke finished. "Well, it does! That is why, my darling, I brought you here—to tell you that I love you!"

He saw her eyes widen and a radiance sweep over her face, transforming it.

Then, as if she thought she must be dreaming, she said a little incoherently:

"What . . . are you . . . saying to . . . m—me?"

"I am saying it in words," the Duke said, "but I would much rather say it a different way."

He put his arms round her as he spoke and very gently drew her closer to him.

Then as she stared up at him as if she could not believe that this was really happening, his lips found hers.

He knew it was the first time she had ever been kissed.

He was very gentle and he thought nothing could be more wonderful than the softness, the sweetness, and the innocence of a kiss that was different from any other kiss he had ever known.

Then because he could not help himself his arms tightened and his mouth became more possessive, more demanding.

He knew that this was what he had been seeking all his life and had thought he would never find.

He raised his head, and when he looked at Anita he thought that no-one who was human could look more beautiful, more part of the Divine.

"I . . . love you," she whispered.

"As I love you. Tell me, my sweet, was your first kiss what you expected?"

"It was wonderful . . . marvellous. . . I did not know a kiss could be like . . . that!"

"Like what?"

"All the things I have dreamt about . . . like the moonlight . . . the stars . . . the sun coming through the clouds. . . and like Heaven!"

"My precious, that is what I wanted you to feel."

"Was it . . . like that . . . for you?"

"It was perfect and more wonderful than any kiss I have ever known."

"Ooooh!"

He understood that there were no words with which she could express her joy at what he had said, and he kissed her again.

What seemed a long time later the Duke raised his head to look down at the stars in her eyes.

"I adore you, my precious!" he said in a voice that was curiously hoarse. "How soon will you marry me?"

To his surprise he felt Anita stiffen. Then she said:

"I . . . love you. . . and I did not . . . know that . . . love could be so . . . glorious . . . but I cannot m—marry you!"

If Anita had been surprised, it was certainly the Duke's turn now.

Never had he imagined that any woman to whom he proposed marriage would refuse him.

For the moment he felt he could not have heard correctly what she said.

"I asked you to marry me, my lovely one," he said after a moment.

"I know . . . you did . . . and I shall always be . . . very . . . very . . . proud," Anita said, "but I . . . cannot marry you . . . you must realise that."

"Why not? I do not understand!"

To his surprise, Anita moved from the shelter of his arms and turned away from him towards the orchids so that he could not see her face.

"Did I hear you say you loved me, Anita?" the Duke asked.

"You heard me . . . say so," Anita replied, "and I never thought . . . I never dreamt that you would love me. I think now I have . . . loved you for a very long time."

"How long?"

"I think . . . really since the first time . . . I saw you. I thought you were L—Lucifer but that did not prevent me from loving you . . . and perhaps really I loved you before that . . . when I dreamt of you as an Archangel in Heaven and was worried because you fell and were unhappy . . . amongst the other souls who were . . . damned."

"I am not damned now," the Duke said. "I am the most blessed and fortunate man in the world because I have found you. You are everything I have ever wanted and ever longed for. Only I was too foolish in that I did not realise it at first."

He paused, then went on with a smile:

"Then I discovered that you were everything I wanted, everything that was different from any other woman I have ever known."

"That is . . . why I cannot . . . m—marry you," Anita said, and there was a sob in her voice.

"Do you really think I would let you refuse me?" the Duke asked, "But you must explain to me why you wish to do so."

He turned her round as he spoke and saw the worry in her blue eyes and that the radiance had gone from her face.

"How can you think for a moment that you would give me up when you have said already that you love me?"

"It is because I love you so much . . . that I cannot make you . . . unhappy."

"Unhappy?" the Duke enquired. "Why should I be unhappy?"

"Because you must see I am . . . wrong for you . . . and if we married . . . I would always be waiting for the day when you would be . . . sorry you . . . had done so."

The Duke smiled.

"Do you really believe I could ever be sorry you were mine?" he asked. "I have already told you, Anita, that I love you as I have never loved a woman in my whole life, and never will again."

"B—but when you . . . look at me . . . you will be . . . disappointed."

"Are you telling me," he asked, "that you are refusing me because you do not measure up to those absurd, nonsensical conditions I set down for the appearance of the Duchess of Ollerton?"

As if she did not trust her voice, Anita nodded.

"Oh, my darling, my precious little angel," the Duke said, "do you not realise that I was being a pompous fool in thinking for one moment that one could buy a wife, as it were, out of a shop-window?"

"That . . . is what you . . . said," Anita said childishly.

"I did not know then that I would fall in love with somebody so adorable, so sweet that she fills my whole heart, my mind, and my soul, and I find her completely and absolutely perfect."

He saw the sudden light come into Anita's eyes and for a moment she looked at him as if she reached towards him from across eternity.

Then she looked away again.

"I . . . I could not . . . wear the sapphire . . . tiara, or the . . . diamond one."

The Duke laughed and it was a very warm and loving sound.

"That is true, my precious," he said, "so we will have another one made especially for you, perhaps a wreath of flowers, or you may prefer the small halo you wear when you are acting 'as sentinel for the immortal souls.' "

Anita gave a little chuckle as if she could not help it.

"Perhaps if I am . . . with you I would not be able to . . . take it with . . . me."

The Duke laughed before he said:

"Whether I am in Heaven or Hell, you will be with me. That is one thing of which you can be absolutely sure."

He pulled her into his arms.

"Is that your only objection to marrying me?"

"You wanted someone tall . . . stately . . . and beautiful like your . . . mother."

"Instead I have found someone so lovely that she is in my heart and *is* my heart and nothing else is of any consequence."

Anita gave a little cry and hid her face against him.

"I love you so . . . much I . . . want to . . . marry you," she whispered.

"And that is exactly what you are going to do," the Duke said, "and however many excuses you may find for not doing so, I have no intention of listening to them."

"Suppose," Anita said in a very small voice, "I . . . make you . . . angry?"

The Duke put his fingers under her chin and turned her small face up to his.

"I will tell you why I was angry," he said. "I was angry that you should have found out, as I should have found out for myself, that the girl I intended to marry was a human being with human emotions."

His voice was hard as he continued:

"When you told me that she was in love with someone else, I was

247

shocked and disgusted that I should have just taken for granted that she would marry me, whether she wished to do so or not, because I am a Duke! I was ashamed of myself, Anita, and as a kind of defensive action I raged at you. Then when you left me, I realised what I had done."

With his lips against her forehead, he said very softly:

"I have said I am sorry and I promise I will never speak to you like that again. Do you believe me?"

"Are you quite . . . quite certain you . . . love me . . . enough? Perhaps you should . . . have another look round in case . . . you find someone . . . better than . . . me."

"Do you think that possible?" the Duke asked. "I have to make you understand, my sweet love, that it was due to my stupidity and obstinacy, and because I am spoilt and selfish, that I nearly lost you. I will never take such risks again with you or with any own happiness. Do you believe me?"

"I want to . . . desperately."

"We will be happy, my darling. I promise you that. There are so many things for us to do together; so many things about which we think the same and feel the same."

The Duke paused, then he said:

"I know that you are going to inspire me to be a better man than I have been in the past. In fact, my darling, if you will help me I feel you will not be marrying Lucifer, as you think you are, but an Archangel who has somehow found his way back into Heaven entirely because a small angel has guided him there."

Anita gave a little cry of sheer joy.

"You say such wonderful . . . wonderful things to me. If you are really certain you want me . . . then please . . . I want . . . to be . . . with you and to love you forever!"

"That is exactly what you will be," the Duke said, "for our love will be eternal and even when we die we shall be together, and nothing will separate us."

He spoke in a solemn voice which Anita had never heard before, and somehow the lines of cynicism had gone from his face and his eyes were no longer mocking.

In fact he looked very different from the way he had ever looked before, and she knew it was because of love. The love she felt pulsating through her own body; the love which made her feel as if they were flying towards the sky, from which they had come.

She saw again the shaft of light which had come between the dark clouds which had made her think of Lucifer in the first place.

But she knew now that instead of him falling down from Heaven, they were both moving upwards towards the light which was all-embracing, all-enveloping.

Then, because there were no words in which to express her thoughts, she could only reach up her arms towards him, saying as she did so:

"I love you! I . . . love you! I will . . . try to make you . . . happy."

The Duke crushed her against him.

"You have made me happy!" he exclaimed. "I love you, my precious little angel, and until the stars fall from the sky and the earth no longer exists you are mine! My angel, who has been sent to bring me a happiness I do not deserve but which I have always longed to find."

"Let me . . . give it to you . . . please . . . please!" Anita whispered against his lips.

Then it was impossible to say any more, but only to feel the sunshine overhead which had become part of them both and was burning fiercely within them, drawing them closer and closer to the heart of love, which is Heaven.

The Wings of Ecstacy

AUTHOR'S NOTE

Although Wiedenstein is a fictitious country the details about Paris during the Second Empire are correct.

The word *demi-mondaine* was coined by Dumas *fils* to describe the world of the *déclassés*—a world which began where the legal wife ends and finishes where the mistress begins.

In a play by Barrière one of the characters says: "It is neither the aristocracy nor the bourgeoisie, but it floats on the ocean of Paris."

There were a dozen courtesans, the Queens of their profession, who were known as *le garde*. Each woman considered her beauty her capital and made it pay fantastic dividends. La Païva, born in a Moscow ghetto, wore two million francs worth of diamonds, pearls and precious stones and was called the "great debauchée of the century."

In March 1871, one year later than this novel, when the Prussians entered Paris, La Païva's lover Prince Henchel von Donnersmarch, in full uniform, watched his compatriots march past.

CHAPTER ONE

1869

*T*HE ARCH-DUKE OF WIEDENSTEIN was engrossed in the newspaper and the rest of his family who were breakfasting with him were silent.

It was always a somewhat uncomfortable meal as they were never certain in what sort of mood their father would be.

Prince Kendric took the last piece of toast and having piled it with butter and marmalade, English fashion, ate it quickly and pushed back his chair.

As he did so his mother, the Arch-Duchess, looked up from the letter she had been reading, and gave a significant cough.

She also looked fixedly at the newspaper which concealed her husband, but there was no response.

"Leopold," she said in a voice that was bound to attract his attention.

The Arch-Duke looked over his newspaper in a manner which showed he was irritated at being interrupted, caught his wife's eye and said:

"Yes, yes, of course!"

Prince Kendric and his twin sister, Princess Marie-Thérèse, who in the family circle was always called "Zena," stared at their father apprehensively.

They had the feeling that they were about to be given a lecture, which was nothing unusual.

The Arch-Duke put the newspaper down slowly on the table and took off his spectacles.

He never wore them in public if he could help it because he thought they spoilt his image.

He had been, and still was, a very handsome man. In fact, the coins of Wiedenstein hardly did him justice.

All his life there had been women to tell him that his looks were irresistible, which was something he had attempted unsuccessfully to keep secret from his wife.

"Your father wishes to speak to you," the Arch-Duchess said unnecessarily in a low tone.

Prince Kendric wished he had left the room earlier, but even if he had tried he was certain his mother would have prevented him from escaping.

The Arch-Duke cleared his throat.

"I have received," he said slowly and ponderously, "a report from your Tutors on your educational progress over these last three months."

He paused because he was looking at his daughter and thinking that she was looking particularly attractive this morning, and it diverted his mind from what he was about to say.

Then his eyes crossed the table to look at his son and the expression in them hardened.

"Your report, Kendric," he said, "is not what I hoped or expected. With one accord your Tutors say you could do better if you tried, and it is beyond my comprehension why you do not do so."

"I do, Papa," Prince Kendric said defiantly, "but if you ask my opinion the way we are taught is old-fashioned and, frankly, extremely dull."

This was such plain speaking that the Arch-Duchess drew in her breath and Zena looked at her brother nervously.

"It is a bad workman who complains of his tools," the Arch-Duke said sharply.

"If you had allowed me to go to University . . ." Kendric began.

This was an old argument and the Arch-Duke interrupted:

"You are to go into the Army. It is essential that when you take my place you should be able to command our troops, and God knows the discipline will be good for you!"

There was a pause and it was obvious that Prince Kendric was biting back the words he wanted to utter. As father and son glared at each other the Arch-Duchess interposed:

"Do continue and tell the children your plans, Leopold. That is what they have to hear."

Almost as if she called him to attention the Arch-Duke continued:

"Your mother and I have discussed the reports in detail and yours, Zena, are no better than Kendric's, especially where German is concerned."

"I find the grammar very difficult, Papa," the Princess replied, "and Herr Waldshutz is, as Kendric says, so long-winded and so slow that it is difficult not to go to sleep."

"Very well, I take your point," the Arch-Duke said, "and that is why we have decided to send both you and Kendric to Ettengen."

"To Ettengen, Papa!" Zena exclaimed in astonishment.

"It is essential that Kendric's German should improve," the Arch-Duke said, "before he goes to Düsseldorf."

There was an audible gasp from Kendric before he asked, with his voice rising:

"Why should I be going to Düsseldorf and what for?"

"That is what I am about to tell you," the Arch-Duke said. "Your brother-in-law has suggested, and I think it is an excellent idea, that you should spend a year in the Barracks there and thus have the chance of joining in the intensive training which is given to the Officer Cadets of the Prussian Army."

"A year with those bloodthirsty warmongers!" Prince Kendric exclaimed. "I cannot imagine anything more like the terrors of hell!"

"It will be good for you, and you will do as you are told," the Arch-Duke replied.

"I refuse! I absolutely refuse!" Prince Kendric muttered, but besides the defiance, there was a note almost of despair in his voice.

"As for you, Zena," the Arch-Duke went on, turning again to his daughter, "as you two make such a fuss at being parted from each other, you will go with Kendric to Ettengen and try to improve your German, after which, when Kendric goes to Düsseldorf, your mother and I have planned your marriage."

If Kendric had been astonished it was now Zena's turn.

"Married, Papa?" the Princess questioned, and there was no mistaking the expression of horror in her eyes.

"You are eighteen, and we have been thinking for some time about finding you a suitable husband," the Arch-Duke said. "I personally hoped there would be a reigning Prince in one of our adjacent States, but unfortunately they are either married or too young."

Zena gave a little sigh of relief and her father continued:

"It was then your mother thought that it might be a good idea for you to marry one of her own countrymen. After all, I was very fortunate in having a relative of the Queen of England as my wife."

The Arch-Duchess inclined her head at the compliment. Then as if she could not forbear to join in she said:

"You must understand, Zena, that it would be impossible, as you are only a second daughter, for us to find a Royal Prince as your husband or, as I would have liked, a reigning Sovereign."

"But I have no wish to be married to . . . anybody, Mama!"

The Arch-Duchess frowned.

"Do not be so ridiculous!" she said sharply. "Of course you have to be married, and with Kendric away at Düsseldorf the sooner the better, as far as I am concerned. I know how tiresome you will be without him."

As this was true Zena looked across the table at her twin, only to find he was scowling at a silver mustard-pot in front of him and obviously engrossed in his own troubles.

"I have written to my sister Margaret," the Arch-Duchess went on, "who is, as you are aware, a Lady of the Bedchamber to Queen Victoria and enjoys Her Majesty's confidence. We are in fact very fortunate and grateful to have her advice."

"And what is that, Mama?" Zena asked, feeling as if her lips were too dry for the words to pass through them.

"My sister Margaret replied that since there were no Royal Princes available at the moment of the right age, she had suggested to the Queen, who gave her approval, that you should marry an English Duke."

The Arch-Duchess paused, but as Zena did not speak, she continued:

"There are in fact two at the moment whose families on the maternal side have some connection with the Royal Family, and both my sister and the Queen thought that being the case that an alliance between one of them and us would be advantageous to both countries."

"But . . . I do not wish to marry an . . . Englishman, Mama."

"What possible objection can you have to the English?" the Arch-Duchess asked angrily.

It struck Zena that whatever she replied would inevitably entail being rude to her mother. She therefore merely looked down at her plate.

"I will ignore that exceedingly childish remark," the Arch-Duchess said scathingly.

"Get to the point, my dear," the Arch-Duke interposed. "We cannot stay here all day."

"That is just what I am trying to do, Leopold," his wife replied coldly, "but the children keep interrupting."

"They are quiet enough now," the Arch-Duke remarked.

"To get back to what I was saying," the Arch-Duchess continued without hurry, "my sister Margaret said there were two Dukes we might consider as your future husband, although she thought in fact that the Duke of Gatesford was too old, although he has recently become a widower."

The Duchess waited as if she expected Zena to ask his age, and as she did not do so, she went on:

"His Grace has turned sixty, and while he is of great importance and has a most commendable character, your father and I have decided that my sister is right and that he should not be approached."

"I could hardly marry a man who is older than Papa!" Zena said.

"You will marry who we tell you to," the Arch-Duchess replied repressively, "and we have therefore chosen, though somewhat reluctantly, the Duke of Faverstone who is only thirty-three. His mother was a second cousin of the Queen and was also distantly related to Her Majesty's uncle, the Duke of Cambridge."

"There is nothing wrong with the fellow's antecedents," the Arch-Duke remarked.

"Of course what you say is true, Leopold," the Arch-Duchess agreed. "At the same time I would have wished Zena to marry an older man who would not only have controlled the regrettably frivolous side of her nature, but also given her a greater sense of responsibility towards the position into which she has been born."

"She will learn all that sooner or later," the Arch-Duke growled.

He was exceedingly fond of his second daughter and thought she resembled him more than any other of his children did. He was therefore always inclined to defend her against the criticism and fault-finding of her mother.

The Duchess favoured her oldest son, but her real affection was for her younger son who was not yet fourteen.

There was something about Prince Louis that made him appear more English than the rest of her children, and he was therefore automatically very close to the Arch-Duchess's heart.

She was a cold woman, brought up austerely in England in a household where it was considered vulgar and ill-bred to show one's emotions.

When she had been married off, because of her Royal connections, to the Ruler of Wiedenstein, she had fallen in love with her handsome husband on sight, but found it impossible ever to express her feelings.

The Arch-Duke in those days had been a romantic Romeo who loved pretty women and who had indulged in a great many fiery love affairs before he was married.

He did not understand his wife but he treated her with respect and even grew to have some affection for her sterling qualities.

He would, however, have been astonished if he had known how wildly jealous she was of the women he favoured or how much she suffered from knowing that he did not admire her cold statuesque looks.

Nevertheless they had produced between them a family of outstandingly beautiful children.

It was, however, the Arch-Duchess thought, extremely unfortunate that her three daughters should take after their father in looks and in temperament, while her eldest son, Prince Kendric also leaned more towards Wiedenstein than the English side of his birthright.

She therefore hoped that her two younger children would be different and so far Prince Louis seemed more likely to fulfil her fondest hopes.

Zena was thinking over what her mother had said and while she thought the Duke of Faverstone sounded more hopeful than the other candidate, she had no wish to marry an Englishman.

She had never, even when she was small, found a soft spot in her mother's character to make her feel warm and cosseted.

In fact, the Arch-Duchess's continual scoldings, the severe punishments she had received as a child, and the way in which her opinions were always swept to one side, made her feel the whole English race was arrogant, dictatorial and heartless.

When she had thought about being married she had hoped, dreamed and prayed that she might marry a Frenchman.

The small Kingdom of Wiedenstein was situated West of Bavaria, with which one of its boundaries marched.

On the North there was the Province of Heidelburg belonging to Prussia, and on the West there was just a short frontier with the Alsace Region of France.

The majority of the population of Wiedenstein was of French origin who had intermarried with Bavarians.

Zena and her brother were therefore bilingual in French and German but their Tutor who was a Prussian continually found fault with the soft-spoken colloquial German of the Bavarians.

English was always spoken by the family in the Palace out of respect for the Arch-Duchess.

It was inevitable, as Zena had said when she was out of hearing of her father, that the Wiedensteins should be a nation of mongrels, and moreover in their own family their father's mother had been half-Hungarian.

"Everybody knows," Kendric had once said to his sister, "that accounts for the wild streak in both of us."

"We have not had much chance of showing it," Zena replied resentfully.

"We shall have to wait until we are grown up," Kendric answered.

Now that he had left School and she was free of the School-Room except for visiting Tutors, they were to be separated and Zena's heart cried out at the idea, for she was sure that when she lost Kendric she would lose half of herself.

The family were at last allowed to leave the Breakfast-Room and Zena had to listen to Kendric's account of the horrors to which he would be subjected in a German Barracks.

"I have heard of the Cadets being ordered about like animals," he said. "When they have any free time they are forced to duel with each other, and the more scars they get on their faces, the prouder they are.''

Zena gave a little cry of horror.

''Oh, Kendric, that must not happen to you!''

''It will,'' Kendric replied grimly.

He was an exceedingly handsome young man who enjoyed his good looks, and to Zena the idea of his being deliberately disfigured was terrifying.

They had rushed to their own private Sitting-Room as soon as they could get away from their parents, and now they looked at each other despairingly.

It was as if their whole world which had seemed safe and secure had collapsed and tumbled them into a slough of despond from which there was no escape.

''What shall we do?'' Zena asked. ''What can we do, Kendric? I cannot lose you for a whole year!''

''It is not only for a year,'' Kendric corrected, ''but for life!''

Zena gave a cry.

''I shall have to marry that horrible Duke and it will be even worse than what poor Melanie has to endure with Georg.''

The twins were silent, both thinking of the unhappiness of their older sister. She was married to the Crown Prince of Fürstenburg which was an allegedly independent State in the North of Germany, but was actually under the heel of Prussia.

Melanie had hated the Prince from the very moment she first saw him, but the marriage had gone ahead as arranged and when she occasionally came home she told the twins how unhappy she was.

''I loathe Georg,'' she had said over and over again. ''He is pompous, obstinate and extremely stupid!''

''Oh, Melanie, I am sorry!'' Zena cried.

''He listens to nothing anybody says except himself,'' Melanie went on, ''with the result that everybody at Court is so deadly dull that I feel as if I am buried alive.''

Her sister's words came back to Zena now, and she thought that was what would happen to her.

If all the English were like her mother, she would be suffocated by them.

She had actually met very few English people except for her mother's relations who came to stay from time to time.

The Arch-Duchess had been the youngest of a large family and her sisters and brothers had all married Royalty. They gave themselves, Zena thought, more airs and graces than any Wiedenstein ruler would think of doing.

The only time they were in the least human was when they were talking about horses, and what her father had said before they left the Breakfast-Room made Zena sure that the Duke of Faverstone would be exactly like them.

"Your mother suggested, Zena," he had said to his daughter, "that we invite the Duke of Faverstone here next month for the *Prix d'Or.*"

This was the most important race-meeting of the year, and owners brought their horses from all over Europe to compete for the main prize.

Zena did not answer and her father had continued:

"Faverstone will thereby see us at our best and will meet the élite of the country. We will entertain for him in a manner which will make it quite clear he would have no grounds for thinking, because he is related to the Queen of England, that he can treat us condescendingly."

"You have no reason to imagine he will do that, Leopold," the Arch-Duchess had said defensively.

"I know the English," the Arch-Duke had replied, and Zena thought he had merely said aloud what she was thinking.

"What can we do to prevent these horrors from happening to us?" she now asked her brother.

Kendric did not reply and she went on:

"It is appalling that we are to be separated in addition to having to go to Ettengen and mug up that ghastly German."

"I hate that language too," Kendric said, "and from all the Baron tells me the Professor is even more boring than he is."

"You can be quite certain of that," Zena agreed. "After all, he must be a hundred and eighty, otherwise we would not have to go to him."

The Arch-Duke's last announcement had been that they were to leave in three days time for a small village where they were to stay with their Tutor, Professor Schwarz, because he was too old to come to them.

"You will be accompanied," their father had continued, "by Baron Kauflen and Countess Beronkasler, who will see that you two behave yourselves and apply yourselves to your studies. Otherwise, when you return, I will be extremely angry!"

"Fancy having to stay for three weeks with those old bores!" Kendric said now.

"I feel like running away," Zena said gloomily. "The only difficulty is . . . where could we . . . run to?"

There was silence, then Kendric suddenly said:

"I have an idea!"

Zena looked at him apprehensively.

"If it is going to get us into more trouble with Mama, I do not think I could stand it!" she said. "You know what happened the last time you had one of your brainwaves."

She was however not speaking severely, but smiling.

The twins had always got into mischief ever since they were born and it was Kendric who with his vivid imagination thought out the outrageous pranks which inevitably brought retribution down on their heads.

But Zena would slavishly do whatever he wanted her to do simply because she loved him.

Kendric jumped up to walk across the room.

Their private Sitting-Room was very untidy simply because the servants had given up trying to create order out of chaos.

Kendric's guns, rackets, riding-whips, footballs and polo-sticks were all muddled up with Zena's paintbrushes and palettes, her embroidery which she thought a boring pastime, but on which her mother insisted, and the books which she loved and which increased in number almost daily.

Books filled the shelves around the room, there were books on the table, on the chairs and on the floor.

There were also flowers which Zena had picked herself from the Palace garden and arranged with an artistry that was seldom shown in other parts of the Palace.

There were dolls she had loved as a child but which she now kept as ornaments and dressed them in beautiful gowns embroidered with jewels to brighten the severity of the panelled walls.

It suddenly struck Zena looking round the room that anyone seeing it for the first time would have a very clear insight into not only hers and Kendric's interests, but also their personalities and characters.

Quite suddenly Kendric gave a cry, jumped up and ran to the door. He opened it, looked outside, and shut it again.

"I am just making sure," he explained, "that there is nobody lis-

tening outside. I feel certain that on two or three occasions one of the
maids or a footman has overheard our conversations, related them to
Mama's lady's-maid, who in her turn wasted no time in passing on the
information to Mama."

"So that is how Mama knew about your pretty little dancer!" Zena
said.

"There is no other possible way she could have known!" Kendric
replied.

There had been an appalling row because the Arch-Duchess had
learnt that Kendric had been out at night alone.

He had somehow evaded the sentries at the gate and gone to the
Theatre where he had not only enjoyed, night after night, the performance of a very attractive Russian ballet dancer, but had also taken her
out to supper afterwards.

After the roof had nearly been taken off the Palace over his "outrageous behaviour," Kendric had decided that the only possible way
his mother could have discovered his escapades was that he had ex-
tolled the dancer's charms and the fun they had together to Zena in
the privacy of their Sitting-Room.

That was why now, to make quite certain there was nobody listening,
he took the precaution of lowering his voice, and he sat down beside
Zena before he began.

"Now listen," he said, "I have an idea and you must help me work
out every detail."

"What is it?" Zena asked.

"You know where the Professor lives?"

"I know the direction on the map," Zena said.

"Well, to get there we have to change at the Junction of Hoyes."

Zena was now looking at her brother in a puzzled fashion.

He had a sudden light in his eyes which had replaced the expression
of dull despair, as if his plan was already exciting him, but at the same
time she was afraid of what it might be.

"You know what happens at Hoyes," he went on.

"You tell me," Zena answered.

"Express trains from many parts of Europe stop there on their way
to Paris."

The way Kendric spoke made Zena sit up sharply and look at him
with startled eyes.

"What do you mean? What are you suggesting?" she asked.

"I am planning," Kendric said slowly, "how we can escape from our watch-dogs at Hoyes and spend a week of our tutorial in the gayest city in the world."

"You must be mad!" Zena exclaimed. "If we ran away from them they would come straight back and report to Papa, and he would have us arrested."

"I do not think so, for he would do nothing to cause a scandal," Kendric said. "At the same time, we have to be clever enough, Zena, to prevent those gloomy old vultures telling him anything for fear they will get into trouble."

There was a sparkle in Zena's blue eyes.

"Are you really saying, Kendric, that you think we can go to Paris instead of to that boring old Professor?"

"It is not what I *think* we can do," Kendric replied, "it is what I intend we shall do!"

"I think Papa and Mama will kill us!"

"Only if they find out."

"How are we going to prevent them? And supposing people recognise us?"

"Once we reach Paris nobody will recognise us, or know who we are," Kendric replied.

"You mean we will be disguised?"

"Of course we will! You do not suppose I am going to arrive as 'Crown Prince Kendric of Wiedenstein,' and have our Embassy preventing us from doing anything except look at Museums."

"But, Kendric, it is too dangerous, too outrageous!"

"God knows, I am entitled to do something outrageous if I am to spend a year clicking my heels and obeying orders at the double!" Kendric said bitterly.

"It is cruel of Papa to send you to such a place, and I am sure he is only being persuaded into it by our ghastly brother-in-law!"

"It is the sort of place that Georg would think enjoyable," Kendric said.

"But . . . can we really get to Paris?" Zena asked.

She knew that if once Kendric began a tirade against Georg whom they both disliked, it would depress them more than they were already.

Sometimes Zena would lie awake in tears when she thought of what her sister was suffering with such a man.

The thought of Georg made her remember that she was to marry an Englishman and because the idea was so horrifying she said quickly:

"Go on with your plan of how we can get there, how we can manage it, and who we shall say we are."

"We will escape from the old crows at Hoyes," Kendric said. "Once we are in the Express nobody will be able to stop us from reaching Paris. Of course they could telegraph a description of us down the line, but I think I can prevent them from doing that."

"How?" Zena asked.

"I will tell you that later," Kendric replied. "It is not yet quite clear in my mind."

"Then go on about when we reach Paris."

"From that moment Prince Kendric and Princess Marie-Thérèse will no longer exist."

"Then who shall we be?"

Kendric looked at her somewhat quizzically.

"It is going to be very restricting for me if I arrive in Paris with a sister who has to be looked after and chaperoned."

"It might be worse if I pretend to be your wife," Zena retorted.

"Exactly," he answered, "and that leaves only one alternative."

"What is that?"

"You must become my *'Chère Amie'*. It will be rather like taking an apple to a Harvest Festival, but I could not be so unkind as to go to Paris without you."

Zena gave a cry.

"How could you even think of anything so selfish, so utterly disloyal and cruel? Of course you must take me with you!"

Kendric put his hand on hers.

"We have always done everything together, and as this will be the most outrageous and our last escapade, even if we are discovered, it will have been worth it."

"Of course it will!" Zena said loyally.

"Very well," Kendric said, "and actually it will be a very good disguise."

"What will?"

"The part you will play as my lady-love."

Zena threw back her head and laughed.

"Oh, Kendric, do you think I dare? Think what Mama would say if she knew!"

"Let us pray that she never finds out!" Kendric said firmly. "But you do see that if you are thought to be a *demi-mondaine*, as a newly coined word expresses it, you will be able to come with me to all the places where ladies are not allowed to go?"

Zena clasped her hands together.

"That will be thrilling, only you will have to tell me how to behave."

She paused before she said provocatively:

"I am quite certain that is something you know all about!"

"Of course I do," Kendric boasted.

"And you also know where we should go in Paris?"

"I have a pretty good idea," he replied. "As you are aware, I have not been to Paris since I was grown-up and the last time was two years ago, but my friends at School, several of whom were older than me, talked of little else."

He smiled as if at the remembrance of what he had heard and went on:

"And Philippe, whose father was in the Diplomatic Service, has told me all about the women who are under the protection of the Emperor, the Prince Napoleon and every important Statesman and aristocrat, and who charge astronomical sums for their services."

Zena looked puzzled.

"What services?" she asked.

Kendric realised he had been carried away by his enthusiasm and replied hastily:

"Because the gentlemen with whom they are—friends show them off to each other, they expect to be bedecked in jewels."

"You mean it is a sort of competition, like who has the best horses?" Zena asked.

"Exactly!" her brother replied. "And you will have to dress yourself up and of course use cosmetics, otherwise I shall lose a great deal of face when I produce you."

"That will not be difficult," Zena said, "for as you know Mama has always said that my looks are 'regrettably theatrical'!"

Kendric laughed.

"I have heard her say that often enough. It is the effect of your hair and your eyes, but there is nothing you can do about it."

"Nothing," Zena agreed, "but now perhaps the combination will come in useful."

Kendric looked at her as if he had never seen her before.

"You know, Zena," he said, "I think if you were not my sister I would be bowled over by you."

"Would you really, Kendric?" Zena asked with interest. "Well, I will certainly try not to shame you in Paris, and I have some new gowns that I think should be smart enough."

"You had better doll them up a bit," Kendric said. "From all I have heard the women who set the pace are 'dressed to kill'. Somebody was saying to Papa after dinner the other night that the Empress spends 1,500 francs on a gown."

"Good gracious!" Zena exclaimed. "I can hardly be expected to compete with that!"

"No, of course not," her brother replied, "but if we take enough money with us perhaps you will be able to buy one gown that will not look out of place, and at least you have some good jewellery."

"You mean what my grandmother left me?" Zena asked. "It is kept in the safe, but I expect I could get hold of it."

"I shall not appear to have been very generous unless you do," Kendric said.

He looked at his sister again. Then he said:

"You will be all right if you mascara your eyelashes and put on a bit of paint and powder. After all, not every man in Paris can have a million francs to throw away on a woman."

"Is that what they usually spend?" Zena asked in a low voice.

"I have heard of one woman called 'La Païva'," Kendric replied lowering his voice again, "who has millions of francs spent on her by every man she meets!"

"Why? Is she so beautiful?" Zena enquired.

It passed through Kendric's mind that as his sister was so innocent it was going to be difficult to answer her questions without embarrassing explanations which he felt it was not his business to make.

At the same time he knew, as Zena had said, he could not be so cruel as to leave her behind.

With his usual happy-go-lucky attitude he thought it would somehow work out all right in the long run.

If Zena guessed the reason for the notorious Courtesans' appearance and behaviour it would not eventually matter very much, while if he said as little as possible she would doubtless remain in happy ignorance of the reality of their behaviour.

Actually he was feeling rather ignorant himself.

He had had two very minor love-affairs, one of which was with the dancer before he had been strictly forbidden to see her again, and one which had been able to last much longer when he was at School.

His parents would have been horrified if they had realised that the older boys considered themselves men, and there were certainly young women from the town in which the School was situated to tell them they were.

But such affairs, Kendric knew, were very different from the methods by which the Courtesans, who were the Queens of their profession, ruled Paris.

The stories of their wild extravagance and the way they were fêted and acclaimed lost nothing in the telling.

Kendric had had an irresistible desire to visit Paris for the last year and he had suggested it again and again to his father. But the Arch-Duke had said:

"I would dearly like to take you there, my boy, but you know the fuss your mother would make if I suggested that we went for pleasure, and at the moment, since politically we are somewhat at loggerheads with the French Government, I cannot think of a really good excuse."

He had seen the disappointment on his son's face, and smiled understandingly.

"I will tell you what we will do, Kendric," he said. "Give it another year, and then when your mother will have no more jurisdiction over you we will get there somehow. I do not disguise the fact that I should enjoy it myself."

He gave a little sigh as he said:

"I often sit here wondering if 'La Castiglione' is still as beautiful as she is reported to be. I know that she is now the mistress of the Emperor."

"Was she a 'love' of yours, Papa?" Kendric asked.

He thought for a moment his father was not going to reply. Then he said:

"Very briefly, and although when she was young she was the loveliest thing I have ever seen she was actually somewhat boring."

He laughed before he added:

"But then, *les expertes ès Sciences galantes* are there to be looked at and loved, and why should we ask for more?"

"Why indeed, Papa?" Kendric had agreed.

If we are caught, he thought now, *Papa will understand.*

But he knew neither his father nor his mother would ever understand or forgive him for taking Zena with him into what the Arch-Duchess considered a "cesspool of wickedness."

Kendric knew without Zena having to tell him how much she dreaded having to marry anybody, let alone an Englishman.

They were both of them deeply distressed about Melanie's unhappiness and the fact that the husband chosen for her was a man without a vestige of sensitivity or kindness.

From a social point of view it was a brilliant marriage, and as Fürstenburg was a far larger and more important country than Wiedenstein, Melanie would eventually be a Queen.

But as Zena had once said to her twin:

"Who in their senses would want to be a Queen except on a pack of cards? And if one was a man, one would rather be the Knave."

Kendric had laughed and agreed with his sister, but he thought now that just as no young man in his senses would want to go to the Barracks at Düsseldorf, so nobody as spirited and warm-hearted as Zena would wish to marry an Englishman.

"We both of us deserve a visit to Paris first," he told himself firmly.

And if his conscience pricked him he was determined not to listen to anything it said.

CHAPTER TWO

*I*N THE TRAIN WHICH WAS CARRYING THEM to Hoyes, Zena was aware that her heart was beating nervously and she found it impossible to read the book which the Countess Bernkasler had bought for her edification on the journey.

It was only a two-hour ride from the Capital to Ettengen and the Arch-Duke had not bothered to provide his children with a Royal coach.

Instead a carriage was reserved on the train and they were seen into it by a Lord-in-waiting, the Station Master and a number of other railway officials.

They were in fact, travelling incognito. This was an excuse for the Arch-Duke not to send a military escort with them on the train or to have sentries posted outside the Professor's House in Ettengen.

As soon as they left the Capital, therefore, Kendric became the *Comte* de Castelnaud and Zena the *Comtesse*. It was actually one of the Arch-Duke's minor titles.

When the train left the capital, Kendric had looked at his sister meaningfully and she knew their escape depended not only on her following his instructions to the letter, but also a great deal on chance.

If the Express to Paris was late, the slow train in which they were travelling might leave Hoyes before it, and they would be carried on to where the Professor was waiting to give them three weeks of unutterable boredom.

In the days before their departure, Kendric talked of nothing else when they were alone, and he was also managing, Zena knew, to see his French friend, Philippe, who he told her was a mine of information.

Both the Countess and the Baron were elderly and having settled themselves down comfortably in the carriage they made no attempt at conversation, but closed their eyes and apparently dozed off into unconsciousness.

Zena and Kendric knew they dare not assume that they were really asleep, and they therefore did not talk. But because they were twins they were each aware of what the other was thinking.

Finally when they had travelled for an hour and a quarter the train puffed slowly into Hoyes.

They had already stopped three times at wayside stations to pick up other passengers, mostly farmers and their wives or students. At the last of these stations Kendric had said:

"I must stretch my legs."

Baron Kauflen had opened his eyes.

"Do you wish me to accompany Your Royal Highness?"

"No, no, of course not," Kendric replied. "I am going to walk very quickly to the end of the platform and back again. You just stay where you are, Baron."

The Baron had given a sigh of relief and Kendric hurried away.

Zena knew he had gone to arrange for their luggage to be taken from the Guard's Van at the end of the train and placed in the Paris Express.

The luggage had been another problem which, on Kendric's instructions, she had managed with what she thought was extreme cleverness.

"You can hardly be expected to take your best Ball-gowns and your more elaborate dresses to Ettengen," he said. "You must therefore have another trunk which you must pack yourself and I will tear off the label when we reach the station before Hoyes and tie on another one which I shall have in my pocket."

"Oh, Kendric!" Zena had exclaimed, "things become more and more complicated at every moment. Surely my maid will think it very strange if I pack a trunk myself?"

"You will just have to think of some excuse," Kendric said firmly. "Anyway, Maria is devoted to you, and if you swear her to secrecy I do not believe she will sneak to the other servants or, worst of all, to Mama."

Zena was certain this was true and she told Maria that she wished to take some of her more attractive gowns with her just in case she was asked to a dance.

271

"Please, Maria, do not say anything about it to anybody," she begged, "because as I have told you, His Royal Highness and I are being sent to Ettengen to study, but three weeks is a very long time to look at nothing but books."

Maria had been sympathetic.

"My mother's always said, Your Royal Highness, that one's only young once, and I'll do nothing to spoil your fun."

"I trust you Maria."

To make sure she kept silent Zena gave her one of her gowns which she knew Maria had always admired, and the maid had promised to help her in every way she could.

In the end Maria had packed the extra trunk far more skilfully than Zena could have done, and also insisted that she take two hat-boxes, one of which contained her more elaborate bonnets which she only wore on public occasions.

When Kendric came back to the carriage after his supposed walk he had winked at Zena, and she knew he had been successful not only in changing the labels, but in tipping the Guard enough to ensure that the luggage would be transferred to the Paris Express.

There was, however, no sign of the fast train when their own train came to a standstill in the station.

A number of people alighted and Kendric opened the window to lean out, apparently watching them.

Zena began to grow afraid that all their plans would be circumvented at the last moment.

Then seeing Kendric's head turn she knew that he was suddenly alert and there was no need to tell her that the Express was in sight.

Porters hurried across the platform to where the train would wait for only a few minutes before it proceeded on to Paris.

Ostentatiously, Kendric yawned.

"I am bored with having to wait about," he said to nobody in particular. "I think I will go to the bookstall and see if I can buy some more newspapers."

"Shall I do that for Your Royal Highness?" the Baron asked.

"No, I would rather choose them for myself," Kendric answered in an indifferent tone.

He opened the carriage door and stepped down on to the platform, leaving the door open.

This was the moment, Zena knew, when she had to be ready.

After a second she rose to her feet to stand as her brother had done at the window, apparently watching the activity on the platform.

Then she saw Kendric beckon to her and she said to the Countess:

"His Royal Highness wants me, I will not be a moment."

As she spoke she put a letter she was holding in her hand down on the seat she had just vacated and jumped down on to the platform.

She heard the Countess expostulate as she ran to her brother's side. He took her hand and without pausing they ran to the Paris train.

The Porters were just slamming the doors of the carriages and the Guard had the whistle between his lips.

Kendric pulled open the door of a First Class carriage and pushed Zena into it.

The train was already moving as he jumped on the running board himself, and a Porter shouted at him for leaving things so late and slammed the door shut behind them.

They threw themselves down on the carriage seats, for the moment too breathless to speak.

Then as the train gathered speed they realised they had done it— they had got away and there was nothing their attendants could immediately do about it.

The carriage they were in was empty and Zena guessed that while Kendric was waiting to signal to her he had chosen it with care.

Now he looked at her and burst out laughing.

"Tell me I am a genius!" he said. "Everything has gone like clockwork! The luggage is in, I saw the Guard carrying it himself, and here we are, embarking on an adventure that will enthrall our grandchildren when we tell them about it."

Zena laughed.

"I am not concerned with my grandchildren," she replied, "but with Papa and Mama."

"There is no need to worry," Kendric said soothingly. "When the Baron reads the letter I have written to him he will not dare to tell Papa. He will be too afraid of losing his job."

"What did you put in it?" Zena asked.

"I told him we have decided to stay with a friend of mine for one week before we start our lessons. I told him we should be completely safe and there is no need for him or the Countess to worry about us."

"They will do so all the same," Zena murmured.

"I pointed out," Kendric went on, as if she had not spoken, "that if they tell Papa he will undoubtedly vent his rage not only on us, but on them for not taking us safely to our destination as they had been told to do."

"Poor things," Zena said, "they did not have a chance!"

"Nevertheless, Papa will hardly consider that an excuse, and I know what Mama would say. So I am quite certain they will keep mum."

"I sincerely hope so," Zena said nervously.

"Even if they do return to the Palace and tell Papa they have lost us," Kendric continued, "he will have a job finding us in Paris. In fact it will be like looking for two needles in the proverbial haystack."

"All I want now," Zena said, "is for you to tell me who we are and what are our names."

As she spoke she opened her handbag and drew out a small pot.

"And I think," she added, "I should start altering my appearance right away."

"You might as well," Kendric agreed.

"Mama was surprised to see me wearing so smart a dress just to travel to Ettengen."

Zena gave a little laugh.

"She scolded me for my extravagance, and said that this dress and pelisse were intended to be worn when the Duke of Faverstone arrived."

She had started to speak lightly, but as she said the Englishman's name her expression altered.

"Forget him, anyway for the next week," Kendric said quickly. "Remember only that you are my *Chère Amie* and you do not have to marry anybody."

"How lucky those ladies are!" Zena said beneath her breath.

As she spoke she had turned round to look in the little mirror which was fixed above the seats and was undoing the ribbons of her bonnet which were tied beneath her chin.

She had done her hair a little more elaborately than usual with curls falling down the back in the very latest fashion.

Wiedenstein prided itself in not being far behind Paris, and because most of its citizens had French taste the dressmakers slavishly followed the latest fashions in the French Capital, while the *coiffeurs* were always ready to introduce a new style to their clients.

Because the hairdresser who had been in attendance on the Palace for nearly twenty years had died, his son, who had taken over the business, was determined that Princess Marie Thérèse should be a good advertisement for him.

The Arch-Duchess had protested at the way in which he had dressed her daughter's hair because she considered its colour was flamboyant enough without it being arranged except in a ladylike manner.

But the Arch-Duke had supported his daughter when she had said:

"I have no wish to lock a dowd, Mama, and I am sure you do not want your Court to be as dull and lifeless as poor Melanie's."

She knew as she spoke that even her father and mother had found their visits to the Palace of Fürstenburg extremely boring and the Arch-Duke in his usual outspoken way had replied:

"My God! If I thought we were going to be like that I think I would abdicate!"

The Arch-Duchess had looked disapproving at his language but had said nothing, and Zena's new hairstyle had been forgotten.

Now watching her, Kendric thought that in her silk gown swept to the back in the new fashion, with a bustle trimmed with pleats and frills, she could easily pass for the *Chère Amie* she was pretending to be.

As if she knew what he was thinking, she turned round and he saw that she had applied a red salve to her lips and also powdered her already pearly white skin.

"How do I look?" she asked.

"Sensational!" Kendric replied. "In fact, you not only look the part, but extraordinarily pretty!"

"Thank you!" Zena said. "When we reach Paris I will blacken my eye-lashes, but I cannot do it in the train because the mascara might run into my eyes and make them smart."

She sat down opposite him and went on:

"Now tell me where we are going and what we are going to do."

"First of all," Kendric said dramatically, "let me introduce you to the *Vicomte* de Villerny."

Zena stared at him.

"But . . . he is a real . . . person!"

"Yes, I know," Kendric agreed, "and that is why it is clever of me to impersonate him."

"I know that the present *Vicomte* is somewhere out in the East," Zena said, "but suppose somebody knows what he looks like?"

"I think that is unlikely," Kendric replied, "and you know as well as I do the French are terrible snobs and sleep with the *Almanach de Gotha* under their pillows. If I had given a false name as I first intended, I might have been quickly exposed as an imposter."

"I see your point," Zena replied.

The late *Vicomte* de Villerny had been a friend of their father's.

He was a distinguished man in his own field who had spent his life collecting shells of every sort and description, and writing books about them which were only read by conchologists.

Because his collection was world famous, the children from the Palace were allowed frequently to visit him to see his latest acquisitions.

What they enjoyed more than the shells was the fact that the *Vicomte* was also a gourmet who had given them delicious *patisseries* to eat and also insisted, even when they were very young, that they should drink a glass of wine with him.

When the *Vicomte* had died two years ago Zena had been genuinely sorry.

His son had inherited the title and, of course, his collection of shells, but he preferred to live in the East where he had strange interests that were spoken about in Wiedenstein only in lowered voices.

Now she thought about it, Zena realised that Kendric was right in assuming a title that would not be questioned, and they were very unlikely to meet anybody who knew the present *Vicomte*.

"And who am I?" Zena asked now.

"You of course, are of no particular consequence," Kendric replied. "Although doubtless there will be a large number of men who will look at you, and look again."

He saw the smile on his sister's red lips and added quickly:

"Now you are to behave yourself, Zena! You know as well as I do that I have no right whatever to involve you in this escapade, and if you get into any trouble in the process God knows what will happen to me if Papa hears about it!"

"Why should I get into trouble?" Zena asked. "And of course I will behave myself properly! All I want to do is to see Paris and have some fun."

It crossed Kendric's mind that that was the last thing she should be wanting in Paris of all places, but it was far too late to have regrets, and as he had said before, he could not have been so cruel as to leave his twin sister behind and enjoy himself on his own.

"I have been thinking of a name for you," he said, "and it ought to sound theatrical."

"Then I can keep my Christian name, at any rate," Zena said.

"Of course! Zena is very appropriate, and I could not risk your not answering when I speak to you."

"No, of course not," she agreed, "and what is my other name to be?"

"I thought of Beauchamp," Kendric replied.

Zena put her head on one side as she considered it.

" 'Fairfield,' " she said. "It sounds rather engaging, but 'Bellefleur' would be even better."

"Of course! You are right!" Kendric agreed.

Zena chuckled before she said in French:

"*Mademoiselle* Zena Bellefleur at your service, *Monsieur*!"

She looked so pretty as she spoke that once again her brother felt apprehensive about what her impact would be on Paris.

Then he remembered it was a City where lived some of the most beautiful as well as the most notorious and outrageous women in Europe, and he told himself that among them Zena would pass unnoticed.

Because the Express was so fast it was only a two-hour journey from Hoyes to Paris, and as they came into the huge arched station Zena felt as if she was stepping into a new world, and she had never known such excitement before in her whole life.

They collected their luggage, which was clearly marked: THE PROPERTY OF THE VICOMTE DE VILLERNY, and a porter loaded it on to a *voiture*.

As it set out over the cobbled streets, Zena saw the tall grey houses with their wooden shutters, the Cafés in the Boulevards with the customers sitting outside on the pavement, and felt as if the curtain was rising on an enthralling drama.

She found that her resourceful brother had already obtained accommodations for them.

"Philippe has a friend," he said, "who has a very comfortable apartment in the Rue St. Honoré. He is in Italy at the moment, and he told Philippe that any time he wished to go to Paris he could use his apartment."

"So he has actually offered it to us?" Zena asked.

"He has not only done that, but he has written to the caretaker to say that we are his guests, and everything is to be done for our comfort."

"How kind!" Zena cried. "It is very lucky you are such friends with him."

"I have often thought such a friendship might come in useful one day," Kendric confessed.

"We must certainly do something for him when we get home," Zena said.

She saw by the expression on her twin's face that he was thinking it would be over a year before he was able to entertain his friends or in any way recompense Philippe.

Because she had no wish to depress him Zena quickly changed the subject, pointing out the new Opera House which had not been finished when she had last been to Paris. Soon they were passing down the Rue de la Paix where all the important dressmakers had their Salons, including the famous Frederick Worth.

"That is where I want to buy a gown!" she said in a rapt voice.

"We will have to see what our expenses are first," Kendric said in a practical tone. "I have brought a lot of money with me but I know Paris is very expensive."

"At least we will not have to pay rent," Zena reminded him.

"No, but if we are going to enjoy ourselves we must entertain. Philippe has already written to some of his friends."

"He has not told them who we are?" Zena asked in horror.

"No, of course not!" Kendric said. "He merely said that I am the *Vicomte* de Villerny who lives in Wiedenstein and who is visiting Paris with a very lovely lady-friend."

Zena laughed.

"Oh, Kendric, you are wonderful! Nobody else could have planned anything so clever, or indeed so thrilling."

"That remains to be seen," Kendric said cautiously, but Zena saw that his eyes were shining.

The apartment was charming and was on the first floor of a large house at what Kendric said was "the right end" of the Rue St. Honoré.

There was a large Sitting-Room, three bedrooms and, to Zena's surprise, a small kitchen.

"Why should the owner want a kitchen?" she asked. "Surely he would go out for his meals?"

FIVE COMPLETE NOVELS

"I expect he thinks sometimes it is more convenient to dine at home," Kendric answered, "and if the Caretaker is not prepared to cook for him, I am quite certain he would have a delightful *Chère Amie* who would be only too willing to oblige."

His eyes were twinkling as he spoke and Zena replied:

"You know as well as I do that I am a good cook, but I have no intention of cooking while we are in Paris! I want to visit all the Restaurants, if for no other reason because Mama says Royalty can never be seen in one!"

"You shall eat in all the most famous of them." Kendric promised. "I have a list."

"Then what are we waiting for?" Zena asked.

"For you to change your clothes," Kendric replied, "and there is no hurry. Nobody eats early in Paris, so you can forget your Provincial ways."

Zena made a grimace at him and went to the bedroom she had chosen for herself which was the largest and most attractive, where she found a young girl who she assumed was the caretaker's daughter unpacking her trunk.

"*M'mselle's* gowns are very beautiful!" the girl said. "Are you going to the Artists' Ball?"

"Is it taking place tonight?" Zena enquired.

"*Oui, oui, M'mselle* and all Paris enjoys the gayest and most noisy Ball of the year. Everybody will be there, except perhaps the Empress who does not approve."

She paused to note that Zena was listening intently and went on:

"The Emperor is sure to attend. He enjoys seeing the pretty women who make each Ball more successful than the last."

Zena ran from the bedroom and across the Sitting-Room.

"Kendric!" she cried as she opened her brother's bedroom door. "Did you know that the Artists' Ball is taking place tonight? Please, let us go!"

"Of course we are going," Kendric replied. "I have not told you because I wanted it to be a surprise."

Zena looked at her twin who had just taken off his coat and tie. Then she flung her arms around his neck.

"Oh, Kendric, you are wonderful!" she said. "Who could have a more fabulous brother than you?"

279

Kendric smiled. Then he saw that the door was open and frowned.

"Hush," he said. "Have you forgotten I am not your brother? Even when we are here by ourselves we must be careful."

"I am sorry. It was stupid of me."

Zena spoke in a contrite tone.

"I do not suppose any harm has been done," Kendric said, "but do be on your guard. We must not arouse the slightest suspicion. Looking at you, I am quite certain a number of men will be very curious."

Zena kissed his cheek as she said:

"And as you are so handsome I am equally certain a large number of women will be curious about you."

"That is the sort of thing I expect to hear," Kendric said complacently.

"You are abominably conceited," Zena teased.

Then because she was in a hurry to get ready she went back to her own room.

As Kendric had said, there was no hurry, but by the time Zena had unpacked, had a bath, arranged her hair and made up her face in what seemed to her to be a very lurid fashion, nearly three hours had passed.

She put on a gown which the Arch-Duchess had complained when she bought it was far too elaborate for a young girl.

It was in fact a copy of one of Mr. Worth's creations, which the dressmaker in Wiedenstein had seen when she was in Paris, and she had actually brought back the same material which Mr. Worth had used.

It was of blue shot with silver, which accentuated the red-gold of Zena's hair and made her blue eyes seem even larger and more brilliant than usual.

It was not surprising that she should have blue eyes, considering that her father's eyes were blue and so were her mother's.

But Zena's were the colour of the gentians she had seen growing in the mountains when they had visited Switzerland, and the combination of them with her white skin and her red hair was positively sensational or, as the Arch-Duchess had said, "regrettably theatrical."

Zena had mascaraed her eyelashes to make them appear even longer than they were already, and reddened her lips.

Having done so, she felt as if the Princess Marie-Thérèse had really ceased to exist and that she was now a *demi-mondaine,* a word she was sure would never soil her mother's lips.

She was still not certain why the *demi-mondaines* of Paris were considered so outrageous.

She supposed they were like actresses, remembering her mother had always said firmly that no decent woman would parade herself in public so that anybody could pay to watch her.

When she and Kendric entered the *Café Anglais,* which her brother told her was the most fashionable and the most acclaimed Restaurant in all Paris, Zena felt as if she stepped on a stage.

It was very large, which she had not expected, and she gathered there were a number of different rooms in it, though she did not quite understand what that involved.

Le Grand Seize, in which they were dining and which was downstairs, was not full when they had entered but now began to fill up minute by minute until there was not an empty table in the whole place.

It was then that Zena was aware why Kendric had told her she must doll herself up and try to look her best.

Never had she imagined that women could be so fantastically gowned, or bedecked with so many jewels.

She found herself staring at them one after another as they came sweeping in from the *Vestibule,* their bustles moving behind them like the wake of a ship at sea.

Their hair fell in long ringlets behind their swan-like necks, and their bare chests and arms literally blazed with gems.

Kendric had ordered some of the specialties that were more delicious than any food Zena had ever tasted before, but it was difficult to appreciate such cuisine when all she could do was stare around her at the other diners.

"I wish we knew who all these people are," she said to Kendric.

"We will soon be told," he replied. "I found quite a number of invitations waiting for me at the apartment, and Philippe's friends seem glad to entertain us to luncheon, dinner, and of course, supper."

The way he said the last word made Zena look at him enquiringly.

"Is there something special about supper?" she asked.

"Of course," Kendric replied. "That is when we shall see the bright lights of Paris and visit the places where no 'nice girls' would go."

"It sounds thrilling," Zena said, "but tonight we are going to the Ball."

"We are joining some of Philippe's friends in a box," Kendric said, "but I warn you it may be rowdy, so do not be surprised."

It was so exciting that Zena could not make up her mind whether to stay on at the *Café Anglais* where there was so much to see, or whether they should hurry to the Ball.

Finally, when she felt it was growing late, although Kendric had laughed at her for thinking so, they set off for the Ball, and she thought that nobody could be more fortunate than she was, and that whatever happened in the future with the dull and doubtless incredibly boring Duke, she would have this to remember.

When they reached the Artists' Ball the lights, the music and the wild dancing of hundreds of guests were dazzling.

They were shown up to the second tier of boxes and Kendric soon found the box where they were to meet Philippe's friends.

They were obviously expecting him and he was greeted with an exuberance which Zena thought was rather overdone, until she realised that the gentlemen in the box had all imbibed a great deal from the innumerable bottles of champagne stacked on a table just inside the door.

"Come in! Come in!" they shouted. "Philippe has asked us to look after you and that is what we are delighted to do."

Kendric shook them by the hand and was introduced to four young women who were with them. Then he introduced Zena.

She thought the women were over-painted and under-dressed. In fact, she felt embarrassed at the lowness of their décolletage and the way, when they were sitting, they exposed their silk-stockinged legs.

Two of them, on being introduced to Kendric, kissed him effusively and when he had sat down one of them put her arm around his neck.

"You are very handsome, *mon cher*," Zena heard her say to him, "and I adore handsome men!"

She thought this was a strange way to behave, then told herself she must not be critical. This was the world she wanted to see, and whatever happened she must not appear embarrassed.

One of the gentlemen put a glass of champagne into her hand, then filled up everybody else's glass to the brim.

Down below them on the dance-floor, Zena could see that a lot of the dancers were wearing fancy-dress and she guessed those were the students who would later in the evening produce tableaux and floats which they had constructed in the different Art Centres to which they belonged.

She had often read about this Ball in newspapers and magazines but although she had tried to visualise it, she found now that her imagination had fallen far short of the reality.

It was certainly very gay and as the Band played louder and faster, everybody swung round and round the floor in a Waltz Zena felt almost dizzy as she watched.

One of their hosts, whose name Zena gathered was Paul although she had no idea what else he was called, said he wanted to dance and his friends agreed that they should go down below and join in the general *mêlée* on the dance-floor.

Kendric would have stayed behind but the lady who had already attached herself to him pouted provocatively and said she had every intention of dancing with him.

"I want your arms around me," she said, "and what could be a better excuse?"

"I assure you I do not need one," Zena heard her brother say.

They disappeared together from the box with the rest of the party, leaving Zena alone with a young man who she realised was looking ill.

"Are you all right?" she asked as he sat down gingerly on the edge of a chair.

"I—will be all right," he answered, slurring his words. "I—will go and get—some fresh air. It is too—hot in here."

He went from the box to leave her alone.

Zena was quite content to sit leaning over the edge of it so that she could watch without interruption the dancers down below. She could see Kendric with both his partner's arms around his neck moving amongst the throng.

There were men dressed in ancient armour, or in nothing but an animal's skin, women in indecently transparent Grecian robes, an innumerable number of Pierrots, and some very dubious Nuns.

It was all fascinating and she did not want to miss anything, even the scuffles that seemed to break out in various parts of the dance-floor when a man wished to dance with a woman who was dancing with another man who had no intention of relinquishing her.

One man who was more importunate than the rest received a blow on the chin which sent him sprawling on the polished floor and Zena gave a little chuckle to herself.

Then a voice beside her said:

"I see you are amused, *Mademoiselle,* and I am not surprised. I always think there is no spectacle as extraordinary as this."

Zena turned her head in surprise and realised that she had been spoken to by a gentleman in the box next to the one in which she was sitting.

There was only a thin partition between them, and the red velvet ledges of their box formed one piece.

The gentleman in question was dark, and from where she was sitting she felt, because he was so broad-shouldered, that he must be tall. He was also extremely handsome, but in a different way from her brother or her father.

He had spoken to her in French, but he looked different from the three young men who were Philippe's friends.

She thought it was because he was older and more distinguished-looking.

Realising he was waiting for an answer to his remark she said:

"This is the first time I have seen the Ball, so I find it fascinating."

"And is it also your first visit to Paris?"

She was just about to reply that she had not been there for many years when she thought it a strange question to ask.

After all, as she spoke French, why should he think she was anything but French?

Then she remembered that Kendric had said:

"It is always wise when you are in disguise to tell the truth as near as it is possible to do so."

"What do you mean by that?" Zena had questioned.

"If you are asked, you must say you have a French friend, but that you yourself come from Wiedenstein."

Zena had looked at him apprehensively.

"Why should I do that? Would it not be dangerous?"

"You do not look French," Kendric had said simply, "having far too much of Papa in you. At the same time you do not look Bavarian either, and after all there are a lot of women, one way or another, in Wiedenstein."

Zena laughed.

"Yes, of course," she had said, "I am just nervous of being denounced as an imposter, and I would much prefer to say I am from Wiedenstein."

284

"On that at least we agree," Kendric had replied, and they had both laughed.

Zena now realised there had been quite a considerable pause before she said:

"I feel I should be insulted that you think I do not look smart enough to be French!"

The gentleman smiled.

"I assure you, I have no thought of insulting you. In fact, if you are looking for compliments, may I tell you you are very lovely, the loveliest woman here this evening."

"Thank you," Zena replied.

She told herself she must not look embarrassed but behave as if she received such compliments every day of her life.

"Let me continue by saying," the gentleman went on, "that your hair is the most unusual and ravishing colour I could possibly imagine. How can you be so original in the City of Originality?"

Zena laughed.

"I am not certain that is not another insult in that you are suggesting that I have created the colour of my hair."

"No, I know that would be impossible," the gentleman said. "Only a great artist could have done that, and who could be greater than God."

Zena looked at him wide-eyed.

"I adore your hair and also your straight little nose and your incredibly beautiful blue eyes," the gentleman continued.

Quickly Zena remembered that as a *Chère Amie* she could not expect men to treat her with the respect and formality she had always received in the past.

Then when she looked into the dark eyes of the man to whom she was talking, she suddenly felt shy in a way she could not understand. She wanted to go away from him, and yet at the same time she wanted to stay.

"Shall we introduce ourselves?" the gentleman asked, "and perhaps to do so it would be more convenient if instead of talking with this barrier between us either I join you, or you join me."

Zena found his invitation somewhat startling. At the same time she thought it was a commonsense suggestion that she should not query.

After all, she had learned that the Artists' Ball was a place of licence, gaiety and good comradeship, and without a chaperon there was nobody to introduce her to this stranger.

"Perhaps," she said after a moment, "you should come into . . . this box, although my friend and I are only . . . guests and I have no . . . authority to . . . invite anybody else to join us."

"Then as I am alone in my box and it belongs exclusively to me," the gentleman answered, "may I suggest we should be more comfortable and less overcrowded here."

This seemed even more sensible, Zena thought, and she was also aware that if the young man who felt ill returned she might have to talk to him or worse still to dance with him.

She was not so foolish as not to realise that he was ill because he had drunk far too much, and she had no wish to see any more of him.

"When your friend returns," the gentleman said, "it will be quite easy for you to see him over the partition, and he will not have to look far to find you."

"Yes, of course."

Zena rose from the chair in which she was sitting and moved towards the door of the box, having to negotiate not only some chairs to do so, but also a number of empty champagne bottles which had been thrown down on the floor.

Before she reached the door it opened and the gentleman from the next box was standing there.

She had been right, she thought, in thinking that he was tall and broad-shouldered, and his eyes, seeming darker than they had before, looked at her in a way which she felt was slightly embarrassing.

At the same time, because it was undoubtedly a look of admiration, she could not help feeling pleased.

It was only a few steps to the next box and as Zena went into it, because it was empty and tidy, it seemed infinitely preferable to the confusion she had just left behind.

The gentleman held an armchair for her to seat herself and she thought it was tactful of him to offer her the one in which he had been sitting, and which was next to the partition which divided the boxes.

"Thank you," she said.

He pulled up a chair next to hers to say:

"Now tell me about yourself. I was feeling lonely and a little bored until I saw you, but now my evening is beginning to sparkle and I can feel the enchantment of Offenbach's music, which was missing before."

"I heard somebody say that it typified the spirit of Paris."

"I would say that so do you, except that I am convinced you are not French even though your accent is perfect."

Zena thought with a smile that this, if nothing else, would please her father who was always so insistent that she should speak with a Parisian accent.

"Are you prepared to guess to which country I belong?" she asked.

The gentleman shook his head.

"No, because I have been trying to puzzle it out for myself ever since I saw you, and have failed dismally to find an answer."

"Perhaps I should leave you guessing," Zena said. "A puzzle is no longer interesting once one has finished it."

She thought as she spoke that it was a rather clever remark, but her companion leaned forward in his seat to say:

"This puzzle will not be finished when you tell me where you were born. There is so much more I want to know; so much about you I find intriguing and, if I am honest, very exciting."

There was a note in his voice which again made her feel shy, and she told herself this was exactly the way she thought gentlemen would talk to the beautiful ladies she had heard about and whom she had seen tonight at the *Café Anglais.*

It was as if she was taking part in a performance on the stage, and she thought she would be very naïve and gauche if she missed her lines and behaved like an inexperienced and rather stupid schoolgirl.

"I think, as you spoke to me first, *Monsieur,*" she said, "you should introduce yourself as there is nobody to do it for you."

"Very well," he replied. "My name is Jean, and if I am to present myself formally, I am the *Comte* de Graumont."

"I am delighted to meet you, *Monsieur,*" Zena said formally, "and I am Zena Bellefleur."

"*Enchanté, Mademoiselle,* and what name could be more appropriate?" the *Comte* said.

He took her hand in his as he spoke and lifted it to his lips.

She had taken off her gloves as she was watching the dancers and when he kissed her hand she thought he would do it perfunctorily in the manner in which gentlemen bowed over her mother's and occasionally hers.

Instead, the *Comte* actually kissed her skin and she thought this a strange thing to do. At the same time, it was a rather exciting one.

Because she felt a little embarrassed she took her hand away from him and looked again at the dancers below them.

"Well, I am waiting," he said after a moment.

"For what?" she asked.

"For you to tell me where you come from, unless of course you have stepped down from Venus, or one of those other planets which I suspect are inhabited by goddesses as lovely as you."

Zena chuckled.

"I wish I could answer truthfully that I have just flown here on wings from the Milky Way. It would sound so much more alluring than coming from a mere European State."

"Whichever one it may be, it is exceptional if it is yours," the *Comte* said.

Once again Zena felt they were speaking the lines of the leading characters in a play.

They had their own Theatre in the Palace and, although the Arch-Duchess arranged that plays produced there were all classical dramas and anything that was not exceedingly proper was forbidden, Zena still found the world of imagination behind the footlights a joy of which she never tired.

"Why are you smiling?" the *Comte* said.

Zena told him the truth.

"I was thinking we are behaving as if we are performing a drama on the stage," she said, "and tonight, because it is so exciting to be here, I feel as if I am a leading lady."

"Of course and a very beautiful one," the *Comte* said, "and I am very honoured that I should be playing opposite you or, should I say, with you."

Again there was a note in his voice that made Zena feel he was being intimate. Perhaps it was also the expression in his eyes, or that as he talked to her he seemed to be very close.

Finally, because it seemed stupid to prevaricate, she said:

"I come from Wiedenstein."

The *Comte* raised his eyebrows.

"Are you sure?"

"Of course I am sure. I must know where I belong."

"I am only surprised," he said, "because I thought that the Citizens of Wiedenstein would be very French. Frenchwomen are usually dark and somewhat sallow-skinned and although they are exceedingly vivacious and entertaining, they do not look like you.''

''Not everybody in Wiedenstein looks like me,'' Zena smiled.

''I can well believe that,'' the *Comte* replied, ''otherwise every man I know would be visiting Wiedenstein and the place would be overrun with eager Don Juans.''

Zena laughed.

''What a lovely idea!''

''But I am afraid,'' the *Comte* went on, ''you are unique, in which case, although my whole idea of Wiedenstein has changed, I cannot expect there to be thousands of Wiedenstein women looking like you.''

His voice dropped, then became deeper as he said:

''As a thousand men or more must have told you already, you are very, very lovely!''

The compliment took Zena by surprise, and because the way the *Comte* spoke seemed to vibrate through her, she forgot for a moment who she was meant to be.

She looked into his eyes, then looked quickly away again.

''I do not . . . think,'' she said in a very small voice, ''that you should . . . speak to me . . . like . . . that.''

''Why not, when it is true?'' he asked.

She did not answer him and after a moment he said:

''What you are really saying is that your friend with whom you came here would resent it and perhaps call me out.''

''No!'' Zena said quickly. ''Of course he would not do that!''

''What I do not understand,'' the *Comte* went on, ''is why he has left you alone. He must realise that if a man leaves a treasure of great value unguarded he runs the risk of somebody stealing it from him.''

Zena smiled.

''I do not think Kendric will worry about that, although I like to think I am a treasure of great value.''

''There are so many other ways in which I could describe you, the *Comte* said, ''but this is not a place in which I find it easy to do so.''

As he spoke there was a sudden noise of voices and laughter in the box beside Zena and she looked over the partition to see that Kendric had come back with the girl with whom he had been dancing.

There were also the other gentlemen accompanied by women, and several men whom she had not seen before.

They were all intent on pouring out the champagne, and as she looked at them Kendric saw her in the corner of the other box and came towards her.

"Are you all right, Zena?" he asked.

"Yes, of course," Zena replied, "shall I come back?"

As if Kendric suddenly realised that she was not where he had left her he looked surprised, but before he could speak the *Comte* said:

"May I introduce myself? I am Jean de Graumont, and I invited *Mademoiselle* to join me as she was alone."

Kendric looked slightly shame-faced as he said to Zena:

"I thought there was somebody with you."

"There was," she agreed, "but he felt ill and went to get some fresh air."

"I thought I could take good care of *Mademoiselle* in your absence," the *Comte* said.

"That was very kind of you," Kendric replied. "My name is de Villerny."

The *Comte* gave an exclamation.

"Do you mean the *Vicomte?* I heard that your father was dead."

"You knew him?" Kendric asked and Zena knew he was nervous.

"My father was extremely interested in shells," the *Comte* replied, "and he talked so much of the de Villerny collection that I almost feel as if I have seen it, though actually I have never been to Wieden-stein."

"Then I hope one day I may show it to you," Kendric answered and Zena thought how clever he was to speak so calmly.

"Thank you," the *Comte* said. "Perhaps one day I shall have the opportunity of accepting your invitation."

There was a pause. Then Kendric said as if he felt he ought to do so:

"Would you like to dance with me, Zena?"

"I think really I would rather watch from here," she replied. "It looks a little rough down there."

"It is," Kendric said ruefully.

He was just about to say more when the girl with whom he had been dancing came to his side and put her arms around him.

"You're neglecting me," she said, "and I think it's unkind of you.

Get me a glass of champagne, then we must watch the Show which is just starting, after which we can go on somewhere else."

"No, I cannot do that," Kendric replied. "I have my friend with me."

"Then you'll have to bring her too, although three is a crowd," the woman said.

Kendric looked uncomfortable and the *Comte*, almost without a pause as if he came in on cue, said:

"Perhaps you would permit me as I am alone to make up the party."

Before Kendric could speak the girl, who by now had her arm around his neck, said:

"That's perfect! You come along, then we can all enjoy ourselves. I want to dance where it is not so crowded and with you, *mon cher*."

She kissed Kendric's cheek, holding on to him in a way which made it impossible for the moment for him to release himself.

Zena realised she was staring, and because she had no wish to embarrass her brother she looked away.

She realised that the *Comte* was watching her and because there was an expression in his eyes which she also found embarrassing, she deliberately looked over the edge of the box down at the dance-floor.

"The Show is going to start," she said, and knew that despite everything that was strange and made her feel shy it was very exciting.

At the same time it flashed through her mind that if her mother knew what she was doing the Arch-Duchess would undoubtedly have a heart attack.

CHAPTER THREE

*I*T MUST BE VERY LATE, *or rather very early in the morning*, Zena thought to herself.

Strangely enough she was not tired, but still excited and exhilarated by the whole evening.

The Show which the students put on at the Ball had taken a long time, but had been extremely amusing.

They brought in strange creations which they had made in their various Studios, and when a prehistoric animal collapsed with dozens of students on top of it, everybody in the Ball-Room screamed and shouted their applause and Zena had found it very funny.

She was laughing at the chaos on the floor below when she realised that the *Comte* was watching her rather than the spectacle.

"Do look!" she said. "You have never seen such a mess!"

"I would rather look at you," he said in a low voice, and she hoped nobody had overheard him.

Actually there was no danger of that for the party which had returned to the box had not only increased in number but the women who joined it had drunk as much as the men and were very noisy about it.

Kendric did not seem surprised to find her with the *Comte* instead of the ill young man who had not returned at all and, as he was completely engrossed with Nanette, as Zena found the effusive young woman was called, she was extremely grateful that she had somebody to talk to.

Because she thought it was right, when Kendric returned she had moved back into the box with his friends, but she soon began to regret she had done so.

Everybody was jostling and trying to get to the front of the box to watch what was happening on the dance-floor, but in doing so they seemed at times in danger of falling over the edge, and Zena looked at them apprehensively.

She was glad when Kendric decided they should leave, but although she expected them to be a party of four as he had originally said, by the time they reached the *Chat Noir* in Montmartre, the party had an addition of several strangers who were friends of Philippe's friends.

The *Chat Noir* was interesting but very noisy and they did not stay long since they found it was too crowded to dance.

The next place they went to had more room for dancing and there were women who appeared to behave in quite an outrageous fashion, dancing alone and showing an unseemly amount of leg and frilly petticoats.

"I have a feeling," the *Comte* said, "that you are shocked by what you are seeing."

Zena was just about to say that was true when she remembered that as a *Chère Amie* and a *demi-mondaine* she should accept such behaviour.

"No, of course not," she said, "but it is very noisy here."

The *Comte* had suggested they should go elsewhere and whether it was because she wished it or that several men asked her to dance, Zena could not decide.

She had no wish to dance with any of the rest of the party because they were not only unsteady on their feet, but they shouted to each other on the dance-floor or tried to change partners with their friends, often when such an overture was unwelcome.

When one man asked her to dance and she refused, he had insisted, and the *Comte* had said:

"*Mademoiselle* is my partner," in a meaningful manner.

"*Pardon,*" the man said immediately, "I did not realise she was your *petite poulé.*"

He walked away and Zena tried to remember what *petite poulé* meant.

It was not a phrase that had entered her vocabulary so far.

It was obviously effective, for after that the men in the party left her alone and she noticed they danced with other women in the room.

When finally they left this place Zena saw with surprise that Kendric was no longer with Nanette, but with another much more attractive French girl whose name was Yvonne.

He obviously found her very alluring and as they talked to each other in low, intimate whispers she realised that Kendric was holding Yvonne's hand.

This time, perhaps on the *Comte*'s suggestion, they went to a dance-hall in the *Champs Élysées* where the Band was playing a spirited Polka in a garden and the dancers were very mixed.

There were not only gentlemen in evening-dress like the *Comte* and their new friends, but there were also men in velvet coats and flowing ties who looked like artists, clerks in neat suits, and pretty *midinettes* in flower-decorated hats and with full skirts that swung round and round as they danced.

It was all very gay and the music was infectious. For the first time in the evening the *Comte* said to Zena:

"Shall we dance?"

She was aware that he had not asked her before because everywhere else they had been was so overcrowded that she felt it would be a case of barging around the room.

Now as she smiled her acceptance he drew her on to the floor and the Polka having come to an end the Band started to play one of Offenbach's dreamy romantic Waltzes.

Zena knew she could dance well, but dancing in the Palace Ballroom with Courtiers whose duty it was to partner her was very different from dancing with the *Comte*.

When he put his arm around her waist she thought he held her rather too closely and proprietorially, but again she told herself she must not complain.

As they started to move she realised that he danced extremely well and was easy to follow.

They danced without speaking, and Zena thought that the stars overhead and the glow of the gaslamps made the dance-hall the enchanted Paris she had wanted to find.

"I must enjoy every moment of it," she told herself, "so that I can remember it when everything is stiff, formal and pompous either at home or in England."

She gave an involuntary shiver as she thought of what she would find in that cold repressed country, and the *Comte* asked:

"What is troubling you? I want you to be happy this evening."

"I am happy."

"But just now you were thinking about something unpleasant."

"How could you know that?"

"Shall I say that your eyes are very revealing, or perhaps, more surprising, I can read your thoughts."

"But you must . . . not do . . . that."

"Why not?"

"Because it is an intrusion and I have no wish for anybody to know what I am thinking."

"Then tell me what I am thinking," the *Comte* suggested.

She looked up at him, saw the expression in his eyes and felt that if she put it into words it would sound very immodest and fast.

As if she had spoken the *Comte* said:

"Exactly! And there is no need for us to speak of what we both know."

Because she was so surprised by what he was saying Zena stumbled and missed a step.

"You are upsetting me!" she said accusingly.

"I have no wish to do that," the *Comte* replied. "Actually I am being very restrained, but needless to say every moment we are together I am growing more and more curious about you."

"That is ridiculous! This is supposed to be a light-hearted evening in which you just have to enjoy yourself."

"I am enjoying myself," the *Comte* insisted, "more than I thought possible and far more than I expected to do."

He smiled as he said:

"I arrived in Paris tonight feeling bored and thinking that although I had time to make contact with my friends I should be wise to go to bed early and start the social round of old acquaintances tomorrow."

His arms seemed to tighten for a moment around Zena's waist as he said:

"On an impulse I went to the Artists' Ball, and from that moment everything changed."

There was no need for her to ask what he meant, but because she felt she must say something she remarked:

"I am glad you have found it amusing, and tomorrow you can start being social."

"Tomorrow I am going to see you," the *Comte* replied. "Can we have luncheon together?"

It flashed through Zena's mind that it would be very exciting to do so, but aloud she said:

"I must ask Kendric what our plans are. I really have no idea."

"Perhaps the *Vicomte*'s plans will not include you," the *Comte* suggested.

As he spoke Zena followed the direction of his eyes and saw, with a little sense of shock, that sitting at the end of the long table they had just left Kendric had his arms around Yvonne and was kissing her passionately.

It was in fact what the rest of the party had been doing all the evening, but Zena had felt it was a very strange way of behaving in a public place and had not expected it of her brother.

She looked away quickly and the *Comte* said:

295

"I am making plans to show you Paris because I am quite certain there is a lot we can see together that you would enjoy."

Zena did not reply and when they had been round the dance-floor once more the *Comte* took her back to the table and to her surprise left her while he went to speak to Kendric.

He talked to him for several minutes, then returned to say:

"The *Vicomte* has agreed that I should take you home. I think you are tired, but he has no wish to leave."

"You are quite certain that Kendric does not wish me to stay until he is ready to go?" Zena asked.

The *Comte* smiled in a way she did not understand before he replied:

"Yes, in fact he was grateful to me for suggesting that I should look after you."

There was nothing Zena could do but agree, and while she was surprised that the *Comte* should be so solicitous, she was in fact growing a little tired because she had not slept much the night before.

She had been too excited and at the same time apprehensive in case Kendric's plans did not come off.

What was more, she had no wish to be so tired tomorrow that she would waste some of their precious free hours in sleeping.

The *Comte* put her wrap around her shoulders, and she was just about to walk to Kendric's side to say goodnight to him, when to her astonishment she saw that he too had risen from the table and was leaving through an exit at the end of the Dance-Hall which led into the Champs Élysées.

As she watched him and Yvonne climbing into one of the *fiacres* that were waiting for customers, she and the *Comte* followed them slowly and she saw the *fiacre* drive away.

"I wonder why Kendric is going on somewhere else," she said. "It was so pleasant here and much nicer than any other places we have been to."

She thought the *Comte* looked at her sharply, but he merely said:

"He asked me to say goodnight to you."

There was no need for Zena to reply because the *Comte* was hailing another *fiacre,* then helping her into it.

The roof was open and as they drove away Zena looked up at the stars to say:

"I always thought there would be a magic about Paris, and it is even more beautiful and more exciting than I imagined."

"I did ask you before if this was your first visit to Paris," the *Comte* said, and this time she answered quickly:

"My first since I was grown up."

"Which has not been very long," the *Comte* remarked.

Because she realised he was being inquisitive again she stopped looking up at the sky and said:

"You are trying to guess my age. I have always been told that is a rude and indiscreet thing to do."

"Only when women wish to conceal how old they are," the *Comte* replied, "and I know without your telling me that you are very young, both in years and experience."

"Now you *are* guessing," Zena said feeling she had to answer this assertion.

"I think, if the truth is known, I am reading your thoughts and using my instinct," the *Comte* said.

"I do not wish you to do either."

Although he had not moved, she felt in some way that he was encroaching on her, becoming too intimate and, although she could not explain it, too possessive.

It was fortunately only a very short distance from where they had danced to where she and Kendric were staying, and as the horses stopped outside the tall mansion at the end of the Rue St. Honoré the *Comte* said:

"As these are private apartments, I imagine you and the *Vicomte* are staying with friends."

"We have been lent an apartment," Zena replied.

The *Comte* made no effort to open the carriage-door. Instead he turned sideways to say:

"Because I think you should go to bed quickly, I am not going to suggest that I escort you to the door of your apartment. Instead, because as you well know, we have a lot more to say to each other than we have been able to say tonight, I will call for you at half-after-noon tomorrow and we will have luncheon at a quiet Restaurant where we will not be disturbed."

Since this was something Zena was more than willing to do, she was just about to accept eagerly when she remembered Kendric.

"I must first ask . . ." she began.

"The *Vicomte* is of course included in my invitation, if he wishes to join us," the *Comte* said, "but I have a feeling that he may be entertaining somebody else."

In view of the way he had been behaving with Yvonne, Zena thought this was very likely, and as she had no wish to be left alone in the apartment with nowhere to go she said quickly:

"Then I should like to have luncheon with you. Thank you very much for asking me."

She put out her hand as she spoke and the *Comte* took it in both of his.

He did not speak, but he sat looking at her and she had a strange feeling that he was turning over in his mind whether he should say or do something or not.

Then as if he had come to a decision he raised her hand to his lips and kissed it as he had done before.

"Goodnight, Zena," he said. "I am glad I have been a part of your first night in Paris, and I intend to make sure that this is the first of many."

He kissed her hand again, his lips moving insistently on her skin.

Then he opened the carriage-door, helped her down on to the pavement and woke the Nightwatchman who was asleep in the Concierge's office.

Drowsily he handed Zena the key of the apartment, then went back to his chair, settled himself into it and closed his eyes.

Zena stood in the dark Hallway and the light from the one gaslight made her hair shine as if it consisted of little tongues of fire.

The *Comte* looked at her for a long moment.

"Goodnight," he said and his voice was very sharp.

"Goodnight and . . . thank you," Zena replied and turned away.

As she ran up the stairs without looking back she had the feeling that he was standing watching her go and wishing, as she did, that the evening had not come to an end.

Zena awoke and knew because the sun was shining golden into her room that it must be very late in the morning.

She could hardly believe it was true when she looked at the clock on the mantelpiece and saw it was nearly eleven o'clock. She could never remember sleeping so late before.

She remembered that when they arrived at the apartment the Concierge had said that when she wanted *petit déjeuner* she was to ring the bell, and either she or her daughter would bring it upstairs.

Zena was just about to ring the bell when she thought that perhaps Kendric had ordered his breakfast already and she opened the door into the Sitting-Room to go and ask him.

She wondered what time he had got back and was glad he had not awakened her.

She walked through the Sitting-Room and knocked on the door of his bedroom.

There was no response and she opened the door.

The first thing she saw was Kendric's clothes thrown untidily over a chair, some of which had slid onto the floor.

Then she saw that he was in bed, fast asleep.

For a moment she hesitated as to whether she should waken him, then she thought it would be a mistake to do so.

Instead she went from the room, closed the door and rang for her own *petit déjeuner* wondering, if they should bring up breakfast for two, how she could keep Kendric's coffee hot until he awoke.

It was actually a long time before the Concierge's daughter Renée appeared carrying a tray.

There was steaming hot coffee in an open jug, croissants that were warm from the oven, butter, and jam made from *fraises des bois* to spread on them.

"*Bonjour, M'mselle,*" Renée said. "Did you have a nice time last night?"

"Wonderful, thank you," Zena replied.

"I heard you come in at four o'clock," Renée went on as she set the tray down on a table in the window, "but *Monsieur* was very, very late. He did not come back until seven o'clock this morning, and I guessed he would still be asleep."

"Seven o'clock!" Zena exclaimed. "I did not think even in Paris dancing went on so late."

She thought Renée looked at her in a rather strange way. Then she said with a little laugh:

299

"I do not think *Monsieur* was dancing, *M'mselle!*"

She left the room and Zena puzzled over her words.

If Kendric was not dancing then where could he have been, she wondered.

Then she told herself that he was obviously taking that attractive Frenchgirl home and she supposed they had stayed talking and perhaps drinking in her apartment until the morning.

Zena of course had not known the details of Kendric's escapade at home with the dancer, and she imagined her father and mother were so angry with him because he had left the Palace without anybody being aware of it.

Also a dancer would be considered by her mother to be very unsuitable company for a Crown Prince.

If Kendric had behaved with the dancer in the same manner as he had behaved with Yvonne last night, Zena could understand that her mother had been shocked.

If Mama ever hears how Kendric is behaving in Paris, she thought, *she will be absolutely furious!*

The she realised that also applied to her. She had danced with a man to whom she had not been formally introduced and what was more, she intended to have luncheon with him today alone, unless Kendric wished to accompany them.

The idea of her mother's anger was very intimidating. Then Zena told herself there was no reason why their behaviour should ever be discovered unless at this very moment the Baron and the Countess were bewailing their disappearance at the Palace.

"I am sure Kendric is right and they will not risk losing their positions by admitting their incompetence," she told herself consolingly.

At the same time, even to think about it was frightening.

She finished her breakfast, then went to her room to start dressing.

It was quite difficult without a maid to fasten her small corset which laced up at the back and she was certain that she would not be able to manage the buttons on her gown.

She therefore left it until the very last moment, thinking that Kendric must wake soon.

If she left him sleeping until twelve o'clock he would still only have had five hours, and if he had been awake all night she was sure he needed more.

She dressed her hair as best she could, thinking as she did so, that if they were to go out this evening she must ask the Concierge to engage a *Coiffeur* to call at the apartment.

She then chose one of her prettiest and most elaborate gowns to wear for luncheon with the *Comte* thinking as she did so that it was amusing to recall that it had been intended to be worn at the Royal Garden Party which took place every summer at the Palace.

Also, the Arch-Duchess had said it would be suitable for the day of the *Prix d'Or* when the Duke of Faverstone's horse would be running.

He would certainly be surprised if he was told I had worn it before in Paris when I was lunching alone with a French Comte whom I had met without any proper introduction at the Artists' Ball, Zena thought.

It struck her that if the Duke became aware of her behaviour he might refuse to marry her.

That would be one way of getting rid of him. At the same time, if it was not the Duke, it might be some horrible German Prince like Georg and then her fate would be even worse.

I am not going to worry, she told herself. *Just for these few days I will be simply Zena Bellefleur, and because I am of no social consequence whatsoever, I can behave as I wish.*

She wondered whether as a *demi-mondaine,* which Kendric had said she was, she should behave as Yvonne had done, but she knew that as far as she was concerned it would be impossible.

How could she throw her arms round a man and kiss him and how could she dance in such an abandoned way?

How could she even flirt provocatively as she had noticed the women in the party doing last night with every man who talked to them?

She thought of the women she had seen at the *Café Anglais* who she suspected were of a far higher class than the girls at the Ball.

I am sure they just sit and look beautiful, she thought, *while men pay them compliments and give them jewellery because they are like magnificent pictures which they can hang on the walls and enjoy.*

She had an idea that perhaps they did something else, but she did not know what it could be.

The clock on the mantelpiece had just struck twelve and she was thinking she would have to wake Kendric and ask if he wished to come out to luncheon with her and the *Comte* when she heard his door open and realised he was awake.

She had left her own door ajar so that she could hear him, and as he came into the Sitting-Room she gave a cry of delight and jumped to her feet.

"You are awake, Kendric! I am so glad! I thought you would sleep for ever!"

Kendric rubbed his eyes.

"That is what I would like to do," he yawned. "What time is it?"

"It is after twelve o'clock. Shall I ring for your breakfast, or will you wait until luncheontime?"

"I had better have some coffee," Kendric replied. "I drank so much last night that my head aches like hell!"

"Oh, Kendric, I am sorry!" Zena said. "I have some *Eau de Cologne* with me. I will put some on a handkerchief and perhaps that will make you feel better."

Kendric groaned and sat himself down in a chair by the window.

With his fair tousled hair he looked very young and almost as if he had just come from school.

Zena rang for his *petit déjeuner* and fetched a small bottle of *Eau de Cologne* and a handkerchief from her bedroom.

She put it against his forehead and he lay back in a chair with his eyes closed.

"Listen Kendric," Zena said, "the *Comte* has asked us out to luncheon and he will be here soon, but if you have no wish to come, he will take me alone."

Kendric opened his eyes.

"I have just remembered," he said, "I have promised to give Yvonne luncheon."

"Then you will not want me!"

Kendric gave her one of his mischievous smiles.

"To tell you the truth, I was wondering what I could do about you."

"Oh, that is all right," Zena said. "I will have luncheon with the *Comte* and I am glad he has asked me since I have no wish to interfere in your amusements."

"That is the right word for it!" Kendric said sitting up and looking much more like his usual self. "I do not mind telling you, Zena, I am rather smitten with her."

"I thought she was much more attractive than that other girl, Nanette."

"Of course she is, and certainly a cut above that riff-raff we had in the box with us last night."

Zena had thought the same thing and she said a little tentatively because she did not wish to seem as if she was prying:

"Is Yvonne an . . . actress?"

There was a pause before Kendric answered:

"I believe she has been on the stage at one time or another."

"And what is she doing now?"

Again there was a pause before her brother replied:

"I really have not had time to ask her a lot of questions."

"No . . . of course not," Zena said, "and it was very difficult to talk to anybody last night. The bands were so noisy, especially at that place in Montmartre."

"It was not the sort of place I should have gone to when you were with me," Kendric said, "but I had no idea it would be like that until we got there."

"I thought the last place in the Champs Élysées was lovely!" Zena said, "but I was surprised you did not say goodnight to me."

Her brother looked shame-facedly.

"To tell you the truth, Zena," he said, "I forgot."

He took the handkerchief from his forehead and added:

"The trouble is, I ought not to have brought you with me, but it is too late now."

"Of course it is!" Zena agreed. "Do not worry about me, I am enjoying every moment, and the *Comte* was very kind."

She thought Kendric looked at her suspiciously.

"He behaved properly towards you?" he asked sharply. "He did not try to kiss you, or—anything like that?"

"No, of course not!" Zena said. "He kissed my hand, but there is nothing wrong in that."

"No," Kendric agreed a little doubtfully, "but keep him at arms' length. You know what these Frenchmen are like."

Zena smiled.

"Actually, I have no idea what Frenchmen are like, but it is rather exciting to find out!"

Kendric groaned.

"Now, Zena, I warn you! If you do anything outrageous, I swear I shall take you straight to Ettengen!"

"Oh, Kendric! No! As though I would let you do that! I promise you
I will never do anything of which you would disapprove, and you are
very lucky I do not extract the same promise from you."

"*Touché!*" Kendric laughed, "but I am thinking of that ghastly Barracks and storing up a few memories with which I can cheer myself
up."

"I am doing exactly the same thing!" Zena said.

They smiled at each other as if there was no need to put it into words
that twins always thought alike.

Then Kendric's *petit déjeuner* appeared.

As Renée set it down in front of him, Zena asked:

"Please, while you are here, would you be kind enough to do up my
gown?"

"Of course, *M'mselle*. Which one are you going to wear?"

She went towards the bedroom and when Zena would have followed
her Kendric gave a low whistle which made her stop.

"You must tip her," he whispered.

Zena looked surprised, then she realised it was something she should
have done before.

"Yes, of course," she said. "How much?"

Kendric shrugged his shoulders.

"Two or three francs."

Zena nodded and went into the bedroom.

When Renée had helped her into her gown and buttoned it down
the back she fumbled in her handbag and produced three francs.

"Thank you very much for helping me," she said.

She felt a little shy as she gave the girl the tip, having never in her life
tipped anybody because whenever they travelled or went anywhere
there was always the Countess or another lady-in-waiting to do it for her.

Renée seemed almost to snatch the tip, saying as she did so:

"*Merci beaucoup, M'mselle!*"

When she had left her Zena put her head round the door of the
Sitting-Room to say to her brother:

"You must remember to tell me the things I have to do as a . . .
commoner. That was the first time I had ever tipped anyone."

"Well, remember you must tip for any service, however small," Kendric said, "and if you do forget, the French will not be slow in remind-
ing you."

The way he spoke made Zena ask:

"What did last night cost you?"

"I had to pay my share everywhere we went," Kendric replied, "and it came to more money than I expected. It is doubtful if you will be able to visit Worth."

"I would rather visit the Restaurants and Dance-Halls," Zena replied, "and don't forget I have a little money with me, and of course my jewellery."

"If you sold any of that you would be mad!" Kendric exclaimed. "If anything was missing it would be noticed as soon as you returned, and there would be an inquisition! You would soon find yourself confessing everything we have done."

Zena gave a cry of horror and disappeared back into her bedroom.

She put on the bonnet which went with her gown and thought as she looked at herself in the mirror that with her red lips and her darkened eyelashes it would be difficult for anybody in Wiedenstein to recognise her.

"Nobody will ever know," she told her reflection consolingly.

As she did so she heard the door of the Sitting-Room open and Renée's voice say:

"A gentleman to see you, *Monsieur!*"

Zena's heart gave a leap because she knew who it would be before she heard the *Comte*'s deep voice say:

"Good-morning, Villerny, I see you slept late."

"Yes, very late," Kendric replied, "and thank you for taking my . . ."

He hesitated and Zena held her breath.

She knew that without thinking, and perhaps because he was sleepy, Kendric had been about to say "my sister."

Then he substituted "Zena" and as he said the rest of the sentence she moved into the Sitting-Room.

The *Comte*, looking even more impressive than he had last night, was standing at the window beside Kendric.

Because the sunshine was behind him she felt that he was enveloped in light.

"*Bonjour Monsieur!*" she said demurely.

The *Comte* turned to face her, and she thought from the expression in his eyes that he appreciated her gown, her bonnet and her skilfully painted face.

"Good-morning, Zena," he said. "There is no need for me to ask you if you slept well! You look like Spring itself!"

"That is how I feel," Zena replied, "but poor Kendric has a headache, and therefore has no wish to accompany us."

"I am sorry about your head, but it is not surprising. If you drank the champagne in that low Dance-Hall in Montmartre," the *Comte* said, "it is only a miracle you are alive!"

"I was foolish enough to drink at least two glasses," Kendric said, "but I was thirsty."

The *Comte* smiled in what Zena thought was a slightly superior manner, and she said quickly:

"Kendric was saying just now that we should not have gone to such a place."

"*You* certainly should not have done so," the *Comte* answered, accentuating the first word.

"You are preaching at me in a somewhat obscure fashion," Kendric interposed. "I must leave you or I shall be late for my own luncheon date."

He rose and as he walked towards his bedroom Zena said:

"What time will you be back here? When shall I see you again?"

"I will be back before dinner," Kendric said carelessly. "I have not yet decided where we shall dine. I have had various invitations, but I have not yet answered any of them."

"I was hoping," the *Comte* said, "that you and Zena would dine with me."

Kendric reached his bedroom door and turned round.

"May I leave the invitation open until later today?" he asked.

He did not wait for an answer but smiled at his sister and went into his bedroom. Only as Zena turned back to the *Comte* did she see that he was looking surprised.

Because she felt he might ask her questions she did not want to answer, she said:

"Shall we go? It seems a pity to be indoors when the sun is shining."

She picked up the handbag which matched her gown and started to put on her long kid gloves as she walked ahead of the *Comte* towards the door.

He hurried to open it for her and as he did so, he said:

"Shall I tell you how lovely you are looking, or shall I wait until we are at the place I have chosen for us to have luncheon?"

"I am quite prepared to wait," Zena replied, "but I find compliments embarrassing and I would much rather you did not make them."

As they went out of the apartment closing the door behind them he asked:

"If what you have said about compliments is true, then you are very different from any other woman in the whole of Paris!"

"I have always heard that compliments from Frenchmen are too glib to be sincere," Zena said, "and I am beginning to think that is true."

The *Comte* did not answer, and as she went through the door into the street, she saw in surprise that there was not an ordinary *voiture* waiting for them, but a very elegant private carriage with a coachman on the box and a footman to open the door.

Zena stepped into it and sat down on the soft cushioned seats.

"This is very grand!" she exclaimed.

"It is a very much more suitable conveyance for you than those in which we travelled last night," the *Comte* replied.

She wanted to ask him if he owned it or had hired it, then thought that would seem impertinent, but as if again he was reading her thoughts the *Comte* said:

"I have borrowed it from one of my friends, and I am glad you appreciate it."

Because she thought that he was insinuating that because she was of no social importance she usually travelled behind inferior horses, Zena longed to tell him she was used to Royal Carriages, and that her father's stable was famous in Wiedenstein.

Then she told herself that if the *Comte* had the slightest suspicion of who she was the whole excitement of being alone with this man who treated her as an ordinary woman would be changed.

After the formality of the Court and the way the Countess, the Statesmen and the Courtiers spoke to her, it was fascinating to find the *Comte* addressing her as she supposed Kendric addressed Yvonne and the other women with whom he associated.

Because she too was for the moment free of Royal restrictions, she smiled at the *Comte* and said with a little lilt in her voice:

"It is very exciting to be in Paris and to be with you. Please tell me where we are going."

"To a small Restaurant in the Bois which has only just opened," the *Comte* replied, "and has not yet become fashionable. The big ones where we would see all the world and his wife are not for us, not today at any rate."

She looked at him enquiringly, and he said:

"I would like to go to them to show you off, but I might meet friends who would want to talk to me and to you, and today I want a *tête-à-tête* where there are no interruptions, except for the song of the birds."

"It sounds very romantic!" Zena said without thinking.

"That is exactly what I intend it to be!" the *Comte* agreed in his deep voice.

CHAPTER FOUR

AFTERWARDS ZENA WAS TO THINK that her luncheon in the Bois with the *Comte* were the most enchanting hours she had ever known.

The Restaurant to which he took her was small, in a little one-storey house which was surrounded by a garden filled with shady trees.

There were only about a dozen tables among the flowers, and the Proprietor, who was also the Chef, took the orders himself and spent a long time explaining which specialty would be the best for his clients on that particular day.

His wife, buxom in black, made out the bills, and their two sons were the waiters.

There was a happy atmosphere about the whole place and to Zena it was something she had never experienced before and felt despairingly she would never do again.

When the *Comte* had ordered and the wine was brought in a bucket filled with ice he turned to smile at her and said:

"Now all we have to do is to enjoy eating what I am sure will be an extremely good luncheon, and being—together."

The way he spoke made Zena feel excited and she answered:

"I am enjoying every moment of my visit to Paris, and you know I want to thank you for looking after me last night."

"I am determined that you will not go to such places again or meet the dregs of Paris," the *Comte* replied, and there was a hard note in his voice.

Zena did not reply and he went on:

"I intend to speak to the *Vicomte* about it and I hope you will not try to prevent me."

Zena gave a little cry.

"Please do not speak to Kendric!" she said. "He was, I think, a little ashamed of himself this morning, besides feeling ill from the bad wine he drank, and as I was with you I did not mind seeing how those older women behaved."

"All the same," the *Comte* said, "you are too good for this sort of thing."

"I am glad you think so."

"What I cannot understand," he went on, "is why de Villerny brought you to Paris in the first place if he did not intend to spend his time with you."

Zena looked away across the garden.

She was afraid this was one of the things the *Comte* would ask.

She knew that it must seem strange, if she was Kendric's *Chère Amie*, that he should be prepared to leave her at the Dance-Hall without even saying goodnight.

Now, because she thought that anything she might reply would make matters sound even stranger than they were already, she said quickly:

"Please ... can we talk about more ... interesting things? It is so exciting to be here with you, and it is something I will want to remember when I have gone home."

The *Comte* stiffened.

"You are thinking of leaving?"

"We shall have to go in a day or two."

"You mean the *Vicomte* will have to leave. But surely you are not compelled to go with him?"

"If he leaves, I must leave," Zena said firmly, "but I do not want to talk about it. I want you to tell me about yourself. Do you realise I have no idea where you live or even where you are staying in Paris?"

309

The *Comte* smiled.

"I am glad it is of interest to you. I am staying in Paris in a very beautiful house on the Champs Élysées belonging to the *Duc* de Soissons. I wish I could show you his pictures. He has the most famous collection in France."

"I would love to see them," Zena said, "and while I am here I must visit the Louvre. I always think Fragonard and Boucher painted the most romantic pictures anyone could imagine."

"You have obviously seen some of their work already," the *Comte* said.

Zena looked at him almost defiantly.

"We are not entirely uncivilised in Wiedenstein."

He laughed softly.

"So you are a patriot! I like people to be patriotic and proud of their own country."

"I am very proud of mine," Zena said, "even though it is small and not a great nation compared to France or Prussia."

"And yet it is at this moment of considerable importance in Europe," the *Comte* said. "Do you know why?"

"Of course I do," Zena replied. "If Prussia invades France, which many people are afraid may happen, then Wiedenstein, like Switzerland, must be neutral, which may be difficult."

She spoke positively because she had heard her father and the other Statesmen in Wiedenstein discuss this subject so often. Then as the *Comte* did not speak she went on:

"I cannot bear to think of the Prussians marching into France. Suppose they tried to destroy this beautiful city?"

"I feel exactly the same way," the *Comte* said, "and I wish you could speak to the Emperor as you are speaking to me."

"Papa says he is under the thumb of the Empress who is great friends with the Foreign Minister who hates Bismarck so bitterly that he is longing to fight him."

She spoke without thinking, then she gave a sudden exclamation:

"I have just realised that the Foreign Minister is the *Duc* de Graumont, and that is your name!"

"That is true," the *Comte* replied. "But the de Graumonts are a very large family and I am only a very distant cousin of the *Duc*."

There was a pause. Then Zena said:

"Perhaps I have been . . . indiscreet. I apologise . . . please forget what I have . . . said."

Even as she spoke she realised that an apology was quite unnecessary.

It would have been very reprehensible for the Princess Marie-Thérèse to have made such remarks, but anything Zena Bellefleur said or thought was not of the least consequence.

"I hope we may always be frank with each other," the *Comte* answered, "and I was just thinking that it is quite unnecessary for you to be clever as well as beautiful."

Zena gave a little laugh.

"What you are really saying is that you like women who are pretty dolls . . . playthings which are easily discarded when you have no further use for them."

She was thinking of how Kendric thought that the only important thing about a woman was that she should be pretty.

Once, when Zena had asked him what he talked about with his dancer, he had replied scornfully:

"Talk? Why should I want to talk to somebody like that? All that mattered was that she was pretty, and I wanted to kiss her."

Now, as if the *Comte* realised she was thinking of Kendric, he said:

"What do you talk about when he is not making love to you?"

Zena felt herself stiffen, and instinctively she felt insulted that he should say anything so personal to her or suspect that she allowed any man to talk of love as he had done last night.

Then once again she remembered who she was supposed to be.

"We were not talking about Kendric," she said aloud after what seemed a long silence, "but about you."

"But I would much rather talk about you," the *Comte* replied, "and before you interrupt me I am going to say again that I have never met anybody so lovely, or so enchanting."

Enchanting was the right word for everything they said and everything they did, Zena thought as they drove home.

They had sat over luncheon until everybody else had left the Restaurant, then sitting in the comfortable open carriage which Zena now guessed belonged to the *Duc* de Soissons they drove along the side of the Seine as far as Notre Dame.

Then they returned through the small narrow streets of old Paris

311

until they reached the impressive boulevards which had been built by Baron Haussmann.

It was so beautiful and so exciting that it seemed quite natural that the *Comte* should hold her hand while Zena looked around her.

She thought perhaps she should prevent him from doing so, but to do so seemed rather childish and so they drove side by side and hand-in-hand until the horses drew up outside her apartment.

"May I come in?" the *Comte* asked. "And if de Villerny is back, I can ask if he has made up his mind whether you will dine with me this evening."

"Please do that," Zena replied, "and I do hope Kendric says yes."

"You cannot possibly want it as much as I do," the *Comte* smiled.

The Concierge gave them the key of the apartment which meant that Kendric was not yet back, and they went up the stairs to the first floor.

The *Comte* opened the door for Zena and they went into the attractive Sitting-Room where the sun was shining through the windows.

"Kendric is not yet back," Zena explained unnecessarily, "but I hope you will wait here with me."

"I have every intention of doing so," the *Comte* replied.

Zena put down her gloves and handbag on a chair, then pulled off her fashionable bonnet.

Then as she turned she found that the *Comte* was standing just beside her and as once again he had his back to the sunlight he looked, as he had this morning, as if he was enveloped with light.

They stood looking at each other, and Zena had no idea how it happened, whether she moved or he did, but some strange power that was outside themselves and their minds drew them together.

The *Comte*'s arms went round her, and as she looked up at him wonderingly his lips came down on hers.

She had never been kissed, but she had often thought that if she loved somebody it would be very wonderful, and the feeling of the *Comte*'s lips was indeed wonderful, but so much more.

They were magical, enchanted, and his kiss seemed an extension of the strange sensations he aroused in her ever since they had first met.

And yet, in a way she could not explain to herself, although her feelings had been strange, they had yet been part of her dreams, and what she had always sought.

312

Now as his arms tightened around her and his lips became more insistent, she knew this was what she had always wanted in life and it was, although she was afraid to admit it . . . love.

It was love that had nothing to do with position or advantage, but was instead the meeting of a man and woman who belonged to each other and while their hearts and their spirits merged there was no need for words.

The *Comte* drew her closer still and now Zena felt as if her whole body vibrated to his and a rapture that was inexpressible seemed to run through her like the warmth of the sun and sweep up through her breasts to move from her lips to his.

The room swung round them and she felt as if her feet were no longer on the ground, but that the *Comte* was carrying her on the shaft of sunlight into the glory and wonder of Heaven.

Only when Zena felt as if she was no longer herself but his, and it was impossible to think but only to feel, did the *Comte* raise his head.

For a moment he looked down at her eyes shining with a radiance that seemed almost blinding, her cheeks flushed against the whiteness of her skin, and her lips parted from the insistence of his.

There was no need to speak; the *Comte* knew that Zena's heart was beating tumultuously against him.

He knew too that this kiss was very different from any kiss he had ever known before.

Then he was kissing her again; kissing her with long, slow, passionate kisses which left them both trembling, and at the same time ecstatic, and once again journeying towards the heart of the sun.

A long time later, as if the *Comte* felt they could no longer stand locked in each other's arms but needed support, he drew Zena to the sofa.

As they sat down she raised her eyes to his and he said:

"Could anybody be more perfect, more alluring? But, my precious, I must talk to you."

Even as he spoke they heard footsteps outside the door and as it opened and Kendric came in, the *Comte* moved a little way from Zena.

"I am sorry to be late," Kendric exclaimed, throwing his top-hat down on a chair, "but I have been seeing a number of Philippe's friends, and I have a marvellous invitation for us this evening."

"Invita . . . tion?" Zena asked in a voice that did not sound like her own.

The *Comte* rose slowly to his feet.

"That sounds as if you do not intend to accept mine," he said.

"I am sorry, de Graumont," Kendric replied, "perhaps we can dine with you tomorrow night, but we have been asked, Zena and I, to have dinner with Prince Napoleon, which as you are aware, is a Royal Command, and to go on later to a party to be given by *La Païva* at her house in the Champs Élysées, and that too is something we cannot miss!"

The *Comte* frowned.

"I did not think you knew the Prince Napoleon."

Kendric laughed.

"I met him today for the first time with one of Philippe's friends. He told me he was giving a dinner-party tonight at his house and he had been informed I had a very beautiful lady-friend whom he was anxious to meet."

Kendric looked at Zena as he spoke and added:

"I could hardly say to the Prince that you would prefer to dine with somebody else."

"N—no . . . of course not," Zena agreed.

"At the same time," the *Comte* said, "you know the Prince's reputation with women? I do not feel he is the right sort of man for Zena."

Kendric shrugged his shoulders.

"I will look after Zena," he said, "and it would be impossible, as I have accepted His Royal Highness's invitation, to back out now."

Zena was aware that the *Comte* was apprehensive and it was with difficulty that he did not make any further protest about Kendric's arrangements.

Because she felt it might be uncomfortable if he did so, she held out her hand.

"I am so sorry we cannot dine with you tonight," she said, "but please, I would like to accept for tomorrow evening, if you will have us."

"I will see you before that," the *Comte* answered. "You have already promised that you will let me take you to the Louvre tomorrow morning."

Zena's eyes lit up.

"Yes, of course," she said, "and I know Kendric does not like Museums or Picture Galleries, so we can start early."

"I will call for you at eleven o'clock," the *Comte* promised, "and thank you for a very happy day."

He raised her hand to his lips and she thought as he kissed it he said without words how much he minded leaving her and how very wonderful their day had been.

Then there was nothing the *Comte* could do now but leave, and when he had gone Kendric exclaimed:

"Zena! I have so much to tell you! Tonight will be extremely interesting even though your friend de Graumont disapproves."

He did not wait for Zena to make any remark, but went on to explain that the Prince Napoleon's parties, which he had always longed to attend, were the most sought after in Paris.

"He can only give them at his home while his wife is away in the country," Kendric explained, "and then he invites all the most famous women in the city."

"Women like those we saw at the *Café Anglais*?" Zena asked.

"Exactly!" Kendric agreed. "And although I suppose it is wrong for you to do so, you will see the most celebrated of the Courtesans who have made Paris the El Dorado of every man in Europe, although their wives and mothers call it something very different!"

"And that, I am sure, includes Mama!"

Kendric flung up his hands.

"She would kill me if she ever finds out where I have taken you!" he said. "But what you will see tonight and the women you will meet will certainly be an education in itself, although it is something you have to forget the moment you go home."

When she was dressing for dinner, Zena admitted to herself that she not only much preferred to be with the *Comte* but also that she loved him.

The word frightened her, and yet she knew he had stolen her heart, and it would never again belong to her or to any other man.

"I love him!" she whispered, and knew that her love was hopeless and could end in nothing but heart-break.

Yet it was an ecstasy to know that he could arouse her to such an inexpressible rapture and that tomorrow she would see him again.

Tomorrow and for five more days!

Then for the rest of her life she would have nothing but memories and the misery of knowing that although they were both in the same world they were divided by a chasm as deep as the English Channel and there was nothing they could do to bridge it.

Perhaps one day, when I am miserable and lonely in England, she thought, *I may see him again. But if I did what would it do except make me more unhappy than I was already?*

Then she told herself that somehow after tonight she would contrive to be with the *Comte* every moment they were in Paris and she would tell Kendric to accept no more invitations on her behalf.

When she was dressed in one of the gowns that the Arch-Duchess had bought for her to wear at the Ball which would be given in race-week, she thought when she had mascaraed her eyelashes and reddened her lips that she would not look too insignificant among the Prince Napoleon's other lady guests.

She had no wish to arouse his admiration, or that of any other man present, but she did not wish to let Kendric down or make those who had arranged to have them both invited to the Prince's party think that his interests in women were inferior to theirs.

She knew as she went into the Sitting-Room that Kendric was nervous in case she would look too ladylike.

His eyes went first to her head.

The Coiffeur had fortunately arrived when Zena was nearly dressed and had made her red-gold hair even more sensational than it usually was.

He had also arranged in it three diamond broaches in the shape of stars and they glittered with every movement she made.

She had clasped around her neck a diamond necklace which her mother had told her not to wear until she was married, as it was too large for a young girl.

Kendric's eyes lingered on the necklace and he said with a smile:

"When you are asked, do not forget to say that I gave you that! It will certainly enhance my prestige, although if anybody knew me well they would wonder how I could afford it!"

Zena was just about to ask him if he had given Yvonne a present. Then she thought he might think she was questioning his generosity and decided that in any case there would be no necessity for it as he had known her for only a short time.

Therefore she said nothing and Kendric, afraid of being late, hurried her downstairs.

To her surprise she found that her brother had hired a carriage to take them to the Prince Napoleon's house.

"You are being very grand!" she said.

"It is expensive but worth it," Kendric replied, "I dislike seeming like a poor relation and I do not mind telling you that some of Philippe's friends, because I am from Wiedenstein, are rather patronizing."

Zena laughed.

"They would not be that if they knew who you were!"

Kendric laughed too.

"I almost feel like telling them."

"Do be careful!" she begged.

"Do not worry, drunk or sober, that is one secret I shall not reveal!" Kendric said. "And you be careful too what you say to de Graumont. I have a feeling he is growing rather fond of you."

"Why should you think that?" Zena asked.

"I thought he was jealous because I was taking you to dine with the Prince, and the way he looked at you might have been admiration, or it might have been something else."

"He has been very kind," Zena said quickly, "and we had a very interesting talk at luncheon."

As she spoke she realised it was the first time in her life she had had any secrets from her twin brother.

She did not want Kendric to know that the *Comte* had kissed her, or in fact that she loved him.

Never had Zena thought that women could be so beautiful, so superbly gowned, or wear so many expensive jewels.

But, and it was a very large "but," she was absolutely astounded how common was their manner of speaking.

The men were all distinguished with high-sounding titles, and Zena did not have to hear them speak to know that they represented the cream of the French aristocracy as well as holding important posts in the Government.

But the women were not all of French origin; there were also two English women and a Russian.

Zena could not tell from the way the Russian spoke if she was cultured or not, but the Frenchwomen did not only speak without Parisian accents, but in their conversation used an argot that was incomprehensible to her, while the two English women spoke in a manner that would have made her mother refuse to engage them as kitchen-maids.

For the first time Zena thought she understood why Kendric had said that while he was with the dancer he did not talk to her.

What could these distinguished and obviously very intelligent men have in common with such women who mispronounced the most ordinary words and who had only to open their red lips to sound vulgar?

She was so bemused while at the same time curious about them, that she sat at the dinner-table looking round, forgetting for the moment to be polite and talk to the gentleman on her right.

Kendric was on her left and she realised they were seated together because the men and women who had been announced after their own arrival were also paired round the dinner-table.

The Prince's partner was obviously prepared to act as hostess, and she looked so sensational and was so loaded down with jewels that Zena thought she was like a Prima Donna on a stage, determined to take all the applause for herself.

"Will you tell me your name, pretty lady?" Zena heard.

She turned to see there was a middle-aged man beside her who had an interesting but, she thought, rather debauched face.

There were lines of dissipation under his eyes that were dark and penetrating and although he had a clever forehead below slightly greying hair, that too was lined with age.

"My name is Zena, *Monsieur.*"

"Why have I not met you before?" the gentleman asked.

"I have only just come to Paris."

"Then that accounts for it. I may tell you that my parties, and I am the *Marquis* de Sade, are as famous as our host's, and I hope you will do me the honour of being my guest."

"That is very kind of you, *Monsieur.*"

As Zena spoke she was quite certain she had heard of the *Marquis* de Sade but in what particular connection she could not be sure.

He bent nearer to her and as she met his eyes she decided she did not like him.

She could not explain why, but the feeling was there that he was a man she should not trust.

"Am I to understand that you are under the protection of de Villerny?" the *Marquis* enquired.

Zena avoided replying to his question by sipping her wine from the twisted glass engraved with the Prince Napoleon's insignia.

"He is too young for you," the *Marquis* went on. "With your hair I know that, when a man can ignite them, the fires of love can burn fiercely and all-consumingly, but it is unlikely that de Villerny is the right man to do so."

"What I would like you to do," Zena said, "is to tell me the names of these outstanding people around the table. Being a stranger I should love to know who they are."

She thought she was very clever in side-tracking the *Marquis* into a different subject, but he merely smiled and replied:

"I want to talk of you, and of course, myself. Tell me how long you have known de Villerny?"

"For a very long time," Zena said defiantly, "and we are very happy together."

Both those things were true, she thought, and as she spoke she could hear her voice ring with sincerity.

"I have a very charming house near the Bois which is empty at the moment," the *Marquis* said. "I want to show it to you."

Zena did not reply and he went on:

"Tomorrow we will go together to Oscar Massin's, and you shall choose for yourself one of his flower-jewelled brooches which are without exception the finest in the world."

Because the way he spoke made Zena feel not only uncomfortable but a little afraid, she said:

"I do not . . . understand what you are saying to me, *Monsieur le Marquis* and if I try to do so . . . I think . . . perhaps it will make me . . . angry."

The *Marquis* laughed.

"You are very young, but you are intelligent enough to know that I am suggesting you change your present protector for one who will make you one of the most famous women in France, in fact a Queen of your own profession."

Zena felt she could not have heard him aright.

319

Then she thought that just as Kendric had explained to her that the women of Paris received jewels and gowns from men so that they could parade them like racehorses to arouse the envy of their friends, so the women were prepared to accept such gifts from the highest bidder.

I must not be angry, she told herself, *I must merely refuse the* Marquis's *offer politely, but firmly.*

That was however easier said than done, for she realised that the *Marquis* had apparently made up his mind the moment he saw her that he wanted her, and that he was a man who always got what he wanted in one way or another, and who had no intention of accepting a refusal where she was concerned.

Whatever protests she made to him he did not listen, and when finally they left the Dining-Room she found not only his behaviour incomprehensible but also that of the other guests at the Prince's table.

As the meal progressed she realised that all the men present were behaving in a more and more familiar manner with the women next to them, and the only odd man out appeared to be Kendric who had become absorbed with the lady on his left.

This was possible because the Prince Napoleon had two women to amuse him, not only the one who was prepared to act as hostess, but also a very celebrated actress whose witty remarks managed to keep her host laughing and also to hold enthralled the gentleman on her other side.

This left his partner free for Kendric and he was certainly making the most of it.

In the French fashion, both men and women left the Dining-Room together and Zena took the opportunity of keeping close to the other ladies as they went up the stairs to collect their wraps, for they were all going on to the party given by La Païva.

When she came downstairs again, to Zena's relief she saw Kendric standing alone and reached him before any other woman could do so.

"Do not leave me alone with the *Marquis* de Sade," she begged. "He is being rather tiresome."

"I have heard about him," Kendric said. "Have nothing to do with him! If he gets difficult I shall take you home."

Zena was just about to say that perhaps that would be a good idea anyway when all the other women appeared.

Before it was possible to say anything more to her brother she found they were squeezed into a carriage with two other people and could not have a conversation without being overheard.

Fortunately the other couple were immersed in each other, and as the man kissed and fondled the woman in a way that Zena found most embarrassing, at least, she thought, she was free of the *Marquis*'s attentions.

When she had refused to hold his hand at dinner she had felt his knee pressing against hers, and had to twist herself to avoid such advances.

It was not a very long distance to La Païva's house and Kendric told her that it was the most luxurious private mansion in Paris and had taken ten years to build.

When they entered it there were loud voices and the fragrance of expensive perfume seemed to make it different from any house Zena had ever been in before.

There was a vast Salon lit by five tall windows, with a magnificent ceiling depicting "Night" chasing "Day" away. The walls were hung with crimson brocade and it seemed almost like a Temple dedicated to pleasure.

Before this Zena had followed the other ladies up the stairs which were lit by a massive lustre in sculptured bronze, and she saw to her astonishment that the steps and bannister were made entirely of onyx.

They left their coats in a bedroom where the bed was inlaid with rare woods and ivory, and stood like an altar in an alcove.

"That cost 100,000 francs!" she heard one of the guests say, and the voice was sharp with envy.

There were many other things that Zena would have liked to look at, but she was afraid that if she was away from Kendric for too long she would find that the lady who had been his neighbour at dinner might once again monopolise him.

She therefore hurried down the onyx staircase and when she reached the Salon she saw to her consternation that the *Marquis* de Sade and Kendric were speaking angrily to each other.

She hurried to her brother's side and as she did so he said:

"I have told you, *Monsieur le Marquis,* that Zena is mine, and I have no intention of giving her up to you, or to anybody else!"

Zena's heart missed a beat, and because the *Marquis* looked not only extremely angry but also overpowering, she slipped her hand into Kendric's.

"I have already told him, Kendric," she said in a low voice, "that we belong to each other, and that I will never leave you."

"Then surely that is decisive enough for you?" Kendric said to the *Marquis*.

He spoke in rather a loud voice and Zena realised that he had had a lot to drink and was annoyed and affronted by the *Marquis*'s behaviour.

There was a Band playing, and Zena said, pulling at her brother's hand:

"Let us go and dance, Kendric."

"Not so fast!" the *Marquis* de Sade said. "I have already made an offer of jewellery to this pretty songbird and I presume you are expecting me to ante-up on the original sum I had suggested! Very well then, I will double it!"

"I consider that an insult!" Kendric said.

The *Marquis* smiled, and it was a very unpleasant sight.

"If I have insulted you, it will be quite easy for you to obtain an apology in the time-honoured manner."

As he spoke Zena knew exactly what he was suggesting, and gave a cry of horror.

Even as she did so, she was aware that somebody had come to her side, and without even turning her head she knew who it was and felt a sense of relief that was also an indescribable joy.

Without pausing to think she turned to move close to the *Comte* and say in a whisper she thought only he would hear:

"Stop him! Please . . . stop him! Kendric must not fight a duel with him! Please . . . please . . . prevent it!"

There was a note of agony in her voice as she realised in terror what it would mean if Kendric fought a duel and was wounded, and it was discovered who he really was.

Because she was quick-witted, even as the *Marquis* had spoken and she had seen the smile on his lips, she knew he had been thinking that if he disabled Kendric it would be easier for him to take her from him.

As if he understood what she was feeling the *Comte* moved closer to the *Marquis* and said:

"I must request you, de Sade, to stop making yourself objectionable to these young people who are friends of mine."

"How dare you interrupt?" the *Marquis* said, diverted for the moment from his anger with Kendric. "What has it got to do with you?"

"It has a great deal to do with me," the *Comte* replied, "because I intend to protect *Mademoiselle* Zena from men like you who are treating her as if she was a piece of merchandise to be haggled over in a degrading manner which any decent man would resent!"

The way he spoke was even more forceful than what he said and the *Marquis* seemed to go almost black with rage as he snarled:

"How dare you insult me and poke your nose into things which do not concern you!"

"I have already said they do concern me," the *Comte* replied, "and if you are intent on fighting anybody, then it would be more sportsmanlike to choose somebody of your own size, and fight me!"

"I will fight you both, if that is what you want," the *Marquis* shouted, "and when I have done so this young woman will be mine without any more argument about it."

"That is something she will never be!" Kendric said furiously.

Zena realised that it was a mistake for him to say anything, and as her fingers tightened on the *Comte*'s she knew he understood.

"I think the best thing I could do would be to take Zena home," he said to Kendric. "There is no reason why she should stay here and listen to a man who cannot behave like a gentleman."

"Thank you," Kendric said.

The *Marquis* gave a roar of rage.

"Do not dare to be so high-handed with me!" he said. "*Mademoiselle* Zena has already promised that she will accept my protection and I will therefore take her home."

He held out his arm as he spoke and Zena shrank back against the *Comte*.

"Come," the *Comte* said, and turned towards the door drawing her with him.

The *Marquis* however prevented her.

He seized Zena by the wrist and put his arm around her waist.

"You know on which side your bread is buttered, my pretty one!" he said. "Now tell these *imbeciles* once and for all that you have made your choice."

"No . . . No!" Zena cried and tried to release herself from the *Marquis*.

Now she was thoroughly frightened not only for herself, but for

Kendric who had moved forward angrily to push the *Marquis* away from her.

"How dare you touch Zena!" he said. "Surely you realise she does not want you? If you do not leave her alone I will kick you out into the street!"

The *Marquis* turned round furiously and raised his arm as if he would hit Kendric.

Then as it flashed through Zena's mind that a duel between them was inevitable, the *Comte* acted.

"Kindly learn to behave yourself, *Monsieur* le Marquis!" he said, and slapped him across the face.

Now the *Marquis* seemed to go pale with anger.

"I will meet you at dawn," he said, "in the usual place, and when I have disposed of you I am perfectly prepared to take on this young jackanapes!"

"I accept your challenge!" the *Comte* said, "and what happens afterwards remains to be seen!"

The *Marquis* drew himself up with a look which told Zena he was very sure of victory.

"At five o'clock then," he said and walked away.

Zena gave a little murmur of horror, but it was impossible to speak because the *Comte* was moving her down the steps from the Salon into the Hall.

When he reached it he said to a servant:

"Fetch this lady's wrap."

The man bowed and waited for Zena to explain what it looked like.

Then as he hurried up the stairs she turned to the *Comte*, holding on to his arm with both hands.

"It is all right," he said softly. "Say nothing until we are away from here."

Zena therefore remained silent until the servant returned with her cloak and she stepped into the *Comte*'s carriage that was waiting outside.

As they drove away she threw herself against him, and his arms went around her as she hid her face against his shoulder.

"What can I say . . . how can I thank . . . you?" she asked. "It would be . . . impossible for Kendric to fight a duel . . . and anyway, I am certain that the *Marquis* would have been too . . . good for . . . him."

"The *Marquis* is considered one of the best shots in the country," the *Comte* said.

"Oh . . . no!" Zena cried, "in which case you must not fight him either!"

"That is something I must do," the *Comte* said.

"B—but . . . he may . . . injure you."

"That is a risk I have to take, but let me tell you that I am not afraid."

"No, of course not," Zena said, "but I should not have . . . involved you in this. It was only that I was so desperately . . . worried for . . . Kendric."

She thought as she spoke that if only she could explain that Kendric was the Crown Prince of Wiedenstein it would be easier.

"He is far too young to be involved with a man like de Sade," the *Comte* said. "He is a very quick shot which is why he always wins his duels."

"But you . . . ?" Zena asked in a whisper.

"I can only hope that I am swifter."

"What can I . . . say to you? It was . . . wrong of me . . . very . . . very wrong to ask your help . . . but when you . . . appeared at that very moment it seemed as if you had been sent by . . . God to help . . . us."

"Perhaps that is what happened," the *Comte* said with a smile. "When I heard you were coming to La Païva's tonight I obtained an invitation for myself, and whatever happens I am very glad I did so."

"Do you mean that?" Zena asked.

"Perhaps it is another way of proving how much you mean to me."

"If he . . . hurts you . . . I will never . . . forgive myself."

"Do not think of such things," the *Comte* admonished. "Believe instead that because what he was doing was wrong, overbearing and insulting, good will triumph over evil, and I shall be the victor."

"I shall pray. I shall be praying with my heart and soul," Zena said.

The *Comte*'s arms tightened around her, but he did not kiss her, and they drove in silence back to the Rue St. Honoré.

When they reached it the *Comte* obtained the key from the Concierge and took Zena to the bottom of the stairs.

When she expected him to climb up them with her he said instead:

"Go to sleep, my darling. Try to think of nothing but the happiness we shall enjoy together tomorrow when I show you the pictures in the Louvre.''

Zena did not speak and the *Comte* went on:

"I am going back now to see that de Villerny gets into no more trouble and to arrange my seconds. After that I shall rest.''

"How can I tell you how . . . wonderful you are to . . . me?'' Zena asked.

"I hope that you will be able to do that tomorrow,'' the *Comte* replied.

He took both her hands, and raised them one after the other to his lips. Then he said very quietly:

"Goodnight, my precious love. Sleep well, but remember me in your prayers.''

The way he spoke brought the tears to Zena's eyes, but before she could answer or try to find words in which to express her feelings he disappeared through the outer door into the street.

Slowly she went up the stairs feeling as though when she had least expected it the roof had caved in and her dreamworld was in ruins about her feet.

CHAPTER FIVE

Zena TOOK OFF HER BALLGOWN and her evening slippers but did not undress any further.

She lay down on the bed waiting with the door open for Kendric to return.

She kept wondering how they could have got into such an impossible position as they were in now.

It seemed cruel and inexcusable that she should have involved the *Comte* to the point where he was fighting the *Marquis* to save Kendric without understanding why Kendric had to accept it.

The idea of Kendric being wounded and perhaps even killed in a duel in Paris was so horrifying that she found it difficult to think straight.

She was quite certain that if he fought a duel, even if he was victorious, somebody would become aware of who he was, and they would then have to explain not only to their father, but to the whole Court in Wiedenstein what they were doing in Paris.

Zena could not bear to think of what her mother would say if she ever learnt the part she was playing. She could only lie tense, praying fervently that everything would be all right, that Kendric would escape recognition and the *Comte* would not be hurt.

To know that he was fighting the most notoriously dangerous shot in France was an agony in itself.

Supposing he was killed? Supposing he survived, but never forgave her for involving him in such a perilous situation?

Then she remembered that anyway he would have to forget her, and although she could never forget him, once they had left Paris she would never see him again.

Everything was frightening, horrible and depressing to the point where Zena felt she must almost go insane because she could find no way out of their difficulties.

Slowly the hours dragged by and it was nearly four o'clock when at last she heard the outer door open and Kendric come into the Sitting-Room.

She jumped off the bed and ran to him saying as she did so:

"Why are you so late? What has happened?"

Kendric threw his hat and evening-cloak down on a chair, then put his arm around her shoulders to say:

"It is all right. Do not work yourself up, but I admit I am damned glad I am not to fight the *Marquis*."

"The *Comte* is doing it for you."

"I know that, and I am very grateful."

"I asked him to save you, and he did so."

"He is obviously very fond of you," Kendric said, "and I feel I am behaving very badly in letting him take my place. But what else could I do?"

He asked the question pathetically, almost as a small boy might have done.

"I have been thinking about that," Zena said. "I am certain that on no account could you fight the *Marquis*. Whether he wounded you or you wounded him, there would inevitably be a scandal about it. Then Papa would hear about us."

"You do not suppose I have not thought of that?" Kendric asked. "At the same time, to tell the truth I am ashamed of myself."

"I shall pray, I shall pray with all my heart that the duel will not be serious, then everybody will forget it ever happened."

Kendric did not answer and Zena was aware that he was not very optimistic.

He took his arm from her and walked towards his bedroom.

"I have to change," he said. "I am acting as a second for the *Comte* and as he did not seem to wish any of his own friends to be told about it, I have asked one of Philippe's, a man called Anton, to stand in."

"You are going to be with the *Comte!*" Zena said almost beneath her breath. "Then I am coming with you."

"You will do nothing of the sort," Kendric replied. "Ladies never attend duels."

"I am attending this one," Zena said firmly. "How are you getting there?"

"In the carriage I engaged last night," Kendric replied. "I told the coachman to wait so that he could take us home from the party, and he is downstairs now, waiting again."

Kendric took off his evening-coat as he spoke and Zena sat down on his bed too.

"What I will do," she said, "is come with you and stay in the carriage. I shall be able to watch the duel, and then if we drive away immediately afterwards nobody will know I have been there."

"I have already told you that you are not coming," Kendric answered.

As he spoke he looked at his sister's face and said slowly:

"I suppose the worst has happened and you have fallen in love with the *Comte*."

It was inevitable, Zena thought, because they were so close to each other, that sooner or later Kendric would guess her feelings.

"I love him!" she said simply.

"Oh, God!" Kendric exclaimed. "That is all we want to make the whole situation completely impossible!"

"I cannot help it."

"Is he in love with you?"

"He says he is."

"Then swear to me on everything we hold holy that you will not tell him who we are," Kendric said. "I know he is a gentleman and I am sure he will behave like one, but you do realise that if inadvertently he revealed our secret to a friend, his valet, or anyone else, we could be blackmailed in a very unpleasant manner."

Zena was silent. Then she said:

"There is no point in my telling the *Comte* anyway. I realise that when we leave Paris I shall . . . never see him . . . again."

There was obviously a sob in her voice as she spoke the last words, and as if she was afraid of crying she ran from the room into her own.

She dressed hastily in the plainest of the gowns she had with her and covered it with a cloak that was of a dark green velvet and therefore not at all conspicuous.

She pulled the stars from her hair and because she still felt like crying washed her face in cold water before she went into the Sitting-Room.

Kendric was ready almost at the same time, and when he saw Zena's expression he put out his hand in a gesture of affection.

She took it in hers and he said as he drew her towards the door:

"Cheer up, dearest, things may not be as bad as we anticipate, and as we have both always known, one pays for one's fun in one way or another."

They walked down the stairs hand-in-hand and when they got into the carriage, Kendric directed the coachman to where they wished to go in the Bois.

It seemed as if the man knew the exact spot, and Zena had the uncomfortable feeling that it would be impossible in Paris to keep a duel of any sort secret from the gossip-mongers.

She did not say so to Kendric, but slipped her arm through his, feeling she needed the comfort of being close to him.

"The *Comte* will be all right," he said as if she had asked the question.

"What shall we . . . do if he is . wounded?" Zena asked.

"He has arranged for a doctor to be present, and doubtless the *Marquis* will do the same," Kendric said. "Whatever happens, they will both have proper medical attention."

That would not be of much use, Zena thought, *if the* Comte *was killed.*

She knew, because her father had often discussed what happened in duels, and she had also read about them, that it was customary for the duel to be more a ritual of honour than anything else.

A very slight wound was considered satisfaction for the insult in most cases, and as far as aristocrats were concerned, it was considered both unsporting and ill-bred to injure a rival seriously.

But she did not trust the *Marquis* knowing instinctively that he was both evil and dangerous, and she had the terrifying feeling that he would do anything, however outrageous, to get his own way where she was concerned.

If the Comte *loses the duel,* she thought, *Kendric and I will have to go home to . . . avoid him.*

It was agonising to think that she might have to leave the *Comte* even sooner than she had expected, and as the carriage drove towards the Bois she tried not to think about it.

When they reached the place, which was a small clearing in the middle of a wood, Zena could see in the dim light there were already some men standing about.

Dawn was just breaking and a few minutes ago the first rays of the sun had come up over the horizon.

"Now swear to me," Kendric admonished, "that you will make sure that nobody sees you. We shall be in worse trouble than we are already if anybody realises that I have brought you with me."

"You could not have stopped me," Zena replied.

He touched her shoulder gently, then he stepped out of the carriage and shut the door carefully behind him.

Zena watched him walk away, then with a leap of her heart she saw the *Comte* come through the trees on the other side of the clearing and meet Kendric.

There was another man with him whom Zena thought must be Anton and a few seconds later an elderly man carrying what was obviously a doctor's bag joined them.

It was difficult for her to take her eyes from the *Comte* but she looked to where at the other end of the clearing the *Marquis* was talking to his two seconds and another doctor.

As the sky rapidly grew lighter she could now see them clearly, and she thought the *Marquis* looked particularly unpleasant and even more debauched than when he was at La Païva's house.

His eyes seemed dark and sinister and his lips were set in a cruel line, which convinced her that he was determined to injure the *Comte*.

Her eyes returned irresistibly to the man she loved and she found herself praying with a fervour which came from her heart and soul.

"Please . . . God . . . save him! Please . . . God let him . . . win. Do not let him be hurt. Please . . . God . . . help us."

She repeated the words over and over, feeling as if they were carried on wings into the sky and God who had given her love must understand and listen to her plea.

Nothing seemed to be happening and she wondered why they did not get on with the duel.

Then, as another man appeared and walked into the clearing, she understood that they had been waiting for the Referee.

He was much older than either of the contestants and looked extremely distinguished. He beckoned to them both and spoke to them for some seconds. Zena was certain he was admonishing them as to their behaviour.

Then the box containing the duelling-pistols was opened, and as the *Marquis* considered he was the person who had been insulted he had the first choice of weapons.

Then obviously on the Referee's instructions the duellists walked into the centre of the clearing to stand back to back waiting for the contest to begin.

Both men were wearing smartly cut day-coats and top hats.

The *Comte*, Zena noticed, as she had yesterday when they had driven in the Bois, wore his hat at a somewhat raffish angle, and it gave her the impression that he was confident that he could defeat the *Marquis* despite the latter's reputation.

Because she was so afraid she intensified her prayers feeling that somehow she could give him extra support and extra strength, and perhaps intensify his skill in handling his weapon.

Then as if she could not bear the tension of only watching and not hearing what was happening, she let down the window and as she did so she could hear the Referee begin to count.

"One . . . two . . . three . . ."

As each number was called the two contestants moved a pace away from each other and went on walking.

"Four . . . five . . . six . . . seven . . . eight . . . nine . . . ten!"

At the last word the *Marquis* and the *Comte* turned and Zena thought she must close her eyes because she could not bear to see what happened.

Two shots rang out almost simultaneously, then as she looked only at the *Comte* she saw as the smoke came from his pistol that he staggered.

She could not control her fear any longer and flinging open the door of the carriage she ran towards him as swiftly as her feet could carry her, knowing that nothing and nobody should stop her from reaching the man she loved when he had been wounded.

Finding that the *Comte* was still on his feet when she reached him she flung her arms around him saying frantically:

"You are . . . hurt! Oh, darling . . . darling . . . I cannot . . . bear it!"

She thought the *Comte* looked at her in astonishment, then one arm went around her.

"What are you doing here?" he asked.

Before Zena could reply a voice said:

"Let me see, *Monsieur,* if the bullet penetrated your arm."

Zena gave a little cry of horror and moved away a little as the doctor began gently to inspect the *Comte*'s arm.

"The shot was a little wide," the *Comte* said.

"It was you, *Monsieur,* who hit *le Marquis,*" the doctor replied.

For the first time Zena looked away from the *Comte.*

She could see three men bending over something on the ground, and she realised that it was the *Marquis.*

She drew in her breath, but before she could speak Kendric was beside her.

"I told you to stay in the carriage!" he said sharply.

"I thought the . . . *Comte* was . . . hit," Zena murmured, but Kendric was not listening.

"You were magnificent!" he said to the *Comte.* "I have never seen such a fast shot!"

"I have had quite a lot of practice," the *Comte* replied, "not at men but at game birds."

The doctor had pulled his coat from his shoulder and now Zena could see that the *Marquis*'s shot had passed through the sleeve of the coat and through his shirt leaving a long red weal across the surface of his arm.

It was bleeding but not badly, and the doctor bandaged it as she stood watching.

"I think you would do well to enquire as to the condition of *Monsieur le Marquis*," the *Comte* said to Kendric.

"I hope you have made it impossible for him to go on making a nuisance of himself," Kendric answered.

"Let us go and find out," Anton said beside him.

Kendric looked at Zena.

"I will take Zena home," the *Comte* said before Kendric could speak, "and perhaps you will follow in your own carriage."

The way he spoke was so decisive that Kendric after a moment's hesitation walked away with Anton.

The *Comte* thanked the doctor, gave him what seemed to Zena to be an enormous number of francs, and then with his coat slung over one shoulder he said:

"Shall we go? As you are well aware, you have no right to be here."

"I am . . . sorry," Zena said in a contrite tone. "I promised Kendric I would not leave the carriage . . . but when I saw you . . . stagger I could not . . . help it."

"I am glad I did not know you were watching me," the *Comte* said. "It was very brave and very touching of you to come."

The *Comte*'s carriage was waiting on the other side of the trees and Zena got in, choosing her position on the seat carefully so that she would not be on the side of his injured arm.

The carriage started off and as she looked at him pleadingly the *Comte* said:

"My darling, you look tired."

"How could I sleep when I knew you were in . . . danger?" Zena replied.

"I feel you were praying for me."

"Desperately . . . and my prayers were . . . answered. I am more . . . grateful than I can possibly . . . say."

She gave a little sigh, then she said anxiously:

"You do not think you will run a temperature and become feverish?"

"It is only a scratch," the *Comte* answered, "and to tell the truth now it is over I feel rather elated that I have managed to defeat a man with such a formidable reputation as a duellist."

"You were wonderful!"

"Perhaps I had an unfair advantage with your prayers and my love for you to support me," he said gently.

333

Zena made an inarticulate little sound and put her head against his shoulder.

"Look at me, my darling," the *Comte* said.

She raised her face obediently and he looked down at her in the light of the pale morning sun coming through the windows of the carriage.

"You are even more beautiful that I have ever seen you before, without all that paint and powder on your face," he said.

Zena gave a little start.

She remembered how she had washed in cold water before she left the apartment, and because she was so unused to cosmetics she had not remembered to mascara her eyelashes or redden her lips as she had done ever since she came to Paris.

"As you are now," the *Comte* went on, "you look very, very young, innocent and—untouched."

It was as if he was speaking to himself rather than to her.

Then as Zena was wondering what she could say in reply, his lips found hers and he was kissing her gently and tenderly, without passion, but it was very marvellous.

He kissed her until the horses turned into the Rue St. Honoré and as he raised his head Zena said as if the words burst from her:

"I love . . . you! I love you until it is . . . difficult to think of . . . anything else but you in my . . . life."

"Just as I think of you," the *Comte* said, "and, my darling, when I come back and fetch you at luncheontime we have to talk about our future together, for I know now I cannot live without you."

"Our . . . future," Zena stammered.

It was as if an icy cold hand suddenly clutched at her heart.

"We have to be together," the *Comte* said. "Although we have known each other only a very short while, you fill my heart until I know that nothing else is of any importance except you."

He kissed her again, and as he did so the horses came to a standstill. The footman got down to open the door and the *Comte* said:

"Do not worry about anything, my darling. Leave everything to me. Go to bed and sleep as I intend to do. I will fetch you at one o'clock and then we will discuss everything which concerns ourselves."

Zena gave him a smile, then as she saw he was about to follow her out of the carriage, she said:

"Please . . . stay where you are. You know as well as I do you should move your arm as little as possible until the ... bleeding has ... stopped.''

"Are you taking care of me?" the *Comte* asked with a smile.

"It is ... something I would ... like to do."

Their eyes met and it was hard to look away.

Then quickly Zena got out of the carriage, and in case he should follow her she ran through the outer door without looking back.

Zena was fast asleep when she heard Kendric calling her.

It was difficult to come back to consciousness and she hoped that he would go away and she could go on sleeping.

Then she felt his hand on her shoulder.

"Wake up, Zena! Wake up!"

"What ... is it?" she asked.

She was so sleepy that for a moment it was difficult even to focus her eyes. Then she saw he was standing beside her bed, dressed as he had been when they went to the duel.

"Wake up, Zena!" Kendric said insistently. "We have to leave here at once!"

"L—leave ... where for?"

"For home!"

As if he had thrown cold water on her face Zena sat up abruptly and opened her eyes.

"What is wrong ... what has ... happened?"

"We have to leave Paris at once," Kendric said, "and if you hurry we can catch a train to Hoyes which leaves at eleven o'clock."

"But ... we cannot go ... why should we?"

Kendric sat down on the side of the bed and pulled off his top-hat.

"The Press are asking questions," he said, "and you know what they are like when they sense there is a story which might cause a sensation."

"You mean ... they intend to ... write about the ... duel?"

"Not because it is an ordinary duel of which there are plenty," Kendric replied, "about one a day I should think, but this one, for the Press, is exceptional."

"Why? Why?" Zena asked.

"Because it really is news that the *Marquis* should have lost a duel, with a serious injury to his arm."

"How serious?" Zena asked.

"He will not have to have it amputated or anything like that," Kendric replied, "but the fact that he has been injured in a duel over a woman and lost it is the sort of story all Paris will enjoy, especially when they know the name of the woman."

Zena gave a little cry of horror.

"So . . . that is . . . what they are . . . trying to find . . . out!"

"Exactly!" Kendric replied. "They already know that you came to Paris with me, and that I am supposedly the *Vicomte* de Villerny."

"But Kendric, how can they have found that out?"

"How should I know. I expect the *Marquis* talked. He had a great deal more to drink after you left La Païva's house last night, and I heard him saying in a loud voice that he would not only fight the *Comte* but me, to make sure he got you."

Zena gave a little groan.

"It is . . . all my . . . fault."

"You cannot help looking as you do," Kendric said. "I suppose it is something we might have anticipated when we came to Paris."

"What can we . . . do to . . . prevent them from . . . finding out . . . who we are?" Zena asked in a frightened voice.

"There is only one thing we can do," Kendric answered, "and that is to disappear."

He paused before he said:

"If we stay it is quite obvious they will ferret out that I am not de Villerny, and if they start making enquiries in Wiedenstein there is always the chance that your extraordinary likeness to the Princess Marie-Thérèse will be noticed."

Zena gave an audible cry of horror and Kendric stood up.

"I have already told Renée to come upstairs and start packing for you," he said, "and I have also ordered a carriage. You have only an hour in which to be ready to leave for the station."

"But . . . Kendric . . . what can I do about . . . the *Comte*?" Zena asked.

"Forget him!" Kendric replied.

Zena started to dress as Renée quickly, but not very skilfully, packed her gowns in the trunk in which they had come.

"It is sad that you must leave us, *M'mselle*," she said. "It has been a pleasure having you here."

"Thank you," Zena replied absent-mindedly. Then she added:

"Renée, will you do something for me?"

"Or course, *M'mselle.*"

"When *Monsieur le Comte* comes to call for me as he has promised to do, will you hand him a letter?"

"*Oui, M'mselle.*"

Zena at first thought it would be wisest to go away without making any explanation. Then she had known it was something she could not do.

She loved the *Comte* and he loved her.

Before she went to sleep she had thought despairingly it would be very difficult to listen to him trying to make plans for their future and not to confess the truth.

She thought that perhaps Fate had taken a hand, and to go away without explanation was better than having to lie.

At the same time, every instinct in her body which loved him told her she was being a fool.

But what could she say?

How could she confess there was no possibility of any future for them together and that their love was just something wonderful and glorious which had come into their lives for a fleeting moment.

When she was dressed for the journey and Renée was packing the last few things into her bag Zena ran into the Sitting-Room and taking some pieces of writing-paper and an envelope from the *Secretaire* carried them with her to her bedroom.

She had the feeling that if Kendric saw her writing he would think it a mistake and perhaps argue with her, which she could not bear.

Then as she sat down at her dressing table and wrote the first words she heard his voice talking to Renée's father who had been helping him pack.

Quickly, because there was now no time, she scribbled:

I love you, I love you! But I have got to go away. And yet because I must tell you how kind and wonderful you have been and that I shall never forget you, I will write to you once again when I reach my destination.

My Love and my Prayers,

Zena.

As she finished and folded the letter into the envelope Kendric was at the door.

"Are you ready, Zena! We must go!"

"Everything is packed, *Monsieur,*" Renée replied.

The maid diverted his attention from his sister and while he was giving instructions to the Concierge to carry the trunk downstairs Zena managed to give the letter to Renée and with it a ten-franc note.

Renée slipped both into the pocket of her apron.

"*Merci, M'mselle,*" she said in a voice that Kendric could hear. Then she added quietly: "I will not forget to do what you have asked, *M'mselle.*"

The luggage was piled on the roof of the carriage, and as they drove away down the Rue St. Honoré Zena looked up at the windows of the Sitting-Room.

She was thinking of how the *Comte* had kissed her and how she had never guessed how perfect and glorious a kiss could be. She knew she would never forget the rapture and the ecstasy which had made her feel he carried her to the heart of the sun.

How can I live and never know such happiness again? she asked herself and felt as if the whole world was dark.

It took them nearly two hours to reach Hoyes and there they had to wait for the slow train to carry them on to Ettengen.

They had picked a compartment to themselves when they left Paris, but Zena had said very little to Kendric because he was tired after not being able to go to bed all night, and he soon fell asleep.

She too felt tired, but she could only think of the *Comte* and wonder what he would think and feel when Renée gave him her note and he learnt that she and Kendric had left Paris.

She remembered all the words of love he had ever spoken to her, and she knew that she would repeat them and repeat them all her life and they would be her only comfort and help in the years of misery which lay ahead.

At Hoyes, Kendric, as if he needed exercise, began to walk up and down the platform.

Zena sat on the hard wooden seat feeling no impatience to continue their journey, but only a dull disinterest in everything that happened.

Finally the slow train from the capital arrived and Kendric found an empty first class carriage and Zena stepped into it.

Then, as Kendric tipped the Porter, the man said:

" 'Scuse me, *Monsieur,* but has anybody ever told you you've a strik-ing resemblance to our Crown Prince?"

Kendric smiled.

"I believe I have heard that before."

"Uncanny it is, *Monsieur,* you might be almost his double."

"I will take that as a compliment," Kendric joked.

"He's a very fine young man, and we're exceedingly proud of him," the Porter said. "In time he'll make us a good ruler."

"I hope he does not disappoint you," Kendric remarked.

As the train moved off he said to Zena:

"It is always pleasant to receive an unsolicited testimonial. Do you think I will make a good Arch-Duke?"

"Not if you behave as you did in Paris!"

Kendric laughed.

"I suppose I should apologise to you. At the same time, I enjoyed myself, and it will be something to remember when I am at Düssel-dorf."

The way he spoke made Zena realise again how much he was dread-ing the thought of a year under Prussian military authority.

She put out her hand to say:

"We must neither of us regret anything we have done, but just be glad that we were lucky enough to know such happiness."

The way she spoke made her brother aware how much she was suffering, and after a moment he said:

"If I were on the throne, I swear Zena, I would make it possible somehow for you to marry the *Comte* and live happily ever afterwards."

"Thank you, Kendric," Zena said, "but although it is an agony to know that I will . . . never see him again . . . I shall always be glad that I knew and loved such a . . . wonderful man . . . and he loved me."

Kendric sighed, and there was nothing he could say to com-fort her.

After they had travelled for some miles in silence Kendric said:

"Do not forget we are now the *Comte* and *Comtesse* de Castelnaud."

"I had forgotten," Zena replied and wished she could continue to be Zena Bellefleur.

When they reached the Professor's house which was on the outskirts of the small village of Ettengen, a tall red-brick ugly building which looked, Zena thought, rather like a School, they were both wondering what the Countess and the Baron had done about their disappearance.

"I can tell you one thing," Kendric said as they drove from the station in a hired carriage, "our watch-dogs, if they have not run tittle-tattling to Papa, will be waiting to bite us. So be prepared for a very uncomfortable reception."

He had not exaggerated and the only thing that mitigated the anger of those waiting for them was that they had arrived sooner than they had said they would.

When they walked into the house and were shown into the room where the Countess and the Baron were sitting with the Professor, the exclamations at their appearance and the recriminations they received made it impossible for them for sometime to make any explanation.

Then at last with an authority which Zena thought Kendric had never shown before he said sharply:

"That is enough. My sister and I have not returned to be scolded as if we were schoolchildren!"

He looked towards the Professor before he said:

"First, *Mein Herr,* I must apologise to you for not arriving when we were expected. But Her Royal Highness and I have missed only a few days of our tuition, and we can easily make up the time lost if we apply ourselves to our studies as we both intend to do."

Zena saw at once that the Professor was somewhat mollified, and thinking that Kendric had started off on the right foot she said:

"As I am tired after my journey, I should be grateful, Herr Professor, if somebody could show me to my bedroom, and, if it is possible, I would like a cold drink. It was exceedingly hot in the train."

The Professor hurried to give the orders and the Countess with her affronted dignity showing itself with every word she spoke showed Zena upstairs to a quite pleasant room overlooking the garden at the back of the house.

"Your clothes have been unpacked, *Mademoiselle la Comtesse,*" she said, "but before I ring for the maid I would like to tell you . . ."

"I am very fatigued," Zena interrupted, "and as I have no wish to sit through a long-drawn-out dinner please have something brought to me on a tray."

The Countess was astounded.

"Your Royal—I mean *Mademoiselle la Comtesse*, must be ill!"

"Only tired," Zena said, "and please be so obliging as to give the orders for what I require . . ."

She thought as she spoke that if Paris had given Kendric a new authority it had made her feel as if she was no longer a child, but grown up.

"I am old enough to be loved," she told herself, "and that makes me a woman, and as a woman I will no longer be imposed upon by people who should obey my orders rather than I should obey theirs."

As a matter of fact she was definitely too tired to wish for arguments or to do anything but rest.

But there was one thing she knew she had to do first—for she would be unable to sleep otherwise—and that was to write again to the *Comte*.

She waited until she was in bed, then writing with a pencil instead of pen and ink she covered three pages of writing-paper with the expression of her love.

Finally she wrote:

You have given me something so priceless, so perfect, that it will shine like a light to guide me all through my life.

Although I can never see you again, and it breaks my heart to write this, I know, because I have loved you, I will become a far better person.

I think love—true love—makes those who find it want to be good, and to inspire others. That is what I shall try to do because you have inspired me and your love is like a guiding star.

It will be always out of reach, yet it will be there, shining in the Heavens above me, and I will follow it, as the Wise Men followed the Star of Bethlehem.

I know too that although you may not be aware of it, I shall sometimes be near you in my dreams, and my love will reach out to protect you as it did when you were fighting the Marquis.

There is nothing more I can say, nothing more I can tell you, except that now and for all eternity my heart and soul are yours.

Zena.

She did not read the letter through but put it straight into an envelope.

She knew that if she addressed it to: *Le Comte Jean de Graumont c/o Le Duc de Soissons, Le Champs Élysées, Paris,* the letter would find him.

341

She rang the bell and when the maid answered it she asked her if she would take the letter at once to the Post Office.

The maid, who was German like the Professor, looked at Zena a little doubtfully, and Zena said:

"As it is very important, if you will go at once, I will of course pay you for your services. Please give me my handbag."

She thought as she spoke that the woman's eyes glinted greedily, and when she drew a ten-franc note from her bag and handed it with the letter and another note of a smaller denomination with which to buy the stamp the servant curtsied.

"I will take it at once, *Mein Fräulein*," she said in her gutteral voice. Then she added as if perceptively she guessed what Zena wanted to hear: "and no one will know I have left the house."

"Thank you," Zena said.

Then, as if at last she was free to rest, she put her head down on the pillow and closed her eyes.

Just for a moment she wanted to cry for her lost love and for the *Comte,* wondering despairingly why she had left him.

Then instead she imagined his arms were around her, and he was holding her close, his lips seeking hers.

She felt her love rising within her and the happiness he had given her seemed to seep over her like sunshine.

Because it was so wonderful, so perfect, and she loved him so much, she fell asleep.

CHAPTER SIX

ZENA WALKED SLOWLY down the stairs to the Library.
They had now been four days at Ettengen and she felt as if four
centuries had passed and that every day her yearning for the *Comte*
grew more intense, more agonising.

She thought that perhaps at first she had been almost numbed by
the shock of the duel, of leaving Paris in such a hurry, and being
plunged into the intolerable boredom of the companionship of the
Baron and the Countess.

Every night as she cried herself to sleep she thought she had lost the
sunshine from her life, and she would never again know anything but
darkness and misery.

Last night she had felt it was too heart-rending to bear any longer,
and after they had all retired to bed she had gone to Kendric's room
to tell him she must run away.

"It is no use, Kendric," she said, "I cannot face life without the
Comte. In fact, I would rather be dead!"

"Things will get better as time goes by," Kendric said soothingly.

He was lying back against the pillows, in his bed reading a book, and
now as he looked at his sister sitting on the mattress facing him he
knew how deeply she was suffering.

He thought she was already beginning to look like Melanie, although
otherwise there was little resemblance in their appearance.

"I am sorry, Zena," he said impulsively, "I should never have taken
you to Paris."

"I shall never regret it," Zena replied fiercely. "I would not have
missed meeting the *Comte* for . . . anything in the world, but why should

343

I . . . suffer like . . . this? Why should I marry a man I will . . . hate?"

She paused, then she said slowly and distinctly:

"I am going back to Paris to find the *Comte,* and as far as Wieden-stein is concerned, I am dead!"

Kendric put out his hand to take hers.

"Now listen to me, dearest. You will not be dead, but the *Comte* will."

Zena stiffened.

"What do you mean?" she asked.

"I mean that Papa will find out where you are and the *Comte* will either be put in prison on some trumped up charge, or, if they feel he is too important for that, he will have a 'regrettable accident'."

"I do not believe it!" Zena cried. "You are just trying to frighten me into not going back to Paris!"

Kendric's fingers tightened on hers.

"You know I want you to be happy," he said. "Do you remember our Cousin Gertrude?"

Zena thought for a moment.

"Do you mean . . . the one who is now the Queen of Albania?"

Kendric nodded.

"Yes. Like you, when she was told she had to marry a rather coarse, uncivilised King and live in Albania, she rebelled."

"What happened?" Zena asked in a low voice.

"Gertrude had fallen in love with one of the Diplomats at her father's Court. He was a Frenchman and as they loved each other passionately they felt the world was well lost for love."

"That is what I . . . feel," Zena said beneath her breath.

"They arranged to run away together and Gertrude made plans to creep out of the Palace and join him. They thought they would leave the country before anybody was aware of what was happening."

"Why were they . . . unable to . . . do so?" Zena asked.

Her voice was hardly above a whisper and her eyes were apprehensive.

"The day before they were due to leave, when they were quite certain that nobody had the slightest idea of their plans, the Diplomat went out riding as he did every morning, was thrown from his horse and broke his neck!"

There was a long silence. Then Zena said:

"Was it not really an accident?"

"He was an expert rider," Kendric replied, "and it is very unusual for any man to die if he is bucked off his horse or even thrown over its head."

There was another long silence. Then Zena said:

"And you think ... something like ... that might ... happen to the ... *Comte?*"

"I am certain of it," Kendric replied. "That way there would be no scandal, and nobody would know except Papa and Mama. You would be brought back, and the *Comte* would be dead."

Zena put her hands over her face and her brother knew that she was crying.

He put his arms around her and said:

"This is the penalty we both pay for being who we are, and you surely do not suppose that when the time comes I will be allowed to choose my own bride? I will have to marry some boring Princess who will be chosen for me, and I shall have to make the best of living with her, whatever she is like."

"At least you will be ... able to get ... away ... sometimes," Zena said in a muffled voice.

"I hope so," Kendric replied.

He was thinking of how his father had said he would like to go to Paris but found it impossible.

Zena took her hands from her face and wiped her eyes.

"I will ... try to be ... brave," she said, "but it will be ... worse when ... you are not ... here."

"It will be very much worse for me also!" Kendric said grimly.

They talked for a long time, but could find no way out of a future that was looming nearer every day that passed. For the moment the only mitigating factor was that they could suffer together.

When Zena went back to bed she had cried not only because she had lost the *Comte* but also because she must lose her twin.

As if in tune with her feelings the day had started misty and dull, but the sun had come out while they were working with the Professor in the room he called the Study. It made the lessons, which were excruciatingly dull, seem worse than they usually were.

The Professor was a perfectionist. He corrected every mispronunci-

BARBARA CARTLAND

ation, every intonation, every grammatical mistake, until Zena felt she must scream.

What made the lessons even more intolerable was the fact that, because they had escaped their watch-dogs once, the Countess and the Baron sat in the Study all the time they were being taught.

They also accompanied them, as Kendric said angrily, every time they moved, in case they should run away again.

"It is our own fault," Zena told him listlessly, and knew the only way she could escape now was in her thoughts.

When luncheon was over, a heavy German meal which was very unlike the French cuisine they had at the Palace, the Professor retired for a rest.

He was an old man and everyone knew that for two hours after luncheon he would sleep.

As they started their lessons quite early in the morning this seemed such an excellent idea to the Baron and the Countess that they too insisted on a *siesta,* and told Zena and Kendric they should do the same.

Because they were so frightened that their charges would vanish for a second time each day they extracted from them a promise on their word of honour that neither of them would leave the house or the garden.

"I am so relieved to get rid of the old crows I would promise to do anything!" Kendric said when their attendants had left them alone.

"I suppose they are only doing their duty," Zena replied, "and we certainly frightened them."

Kendric picked up the newspapers.

"It is too hot to stay in the house," he said. "I am going to read in the garden under the trees. Come and join me."

"I will in a minute," Zena replied. "But I must first find something to read."

"I do not think you will find much in the Professor's Library, except history books," Kendric scoffed.

Zena felt that even that would be better than having nothing to do but think, which inevitably led to her crying for the *Comte.*

Kendric picked up the newspapers and went off into the garden, while Zena went to the Professor's Study where the walls were lined with books.

She found some on one shelf which were in French, and she was taking them out one by one to see if there was anything she wanted to read, when the door opened behind her and she thought Kendric had come back.

"You were right!" she said. "Everything here is so unutterably dull."

"Perhaps you would prefer to talk to me," a man's voice said.

Zena started so violently that she almost dropped the book she was holding in her hands.

Then, as she turned round, she saw in amazement that it was the *Comte* who was standing inside the door.

He looked so handsome, so tall and elegant, that for a moment she thought she must be dreaming and she was seeing a vision of him as he had looked when he took her to luncheon in the Bois.

He shut the door behind him and came forward into the room.

It was impossible for Zena to move and she was holding her breath.

Then, as she longed to run to him, to touch him, and make sure he was really there, she said in a voice that trembled:

"W—what has . . . happened? Why are you . . . here?"

"I am here," the *Comte* replied with a smile, "because they informed me at the *Gendarmerie* that the only beautiful young woman in Ettengen with red-gold hair and blue eyes was the *Comtesse* de Castelnaud."

"You were . . . looking for . . . me?" Zena asked in a voice that did not sound like her own.

The *Comte* came nearer and when he reached her side he said:

"You have driven me nearly mad by disappearing in that cruel fashion and leaving me no address and no idea how I could find you."

"I told . . . you that I could never . . . see you again."

"I was in despair, utter and complete despair!" the *Comte* said, "in fact I have never been so unhappy in my whole life."

"But . . . you are . . . here."

"I am here," he repeated, "thanks to the second letter you wrote to me."

"I did not put any address on it," Zena said quickly.

"The Post Office did that for you," the *Comte* replied. "When I saw the letter was stamped 'Ettengen' I took the first train from Paris that would carry me to Wiedenstein."

Zena put down the book she was carrying as if it was too heavy to hold.

"So that is . . . how you . . . found me."

She could not help the lilt in her voice or the fact that her eyes were shining radiantly in her pale face.

"That is how I found you!" the *Comte* confirmed.

As he spoke he put his arms around her and drew her against him.

Zena felt her heart turn over in her breast and she lifted her face up to him.

He did not kiss her, he only looked down at her for a long moment before he said:

"I have found you, and now I want to know how soon you will marry me, for I have discovered, my darling, that I cannot live without you."

He pulled her almost roughly towards him, then his lips were on hers.

Now he kissed her in a very different way than he had done before. His lips were passionate and demanding, and there was a fire in them which told Zena that, because he had suffered, he could no longer control his feelings.

It flashed through her mind that if the first kiss she had received from him had been like this, she might have been frightened. But now something wild and wonderful within her leapt to meet the fire in him.

Once again he carried her into the sun, and the light of it seemed to blaze around them as she knew this was another side of love which was wonderful, exciting, demanding, and she gloried in it.

He kissed her until Zena felt her misery and depression was swept away, and her whole body vibrated to a force that was stronger and more vital than anything she had ever known before.

She felt as if she had suddenly come alive, and no sensation she had ever known in the past had been so rapturous, so ecstatic as what the *Comte* was making her feel now.

His heart was beating tempestuously against her own and she knew the sensations he was giving her he was feeling himself, and it made them one person as truly as if they were married and nothing could divide them.

When at last the *Comte* raised his head Zena felt that if he were not holding her in his arms she would have fallen to the ground.

Because she was pulsating with emotion she could only hide her face against his shoulder and say in a breathless little voice:

"I . . . love you . . . I love . . . you and I thought I would . . . never see you again."

"And I love you!" the *Comte* said. "Never again my darling, will I lose you. Nothing shall prevent you from being mine."

He spoke with a violence that seemed to echo his kisses, and it was only with a superhuman effort that Zena remembered that what he was saying was impossible.

"I . . . must talk to . . . you," she said.

The *Comte*'s lips were pressed against her forehead.

"What is there to talk about?" he asked. "I have learnt that you are not who you pretended to be, and the *Vicomte* de Villerny is really the *Comte* de Castelnaud."

Zena raised her face to look up at him.

"You . . . know who Kendric . . . is?"

"They told me at the *Gendarmerie* that he was your twin brother," the *Comte* smiled. "I was so overwhelmingly glad at the news that I would have given my informant several thousand francs if I had not been afraid of being arrested for bribery!"

He looked so happy as he spoke that Zena felt she could not bear to tell him the truth.

His arms tightened around her.

"How could you do anything so disgraceful as to come to Paris disguised in such a manner?" he asked. "I suppose I should be very angry with your brother for taking you to places where no lady should go, and letting you meet people who might have involved you in a great deal of trouble if I had not been there."

"But . . . you were . . . there," Zena said, "and you . . . saved me from the *Marquis*."

"If I had not been able to do so, I hate to think what would have happened," he said and his tone was grim.

"I was . . . always aware that I . . . could run . . . away," Zena said feeling she should make some explanation.

"You might not have been able to escape from the *Marquis* as easily as you escaped from me," the *Comte* said.

"I did not . . . want to . . . escape from . . . you," Zena said in a whisper, "but Kendric said the Press were making 'enquiries' about us."

"I cannot help feeling you will get into a great deal of trouble if your parents, provided they are alive, discover your extremely improper masquerade," the *Comte* remarked.

The way he spoke told Zena now quite clearly that she must tell him who she was.

Just for a moment she played with the idea of persuading him to carry her away now, at this moment.

Perhaps they could find somewhere in the world where they could hide and where nobody would find them, where they could be together, and if his love was as great as hers nothing else would be of any consequence.

Then she remembered what Kendric had said last night and knew she loved him too much to risk his life, even though she might as well die without him.

The *Comte* put his fingers under her chin and turned her face up to his.

"You are so beautiful, so ridiculously, adoringly beautiful," he said. "How could you not expect in that ridiculous guise of pretending to be a *demi-mondaine* that every man who looked at you would not wish to possess you!"

Now there was a scolding note in his voice which she knew was because he had been frightened for her.

"It may . . . seem to you very . . . wrong," she said, "and perhaps . . . immodest . . . but if I had not . . . gone to Paris I would not have . . . met you."

There was a smile on the *Comte*'s lips as he said:

"That is a very plausible excuse, my precious one. At the same time it is something that can have a lot of unpleasant consequences in the future."

Seeing she did not understand he explained:

"I shall not be able to take you to Paris again, until not only the Prince Napoleon has forgotten what you look like but also the *Marquis* de Sade."

"That would not . . . matter to . . . me if I could be . . . anywhere else with you," Zena said, "but . . . there is something I must . . . tell you."

Her voice trembled and the *Comte* looked at her searchingly.

"What is wrong?" he asked. "I love you, and I know that you love me. All I want, my precious, beautiful little Wiedensteiner, is that we should be married, and as quickly as possible."

"What is . . . what I have to . . . tell you," Zena said. "I . . . cannot marry you."

"Why not?"

The *Comte's* voice was sharp and seemed to ring out.

Because she felt she could not bear to wipe away the love from his eyes or the smile from his lips Zena gave a little cry and said:

"Before I tell you, will you . . . kiss me once . . . again as you did . . . just now?"

"You are making me nervous," the *Comte* complained. "Now I have found you, nothing matters except that to love you and look after you, and above all prevent you from doing dangerous and unpredictable things like pretending to be a *demi-mondaine*!"

The smile was back on his lips as he said:

"I think I felt from the first moment I looked at you that your darkened eyelashes and red lips were wrong, and when I talked to you I realised quickly how innocent you were, unless of course you were the most brilliant actress who ever performed on any stage."

"Did you really . . . think that?" Zena asked. "And it did not . . . shock you?"

"I was very shocked that you should have been to that low Dance-Hall in Montmartre and that you agreed to have luncheon alone with a stranger in the Bois."

He paused and Zena said in a voice he could hardly hear:

"I . . . I did not mean to let you . . . kiss me . . . but it was . . . so wonderful . . . so perfect that I cannot . . . believe even now that it was . . . wrong."

"It was the first time you had ever been kissed?" the *Comte* asked.

"Y—yes."

"I knew it!" he exclaimed. "I knew when my lips touched yours that they confirmed what I had already thought, that you were pure and innocent."

"I am . . . glad you thought . . . that."

"At the same time it is certainly something which must never happen again," the *Comte* said, "and it never will when I am looking after you."

His words brought back to Zena's mind what she had to tell him and because she was afraid she felt herself trembling.

"What is upsetting you?" he asked. "Tell me, my darling, and let us get it over. Then we can make plans for our future."

351

It was what he had said before, and she remembered when she left Paris she had known there was no future with him.

Then, as the tears would have swept over her in a floodtide, she shut her eyes.

"Kiss me . . . please kiss me," she pleaded, "then I will tell you . . . what you . . . have to know."

The *Comte* held her so closely against him that she could hardly breathe. Then he kissed her at first gently, then compellingly and possessively.

He took his lips from hers to kiss her eyes, her nose, then the softness of her neck beneath her ear.

She was surprised he should do so and she felt rising within her a strange and exciting feeling which was different from anything she had ever felt before.

It made her feel wild and for some reason she could not understand it was hard to breathe, and when she did, her breath came in little gasps from between her parted lips.

Once again the *Comte* kissed her lips, and she wished she could die before she must tell him who she was, and know they must say goodbye again.

When finally he released her, her cheeks were flushed, her lips were red from his kisses and her eyes seemed to hold all the sunlight in them.

"I . . . love . . . you . . . Jean."

It was the first time she had ever used his Christian name and somehow it made her feel as if she belonged to him so completely that there were no titles or rank to divide them.

They were just a man and a woman in love—Zena and Jean.

He looked down at her and there was a smile of triumph on his lips as if he felt he had won a battle and the enemy had surrendered.

"Now tell me what you have to say," he said.

As if she could not bear to do so while he was touching her, Zena moved away from him to stand at the window looking out into the garden.

She did not see the sunshine, the trees, the flowers, or Kendric in the distance lying on the grass reading the newspapers.

Instead she only saw the grandeur of the Palace, the Throne Room where her father and mother sat on official occasions and the smaller chairs on either side of them which were also ornate and rather like thrones for Kendric and herself.

She must have stood silent for several seconds before the *Comte* said:

"I am waiting!"

"I . . . I . . ."

Zena's voice seemed to come from a very long way away and be almost inarticulate.

"I am not . . . who you . . . think I . . . am."

"Not the *Comtesse* de Castelnaud?"

"N—no."

"Another disguise?" the *Comte* asked.

Zena nodded.

"Then who are you?" he asked. "Let me say before you tell me, that whoever you are—Zena Bellefleur or *La Comtesse* de Castelnaud or whoever else—to me you are the woman I love and whom I will make my wife."

"If only . . . I . . . could be . . . married to you, I would be the . . . happiest person in the . . . whole world."

The way she spoke was so poignant that even the *Comte* was startled.

"Why can you not marry me?" he asked. "You cannot be married already?"

"N—not . . . exactly."

"Then if you are engaged," the *Comte* replied, "forget it! I suppose, as in all French families, you have been affianced to some suitable young man by your parents and you have no choice in the matter. Then let me make it clear before we go any further—you will marry me!"

Once again Zena wondered if she should agree to do as he wished, on condition that he took her away immediately.

She was sure she could persuade Kendric to help them, and it could actually be quite easy to escape from the house at night, climb over the garden-wall and be over the border into France long before dawn.

It might take them a week or longer to find out that it was the *Comte* who had spirited her away and by that time they would be married and legally she would be his wife.

That is what we will do, she thought. *I will pretend that all I was going to tell him was that I am engaged.*

As this was going round in her head she remembered Cousin Gertrude and what had happened to the man she had loved.

Would this be different? Zena knew she dare not risk it, and she must tell the *Comte* the truth.

As if he was reading her thoughts, which he had told her before he could do, he said:

"You must tell me the truth, Zena, however difficult it may be. To have secrets from each other would spoil our love and raise reserves and barriers between us."

Zena knew he was right.

However hurtful it might be for her, he must know the truth, and she could not sacrifice him to her love, however great it might be.

She took a deep breath. Then she said, slowly and in a voice that trembled on every word:

"I . . . am the . . . Princess Marie-Thérèse . . . of Wiedenstein!"

There was a long silence.

Zena felt the tears come into her eyes and she clasped her hands together so tightly that she squeezed the blood from her fingers.

"Is this true?" the *Comte* asked at length.

Zena was unable to speak, but she nodded her head.

"And as the daughter of the Ruler of this country you dared to go to Paris pretending to be a loose woman of a kind you should know nothing about?"

"K—Kendric was . . . upset and . . . unhappy," Zena said, "because . . . Papa had told him that he is to go to Düsseldorf for a year to train with the Prussian Cadets."

"I can understand his resenting that!" the *Comte* agreed. "But if he decided to go to Paris, how could he have dared to take you?"

"We have always . . . done everything . . . together," Zena answered, "so it would have been very . . . cruel of him to . . . leave me behind."

"He could have taken you as his sister."

"If he had done so he thought it would prevent him from enjoying himself because I would have to be chaperoned. So I . . . became his . . . *Chère Amie*."

"I can follow his thinking," the *Comte* said. "At the same time it was a mad, crazy idea from the start, and I cannot understand what your attendants did when you had run away."

"We managed it because we were coming here," Zena said. "The Paris Express stopped at Hoyes while our train was in the station. We jumped into it leaving a . . . letter for the two . . . old people . . .

escorting us telling them that if they told . . . Papa we had . . . disappeared he would be very . . . angry with them.''

"It was quite ingenious, I admit,'' the *Comte* said, "but now the day of reckoning has come, Zena, what do you intend to do about us?''

Zena turned from the window.

"I want to marry . . . you,'' she said, "I would . . . give up my . . . hope of Heaven to be your . . . wife, to live with you and . . . love you. But it is . . . something that I . . . cannot do.''

"Why not?'' the *Comte* asked. "Is the pomp and circumstance of being Royal more important to you than our love?''

Zena walked towards him and put her two hands flat on his chest.

He did not put his arms around her, and she thought the way he looked at her was cold and critical.

"I love . . . you and I . . . swear to you I . . . love you more than . . . life itself,'' she said, "and if you were to marry me . . . I would go with you . . . anywhere in the . . . world.''

"But it is something you will not do because you are a Royal Princess!''

"I want to . . . do it,'' Zena answered, "and if in order to hide we could only live in a hut I would . . . wait on you and . . . love you . . . and nothing else would . . . matter.''

"And yet you still intend to send me away?''

"I have . . . to.''

Her voice broke on the words.

"Why?''

She thought now there was a definite hardness in his eye. Because she had to make him understand she looked up at him pleadingly before she answered:

"Last night I told Kendric I could not . . . bear losing you . . . and I intended to run away . . . to go . . . back to Paris to . . . find you.''

"But Kendric, very sensibly, persuaded you against it,'' the *Comte* said.

"He told me that if I did so,'' Zena replied, "you would . . . die!''

She felt the *Comte*'s body stiffen against her fingers.

"Why should he say that?''

"Because that had happened to one of our cousins. She was in love with a Diplomat but was told she had to . . . marry the King of Albania.''

"What did she do?" the *Comte* asked.

"She was going to run away with the Diplomat, and they thought nobody knew about it. But he had what was called 'an unfortunate accident' when he was out riding and was found with a . . . broken neck!"

"And you think that kind of thing might happen to me?"

"Kendric is . . . sure of it, or else if you are not of . . . great importance you would be . . . imprisoned on some trumped up charge . . . perhaps for spying."

"In which case I would be shot," the *Comte* said reflectively.

Zena gave a little cry.

"How could I . . . allow it . . . how could I be . . . responsible for . . . that?"

She felt somehow that he was not convinced and she said:

"I love you! I love you so . . . desperately that if there were no . . . danger for you, I would pack my things and come away with you . . . now. But if we did that and you died, I would . . . kill myself!"

The last words were very low, but the *Comte* heard them.

It was then he put his arms around her and as he did so Zena burst into tears.

"I love you . . . I love you," she cried. "To be without you is like having a . . . thousand knives . . . driven into . . . my heart! But what . . . can I do? I cannot live . . . without you . . . but I cannot let you . . . die for my . . . sake!"

The tears became a tempest and now she sobbed despairingly against the *Comte*'s shoulder.

His arms tightened, they were very comforting and she felt his lips on her hair.

"Do not cry, my beautiful one," he said. "Our love should be happy and even though we met in extremely reprehensible circumstances I would not wish you to regret it."

"I do not . . . regret it! It was the most . . . wonderful thing that ever . . . happened to me," Zena sobbed, "but you might have been . . . injured or killed by the *Marquis* and now we have to say . . . goodbye to each other . . . and in a way . . . everything is my . . . fault."

"I think we should rather blame Fate," the *Comte* said. "Fate made you and your brother brave enough to run away, Fate put us next to each other at the Artists' Ball, Fate made me able to find you after I thought I had lost you for ever."

"But you . . . still have to . . . leave me."

She looked up at him as she spoke and he thought that even with the tears running down her cheeks and her lips trembling she was still the most beautiful person he had ever seen.

"I love you!" he said. "God, how I love you, but you have to be brave, my precious one."

"It is ... not going to be ... easy," Zena said, "and there is ... something else I have not ... told you."

"What is that?" he asked.

"Papa and Mama have arranged my marriage."

The *Comte* was still, then he asked:

"You are to be married—to whom?"

"To an ... Englishman!"

"Does that horrify you?"

"Of course it ... does! The English are ... cold, arrogant and insensitive, and I shall have to live among ... people who never laugh ... without love and ... without ... you."

"And who is this Englishman?"

"His name is the Duke of Faverstone, and he is coming to stay for the *Prix d'Or.*"

She thought the *Comte* did not understand and added:

"It is our most important race-meeting."

"I have heard of it," the *Comte* said. "But why should you marry an English Duke?"

"Because there are no Royal Princes available, and he is a relative of Queen Victoria."

"And you think you will be unhappy with him?"

"How could I be ... anything else?" Zena asked. "Especially ... now that I have ... met you."

She gave a deep sigh.

"My sister Melanie is desperately miserable with the Crown Prince of Fürstenburg, and I shall be the ... same."

The *Comte* was silent. Then he said very quietly:

"Then as I cannot bear to see you unhappy I shall have to save you, my darling."

"Save me?" Zena asked with an eagerness and for a moment there was a light in her eye.

Then she said, and her voice was dull again:

"There is ... nothing you can do. Kendric was not speaking ... lightly, and I know Papa would never ... tolerate the scandal of my ...

357

running away so I would always be afraid that something . . . terrible would happen to you.''

"Are you really thinking of me?'' the *Comte* asked. ''Or do you think life with your Duke in England would be preferable.''

He did not wait for Zena to reply but went on:

"As you say, if we went into hiding, you and I might be very poor. Could love really mean enough to a woman to make her willingly give up her beautiful gowns, her jewellery, the comfort of having a lot of servants, just for one man?''

"I would wear rags . . . scrub floors and . . . beg for our food if I . . . could be with you.''

Because there was a note in Zena's voice that had not been there before the *Comte* looked at her for a long moment before he pulled her against him and kissed her.

When once again she was pulsating with the wonder and rapture of his kiss, he said:

"I am going to find a way out of the *impasse* and it may not be as frightening as you anticipate it will be.''

"You mean . . . I can be with . . . you?'' Zena asked.

"I mean that I intend to marry you,'' the *Comte* said. ''It is the first time—this is the truth, Zena—I have ever asked a woman to be my wife, the first time I have ever found a woman I knew I would be happy with for the rest of my life.''

"As I would be . . . happy with . . . you.''

"I will make sure of that by making you love me until no other man will ever matter to you.''

"No other . . . man ever . . . will.''

As Zena spoke she thought of the Duke and shivered.

Then in a voice that sounded desperate she asked:

"What can we do . . . what can we . . . do?''

"I have asked you to leave that to me,'' the *Comte* said, ''and because I want to be sure of success I prefer not to talk about it.''

"But . . . supposing you . . . fail?''

"Will it sound very conceited if I say I never fail in getting what I want in life?'' the *Comte* replied. ''And I want you, Zena, as I have never wanted anything else.''

"I shall pray . . . I shall pray . . . desperately . . . as I prayed . . . before the duel,'' Zena said. ''At the same time . . . I am . . . frightened.''

"I am frightened too that I may lose you," the *Comte* said, "and now that you have told me who you are, perhaps I should leave."

Zena flung her arms around him.

"How can I let you . . . go?" she asked. "Supposing I never . . . see you again? I cannot . . . imagine what I would do! Oh, dearest, dearest Jean, I cannot lose you!"

"Nor I you," the *Comte* said. "That is why, my precious, you have to trust and believe in me."

"I know already that you are the most wonderful man in the whole world," Zena cried, "but it is still a question of Papa and the whole might of the Palace and the country which is involved. How can you . . . defeat all of them?"

"Love conquers all," the *Comte* said softly, "and we must believe that our love is big enough to do so."

"Mine is . . . I swear to you, mine is!" Zena said. "I love you until you fill the whole world. There is no sky, no sea, sun, moon, or stars. There is only . . . you."

The *Comte* put his cheek against hers.

"I adore you!" he said. "One day I will be able to tell you how much. Then we will be married."

"If . . . only I could . . . believe you."

"Half the battle is always to believe that you will win," the *Comte* said. "So I am asking you, Zena, to believe in me."

Zena drew in her breath.

"I do . . . and I . . . will."

"Then we will win, my lovely one."

She could not reply for the *Comte* was kissing her again, kissing her until the rapture he always aroused in her swept through her and she knew that there was no need for words to tell him that she believed in him.

If her logical mind was still unconvinced she believed with her heart, her soul, her body, and her faith in God.

It was God who had brought them love and she knew indisputably that God would somehow make their dreams come true.

CHAPTER SEVEN

$\mathcal{A}$s THE TRAIN LEFT Hoyes it began to gather speed towards the Capital.

Zena looked across the carriage at Kendric and knew that he was as apprehensive as she was.

When yesterday a Courier had arrived from the Palace to say they were to return immediately, they could only guess at the reason for their father's command and were both much alarmed by it.

As soon as she could be alone with Kendric Zena asked:

"Do you think Papa has found out that we went to Paris? Who could have told him?"

"God knows, but that may not be the reason he has sent for us."

"Then why should he want us back in such a hurry?"

"I cannot think," Kendric said.

It was then that Zena told her twin the secret she had kept from him for two days, that the *Comte* had been to see her.

"He came here?" Kendric exclaimed incredulously.

Zena nodded.

She went on to say that she had told the *Comte* the truth as to who she was and he had said whatever the obstacles, whatever the difficulties, he would marry her.

"You must be crazy if you believe him," Kendric said sharply.

"He told me to believe in him," Zena replied unhappily.

Kendric put his arm around her shoulder.

"Listen, Zena, I know what you are feeling, I know how unhappy you are, but I do not want you to have false hopes. They will only leave you more miserable than you are already."

"I love him!" Zena said. "Oh, Kendric, I love him so desperately."

"I know you do," Kendric answered soothingly, "but believe me when I tell you there is nothing you can do. If the *Comte* approaches Papa as a suitor for your hand, he will find himself in a great deal of trouble."

"I warned him of . . . that."

"Then if he is wise he will listen and go back to Paris," Kendric said. "I only wish I could do the same thing."

"So do . . . I," Zena murmured, and her voice broke on a sob.

The train reached the Capital late in the afternoon, and when Zena saw the Lord-in-Waiting on the station and a number of the Palace servants to attend to their luggage she felt as if the prison-gates of protocol and pomposity were waiting to close behind her.

Now she was no longer *la Comtesse* de Castelnaud, but Her Royal Highness Princess Marie-Thérèse.

They were escorted to their carriage by a number of the Railway Officials and drove away watched by a crowd which had assembled when they saw the Royal carriages.

As soon as she had the opportunity Zena said to the Lord-in-Waiting:

"Why has Papa sent for us? We did not expect to return for another ten days."

"I think His Royal Highness will wish to explain that to you himself," the Lord-in-Waiting replied, "but Your Royal Highness I am to ask you and Prince Kendric as soon as you arrive at the Palace to go straight to your rooms to change your clothes."

Zena looked surprised and the Lord-in-Waiting explained:

"Their Royal Highnesses are entertaining guests and you will find them in the Red Drawing Room."

Hearing that was where they were to meet, Zena knew that the guests were of some importance and wondered which of their neighbouring Rulers was being entertained and if there was any particular significance in their visit.

Because she knew it was useless to ask questions she kept silent and concentrated on acknowledging those who waved to her from the sides of the road as they passed by.

"What do you think is happening?" she asked Kendric in a low voice as they went up the stairs of the Palace side by side.

"I have no idea," he replied. "But I am thankful for anything which

361

delays the storm which I fancy will break over our heads at any moment.''

Because Zena felt frightened she changed her clothes as quickly as possible, paying little attention to the gown her maid chose for her to wear.

It was in fact a very pretty one, not so elaborate as those she had taken with her to Paris, but because it was more simple it made her look very young and spring-like.

Kendric came to her room to tell her he was ready, and feeling rather like schoolchildren who had been caught out playing truant they went down the stairs together and a footman opened the door of the Red Drawing-Room for them.

They entered to find there were quite a number of people with their father and mother.

The Arch-Duke detached himself to walk towards them as they approached and Zena lifted her face to kiss him.

"We are home, Papa!"

"I am delighted to see you, my dear!" the Arch-Duke replied.

The tone of his voice and the expression in his eyes made Zena know that their fears were unfounded, and whatever the reason they had been summoned back to the Palace, it was not because he was angry.

"How are you, my boy?" he asked Kendric.

"Very glad to be home, Sir," Kendric replied.

The Arch-Duke smiled as if he understood that his son had found Professor Schwarz extremely boring.

He then took Zena's hand in his.

"I brought you home," he said, "because the Duke of Faverstone has arrived sooner than we expected. He is talking to your mother, and I will present him to you."

Zena felt herself stiffen but there was nothing she could do but move beside her father through a crowd of Statesmen and politicians to where in front of the mantelpiece she could see her mother talking earnestly to somebody.

It was then she knew that Kendric was right and the *Comte* had talked nonsense when he said he would somehow make her his wife.

She felt the little glimmer of hope that had been in her heart since he had come to Ettengen flicker away as if it was candlelight that had been snuffed out by a heavy hand.

She was lost and nobody, not even the *Comte* could save her from an Englishman and England.

For one despairing moment she felt like running away and refusing to meet the Duke.

She could almost feel her feet carrying her towards the door and she knew the consternation such an action would cause.

But all the years of discipline in doing the right thing made her walk on beside her father until he stopped and she knew this was the moment when her fate was sealed, and the man she loved had failed.

She wished the floor would open up and swallow her, she wished she could die.

Nevertheless she stood there stiff and tense, and because she dared not look at the man she was forced to take as a husband, she could not raise her eyes.

"So here you are, Zena!" she heard her mother's voice say.

Then a reply was unnecessary because her father interposed before the Arch-Duchess had even finished speaking by saying:

"Let me present, Zena, the Duke of Faverstone, who is an unexpected but very welcome guest."

Automatically Zena put out her hand.

She felt it taken in a strong grasp, and a deep voice said:

"I am enchanted to meet Your Royal Highness!"

There was something familiar in the tone and the fingers holding hers seemed somehow significant.

Slowly, as if she was compelled to do so, Zena raised her eyes.

Then she knew that she was either dreaming or had gone mad.

It was Jean she was looking at, Jean tall, dark and handsome with a smile on his lips and his eyes looking into hers with an expression of love which only she would understand.

For a moment she felt as if she had stopped breathing.

Then because it was so incredible and overwhelming she felt as if everything swam dizzily round her and she must faint.

With his hand still holding hers firmly, he said almost beneath his breath, and yet she heard:

"I told you to believe in me."

~

The platform was covered with a red carpet and the Royal Train gleaming white and red with new paint was waiting.

The applause of the crowd which had been deafening all the way from the Palace to the station could still be heard as the Royal Party accompanied the bride and bridegroom to the train.

Outside the door leading onto the platform Princess Marie-Thérèse, Duchess of Faverstone and her husband started to say goodbye to their relatives and the other Royal guests who were waiting to see them off on their honeymoon.

They were "going away" much later than was usual because they had stayed for the Royal Banquet which had followed the marriage.

The Banquet should have taken place according to custom on the previous evening, but the Duke's horse had won the *Prix d'Or* on that afternoon and as was traditional he was the guest of honour at the Jockey Club Dinner which was always held after the race-meeting.

It had been anticipated that this might happen and therefore the Banquet which had to be held while the visiting Royalty was still in the Capital had been postponed to the next evening.

It had been a long day of ceremony, and yet Zena was not tired.

She was so happy, so excited and thrilled that she felt as if she was flying on wings of ecstasy, and it was all part of a rapturous dream.

She had hardly had a chance of being alone with the Duke since she had discovered that he was the *Comte*.

She had a thousand questions to ask him once they could be together and not feel they were being chaperoned and watched so that it was difficult to talk about anything but commonplace subjects which could be safely overheard.

The Duke had spent two nights in the Palace after she had learnt who he was before returning to England to inform the Queen and his other relatives of their engagement.

They had actually been allowed only five minutes alone in which he was supposed to ask her formally to marry him.

How could they spend those few precious seconds talking when he could be kissing her?

"Is it true ... is it really ... true that you are the ... Duke of Faverstone?" Zena managed to gasp disbelievingly as he took his lips for one second from hers.

"I asked myself very much the same question when Zena Castelnaud told me she was the Princess Marie-Thérèse," he replied.

Then he was kissing her again and explanations were unnecessary.

As Kendric said goodbye to his sister he said in a mischievous whisper that only she could hear:

"I bet you are thanking your lucky stars that you came with me to Paris!"

"I shall always be very, very grateful to you for thinking of such a reprehensible escapade," Zena replied.

The twins smiled at each other and Zena was grateful that Kendric was happy too.

The evening they had arrived back from Ettengen, when the guests in the Red Drawing-Room were proceeding upstairs to change for dinner, the Arch-Duke had said to him:

"By the way, Kendric, our plans have changed. You are not to go to Düsseldorf after all!"

Kendric had looked at his father hopefully.

"The Minister of Defence thinks that Germany is determined sooner or later to invade France, and it is essential for us not to appear to give Bismarck any encouragement."

"I certainly agree with that, Papa!" Kendric said.

"What we have therefore decided," the Arch-Duke went on as if he had not spoken, "is that we should send a Military Mission under General Nieheims to visit England and various countries in Europe, and you will accompany the General."

He saw the excitement in his son's face and there was a smile on his lips as the Arch-Duke added:

"I think you will be glad to hear that the General's first visit will be to Paris."

"That is marvellous news, Papa!" Kendric exclaimed.

The Arch-Duke put his hand on his son's shoulder.

"I knew that would please you, and I wish I could come too."

"Perhaps it would be a good idea, Sir, if you joined me while I am there, to see how I am behaving on such an important mission."

The Arch-Duke laughed.

"I see, Kendric, you already have the makings of a Diplomat. I shall certainly consider your suggestion."

Father and son smiled at each other in conspiratorial fashion, then Kendric ran up the stairs to burst into Zena's bedroom to tell her his good news.

Because they had both been so happy they hugged each other as they had done when they were children.

"Will you see Yvonne in Paris?" Zena asked.

"I may set my sights somewhat higher," Kendric answered.

"But I am sure you will not be able to afford jewels from Massin's," Zena said and they both laughed.

Now after Zena had said goodbye to Kendric she kissed her mother, then her father.

"I wish you every happiness, my dearest," the Arch-Duke said.

"I am already happier than I have ever been in my whole life, Papa!" Zena replied.

He looked a little surprised, but her answer pleased him.

He supposed there was no point in saying so, but he had always bitterly regretted that his oldest child had been obliged to marry a man she disliked and who had made her so unhappy.

But there was no doubt as the train moved out of the station and Zena waved goodbye from the windows of the Saloon that her eyes were shining, and there was a radiance about her that seemed somehow to have transmitted itself to her bridegroom.

When the Royal Party was out of sight Zena turned to look at the Duke.

Their eyes met and she felt as if she was already in his arms.

Then he said without touching her:

"You have had a very long day, my darling. I suggest you go to bed, while I rid myself of this finery."

Zena gave a little laugh.

"You look very magnificent."

The Duke was wearing the uniform of a Colonel-in-Chief of the Royal Horseguards, his chest ablaze with decorations which Zena knew when they had time she must ask him to explain to her.

She thought it was impossible for any man to look more magnificent, more distinguished or more lovable.

"I am not going to tell you what you look like until later," the Duke was saying. "It is however, something I am longing to do, so I beg you to hurry."

She gave him a little smile and moved across the Saloon towards the bedroom coach which it adjoined.

Zena knew the train well because her father always used it when he travelled not only in Wiedenstein, but to neighbouring Kingdoms and other parts of the Empire.

But she had never slept, of course, in the main bedroom which had been redecorated in time for her wedding.

It was the Duke who thought up the plausible excuse that they must be married with such unprecedented speed because his mother was in ill-health. If she died he would be in mourning and unable to marry for a year.

Zena was to find when she reached England that while her mother-in-law was under her Doctor's supervision, she was not on the danger list. In fact it was anticipated that she had many years of useful life in front of her.

Everyone in Wiedenstein was galvanised into immediate action by the Duke's insistence.

Zena watched the Duke's horse win the *Prix d'Or* then married him the next day and the whole country was wildly excited with the speed and thrill of it all.

At first her father and even more her mother had disapproved of what they called "this very unseemly haste." But that morning as Zena drove beside him in the State Coach to the Cathedral the Arch-Duke had said:

"If you ask me, it has done the whole of Wiedenstein good to be shaken out of their usual lazy lethargy by your wedding."

Zena turned her head for a moment to look at her father.

"Do you mean that, Papa?"

"I do," the Arch-Duke replied, "and because they have had to hustle and bustle to put up the decorations and to accommodate the huge crowds that have come into the Capital, I think we as a country have entered a new era of increased productivity."

Zena drew in her breath.

"It is all due to Jean," she wanted to say or rather "John" as she was now told to call him.

Then she thought he could not take all the credit, only love could do that.

Now, as she entered the State Bedroom which had gold and white walls and blue silk curtains which matched her eyes, she felt like blushing.

The bed seemed to fill the small compartment, and as the lady's-

367

maid took off her tiara and removed the glittering silver and diamanté gown she had worn for the Banquet, Zena's eyes kept straying to the lace-trimmed pillows bearing the Royal Insignia.

She was thinking she was glad they were to spend tonight in the train instead of in the *Duc* de Soisson's Chateau which had been lent to them for their honeymoon in France.

At the Chateau, although they would be alone, there would be servants to wait on them, and inevitably when they arrived there would be a long line of officials and staff to be presented.

But tonight there was only a lady's-maid for her and a valet for the Duke and when they had retired to the coach where the other servants slept, she would be alone with her husband.

Zena knew too that the train was travelling for only a short distance before it stopped in a siding for the night.

Then there would be no rumble of wheels to prevent her from hearing the words of love which she knew the Duke was longing to say to her, just as she had so much to say to him.

Wearing a diaphanous nightgown of chiffon trimmed with lace which had come from Paris, and which the Arch-Duchess had said she considered extremely immodest, Zena got into bed.

It was very soft and comfortable and the sheets felt cool after the heat of the day.

The maid picked up her gown and looked around to see that everything was tidy before she curtsied.

"*Bon soir*, Your Royal Highness!"

"*Bon soir*, Louise," Zena replied.

Now she was alone, and there was only one shaded light left by the side of the bed.

She waited, her heart beating frantically in her breast, as the door opened and the Duke came in.

She felt as if he was enveloped with light as he had been when she had seen him standing against the sunshine in the Sitting-Room in the Rue St. Honoré.

She knew now that it was the light of love which seemed to burn through them both.

With her red-gold hair falling over her shoulders, her blue eyes very wide and shining in her small face, the Duke thought it was impossible for anybody to look lovelier, and at the same time so pure and untouched.

He could see very clearly the outline of her breasts beneath the chiffon of her nightgown, but he knew that his feelings were at the moment more spiritual than physical, even though he desired her wildly as a woman.

She had aroused in him feelings of reverence and inspiration which had never happened with any woman he had known before.

It was not something that could be put into words: it was something they both knew vibrated from each to the other.

It lifted their souls towards the sky, and would, the Duke knew, make them better and finer people because they had found each other.

Zena was waiting for him to speak and after a moment he said:

"Have you any idea how beautiful you are?"

"That was what I . . . wanted you to say," she answered. "I wanted you to tell me how . . . glad you . . . are that I am . . . your wife."

"Let me try to put it into words, my darling," the Duke said. "I feel as if I have moved Heaven and earth to make you mine, and yet really I have done nothing. Fate did it for us."

"The fate which . . . took me to . . . Paris to find . . . you," Zena said.

She put out her hands to clasp his as she said:

"Do you realise that if we had not met in such a strange way which I know . . . shocked you . . . I would perhaps be . . . hating you at this . . . moment because you are English . . . and it might have taken me a very long time to realise that you were very . . . very different from what I . . . expected."

The Duke smiled.

"I am quite certain that the moment I saw the Princess Marie-Thérèse I should have fallen in love with her," he said, "as I fell in love with a lovely red-lipped Zena Bellefleur."

"If we are honest," Zena said, "what you felt for the girl in the next box was not the . . . love we have for . . . each other now."

"Perhaps not," the Duke conceded. "At the same time the moment I looked at you and heard your voice, something very strange happened to my heart."

"Is . . . that . . . true?"

"It is the truth," he said firmly. "But you have not yet asked me why I was in Paris and not under my own name."

"I have never had the chance," Zena answered.

The Duke laughed.

"When I see how wrapped around you were at home with chaperons, ladies-in-waiting and protocol," he said, "I find it understandable that you wanted to run away."

"I never expected that an Englishman would . . . understand that," Zena teased. "But then how many Englishmen would . . . pretend to be French?"

"What I have not had time to tell you," the Duke said, "is that my father's mother—my grandmother—was French. As you can guess she was a de Graumont."

He smiled before he went on:

"Whenever I wished to leave England, I have always stayed with one of my many de Graumont relations in France, as I used to do when I was a boy, or I have called myself '*le Comte de Graumont*'."

"So you could have fun!" Zena finished.

"It made it possible to avoid having to spend hours of boredom at the Tuilleries Palace with the Emperor and Empress. An English Duke suffers nearly as much as a Royal Princess!"

"So, like me, you were escaping when you went to the Artists' Ball."

"Exactly!" the Duke said. "And do you know from whom on that occasion I was running away?"

"Who?"

"Somebody called the Princess Marie-Thérèse of Wiedenstein," the Duke replied.

Zena looked at him wide-eyed and he explained:

"When I was told it was the wish of the Queen that I should marry a somewhat obscure European Princess, I was horrified!"

"You had no . . . wish to . . . marry?"

"Of course not!" the Duke replied. "I was perfectly happy as a bachelor, and although I would not pretend that I have not enjoyed many love-affairs, I had never met a woman I wanted to be my wife."

"Why could you not have . . . rejected the proposal of . . . marrying me?" Zena asked.

"You will find when we reach England that it is very difficult to refuse anything the Queen desires," the Duke said with a twist of his lips. "But I was indeed longing to defy Her Majesty and in order to think out how I would do so, I escaped to Paris."

"And what did you intend to do in Paris?" Zena asked.

The Duke's eyes sparkled as he replied.

"I will confess that I was looking for amusement."

"The sort of . . . amusement you would find with . . . a *demi-mondaine?*"

"Exactly!"

Zena gave a little cry.

"Suppose I had met you too late and you had already found someone else to amuse you like the women who dined with the Prince Napoleon, then you might never have come to Wiedenstein!"

"I had decided after I had met you that one way I could avoid being forced to marry Princess Marie-Thérèse," the Duke replied, "was to accept your father's invitation but ask if I could bring my wife to watch the *Prix d'Or.*"

Zena laughed and said:

"I am so . . . glad, so very . . . very . . . glad that you fell . . . in love with me!"

"How could I help it," the Duke asked, "when not only are you the loveliest person I have ever seen in my life, but there is something more than that? Perhaps it is that we have been together in other lives or quite simply that we are each the other half of the other."

His voice deepened as he said the last word and now he bent forward to put his arms around Zena to kiss her.

Her lips were waiting for his and as he felt the softness and warmth of her body beneath his hands he drew her closer and still closer.

To Zena it was as if the Gates of Heaven opened and she stepped inside.

Thrill after thrill rippled through her until they were so intense, so vivid, that they were almost in pain.

Yet it was a wonder of wonders and everything she had longed for and prayed she might find.

Then the Duke released her and as she gave a little cry at losing him she realised he had pulled off his robe and lifted the sheet and was getting into bed beside her.

The train had come to a standstill without their realising it. Everything was very quiet and as the Duke put his arms around Zena again and drew her body close against him she said breathlessly:

"I feel . . . this is like the . . . little hut where I thought we could . . . live if we . . . ran away together, and where I would . . . look after you and . . . love you."

"It does not matter where we are," the Duke answered. "I want your love, my darling, and I will look after you now and for the rest of our lives."

He pulled her closer as he added:

"Never again, my precious, beautiful little wife, will you do anything outrageous, because I shall not only be afraid of losing you, but I shall also be a very jealous husband."

"As I shall be . . . a jealous wife," Zena said. "Suppose after we have been married for a while you . . . go to Paris to find . . . one of those . . . beautiful women whom you will . . . bedeck with jewels because she . . . amuses you?"

"If I go to Paris," the Duke said, "you will come with me. Then, my darling, I shall not go through the agonies of having to leave you at the door of your apartment."

"Was it . . . agony?"

"I wanted you and you excited me," the Duke said. "But there was something very pure about you, my darling, despite your red lips, which made me feel it was like an armour protecting you."

"Oh, Jean, you say such wonderful things to me," Zena cried, "and I am glad that I made you . . . feel that way."

"You still do," the Duke said, "and so my precious, now you are my wife I will be very gentle and will try not to hurt or shock you."

"How . . . could you do . . . that when I . . . love you and I . . . belong to you," Zena asked.

She paused for a moment before she said in a whisper hiding her face against his neck:

"I know I am . . . very ignorant and you will have to . . . tell me what a . . . man and a . . . woman do when they . . . make love . . . but whatever it is . . . because it is you . . . it will be . . . glorious and . . . wonderful . . . like when you kiss me . . . and I feel as if it is . . . part of the sunshine and . . . God."

She felt the Duke draw in his breath.

Then very gently he kissed her eyes, her straight little nose and the softness of her cheeks.

Her lips were ready for his, but instead the Duke kissed her neck and when he felt Zena quiver with the sensations he aroused in her he pulled her nightgown off her shoulder and kissed it.

His lips moved over her skin lower and lower until he found her breast.

His mouth made Zena feel so wildly excited that her whole body moved against his as if to music.

He raised his head to look down at her.

"Am I arrogant or insensitive?" he asked and his voice was very deep and passionate.

"N—no . . . no," Zena answered.

"Am I cold?"

She gave a cry that was half a laugh and put her arms round his neck.

"You are . . . warm . . . marvellous . . . wonderful . . . and very . . . very . . . loving."

Then the Duke took her lips captive, kissed her possessively, demandingly and passionately. Yet at the same time there was an underlying tenderness she could not explain, but knew was even more wonderful than his kisses had been before.

She could feel his hands touching her body, arousing in her unknown thrills which swept through her like shafts of sunlight, growing more and more intense until they turned from the gold of the sun to the crimson of fire.

Then as she felt the fire on the Duke's lips a flame rose within her and she wanted him to hold her closer and still closer.

She did not understand what she wanted but she knew that without it she would feel incomplete and not entirely his.

"Love me . . . I . . . want you to . . . love me," she cried. "Please . . . please . . . teach me about . . . love."

Her words made the fire in the Duke and within herself burn more fiercely and its flames leapt higher and higher.

It carried them both on the wings of ecstasy towards the heart of the sun and they were one.

The River
of Love

AUTHOR'S NOTE

Many Greeks visited ancient Egypt, but it was the Romans who began collecting Egyptian antiquities, and Sphinxes and statues of the Pharaohs adorned the Palaces of the Roman Emperors.

Demand for antiques from Europe in the early 1830s encouraged tomb-robbing. In this way, the great collections of the British Museum, the Louvre, Berlin, etc., were built up. The Valley of the Kings, however, aroused only a lukewarm interest until in 1922, when Howard Carter, financed by Lord Carnaervon, discovered the tomb of Tutankhamen.

On my first visit to Luxor in the '20s, I met Howard Carter at the Tomb and saw the dazzling display of treasures it contained.

The magic I felt then in Luxor was intensified on my second visit, over thirty years later, into a spiritual awareness which I have tried to portray in this novel.

CHAPTER ONE

1892

"*I* HAVE SOMETHING to tell you."

The Duke of Darleston, who was just thinking sleepily that he should return to his own bedroom, roused himself to ask:

"What is it?"

"Edward Thetford has asked me to—marry him!"

There was silence before the Duke said:

"I think you would be wise to accept him, Myrtle. He is slightly pompous but rich and good-natured."

There was no response for a moment. Then Lady Garforth said hesitantly:

"I suppose—you would not—marry me?"

The Duke smiled.

"I cannot remember if it was Oscar Wilde or Lillie Langtry who said that a good lover makes a bad husband."

"It was the Prince of Wales!" Lady Garforth replied. "And it is certainly true where he is concerned."

"As it would be for me."

"We have been so happy," Myrtle Garforth said with a little sob in her voice, "and I love you, Dasher, as you well know."

"Thetford will make you a good husband. Does he know about us?"

377

"I am quite sure he suspects, but it is not something he would put into words, and he certainly would not embarrass me by asking questions!"

The Duke laughed.

"If I know Thetford, he will know only what he wants to know and will ignore the rest. Marry him, Myrtle. You will be able to twist him round your little finger, and the Thetford diamonds, which I believe are very fine, will become you."

There was silence again.

Then Lady Garforth exclaimed tearfully: "Oh, Dasher!" and turned to hide her face against his shoulder.

The Duke held her close and thought as he did so that she was a very sweet person and he was very fond of her.

They had enjoyed a fiery but at the same time an amicable relationship for the last five months. Inevitably, however, he had found himself thinking that Myrtle's love tied him to her, and if there was one thing of which he was afraid, it was of being tied.

The Duke's nickname of "Dasher" was an extremely apt one, and he had earned it from the moment he was born.

His father, the fourth Duke, had just watched his horse *The Dasher* pass the winning-post on the Epsom Race-Course a length in front of the rest of the field, when his Comptroller, pushing his way through the crowds outside the Jockey Club, came to his side.

For a moment it was difficult to speak to his Master because his friends were congratulating him on his win.

"Well done!"

"A tremendous victory!"

"The Blue Riband of the Turf, and nobody deserves it more!"

The Duke was just about to move away to see his jockey weigh in, when he found his Comptroller at his elbow.

"Excuse me, Your Grace."

"What is it, Hunter?" the Duke asked testily.

"Her Grace has just been delivered of a son!"

"A son?" The Duke roared out the word and his voice arrested the attention of quite a number of men near him.

"A son! At last!" he ejaculated.

His closest friends echoed the cry, well aware that after four daughters, a son was what the Duke wanted more than anything else in the world.

Then he laughed and it shook his large frame.

"A son, and three weeks early!" he cried. "It seems to me he intends to be a bit of a Dasher too!"

From that moment, the Marquis of Darle was never known by any other name.

He was duly christened after his grandfather, his God-parents, and his mother's favourite brother, but he became The Dasher by name and inevitably The Dasher by nature.

Extremely good-looking, by the time he left Eton it seemed as if few women could resist his engaging smile and what was undoubtedly a raffish face.

It was easy to understand why he was so irresistible.

It was not only his good looks, his social position, and the immense wealth of the Darleston family. It was because he found life an exciting, amusing adventure.

"What the hell have you got to be so happy about?" his friends would sometimes ask, when he seemed to radiate a joy of living which they somehow missed.

But it meant that nothing lasted permanently where The Dasher was concerned, least of all women.

As he grew older, they came into his life in such numbers that even the most inveterate gossips lost count.

The strange thing, unusual in most men's *affaires de coeur,* was that the women he loved so fleetingly were seldom bitter or even resentful when he parted from them.

Undoubtedly many of them had aching hearts, but in some extraordinary and quite unusual way they thought of The Dasher with gratitude for the happiness he had given them and were prepared to defend him against his enemies.

It was inevitable that quite a number of people, especially men, were jealous and envied him, but he also had many friends who were concerned with him as a person and with his sporting rather than his amatory activities.

There was little in the Sporting World which The Dasher had not attempted. He raced his own horses, riding even in the Grand National, and had made his name in the Polo-Field.

He had sailed his own yacht in the races at Cowes, and had nearly been drowned trying to beat the record when paddling a light canoe.

As a fast bowler he had captained the First Eleven at Eton, owned the champion greyhound for two years, and naturally was Master of his own foxhounds.

The shooting on his Estates had been greatly improved since he had inherited the title, and the Prince of Wales had said only the previous year that he would rather shoot at Darle Castle than anywhere else.

All these interests, numerous though they were, seemed to leave The Dasher time to want more and yet more out of life.

"It is almost," somebody had once said, "as if he is racing against time, or perhaps seeking something that he is afraid he may miss if he does not hurry."

It was as if this idea came to Myrtle Garforth's mind now, as she asked:

"What are you looking for in a wife, Dasher?"

"I have no intention of getting married," the Duke replied.

"But you will have to sooner or later. Do not forget, your father had four daughters before you arrived."

"My relatives leave me no choice of forgetting that!"

He was thinking, and he was very honest with himself, that it was not surprising that he had been spoilt as a child.

His four sisters had adored him, and as far as his father was concerned the sun and the moon rose for him alone.

He remembered his mother, when he was very small saying:

"You must not spoil him. If you give him his own way in everything, he will be impossible by the time he grows up."

What had saved the Duke from becoming impossible was the fact that he was extremely intelligent.

He was well aware of his good fortune in being born into a family which was respected and admired by everyone from the Monarch downwards. Even the Queen, extremely critical of the nobility, especially those who surrounded her son, had no fault to find with the fourth Duke and his wife.

And although some of the present Duke's more outrageous exploits must have been repeated to her, she treated him with an indulgence that she seldom granted to any other young man of his age.

The Duke's critics said sourly that Her Majesty had always been susceptible to flattery.

But actually the Duke did not flatter the Queen. He merely talked to her, as he talked to every women, as if he found her both attractive and interesting.

And like all women the Queen responded to it like a flower opening its petals to the sun.

In fact, the only problem in his life, if you could call it that, was how to avoid being married to one of the innumerable females who were determined by hook or by crook to shackle him for life either to themselves or to their daughters.

"One day, Dasher," Myrtle Garforth said now, "you will fall in love."

For once she actually surprised the Duke.

"Are you suggesting," he enquired, "that I have never been?"

"I am not suggesting it. I am stating a fact!"

The Duke was about to laugh at her for saying something so absurd, when it suddenly struck him that it might be the truth.

He had always thought himself to be in love when he was attracted by some beautiful face turned towards his and saw two eyes looking at him with an unmistakable invitation in their depths.

Whenever he felt a response within himself and knew an irrepressible desire to kiss a pair of provocative lips, he would tell himself that Cupid had struck again and he was in love!

Now, looking back at what had invariably been a short-lived rapture, an ecstasy which had slowly but inevitably subsided, he wondered if Myrtle was right.

She was aware that she had made him think, and, settling herself a little more comfortably, she said:

"I love you, Dasher, and I know I shall love you all my life, and there will never be another man to compare with you. But I am not so foolish as to think that what you feel for me is something which will last."

"How do you know that?" the Duke enquired.

"Because, darling, you have never been in love in the way that has inspired men and women since the beginning of time so that if necessary they would be prepared to die for it."

"I understand what you are trying to say," the Duke remarked, "but do you really think that sort of love—the love of the poets, the musicians, the romantics—is likely to happen to a man like me? I am a roamer."

"Of course you are," Myrtle agreed. "But that is because you have not found what you seek."

"I am certainly not seeking love, if that is what you mean," the Duke answered sharply. "I am quite prepared to admit that what you are talking about exists, but I am very content with what I find and— enjoy."

His arm tightened round Myrtle's soft body as he said the last word, and she responded by putting her arm round his neck as if to pull his head down to hers. Then she changed her mind.

"Because I love you, Dasher," she said, "I would like you to find real happiness. And I have the feeling, although I may be wrong, that one day you will find it."

"When I do, I will let you know!" the Duke said lightly.

"No, I am serious. You give so much happiness to others, in all sorts of different ways, that I want you to find the greatest happiness which human beings can attain, and that is—real love."

"You are trying to make me dissatisfied," the Duke complained, "and I understand you think I am missing something! In which case, you know as well as I do that I shall do everything in my power to find it—and win it!"

"I hope what you are saying is true," Myrtle said, "but perhaps it would only be fair if you failed. You have too much already."

"Now I am quite certain that you are trying to punish me for saying you should marry Thetford!" the Duke exclaimed.

"That is unkind," Myrtle protested. "I only want you have the best out of life."

"That is what I thought I had already."

There was silence as the Duke thought over what she had said.

In a way it annoyed him to think she might be right.

He had always been so sure that everything he wanted was within his reach, and while he enjoyed having to strive for what he wanted, deep down he always had the conviction that sooner or later he would be the victor.

Even now it was impossible for him to believe that there was some strange sort of love which so far had evaded him.

He thought of the women with whom he had been infatuated, if that was the right word, and the pleasure they had given him and he had given them.

The excitement they had engendered together had sometimes been like fireworks sparkling against the darkness of the sky, at others like flowers growing at the water's edge and the lap of waves on golden sand.

Love, many diverse and different types of love, but always the initial fiery flames dying down to a mere glow.

"Why should I want anything different?" the Duke asked defiantly.

"I have made you think," a soft voice broke in on his thoughts, "and that is an achievement in itself."

"You are making me feel as if I were abnormal," the Duke said crossly.

"Not abnormal," Myrtle protested, "but different! A King, a Chieftain, a Pharaoh, and very different from any ordinary man I have ever known."

There was a little pause. Then the Duke said:

"Is that really the truth?"

"Of course it is," Myrtle replied. "You must be aware, Dasher, that there is nobody like you. That is what makes you so exciting. You make one feel almost as if you do not belong in these modern times but have stepped out of history or perhaps a different planet."

She gave a little laugh before she went on:

"Perhaps you have been—what is the word for having lived before and being reborn?"

"Reincarnated."

"Yes, that is it," Myrtle agreed. "Perhaps you have been reincarnated after being, as I said just now, a King in some Eastern country, or a Pharaoh in Egypt."

"Or a slave, a monkey, or a reptile!" the Duke said teasingly.

"No, that would be impossible!" Myrtle cried. "Your talents, or whatever they are, are far too developed."

In his determination not to be serious, the Duke said:

"And all this because I suggested you should accept Edward Thetford's proposal of marriage!"

"And you—refused to marry—me!"

"I want you to continue to love me," the Duke said, "and that is certainly something you would not do if I were your husband."

"It would almost be worth the—unhappiness of being—jealous like—Princess Alexandra, rather than—lose you—altogether."

The Duke did not answer, and after a moment she said:

"Very well, I shall marry Edward. But please, Dasher, let us forget him for just a little while longer."

The Duke could not resist the pleading in her voice. He turned round, pulled her nearer to him, and his lips were on hers.

But even as he kissed her, he was asking himself:
Where is the love that I am missing?

Harry Settingham was fast asleep when he became aware that some-body was pulling back the curtains over the windows, and thought before he opened his eyes that he was very tired.

He had certainly gone to bed late, and perhaps he had drunk too much of Dasher's excellent wine, for he certainly had no wish at the moment to face another day.

He suddenly realised that it was not his valet who had opened the curtains to let in the daylight, but somebody very much larger, who now advanced to sit down on the end of his bed.

"Dasher!" he exclaimed. "What do you want so early?"

"I want to talk to you, Harry."

With an effort, Harry opened his eyes wider.

"What about! What time is it?"

"About six o'clock, I think."

"Six o'clock? Good Heavens, Dasher, what has happened?"'

"I have decided to go exploring and I want you to come with me!"

"Exploring?"

With an effort, Harry Settingham moved himself higher against his pillows before he asked:

"What has upset you?"

"Nothing has upset me," the Duke replied. "I have merely decided that I want to get away from all the things we have been doing week after week, month after month, with monotonous regularity."

"I think you are mad!" Harry Settingham exclaimed. "Anything less monotonous than your life I cannot imagine! You were hunting in Leicestershire last week, and we were supposed to be hunting to-morrow, if the ground is not too hard, and yet you talk of going away!"

"I am leaving for Egypt immediately!"

"Egypt!" Harry cried. "What on earth for?"

"I think it will be interesting, and I want to see the land of the Pharaohs."

"I am not sure I wish to look at a lot of old ruins," Harry said.

"Bertie went there last year and said it was a 'dead and alive' place, except that there were some pretty dancers in Cairo."

"I am not going for that sort of thing," the Duke said. "I am serious, Harry. I want to look into the past of Egypt, and see other parts of the world."

"Are you bored with Myrtle?" Harry asked, as if the idea had suddenly come to him.

"I am very fond of Myrtle," the Duke said firmly, "but Thetford has asked her to marry him and I have advised her to accept."

"So he has come up to scratch, has he?" Harry remarked. "The betting at White's since you took over was that he would cool off."

"You can always be quite certain that any conclusion reached by members of White's, who have nothing else to do, is invariably wrong!"

Harry laughed.

"What you are really saying is that you dislike their talking about your private affairs. Good Heavens, Dasher, you must be aware that you bring light and laughter into their otherwise rather dull lives."

The Duke laughed too, as if he could not help it.

"I suppose in that case I must be willing to oblige," he remarked. "But you have not yet accepted my invitation."

"To come to Egypt with you? Of course, if you want me. Who else are you thinking of taking?"

"I am not quite certain," the Duke said. "It is something I want to discuss with you."

"At this hour of the morning?"

"As I wish to leave as soon as possible, the invitations will have to be sent out immediately."

Harry put back his head against the pillows and laughed.

"That, Dasher, is exactly like you! Most people, if they are going abroad for any length of time, especially to places they have never visited before, spend months preparing for it. All right, you win! And I will not protest about losing my 'beauty sleep.'"

"You can make up for it on the voyage," the Duke said unfeelingly. "Now, who will be amusing for what may be quite a considerable length of time?"

There was an hour's discussion before finally they chose four people.

Harry Settingham had been the Duke's closest friend all through his life. They had been at Eton together, had gone up to Oxford together, and both had served for three years in the Household Brigade until the Duke had inherited the title.

Although he had enjoyed the comradeship in his Regiment, he had longed for the activity of war, which had not come their way, owing to the fact that the Household Brigade was so seldom sent abroad.

Camps and manoeuvres were not the same thing, and Harry had been aware that The Dasher was already champing at the bit when, on his father's death, he could resign with dignity and without reproach.

Because the two men were such close friends, it had been assumed that Harry Settingham would follow the Duke's example.

It was also generally accepted that Harry had a restraining influence on The Dasher, but only he knew that actually nobody had any influence on a man who was unique, especially when it came to intellect.

If Myrtle Garforth thought the Duke had never been in love, Harry was sure of it.

He told himself it was unlikely that the Duke would ever find any woman to satisfy him while there were so many who could offer him the physical attractions of Venus but who could not hold his mind as well as his body.

Now as he listened to the Duke planning their trip to Egypt, he told himself that he might have expected it, since he had been aware that The Dasher's interest in Myrtle Garforth was inevitably waning.

He had always liked Myrtle and thought her one of the nicest and most understanding of the many lovely women with whom the Duke had been enamoured.

She was kind to other women, pleasant to the Duke's friends, and he had never heard her say anything spiteful or unkind about anybody.

At the same time, while she had an average intelligence, she was not well read.

Very few women were, when inevitably their education had been entrusted to one badly paid Governess who had been expected to teach every subject in the curriculum.

This was the ordinary, accepted pattern in any aristocratic household, where every penny was expended on the sons and as little as possible on the daughters.

Kept in the School-Room, out of touch with ordinary everyday life until the moment they made their début, the girls were then supposed to blossom like flowers and make a distinguished Social marriage within the first two years of their "coming out."

This was, of course, arranged by their mothers with little or no regard for the daughters' feelings in the matter.

Only when they had the ring on their finger and were able to enjoy the company of other young married women did they develop the sophistication and poise expected of them.

The extraordinary thing, Harry had often thought, was that they did in fact become elegant and witty, with a polish and a sophistication that made them outstanding even in other countries.

The ladies who centred round the Prince of Wales were obvious examples of those qualities, and although The Dasher and Harry were almost a generation younger, they expected the same standard from their contemporaries.

It is a pity about Myrtle, Harry thought now, *but doubtless her place will soon be filled.*

Aloud he asked:

"Are you really intending to include Lady Cairns in your party?"

When the Duke had first mentioned her name, Harry had hesitated because he thought that although she was extremely beautiful, she might not have the same kind nature as Myrtle.

Lily Cairns had obviously aroused the Duke's interest the previous week when he had been introduced to her at Marlborough House.

Because she had been living in the North, she was new to London, but there was nothing countrified about her appearance.

With her auburn hair, her white skin, and a slightly enigmatic look in her eyes, she had caught everybody's attention when she had appeared, including that of the Prince.

"This is your first visit to Marlborough House?" Harry had heard His Royal Highness ask in his deep, rather guttural voice. "I understand you have only just arrived in London."

"I have been living in Scotland, Sire."

"And has the 'Land of the Haggis' so much to offer that it has made you neglect us here in the South?" the Prince enquired.

The smile that Lily had given the elderly Prince was very enticing.

"I have merely returned home, Sire, now that I am a widow."

Later in the evening Harry had seen the Duke gravitating irresistibly towards the corner of the room where Lady Cairns was undoubtedly "holding court."

Although he had not realised it at the time, he knew now that it had been the moment when Myrtle's fate was sealed, for The Dasher was once again drawn to a new and lovely face.

In answer to Harry's question, the Duke said now quite seriously:

"Lily Cairns has lived in Scotland for so long that she should be used to a certain amount of hardship, not that I expect there will be much aboard *The Mermaid*."

"I hope not," Harry said. "If I am to be uncomfortable, I have no intention of going with you."

"After that extremely selfish remark," the Duke said, "I shall take you riding in the middle of the desert on a camel. You are getting soft, Harry, and it would doubtless do you good to climb to the top of one of the pyramids."

"I refuse to talk about this absurd trip any longer," Harry complained. "I want to go back to sleep. Arrange anything you like—bring anyone with us who will amuse you, not me, so that you will not be bored stiff within twenty-four hours, and I am prepared, O Master, to obey thy command!"

The Duke laughed.

"All right, Harry, go to sleep. I will have everything arranged, including an alluring houri to keep you amused."

"You can pick one up in Cairo," Harry replied. "Remember, Dasher, most women do not look their best when they are being seasick!"

The Duke laughed again, walked to the window to flick back the curtains, and left the room.

Harry shut his eyes, but, not unnaturally, he did not fall asleep immediately.

Instead, he was thinking that it was very like the Duke suddenly to move to pastures new.

It was in fact one of the things that made him so interesting, when like a small boy he would play truant on all his responsibilities and embark on some new adventure without the slightest hesitation or any anticipation of whether it would be a success or a failure.

It was what made life with him so interesting, Harry thought. Then he came to the conclusion that it was surprising that it had not happened earlier.

It was now nearly a year since the Duke had rushed off at a moment's notice to do something entirely different from what anybody might have expected of him.

The reason for his being almost static was that before Myrtle he had had an extremely passionate love-affair, which had lasted for seven or eight months, with the wife of a famous Politician.

The reason that it had lasted so long was that they could not be together as much as they wished.

Although the lady's husband was conveniently kept busy at the House of Commons, she also had to spend quite a considerable amount of time with him in his Constituency and accompanying him on occasional trips abroad.

Surprisingly, because it was unusual, The Dasher's heart seemed to grow fonder in her absence, and he was awaiting her eagerly on her return.

She was certainly, Harry had thought at the time, well worth waiting for.

Her beauty at twenty-seven was at its height, and she was half-Russian, which gave her a mysterious allure that seemed to hold the Duke as if it were a magnet.

And yet, even with her the affair, as happened with all his other loves, had ground to a halt, and although nobody was surprised, Harry had anticipated the inevitable.

The Dasher had found that there was nothing more to know or to discover about the lady in question, and therefore he was no longer interested.

It was Harry who was aware that the Duke really took from the women who loved him all they had to give, then when his curiosity was assuaged he needed fresh stimulus from someone else.

Although he had the greatest admiration and deepest affection for his friend, he sometimes wondered if the Duke was too richly endowed by nature.

It was not fair for one man to have so much and to expect to find the counterpart of himself in a female body.

But there was certainly no point in worrying about a man who seemed so happy and who enjoyed life with an exuberance which everybody with whom he came in contact found infectious.

When the Duke entered a room, the tempo seemed to quicken.

Women became brighter and more animated, men wittier and more amusing.

Harry often thought that the most ordinary, boring party could be transformed when the Duke was a guest.

It was one of the reasons why every hostess prayed that he would accept her invitation and was genuinely elated by the sight of him when he appeared.

"Egypt!" Harry exclaimed to himself. "Now, why on earth would The Dasher want to go there, of all places?"

He felt personally that ruins were invariably depressing, and the Mummies of those who had been dead for centuries were not the sort of women the Duke would find interesting.

Still, it was something new!

He had never been to Egypt, nor had the Duke, and the idea of steaming up the Nile in *The Mermaid* would certainly be different from chasing a fox or watching The Dasher's superb horses moving far too easily in the Spring Steeple-Chases.

"Anyway, we will have Lily!" Harry said to himself.

He closed his eyes and fell asleep.

CHAPTER TWO

*L*ILY CAIRNS STEPPED OUT of the old-fashioned carriage in which she had been driving in the Park, and, carrying her muff which was of sable, walked slowly up the steps and into the Hall of the house in Belgrave Square.

The Butler, grey-haired and slightly bent with age, said in the loud voice of someone who is deaf:

"The Duke of Darleston has called to see you, M'Lady!"

Lily stood still for a moment. Then with a composure which she was far from feeling she asked:

"Is His Grace in the Drawing-Room?"

"Yes, M'Lady."

Lily hesitated, then with a swiftness which was echoed by the beat of her heart she ran upstairs to her bedroom, pulling off her long fur-trimmed coat before she reached the door.

She flung both her coat and her muff down on the bed and moved quickly to the dressing-table to remove her very attractive bonnet.

As she did so, she looked at her reflection in the mirror, and her eyes, which had been wide with excitement, narrowed a little as she concentrated.

This was what she had expected. This was what she had prayed for!

Now the Duke was waiting for her downstairs, and she had taken the first step towards her goal.

Lily Cairns was shrewd, calculating, and insatiably ambitious. She had determined since the age of fifteen not to be crushed by poverty or to live a nondescript life as a nobody in the wilds of Perthshire.

Her father, Roland Standish, who was a gentleman but an impoverished one, had, because he was keen on sport, accepted the position of Agent on the large Estate of Sir Ewan Cairns when Lily was twelve years old.

Before that they had lived in the South, but her father had disliked being too poor to afford horses for riding and hunting, and he found it more and more difficult to patronise the best Clubs or even to pay the rent for his lodgings in London.

Lily's mother had fortunately died when she was very young.

Being a sharp-witted child, Lily had soon learnt that there was some mystery about her mother, and her father's relatives spoke of her with pursed lips.

Other people insinuated, although they did not actually say so, that it was lucky for Lily and her father that she was no longer with them.

When Lily questioned her aunts, all they said was that her mother had "gone to God."

But it was obvious from the tone of their voices and the expression in their eyes that they thought she was far more likely to be in a very different place.

It was only when she was much older that Lily learnt that her mother had been the daughter of a Wine Merchant to whom her father had owed money.

She had been exceedingly attractive, and when the Wine Merchant learnt that his daughter had been seduced by one of his largest debtors, it was not surprising that he had brought pressure to bear on him to make her an honest woman.

He also offered to write off or cancel a debt which had been outstanding for far too long.

Unfortunately, the money the Wine Merchant contributed towards the marriage came to an end with his daughter's death.

It was then that Roland Standish found the suggestion that he should go and stay with Sir Ewan Cairns in Scotland as an excuse for foisting his daughter on one of his relatives, while he tried a different life from the one he had been leading up until then.

He was in fact by nature a sportsman, and although as a game-shot he was at first, through lack of practice, not very proficient, he soon improved.

At the same time, he appreciated the large, comfortable grey-stone house on the edge of the moors and the companionship of his host.

They shot over the Estate, caught salmon in the river, and entertained the local Lairds and their wives, who were prepared to travel long distances in any sort of weather in order to enjoy congenial company.

It was only when Roland Standish suggested that he should return South that Sir Ewan offered him a house on the Estate and a salary which he felt he would be stupid to refuse.

It meant giving up the friends he had known in London, but that loss was offset by the fact that he still had a number of outstanding debts there which might be forgotten if he stayed long enough in the North.

Finally having agreed, he sent for Lily, and on her arrival was pleased to find that she had not only grown taller in her absence but had become exceedingly attractive.

To Lily, who had hated the restrictive life she had lived with her father's cousin, who seemed intent on finding fault with everything she did or thought, life in Scotland meant a new freedom and to begin with was sheer delight.

Then as the years passed she began to understand how everything depended on the whim and goodwill of her father's employer.

At over fifty, Sir Ewan was, thanks to the life he led, still a healthy, active man, and he was also an autocrat, very conscious of his ancient Scottish lineage.

Like the ancient Chieftains, he expected not only obedience but an adoration which was not so readily given as it had been in the past.

But no longer, although the change was slow in coming to the Highlands, were the servants prepared to be as subservient as they had been over the years.

Lily soon realised that Sir Ewan liked feeling that her father was completely dependent on him, and that also included herself. It became obvious that if she wanted anything special, it was not her father who provided it but Sir Ewan.

She was also aware that since his wife had died some ten years earlier, he was in many ways a lonely man.

Periodic trips occurred, which Lily understood later were to see an old friend of many years' standing who supplied the only feminine influence in his otherwise strictly masculine life.

By the time she was nearly seventeen she was aware that Sir Ewan was thinking of her not as a child but as a woman.

When her father died from pneumonia caught after being lost on the moors in a thick fog one freezing November night, Lily had decided to marry Sir Ewan long before he made up his mind to propose to her.

When the Funeral was over, looking sad but exceedingly beautiful in her black gown which had hastily been procured from Perth, she looked at him with misty, tearful eyes and asked in a low, childish voice she was often to use in the future:

"I know Papa has left—no money—and you will—want the house for another Agent—so perhaps I can find some sort of work in—Perth, if you will—help me."

It was then that Sir Ewan had offered her a wedding-ring and bought her a trousseau which had left her ecstatic with joy.

Never had she expected to own such lovely gowns, and she was not in the least fastidious about wearing the furs and jewellery which had been owned by the previous Lady Cairns.

They went to Edinburgh for three weeks, where Sir Ewan introduced his young bride to his shocked and disapproving relatives, but they were too much in awe of him to express their feelings openly.

Only Lily sensed what they were thinking, and it amused her.

There was Theatres to attend, besides Balls, Assemblies, and Receptions.

She also persuaded her husband to buy her more clothes and jewellery that was larger and more spectacular than any the first Lady Cairns ever owned or would have considered tasteful.

It was after three years of marriage that Lily began to think of her future.

She had known when she married that Sir Ewan had a son by his first wife, and although Alister had quarrelled with his father and lived in the South, he was heir to the Baronetcy and to the Estate.

It had not worried Lily at first, in fact she had not even thought about Alister Cairns, whom she had never met, as having any particular impact on her own life.

But when her husband was laid up with severe influenza after getting soaked to the skin while fishing, she was suddenly aware that if he died as her father had done, she would once again be penniless.

He had been quite frank with her soon after they were married.

"I have made a new Will," he had said, speaking in a somewhat grudging manner because he always disliked discussing his private affairs with anybody, least of all a woman. "I cannot leave you much. Everything is entailed onto Alister, and I am not a rich man."

Lily had not answered for a moment, then before she could do so Sir Ewan had continued:

"You shall have everything it is possible for me to leave you, but you will have to be frugal, which is something you do not seem capable of doing at the moment."

"I am sorry if I have done—anything—wrong," Lily said in the childlike voice which never ceased to have the right effect.

"Not wrong," Sir Ewan replied, "but you are an extravagant young puss!"

The words were not a reproof but a caress. Then he said sharply in a very different voice:

"I suppose you will marry again, and you had better see that he is a rich man."

It was perhaps that more than anything else which made Lily realise that when she was a widow she would have to find a husband, and one rich enough to keep her in the manner to which she had become accustomed since her father had died.

Edinburgh had given her a taste of Society, but by now she was well aware that what she really craved was not the Scottish Capital but the English one.

She read every magazine and the social-column of every newspaper and she also listened to what the women said, which was far more informative on this score than any information she could glean from the men.

London Society had no idea how interested other parts of the country were in its doings.

Lily learnt about the mistresses of the Prince of Wales, the fascinations of the Professional Beauties, the noblemen who surrounded His Royal Highness and who vied with one another in entertaining him at their country houses and at their shoots.

It was actually somebody talking with her husband who had first mentioned the Duke of Darleston.

"The bag at Darle Castle last week was over twenty-six hundred pheasants, Cairns!" he said. "I wish I had been there."

"I hear the new Duke has improved the shoot out of all recognition since he inherited," Sir Ewan replied. "But it is a long time since I shot a pheasant."

"How are your grouse this season?" his friend questioned, and the talk became exclusively Scottish.

Other people had talked about the Duke.

"I have never seen such an attractive man in my whole life!" Lily heard one pretty married woman say to another. "I saw him at several Balls when I was in London, and it does not surprise me that he is nicknamed 'The Dasher.' He is in fact the most dashing and exciting man one could dream about."

When on Lily's insistence Sir Ewan had taken her back to Edinburgh year after year, staying each time, because she pleaded with him, a little longer than the time before, she increased her knowledge of the Duke of Darleston.

The stories about him were stored away in her mind as a magpie hides its treasures in its nest.

She began to look for his name in the social-papers, the races in which his horses ran, and the Balls where his name was listed among the guests.

Even the Funerals where he occasionally represented either the Prince of Wales or occasionally the Queen did not escape her.

"If I ever go to London," Lily promised herself, "the first man I shall try to meet will be the Duke of Darleston!"

When Sir Ewan died after they had been married for nine years, she had everything planned.

She had been clever enough, when she realised that her husband was growing old and the snow and the cold winds in the winter often forced him to stay in bed, to accumulate everything she could against the future.

Although he had never mentioned it again, she had not forgotten that he had said he could leave her very little in his Will, and when it was read she found that that was undoubtedly the truth.

She had approximately five hundred pounds a year, while everything else in the Castle belonged to Alister, who appeared at his father's Funeral and instantly took over in a manner which told Lily without words that her days there were numbered.

Fortunately, she had anticipated what would happen, and she had already made plans for where she could stay in London.

She had learnt after she was married that Sir Ewan had a sister who had married one of the Senior Officers who had been stationed in Edinburgh Castle.

When General Sir Alexander Rushton retired, he and his wife had gone South to London, where Lily knew they had a house in Belgrave Square.

She had persuaded Sir Ewan, who did not particularly like his brother-in-law, to invite them to the opening of the grouse season on the twelfth of August.

The first year they had refused but the second year they had come, and Lily had exerted herself in every possible way to please and charm her sister-in-law.

There was no doubt that Lady Rushton had disapproved of her brother marrying again and a girl young enough to be his grand-daughter.

But Lily's deferential manner, her obvious and grateful adoration of her husband, and her desire to please would have melted a far harder heart than that of a woman who had no children of her own.

"You have been so kind—so wonderful to—me," Lily said, using again her childish voice when it was time for Lady Rushton to depart.

"I shall miss you," she added with what sounded curiously like a sob."

"And I shall miss you, dear," Lady Rushton said. "I will ask Ewan to bring you to stay with us in London. If that is not possible, I will try to persuade my husband to come back here another year."

"Oh, please—please do that!" Lily had begged.

She had sounded so sincere and in a way pathetic that Lady Rushton's maternal feelings had been aroused, and for years she replied regularly to Lily's effusive letters from the North.

After Sir Ewan's death, Lily had written to Lady Rushton asking if she could come and stay with her in London, and the answer was a spontaneous invitation to stay as long as she liked.

Lily had not rushed. She had got exactly what she wanted, and she had no intention of arriving in London wearing black, in which she always felt depressed.

She had gone instead to Edinburgh to stay with some rather dull friends she had made on her various trips who respected her for being self-effacing and very quiet in her appearance and had understood that she had no money to spend on herself.

The presents they have given her had been so enthusiastically received that both her host and hostess and a number of their friends had found themselves being unexpectedly generous to the "poor little widow."

Six months had passed quickly, and once Lily could be in half-mourning she shook the dust of Edinburgh from her feet and set off with a thrill of excitement to the South.

Lady Rushton received her with open arms.

The General was by this time practically bedridden, and she looked forward to the companionship of another woman, even one so much younger than herself.

What she had not expected was that Lily had no intention of sitting chatting or knitting by the fireside but was determined to storm Society.

By this time she had a very good idea of her own attractions.

Having no longer to act the part of being crushed by fate and perpetually on the verge of tears, she could hold her head high and demand the attention to which her lovely face entitled her.

She had spent every moment of her six months of mourning in learning all she could about the social life in which she intended to shine.

The story that Mrs. Langtry had captured first the attention of the artistic world by her beauty and finally the heart of the Prince had pointed for Lily the way to her own success.

She was not so foolish as to try to copy Mrs. Langtry in having only one black dress, but had decided she would dress entirely in white, which she knew with her red hair would look fantastic.

She was far too astute to pretend a sophistication she did not possess.

She had already learnt that everybody, men and women, like to patronise somebody they thought was humble and subservient.

Lily flattered Lady Rushton by imploring her to help in finding her another husband.

"I am so stupid and untalented," she said sadly. "I know I ought to be able to earn a little money somehow, but as that seems impossible, I must find myself a man who is kind enough to ask me to be his wife."

"That should not be difficult," Lady Rushton said, looking at Lily's pleading eyes and white skin.

"Unfortunately, I know no young, unattached men," Lily went on, "and of course when we stayed in Edinburgh we were always with dear Ewan's friends—not that I would ever have looked at anybody but him!"

"I am afraid I have been rather remiss in not attending any parties since Alexander has been ill," Lady Rushton answered. "But now, for your sake, I must make an effort, and I am sure my friends will help me."

Because Sir Alexander had been an extremely distinguished soldier, it was not difficult for Lady Rushton to call on the wives of his brother-officers and arrange for Lily to be asked to Balls, parties, and Receptions.

Lily went on a shopping expedition and bought gowns that revealed her exquisite figure and bonnets which accentuated the colour of her hair.

Lady Rushton would have been surprised if she had known how much Lily had in a secret Bank-account.

She had been systematically stealing from her husband ever since the first time he had been taken ill.

She did it so cleverly that he never suspected for an instant what was happening.

She had also insisted on having a Solicitor. He was young and impressionable, and when she told him wistfully that her elderly husband could leave her little money when he died, he was very helpful.

She offered to pay him, but instead he kissed her passionately before she left, and she enjoyed it.

On his advice, when Sir Ewan was dying she ran up huge bills in his name, which were the first call on the Estate when it was handed over to his son.

At every party men flocked to Lily's side, gazing at her with an undisguised admiration that was like sunshine breaking through the dark clouds after so many years of waiting.

Lily was wise enough to realise that for the moment women were more important than men, and she made herself so charming and again so pathetic that the Society matrons who might easily have closed their doors to her made sure that she was included in all their entertainments.

The Social World was a small one and the advent of a new face and a new beauty was passed from mouth to mouth from Belgravia to Mayfair, from Mayfair to St. James's.

Lily became a name to be mentioned in the same breath as the Professional Beauties such as Lady Randolph Churchill, Mrs. Cornwallis West, and Lady Dudley.

It was therefore inevitable that as she moved up the social ladder she should eventually meet the Prince of Wales.

At an afternoon Reception, accompanied by Lady Rushton, she was talking to somebody else when she heard a rather guttural voice ask:

"And how is your husband, Lady Rushton?"

She turned her head and saw her hostess sweeping to the ground in a low curtsey as she replied:

"A little better, Sire, and he will be very honoured that you have remembered to ask after him."

"Give him my kind regards and say I hope to see him at my next Reception."

Then the Prince of Wales's eyes were on Lily, and she was well aware why he had crossed the room to speak to her sister-in-law.

When she curtseyed with a grace that she had practised for long hours in front of the mirror, she saw that flicker of admiration in his eyes that she had expected, and she was aware that he held her hand a little longer than was necessary.

As she went home with Lady Rushton she felt as if she were dancing on air, for she had received the invitation she coveted to Marlborough House, and she thought it was possible, indeed probable, that the Duke of Darleston might be there.

She had studied *Debrett* with great care, and she had also compiled a list in her mind of a number of eligible men who might become her husband.

There were not a great many.

It was fashionable for noblemen to be married off when they were young to some eminently suitable young woman, and, having provided an heir to their title and Estates, they could then enjoy themselves, as the Prince of Wales did, with the sophisticated beauties who, Lily thought scornfully, were waiting like cormorants for a fish.

She had no intention of joining their ranks. It was not a lover she wanted, but a husband, and a husband she intended to have.

When she met the Duke she knew that her choice, which she had made many years before, was an admirable one.

By this time she was aware that his love-affairs never lasted long, but she told herself she would marry him before he grew bored, and what he did after that would not be important.

When she was in Edinburgh it had been fashionable amongst the younger women to visit a Fortune-Teller.

"She is uncanny," one of her friends had told her. "She can see things in one's past that are so secret that one has never breathed them to a living soul."

"But what about the future?" Lily had asked.

"She is infallible! Every word she says comes true!"

Lily had visited Mrs. McDonald in a back street where she received her customers.

She was an elderly Scottish woman who looked "fey" and undoubtedly had some clairvoyant ability, but Lily decided she made up what she could not "see."

At the same time, Mrs. McDonald reiterated over and over again that she had a great future in front of her.

"Ye'll walk with th' greatest in th' land," she said, rolling her *R*'s which made what she said more impressive than it might have sounded otherwise. "Ye'll glitter with jewels like a Queen, an' there'll be men, always men tae acclaim yer beauty."

She elaborated on this prophecy a little, then asked:

"Have ye a question tae ask me?"

Lily shook her head.

"I think not," she replied. "You have told me all I want to know."

The old woman look surprised.

"Wot aboot love? Theer's nay a lassie comes here as does nae wish tae talk aboot love."

Lily smiled and she went on:

"Noo look, ma dear, hearrts will be thrown at yer feet, but ye'll gie yer own, sooner or later, an' there'll be nae taken' it back."

She shut her eyes in concentration before she said:

"Noo yer heed rules yer hearrt, bu' one day yer hearrt'll win th' battle, an' ye'll find oot which is th' strongest."

The old woman looked at her.

"Remember all Ah've told ye, an' for what ye've set oot tae do, ye'll need all yer wits aboot ye."

"I will remember," Lily replied in an uninterested voice.

She put a half-guinea down on the table, thinking as she did so that it was a lot of money to spend on what her brain told her was really thought-reading, but at the same time it contributed to her self-assurance.

Now as she came down the stairs from the Second Floor to the large Drawing-Room which overlooked the trees in Belgrave Square, she told herself that everything she had planned and had worked for was coming true.

The Duke of Darleston was waiting for her and she was determined, with a cast-iron determination that had driven her to get what she wanted since she was fifteen, that he would be her husband.

The Fortune-Teller in Edinburgh had made Lily think of another way in which she could help herself.

If an old woman living in the back street could sense things about people in a way which the Scots called "fey," she was quite certain it was a power that everybody could use.

She thought it was just a question of developing it, and she had lived in Scotland for long enough to know that in every village there was some old body who was consulted about the future because she had what people called "second sight."

To Lily it was a gift which she thought she could use to further her ambitions.

If she could sense what a man was feeling and thinking, then her power over him would be even more effective than if he was just beguiled by her beauty.

She trained herself to try to see perceptively into the minds of almost everybody she met, and she thought that on a number of occasions she had been extremely successful.

At any rate it made her find out quickly what were a man's habits and interests.

Where women were concerned she had usually encouraged them to speak of their sensitivity and perhaps a secret unhappiness, and they would confide in her in a manner which certainly gave her an insight into their frustrations and miseries.

Now she told herself that if she was to captivate and hold the Duke, she must from the very beginning make him realise that she was different from all the other women with whom he had associated and of whom she had learnt he tired remarkably quickly.

She went to the Drawing-Room door.

The Duke, looking very attractive and extremely raffish, was standing amongst the old-fashioned furniture and seeming to dominate the whole room.

She stood for a moment in the doorway, conscious that with her white gown and her red hair, fortunately dressed only that morning by the hairdresser, she looked very lovely.

Her eyes were rounded with astonishment before she moved towards him.

"This is a surprise, Your Grace," she said, "and I regret to tell you that my sister-in-law is not at home."

"I came to see you," the Duke replied.

He took her hand in his and held it for a moment while he looked into her eyes, before he raised it to his lips.

"To see me?" Lily asked ingenuously.

"I think you are as aware as I was that we had not finished our conversation last evening at Marlborough House. In fact, His Royal Highness interrupted us to sweep you away from me, and I hoped you would be aware that I had not even begun what I wished to say."

It was not only what the Duke said which Lily found so enlightening, but the fact that his eyes were, she knew, taking in every facet of her face and the sweep of her long eye-lashes, and she dropped them rather shyly, as if his admiration embarrassed her.

She took her hand from his and he said:

"Come and sit down. I have an invitation to offer you which I hope you will accept."

She did not answer, but she thought that an invitation to Darle Castle was exactly what she wanted.

It would give her the chance to see the house that one day would be hers, where she would act as hostess to the whole of the Social World.

She gave him a faint smile that was a little unsure and a little questioning, as if she was not certain what his invitation would be and was already wondering how she could accept it.

She sat down on the sofa, sitting upright with her hands clasped in her lap and her face turned towards the Duke.

As she sat, she knew that her hair would be haloed by the pale winter sunshine coming in through the window behind her.

"I have decided," the Duke said, "to leave almost immediately for Egypt in my yacht, and I hope that you will join me as one of my guests."

"To Egypt?" Lily questioned.

This was something she had certainly not expected, and, being unprepared, she was not quite certain how she should reply.

At the same time, she knew with a leap of her heart that if she was alone with the Duke in his yacht on such a long voyage, it would be impossible for him to escape from her.

As she looked at the sun that had no warmth in it, the Duke said:

"I want to travel up the Nile, and I only learnt this morning for the first time that it never rains in Egypt!"

He laughed as he spoke, and Lily thought it made him even more attractive than he was before.

"You will come?" he asked.

She did not reply, and after a moment he went on:

"I have asked Lord and Lady Southwold, of whom you may have heard, and two men, James Bushly and a very old friend of mine, Harry Settingham, whom you met last evening at Marlborough House."

"Yes, of course!" Lily said.

"We will be six," the Duke said, "and I think I can promise you, Lady Cairns, a very happy and a very comfortable voyage."

There was a little pause, then Lily rose to her feet to walk to one of the windows and look out at the Square.

The sun had just disappeared behind a cloud and in consequence everything looked drab and grey and wintry.

The Duke had risen when she did but he was still on the hearth-rug, watching her and waiting for her to speak.

403

"I—I do not know what to—say," Lily said hesitatingly.

"What is the problem?" he enquired.

"I am still in—half-mourning." Lily replied, "and I feel perhaps it would be—wrong to enjoy myself so much as I would with you when I am still—missing my dear—husband."

As she spoke she thought she had said it well and in a voice that any man would find extremely moving.

"I think what you need," the Duke said, "is a holiday away from the past, if you like, with new faces and new people to occupy your mind."

"You make it sound very fascinating," Lily said without turning her head.

"That is what I want it to be," he said, "and because I know what is best for you, I do not intend to take 'no' for an answer."

She turned round then and there was a smile on her lips.

"I—I hope it is the—right thinking for—me—to do."

She thought he was waiting for an explanation, and she went on: "My husband was a very autocratic and authoritative man. I am not—used to making—decisions for myself."

"Then I will certainly make them for you," the Duke replied. "Can you be ready the day after tomorrow?"

She moved from the window towards him.

"I suppose if you tell me so—I shall have to be."

"Then that is an order!" he said. "And your brother-in-law will tell you, if you ask him, that orders have to be obeyed!"

"I will be—ready!" Lily said meekly.

"I cannot tell you how happy you have made me!"

She raised her eyes to his.

"That is what I want to do—make you happy—but I am told that happiness is what you give other people."

"That is the sort of compliment I like to hear," the Duke said with a smile.

He continued to look into her eyes, and once again Lily's lashes, which were a little darker than nature intended, were silhouetted against her white skin.

Then she settled herself down on the sofa again and the Duke said:

"I have decided that as the Bay of Biscay can be very unpleasant at this time of the year, we will go overland and join my yacht at Marseilles. *The Mermaid* has in fact already left harbour and is on her way."

"*The Mermaid?*" Lily repeated. "What a lovely name, and so very—romantic."

"That is what I thought when I christened her. Do you play Bridge?"

"Yes—yes, of course!" Lily replied.

She was glad now that she had paid for lessons while she was in Edinburgh, knowing that Bridge was the latest craze, although the Duchess of Devonshire insisted on playing the old-fashioned Whist.

"There will be plenty to amuse us if it is too cold to be on deck," the Duke remarked, "but once we reach Egypt I am certain you will be as entranced by the Temples as I shall."

For a moment Lily wondered what the Temples in Egypt would be like.

She had never met anybody who was in the least interested in that far-away country, and although she had been taught about the Pyramids and the Sphinx, she had always somehow connected Temples with India rather than with Egypt.

"It will certainly be—fascinating," she said.

"I have sent my Comptroller," the Duke went on, "to purchase every book on Egypt that is obtainable from the Libraries, and we can spend some of the time when we are in the Mediterranean finding out about the Pharaohs."

"And of course Cleopatra," Lily said, remembering that she had been a beauty like herself.

"I shall not want to look at her when you are there," the Duke said.

Lily was not certain whether the words came automatically from long practice.

At the same time, there was no doubt from the expression in his eyes that he was finding her as beautiful as she believed herself to be.

Before he left she said hesitatingly:

"You are—quite, quite sure you want me to—come with you? After all, Your Grace—since I have lived so long in the North, you may find me—rather dull, and very—ignorant about the things that—interest you."

"I will tell you exactly what interests me when we have more time," the Duke replied.

He kissed her hand again on leaving, and only when the door of the Drawing-Room shut behind him did Lily turn to the looking-glass over the mantelpiece to stare at her reflection.

She thought as she did so that it would be impossible for any woman to look lovelier or indeed more fascinating.

"I am beautiful, and already he wants me!" she said beneath her breath. "But I have to play my cards very, very carefully if he is to offer me marriage, as I intend him to do."

She resisted an impulse to go to the window and watch the Duke drive away in his carriage which had been waiting across the Square.

Nevertheless, she sent her thoughts after him, saying:

"You are mine! My husband! Mine!"

Then the intensity of them turned to a cry of sheer delight and triumph.

"Egypt!" she cried, and flung her hands high in the air. "Egypt! And there will be no other distractions besides me!"

CHAPTER THREE

*T*RAVELLING ACROSS FRANCE in the Duke's private railway-carriage, which was attached to the Express to Marseilles, Lily though that the luxury and the comfort were beyond anything she could have imagined.

This is what it means to be really rich! she thought with satisfaction.

She thought that when she married the Duke she would feel as if she floated on a golden cloud and that the stars were made of diamonds.

It was impossible not to feel romantic when she looked at him, while at the same time his attractions were framed and gilded by his possessions.

Almost every conversation told her more about the wonders of Darle Castle and what the Duke owned in other parts of the country.

But apart from him, Lily found that all the other guests lived a life of luxury that was very different from her life with Sir Ewan.

Lady Southwold was the only other woman, and Lily had been a little apprehensive as to what she would be like.

They had met first in the Drawing-Room compartment of the train at Victoria, and a first glance told Lily that she was well over thirty and there was no reason for her to fear any competition from Amy Southwold.

Then when the journey started, she found that although Lady Southwold might not be beautiful, she had an unmistakable fascination and was also extremely witty and amusing.

This actually was the reason why the Duke had invited her and her husband, with Harry's full approval, to join the party.

Lord Southwold, who had only recently been raised to the Peerage, thanks to his friendship with the Prince of Wales, was an extremely intelligent man who had inherited one fortune, then doubled and trebled it by his own expertise.

Those who invariably criticised the Prince of Wales hinted that Lord Southwold was one of the Financiers who helped him invest his money and took particular care that he did not lose it.

That put him in the same group as the Rothschilds, but everybody who knew Charles Southwold liked him, and although he was older than the Duke and Harry, they counted him as one of their closest friends.

Amy had laughed her way into Society and the Duke knew that she could always be relied on to make any party, however heavy, a success.

When he had invited her to come with him to Egypt she had exclaimed:

"Oh, Dasher, you are the answer to my prayers, as you have been before! Charlie has been over-working lately and I was wondering where we should go so that he would be able to do nothing but eat, drink, and enjoy the sunshine."

"That is exactly what he can do on *The Mermaid*," the Duke had replied.

"He will love being with you and Harry, and so shall I," Amy Southwold had said. "You are not only the most attractive man I know, but also the kindest."

"You are embarrassing me," the Duke had replied, "but I also want to get away to the sunshine, and I am very grateful to you and Charlie for accompanying me."

407

Amy was certain that his insistence on leaving was due to the rumour, which of course had reached her ears, that his affair with Myrtle was over, but when she saw Lily she thought there was obviously a new reason as well.

The Duke's fourth guest, James Bushly, had been in the Regiment with him and was a perfect guest in every house-party, so that hostesses fought to include him and those who were unkind said that he had so many beds to choose from that he had no time to fill his own with a wife.

He often said that he, the Duke, and Harry were the "Three Musketeers."

"Three bachelors in search of adventure!" he elaborated. "And so far I do not remember our ever being disappointed."

Jimmy Bushly's love-affairs lasted longer than the Duke's, but he still evaded with some dexterity the traps set for him by ambitious Mamas.

He was likely one day to become the Earl of Thame, if the present holder of the title did not produce an heir, which appeared to be unlikely, and when his father, a comparatively young man, died.

However, his future prospects did not worry Jimmy, although they were duly noted by the Social World.

Like the Duke he always said that he had no intention of marrying, and like the Duke he always received the answer that sooner or later he would have to produce an heir.

In the meantime, he enjoyed life, and although he had not the intelligence of The Dasher, he was an excellent audience and could always be relied upon to take part in any activity in which the Duke was particularly interested.

When Jimmy saw Lily, there was a twisted smile at the corners of his mouth, and he said to Harry in a voice that only he could hear:

"Now I understand the rush to leave England!"

Harry's eyes twinkled but he did not reply.

He was thinking that Lily was undoubtedly one of the loveliest women he had ever seen, and because he was so fond of the Duke, he only hoped the inside of the parcel was as attractive as the outside.

Once they reached Calais and the Duke's private coach was attached to the Express, they all settled down as if prepared to make a "home away from home" wherever they might find themselves.

The food which was served by the Duke's servants was superb because it was cooked by one of the Duke's Chefs, the wines were outstanding, and Lily was to sleep in a large, comfortable bed made up with linen bearing the Duke's coronet.

She told herself it would be like having a *genie* who could magically produce everything one could wish for.

She could not help wondering how soon the Duke would approach her as a lover.

She was considering whether she should look shocked and say that she could not contemplate any liaison which did not involve a wedding-ring.

Then she told herself that in that case she might frighten him off from the very beginning.

She was not a young girl whom he would think it wrong to seduce, but a widow who was, in the parlance of the Clubs, "fair game."

Having seen the rest of the party, Lily was well aware of the part the Duke expected her to play and that she was to be the main factor in keeping him amused.

At the same time, unlike any other man she had known, he enjoyed life so tremendously that he was the one who stimulated the laughter and who encouraged Amy Southwold to be witty with words as sharp as pointed arrows. To listen to him sparring verbally with Harry and Jimmy was almost like watching a performance on the stage.

It made Lily realise that only an exceptional woman could keep up with the rest, and she knew that first evening that with her limited knowledge of the life the other guests lived, she had no chance of being the star when they were all together.

She thought things over and decided she could hold the Duke simply by her beauty, and hoped that as there would be no competition, he would concentrate on her until she knew him well enough to enslave him.

She had it all worked out in her mind, and as they travelled through France she was aware that his desire for her was growing and she saw by the expression in his eyes that it would not be long before he made a move.

She expected it would happen when they reached the yacht at Marseilles.

Having listened attentively to everything everybody was saying, she tentatively tried a new approach which she had formulated in her mind.

It was at dinner that she said to Lord Southwold:

"Do you use your instinct when you are buying shares on the Stock Exchange?"

"My instinct?" he repeated. "No, not often, although I sometimes have what you might call a 'hunch.' "

"That is what I meant."

"And your 'hunches' certainly pay off, Charles!" Harry said with a laugh.

"I was once told about a man," Lily said, "who made a fortune because he followed the signs of the stars."

"How interesting!" Amy exclaimed. "But how did he do that?"

"An Astrologer worked it all out for him."

"The Egyptians believed in Astrology," the Duke said. "In fact the Pharaohs did little without consulting the Palace Astrologers, who, from all I can ascertain, were kept very busy?"

"I wonder if we will find one there now?" Amy questioned.

"I am quite certain there will be a horde of charlatans only too willing to tell your fortune," Harry said. "Everybody who comes back from India says the 'Gully-Gully' men in Alexandria are a perfect nuisance, besides being cruel to the chickens they use in their prognostications."

"I did not mean that sort of thing!" Lily protested. "I was thinking really of people who are 'fey,' like the Scottish."

"But of course! They can really 'see,' " Amy agreed.

"Yes—I know!" Lily said in a low voice.

The way she spoke made Charles Southwold look at her sharply.

"Are you telling us," he asked, "that you are 'fey'?"

"Sometimes. It always seems incredible at first, but eventually things come true, and it surprises me as much as it does everybody else!"

"Well, I must certainly ask you to use your power on my behalf," Charles Southwold said. "I have three deals in question at the moment, and I should be very interested to hear any advice as to whether or not they are likely to be a success or a failure."

"I will—try to tell—you," Lily said a little shyly.

Amy gave a cry of excitement.

"But this is fascinating! Of course you must tell us all what we shall find in the future."

"Now you are frightening me!" Lily protested. "If I tell you that something is wrong, you may be angry, or even leave me stranded in the desert while you steam away!"

"I promise you that is very unlikely," the Duke said.

Lily saw the expression in his eyes and felt her excitement grow.

He wanted her. There was no doubt about that, and in her plan to make him interested not only in her face but in something mysterious and elusive, she felt quite certain that she was on the right track.

Marseilles was bathed in sunshine but there was a nip in the wind and at night darkness came early.

The Mermaid was larger and more impressive than Lily had imagined it would be. It was the Duke's latest acquisition and he was very proud of it.

What was more, it was, with the exception of the Royal Yacht, the largest yacht in the private possession of any British citizen, and he had supervised the building of it so that in a way it was more exclusively his than were any of the houses he had inherited.

Every gadget ever invented had been incorporated, and the decorations, chosen by the Politician's wife, who had extremely good taste, were very attractive.

The stewards were augmented by some of the Duke's personal servants who travelled with him, and his Chef took over the Galley.

Lily found with a little smile of satisfaction that her very large and comfortable cabin was next to the Master Suite, which was what she had expected.

The first night they did not move from the harbour and dinner was a very enjoyable meal, with Lady Southwold and Lily dressed in their prettiest evening-gowns with jewels flashing on their bare necks.

They talked for a long time at the dinner-table, and when they moved from the Dining-Saloon into another extremely comfortable Saloon, Lady Southwold said:

"I hope, Lady Cairns, you will show us tonight some of your powers of 'second sight.' At least it is quiet and peaceful here."

On the train when they had asked her to tell their fortunes, Lily had made the excuse that the rumble of the wheels was too disturbing and the movement made it difficult to concentrate.

Now she smiled and said:

"I will certainly try, but I wish I had not mentioned it in the first place. I have always found that clairvoyance is not something you can order or perform at will. It has to come to one like a shaft of moonlight, and is impossible to control."

While they were talking, the gentlemen joined them and Amy South-wold said:

"It is so exciting! Lady Cairns says she will try her powers tonight. I know it is something which will really interest us all."

"Do you need any 'props' for your exhibition?" Harry enquired.

There was something in the way he spoke and in the laughter in his eyes which made Lily suspect that he thought what she was doing was designed to draw attention to herself.

But what he thought or did not think was unimportant, and as she looked at the Duke a little pleadingly he said:

"You must not let Harry tease you. I am sure being 'fey' is to you something serious and not to be treated lightly."

"You—understand," she said.

"I want to."

For a moment she looked into his eyes and the rest of the party was forgotten.

Then as if she felt she must prove herself she said:

"It is easier if I have something with which to concentrate, and the same applies to whomever I am helping."

"What do you need?" the Duke asked.

"It is unlikely that you have a crystal ball on board," Lily answered, "so a pack of cards will do."

After she had been to Mrs. McDonald in Edinburgh, she had searched the Libraries for books on clairvoyance and Fortune-Telling, and to her surprise she had found quite a number, most of which she thought were rubbish.

At the same time, they told her what she wanted to learn, which was what each card was supposed to predict. She learnt, however, that what had been used through the centuries for more advanced clairvoyance was the Tarot-cards.

As these seemed rather complicated, she decided that playing-cards were something with which she could show off her hands while using what she called her "instinct" to tell the person who was consulting her what they wished to know.

She was certain that imagination was the secret of Mrs. McDonald's success, and she had also collected every possible detail from Lady Rushton about the Duke's friends before they had left London.

Unfortunately there had not been much time, but she had also looked them up in *Debrett* and the night before she left for Egypt was at a dinner-party where fortunately she was seated next to a well-known gossip.

When she told him she was to be a guest of the Duke of Darleston and who were to be the other guests, he told her a great many things she was certain would now come in useful.

"I will try to consult the fates for Lord Southwold," she said, "but only if he promises that if he loses money as a result of my advice, he will not expect me to make good any deficiency in his Bank-account!"

There was laughter over this and Harry remarked:

"If Charles loses money, he puts it down to experience, and that is what you will undoubtedly give him, Lady Cairns."

The Duke brought Lily a pack of new cards and she seated herself at a card-table.

Then she said:

"I think it would be embarrassing if you are all listening, and besides you will laugh and disturb my train of thought. Could the rest of you play Bridge and forget Lord Southwold and me?"

"A good idea!" the Duke commended. "Lady Cairns can take us one by one when we are sitting out, and afterwards we can repeat the less personal revelations!"

There was a good deal of laughter and Jimmy said:

"If Lady Cairns has any revelations to make about The Dasher, it will undoubtedly take all night—in which case he had better be last!"

They all agreed to this, and as the others seated themselves at another card-table which a steward erected for them, Lily opened the pack of cards she held in her hand, shuffled them, and held them out to Lord Southwold.

"Do you really think these are necessary?" he asked.

"As I have said, they are helpful," she said, "but I do not need these cards to know that you yourself have a strong, very clear intuition which you must never deny."

She made a quick sketch of his character, which, as it was extremely flattering, he made no effort to contradict. She then managed to make an intelligent guess about the propositions of which he had spoken.

"Two," she said, "will turn out to be all you expect of them, but beware of one which appears extremely attractive but is fundamentally unsound."

She gave him a beguiling smile as she said:

"It seems unnecessary to say this to you, and I am sure you are so

413

clever you know already where there is something wrong, and that you judge your investments as you judge people."

"What do you mean by that?" he asked.

"I think you have an analytical mind," she replied, "and it would be very difficult, in fact almost impossible, for a person whom you knew well to deceive you. You merely extend that knowledge when you deal with stocks and shares."

"I believe you are right!" Lord Southwold said reflectively.

"I am sure I am," Lily answered. "Because in many ways you are very modest about your own brilliance, you think that what happens in business is just the reward of efficiency, when actually it is so much more."

By the time the first hand had finished at the other table and Harry, who was dummy in the second hand, crossed to where Lily was still talking to Lord Southwold, she was aware that she had achieved her first success.

"You are a very clever woman!" Charles Southwold said as he rose somewhat reluctantly from his seat opposite her. "They say Napoleon never moved without consulting an Astrologer and several Fortune-Tellers, and I am tempted to ask you to join my staff."

"Be careful," Lily warned. "I might accept!"

Harry sat down opposite and she knew that he was unimpressed and she thought, although she could not be sure, a little hostile.

She made him shuffle the cards, then picked out twelve of them which she arranged in a pattern with one, which represented himself, in the centre.

Then she said:

"It is very difficult to tell you, because you have erected a barrier round yourself. Tonight I shall not attempt to climb it, but wait until you open the door to me, which is at present closed."

"Are you saying that you have nothing to say to me?" Harry asked.

"Yes, Mr. Settingham," Lily replied, "for reasons I have just explained."

"A barrier? What barrier?"

"That is for you to say. I only know it is there."

She looked at him across the table and felt as if he was sizing her up like a duellist calculating the dexterity of his opponent.

Then he smiled.

"I hope you will be kind to me another evening," he said. "But I realise that an unbeliever always causes trouble."

"Invariably!" Lily agreed.

Harry rose and Lady Southwold exclaimed:

"You cannot have finished already! Or has Lady Cairns nothing to tell you?"

"She turned me away from the temple of knowledge," Harry replied lightly. "She says I am an 'unbeliever.' "

"Then I shall take your place," the Duke said. "Personally, I am prepared to believe anything Lady Cairns tells me!"

Without arguing, he sat down in the seat which Harry had just vacated.

Because they knew he expected it, the others went on with their Bridge, talking amongst themselves, and the Duke said in a low voice:

"Only you can tell me if the future holds what I want more than anything else."

"Will you shuffle the cards, Your Grace?"

"There is no need for cards," he said. "Look at me, Lily, and tell me the answer to my problem, which quite simply I hope is . . . 'yes'!"

She did not pretend to misunderstand what he was saying, she only looked across the table into his eyes and felt the excitement within herself rising until she felt it overwhelmed her.

It was impossible not to be aware of the light in his eyes and the invitation on his lips.

He was the Duke of Darleston, the man she had thought about and dreamt about for years, the man whom she intended to marry.

Because her astute mind told her it would be a mistake to surrender too easily, she said:

"Have you ever dreamt that you were standing on a very high mountain or on the top of a lofty tower and you wonder whether if you jump you will fall crashing to the ground, or by some miracle be carried safely on wings?"

"Do you mean the wings are there if you desire to use them?"

"Yes."

"Then you will not be flying alone."

His voice was soft and beguiling and, Lily thought, irresistible.

"I want you to answer me, Lily," he said.

She looked at him without speaking and he added:

"The question is no longer there, and to save you from giving me the answer, I will make it for you."

"Thank—you," Lily whispered.

~

Later that night, when she lay in his arms, she told herself that it was easy to think she had won the battle, but she had a long way to go before she was victorious.

The Duke had exclaimed over her beauty, she knew she excited him, but she was well aware that the question of marriage had not entered his mind.

She had also learnt at the party her last night in London that it was a surprise that Lady Garforth was not going to Egypt.

"Did I hear you say Egypt?" she heard her dinner companion remark to Lady Rushton. "Good Heavens! Why on earth should Darleston want to go there?"

"It is not a bad idea to seek the sun in this weather," a man said. "Who is going with him?"

"My sister-in-law, for one," Lady Rushton replied.

"Your sister-in-law?"

The first speaker seemed astounded. Then he had said:

"But I thought Lady Garfor . . ."

He realised he was being indiscreet and bit back the words, but Lily knew what he had intended to say.

She remembered then that Lady Garforth had been at the Duke's side when they were at Marlborough House.

There had been another man with them but Lily had noticed the expression in Lady Garforth's eyes when she looked at the Duke, and although it had meant nothing particular at the time, she remembered it now.

So it was she with whom he had been associating before he had met her!

On the way back from the party she had learnt that Lady Garforth was a widow like herself, and there was therefore no reason why the Duke, if he wished to do so, should not marry her.

I must be careful! Very careful! she thought.

But it was difficult to think when the Duke's lips were seeking hers, his hands were touching her body, and she knew that the women who had said he was a fascinating, exciting lover had told the truth.

As Lily put her arms round his neck to draw him closer still, she told herself fiercely that she would never let him go and would make it impossible for him to escape her.

~

The following day they were in the Mediterranean and the Duke made it very clear to the rest of the party to whom he wanted to talk.

He took Lily up on the bridge and walked with her on the deck, and she joined him in his private cabin where none of his guests ventured unless they were particularly invited.

"You are beautiful!" he said to her. "I was wise to bring you away from London before you were spoilt by the adoration which sooner or later is bound to turn your head!"

"I deserve it!" Lily replied. "Although the grouse, the eagles, and the blackbirds may admire me, they are not very articulate in saying so."

"I will make up for them," the Duke answered.

He pulled her into his arms and kissed her until she felt dizzy with the joy of it.

"I do not believe Cleopatra could have been any lovelier than you," he said the next day.

Once again they were in his private cabin, and she was leisurely turning over the books he had been reading about Egypt.

"I am glad she is dead."

"Why?" the Duke enquired.

"Because otherwise you would prefer her to me. After all, what man could resist a Queen and one who could offer him all the mysteries of Egypt?"

"I am quite content with your mysteries."

"I have not yet told you about myself."

"I have no wish to know the future," the Duke said. "If you told me what races I was going to win they would lose their excitement, and also it is distinctly unsportsmanlike to bet on a certainty."

"I am not thinking of races."

"Then what?"

"Of you, of your feelings and your emotions."

"That is quite easy," the Duke said. "I do not need cards to know that you excite me, and all I am concerned with at the moment is exciting you."

He kissed her again, and it was impossible to go on talking and Lily told herself there was no point in it now.

417

But the others were not put off so easily.

Lady Southwold insisted upon having her fortune told, and so did James Bushly, while Lord Southwold continued to sing her praises as being extraordinarily accurate and astute.

When he had a chance to speak to Lily alone, he said:

"I want to use your 'second sight' again, but at the moment our host appears to have made a 'take-over bid' in a big way."

"I always have time for you, Lord Southwold."

"Thank you for saying that," he replied. "I am well aware that I must take my turn."

She smiled at him beguilingly, and he said:

"I have a deal in mind on which I want your advice, or rather, to use your 'eye.' If it comes off, you shall tell me which are your favourite stones, which I imagine are emeralds."

"They are my birth-stone," Lily said softly.

"Then I think it is time you had a birthday."

Lily shut her eyes for a moment. Then she said:

"I think you ought to go ahead with what you are planning, but cautiously. There is one man whom I do not trust. You should consider everything he suggests to you very, very carefully. Weigh it up and use your own intuition, which I have told you is unusually perceptive, before you make any move, however hard he may try to persuade you."

She paused, and although she did not open her eyes she knew that Lord Southwold was watching her intently.

"What else can you see?" he asked at length.

"I see you attaining everything you desire. Failure is impossible. You are omnipotent and infallible, but at the same time—be cautious!"

"That is exactly what I felt myself," Lord Southwold remarked, and Lily, opening her eyes, thought it was all too easy.

The only person in the party who did not show an almost abject respect for her powers as a "Seer" was Harry.

When she met his eyes across the table at meals and when Lord Southwold spoke of her powers with a note of reverence, she was aware that Harry was not deceived.

She felt somehow as if he could, if he wished, expose her as a cheat, a charlatan, and a fraud.

Then she told herself that she was being ridiculous and needlessly apprehensive.

She had not done or said anything wrong, she had merely planted in people who had an almost childish belief in good luck the idea that she could see their future.

As far as she was concerned, that could not be anything but the primrose path and the crock of gold at the end of the rainbow.

"They are so rich, they are so important," Lily told herself when she was alone in her cabin. "It makes them safe from poverty, loneliness, and fear."

She felt a little shudder go through her as she remembered how poor she and her father had been, and she remembered too how nervous she had been of the future as she realised that Sir Ewan was likely to die and how little money he could leave her.

She had certainly improved the situation once he was tied to his bed, by going round the Castle collecting everything that was not likely to be entailed and sending it to Edinburgh.

When she had been staying there with her husband's relatives she had made contact with a man who dealt in antiques.

She had told him a long and complicated story of being left by her family a large number of small objects which they wanted her to keep and treasure for sentimental reasons, but which she had found an encumbrance.

"I could not bear to hurt them after all their kindness," she said, looking pathetic and speaking in her childish voice. "But because I am desperately in need of money, I must sell something from time to time, but of course the transactions must be kept entirely secret."

"I understand," the Dealer replied, "and I promise you, anything you sell me will be conveyed as quickly as possible to a shop I have in London."

Lily sent him snuff-boxes which fetched a surprisingly large sum, small items of table-silver from the safe which she thought would not be missed as they were unable to entertain, and even a few small and minor paintings that she could not find included in the catalogue which listed the contents of the house.

When Sir Ewan was dead and she went to stay in Edinburgh, she sold his gold watch and chain, several pairs of his cuff-links, and some very fine pearl studs that he always wore in the evening.

Alister had actually asked her what had happened to them.

"I have no idea," she answered, "but your father's old valet died five years ago, and he did not like the man he engaged to succeed him, so when he left he preferred to be looked after by the Butler and the footman.''

Alister Cairns had pursed his lips into a hard line.

''I suppose it is no use asking the Police to make enquiries about the man?''

''He told me when he left that he intended to go to Australia,'' Lily replied. ''He said he had relatives there.''

She knew that Alister was not likely to pursue the matter further, and the money went into her secret account at the Bank, which she had transferred to London as soon as she went South, still using the fictitious name that she had used in Scotland.

Yet, whatever she had accumulated, by fair means or foul, was a mere drop in the ocean compared to the great fortunes enjoyed by the Duke, Lord Southwold, and, as far as she could make out, the majority of their friends.

Harry was teased by Lady Southwold as being a ''rich bachelor who spent money on nobody but himself,'' and Jimmy, although he did not appear to have much money at the moment, obviously had big expectations.

They made Lily feel as if she had stepped into an Aladdin's cave and everything round her glittered blindingly, especially the Duke. She felt as if his strong, athletic body shimmered with gems and his coronet was ablaze with them.

That is what I want on my head, Lily thought.

She had a picture of herself moving amongst the Peeresses, a huge tiara on her red hair, a necklace of diamonds encircling her white throat, and her bracelets shining dazzlingly with every move she made.

''The Duchess of Darleston!'' That was what she would be, and besides having the title she would be married to the most alluring, most fascinating man she had ever imagined.

Then she was suddenly aware that there was another adjective that was often used when people spoke of him—the most raffish!

As she waited for him to come through the door of her cabin, she was afraid that after all her calculations her heart might betray her!

CHAPTER FOUR

———— ❧ ————

THE DUKE STOOD on deck alone.

It was very early in the morning, and the sun rising in the cloud-free, mist-free sky threw a strange, mystical light, first red, then yellow, lastly a blinding white, over the landscape.

"No wonder," he thought, "the ancient Egyptians worshipped, above all other Deities, the God of the Sun."

Every mile they travelled since they had left the Mediterranean for first the Nile Delta, which was like a lotus, and then the river itself, he had felt more and more fascinated by the country he wished to see.

Now the river moved through mile after mile of green, with cotton and tobacco fields, palm groves, and plantations of beans and peas springing from the rich, red-brown mud. In the distance, waterless and sun-dried, was the golden desert.

As they went farther South, the river itself was surprisingly empty. Sometimes the Duke would see the lateen sail of a felucca and an occasional barge moving slowly through the brown water, but otherwise there were only the birds.

But the view was often of mud-built villages with their flat roofs shafted by palm trees, patient plodding donkeys carrying huge loads, and men in long white galabiehs labouring in the fields.

They used hoes and dibbers which the Duke thought were the same shape and type that their ancestors had used over five thousand years earlier.

He was intensely interested in the creaking, groaning Shaduf, or water-pump, a primitive apparatus of water-buckets attached to a vertical wheel and operated by a circular wooden treadmill round which oxen or donkeys endlessly revolved.

But what really thrilled him was that soon he would have a sight of the Temples and the statues which had been left by the Pharaohs at Thebes.

He could not explain to himself why he was so intrigued or why he felt a new and very different excitement from anything he had ever known before. It was almost, he felt, as if there was a familiarity not only about what he saw but what he felt about the country.

It was this which made him resist the pleading of his party that they should make a stop at Cairo and enjoy the gaieties of belly-dancers and other exotic entertainments instead of pressing on toward Luxor.

There had been a brief glimpse of the great Pyramids, but the Duke refused to change his plans.

Only Amy Southwold had been delighted with his decision, because it meant that Charles would continue to take things easy and spend most of the time on deck under the awning, reading or sleeping.

He roused himself in the evenings to join in the laughter and chatter at dinner, and he insisted that Lily should use her "eye" to look into the future of his financial operations.

"I only hope she has a stake in the great fortune she is making for you!" the Duke had said. "But take warning, Charlie, when you look round you, note that even the greatest Empires can crumble away and leave nothing but rocks and stones behind them!"

"It will be a long time," Lily said in an intense voice, "before Lord Southwold's Empire vanishes. In fact it has not yet reached its zenith."

She found that when she spoke in a certain voice, with her eyes misty and vacant as if she looked into the future, Lord Southwold listened to her raptly, and the others seemed impressed.

As far as the Duke was concerned, she was so beautiful that it did not matter to him what she said, for he liked the movements of her lips because they were kissable rather than because they mouthed prophecies which only time could prove to be right or wrong.

Although Lily tried to pretend that she understood his desire to move South without lingering on the way, she privately thought it a pity that they did not have a chance to visit the shops in Cairo, especially those which sold jewellery.

Lord Southwold had referred several times to his promise to give her emeralds, and the Duke, realising how little jewellery she had and that what she did wear was very inferior to the necklaces, earrings, and bracelets which adorned Lady Southwold, had promised her diamonds to echo the light in her eyes.

"I cannot imagine why you should be so beautiful," he said more than once. "What did your mother look like?"

Lily felt a touch of fear as she thought how horrified he would be if she told him the truth. Instead she said sadly:

"Alas, I cannot remember. She died soon after I was born, but my father always said she was very lovely."

"Then you must be like her," the Duke said. "But as your father was an Englishman, how did you meet your husband?"

"My father always went to Scotland for the grouse-shooting," Lily replied, "and when I was seventeen he took me with him. My husband always said that he fell in love with me the moment he saw me."

"That is not surprising."

"He was a Chieftain and he appeared very romantic."

"He was very much older than you," the Duke commented.

"Much older, and I suppose in a way he was a father-figure, which means I had never—loved anybody—properly—until I met—you."

The way she spoke with a little hesitation over the word "properly" made the Duke's lips seek hers, and to her relief there was no further conversation about her past.

She knew, however, that it was extremely important, if she was to be a Duchess, to establish the fact that her antecedents were impeccable, for she knew that the Duke would be unwilling to marry beneath him.

She therefore invented a number of distinguished relatives who were of course dead, and who, when they were alive, had lived in obscure parts of the British Isles so that the Duke and his friends were not likely to have heard of them.

"My mother's family was always supposed to be descended from the Kings of Ireland," she said once at the dinner-table, "which caused an endless conflict with my husband, who believed the Cairns are descended from one of the Kings of Scotland."

"It is not surprising that you are 'fey'!" Lord Southwold remarked. "A mixture of Irish and Scottish is bound to have an explosive quality about it!"

"Which is certainly true when you drink it!" Harry said drily.

Everybody laughed, and Lily told herself that she was beginning to dislike Harry more and more.

She was quite certain that he was the one person aboard who was skeptical about her powers of clairvoyance, and she suspected too that he did not approve of her liaison with the Duke.

Yet she felt that he would not say anything to his friend, and she was shrewd enough to go out of her way to tell the Duke how much she liked all his friends, especially Harry.

She was not yet aware that much of what she talked about when she was with the Duke "went in one ear and out the other," as his Nanny would have said.

He found Lily so lovely that she was part of the beauty of Egypt, the mysterious world of hot, dry sunlight and black shadows, which as they steamed South made him feel as if he were stepping back in time.

He had read many of the innumerable books that he had brought with him, but although nobody aboard noticed it, he had ceased to talk about what he had read.

If Lily had been more astute she would have thought it was significant, but, satisfied as long as he was excited by her beauty, she did not understand that his mind was probing deeper all the time into something new, something fundamental, and in every way the opposite of anything that had interested him before.

He found that the books he read left him with hundreds of questions to which he did not know the answers, and he decided that when he returned to England he would visit the British Museum and find an Egyptologist who could explain many things that puzzled him.

But if everything else was a mystery, one thing he had learnt was that the place of most importance in the days of the most powerful Pharaohs was Thebes. It might be in ruins, but on the opposite bank was Luxor, where they were going.

He had in fact insisted that the yacht, which lay at anchor all night so as not to disturb the sleeping passengers, should leave very early this morning so that he could see Luxor at dawn.

Now as the sun rose a little higher, throwing a rose-coloured light over the cliffs of the Theben hills, the Duke knew he was looking at the burial place of the Pharaohs, known as "The Valley of the Kings."

On the east bank, the pillars of two Temples were silhouetted against the blue of the sky and they had all the magnetic appeal that he was seeking.

He had been told before he left London that at Luxor the Egyptians had been building a luxurious Winter Palace Hotel for tourists from Europe and America, who found the warm climate an attraction in the cold months of the year.

The Duke was not concerned with this, even though he thought it would doubtless amuse his guests.

But as the yacht drew a little nearer he saw a flight of white steps leading from the river up to a Temple whose pillars gleamed brilliantly in the morning sunshine.

He stood looking at it and felt an irresistible desire to enter the Temple, but even as he did so, he knew that more than anything else he wished to go there alone.

He could not explain why he had no desire to be accompanied by anybody, except somehow he felt it would disturb the atmosphere and perhaps himself.

He therefore ordered the yacht to drop anchor on the opposite side of the river.

Although the Captain thought it strange that the Duke did not wish to be beside the Hotel and Temples on the other bank, he was too well trained to question his Master's decision.

When the others appeared later in the morning they exclaimed with delight at the view opposite them, the high palm trees shading the banks of the river, and the feluccas with scimitar-like sacks everywhere round them on the Nile.

The Mermaid, being so large, was regarded with admiration and curiosity by numbers of small, dark-skinned children splashing about naked in the water, and along the side of the river under the palm trees there were the inevitable small donkeys drawing *arabiyas* and clopping along with sight-seeing visitors.

Because it was very hot, everybody felt relaxed and lazy and they agreed to the Duke's suggestion that they should not move until after luncheon, and then if they wished they could be rowed across the river to the Winter Palace Hotel.

Lily, looking cool and alluring in a white muslin and lace dress and a large white hat that shaded her beautiful face, was only too happy to agree to anything which did not require a great deal of movement.

She disliked getting hot, and if her white skin was flushed she was always afraid it might clash with her hair.

When finally they were rowed ashore in the ship's dinghy, she sank down in one of the wicker armchairs on the verandah of the Winter Palace to be waited on by a tall Sudanese waiter in a white galabieh with a red sash, and she had no wish to go any farther.

"What about a bit of exploring?" she heard Jimmy say to the Duke.

"Tomorrow," the Duke answered. "There is no hurry. I intend to say here for a few days, and if you want a change of cuisine, we might dine at the Winter Palace one evening."

"That would be fun!" Amy exclaimed. "I was looking at the guest-list, and although they have not yet arrived, I know the names of quite a number of people who will be staying here later on in the week."

"Then we must certainly ask them on board," the Duke said. "The last thing I would wish you to do is to get bored with your own company or mine."

"How could we do that?" Lily asked softly.

The way she looked at the Duke told him that it would be impossible for her ever to be bored with him.

It was cooler and the shadows were growing deeper and longer when they returned to the yacht.

Only when everybody was seated in the boat which would carry them across the river to where the Duke's staff were waiting to help them on board did he say unexpectedly:

"Go ahead. I will join you later, but I must first stretch my legs."

"Do you want me to come with you?" Harry asked automatically.

"No, Harry. Please look after the party for me."

He walked away quickly before Lily could say anything, and she frowned at the idea of his being alone.

Then she told herself that she had no wish to walk in the dust, and although it was certainly cooler than it had been an hour ago, she would find that any movement, however slow, would be exhausting.

She was well aware that the Duke needed exercise. He had swum every morning from the yacht while they had been moving up the Nile, and although they had teased him and told him he would be attacked by crocodiles, he had continued to dive off the stern.

He also played strenuous Badminton every day with Harry and Jimmy. Occasionally, when Charles could be persuaded to join them, they had a foursome.

"It will do him good," Lily consoled herself, "and he will find me even more alluring when he returns."

426

As soon as they reached the yacht, she went to her cabin to change into a diaphanous gown that revealed every line of her perfect figure.

Then, instead of joining the others, she went to the Duke's private cabin to lie on the sofa and wait for him.

~

Alone, the Duke walked briskly along the riverside, knowing that this was what he had been waiting for all day. He was trying to remember what he had read about "The Temple of Luxor," as it was called in the Guide-Books.

He guessed that because he had waited until late in the afternoon, everybody staying in the Hotel would have already visited it, and as he approached the Temple he saw to his relief that there was nobody about.

The massive entrance pylons were flanked outside by six colossal statues of Ramses II in a marvelous state of preservation.

Through these he entered the great pillared Courtyard of Ramses II surrounded by double rows of massive columns, and as they towered above him as he walked between them, the Duke felt not as if he had stepped back into the past but as if he had never left it.

On the far side he could see an impressive colonnade with columns each capped by an "open flower" papyrus capital, which he knew from his reading led into another great open Courtyard.

For some minutes he stood enveloping himself in the atmosphere, almost as if he was listening and using not only his eyes but some inner sense.

Then he moved on silently over the soft sand to where the shadows seemed almost black in contrast to the white of the pillars.

It was then as he looked from the inside of a small chamber toward the river that he saw the profile of a woman.

For a moment, bemused by his own thoughts, he was not certain whether she was real or engraved on one of the pillars.

He only knew that her straight nose and pointed chin were part of Egypt and what he was seeking.

He stood looking at her, his thoughts refusing to materialise in his mind, at the same time vividly conscious that this was the beauty of the ages.

Then she moved and he realized that she was in fact a real person, although her body had been in the shadows and he had been aware only of her face.

He came nearer, and now, coming as it were back to reality, he saw that she was a young woman, or rather a girl.

Her gown, which had melted into the shadows, was a soft shade of blue, and her hair was neither fair nor dark but a colour which blended into the sun-kissed stone.

As he nearly reached her, as if she had not heard him but was aware of his presence, she turned her face and he found himself looking at a pair of eyes that were startlingly blue.

Instinctively he moved no farther but stood still.

They looked at each other until, as if he were speaking across a chasm instead of the short space which divided them, he said:

"Forgive me if I startled you. I was not aware that there was anybody else here."

For a moment he thought she would not reply. Then she said in a low, musical voice:

"There are few visitors at this time of the evening."

"That was what I had hoped."

He moved nearer and now he saw that she had been looking from between the columns to where in the distance there was an exquisite view across the river toward the Valley of the Kings.

Because he felt he must say something, he remarked, and somehow it was difficult to speak lightly:

"You are too young to be interested in death."

She looked away from him once more towards the distant mystery of the hill-tops which the setting sun was turning to a deeper pink.

"The Egyptian word for 'tomb,' " she said after what seemed to the Duke to be a long pause, "means 'the House of Eternity.' "

"They believed in life after death?"

"Of course," she replied, "and as they had a very clear idea of what it would be like, they took with them everything they thought they would need in the new world to which they were going."

The Duke thought this was what he wanted to learn and had not found in the books he had read, which had merely contained a long list of the Pharaohs and an even longer description of the gods they worshipped.

"Tell me what the Egyptians did believe."

"The survival of the soul was dependent on the preservation of the body," she answered. "If the physical body perished, then so would the spirit."

The Duke thought this explained many things he had not understood before.

Now he knew why the ancient Egyptians had hidden their Pharaoh away in secret Tombs, and why they had taken with them their personal possessions, clothes, jewellery, furniture, their weapons, their chariots, and even food.

"They were a happy people," the girl said quietly. "People have depicted them as being cruel to the slaves who were building the Pyramids, tyrants to those who served them, and sinful in their private lives . . . but they are wrong."

"How do you know so much about them?" the Duke enquired.

She smiled, and he realised as she did so that she was very lovely, lovelier than anyone he had ever seen before, but also completely different from what he had thought of as his ideal of beauty.

There was a rightness about her in this particular place, as if she belonged as he had thought she did when he had first seen her.

"I live here," she said in answer to his question, and he looked at her in surprise.

"All the year round?"

"Yes. At least since my father came to Luxor."

"And before that?"

"We were moving about the country, sometimes camping in the desert."

He looked at her in astonishment.

She appeared so refined, so fragile with her delicate features and small hands with long thin fingers, that he could not imagine her enduring the heat and hardship of the interminable sands.

"Your father is an Egyptologist?" he asked, as if that must be the explanation.

She smiled again, and he wondered why the question amused her. Then she said:

"That is what he is at heart. But he came to Egypt years ago as a Missionary, and that is his real work."

"A Missionary?"

The Duke could hardly imagine that she was speaking the truth.

He had always thought of Missionaries as tiresome men who interfered with the established religion of the natives and generally made a nuisance of themselves in countries where they were not wanted.

Anyone less like his conception of a Missionary's daughter than this lovely creature beside him he could not imagine.

"You speak as if your father is not a very successful Missionary," he said at length.

She gave a little laugh, and it was a soft, musical sound that seemed part of the movement of the pine leaves that had just caught the evening breeze coming upstream from the river.

"Papa unfortunately fell in love with Egypt," she said. "It is something people often do, and they find its history so entrancing that it is like a dream from which they cannot awaken."

The Duke thought that was exactly what he was beginning to feel himself.

"I would like to meet your father. I feel he could tell me many things I want to know but do not understand."

"I wish that were possible, but Papa has been ill for two weeks with a fever."

She looked at the Duke, then as if she felt she ought to make some explanation she said:

"I stay with him at night and our servant looks after him in the day while first I sleep, then I come out here."

"You have had a Doctor to see him?" the Duke asked.

The girl shook her head.

"Papa is a Medical Missionary and I know about medicines too. We have done everything that is possible, but Nile fevers are very unpleasant. That is why you must not come in contact with him."

When she looked at the Duke and thought perhaps he was nervous that she might be infectious, she explained:

"I think I am immune. I have nursed so many children with fever, and women too, but I have never caught one."

"I cannot imagine you doing such things," the Duke remarked. "When I first saw you I thought you were not real and that your face was carved on the pillar against which you leant, and that you really had lived thousands of years ago."

He spoke lightly, but as she did not answer he added after a silence which seemed to last for a long time:

"Perhaps you did live here in the past!"

As he spoke he thought it was a very strange thing to say and perhaps she would not reply, or would laugh it away. Instead she said:

"I know . . . I did . . . and so . . . did . . . you!"

The Duke stiffened. Then as he looked at her incredulously she said quickly:

"I should not have said that. Forgive me . . . I must return to my . . . father."

She moved away from the pillar and now the Duke saw that she was slender and her waist was very tiny. But she was not short, and she had, he thought, the lithe grace of one of the engraved figures he had noticed when he had first entered the Temple.

She was wearing a gown that was not in the least fashionable, but-toned up to the throat and down the front of the bodice, with a full skirt, plain and unadorned.

Yet, simple though it was, on her it had a grace that was again part of the beauty round them.

"Please do not leave me," the Duke said. "If I cannot see your father, then I want you to answer the questions that trouble me. I promise you I am a very serious student of the land that has drawn me irrepressibly for no reason I can understand."

Because he so desperately wanted her to stay, the Duke exerted all the charm that had never failed him in the past.

He knew as she stood looking at him indecisively that she was trying to make up her mind as to what she should do.

"Tell me about the Temple," he begged.

He felt as he spoke that what was worrying her was that inadvertently she had said something too personal, and now, like a child who has done something wrong, she wanted to run away and forget it.

"How much do you . . . know about it . . . already?" she asked.

He thought from her tone that she was attempting to sound matter-of-fact and speak as if it were of little importance.

"I must confess an abysmal ignorance," the Duke replied.

She gave a little laugh. Then as she walked back into the Courtyard he said:

"I think perhaps we should introduce ourselves. I am the Duke of

Darleston, and I arrived only this morning in the yacht which you can see moored on the other side of the river."

"I noticed it."

As if he could read her thoughts, he knew she was comparing it somewhat unfavourably with the barges that had been used by the Pharaohs, or perhaps the one with the silken, scented sails which had carried Cleopatra down the Nile to Mark Antony.

He also felt that a Duke was hardly in the same category as a Pharaoh.

"Now tell me your name," he said.

"Irisa," she replied, and he smiled.

"It suits you. And your other name?"

He thought she hesitated for just a moment before she said:

"Garron."

As if she had no wish for him to comment, she pointed out to him some of the details of the Great Court.

The Duke was interested, but he had a feeling that she was talking almost like a Guide rather than as she had spoken before, as her own person.

"They have been doing some excavations here," she said, "and there is a great deal more to do. As you see, the Temple has, over the centuries, been built on by other religions."

As she spoke she pointed, and the Duke saw a small Mosque built onto the wall of the Courtyard from the outside and perched high above the original ground level.

"A strange contrast," he said, "and yet I believe that all religions are good for the people who believe in them."

"Of course they are!" Irisa replied. "So it is ridiculous for outsiders to try to force another religion on people who have their own."

"If your father feels the same way, I can understand why he has given up being a Missionary to concentrate on Ancient Egypt," the Duke commented.

"I did not say he had done so," Irisa said quickly.

"Then perhaps I read your thoughts."

"It is something you . . . must not . . . do!"

"Why not?"

"Because thoughts are a very intimate part of oneself and to read them would be an intrusion."

"I do not think I have ever before been able to do so," the Duke replied, "but when you were speaking just now I was aware of a great deal you did not say, just as I think you feel the same about me."

As he spoke he was astonished to hear the words that seemed to have come involuntarily to his lips and the voice that spoke them was his own.

"Why should you . . . say that?"

"Perhaps you have cast a spell over me," he answered, "or perhaps it is the Temple itself. I only know that I feel as if I have stepped through the veil that parts one world from the other, and now this is just as real to me as the world I have left."

She turned quickly to face him, and now as the setting sun turned everything to a deep gold, her hair seemed to glow as it had not done before and her eyes were vividly blue.

"You frighten me," she whispered. "I thought when I first saw you I was dreaming and when we spoke to each other I was still asleep. Now I am awake and I want you to go . . . away and . . . forget you have . . . met me."

"Why should I do that?" the Duke asked. "I want to talk to you. If you believe in fate, as I know you do, then you believe it was not by chance that I came here tonight alone to the Temple and that you were here waiting for me."

"I was not . . . waiting . . ." she began.

Then her voice died away and she made a helpless gesture, as if it was impossible to try to refute what he had said.

"Let us accept," he urged, "that the gods, or whoever is watching over our destiny, have brought us together for a purpose, and that, as far as I am concerned, is to learn what is hidden from those who write very dull books about Egypt and who think that the past has no bearing on the future."

He realised as he spoke that his words had moved her, and she clasped her hands together as she said:

"I understand, because . . . that is what I . . . too think. There is so much here we could learn if we are . . . prepared to listen . . . so much that would help the . . . people of this nation and . . . others."

"Then begin by teaching me what I should know, and perhaps I shall have the power to bring it to the notice of people who matter."

"Can you do . . . that?"

She asked the question simply, as a child might have done.

"I hope so," the Duke answered, "but first, as you can understand, I have to be utterly and completely convinced that what I am saying is true."

"Yes, of course," she replied, "but perhaps I am not the right person to . . . teach you. If only Papa was here tonight it would be . . . different."

"I think we should take one step at a time," the Duke said. "The first step for me is to listen to a goddess called Irisa."

She smiled as if she understood that he was comparing her to the great goddess Isis who was depicted on so many of the columns.

She led him beyond the Mosque to where there were eleven red granite statues of Pharaohs and among them a diminutive replica of Queen Nefretiri.

She did not speak, she only stood still, and the Duke looked at the statue as she intended him to do.

The Queen was very beautiful with her luxuriant, thick plaits of hair flowing from her head to cover her breasts. Her lovely face showed no lines of worry and her mouth curved in the suspicion of a smile.

She looked happy, and at the same time she was demure and dignified as befitted a Queen.

"Is this who you were?" the Duke asked softly.

Irisa shook her head.

"No."

"Then who?"

"I do not wish to . . . speak of it . . . now."

"But you will do so another time?"

"P—perhaps."

She hesitated over the word, and he had a feeling that she did not want to tell him because she was shy, but he was afraid to tell her so.

They moved on to look at Temple reliefs which showed the splendour of the processions which had taken place between the Temple of Luxor and that of Karnak.

"I want to see Karnak tomorrow," the Duke said.

He looked at her as he spoke, and she knew he was asking her to show him the Great Temple of Arnon, on which every guide-book expended pages and pages of description.

"I will show it to you," she said after a moment's pause, "but it is not as beautiful as this Temple, and there is not the same atmosphere."

"I will be able to tell you what I feel after I have seen it."

He knew as he spoke that he must make quite certain she did not disappear and he could not find her again.

He realised the shadows were lengthening and growing darker and when the sun sank they would be in darkness, for night would come swiftly.

"I will take you back to where you live," he said.

"There is no . . . need."

"It is something I wish to do. Is it really wise for you to wander about here alone?"

"I will come to no harm," she replied. "The people know me and they respect Papa."

"Even when he tries to convert them?"

"I am afraid he does not try very hard, not nowadays."

"Then what does he do?"

The Duke thought she was not going to answer the question, but after a moment she said:

"Ever since we came here he has been interested in the excavations and the discoveries made in the Tombs."

"I can understand that."

"He believes there is a great deal more that has not been discovered, and thieves are still at work, finding treasures which they sell to the tourists, especially the Americans."

"And yet, I understand that quite a number of investigators have said there is nothing more to be found."

Irisa smiled.

"Papa does not believe that . . . nor do I."

"Why not?"

"Because we know from documents only recently translated that there are a great number of Pharaohs buried secretly in Tombs deep down in the cliffs, which even the robbers have not found."

"But they will eventually," the Duke said.

"So Papa hopes."

"And you?"

"I am quite happy to think back into the past and imagine what those sleeping Kings or Queens were like when they were alive."

"You say they were happy?"

"A very happy people."

"And you are happy too?"

She smiled in answer, and he thought that although it reminded him of the smile on the lips of Queen Nefretiri, it was far lovelier.

"Yes, you are happy!" he said positively.

It was only much later that he thought how strange it was that he should find a Missionary's daughter, obviously poor, living in a strange land, apparently with no friends and her only companion her father, happy in a way which no other woman of his acquaintance ever appeared to be.

Now Irisa was leading the way out to the back of the Temple where there were palm trees in a sandy wasteland.

There were also a few mud huts and the inevitable small, naked children playing games round them.

Then there was a clump of tall palm trees and shrubs vivid with blossom and a house.

Long and low, it was made of wood with a verandah reached by a flight of steps running across the front of it.

Above the verandah there was a small cross and behind it, somewhat incongruously, a ragged Union Jack.

"So this is where you live!" the Duke said.

"I cannot invite you in," Irisa said as they stopped near the shrubs. "I would not wish you to catch Nile fever."

"I am grateful that you are thinking of me," the Duke answered.

He spoke automatically, but as he did so he was aware that it was actually what she was doing.

She put out her hand and he took it in his.

For the first time since their meeting he realised that it was unconventional and certainly unusual for her not to be wearing a hat.

Instead, her hair was drawn back into a large coil at the back of her neck and held in place by hair-pins and a small bow of blue ribbon.

It somehow looked a little frivolous compared to the severity with which she was otherwise dressed.

"I do not know how grateful I am," the Duke said, "for having met you and for what you have taught me so far."

He spoke with an intensity that surprised himself, and as Irisa's eyelashes flickered over her blue eyes he realised that he had made her shy.

"I will wait for you tomorrow at the same place."

For a moment she did not answer, and he said urgently:

"Please do not fail me!"

"I . . . I might not be . . . able to come."

"That is a prevarication and untrue," he said. "You told me you sleep in the daytime, so shall I say I will meet you at the Temple where we met this evening at the same time? Or perhaps just a little earlier, as we have to go to Karnak."

"I will . . . try."

She would have moved away from him, but he held on to her hand.

"I want your promise—a promise you will not break. By whichever god the Egyptians swear at such a moment as this.'

There was a faint smile on Irisa's lips as she replied after a moment's thought:

"Thoth is the God of Wisdom."

"And therefore of the truth," the Duke added. "So swear to me by Thoth that you will come to me tomorrow night and not leave me waiting and wondering if I have been dreaming, and fearing that when I come here in search of you the house will have disappeared."

As he spoke he felt he was being a little unsportsmanlike in threatening her, and as if she understood exactly what he was doing she said:

"It is too . . . trivial a matter with which to . . . worry the gods. I will come if my father is well enough. If he is not, I will send a messenger to . . . tell you that I am . . . detained."

"Thank you," the Duke replied.

Her eyes met his, then as if she suddenly realised for the first time who he was and was conscious of his importance, she dropped him a small curtsey.

"Good-night, Your Grace," she said, and walked through the gap in the shrubs toward the wooden house.

The Duke waited and thought that when she reached the steps and climbed onto the wooden verandah she would turn and look back.

He had never known a woman who did not look back when she had left him, and he waited, ready to smile and wave.

Irisa, however, walked straight across the verandah and in through the half-open door.

She left the Duke with an apprehensive feeling that perhaps what the gods had given, the gods would take away and he would never see her again.

437

CHAPTER FIVE

THE DUKE AWOKE EARLY and lay planning his day as he had started to do last night.

When he got back to the yacht he had found it difficult to adjust himself to the chatter and laughter of his guests.

They were sitting on deck, drinking champagne, and as he saw at once that Lily was not with them, he knew where she would be.

He was aware that he had no wish at the moment either to talk to her or touch her. So he waited until it was time to dress for dinner, then deliberately went straight to his bed-cabin, where his valet was waiting and had prepared a bath for him.

He knew that Lily would hear him talking to the man, if she was still in the cabin next door, and would understand that he was not joining her as she had expected.

If she had waited all that time, Lily was too clever to look reproachful when the Duke joined them all before dinner.

Instead, she had arrayed herself in one of her most becoming evening-gowns. It was white, like all of her clothes, but it was very elaborate and she wore every jewel she possessed so that she glittered like the stars that were coming out overhead.

She planned that she would ask the Duke to take her on deck while the others played Bridge.

But, to her surprise, after dinner was over he sat down at the card-table and challenged Lord Southwold to a game in which they had very large side-bets which did not affect the other players.

Despite everything she tried to do, Lily could not capture the Duke's attention. So instead she flirted with James Bushly, making it appear obvious that she found him attractive, and hoped the Duke would be jealous.

When finally they retired to bed, Lily was sure the Duke would come to her as he had done every night since they had reached the Mediterranean. But as the hours went by she knew that, for some reason she could not ascertain, she had for tonight, at any rate, lost his interest.

The Duke hardly gave a thought to the fact that Lily was waiting for him.

All the time he played Bridge he was longing to be alone so that he could think over the strange and unusual things that had happened at the Temple of Luxor and the girl who had opened the windows of his mind to new horizons which he had not known existed.

It was not only what she had said, it was what she was, or perhaps she had put a spell on him.

He had read somewhere, or else he had known it instinctively, that the Egyptians saw magic in everything round them, and because he was a very intelligent man, he reasoned to himself that they found the life-force, which was for them the Divine Spirit, in every creature and especially in animals.

Why else, he asked, would animals in human form play such a prominent role in their system of worship?

He had seen the gods with animal-heads on the columns in the Temple and had read in one of the books he had studied that the Sky-god Horus had the head of a falcon, the Goddess of War the head of a lioness, the God of the Cataracks that of a ram, and the Moon-god that of an ibis.

He lay thinking, trying to understand, and he thought, although he was certain it must be his imagination, that Irisa was also thinking of him.

She will tell me more tomorrow evening, he told himself, and knew the idea was exciting in a way that was different from any excitement he had felt in the past.

He had told his valet before dinner to arrange for him to have breakfast early alone in his cabin, and to order two horses, one with a Guide, to be waiting beside the yacht.

He wanted to explore and he had no intention of riding one of the small donkeys that were provided for tourists.

It was still very early and he was sure everybody else was asleep in

their cabins when he walked on deck into the already brilliant sunshine and saw the Theban hills glowing pink from its rays.

The horses waiting for him were the small-boned, fidgety little animals which were far stronger than they looked, and they appeared not
to mind the overwhelming heat as a European horse would have done.

The Guide was a tall, dark-skinned man with handsome features,
wearing the usual white galabieh with a black robe over it and a turban.

Having greeted the Duke respectfully, he led off in the direction of
the hills.

The horses were fresh and at first they moved quickly, then the Duke
deliberately drew in his mount because he wished to look round him.

He also felt, as he had yesterday, the spell of the place enveloping
him, and as he saw ahead the mysteries of the Valley of the Kings, he
remembered that Irisa had said that the Tombs were "Houses of Eternity."

Today the Duke had no wish to visit the few empty Tombs that had
already been excavated but wished merely to look at the countryside
and to sense the atmosphere.

The sun rose higher and it was very hot, but he was too intent to
think of what he was feeling physically while he concentrated on what
he felt in his mind.

He had already told his valet to inform the Guide that he had no
wish to talk unless he asked questions, and accordingly they rode in
silence until, as the man had pointed in the direction he wished to go,
the Duke saw on the ground in front of him a huge, dark granite head.

He realised it was a head from the colossus of a Pharaoh which must
once have adorned a Temple.

He was not interested in who had been carved in such gigantic
proportions. But the Guide said quietly:

"Ramses II said: 'I did good to the gods as well as to men and took
possession of nothing belonging to other people.' "

The Duke found the head lying by itself on the ground somehow
moving, as if it typified the end of a Dynasty which in its time had
played a great part in the history of the world but was now forgotten.

He rode on to look at an amazingly well-preserved Temple which the
Guide told him had been built for Queen Hatshepsut.

The man was obviously anxious for the Duke to dismount and inspect the Temple, and he could see that on the walls sheltered by a

many-pillared portico there were many inscriptions coloured flame and turquoise and depicting gods and goddesses with their strange animal-heads.

Again, he was not interested in detail. He only wanted to look, think, and above all—to feel.

~

When Lily learnt that the Duke had left the yacht very early, she was annoyed.

She had been so certain that he found her irresistible, and the ardour of his love-making had lulled her into a false sense of security.

Now she was alarmed.

Then she was sure that such fears were needless.

He had gone riding only with a Guide, and if he found any women in the Valley of the Kings they would either be mummies or engraved on the ruined Temples and were not likely to constitute any danger to their relationship.

She had always heard that The Dasher was unpredictable, and she supposed that after being cooped up in the yacht for so long he wanted to be free and alone.

She told herself that she would be very stupid if she let him think that she was clinging to him or shackling him in any way.

The stories of how he had avoided matrimony for so long had lost nothing in the telling, and the gossips had described in detail the failure of the many women who had tried to capture him.

"I will not fail!" Lily swore.

She thought of the fire in the Duke's eyes when he kissed her, his excitement when he touched her, and his passion, which exceeded anything she had ever known before.

He loved her! She knew he loved her!

But as the Duke was not there, she contented herself with flirting with Lord Southwold, who was only too willing to substitute for his host.

On any other occasion Lily thought such a very rich man would have been useful to her, and she was quite certain that Lord Southwold, given the opportunity, would be an exceedingly generous lover.

But she had come on the trip determined to marry the most elusive and fascinating bachelor in England, and she was not prepared to be side-tracked into doing anything which might conceivably annoy him.

However, because he was not there, she talked to Lord Southwold about his financial interests and beguiled him with her prophecies of huge successes, enormous profits, and even greater developments in the future.

At the same time, while painting such a glowing picture, she added warnings of the necessity for caution, which made him more certain than he had been already that she could really see into the future.

After luncheon they went ashore as they had done the day before, to walk leisurely in the beautiful garden of the Winter Palace Hotel and then to sit sipping deliciously cool drinks on the verandah.

Two people whom the Southwolds knew had just arrived from England, and as they were socially distinguished and obviously very wealthy, Lily was delighted to make their acquaintance.

Only as the afternoon wore on did she say almost involuntarily to Harry:

"What can have happened to His Grace? I do hope he has not met with an accident or fallen amongst thieves!"

"I am sure The Dasher can look after himself."

"I hope so," Lily said. "At the same time, I cannot help feeling there is a chance of danger."

She spoke in the same mysterious voice that she used when speaking to Lord Southwold, then realised that Harry's eyes were mocking as he answered:

"If you want my opinion, the only danger at the moment is that our host will find his voyage of discovery disappointing and want to return home."

Lily gave a little cry.

"Oh, I hope not!" she said. "It is so lovely here that I have no desire to move anywhere else."

"Then it is up to you," Harry remarked.

She knew he was taunting her, and she hated him. Nevertheless, she gave him one of her beguiling smiles as she said:

"I think we must all be very, very nice to our dashing Duke when he comes back from the wilds."

However, she looked, even if she did not sound it, worried by his absence, and she thought as she turned to speak to somebody else that Harry was pleased at her frustration.

~

The Duke had in fact made his return to the yacht when he knew his party would have crossed the Nile. He was hot and hungry, but at the same time he had enjoyed every moment of his ride and the exploration of the Theban hills.

He thought as he looked at them that they had a glory and at the same time a glamour he had never found anywhere else.

Barren and bare as the rocks were, he was sure that Irisa would tell him that they breathed the mystery of eternal life.

He felt too that they stimulated his mind and gave him an impetus to seek and go on seeking until he found the answer that was waiting for him.

He bathed, changed his clothes, had an excellent luncheon which his Chef had started to prepare as soon as he appeared, then was ready to cross the river to the steps which led directly down from the Temple of Luxor to the water.

He was early and he expected to have to wait for some time before Irisa appeared, but she was there exactly where she had been the day before.

She was looking out in the same way, her little straight nose and softly curved chin silhouetted against the same pillar.

He stood watching her for some moments before she was aware of him, then as a faint smile touched her lips he moved towards her and she turned her head.

"You are there!" he said in his deep voice. "All night I have been half-afraid that you were a dream and I would never find you again."

"I promised to take you to Karnak, and I always try to keep my promises."

She walked away as she spoke, and a moment later he understood that she was taking him to Karnak by boat.

He felt that the reason for it was not because it was an easier way of approach but because he would approach the Temple in the manner intended by those who had built it.

As they stood waiting on the white steps of the Temple for the felucca to pick them up, the Duke felt that he was embarking on a voyage to another land.

Everything he had read about Karnak had bewildered him because

443

it was difficult to understand what the author was trying to say, and yet now as they journeyed slowly towards the greatest Temple in Egypt, the Duke began to realise its significance.

He had read that Karnak covered four hundred acres by the riverside, and he knew that brilliant paintings had adorned its walls and steles of lapis-lazuli were set on both sides of the foremost pylon, of which there were ten in all.

Vast quantities of malachite, silver, and gold covered the facade, while over all, glowing with magic, was the colossus of the Pharaoh, hewn from gritstone, soaring sixty-seven feet into the air.

He was not certain afterwards whether Irisa had said it aloud or he had merely read her mind.

It had taken Egyptians eight hundred years to build it, and now the columns were bare of colour. But the moment they entered the Temple with its gigantic columns seventy feet in height, the Duke was conscious that the whole effect was of an overwhelming, mind-crushing power.

The atmosphere was so different from that of the Temple of Luxor that at first it was hard to collect his thoughts.

Then as he walked in silence, with Irisa moving so lightly beside him that her feet seemed to make hardly any impression in the sand, he knew that here the gods had ruled by fear and their majesty had no humanity.

Many of the reliefs on the columns were strikingly beautiful, and he would have stopped to look at them if Irisa had not seemed to wish him to move on.

He was content to follow her, feeling that she had some reason for where she was taking him.

They passed an enormous relief depicting conquests and sacrifices, then she paused and the Duke could see ahead the Sacred Lake, although she evidently did not intend to go there at the moment.

She was looking at him, he thought, in a strange manner, almost as if she was convincing herself that what she was doing was right, and there was also something which made the Duke feel as if she was testing him.

They had hardly spoken more than a few words since they had met, and yet words had been unnecessary, and he knew that they communicated with each other in their thoughts and he was content just to be with her.

Now as the huge columns rising overpoweringly above them made them seem tiny and insignificant, the Duke had an irresistible impulse to cry out that he was alive when the Temple itself was dead.

And yet he knew it was not true. So much that was life still remained within it.

As the thought came to him, he knew that in some strange, mysterious manner he could not explain, it was what Irisa wanted him to feel.

She gave him a little smile and put out her hand, and when he took it in his he felt her fingers tremble as if they spoke instead of her lips.

"Come," she said very softly. "I have ... something to show ... you."

Drawing him by the hand, she walked towards the end of what appeared to the Duke to be a small Temple.

Ahead he could see some very old and dilapidated bronze gates. One of them was open and Irisa drew him through it and with her free hand closed it behind them.

In front of them was a low chamber, and as they walked into it the sunlight vanished, and at first the Duke could see nothing and was conscious only of the damp, chilly darkness.

Irisa was standing quite still and he held on to her hand almost as if he was afraid he might lose her.

Then as his eyes grew accustomed to the darkness, he was aware that there was light filtering through a tiny hole in the ceiling, and he saw that standing quite close to them there was a female figure.

It was the body of a young woman with rounded hips and firm breasts, but the face was that of a lioness.

It was so unexpected, so different from the huge monstrous columns outside with the blazing sunshine gilding everything with a brilliant light, that the Duke could only look at what he remembered now was the Goddess of War.

Then in an unexpected manner the goddess vanished and he saw clearly a vision in the darkness.

He could never determine afterwards whether the scene was in his mind or if it was actually portrayed in the cell-like sanctuary.

He was now a warrior wearing armour and in command of a number of men who were marching beside him.

He knew they had just arrived by river and had disembarked from a ship in which they had travelled a great distance. They were tired after

445

such a long voyage, but at the same time they were elated because they had reached their destination.

He had been given orders to escort and protect someone who was carried on a litter on the shoulders of six strong men. The Duke looked up and saw that the Princess from the land whence they had come was Irisa!

He saw her face framed with jewels, and he knew she was decked in her finest robes because she had come to Egypt as a bride for the Pharaoh.

As they moved on, the Duke knew that he loved with every breath he drew the woman who had been entrusted to his charge, and whom he had brought as the bride of another man.

He was aware that as soon as he had given her into the hands of the Egyptians, he would return to his own country and never see her again. Yet, he would leave his heart with her.

It was an agony as they neared the great Palace of the Pharaoh to know that while he loved the Princess and she also loved him, there was nothing either of them could do about it.

The Duke was not even sure if they had told each other of what they felt, but words were unnecessary.

Their love linked them together as closely as if they were one person, and it was a love which they had known in the past and would never die.

He was aware in his soldier's mind that the Pharaohs usually took as their Great Chief Wife their sisters or even occasionally their own daughters.

In pre-Dynastic times, property and possessions were transferred through the female line—by matrilineal rather than patrilineal descent.

So, to secure his title beyond the faintest shadow of doubt, the Pharaoh married every woman who could possibly lay claim to the throne.

In addition to his principal and much venerated Queen, he would also possess what might be called "Political Wives"—foreign Princesses who were sent by their fathers to marry the King of Egypt in order to cement a diplomatic alliance.

There might also be "wives" who were bought and introduced into the Royal *harim*, but the children of the Great Chief Wife and the

Political Wives were recognised as Princes or Princesses and they were also endowed with some of the great might and majesty and god-like qualities of the Pharaoh himself.

All this flashed through the mind of the Duke as he escorted the Princess on her carved and gilded litter.

Then as he looked up and her blue eyes met his, they both cried out at the cruelty of the separation ahead.

Yet there was nothing they could do but say a silent "good-bye" and try to believe that their love would endure through the rest of their lives or perhaps, by some strange power they did not understand, surmount death and the grave.

Ahead of them the Duke could see the soldiers of the Pharaoh and his servants coming out to greet the new bride. There were women with flowers and children carrying rose-petals to sprinkle on her path.

Once again he looked up into the blue eyes searching his face.

"Good-bye, my love," he said in his heart.

Then there was darkness.

The vision had gone and there was just a light on the lion-headed goddess.

A long time later, or it may have been only a few minutes, the Duke found himself sitting at the side of the Sacred Lake.

Irisa was beside him and as he looked down at the still water where the Priests had reverently lowered the Royal cedar barge containing the body of a dead Pharaoh, he wondered whether he had suddenly become insane or had taken a drug which had induced strange visions.

Never in his life had he ever not been in complete control of his mind and his body, and he had believed that it was impossible for anyone to hypnotise him.

Now he wondered whether that was what Irisa had done. Then he knew that was not true.

The water touched by the sun was dazzling, and in a voice which did not sound like his own the Duke asked:

"Did you see what I saw?"

There was a little pause before Irisa replied:

"I have . . . seen it in the . . . past."

"You saw how we parted, I suppose in a—previous life?"

"Yes, but there may have been others."

"Other lives?"

"Perhaps . . . I do not . . . know. In Egypt, you will only . . . see the ones that happened . . . here."

"To me it is unacceptable, but you believe it to be true."

The Duke felt as if he forced the question from her and after a moment she said:

"I know you suspect me of trickery in some way, but it would be impossible."

"Where did you take me?"

"To the sanctuary of the Goddess Sekhmet. It is the only sanctuary in the whole of Karnak which still houses the image of a Deity."

"And you found it yourself? Or does everybody know about it?"

"The Guides never take visitors there. They are afraid. But Papa found it soon after we first came to Luxor, and I think it was there that he knew he had been brought here for a purpose."

"What purpose?"

"I would like him to tell you that himself, when he is well enough."

The Duke was silent for a moment. Then he said:

"I am still feeling greatly disturbed by what I have seen, and you can understand that I am trying to find an explanation."

Irisa laughed and it seemed somehow as if the sound rippled across the Sacred Lake and took away some of the overwhelming menace of the great Temple behind them.

"Why are you laughing?" the Duke asked.

"Because you are being so English! You are just like Papa when he first came here and suspected everybody of being a charlatan! 'There must be a reasonable explanation for this!' he would say to me, until he found it was entirely reasonable that we have lived before."

She waited for the Duke to argue with her, and when he did not do so, she went on:

"Just as the Nile never dries up, so life continues, season after season, year after year, century after century."

The Duke was suddenly aware that the sun was deepening red on the horizon and he rose to his feet.

"I must take you home," he said. "Sensible and unimaginative as I am trying to prove myself to be, I do not wish to be lost in Karnak in the darkness.''

"You would not be harmed," Irisa said, "but I agree, it would be frightening.''

They walked back through the rows of pillars which seemed to the Duke to have been placed too close to each other, perhaps in order to proclaim deliberately a power against which there was no defence.

They passed through the Forecourt of Amum and the Temples of various Pharaohs with heraldic pillars until at last they came to the stone steps leading down to the river.

By now the sun was only a streak of burning crimson on the horizon, and by the time they reached the Temple of Luxor the river had turned from gold to purple.

The Temple seemed to welcome them and once again the Duke took Irisa's hand as they moved past the beautiful columns and out on the other side to the waste-land with its mud huts.

There was still enough light to lead them to the wooden house protected by the high palm trees, and when they reached the shrubs Irisa halted.

"We will meet again tomorrow?" the Duke asked.

"Perhaps I have . . . shown you all . . . you wish to . . . see?"

"You know without my saying it that I must see you, and I have only touched the fringe of what I want to know and hear.''

"After what has . . . happened today, you may be disappointed with . . . everything else.''

"That is for me to judge," he replied. "All I want to make certain of is that I shall find you in the same place at the same time. You will promise to come?"

She hesitated, and he was suddenly afraid.

"Please, Irisa, you know as well as I do that I cannot lose you, and you cannot leave me gasping at the incredibility of what you have made me see and feel. You must help me to understand.''

"I do not think you really need my help.''

"I promise you I want it more than I have ever wanted anything before. I am like a drowning man, Irisa, and you have to save me!''

She smiled as if there was something ridiculous in his portraying himself as being so helpless. Then looking up at him she said:

"I was afraid at first that I might be . . . mistaken, but now I am glad,

449

so very glad, that my instinct was right and you are ... who I thought you ... would be."

"What you are saying is that you recognised me when we first met?" She nodded her head.

"I suppose really," the Duke said reflectively after a moment, "that I recognised you when I thought your face was carved on the pillar against which you were standing. It seemed familiar, but it is something which if spoken out loud would seem absurd."

"Of course," she said, "as I have already told you, it is difficult when you first come here to adjust yourself. But in time, as something ... happens every day, it grows easier."

"That is what you have to convince me."

He made an impatient little sound.

"I do not want to leave now, I want to go on talking to you. It is more frustrating than I can possibly explain to have to wait until tomorrow afternoon before I can see you again, but I realise you have to sleep if you watch over your father all night."

It was obvious that he was reasoning it out for himself. Then he said:

"I have had no chance to tell you, but today I rode to the Valley of the Kings."

"Yes, I know."

He raised his eye-brows.

"How do you know?"

She smiled.

"Everybody knows everything in this small place. Ali, one of our servants who works in the gardens, told me you had hired horses, and I thought it very wise of you to do so, rather than go alone."

"I might have gone completely alone," the Duke said, "if I had not been afraid of losing my way, but I told my Guide not to chatter."

"You were sensible in that at any rate. And what did you do when you reached the Burial Ground of the Pharaohs?"

"I only stayed a little while," the Duke said, "as I wanted to go again with you."

"I think ... perhaps it would be ... impossible."

"Why?"

She obviously did not wish to explain. Instead she said:

"Perhaps we can talk about it ... another time."

"And you will come tomorrow?"

She was just about to answer when there was a sudden cry that seemed to echo in the night.

They both turned and saw standing on the verandah a man in white.

He looked about him wildly across the flowers and shrubs, then he saw Irisa and cried:

"Missy, come quick! Come!"

It seemed to the Duke as if Irisa flew from his side. She sped towards the steps leading up to the verandah and climbed them and vanished into the house almost before he could catch his breath.

It was then, slowly and deliberately, that he followed her.

The wooden steps creaked beneath his feet and he walked across the verandah and entered through the open door.

He saw by the faint light coming from another room that he had entered what was obviously a Sitting-Room with windows on both sides of it.

It was already too dark to have an impression of anything but the out-lines of furniture, and he walked towards a light and found himself in the doorway of a small square bedroom on the other side of the house.

Lying on a wooden bed covered only with a white sheet was a man, and kneeling beside him was Irisa.

One glance at the man on the bed told the Duke that he was dead.

He stood in the doorway, not certain what he should do, aware that Irisa's father was, as he might have expected, an exceedingly good-looking man.

His features were clear-cut and very English. The hair at the sides of his head was streaked with grey, and he was extremely thin.

But the Duke was certain that his high forehed denoted intelligence, and he regretted that now it was too late for him to speak to the man who could have told him so much.

There was still Irisa, and he saw that while she was kneeling beside her father, the fingers of one hand were on his pulse, the other hand was on his heart, and she was calm and controlled in a manner that he admired.

Then, as if she recognised that her father was dead, she crossed his hands on his chest and, rising to her feet, drew the sheet very gently over him.

She spoke in Arabic to the servant waiting at the end of the bed. He nodded and the Duke stood aside to allow him to pass through the door, cross the Sitting-Room, and go out of the house.

He waited until Irisa looked at him. Then he said:

"I am sorry. I wished so much to meet your father."

"And I wanted . . . him to know . . . you."

She stood looking down at the body that lay on the bed, then she lifted one of the candles from the table and carried it into the Sitting-Room.

It was a thick white candle in a wooden holder and it illuminated the room, which the Duke could now see was furnished poorly but in good taste.

He liked the simple wicker chairs which were unpretentious but practical in a land where it was always hot.

Then he saw that on the shelves and tables round the room there were pieces of pottery, carvings, and figurines which he was sure had come from the Tombs.

As if he had asked the question, Irisa said:

"They were presents to Papa from those he treated, and, although it seems somewhat . . . reprehensible, they stole what they did not have to give."

"I am sure some of these things are very valuable."

"I would not wish to . . . sell them," Irisa replied, "but I am afraid I shall . . . have to."

As she spoke she sat down in one of the wicker chairs and the Duke thought she had done so because she found she had not the strength to go on standing.

"Now that your father is dead," he said gently. "what are you going to do? You cannot stay here alone."

She made a little sound that was half a sigh and half a sob.

"I suppose not . . . but I would . . . like to . . . stay."

"Unless you have friends who will look after you, you must realise that is impossible."

There was silence and he realised that she was striving desperately to find some way of keeping the house which was, to her, home.

"To whom does it belong?" the Duke asked, and she was aware that he had followed her thoughts.

"The Missionary Society," she answered, "and I suppose now when they learn of Papa's death they will send another man to take his place."

"He will be eager for converts," the Duke remarked, "until the magic of Egypt captivates him as it captivated your father."

He thought he brought a faint smile to her lips. Then she said:

"Perhaps he . . . will need an . . . assistant."

The Duke shook his head.

"He will more likely have a wife and half-a-dozen children!"

"Then . . . I must . . . go . . . home."

He could barely hear the words, and yet she had said them.

"Do you mean to England?"

She nodded as if it was difficult to speak, and after a moment he asked:

"You have relatives there who will look after you?"

"I suppose I must go to my grandfather, but I have not . . . seen him since I was . . . a baby."

"It is not likely he would refuse to have you, considering you are alone."

As he spoke, the Duke thought that Irisa's grandfather or any other relative who might be alive would be surprised at her beauty and also at her intelligence.

How could it be possible that anybody could behave so bravely in such circumstances?

He knew without her telling him that her father had meant everything in her life, and that her security and safety was gone. She was alone in a strange land where it would be impossible for her to look after herself.

It was one thing, the Duke thought, to be the daughter of a Missionary and be protected by the very sanctity of her father's calling, but another to be a very lovely young girl who had barely reached womanhood and must try to cope alone and unprotected.

He felt himself shudder at the thought of what might happen to her, and after a moment he said:

"As you have to return to England, I will take you there."

He knew as she looked at him in a rather startled fashion that the idea had never crossed her mind, and he thought that no other woman, having met him, would have been prepared to let him pass out of her life without even a backwards glance.

"But . . . I cannot—ask you to do . . . that," she said.

"Why not?" the Duke enquired. "There is plenty of room in my yacht, and I am quite prepared to wait until you have packed and tidied things up, and of course buried your father."

453

Irisa clasped her hands together, and after a moment she said:

"I feel I would be ... imposing myself upon you, and I am quite certain your ... friends will not ... want me ... but for the moment ... it is difficult to think of what else I ... can do."

"Then I suggest that you leave everything to me," the Duke said quietly.

Afterwards he realised that it was his attitude of authority that made everything easy for Irisa.

She had sent the servant to fetch embalmers, and while they were working, the copper-maker and the grave-diggers had come from one of the scattered mud huts to await instructions.

He learnt that there was at the moment no Christian Priest in Luxor and it had been arranged that the Services for those who desired them should be conducted by Irisa's father, who had been ordained before he became a Missionary.

There was, however, a small Cemetery which the Reverend Patrick Garron had himself set aside for the burial of the few Christians who followed his creed.

There had been very few, and the Duke suspected that they had paid him lip-service because they liked him as a man rather than because he had lured them away from the gods they had worshipped since they were born.

As was usual in the East, the Duke arranged for the burial to take place early the next morning, and he paid the grave-diggers to work by moonlight.

Then he went in search of Irisa and found that the embalmers had finished their work and she was kneeling beside her father's bed, and he thought she was praying. When he appeared in the doorway, she rose to her feet.

He took her hand and stood looking down at her father, who appeared serene and at peace.

He was dressed in a clean white shirt, with his hands crossed on his chest, and Irisa had placed between his fingers a lotus-flower that was just coming into bud.

As the Duke looked at it, as if once again she read his thoughts she said:

"The emblem of ... love and ... eternal life. Papa is not ... dead, and one day we shall ... meet again."

Her voice broke a little but she did not cry, and the Duke tightened his fingers on her hand.

"I know he would want you to think like that."

"Of course," she answered. "He always believed that death was quite unimportant . . . just the discarding of a body that is worn out and is no longer of any use."

She spoke in her soft voice that seemed almost like music.

Then the Duke drew her from the bedroom and back into the Sitting-Room.

"Will you come to the yacht with me now," he asked, "or do you want to stay here tonight?"

It was something he would never have suggested to any other woman, but he knew already, without even asking the question, that Irisa would not wish to leave her father.

"I will . . . stay here," she said, "and of course . . . if tomorrow you change your mind . . . and do not . . . want me . . . I will . . . understand."

"There is no question of my changing my mind," the Duke replied. "I am only concerned with what is best for you."

"Then you know I cannot . . . leave him."

"Yes, I know," he said, "and I will stay with you."

She looked at him in a startled fashion.

"There is no need for you to do that. I shall be quite . . . safe."

"I would not like to risk it," he said. "By now everybody will know that your father is dead, and there are many things in this room that would interest the Collectors. Robbers who are prepared to rob the Tombs would not hesitate to rob you."

"I have our . . . servants . . . here," Irisa said.

"I feel that in an emergency I would be more protection than they could be," the Duke insisted. "What I would like to do, if you will allow me, is to send your servant to the yacht and tell them I shall not be returning. I will also order something for us to eat."

"I could . . . cook you . . . something," Irisa said a little vaguely.

"What I want you to do," the Duke answered firmly, "is to lie down. You are sensible enough to realise that you have had a severe shock. When the meal is ready I will let you know. In the meantime, rest. Try to believe, as you said just now, that one day you and your father will meet again."

As he said the words he thought that they were very unlike anything he had ever thought or said before, and certainly something he would never have believed if he had not seen that strange vision in the sanctuary in Karnak.

But there was no time to think of that now.

Irisa went to her room, which was situated on the other side of the Sitting-Room. Then the Duke called the servant and, having scribbled his instructions on a piece of paper, sent him off to the yacht.

Only when he had gone and the Duke started to wander round the Sitting-Room, looking at the collection of Egyptian antiques which Irisa's father had accumulated, did he wonder what construction his party would put on his absence.

He had made no explanation in the note he had written to Harry. He had merely said that he would not return as he was staying with a friend who needed him. He had added a list of the food and drink he wanted.

As he could find no envelope on the table which was obviously used as a desk, he merely folded the note, handed it to the servant, and told him to hurry as quickly as he could to the yacht on the other side of the river.

The Egyptian was obviously extremely impressed that the Duke should be the owner of such a large and magnificent craft.

He bowed low, his fingers touching his forehead, and by the light of the stars now coming out the Duke watched him running in his flat sandals over the sand.

Then as he looked round the room again to decide where later he could make himself comfortable, he thought this was an adventure that he had never foreseen and could not possibly have imagined might happen on what was entirely a pleasure trip.

Yet he knew that this small room with its wooden walls, cheap furniture, and priceless relics from the past was also a part of the spellbinding mystery of Egypt which had enthralled and enchanted him ever since he had steamed through the lotus-shaped Delta into the Nile.

He had been propelled relentlessly towards Luxor, where fate, or perhaps one of the animal-headed gods, had decided that Irisa should be waiting for him in the Temple.

CHAPTER SIX

THE DUKE SPENT a far more comfortable night than he had expected, because his valet Jenkins had arrived with the food and had brought what he would require for the night.

Jenkins was always invaluable in a crisis, and without asking any questions except to elicit that the Duke intended to stay in the Mission House, he procured, by some means of his own, a native bed.

It was only the usual structure of a frame on four legs with rope webbing as a support, but when there were blankets laid on it and a pillow it was easy for the Duke to sleep.

Before this he had sent Irisa's servant to the Hotel, and he had come back with the information that among the guests there was a retired Clergyman.

The Duke then wrote a note asking the Clergyman to perform the Burial Service the following morning.

He felt that it was the right thing in the circumstances, although he was aware that Irisa would have been quite content for her father to be buried in consecrated ground without a Service.

When he could think of nothing else for him to do, and the carpenter, having measured the dead man, had promised the coffin would be ready first thing in the morning, the Duke went to Irisa's bedroom to tell her that dinner was ready.

Jenkins had laid everything out on the table in the centre of the Sitting-Room, and he had also found several other candles in their carved wooden candle-sticks, which he had lit so that the room was lighter and without shadows.

When the Duke knocked on Irisa's door she opened it and he saw that she had changed her gown for another made in the same simple way.

He also thought she had been crying, but he could not be sure, since she was still calm and controlled.

"Come and have something to eat," he said, "and for the moment do not worry about anything else."

"I have been writing letters to the Missionary Society in England," she replied, "and also to the Anglican Bishop in Cairo, who asked Papa to take the Services here until the Church they are building is finished."

The Duke told her that there was a retired Clergyman staying at the Winter Palace, and she exclaimed:

"How kind of you to think of it! I thought Papa would have to be buried without any prayers but mine."

"And mine," the Duke said quietly.

She gave him a glance of gratitude, then sat down at the table on the chair that Jenkins pulled out for her.

"Thank you," she said to him. "I can see you have saved me a great deal of work, and I am most grateful."

"It's a pleasure, Miss," Jenkins answered, and went into the small kitchen to collect the first course.

The food the Duke had ordered was cold, but it was certainly delicious, and he was pleased to notice that Irisa ate quite a considerable amount and did not protest when Jenkins filled her glass with wine.

They talked very little while the valet was waiting on them, and only when he had cleared away the dishes and left the room did Irisa say:

"Please . . . do not trouble to stay . . . here tonight. I promise you I shall be quite . . . safe, and I do not . . . wish to take you from your . . . friends."

"My friends will amuse themselves without me," the Duke said, "and I am still concerned with your safety."

He spoke positively, and he liked the way she accepted that he was determined to do what he wished and ceased arguing with him.

Instead she said:

"You will understand that I want to stay . . . with Papa a little . . . longer before I go to . . . bed."

"Of course," the Duke agreed, "and I am quite prepared to sit reading until you are willing to try to sleep."

She thought he was telling her in a subtle way that it would be foolish to stay up all night and that with the ordeal of the Funeral ahead of her tomorrow she should rest.

She hesitated a moment. Then she said:

"I think perhaps it would interest you to read some of the notes Papa made about the Temples and Tombs since he came to Luxor."

"You mean he has written down his findings?"

"His findings and his thoughts, which I am sure one day will be proved true."

"Then there is nothing I would like more than to read them," the Duke said, "and I shall always, Irisa, regret deeply that I did not meet your father."

He smiled before he added:

"You will have to make up for my disappointment by telling me of the things that I want to know but was unable to ask him."

Irisa opened a drawer in the table which the Duke had thought was used as a desk and took out several manuscript-books from what he could see was a large pile of them.

"I think perhaps you will find it best to start with the last one and work backwards," she said. "As I told you, when we first came here Papa was skeptical about many things."

"I will read them in whichever order you tell me to," the Duke answered quietly.

As he spoke, Jenkins came from the kitchen. He had packed up the dishes in a basket and now he set it down on the floor.

"Is there anything else Your Grace requires?" he asked, "I've put Your Grace's razors in the washing-room and I'll be back first thing in the morning."

"Thank you," the Duke said, "and, Jenkins, I shall require two stewards to pack up all the ornaments in this room. It would be best if they could obtain wooden boxes so that nothing will be broken, and they will require plenty of newspaper with which to wrap each object."

Jenkins looked round.

"I'll see to it, Your Grace."

He picked up the basket and bowed to Irisa.

"Good-night, Miss! Good-night, Your Grace!"

When he had shut the door that led to the verandah, they heard his footsteps receding down the wooden steps.

"He is so kind," Irisa said, "but I am giving you all this . . . trouble."

"It is a repayment for what you have given me in the past," the Duke said, "and will, I hope, continue to do in the future."

He spoke lightly, wanting her to smile, and she said:

"I wish I had been able to tell Papa what happened today in the sanctuary. He would have been so interested and he would certainly have written it down."

"I have a feeling that his notes would be of inestimable value to a great number of people if they could read them," the Duke said, "and that means they must be published."

He felt for a moment that Irisa would refuse, thinking that what her father had written would be too personal. Then she said:

"If you could arrange that, it would justify everything Papa did in the life he chose against a great deal of opposition."

As she spoke she became very conscious that her father was separated from them only by a wooden door, and she added:

"I hope he . . . knows what you have . . . suggested."

Without another word she walked into the room where her father lay.

The Duke sat down in a wicker chair, thinking that nobody would believe it if he told them the strange things that had happened to him since he had come to Luxor.

He put the manuscript-books down on his knees and looked round the room. He was quite certain, as he had been when he first saw them, that many of the Egyptian carvings, statues, and bowls were very valuable.

"There are Collectors all over the world," he said to himself, "who would wish to possess that small statue of the Pharaoh with the cobra-sign on his forehead."

There was another of a hawk-headed god which he was certain any Museum would covet.

He decided that before he allowed Irisa to sell even one of them he would not only have them all examined by the best Egyptologist in London, but he would also learn a great deal about such things himself, so as to make certain she was not cheated.

I thought I was a knowledgeable man, he thought with a sigh, *and yet I have just discovered I am a complete ignoramus about a Kingdom which goes back to 3,200 B.C.*

It was two hours before the door of the bedroom opened and Irisa came out carrying the candle which had stood by the bed.

She closed the door quietly, and as the Duke rose to his feet, she did not speak to him but merely gave him a faint smile as she walked past him towards her own room.

He knew, because she did not talk, that she was transported by her prayers and her love of her father until she was with him in the world to which he had gone rather than in the earthly one he had left behind.

As the door of her bedroom closed, the Duke knew that she was aware that he would understand, just as he had known instinctively what she was feeling.

The notes he had been reading were so absorbing, so interesting, that he thought it was a pity to have to go to bed.

Then he knew that because of his long ride during the morning he was physically tired even though mentally he had never felt more alert.

He partially undressed, put on the long blue cotton robe which Jenkins had left ready for him, and lay down on the native bed, finding it surprisingly comfortable.

As he did so, he remembered that on his instructions Jenkins had brought with him a small revolver and placed it in the pocket of his gown.

He drew it out, put it down on a chair beside the bed which also held a candle, and then with a last look round at the treasures he was guarding as well as Irisa, he blew out the light.

He had been asleep for perhaps two hours when he awoke, conscious of danger.

He did not move but only listened, and was sure that something unusual had disturbed his sleep.

At first he could only hear the familiar sounds of the night, an owl hooting, a dog barking in the distance, and indistinct sounds to which it was impossible to put a name but which were doubtless the movements of rats or other small animals which would have gone unnoticed in the daytime.

He thought he heard a child crying, then much nearer, in fact he was certain it was outside on the verandah, there was a sound that could only have been made by a human being.

The door was locked, and after Jenkins had left them and Irisa had gone to her father's room the Duke had pushed home a heavy bolt.

He was sure that the sound he heard came from the window, and it flashed through his mind that that would be the easiest way for a thief to enter the house or even to put in his hand and try to grasp anything within reach.

He considered what he should do, and, sitting up in bed, he swung his feet onto the floor and reached first for his revolver, then for a box of matches.

He managed to hold both the revolver and the box in his left hand, then struck a match. It failed to light and he took out another.

As he did so, he was aware that whoever was outside the window was standing still, and he thought, although it might have been his imagination, that he could hear heavy breathing.

Then as the match flared into flame and he lit the candle, he heard somebody scurrying away down the wooden steps, but so quietly that he was certain the man was bare-footed.

The Duke rose and walked to the window to pull back the curtains. The stars and the moon gave a light by which he could be sure the small garden was empty, but it was impossible to see far beyond the shrubs.

It is a good thing I was here! he thought.

He knew that if he had not been, Irisa would certainly had been robbed of her father's treasures, and if she had attempted to interfere she might have been injured.

The Tomb-robbers were completely ruthless, and he had heard from visitors to Cairo how they had looted the treasures that had been excavated and had not hesitated to murder those who tried to prevent them from taking away their spoils.

The Duke thought that if he had been alone he might have followed the man, who perhaps had an accomplice waiting for him, but he knew that it was more important to keep Irisa safe than to risk leaving her unprotected.

He stood for some time at the window, knowing that anybody watching would be able to see him clearly with the light behind him.

Then, thinking it was unlikely that the robbers would return, he went back to bed.

~

In the morning, thanks to the Duke's organisation, everything went smoothly.

He had paid for the coffin, which he was certain was more expensive than what Irisa would have chosen. By the time she came from her bedroom, pale but composed, her father had been lifted from the bed and into it.

The embalmers had come back to make sure their work had not deteriorated overnight, and had brought with them flowers which the Duke thought should be both inside and outside the coffin.

He saw that Irisa was wearing a gown in which he had not seen her before, again very simple, and the pale blue-grey of a pigeon's breast.

It gave her an ethereal appearance and the bonnet which she carried in her hand had ribbons of the same colour.

Then as if the Duke had asked the question she said as he looked at her:

"I have no black, and Papa always said that if one believed in eternal life either as a Christian or an Egyptian, it was hypocritical to mourn those who had left us but were not dead."

The Duke thought that this was a very different sentiment from that expressed by Queen Victoria, who mourned so excessively that she was still wearing the deepest black for the Prince Consort, who had died twenty-six years ago, but he merely said:

"Everything you tell me about your father, and everything I read last night, makes me realise he was a very exceptional person."

Irisa's eyes lit up and she replied:

"I wish he had known that . . . somebody like you had . . . said that about . . . him."

She did not wait for the Duke to reply but went to the bedroom, and although he did not follow her he could see her through the open door standing looking down at the coffin.

After a few minutes he told the men who were waiting outside to come in, put on the lid, and screw it down.

When they carried the coffin out onto the verandah, the small garden was already filled with people and others were arriving every moment.

The Duke knew they were the men and women whom Irisa's father had served not by trying to convert them to Christianity but by tending them in their illnesses.

He had healed their children of the eye-disease which affected so many Egyptians, and because he had lived amongst them they felt he was always there when they needed him.

Because they loved him when he was alive, they were prepared to revere him now that he was dead.

By the time the bearers had lifted the coffin onto their shoulders and moved away with Irisa and the Duke following, there was a crowd of silent mourners following them all the way to the small Cemetery.

There were half-a-dozen graves of Christians who had died since Irisa and her father had come to Luxor, all marked with cheap little wooden crosses.

The retired Clergyman, wearing a white surplice, was standing by the open grave with a prayer-book in his hand, and as soon as the coffin was lowered he started the words of the Burial Service.

It was very short. At the same time, the Duke could not help thinking it was the sort of Funeral he would like for himself, with no pomp and circumstance, no mourners in black crepe, veils, black morning-coats, and top-hats.

Instead there was just Irisa, looking like someone who had stepped out of a fairy-story or perhaps down from the engravings on a Temple, and the natives with their children standing outside the small Cemetery but watching with reverence all that was taking place within.

As the Service finished, Irisa dropped a lotus-flower, which the Duke realised now came from the Sacred Lake at Karnak, onto the coffin.

Then as the grave-diggers covered it with sand, her lips moved and the Duke knew she was saying good-bye to her father.

After they had both thanked the Clergyman, they walked back in silence to the house while the natives dispersed to their own mud huts.

The children, as if released from the constriction of being quiet, were chasing one another round the palm trees and their voices and laughter seemed to fill the air with joy.

When they entered the house, the Duke saw as he had expected that Jenkins had breakfast ready for them.

Irisa, however, went quickly into her bedroom and he wondered if she was too upset to join him, but again with a self-control that was exceptional she returned in about five minutes to sit down at the table and drink the coffee which Jenkins poured out for her.

Only then did she realise that a great number of the ornaments in the room had gone, and when she looked at the Duke as if for explanation he said:

"Jenkins tells me my stewards have already packed and taken two large boxes to the yacht, and are now procuring more, with which they will return in a very short while."

As he said this, Irisa rose from the table and walked to the shelves where the pottery was arranged. She lifted down three pots and several attractively decorated tiles which were propped against the wall behind them.

"These are fakes," she said, "and I think perhaps they should be separated from the others."

"Fakes?" the Duke exclaimed. "How do you know?"

He thought as he looked at them that they appeared to be very much the same as the others, and in fact they were indistinguishable from the ones Irisa had not moved.

"There are craftsmen working all the time," she explained, "to copy what is to be found in the Museums or a genuine article which has been stolen from a Tomb."

"How do you know which are fakes?" the Duke asked.

Irisa smiled at him for the first time that morning.

"*You* should be able to know by instinct," she replied. "But for ordinary people there are certain tests—quite simple ones—that can be made to determine whether the glazing is hundreds of years old or was put on yesterday!"

She saw that the Duke was interested and added:

"You always have to be on your guard against fakes, whatever you are offered, for the Egyptians are very, very clever at such deceptions."

"You mean they have inherited the craftsmanship of their ancestors?" the Duke replied. "I intend to buy quite a number of objects to take home with me before I leave Egypt, and I shall certainly need your help, Irisa."

"I am sure you will find plenty of connoisseurs in Cairo who will be only too willing to advise you."

"I prefer to trust you."

He thought, although he was not sure, that she was pleased.

He looked again at the genuine pottery on the shelf and saw that beside them there was a flat stone which seemed somehow out-of-place.

Irisa followed the direction of his eyes.

"That is Papa's consecrated stone."

The Duke looked puzzled.

"A travelling Priest," she explained, "cannot expect to find a Church everywhere he goes, but with that stone, any place where he puts it has the sanctity of a consecrated building."

"I have never heard of that before!" the Duke exclaimed.

When breakfast was over the stewards returned with the boxes which they required for the rest of the treasures, which were being carried by native porters.

The Duke said nothing, but he smiled as he thought how quickly the English, whatever their station in life, reacted to being waited on when they were on foreign soil. In England there was no question but that the stewards would have carried the boxes themselves.

While they were carefully packing each object wrapped thickly in newspaper, Irisa went from the room to pack her clothes.

There could not have been many of them, for all she possessed filled only two small leather trunks, which to judge from their appearance had travelled many dusty miles and been somewhat roughly used.

She came into the Sitting-Room to collect her father's manuscript-books, and by that time all the ornaments had gone, including the fakes which the Duke had told the stewards to pack separately.

Then in a voice which sounded a little helpless she said:

"What shall I . . . do with Papa's . . . clothes?"

"I think you might leave them," he replied, "although I doubt very much whether they will still be here when his successor arrives."

She nodded her head in agreement, and he said:

"Does anything else belong to you? I suppose the furniture goes with the house."

"Our servants will be paid for keeping it safe."

"I will give them some money."

She looked at him a little shyly as she explained:

"Papa always . . . saw to those . . . things. I have never . . . worried about it . . . until now."

"Then leave it to me," the Duke said.

"N—no . . . please . . ." Irisa began, but he interrupted:

"We can talk about your financial situation later, but I think now it is best to take you away from here, otherwise you will feel upset."

"Papa hated people who made . . . scenes," Irisa said simply.

The Duke thought there were tears in her eyes as she said good-bye to the servants who he learnt had waited on them ever since they had arrived in Luxor.

One, who was a middle-aged man, obviously had a deep affection for Irisa, calling down on her the blessing of the gods, then as if he suddenly remembered he was a Christian, he added: "And the blessing of the Lord God and His Holy Spirit!"

When finally the stewards, Jenkins, and the luggage had all gone, the Duke and Irisa left too, but not by the shortest way used by the others, but through the waste-land which led to the Temple of Luxor.

The people in the mud huts waved to them and several small children ran up with flowers for Irisa. Then as they stepped through the tall columns they were alone and the atmosphere of the Temple seemed to envelop them as if they belonged there.

They did not speak but went slowly through the great Courtyards and past the red granite statues until they reached the place where they had first seen each other.

The view over the river towards the Valley of the Kings was dazzling in the sunshine, and Irisa stood looking at it for a long time, until the Duke said gently:

"There is no need for you to say good-bye. We shall come here again."

"You are . . . sure? I feel as if I am leaving everything I have ever known and stepping into a strange and frightening world of which I am completely ignorant."

"It is something you have done before," he said, thinking of how he had seen her in the sanctuary raised on a litter and being carried towards the Pharaoh's Palace.

"It is much the . . . same," she said, reading his thoughts, "only then I was saying . . . good-bye to . . . you, but now I have said . . . good-bye to . . . Papa."

"As you said yourself," he answered, "life flows on like the river— the river you are going to cross now. But we will come back."

She smiled at him as if he had suddenly swept away the mist in which she had been enveloped and now it was clear.

"It will . . . be an . . . adventure!" the Duke replied.

467

He put out his hand and she put her fingers in his.

She had taken off the gloves she had worn during the Funeral and now he felt her fingers tighten on his, not from fear but as if she sought his strength and it gave her courage.

They walked down the steps to where the Duke had ordered the dinghy to be waiting for them.

He helped her into it and as they sat side by side in the cushioned stern and the sailors dipped their oars, he said:

"You must not be nervous of meeting my guests. They are all very charming people and you will like them."

He felt it was right that he should reassure her, but even as he spoke he wondered what Lily's reaction would be to having another very lovely women on board.

Irisa gave a little smile.

"I do not suppose," she said, "that they will be more frightening than the cannibals that Papa and I encountered in the Congo, or Mtesa, the King of Buganda, who celebrated any significant dream with a human sacrifice—Christians were the usual choice."

"But you survived."

"Only by the skin of our teeth!" Irisa answered, and the Duke laughed.

It was still comparatively early despite the fact that they had been busy for hours, and when they boarded the yacht there was only Harry seated under the awning and reading the newspapers which were out-of-date.

He rose to his feet as soon as the Duke and Irisa appeared, and exclaimed:

"I am delighted to see you, Dasher! I was rather afraid you had been lost in the desert or incarcerated in the Tomb of some long-dead Pharaoh and we would have to excavate the whole mountain to find you."

"But as you see, I am very much alive," the Duke replied.

He turned to Irisa.

"May I introduce my oldest friend, Harry Settingham—Miss Irisa Garron."

He saw as he spoke that Harry was staring at Irisa with both surprise and admiration in his eyes.

Then he was aware as Harry looked back at him that there was something he wanted to tell him.

"I expect you would like first to go to your cabin," he said to Irisa, "and take off your bonnet."

He did not wait for her answer but began to lead the way down the companionway which led to the cabins.

Then Jenkins appeared and he said:

"Will you show Miss Irisa to her cabin, Jenkins? I want to have a word with Mr. Settingham."

"Of course, Your Grace."

Leaving Jenkins to provide Irisa with everything she needed and doubtless to unpack for her as well, the Duke hurried back the way he had come to find Harry waiting for him.

Because they were so closely attuned to each other, the Duke said without preamble:

"What has happened?"

"A great deal!" Harry replied. "And I know you will be astonished, but I doubt if it will upset you very much."

"What do you mean?"

"Lily has left!"

"Left!" the Duke exclaimed.

This was certainly something he had not expected.

"With Charlie!"

The Duke stared at Harry incredulously.

"What are you saying?"

"That Lily was astute enough to realise she had lost you, and cut her losses somewhat dramatically."

"Did you say she has left with Charlie?"

Harry's lips twisted in a wry smile.

"Ostensibly he has left for England to see to some financial deal that makes it imperative for him to be in London in person."

"And what is the truth?"

"That he and Lily have gone first to Cairo, and then I think they intend to visit Paris."

"Good God! What has Amy to say about all this?"

"I have not dared discuss it with her. I was leaving that to you."

"Thank you!" the Duke answered sarcastically. "But Charlie! I would not have believed it of him!"

"Shall I tell you exactly what happened?" Harry asked. "She saw you yesterday evening with that lovely creature you have just brought aboard."

"Where did she see me?"

"Coming down the steps of the Temple and getting into a boat."

The Duke looked puzzled, knowing it was some little distance from where the yacht was moored. Then Harry explained:

"Charlie, Lily, and I were standing here, and we were watching the birds through a pair of binoculars which he told us were the strongest ever made. They certainly had fantastic magnifying power."

He paused, but the Duke did not speak, so he continued:

"Charlie had been looking at the birds in the palm trees when suddenly Lily gave an exclamation and took the binoculars from his hands. She could see you quite clearly as you walked down the steps and helped a young woman into a boat."

The Duke was still silent as Harry went on:

"I knew Lily had been annoyed all day that you had gone off riding without seeing her, and she dragged us back from the Winter Palace far earlier than we intended, simply because she hoped to catch you as soon as you returned."

The Duke said nothing, but he was thinking that Lily must have been already annoyed the day before, when he had not joined her in his private cabin and that night had omitted to make love to her as she must have expected.

But he was in fact not concerned with Lily's feelings so much as with his own overwhelming relief that he had no explanations to make about Irisa.

Nor was Lily here waiting to continue a love-affair which had, he knew, come abruptly to an end the moment he had arrived in Luxor.

It was not only Irisa who had ended his feelings for Lily but the fact that Lily belonged to a world which for the moment had no interest for him, and her beauty had lost its power even to evoke his admiration, let alone his desire.

He was aware that if she were still on the yacht he would have felt somewhat guilty at expressing the suddenness of the change in his feelings, which he could no more control than the river beneath them could stop flowing.

He knew that he was interested, intrigued, and fascinated by what he had found in Egypt, to the point where it was difficult to think of anything else or to understand how Lily had ever aroused him.

"When we learnt you were not returning last night," Harry was saying, "Lily accepted the inevitable and cut her losses."

"With Charlie," the Duke murmured.

"As you say, with Charlie," Harry repeated.

As if the Duke felt he must help in a mess for which he knew he was responsible, he said:

"I can hardly believe that what you are telling me is the truth, but I am extremely concerned about Amy."

"Charlie was attracted to Lily the moment he saw her."

"I had no idea."

"I know that," Harry said. "You had made it very obvious that she was yours and it was a question of 'Keep off!' But Lily appreciated that Charlie is a very, very rich man."

"I am disgusted by the whole thing!" the Duke exclaimed sharply. "I am going below to have a word with Amy."

As he did so, he knew he was not only disgusted but apprehensive as to what Amy would say or do.

He was extremely fond of her and he had always thought of Charlie as one of his best friends, but that this should happen, clearly through his fault, was very awkward and embarrassing.

He knocked on the door of Amy's cabin and when she told him to come in found her sitting in a chair, writing letters.

"May I come in?" the Duke asked.

"Yes, of course, Dasher," Amy replied. "I am glad you are back. I was beginning to be worried about you."

"I am very worried indeed about what I have just learnt," the Duke said.

He crossed the cabin to sit down in a chair beside her, and after a moment she said:

"I know it must be embarrassing for you. At the same time, let me assure you that Charlie will come back to me."

"You are sure of that?"

"But of course!" Amy answered. "This has happened before, and when the first excitement of feeling young and showing off to a woman young enough to be his daughter is over, Charlie finds that there are two things which matter in his life more than anything else."

"What are those?" the Duke asked.

"His son and me!"

471

Amy gave a little sigh.

"I think Charlie loves Jack, who as you know will be leaving Eton next year, more than anybody else in the whole world. Although I am not and never have been as beautiful as somebody like Lily, I understand him and I also love him, because when he is not playing the part of the Gay Cavalier, he is only a little boy who needs mothering."

The Duke took Amy's hand in his and kissed it.

"You are wonderful!"

"Not really," Amy contradicted. "I want to scratch her eyes out, pull her hair, and scream! But that would do no good, so I am just going to try and amuse myself until Charlie returns."

"He has behaved abominably!" the Duke exclaimed angrily.

"Men are only human," Amy said, "and Lily is very, very beautiful, and I understand she has an appetite for emeralds."

The Duke repressed a laugh.

"That is what Harry said, but how do you know?"

"She has persuaded Charlie to go to Cairo, and if she does not find what she wants there, Paris will doubtless supply everything she needs, and that will include gowns from the redoubtable Mr. Worth."

"I am glad we have found her out," the Duke said. "She certainly took me in."

He realised that Amy was looking at him a little quizzically and with a somewhat twisted smile.

"To me she was always too good to be true," she said after a moment, "and I never did believe all that nonsense about being clairvoyant."

"Of course! It was all a fake," the Duke said.

As he spoke he could hear Irisa saying in her soft voice:

"Always beware of fakes."

If he had been more astute and used his intelligence and instinct, he thought now, he would have been aware from the very beginning that Lily was not what she seemed, and her claim to being "fey" had merely been an act which had unfortunately ensnared poor Charlie.

"A fake!" he murmured to himself, and knew that in contrast he had brought on board what was real and undisputably genuine.

When he left Amy, telling her again how much he admired her, he went back to Harry.

He had waited for him, and as the Duke flung himself down in a comfortable chair he said:

"I am not going to ask any questions. I just want to know what is happening, where we are going, and what you intend to do about Miss Garron.''

"What do you expect me to do?'' the Duke asked.

"Well—and I suppose it is a question—who is she?''

"She is the daughter of a Missionary.''

He saw the astonishment in his friend's face and it amused him.

"Her father is dead,'' the Duke explained. "We buried him this morning, and she wishes to return to England. Is that what you want to know?''

"I never imagined that Missionaries had beautiful daughters. It is usually their wives who cut their way single-handedly through the jungle and rout hundreds of blood-thirsty Zulus!''

"You have been reading too many boys' adventure-stories!'' the Duke remarked. "At the same time, Irisa did say that more frightening than meeting you were the cannibals her father and she encountered in the Congo.''

"I find that easier to believe than Lily's prophecies of rising shares and gigantic profits!''

"Amy says,'' the Duke remarked, "that this is not the first time Charlie has gone off, but he always comes home.''

"I know that,'' Harry replied. "Three years ago he went to the South of France for three months with Philip Goodwin's wife.''

"Good Lord! I had no idea of that!'' the Duke exclaimed.

"Everybody hushed it up for Amy's sake, and when he returned we pretended it had never happened.''

"What happened to Philip's wife?''

"Consoled herself with a Greek ship-owner, I believe. Anyway, Philip refused to divorce her, so they are still married, although he has since involved himself with quite a few attractive creatures.''

"I cannot think why you never tell me these things,'' the Duke complained.

"The answer to that is quite easy,'' Harry answered. "You are not interested.''

The Duke was aware that that was true.

He was not interested in gossip and he did not care who ran away with whom, when he was living his own life to the full and concentrating on the things which he felt at that particular moment were important to him.

Now he had something much more interesting to concentrate on, but in an entirely different manner from anything he had known before.

He suddenly had an urge to be with Irisa, to talk to her, to hear her soft voice telling him things which he found completely and utterly absorbing.

He thought perhaps she was staying down in her cabin because she had sensed that he wanted to talk to Harry alone.

Without explaining his reason for doing so, he got up and walked away to find her. Harry watched him go and for a moment his eyes were puzzled.

Then there was a smile on his lips, as if he had found the answer to a question.

He picked up the newspaper again.

Down below, the Duke found Jenkins coming from his own cabin.

"Where is Miss Irisa?" he asked.

In answer, Jenkins pointed to the cabin next to his, which had been occupied by Lily.

For a moment the Duke felt annoyed.

Then he told himself that it was the second-best cabin in the yacht and, as Lily was no longer using it, it had seemed obvious to Jenkins that he should install Irisa there.

Then as he thought about it, although it had not occurred to him before, it was exactly where he wanted her to be.

She was lovely, far more beautiful than Lily could ever be, and in a very different manner.

She was also, although until this moment he had been too bemused by all she had shown and told him to realise it, very desirable.

There was a light in the Duke's eyes, a light which had glowed over the years a great many times and which Harry would have recognised.

With a smile on his lips he knocked on the cabin door.

CHAPTER SEVEN

THERE WAS NO ANSWER, and when the Duke entered the cabin he found the reason for Irisa's silence. She was fast asleep.

She had lain down on top of the bed, having taken off only her bonnet and shoes, her cheek was turned against the pillow, and she was sleeping the sleep of complete exhaustion.

The Duke stood looking down at her.

Then he crossed the cabin and pulled the curtains over the portholes before he went out, very quietly closing the door behind him.

He found Jenkins and said:

"Miss Irisa is asleep, Jenkins, and I think it would be wise to leave her."

"Of course, Your Grace," Jenkins agreed. "I thought as how she was very brave after her father died, but it always takes it out of one."

"Naturally," the Duke agreed. "See that she is not disturbed, and when she wakes, suggest that she stay in bed until dinner-time."

He went up on deck and found that James and Amy had joined Harry and were sipping from long glasses which contained fresh fruit-juice.

"There you are, Dasher!" James exclaimed. "I was beginning to think you had been eaten by the crocodiles!"

"Not yet," the Duke replied, "and that reminds me—I want to swim this afternoon, but farther up the river. I do not like to be too near to human habitation."

"What has happened to Miss Garron?" Harry asked.

"She is asleep," the Duke replied.

He sat down beside Amy, who said:

"Harry has been telling me that her father was buried this morning. How tragic for her, and she does not sound very much like a Missionary."

"I cannot believe you have often met one," the Duke replied, and Amy laughed.

"No, that is true, but I always think they must be outstandingly brave to go into the wilds, protected only by their faith."

"I have heard that Africa has accounted for the lives of many Missionaries," James remarked, "and I agree with Amy, even if such people are misguided, they are certainly brave."

They had luncheon, and a short time afterwards the Duke was rowed up the river to find himself a place where he could bathe in what he was sure was clean water, and without too many interested observers.

He swam against the stream, feeling he was using every muscle in his body and that it was as good an exercise as riding one of his own horses round the Race-Course, or sparring with Harry, which they often did in his private Gymnasium at the Castle.

The Duke tried not to think of the wonders that were to be found on the banks of the Nile.

He felt it would somehow be unfair to explore them without Irisa, and if he thought about them when she was not there, there would be too many questions in his mind which needed answers.

Feeling pleasantly relaxed after his swim, he was rowed back to the yacht to find that his guests had left a message to say that they had gone to the Winter Palace Hotel, where Amy wished to see some friends who had just arrived from England.

The Duke had no intention of joining them.

Instead he went to his own private cabin and started to read the manuscripts that Irisa had given him, written by her father. He found them absorbing and they explained many things he wanted to know.

Then, because he too had spent a somewhat restless night, he dozed in his armchair, to awake with a start when Jenkins came to tell him that it was time to change for dinner.

"Is Miss Irisa awake?" the Duke enquired.

"Yes, Your Grace. She woke at about four o'clock and I took her some tea and persuaded her to settle down for a few hours longer. Now she's taking a bath, and I'm sure looking forward to joining Your Grace for dinner."

The Duke thought Jenkins sounded like an efficient Nanny, and he thought that any man, whatever his position in life, would feel protective towards Irisa.

He himself certainly did, and as he bathed and dressed he wondered what sort of life she would find waiting for her when she reached England.

It seemed strange that she had not visited the country of her origin since she was a baby. Yet he supposed that having travelled so much and encountered people of such varied kinds, she would somehow be able to take it in her stride.

He found that this supposition was correct when she met his friends.

Thinking she might be shy of meeting them alone, when he was dressed the Duke sent Jenkins to ask if she was ready, and he returned to say that she was.

As the Duke came from his cabin and saw that the door of Irisa's was open, he walked in to see her arranging her hair in front of the mirror.

She turned to smile at him, and he thought that now that she had rested and the lines of suffering were no longer dark beneath her eyes, she looked very beautiful and very spring-like.

"I am ashamed at my indolence!" she exclaimed as the Duke appeared. "Your valet tells me you have been swimming, and I am envious."

"You can swim?" the Duke asked in surprise.

"Like a fish!" Irisa replied. "I assure you if I had not been able to I would have been drowned a dozen times when Papa and I had to cross swollen rivers, and once in a monsoon we were caught in a rising flood which drowned quite a number of native children before we could rescue them."

"I shall insist not only that your father's book must be published but that you should write one yourself."

Irisa laughed.

"Do you really believe that anybody would be interested in the perils of being a Missionary?"

"I would be interested," the Duke answered, and she smiled at him again.

Only as she rose from the stool on which she was sitting did he realise that she was not wearing evening-dress but again one of the simple gowns that he suspected she had made herself.

It was an attractively patterned muslin such as could be bought cheaply in any native Bazaar, but on Irisa it seemed as right as if she were clothed in cloth of gold, and it was difficult to think that anything could be more becoming.

The Duke did not say anything, but with a lack of self-consciousness that he realised was exceptional she said to Amy as soon as they had been introduced:

"I hope you will forgive me for not possessing anything more elaborate in the way of evening-gowns, but Papa and I were never invited out to dinner except with Bedouin Chieftains when they roasted a whole sheep."

"You look charming!" Amy said.

The Duke, seeing the expression in James's eyes, and in Harry's, realised they thought the same.

As dinner progressed, he was aware that Irisa was quiet but attentive, still appearing to be supremely unself-conscious that she was doing anything unusual, and he knew too that Harry approved of her.

The Duke was too close to his oldest friend not to be aware that he had disliked Lily and obviously mistrusted her.

But it was quite clear that his feelings where Irisa were concerned were very different, and the Duke found it rather surprising.

He knew that Harry, like some of his other friends, was always afraid that he would be exploited because he was so rich and of such social importance.

Since Harry knew nothing of his mental affinity with Irisa, he thought that it might be expected that he would suspect her of being a penniless Missionary's daughter intent on making use of him and getting herself invited on his yacht after such a short acquaintance.

But there was not that mocking, sarcastic note in his voice that Harry had used towards Lily, and when after dinner Amy had the chance of speaking to the Duke alone, she said:

"That child is delightful! Do you think she would resent it if I offered to lend her anything she might need while we are on the yacht together?"

"I am sure she would be delighted," the Duke answered.

As they were five, there was no question of their playing cards, so they sat on deck listening to the sound of voices and laughter coming from the other side of the river.

All the time the Duke was vividly conscious of the moonlight on the Temple of Luxor, and he felt as if the mystery of it was vibrating towards him.

Then as if Amy found it difficult to keep up a brave front, and she too felt emotionally exhausted after what had happened earlier in the day, she rose to her feet.

"I am going to bed," she said. "I do not want to break up the party, but I am tired."

"I think I . . . too should go . . . to bed," Irisa said.

She glanced at the Duke as she spoke, as if for his approval, and he answered:

"I think it is a good idea, and I am sure that tomorrow there will be some interesting but quite tiring things for us to do."

"Then come along, Irisa," Amy said. "You and I will leave the men to gossip, we hope about us, but it is more likely to be about horses!"

"Good-night, Your Grace!" Irisa said.

She gave him a little curtsey which was very graceful.

About an hour later the Duke went to his own cabin, where Jenkins was waiting for him.

"It's been very hot today, Your Grace," he said as he helped him out of his tight-fitting evening-coat.

"Yes, and I enjoyed my swim. I have an idea I am losing weight."

"I wouldn't be surprised," Jenkins said gloomily, "and that means Your Grace's clothes'll all have to be altered when we gets back to London."

"There is plenty of time to worry about that," the Duke replied.

He put on one of his thin cotton robes like the one he had worn last night, which in the heat were far more comfortable than silk.

When his valet had left him, he went to the port-hole to look out at the stars.

It was then that he was vividly conscious that he was looking at them alone, and that Irisa was in the next cabin.

As he thought of her, he felt her beauty and her desirability sweep over him and arouse in him emotions that he recognised because they were so familiar.

"She is lovely!" the Duke told himself. "Lovelier than any other woman I have ever seen!"

He did not stop to think or even to consider whether it was right or wrong. He only knew that he wanted to be with Irisa, and he had never denied himself anything he wanted.

Closing the port-hole, he walked across the cabin and a second later he was standing outside her door.

He wondered for a moment whether he should knock, then thought if she was already asleep it would be unkind to wake her.

He turned the handle, then he saw that she was sitting up in bed with one of her father's manuscript-books in her hands.

As he looked at her he realised for the first time that he was seeing her with her hair down, and it was something which subconsciously he had longed to see.

It flowed over her shoulders with just a faint wave in it and made her look like the classical pictures of a nymph or a mermaid.

She was wearing a very simple nightgown of white muslin that was fastened at the neck and had little frills over her wrists.

But the light beside her bed revealed the curves of her breasts and the Duke was aware that she was very human and a woman.

It flashed through his mind that she might be surprised at his appearance, or perhaps shocked, but when she saw him she smiled and exclaimed:

"I am so glad you have come to say good-night to me. I have something very exciting to tell you."

It was not the reception the Duke had expected, but he walked to the bed and sat down on it, facing her.

"I thought you would like to know that I have remembered what your name was when you were a . . . soldier and I was the . . . bride of a . . . Pharaoh."

"I am prepared to believe anything you tell me," the Duke answered.

Looking at her, he thought that nobody could be more alluring, more exciting, and because his whole body was throbbing he found it hard to concentrate on what she was saying.

"Your name was Alexi," she said. "Does that seem significant?"

"No, I do not think so."

"It is Greek."

"Yes, of course," he agreed, "and now that I think of it, Iris is also a Greek name. Do you suppose we might have come to Egypt from Greece?"

"It is certainly possible."

"Then we must go there," the Duke said, "and perhaps we shall see what happened before you arrived here."

Irisa clasped her hands together.

"That would be too ... wonderful to ... contemplate, but ... perhaps ..."

She hesitated.

"Perhaps?" the Duke prompted.

"... you want to go somewhere else with your friends. They were very kind to me tonight, and I think for the first time I realised that in this life you and I live in very different worlds."

"I suppose that is true," the Duke said slowly.

He was thinking of his life in England, his Castle, his horses, of the parties at Marlborough House, of the piles of invitation-cards that arrived every day for him wherever he was.

Then his thoughts came back to Irisa.

She looked like a lotus-bud, but she was alone, and he knew, as surely as if she had said so, that for the moment the future for her was an empty, barren desert stretching away interminably to an indefinite horizon.

Irisa was watching his face and he knew she was reading his thoughts.

"I have no ... wish," she said softly, "to be an ... encumbrance, and perhaps I should ... return to England without ... troubling you."

The words were spoken quite simply and he knew that she was thinking not of herself but of him.

For a moment there was silence. Then he said:

"Will you marry me, Irisa?"

She looked at him as if she did not understand what he had said.

Then there was a light in her eyes that seemed as dazzling as the sun on the water of the Sacred Lake.

The Duke waited, somehow unable to say any more, conscious only of the radiance in Irisa's eyes as she asked almost inaudibly:

"Is ... that what you ... want?"

"I have only just realised, Irisa" he replied, "that I want it more than

I have ever wanted anything in my whole life. After all, it would be a fitting end to our story."

"Not an . . . end," Irisa whispered, "but . . . a beginning."

Slowly, as if he was moving forward in time, the Duke took both her hands in his and raised them one after the other to his lips.

Then, as his mouth felt the softness of her skin, the spell which had made him feel that it was hard to speak and almost impossible to move broke. He put his arms round her, his lips sought hers, and he kissed her.

As he did so he realised that it was very different from any kiss he had ever given or received before. There was none of the fiery passion that he usually associated with desire.

It was something very different, very wonderful, ecstatic and spiritual.

He wanted Irisa not only with his body but with his mind and his soul. At the same time, he approached her with a reverence, as if she were sacred in a way he had never felt about any other woman.

Her lips were very soft, yielding, and innocent, and as he knew he was the first man who had kissed her in this life, he was tender and gentle.

Then when he felt her respond to his need of her, his kisses became more possessive and more demanding.

They were both breathless when he raised his head to say:

"How can this have happened? I know now that you are what I have been looking for and missing all my life, and it was an instinct stronger than thought which brought me all the way to Egypt to find you."

"I love . . . you! Oh, Alexi, I love . . . you as I . . . always . . . have!"

"For how long?"

"From the . . . beginning of . . . time . . . perhaps even . . . before . . . that."

The Duke made a sound of happiness and triumph.

Then he was kissing her again, kissing her until she felt overwhelmed and put up her hands with a little murmur of protest.

Instantly she was free:

"Forgive me, my darling," he said. "I worship you, and at the same time I am reassuring myself that you are human and will not vanish onto one of the columns and another thousand years will pass before I find you again."

"Wherever I . . . am, I shall . . . always love . . . you."

"Is it true, really true, that you loved me before we met?" the Duke asked.

"I have always been aware of you in my dreams. The first time Papa took me to the sanctuary at Karnak, I saw, as we both saw it yesterday . . . my arrival in . . . Egypt."

"Alexi!" the Duke said softly. "So that was my name!"

"You do not mind my calling you that?"

"No, of course not," he answered. "In fact, it is very appropriate that I should have a new name, because, thanks to you, I have been reborn. In the future, 'The Dasher,' as he is known in England, will cease to exist."

Irisa gave a little cry.

"No, I would not have you . . . changed! You have . . . become what you are over . . . thousands of years . . . in perhaps thousands of lives . . . and through your own good deeds you have . . . gained the position you have now."

"And you?"

She gave a little sigh.

"Perhaps I behaved badly or forgot to do good, which is why I have come back as I have."

"I am content for you to be just as you are," the Duke said.

Then he was kissing her again.

It was a long while later when he sensed that while the radiance was still shining in her eyes like the stars that shone in the sky outside, she was tired, and he said:

"I am going to leave you now, my lovely one. Go to sleep and think only that I love you and you are to be my wife."

"I wish I could tell Papa about . . . us," Irisa whispered.

"I am sure he knows," the Duke answered.

He thought it was the most unexpected thing for him to say, and yet he knew it was true.

He kissed her again very gently and tenderly, and when she had cuddled herself down in the bed he pulled the sheet up to her chin.

"Good-night, my precious," he said very softly. "Dream of me."

"It would be . . . difficult for me . . . not to."

He looked down at her for a long moment before he turned out the light.

Then, as he went from the cabin, he felt as if his whole world had turned upside down and he could hardly believe that his feelings were not just a figment of his imagination.

One thing was irrefutably true—he had found the love that was different and for which, although he had denied it, he had always been seeking.

~

The stars were shining in the great arc of the Heavens and a crescent moon was moving slowly up the sky.

The yacht was anchored for the night and everything was still and quiet.

The Duke put his arm round Irisa as they stood on deck, looking out into the star-strewn darkness, knowing that tomorrow they would be seeing the Temples of Abu Simbel.

At the same time, they were finding for the moment that nothing could be more wonderful and exciting than their discovery of each other, and every day it seemed to the Duke they grew closer.

In fact, their happiness increased until he felt as if it vibrated from them like the light which shone from the stars.

To Irisa it was as if she had stepped into a Paradise that she could hardly believe was not just a vision in the darkness and had no substance in reality.

Yet, every time the Duke touched her, she knew it was very real, and although they had loved each other in many other lives, in this they were man and woman, and it was too wonderful to express in words.

"Are you happy, my darling?" the Duke asked.

"So happy," she answered, "that all I want to say is " 'I love you! I love you!' over and over again until you are tired of hearing it."

"I shall never be that," he replied, "and I keep thanking the gods that they sent me anybody so perfect as you."

Irisa thought that the gods had certainly blessed them as she had known they would when they had been married the morning after the Duke had come to her cabin and asked her to be his wife.

She had slept without dreaming, and even while unconscious she had a feeling of happiness that was with her when she awoke to find Jenkins pulling back the curtains over the port-holes.

"It's eight o'clock, Miss!" he said. "His Grace asks for you to be ready for him in a hour's time!"

"But of course!" Irisa exclaimed. "How can I have slept so late? I usually rise at six."

"It's the best thing you could do, Miss," Jenkins said firmly. "I've brought you a small breakfast, but there's plenty more if you're hungry."

Irisa looked at the tray he had put down beside her and exclaimed:

"It is more than enough. Thank you!"

Jenkins went towards the door, and as he did so said:

"I'll have your bath ready for you, Miss, when you're finished, and His Lordship asks if you'll wear the blue gown. He says you'll know the one he means."

Irisa smiled.

She knew it was the gown she was wearing when they had first met. Although it was not one of her newest and the Duke had been right in thinking she had made it herself, she knew that that particular dress would always have a special significance for them.

She enjoyed the cool, scented bath that Jenkins had prepared for her, and she was just ready when he came into her cabin carrying something on a tray.

"I was just going to ask if His Grace wishes to go ashore," Irisa said, "in which case I must wear my bonnet."

"His Grace asks if you'll wear this, Miss," Jenkins said, holding out the tray.

Irisa looked in surprise at what it contained. She saw it was a wreath of lotus-buds, just pink tinged, and skillfully woven together with a few small garden leaves.

For a moment she did not understand. Then suddenly she did, and to Jenkins, watching her, her face seemed transfigured.

She placed the wreath on her head, then as she went a little shyly up the companionway and onto the deck, she found the Duke waiting for her with a bouquet of lotus-flowers.

He handed it to her and there was no need for words.

She only looked into his grey eyes and knew that she loved him overwhelmingly and that he loved her.

They were rowed across the river to the steps which led into the Temple of Luxor, and as the Duke drew her without speaking through the passage of the columns, she knew where they were going.

When they reached the place where they had first met, she saw first a profusion of brilliant flowers which lay at the foot of the pillars, and then the same Clergyman who had buried her father waiting for them in his white surplice.

Behind him on a plinth which acted as an altar was the consecrated stone which had belonged to her father.

The Service was short, and yet as they were made man and wife Irisa felt that the gods were all round them and were giving them their blessings.

Only when they were alone and walking back down the steps to where the boat was waiting did Irisa say a little incoherently:

"How could you have . . . thought of . . . anything so wonderful . . . so perfect as for us to be married in the Temple where we . . . found each . . . other?"

"I could not imagine anywhere more appropriate," the Duke replied, "and, my sweet, as we took our vows, I felt as if it were the gods themselves who gave you to me."

She looked at him with her soul in her eyes because it was what she had been thinking herself.

"Only . . . you would understand," she said.

When they had gone back to the yacht, the Duke took her down to his private cabin to put his arms round her.

"You are mine! My wife!" he said. "Whatever happened in the past, we are now together, and I swear that as long as we shall live, I will never lose you."

Then he was kissing her until Irisa felt that they had found a special Heaven in which there was nobody else, not even the gods but only themselves.

A long time later, when the Duke had sent for champagne with which they could drink their own health, Irisa realised that the yacht was moving.

She had been so bemused by the wonder of the Duke's kisses that she had not realised the engines were throbbing beneath them.

Now she asked.

"Where are we going?"

"On our honeymoon," the Duke replied, "and alone."

She looked at him questioningly, and he explained:

"My friends have tactfully agreed to stay at the Winter Palace Hotel as my guests until we return. Then we will take them as far as Cairo or Alexandria, from where they will make their own way home."

"Do they . . . mind?" Irisa asked.

"No, because they want us to be happy," the Duke replied. "They sent you their good wishes, my darling. But I would not let them see you, because I want you to myself."

"That . . . is what I want too," Irisa said, "but how can you have arranged everything so . . . cleverly and so . . . perfectly?"

"I think you have inspired me to think in a different way from what I have ever done in the past," the Duke answered, "and all I wish to do is to imagine how I can make you happy."

"I am happy, so very . . . very happy!" Irisa cried.

She suddenly put out her hand to touch the Duke.

"You are quite certain you are not just a part of my vision, and in a moment you will vanish?"

"Later I will make you believe I am very real," the Duke said in his deep voice.

For a moment they could not look into each other's eyes. Then Irisa gave a little sigh.

"I am so glad I do not have to go to England . . . alone . . . I was . . . frightened of meeting my . . . grandfather."

"Is he so ferocious?"

"He was to Papa when he became a Missionary! He cut him off without the proverbial shilling."

"Why should he think it so wrong?"

"Because he wanted Papa, who had always wanted to be a Doctor, to take Holy Orders so that he could take over one of the many livings my grandfather has on his Estate."

The Duke looked surprised because it sounded as if Irisa's grandfather was a land-owner. Then suddenly he exclaimed:

"Garron! I thought it sounded familiar! Are you a relative of Lord Tregarron?"

"He is my grandfather!"

"I had no idea. Why did you not tell me?"

"There was no reason to do so," Irisa replied, "and Papa was so hurt by his father's refusal to have anything to do with him that we never spoke of his family."

"I have met Lord Tregarron at Race-Meetings. Now that I think of it, I have always thought him a proud, unbending man."

"I am sure he is, and he expected his sons to obey him. Papa's elder brother went into the family Regiment, as he was told to do, but Papa wanted to see the world, to travel and explore! When his father insisted he should become a country Vicar, he ran away."

"To become a Missionary."

"He saw a lot of the world, if rather uncomfortably. It . . . killed Mama, but Papa was . . . happy after he came to . . . Luxor."

"It was fate," the Duke said, "that I should find you here."

He was perfectly content to marry Irisa even if she was a nobody, but he knew that the fact that she was the granddaughter of Lord Tregarron would make it easy for her to enter the Social World to which sometime he would have to return.

But there was no hurry for the moment. There would be many places for them to see and explore together, the first being Greece.

"I adore you," he said. "And all I can think of is you."

The reality of being in the Duke's arms and learning about love was so rapturous and divine that Irisa was sure they were held in the magic spell in which the Egyptians had always believed.

There was the magic of the Temples, the barren hills, the sunshine, the Nile itself, and now with her head on the Duke's shoulder as she looked at the reflection of the moon and stars on the water, she said:

"This river has meant so much in our lives. It carried me to the Pharaoh, and it took you away from me. Now it has brought you to me again and we are together! And it will flow on, even when we are no longer here."

"It is the river of love," the Duke answered. "And remember, my precious, that love, like life, cannot die."

Irisa smiled.

"Now you are teaching me."

"That is what I want to do where love is concerned," the Duke said, "and because I love you so wildly and passionately, I am at this moment, my adorable one, a man and not a god, and I want you to be closer to me than you are at the moment."

As he spoke he bent and kissed not her lips, as she expected, but the softness of her neck where a little pulse was beating frantically because he excited her.

"I love . . . you . . . oh . . . Alexi," she whispered. "I love . . . you."

"I will worship you," he answered, "from now until the stars fall from the sky and the world ceases to exist."

Then with the smoothness of the river flowing beneath them he drew her from the deck.

He knew that in the secrecy of their cabin they would find a love that was older than the earth, but still young and creative with every new life—the love which is eternity.

A Shaft
of Sunlight

Author's Note

It was after the development of the Sugar Plantations that the slave-trade between the West Coast of Africa and the Americas reached enormous proportions, becoming the most lucrative trade of the time.

The English became the biggest importers of slaves, although the Dutch, the French, and other nations also took part in the trade.

Ships set out first from a home port such as Liverpool, carrying liquor, cotton goods, fire-arms, and trinkets, which were exchanged for slaves right along what was called the Slave Coast—the Gulf of Guinea.

Then came what was known as "the middle voyage" towards one of the Colonies or countries on the American continent. The slaves, closely packed in the hull and often chained to prevent them from rebelling or jumping into the sea, suffered agonies.

Food was inadequate, water was scarce, and mortality often reached the appalling proportion of twenty percent. If it was necessary to reduce the load in a heavy sea, the sick were thrown overboard.

On arrival, slaves were kept in stockades to await a purchaser. The ship was then loaded with another cargo, such as sugar produced on the American plantations, and sailed for home. If all went well, the profit was enormous.

Despite strong protests against this traffic by the Quakers and William Wilberforce, it was not until 1806 that Parliament prohibited British Merchants from providing slaves and the importation of them into British possessions.

The traffic continued, however, until 1811, when slave-trading became a criminal offence.

CHAPTER ONE

1819

$\mathcal{T}$HE BUTLER AT ALVERSTODE HOUSE in Grosvenor Square was surprised to see the Viscount Frome alighting from his Phaeton.

His surprise was not connected with His Lordship's appearance, because he was used to such resplendence, knowing the Viscount's ambition was to be the most acclaimed "Tulip of Fashion" in the *Beau Monde.*

However, what was astonishing was that the twenty-one-year-old Ward of the Duke of Alverstode had appeared so early in the morning.

Barrow was well aware that like the rest of the Dandies the Viscount rose late and spent at least two hours preparing himself to face a critical world.

Yet now when the hands of the clock had not reached nine the Viscount was walking up the steps towards him.

"Good-morning, M'Lord!" Barrow said. "You've come to see His Grace?"

"I am not too late?" the Viscount asked anxiously.

"No, indeed, M'Lord. His Grace returned from riding but ten minutes ago, and Your Lordship'll find him in the Breakfast-Room."

The Viscount did not wait to hear any more, but walked across the impressive marble Hall towards the Breakfast-Room which overlooked the garden at the back of the house.

As he expected, the Duke of Alverstode was seated at a table in the window, with *The Times* propped up in front of him on a silver stand while he ate a hearty breakfast with which he drank coffee.

As the Viscount walked into the room, the Duke looked up with the same expression of surprise as had appeared on his Butler's face.

"Good-morning, Cousin Valerian," the Viscount said.

"Good Heavens, Lucien! What brings you here at this early hour? Can you have been engaged in a duel that you have risen so early?"

"No, certainly not!" the Viscount replied sharply, before he realised that his Guardian was merely teasing him.

He crossed the room to sit down on the other side of the table. Then there was a silence which told the Duke without it being put into words that his Ward was nervous.

"If it was not a duel," he remarked after eating another mouthful of the lamb-chop which was in front of him, "then what can be perturbing you?"

Again there was silence before, almost as if the words burst from his lips, the Viscount replied:

"I am in love!"

"Again?" the Duke exclaimed, pausing in his eating.

"This is different!" the Viscount replied. "I know I have thought myself to be in love before, but this is very, very different."

"In what way?" the Duke enquired.

The tone of his voice made the Viscount look at him apprehensively.

There was no doubt that his Guardian was an extremely handsome man, but he was also an awesome one, and there was nobody in the whole of the *Beau Monde* who did not treat the Duke of Alverstode with respect.

Even the women who pursued him, and there were a great many of them, admitted when they were confidential with one another that they found him a little frightening.

Even The Regent was known to conform to the Duke's opinion and seldom contradicted anything he said.

"I want to marry Claribel," the Viscount said after a pause, "but you made me promise I would not propose marriage to anybody until I had your permission."

"A very wise precaution on my part," the Duke said drily. "I cannot believe you would be very happy if I had allowed you to marry that Don's daughter who took your fancy when you were at Oxford, or that Opera-Dancer who you assured me at the time was the love of your life."

"I was very young then," the Viscount replied hastily.

"You are not so very old now."

"I am old enough to know my own mind!" the Viscount retorted. "I know I shall be exceedingly happy with Claribel, and at least you cannot say she is 'common,' which is how you referred to the other ladies who have engaged my attention."

The Duke raised his eye-brows.

" 'Ladies'?" he queried, and it was an insult.

"Have it your own way," the Viscount said petulantly. "They were not 'up to scratch,' as you pointed out to me in no uncertain terms, but you can hardly cut off my money as you threatened to do then because I want to marry Claribel, because for one thing she has a fortune of her own."

"That is always useful," the Duke conceded, "but tell me more about this new enchantress who has captured your somewhat vacillating heart."

The Viscount needed no encouragement. He bent forward eagerly in his chair, his elbows on the table, to say:

"She is beautiful—so beautiful that she makes me think she has stepped down from Olympus—and yet she loves me! Can you believe it? She loves me for myself!"

The Duke's expression was rather more cynical than usual and he looked across the table thinking that a great number of women had already thought themselves in love with his Ward, and he was certain there would be a great many more.

The Viscount's father was a distant cousin who had been killed at Waterloo, and it had been a distinct and not particularly pleasant shock for the Duke to find that he had become the Guardian of his son.

He was aware that the late Viscount Frome's Will had been made some years earlier while his own father was still alive.

It had simply stated that if anything happened to him while he was on active service with Wellington's Army, his son and any other children he might have were to become Wards of the Duke of Alverstode.

The Duke had often thought it was a careless omission on the part of the Solicitors who had drawn up his cousin's Will not to have named his father as the third Duke.

This would have meant that he himself could have passed on what was undoubtedly a tiresome duty to some other member of the family.

At the same time, because he was legally Lucien's Guardian, he was determined to see that the boy did not make what was in his opinion a disastrous marriage.

There was no doubt that everybody who had engaged or captured the Viscount's attention up to date had been from a social point of view completely unacceptable.

There had been not only the two ladies already mentioned but also, the Duke remembered, a socially ambitious widow several years older than Lucien who had fancied herself a Viscountess.

Besides these there had been a lady of very doubtful virtue who had tried to make a great deal of trouble about her "broken heart," which fortunately had been most successfully mended when she received a large number of golden sovereigns.

"Your eulogy of this mysterious creature of mythology is very touching," the Duke said mockingly, "but so far you have omitted to tell me her name."

"She is Claribel Stamford," the Viscount said in a rapt voice.

He saw the frown of concentration on the Duke's face as he tried to remember where he had heard the name.

"Stamford," he said after a moment. "You do not mean that she is the daughter of Sir Jarvis Stamford, the race-horse owner?"

"That is right," the Viscount said. "I thought you would remember him. He owns some excellent horseflesh, and if you recall he pipped one of your horses to the post last year in the Cambridgeshire."

"Victorious was off-colour that day!" the Duke said defensively, then laughed as he added:

"I remember now that Stamford was certainly remarkably elated at beating me."

"Even so, there is no need for you to be prejudiced against his daughter."

"I have not said I am prejudiced," the Duke protested.

"Then you will allow me to marry her?" the Viscount asked eagerly.

The Duke was silent.

He was thinking that at twenty-one his Ward was still very young and in some ways as ingenuous and, in his opinion, as "hare-brained" as any School-boy.

He had also been very wild and in some people's opinion had sewed a prodigious and unprecedented number of "wild oats."

Not that the Duke thought any the worse of him because of that, for it was what he expected any young man would do when there was no war on which to expend his high spirits, regardless of who was injured in the process.

The Duke was quite certain in his own mind that Claribel, or whatever Lucien's latest infatuation was called, was not likely to prove a more suitable wife than any other of the women who had taken his fancy.

While he was pondering the matter for some time in silence, the Viscount had been watching the Duke's face anxiously, and now he said impetuously:

"If you are going to refuse me permission to pay my addresses to Claribel, Cousin Valerian, I swear I will persuade her to run away with me and damn the consequences!"

The Duke stiffened and said sharply:

"If she is the type of girl you should marry, and certainly the sort of girl to whom I would give my approval, she would refuse to do anything so outrageous!"

He paused before he added:

"No decent girl, and certainly none with any idea of correct behaviour, would contemplate for a moment posting to Gretna Green or being married in some 'hole and corner' manner, which, as you are well aware, is only a type of blackmail on those who hold your best interests at heart."

The Viscount threw himself back in his chair in a sulky manner.

"Now that I am twenty-one I thought I was allowed to be a man, not a puppet tied to your apron-strings!"

The Duke's rather hard mouth twitched.

"A rather mixed metaphor, my dear Lucien," he said, "but I get your meaning."

"You certainly treat me as if I were in petticoats," the Viscount complained.

"Strange though it may seem," the Duke replied, "if I do, I am thinking of your interests and yours only. But I will certainly admit that Miss Stamford sounds a better proposition than anything you have suggested previously."

There was a new light in the Viscount's eyes.

"Then you will consider my request?"

"Most certainly!" the Duke replied.

Once again the Viscount was bending forward eagerly.

"You had best meet Claribel, and then you will understand why I wish to make her my wife."

"That is just what I was about to suggest," the Duke said, "and I always think it is best to see people at their own home and against their natural background."

"You mean . . . ?" the Viscount asked hesitatingly.

"I suggest you ask Sir Jarvis if he is prepared to invite you and me to stay with him for a day or so."

"In the country?"

"Definitely in the country!" the Duke said firmly.

The Viscount looked at his Guardian uncertainly.

"I cannot quite understand, Cousin Valerian, why you think that is important."

"Must I make explanations?" the Duke asked. "I should have thought my reasons were obvious."

"Sir Jarvis has a house in London and Claribel enjoys attending Balls that are taking place there at the moment."

"I am sure she does," the Duke replied, "and as you dance very prettily she doubtless finds you an admirable partner."

He did not make it sound a compliment, and the Viscount, who fancied himself on the dance-floor, flushed a little resentfully. Then he said:

"If I suggest a visit to the country and Sir Jarvis does not wish to leave London, what shall I do?"

"I think," the Duke said loftily, "you will find Sir Jarvis will be only too agreeable to the suggestion of inviting me to be his guest. If, on the other hand, he prefers to wait indefinitely before issuing such an invitation, then, you, my dear Lucien, must wait too."

There was something in the way the Duke spoke which told the Viscount there would be no point in arguing further.

At the same time, he was worried in case Claribel, who loved London, would not wish to return to the country.

His thoughts were very obvious to the Duke, who, however, had returned to his perusal of the *Times,* turning the newspaper over on its silver rack and drinking his coffee as he read it, apparently no longer interested in his Ward.

The Viscount did not speak for a few minutes. Then he said hesitatingly:

"I suppose, Cousin Valerian, I should thank you for not having given me a complete set-down. I am sure when you meet Claribel you will understand what I feel about her."

"I am sure I shall," the Duke replied.

He finished his coffee, put down the cup, and pushing back his chair rose to his feet.

"And now," he said, "I have a great deal of work to do. What really worries me is what you will find to occupy yourself with until your friends, who I believe seldom wake before noon, are capable of receiving you."

"You are laughing at me," the Viscount replied in an annoyed tone.

"Not really," the Duke replied. "I do not think it is a laughing matter that you take so little exercise except on the dance-floor, and the only fresh air you breathe is between your lodgings in Half Moon Street and your Club!"

"That is not true!" the Viscount answered hotly. "Yesterday I went to a Mill at Wimbledon and last week—or was it the week before—I attended the races at Epsom."

"What I was really suggesting," the Duke said patiently, "was that you should ride every morning or, if you prefer, late in the day. I have always told you that my horses are at your disposal."

"I really do not seem to have the time," the Viscount replied.

"Or if you do not want to ride," the Duke went on as if he had not spoken, "a few strenuous rounds at 'Gentleman Jackson's Boxing Academy' will develop the muscles of your arms and doubtless improve your general stamina."

"I loathed boxing at Eton! I have no desire for anybody to knock me about!" the Viscount exclaimed passionately.

Then looking at the Duke he added:

"It is all very well for you, Cousin Valerian, because you are a natural athlete. Everybody says that, and you are better at boxing and fencing—and riding, for that matter, than most other people.''

"I am only better because I have taken the trouble to learn the art of the first two sports you have mentioned,'' the Duke explained, "and I ride because I love horses, besides the fact that the exercise keeps me fit.''

"I prefer driving,'' the Viscount remarked petulantly.

"A lazy sport, but of course you can always have an audience to admire your expertise with the reins.''

"Now you are trying to make a fool of me!'' the Viscount complained bitterly.

The Duke sighed.

Then he said in a very different tone:

"Not really. As a matter of fact, Lucien, I am thinking of you and trying to help you to the best of my ability to be the sort of man your father would have wanted you to be. Perhaps I am making a mess of it, but then I have not had much practice at being the Guardian of anybody!''

The way he spoke without appearing cynical or mocking swept the sulky, resentful look from the Viscount's eyes.

"I am not ungrateful, Cousin Valerian, for the way you have treated me since Papa died. You have been very generous about everything I have wanted to do except where it has concerned marriage.''

"Then let us hope,'' the Duke answered, "that this time I shall be able to give my whole-hearted approval to the lady of your choice.''

"You will—I know you will!'' the Viscount said eagerly. "Wait until you see Claribel! You will be bowled over by her!''

He gave the Duke a somewhat bashful smile as he added:

"What I am afraid of is that when she meets you she may prefer you to me! She has already told me she has admired you from a distance.''

"I am gratified!'' the Duke said drily. "At the same time, Lucien, the one thing that need not trouble you in the slightest is that I shall take Claribel or any other very young women from you. For one thing I find them a dead bore, and secondly I have no intention of marrying, not for many years, at any rate.''

"You have to produce an heir to the Dukedom sooner or later,'' the Viscount remarked.

"There is plenty of time for that when I think I am growing senile,'' the Duke replied. "Then doubtless there will be somebody who will be prepared to provide me with a son and support me in my dotage!"

The Viscount laughed.

"There is no question of that! Your reputation as a heart-breaker, Cousin Valerian, loses nothing in the telling!"

The Duke frowned.

It was the sort of remark that he thought was in extremely bad taste, and he was quite certain that it had been made to Lucien by the women with whom he usually associated.

As if he knew he had presumed on his Guardian's unexpected good humour, the Viscount said hastily:

"If you have work to do, though I cannot conceive what it could be, I will leave you. My Phaeton is outside."

"The new one?" the Duke exclaimed. "I saw the bill for it yesterday. You are certainly determined to cut a dash in more ways than one!"

"Those Coach-builders are all crooks," the Viscount said, "but actually you cannot imagine what a slap-up vehicle it is and how fast it can travel. If you will come and look at it, Cousin Valerian, you will know that what I am saying is the truth."

"I will keep that treat for another day," the Duke replied, "but now Middleton is waiting for me and we have a great deal to do before I have luncheon at Carlton House."

"I am going," the Viscount said. "I will see Sir Jarvis sometime today and try to persuade him to arrange a date for our visit to Stamford Towers."

"I shall be waiting to receive his invitation," the Duke answered. "Until then, good-bye, Lucien!"

He did not listen for his Ward's reply, but walked swiftly from the Breakfast-Room down the corridor towards his Library, where he knew his Secretary and Comptroller would be waiting for him.

For a few seconds the Viscount watched him go, thinking that on the whole the interview had not been as terrifying as he had thought it might be, and also envying almost unconsciously the athletic and co-ordinated manner in which the Duke moved.

It was almost, he thought, like watching a thoroughbred gallop past the Winning-Post, and just for a moment he toyed with the idea of doing what his Guardian suggested and taking more exercise.

Then he was sure that to do so would only prove conclusively what he knew already, that it was impossible for him to excel at sports and he had better spend his time with his tailor and on the dance-floor.

He walked across the Hall to where Barrow was waiting to hand him his tall hat and his riding-gloves.

"Everything all right, Master Lucien?" he asked in the conspiratorial tone of a servant who had known him ever since he was a small boy.

"It might have been worse!"

"I'm glad about that, Master Lucien."

"Thank you, Barrow."

The Viscount smiled at the old retainer and walking down the steps climbed into his Phaeton, which he thought with pride was smarter than anything that could be seen in the Park or anywhere else in London.

It had cost a lot of money, but he could afford it, the only drawback being that all his extravagances still had to be seen and approved by his Guardian before the bills were paid.

The Viscount asked himself as he had a thousand times before why his father had tied up his considerable fortune until he was twenty-five.

Most men, he thought hotly, handled their own money when they came of age! But no, not him! He had to be spoon-fed for another four years! And he found it extremely irksome.

Then he remembered that Claribel would be waiting to hear the result of his visit and he forgot about everything else.

He wished it could be possible to call on her immediately and tell her what the Duke had said, but he knew there could be no possibility of seeing her until nearly luncheon-time and it would be more correct to call later in the afternoon.

"I cannot wait as long as that!" the Viscount told himself, and thought it was agony to hang about in suspense.

It was not surprising that he was enamoured of one of the most beautiful girls who had ever appeared in a London Season.

It was not only, as the Viscount thought poetically, that her hair was like sunshine, her eyes as blue as a thrush's egg, and her skin like strawberries and cream. It was also that she had none of the gaucheness of the usual débutante.

Perhaps it was her beauty that gave her an assurance and a composure that was lacking in all the other young girls he had met.

With my money and heirs, the Viscount was thinking as he drove his horses into Park Lane, *we can live in a really slap-up style. I will be able to give Claribel anything she desires, besides having horses to ride that will be the envy of every man in St. James's!*

~

Seated at his desk in the Library, which was piled with papers, while Mr. Middleton explained some complicated problem which had arisen on one of the Alverstode Estates, the Duke found his mind wandering to Lucien.

He felt, as he had so often before, worried about the boy.

He was convinced that the Viscount's friends were an exceptionally brainless collection of young men, but he recognised that perhaps he was being over-critical because he was so much older than they were.

"I cannot believe I was as bird-witted when I was twenty-one," he told himself.

But he had been in the Army then, and now not every young man with intelligence, drive, and courage had the same chance to excel as he had enjoyed.

As Mr. Middleton finished his long discourse on the necessity for completing a new timber-yard and a road leading to it, the Duke said:

"I am worried about Mr. Lucien. What have you heard about him lately?"

Mr. Middleton had been with the Duke for so long that Lucien was usually still referred to as he had been before he came into the title.

Mr. Middleton paused before he replied:

"I do not think His Lordship has done anything particularly outrageous in the last few months. There have been the usual stories about him and his friends being rowdy in dance-halls."

He paused, saw that the Duke was listening, and went on:

"They were thrown out of one of the more respectable 'Houses of Pleasure' the other evening because they were interfering with 'business,' but apart from a rather dangerous duel between two young-bloods at which His Lordship was a 'second,' there is nothing that need concern Your Grace."

"I suppose you were already aware before I was told about it that Mr. Lucien wishes to get married."

"To Miss Claribel Stamford?"

"Yes. I thought you would be the first to know! But you did not report it to me."

"I did not think it serious enough to worry Your Grace," Mr. Middleton replied. "Miss Stamford has a great many admirers."

"She is a beauty?"

"Undoubtedly, and she has already been acclaimed the Débutante of the Season!"

"An 'Incomparable'!" the Duke remarked sarcastically.

"Not yet," Mr. Middleton answered, "but she may easily receive that accolade when the gentlemen in the Clubs become aware of her."

The Duke looked cynical and Mr. Middleton went on:

"Your Grace must have met Sir Jarvis Stamford on the Race-Course?"

"I believe he is a member of the Jockey Club," the Duke said carelessly, "but I cannot remember actually having made his acquaintance. What do you know about him?"

"Very little, Your Grace, but I can easily find out."

"Do that!" the Duke ordered. "I have a feeling, although I may be wrong, that there was some scandal about him at one time, or was it just a rumour about something that was not particularly sporting? I am guessing! I do not really know."

"Leave it to me, Your Grace. In the meantime, I will also discover why Miss Stamford is favouring His Lordship. When I last heard her name mentioned, it was with someone more important in the running."

The Duke stared reflectively at his Secretary.

"What you are saying, Middleton," he said slowly, "is that Miss Stamford, or perhaps her father, is socially ambitious."

Mr. Middleton smiled.

"Of course, Your Grace. All young ladies are, and as Your Grace well knows, the higher the title the better the catch!"

He saw the Duke's lips tighten and remembered, as the Viscount had, that any mention of his love-affairs annoyed him excessively.

However, he was pursued ardently not only because he was a Duke but because he was an exceedingly attractive man, and his very lofty indifference was a challenge which most women found irresistible.

Surprisingly, in an age of loose talk and even looser morals, the Duke considered it in bad taste to discuss any woman who interested him, even with his closest friends, and this prejudice, which was well known, added to the mystery and the aura which surrounded him almost like a protecting halo.

There was not a woman in the whole of the *Beau Monde* who was not aware that if she could capture the heart of the Duke of Alverstode she would achieve a success greater than that of winning the Derby.

Although the Duke had had many *affaires de coeur,* they were discreet, and even the gossips knew nothing about them until they were over.

Then they could only guess at what had occurred when some well-known beauty retired unexpectedly to the country or went about looking so miserable that it was obvious she had lost something of very great value.

The word "heart-breaker," which the Viscount had injudiciously used, was whispered from *Boudoir* to *Boudoir.*

But because the Duke was so fastidious in his choices, and because the women who loved him were seldom if ever spiteful when he left them, those who were interested in the details of his love-life continued to be frustrated.

Mr. Middleton picked up his papers.

"I will find out everything I can, Your Grace," he said, "and furnish whatever information there is about Sir Jarvis as quickly as possible."

"Thank you, Middleton, I knew I could rely on you."

The Duke rose from the desk at which he had been sitting for nearly two hours and stretched his legs.

"I am going now to Carlton House," he said, "but as I shall doubtless be forced to over-eat and over-drink, which I very much dislike doing in the middle of the day, send a groom to 'Gentleman Jackson's' and tell him I hope to be there about half-after-four and would be obliged if I could have a few rounds with him personally."

Mr. Middleton smiled.

"I am sure he will be willing to oblige Your Grace, despite the fact that I hear you knocked him down last week."

The Duke laughed.

"I think perhaps I was unusually lucky, or Jackson was off his guard, but it was certainly an achievement."

"It was indeed, Your Grace."

As "Gentleman Jackson" had been the greatest boxer ever known, this was undoubtedly true, and there was a reminiscent smile on the Duke's lips as he left the Library.

~

It was much later in the day when Sir Jarvis Stamford returned to his large and extremely impressive house in Park Lane.

As he entered the door, where a Butler and six footmen were in attendance, his Secretary, a small, rather harassed man who always spoke in a somewhat hesitant manner, came hurrying towards him.

"Miss Claribel, Sir, asked if you would see her the moment you returned home."

Sir Jarvis gave his Secretary a sharp look as if he suspected there was some special reason behind the message.

Then as he was about to speak he realised that the six footmen, who had all to be of exactly the same height and who wore a very distinguished livery of purple and black, were listening.

"Where is Miss Claribel?" he asked quickly.

"In her own Sitting-Room, Sir."

Sir Jarvis walked up the stairs, his feet sinking into the soft carpet whose pile was deeper and certainly more expensive than the carpets in most other people's homes.

When he reached the top of the staircase Sir Jarvis found himself facing a painting he had recently bought in a Sale-Room and which he had been assured was a Rubens.

He only hoped he had not been crooked on the purchase, which had been an exceedingly expensive one, and he thought that if he had been, somebody would undoubtedly suffer for it.

He walked down the passage, which was slightly over-filled with expensive furniture, to the very elegant Sitting-Room which adjoined Claribel's bedroom and which had been decorated to be a perfect frame for her beauty.

The white and gold walls, the blue hangings, and the painted ceiling which had been done by an Italian artist would certainly become any woman, and as Claribel sprang from the sofa to run towards her father, he thought she looked like a priceless jewel, with or without the appropriate frame.

"Papa! I am so glad you are back!"

"What has happened?" Sir Jarvis asked almost harshly.

"Lucien has seen the Duke! He has really plucked up the courage at last! But as you know, I have had to bully him into making the effort."

"But you succeeded!"

"Yes, I succeeded!"

Claribel took her father by the hand and led him to the sofa where they sat down side by side.

"Well?" he asked. "What happened?"

Claribel drew in her breath.

"Lucien told the Duke that he wished to marry me."

Sir Jarvis's lips tightened as if he anticipated that his daughter would now say that the request had been refused.

"And what do you think the Duke said?" Claribel asked.

"Tell me."

"He said that he wishes to see me in my home and in the country!"

For a moment Sir Jarvis did not speak. He only stared at his daughter as if he doubted what he had heard. Then he said:

"The Duke wishes to *stay* with us at Stamford Towers?"

Claribel nodded.

"Yes, and I am sure that means, Papa, that he will give his consent. Oh, is it not wonderful? I can be married before the end of the Season, and I shall be able to attend the Opening of Parliament as a Viscountess!"

"And you will be the most beautiful Peeress there, my dearest."

"That was what I thought, Papa, and you must buy me a tiara that is bigger and better than anybody else's."

"Of course, of course!" Sir Jarvis agreed. "But I can hardly credit that the Duke wishes to stay with us."

"Lucien was also surprised, because he told me that the Duke is very fastidious about whom he stays with and accepts the invitations only of his close friends, like the Duke of Bedford and the Duke of Northumberland, and refuses thousands of others."

"We must make sure he does not regret his visit to Stamford Towers!"

"We must make sure that he agrees to my marrying Lucien!"

"Yes, yes, of course, but I think that is what is known as a foregone conclusion."

As he spoke Sir Jarvis thought that Claribel was not so confident.

"Why should he not accept you?" he asked sharply. "You are not only beautiful, my dearest, but you are also rich, and nobody can say that your mother's family are not blue-blooded."

"I wonder if Lucien remembered to tell him about Mama?"

"If he has forgotten I will do it myself," Sir Jarvis said, "and once the Duke is in our home he will have to listen to me."

"Of course, Papa, and send him the invitation right away. Lucien thought it would be a mistake to allow what he called the 'grass to grow under our feet.' "

"I agree with him," Sir Jarvis said. "The sooner the better. In fact, very definitely the sooner."

He spoke as if he was thinking of something other than his daughter. Then he bent forward and kissed her.

"I am very proud of you, my dearest," he said. "This makes it easy to forget that little set-back we had over the Earl of Dorset."

"I am never going to think of him again!" Claribel cried passionately. "He deceived me, and that I will never forgive!"

"Neither will I," Sir Jarvis agreed. "Make no mistake, I will get even with that young man sooner or later, and he will rue the day he behaved to you as he did."

Claribel jumped to her feet and walked to the mantelpiece to stare at her reflection in the mirror above it.

"How could he?" she asked in a low voice, as if she spoke to herself. "How could he have preferred that pie-faced Alice Wyndham to me?"

"Forget it! Forget it!" her father said behind her. "I know young Lucien is only a Viscount, but he is the Ward of the most influential man not only in the Social World but also on the Turf and in the country. The Alverstode Estate is a model for all other great Landowners, and an invitation to stay at Alverstode House is more prized than being asked to any of the Royal Palaces!"

"Then that is where we shall undoubtedly stay not once but frequently," Claribel said in rapturous tones.

"And I hope you will make sure that your poor Papa is included in some of the parties," Sir Jarvis said.

"But of course, Papa! And I feel that once Lucien and I are married, you and the Duke will become close friends. After all, between you, you own all the best race-horses in England."

"Not all, my dear, but certainly a great number of them," Sir Jarvis said complacently.

"And that is a real bond in common, is it not?"

"Of course, of course," Sir Jarvis agreed, "but the closest bond of all will be when you are married to the Duke's Ward, a young man with whom I understand His Grace has deeply concerned himself ever since he was a School-boy."

"That is true," Claribel agreed, "and although Lucien is nervous of the Duke he certainly admires him."

"As do a lot of other people!" Sir Jarvis approved. "I think, my dearest, that your future is exactly as I planned it, and you are a very lucky girl."

Claribel turned round from the contemplation of her reflection in the mirror and walked towards her father.

She lifted her face to his, looking so lovely as she did so that he stared at her as if he had never seen her before.

"I shall enjoy being a Viscountess!" she said simply.

CHAPTER TWO

*L*OOKING ROUND WHAT was more a Baronial Hall than a Dining-Room, the Duke thought that Sir Jarvis Stamford certainly lived in style.

He had not expected Stamford Towers to be quite so big or to find that inside it was furnished opulently but with good taste.

However, he thought there were an unnecessary number of footmen in the Hall and he was quite certain that his valet would tell him about the army of servants that existed in the kitchen-quarters.

At the moment he was sizing up the guests who had been invited for dinner tonight as highly respectable, and Sir Jarvis himself as a very genial host.

The Duke was well aware that for him to stay with somebody with whom he had a bare acquaintance was unprecedented, and the effusive manner with which he was greeted and Sir Jarvis's anxiety that he should be provided with every comfort were no more than he had expected.

When he had seen Claribel for the first time he had understood why Lucien was in love, for she was without a doubt one of the loveliest young women he had ever seen.

At the same time, for his Ward's sake he was determined to be highly critical, as he still thought that Lucien was too young to be married.

If he was, it should be to a very exceptional wife who would help him develop the better qualities of his character and dispense with the undesirable ones.

That, the Duke told himself cynically, would undoubtedly be beyond the powers of any girl as young as Claribel.

However, he had learnt before coming to Stamford Towers that since she was in mourning for her mother, Miss Stamford had not been presented at Court last year but had been obliged to wait until this Season before she could appear and dazzle the Social World.

It was therefore understandable to the Duke that Claribel appeared to have none of the shyness and sense of insecurity that was usual in a very young débutante but had already a poise which would not have been amiss in a much older woman.

But that did not prevent her from looking as fresh as a dew-drop and every young man's ideal of spring.

Her extremely expensive white gown was exactly what a sweet young maiden should wear, and the blue ribbons which crossed over her breasts and cascaded down her back were the colour of her eyes.

As course succeeded course, all brought to the table on gold dishes, the Duke became aware that Sir Jarvis employed an exceptionally good Chef and the wines were superlative.

There was certainly no question, he told himself, of his Ward being married for his money.

But he was still remembering that Mr. Middleton had said that all young girls were socially ambitious and the higher the title the better the catch.

Mr. Middleton had also hinted that there had been a man of greater social importance in Miss Stamford's orbit, and a few discreet enquiries at White's Club had enabled the Duke to learn that this was the Earl of Dorset.

He had met him several times and thought him a well-mannered, rather serious young man who was a credit to the Household Cavalry.

But the Duke had learnt that he had sheered off and married a girl who preferred the country to London and whose father's Estate marched with his own.

That was sensible, he thought.

At the same time, he wondered if there had been some undisclosed reason for the Earl not continuing his pursuit of the exquisitely lovely Claribel.

As dinner progressed, the Duke saw Lucien staring at his young hostess with what he termed "sheep's eyes," and he thought that perhaps he was being too critical in looking for flaws in such perfection instead of giving without more ado his whole-hearted consent to the alliance.

In the years during which he had shown himself to be an outstandingly brilliant soldier, and in the subsequent years of peace, he had learnt to sum up people quickly and to trust his instinct.

Strangely enough, for no apparent reason he could possibly ascertain, his instinct at the moment was giving him warning signals that everything was not quite right.

He had no idea what it was.

He only knew perceptively, as he had known in Spain and in France when he and his men were in danger before there was any evidence of it, that he had to be on his guard.

"I am being ridiculous," he told himself, and concentrated on the conversation of the lady on his right, whom he found attractive and quite surprisingly intelligent.

When the ladies had retired to the Drawing-Room, the gentlemen lingered for only a short time over their port.

The conversation was all on horses, because besides the Duke and Sir Jarvis there were several other distinguished race-horse owners present.

They talked of their triumphs and ambitions, which the Duke found distinctly interesting.

He was actually reluctant to leave the Dining-Room, were it not that he was aware that Lucien was fidgeting to go and Sir Jarvis was only too willing to make it easy for him to be with Claribel.

In the huge Drawing-Room, which was hung with a number of paintings the Duke would have been delighted to add to his own collection, there were card-tables for those who wished to gamble, comfortable sofas for those who preferred to converse, and one of the guests was playing the piano in an almost professional manner.

The Duke saw Lucien gravitating towards Claribel like a homing pigeon, and, not wishing to embarrass them, he walked out onto the terrace.

The sun was beginning to sink in a blaze of glory and the colour of the sky behind the huge oak trees in the Park was very beautiful.

Behind him the Duke heard Sir Jarvis settling the other guests down at the card-tables and decided he had no wish to gamble.

Instead, he walked over the velvet-smooth lawns, finding that the garden, like the house, was almost too perfect to be real, and he wondered vaguely how many gardeners were employed.

"It must cost Sir Jarvis a pretty penny," the Duke ruminated, and made a mental note to find out where so much money came from.

The invitation to stay at Stamford Towers had arrived so promptly that Mr. Middleton had not had time to bring him the information he required.

He decided that there were a great many questions to be answered before he finally made up his mind to allow Lucien to propose to the delectable Claribel.

He walked on, moving between two yew-hedges that were clipped until there was not a twig or a leaf out-of-place, and then he saw ahead of him some steps that led up by the side of a cascade.

Round the pool there was a blaze of flowers, and because it was so skilfully planned, the Duke walked curiously up the steps to find at the top a small path leading through shrubs that were in bloom and whose fragrance filled the air.

It was so beautiful that he could hardly believe Sir Jarvis had planned it without a professional designer, and yet it certainly was a tribute to the character of the man that he appreciated anything so exceptional.

The Duke walked on and now the shrubs gave way to pine trees and the path became a mere mossy track between their trunks.

Through them he could still see the red and gold of the setting sun and thought that having come so far he might as well finish his walk by seeing what lay at the end of the wood.

He had the idea, because Stamford Towers was on raised ground and this was higher still, that there would be a fine view, and as the trees thinned until they were silhouetted against the sky he saw that he had been right.

At the end of the wood the land dropped down several hundred feet and there was a view over the valley which was exceptional.

The Duke stood looking at it, then suddenly he was aware that he was not alone.

Just a little to the right of him, seated on the trunk of a fallen tree there was a slight figure.

The Duke was still sheltered by the trees through which he had been walking, and he realised that the girl, for that was what she appeared, was not aware of him.

He thought at first glance that she was probably some labourer's daughter or perhaps a servant from the house.

She was wearing a grey cotton gown which looked somewhat like a uniform and she was bending forward as she looked at the view.

He thought that it was rather annoying that he was not alone as he had wished to be and that the best thing he could do would be to turn and go back the way he had come.

Then as if she was conscious of his scrutiny the girl turned her face towards him.

He had the quick impression of huge dark eyes in a small, pale face and was aware that he had been wrong, for she was certainly not a servant but somebody refined and in an unusual way very lovely.

Then as he stared at her she exclaimed:

"How magnificent you are! And just as I thought you would be even though I could only see the top of your head!"

The Duke was astonished.

But before he could find words in which to reply, the girl said:

"I am . . . sorry. I . . . apologise. I should not have . . . said that . . . but I was so surprised to see . . . you."

The Duke walked the few steps that took him to the fallen tree-trunk and as he did so the girl rose and made him a slight but very graceful curtsey.

"You obviously know who I am," the Duke said, "so it is only fair that you should introduce yourself."

"That is unnecessary."

The Duke raised his eye-brows, then deliberately sat down on the fallen tree-trunk.

"If I have interrupted your communion with nature you must forgive me," he said, "but it is certainly a very beautiful place in which to see the sunset."

She turned her head to look across the valley.

"It is so lovely," she said, "and when I am here I can believe I am seeing the sun set in India."

"India?" the Duke questioned. "You have been there?"

She nodded.

"Tell me about it."

It was half an order and half a plea in a voice that many women had found irresistible.

He realised that she hesitated before she replied:

"I think . . . I should . . . go away."

"Why?" the Duke enquired.

"Because . . ." she began, then she stopped and said, "There is no . . . need for me to . . . explain."

"There is every need," the Duke contradicted. "You could not do anything so infuriating as to go away without explaining why you have only seen the top of my head."

She gave a little gurgle of laughter before she replied:

"That is all one ever sees when one looks down from a top window."

The Duke smiled.

"So you were peeping at me when I arrived!"

"Yes, and through the bannisters on the second floor when you proceeded into dinner."

The Duke was wearing his decorations on his evening-coat because one of the guests at dinner was an obscure foreign Prince, and as she looked at one of them she exclaimed:

"I am sure that is a medal for gallantry."

"How do you know?"

"My father was at one time in the Brigade of Guards."

"Tell me your father's name."

Once again she looked away towards the sunset and did not reply.

"If you will not tell me your father's name," the Duke persisted after a moment, "tell me yours. I find it irritating to converse with somebody who is entirely anonymous."

"If you are so . . . interested, you had better . . . know that I am the . . . skeleton in the cupboard!"

"The skeleton?"

"Exactly! So please, Your Grace, will you promise me on your . . . honour that you will not mention to . . . anybody that you have . . . seen me?"

"It would be very difficult to explain that I had met somebody who had no name and the only thing I knew about her was that she had visited India."

"But you must not . . . say that! They would know . . . at once who I was . . . and it only . . . slipped out because I was so . . . surprised to see . . . you."

"I will give you my promise that I will tell no-one we have met," the Duke said, "if in return you will relieve my curiosity by telling me who you are and why you are here."

She looked at him with her large eyes which the Duke thought were very expressive, and he was aware that she was deciding whether or not she could trust him to keep his word.

Then as if something about him reassured her, she said simply:

"My name is . . . Giōna."

"Greek!"

"That is clever of you!"

"Not really. I used to be fairly proficient at Greek when I was at Oxford, and I visited the country two years ago."

"Did it thrill you? Did you feel as if the gods were still there and the light had not changed since Homer wrote of it?"

"Of course!"

"I had an idea you would . . . feel all those . . . things," she said almost beneath her breath.

"And now tell me why you are here and what connection you have with Stamford Towers," the Duke said

The expression that had been in her eyes when she spoke of Greece changed dramatically.

"That is a . . . question you must not . . . ask," she said quickly. "I have told you that I am the . . . skeleton in the . . . cupboard."

"In Sir Jarvis's cupboard?"

"Please . . ." she pleaded.

"If you have deliberately set out to intrigue me and make me so curious that I shall not be able to sleep," the Duke said, "then you have, Giōna, succeeded."

"You promised to . . . forget that you had ever . . . met me!"

"I promised nothing of the sort! I merely said that I would not speak of you to anybody else, and I never break my word of honour."

She smiled.

"That I can believe."

"Then be a little more explicit, in fact a little more kind than you are being at the moment."

"You are making everything very . . . difficult for . . . me," she said. "At the same time . . . although I believe I am dreaming . . . it is very . . . exciting to sit here . . . talking to you. When I heard you were coming to . . . stay, I could hardly . . . believe it."

"You have heard of me before?"

"Yes. Papa was interested in your . . . successes on the . . . Race-Course and many years ago he met your father at a Regimental dinner."

"So your father talked about me?"

Giōna nodded.

"Because we lived abroad, he was interested in everyone he had known before he . . . left England."

"Why did you live abroad?"

She did not answer and the Duke said:

"Tell me more about your father."

"What is the point of remembering him now when he is . . . dead?"

There was a tremor in Giōna's voice which was almost a sob.

She turned her face away so that the Duke should not see the sudden mistiness in her eyes.

"Was your father killed in the war?" the Duke asked gently.

She shook her head.

"No . . . he died . . . and so did . . . Mama, of typhoid in . . . Naples . . . two years . . . ago."

"I am sorry."

"If only I had . . . died with . . . them!"

It was a cry that seemed to burst from her lips.

"You must not speak like that," the Duke said. "You are very beautiful, and life can be an exciting thing, even though for everybody there are ups and downs."

"For me it is very . . . very . . . down. I am in the . . . depths of . . . despair and there is no . . . escape!"

"Why?"

There was silence and after a moment the Duke asked:

"Did your father leave you penniless so that you are forced to work for your living?"

He thought that must be the explanation of why he had mistaken her for a servant and why her grey cotton gown seemed very much the sort of dress a maid would wear.

Then as if she had been insulted Giōna answered angrily:

"Papa provided for me! He would never . . . never have left me . . . penniless! In fact he left me very . . . wealthy!"

The Duke raised his eye-brows.

He could not help looking again at the gown she was wearing, and he could see that peeping beneath the hem her black slippers were worn at the toes.

"Do stop asking questions," she said suddenly. "You will . . . leave me . . . unhappy and make me . . . remember the . . . past . . . which I am . . . trying . . . to forget."

There was something very pathetic in the way she spoke, but before the Duke could reply she added quickly:

"I cannot think why we . . . started this . . . conversation . . . and although it has been more . . . wonderful than I can possibly tell you to . . . talk to you . . . please . . . go away."

"I have no wish to do that," the Duke said firmly.

"But . . . you must . . . you must!" Giōna said. "Besides . . . they might . . . miss you."

"If they do, I shall have a very reasonable explanation for my absence."

"Then I must . . . go," she said, "and please . . . if you want to . . . stay, please do not . . . look at me as I . . . go."

The words came hesitatingly and the Duke stared at her in surprise.

"You must first give me an explanation for your asking that," he said.

He thought Giōna was about to refuse, and he added:

"Otherwise you will make me once again curious, and I shall certainly watch you vanishing between the trees."

"Do you . . . always get your . . . own way?" she asked.

"Invariably!" the Duke replied.

"Then it is very . . . bad for you . . . but I suppose it is to be expected . . . since you are so important and so clever."

"Are you flattering me?" he enquired.

She shook her head.

"The opinion of somebody as insignificant as myself would doubt-less be dismissed by a wave of your hand."

The Duke laughed.

"Now you are deliberately trying to provoke me. So let us get back to the question you have not answered—why I should not watch you leave, if that is what you insist on doing."

There was a hint of mischief in Giōna's eyes as if she found it amusing to whet his curiosity even further.

"If you want the truth . . . it is because I have . . . undone the back of my . . . gown and it would be distinctly . . . immodest to move away until I can do it . . . up again."

"Why have you done that?" the Duke asked.

"Are you still . . . interested in hearing the . . . truth?"

"You know I am. Just as you are aware that you are making me more and more inquisitive."

"About a skeleton in a cupboard? Your Grace should have more important things to occupy your mind."

"It would not be so intriguing if it was not so unexpected."

Giōna gave a little chuckle.

"Perhaps that is true. It is the same way that Papa would have thought. Perhaps that was why it was such fun to be with him."

"Then tell me why you have undone your gown."

"I wonder if I do so whether you will be shocked, surprised, or disgusted."

"I will tell you my reaction when I hear your explanation."

"Very well," Giōna said with a sigh. "Some of the weals on my back are bleeding, and when they . . . stick to my . . . gown it is very . . . painful to pull it off. I also find the evening air . . . cooling."

The Duke stared at her incredulously.

"What are you saying?" he asked.

"I am telling you that I have recently been beaten!" Giōna replied defiantly. "It is something that happens frequently since I came here. Now do you understand why I wish I could have . . . died with . . . Papa and Mama in Naples?"

It was impossible to hide the tears in her eyes, and as they overflowed she wiped them away almost angrily with the back of her hand.

"It is . . . your fault for making me . . . talk like this," she said accusingly. "But it is . . . two years since I have . . . spoke to a man like you."

She drew in her breath before she went on:

"Because you have brought back the happiness I have . . . lost . . . I do not know whether to . . . thank Your Grace . . . the fates . . . or the gods who brought you here this evening."

"Who has beaten you?"

The question came sharply in the authoritative voice which, when the Duke used it, invariably commanded obedience.

There was a little pause before Giōna said in a low voice:

"The same person who . . . brought me here . . . from Naples . . . who defamed my darling mother . . . and who hates me!"

Without her saying any more the Duke knew the answer.

"I presume," he said, "you mean Sir Jarvis?"

Giōna did not speak, but he thought there was a slight affirmative movement of her head.

"Why? What is his connection with you?"

"You gave me your . . . word that . . . nothing we have said will go any further . . . but if you do speak of it . . . he will . . . kill me! He will do it anyway . . . with his floggings . . . but it would be a rather quicker death . . . than the way he is . . . doing it now."

The Duke put out his hand and took Giōna's in his.

"Look at me, Giōna."

Again it was a command, and slowly she turned her face towards him.

There were tears on her cheeks and her eyes were misty, but she still looked lovely in a manner that the Duke was sure was not English but Greek.

"Trust me," he said quietly. "You have told me so much. Trust me with the whole story, and I swear that somehow I will help you."

He felt her fingers tighten on his as if she suddenly felt he was a lifeline to which she could cling.

Then she said helplessly:

"Even if I . . . tell you . . . there is . . . nothing you . . . can do."

"How can you be sure?"

"He will . . . never let me go . . . I am not being hysterical or exag-

gerating when I say he . . . wants me to . . . die! Then . . . since Papa is
. . . dead . . . his secret will be safe forever!"

She spoke in a way that told the Duke irrefutably that she was speaking the truth.

He was a very good judge of character, and he knew when a man or a woman was being sincere or was acting or exaggerating in any way.

He was utterly convinced that Giōna was neither acting nor exaggerating, and again he said, as his fingers tightened on hers:

"Start from the beginning and tell me the whole story."

"I cannot really start at the . . . beginning," Giōna replied, "because I do not . . . know it . . . myself."

"Who was your father?"

"Uncle Jarvis's brother."

"So your name is Stamford."

"Yes, but I am not allowed to use it."

"Why not?"

"I am not quite . . . certain. Papa used many names as we . . . travelled about, but I know it was something to do with Uncle Jarvis which made Papa move from country to country and change his name."

"And your mother went with him?"

"Of course Mama went with him. She loved him. They loved each other. She would have walked barefoot to the top of the Himalayas if he had wanted her to."

"But he had no money."

"Papa had plenty of money, in fact he was very rich, but I think most of what he had to spend came from Uncle Jarvis. It was always waiting for him in the Bank of any country we visited, so that we lived very comfortably and were very happy."

"But you did not come back to England?"

"I knew we could not. Sometimes Papa would be restless and look sort of 'far away,' and Mama and I knew that he was missing his friends, his hunting and shooting, and all the other things he had enjoyed before he went abroad."

"Then what happened?" the Duke enquired.

"We had come back to Europe and were in Greece, until Papa thought it would be fun to explore Italy again. But when we arrived in Naples there was an epidemic of typhoid!"

The Duke felt Giōna's fingers tremble again in his before she went on:

"It was . . . horrifying! Everybody was so . . . ill, and before we could . . . move out of the . . . city, first Papa and then Mama . . . collapsed."

"But you survived."

"Unfortunately!"

There was a long silence, then the Duke prompted:

"What happened then?"

"I was so . . . upset when Papa and Mama died that I first stayed in the Villa we had rented. The Bank which handled the money which was waiting for Papa wrote to England to tell Uncle Jarvis what had happened. That was how he knew where I . . . was."

"And I presume he came out to fetch you."

Giōna shut her eyes.

"I do not . . . want to . . . talk about it."

"I can help you only if you tell me everything."

"I have already . . . told you that you . . . cannot help . . . nobody can. But if you want me to go on with this . . . miserable story, I will . . . do so."

"That is what I want you to do."

"Uncle Jarvis arrived and he . . . told me . . ."

She stopped, and the Duke knew she found it almost impossible to say the next few words, and when she did speak it was in a whisper.

"He . . . told me that . . . Papa and Mama were not . . . married . . . I was . . . illegitimate, or as he put it . . . a bastard!"

She suddenly pulled her hand from the Duke's to say furiously:

"It is not true! I know it is not true! Papa ran away with Mama because his father wanted him to marry an aristocrat as Uncle Jarvis had done."

"And he refused?"

"He had become engaged to a nobleman's daughter, but then he met Mama."

"And they fell in love?" the Duke prompted.

"They were deeply and completely in love, and as Papa knew his father would never consent to the marriage, he persuaded Mama to elope with him. But they were married . . . I know they were!"

"There must be some record of it, and it should not be hard to find."

"I have no . . . chance of . . . looking for it."

"I could do that for you."

"You could? Or rather . . . would you?"

"That is another thing I will promise you to do."

"Mama's father was the Vicar of a small Parish in Hampshire. I know he did not marry them because the Patron of his living was a friend of my grandfather's, and Mama thought her father might be made to suffer for it. So she and Papa were married, I am sure, at Dover."

"Why do you think that?"

"Because to escape all the fuss there was about Papa breaking off his engagement they went to France."

"And was there a fuss?"

"I think so. I am sure there was, for while they were in France, Uncle Jarvis went to see them and said that Papa was to stay out of England because of the scandal he had caused . . . and there was some other reason also."

Giōna made a helpless little gesture with her hands.

"But that is what I do not know. Papa never told me, but thinking back to some of the things Mama said, I know it was then that Uncle Jarvis began to send them so much money and they began to change their name as they went from country to country."

"And what happened to all the money?"

"Uncle Jarvis told me I was . . . illegitimate and he was . . . ashamed and . . . disgusted that I should even . . . exist. He said I was not . . . entitled to any of Papa's money and that it was his by law."

"I am sure that is untrue. Whether you were born in wedlock or not, if he made a Will in your favour the money is yours."

"How can I . . . prove that? Uncle Jarvis brought me back to England with him and said that I should live here at Stamford Towers but that nobody must . . . see me . . . and if I ever attracted . . . attention to myself he would . . . beat me until I was . . . unconscious."

"Why did he beat you today?"

"It was yesterday . . . just before you . . . arrived. I very stupidly went to look at the table in the Dining-Room. I had never seen all the gold plate brought out before, and the garlands on the table were the best orchids from the greenhouses . . . but Uncle Jarvis . . . caught me . . . there."

"So he beat you!"

"I think he is glad of any excuse, and he has instructed the servants to half-starve me, so that if I grow weak enough I will . . . die and he will be . . . rid of me!"

The Duke was about to say that he could not believe that any man could be so bestial or so ruthless, when as if overcome by what she was saying, Giōna bent forward to put her hands over her eyes.

As she did so the back of her gown, which was unbuttoned, fell open and the Duke could see that on the whiteness of her skin there was a criss-cross of weals.

Some of them were purple as if they were beginning to heal, but others were clotted with blood and showed that they were of more recent origin.

For a moment he could only stare incredulously as if he could not believe what he saw.

Then he felt an anger rising within him that was like a burning fire.

It was what he had felt when on the battlefields of Portugal he had seen some of the soldiers stripped and mutilated, and had been ready to murder with his own hands those who had perpetrated such atrocities.

Now he knew that his instinct which had told him there was something wrong with Sir Jarvis was not at fault, and he was also aware that somehow he had to save Giōna.

He could see not only the weals on her back but the sharp curve of her spine protruding in a manner which told him all too clearly that she was under-nourished.

Then he knew that it was of first importance to convince her that her confidence in him had not been in vain and that somehow he would save her from the fiend who was attempting to destroy her.

"Listen to me, Giōna," he said.

Obediently like a child she raised her face and he saw that despite the tears on her cheeks she had herself under control.

Once again he took her hand in both of his.

"I want you to trust me," he said very quietly, "and I promise you again on my honour that somehow I will save you and I will prove, because it will make you happy, that your father and mother were married."

For a moment Giōna's eyes were incredulous, then they seemed to catch the last golden light of the setting sun and to shine as brilliantly as the first evening star that was just appearing overhead.

"I knew when I first saw you," she said, "that somehow, in some . . . mysterious way I did not . . . understand, you had been sent to . . . help me."

The Duke, holding her hand, said:

"I am going back to the house, and I will be thinking of what we can do. You must meet me here again tomorrow evening."

"There is a Ball tomorrow evening."

"All the better! It will make it easier for us to meet without anybody being in the least suspicious."

"They might be suspicious if . . . you disappear for a long time. After all, you are the most . . . important guest."

"I think my Ward is that. You know, of course, why we are here?"

"Claribel intends to marry him."

"If I give my permission."

"I gather from what is being said in the house that it is a foregone conclusion."

"On the contrary, I made it clear that I would only consider the question as to whether my Ward should propose to Miss Stamford. I can tell you now quite categorically that there is not the slightest chance of my answer being anything but 'No'!"

"That is wise. She would not make him happy."

"How do you know? Apart from the fact that she is your uncle's daughter?"

"That is a question I would . . . rather not answer."

"I will not press you," the Duke said, "since for the moment my only concern is for you."

"I . . . I did not mean to . . . involve you in my . . . troubles. I had not the slightest idea that I would ever . . . see you except . . ."

". . . From the top window," the Duke said with a smile. "But we have met, Giōna, and I think it was fate."

He knew that she was trembling, but as she did not speak he asked:

"What is frightening you?"

"I was just . . . thinking how . . . furious Uncle Jarvis would be if he knew I had even . . . spoken to you . . . let alone had this . . . conversation."

"He will not know," the Duke said. "That is why we must be careful."

He rose as he spoke, and because he was still holding her hand he drew Giōna to her feet.

"I am going back now," he said, "and I imagine you have your own way of returning, so there is no reason why anybody in the house should know we have been here together."

"I . . . I . . . hope not," Giōna said. "The servants do not like walking in the woods when it is getting dark . . . it seems spooky to them . . . and anyway nobody will miss me."

"Have you had your dinner?"

She gave a little laugh.

"I may . . . or may not find something in my room. I am not allowed to go to the kitchen when there is a house-party for fear the valets and lady's-maids belonging to the guests should see me."

"You are too thin!" the Duke observed abruptly because it upset him to think of her hungry.

Giōna shrugged her shoulders.

"I have been spoilt by the food I ate with Papa and Mama, who thought cooking was an art . . . and I find it difficult to eat the remains of the servants' meals, which is . . . all I have here . . . but there is . . . no alternative."

"There will be in the future," the Duke said, "and when you go to bed tonight remember, Giōna, that the future will be as bright and as lovely as the sun that will rise again in the morning."

"I . . . I want to believe . . . that," she said.

"If you pray, which I have a feeling you do," he said, "pray that the night and the darkness will pass quickly."

"How can you be so understanding?" she asked. "That is the sort of thing Papa would have said to me."

"I think the one thing your father would have wanted," the Duke said, "would be for you to believe that I am here to help you."

"I want to believe that . . . but I am . . . afraid!"

"Of your uncle? Forget him!"

She drew in her breath and he knew that she was thinking of the beating she had received yesterday and of her uncle's anger if he had the slightest idea she had revealed so many secrets to the Duke.

"You promised to trust me," the Duke said quietly.

"I do! I swear I do!" Giōna said. "And thank you . . . thank you for bringing me . . . hope when there was only . . . darkness and de-spair."

"That is over and you will soon forget. In the meantime, we have to be very careful, very cautious."

She nodded.

The Duke released her hand.

Then as if there was no need for any more words, as the last glow of golden light sank over the horizon, he turned and walked back the way he had come, along the twisting path through the pine wood which led first to the shrubs, then to the steps beside the cascade.

Then he moved as swiftly as he could, not straight towards the house but to another part of the garden, so that when he approached the terrace leading into the Drawing-Room he came from a different direction altogether.

Now he walked slowly and casually, as if he was deep in thought, and as he neared the steps which led down onto the lawn from the terrace he was acutely aware that somebody was waiting for him behind the grey stone balustrade.

"So there you are!" Sir Jarvis exclaimed as the Duke slowly ascended the steps. "I wondered what had become of you!"

"I have been admiring your garden, Stamford," the Duke said. "It is absolutely delightful! You must tell me who planned it."

Sir Jarvis laughed.

"I am gratified that it pleases you. Shall I sound very conceited if I tell you that I laid it all out myself? It is one of the achievements of which I feel justifiably proud!"

There was no doubt that his tone of voice echoed that sentiment.

At the same time, the Duke was aware that he lied.

CHAPTER THREE

*I*F GIŌNA STAYED AWAKE, finding it impossible to believe what had happened, so did the Duke.

He had made himself particularly pleasant to Sir Jarvis to eliminate any possible suspicion that might be in his mind, and when finally he reached his own bedroom Hibbert was waiting for him and he undressed in silence.

Only when Hibbert was about to leave the room, holding his evening-clothes over his arm, did the Duke say:

"Tell me what you make of this place, Hibbert. I am interested to hear your views."

His valet looked at him enquiringly, being well aware that he would not have asked the question without there being some good reason for it.

He had been batman to the Duke while he was in the Army and had been exceedingly useful on many occasions by obtaining information when they had captured a town or a village which otherwise would not have been available to the English.

Hibbert, despite his very English name, was a mixture of several nationalities, which meant that he found it easy to speak other languages besides his own, and his proficiency both in French and in Portuguese had been invaluable.

Now he hesitated before he said slowly:

"Sir Jarvis, Your Grace, employs a larger number of people than any house we've visited recently, but as Your Grace has asked me my opinion, it's that they're not happy."

"Why not?"

"I'm not quite certain, Your Grace," Hibbert replied, "but there's a sort of undercurrent about everything that makes me think, although I'm sure it's ridiculous, that they're afraid in some way."

"I do not think it ridiculous," the Duke said, "and I want you to try to find out what makes them afraid and anything else that you think might be of interest to me."

He was well aware that there was an alert look in Hibbert's eyes, like that in the eyes of a terrier who scents a rat.

He had often thought that Hibbert, like himself, found peacetime dull, and when the valet had left him he thought that it was in fact the truth.

The superficiality of the Social World, the way in which party succeeded party, all much the same, and the women showed little originality or individuality, had contrived to make him both bored and cynical.

Now the knowledge that he had not only to save Giōna but to outwit what he was sure would be a formidable enemy resuscitated a feeling he had not known since the defeat of Napoleon had brought an end to the hostilities with France.

He thought over all she had said and built up a picture in his mind.

But he knew that it was not going to be easy to prove why Sir Jarvis had paid large sums of money to his brother to stay abroad unless Middleton could unearth a scandal to account for it.

Try as he would, he could not recall anything other than a vague idea that somehow he had heard something derogatory about Sir Jarvis.

"It must have been a long time ago," he said to himself.

Then he remembered the horror he had felt when he saw the weals on Giōna's back, and he knew that if it was the last thing he did he would save her from a cruelty which must cause her indescribable agony.

For one thing, it had been impossible not to see the pain she was suffering etched on her face, and he wished he could give Sir Jarvis some of his own medicine and whip him until he was unconscious.

He had felt such a wave of hatred well up inside him when he met his host on the terrace that only years of self-control, which was due in part to his Army training, made the Duke respond to Sir Jarvis's geniality with flattering appreciation of his garden, his house, and his daughter.

It had been, the Duke thought in retrospect, a fine piece of acting, and he only hoped he could continue the role tomorrow without Sir Jarvis having the slightest suspicion that he was not favourably inclined towards an alliance between Claribel and Lucien.

Then as he thought of his Ward he was suddenly aware that it was not going to be easy to convince him that the girl he loved was as reprehensible and despicable as her father.

If he had read Lucien's character right, direct opposition to his plans to marry Claribel would only make him all the more determined to press his suit, with or without his Guardian's approval.

It is what I would do myself, the Duke thought with a wry smile.

He knew that in fact it was an admirable trait for any young man to believe in the woman he loved rather than to listen to defamatory hearsay against her.

The Duke was well aware that this constituted another problem and a very definite obstacle which must be overcome if Sir Jarvis was to get his just deserts.

In the same way as he planned every move of his troops before going into battle, the Duke began to think out his moves one by one, and it was a long time before he got to sleep.

~

The Duke had arranged to ride early the next morning before breakfast in the same way that he rode when he was at home in the country or in London.

Hibbert called him at seven and helped him dress, in customary silence, before the Duke said:

"One thing I would like to know, Hibbert—and you might be able to find out from some of the older servants—is why the Earl of Dorset, who was pursuing Miss Claribel a short time ago, cried off and became engaged to somebody else."

"I'll do my best, Your Grace," Hibbert replied, "but the older servants are very closed towards those of us visitors. In fact—what's never happened before in any house we've visited—we eats in a room on our own."

The Duke raised his eye-brows.

He was well aware of the hierarchy in the aristocratic mansions in

529

which there was a protocol below-stairs which was stricter even than that observed in the Dining-Room.

He knew it was usual for Hibbert, being the valet of a Duke, to sit on the Housekeeper's right, unless there were servants of Royalty present.

Following the same tradition, the lady's-maid to his wife, when he had one, would sit on the Butler's right.

Every servant took on the rank of his Master or Mistress, and he knew that at Alverstode there would be no deviation from this rule, although to make it more interesting for his guests he often changed their places at meals so that they would have different people with whom to talk.

"That is certainly strange, Hibbert!" he remarked aloud. "Nevertheless, see what you can find out. I have never known you to fail in matters of this sort."

As he spoke, he knew that he put his valet on his mettle, and he was quite confident that some results would be forthcoming before they left early on Monday morning.

He had in fact been on the point of insisting that they should leave on Sunday, but Lucien had pleaded with him to stay three nights at Stamford Towers, saying anxiously:

"It is only fair to Claribel and me that you should take time to consider your judgement."

The Duke had laughed.

"You make me sound like a Hanging Judge."

"That is what you will be if you do not allow me to marry Claribel," Lucien had replied hotly.

The Duke thought apprehensively that he would undoubtedly have a great deal of trouble with Lucien when he informed his Ward that he would rather see him dead than married to any child of Sir Jarvis Stamford.

As he came in from riding and went into the Breakfast-Room, he found himself wondering what Giōna had had to eat.

He also found it hard, when Claribel appeared later in the morning in a ravishing and extremely costly creation, not to compare it with Giōna's cheap grey cotton gown and worn slippers.

It would have been impossible for Claribel to live in the same house and not know how her cousin was being treated, and he thought that her dewy-eyed, spring-like appearance was a very clever impersonation of what people would expect her to be like, and not what she really was.

Sir Jarvis had been so determined that the Duke should enjoy his visit to Stamford Towers that every moment of the day had been carefully planned.

The ladies did not rise early, but for the gentlemen after breakfast there was an interesting Mill between two local pugilists who the Duke found were unexpectedly fine exponents of the sport he himself enjoyed.

Before luncheon when the ladies joined them, they inspected the stables, and any lover of horse-flesh would have been impressed by Sir Jarvis's Stud.

"I have two horses with which I hope to challenge you next year," Sir Jarvis said complacently to the Duke. "Perhaps together we should challenge the rest of the world and take each prize without having to divide it."

Sir Jarvis spoke with an eagerness which showed the Duke that he was thinking that by next year Claribel and the Viscount would be married.

"It is certainly an idea," the Duke managed to say with a smile, then he changed the subject by admiring the points of a horse they were examining.

After luncheon, at which they were joined by a number of neighbours, there was a Steeple-Chase on Sir Jarvis's private Race-Course which was situated a short distance from the house.

They drove there in Phaetons and brakes, the ladies in their flowered muslins and pretty bonnets holding sunshades over their heads and looking elegant enough for the Royal Enclosure at Ascot.

There was a book-maker to take the gentlemen's bets, not a professional but one of Sir Jarvis's employees, and any profits, they were told, would be shared out at the end of the day amongst the backers.

As this was such an amusing idea the bets were high, although the horses taking part in the Steeple-Chase were so superlative that the Duke acknowledged it was difficult to pick a winner.

It was in fact an entertainment he would have enjoyed if he had not found himself disliking his host more every minute as the day passed and being critical of everything he said, suspecting it to be an untruth.

However, there was nothing untrue about the preparations that were being made for the Ball that was to take place that evening.

The garden was decorated with Chinese lanterns, fairy-lights glittered amongst the flowers and round the edges of the paths, and an Orchestra had been ordered from London which the Duke was aware was the favourite amongst the young women who danced to it every night.

"You must be enjoying yourself, Cousin Valerian," Lucien said to the Duke as they went upstairs to dress for dinner.

"Naturally," the Duke replied.

Lucien followed him into his bedroom and as Hibbert tactfully withdrew he said:

"I suppose it is too soon to ask you if you have made up your mind?"

"About your marriage?"

"I would like to propose to Claribel tonight in the garden."

"If I allowed you to do so," the Duke said loftily, "I think it would be somewhat banal."

"Banal? What do you mean—banal?" Lucien asked testily.

"It is all too obvious, my dear boy; the stars, the moon and the music in the background might all be a stage-set."

"What is wrong with that?"

"If I were going to propose marriage," the Duke replied, "or when I do, I would like it to be in such original circumstances that we would remember it for the rest of our lives."

There was silence. Then Lucien said:

"I see what you mean."

"I have always thought that you would wish to excel in some particular way of your own," the Duke went on, "and I can imagine nothing more important than the moment when you ask a woman to live with you for the rest of your life. It is then that you should show your originality and of course your intelligence."

As he spoke he feared he was rather overdoing the flattery, but to his relief Lucien accepted the idea and was smiling as he said:

"You are quite right, Cousin Valerian, I have never thought of it like that before. Claribel and I have been to innumerable dances and in a way they are all very much the same."

"I have always found that," the Duke agreed.

"Then are you saying that if I can think of some really original way in which I can ask Claribel to be my wife you will give me your blessing?"

"I am saying nothing of the sort!" the Duke answered quickly. "I am merely saying that tonight is too soon and too obvious, and I would like to get to know Claribel a little better before I consider she is really good enough for you.''

"Good enough for me?" the Viscount echoed in astonishment. "But she is the most beautiful girl in London!''

"And you in a great many people's estimation are the most hand-some and certainly the best-dressed young man!''

The Duke was not looking at his Ward as he spoke, but he was aware that he was preening himself.

He thought it a mistake to "over-egg the pudding" and added quickly:

"As it will undoubtedly take time to tie your cravat to perfection, I suggest you go and dress. You must not be late for dinner.''

The Viscount gave a little exclamation of horror and hurried from the room.

The Duke was smiling as Hibbert came back to help him out of his Hessian boots.

Only when he had bathed and was nearly dressed did he ask:

"Any news for me, Hibbert?''

"Nothing concrete, Your Grace, just a conversation I overheard between one of the men who had come in from the village to help.''

"Whom was he speaking to?''

"A footman who's been here for several years and is older than the others.''

"What did they say?''

"They didn't know, Your Grace, that I was listening, but Your Grace's aware I've got sharp ears.''

The Duke nodded, and Hibbert went on:

"The man from the village said: 'Oi hears we be a-havin' a wedding 'ere soon, Oi shall look for'ard ter that. There'll be a feast an' fire-works, no doubt.'

" 'No doubt,' the footman agreed. 'But we was a-countin' on it a month or so ago.'

" 'Oi knows that! What happened?''

" 'None o' your business!'

" 'They says down at th' *Dog and Duck* Jack had stuck 'is oar in.'

" 'Whether he did or whether he didn't,' the footman replied, 'an' keep yer mouth shut or you'll be in trouble.' ''

Hibbert gave a very good impersonation of the country accent of the man from the village, then said simply:

"That was all, Your Grace."

"Have you any idea who this man Jack is?"

"Not at the moment, Your Grace."

"Try to find out."

"I'll do that, Your Grace."

No more was said, and the Duke went downstairs and found, as he had expected, that the largest Drawing-Room in the house where they were gathering before dinner was packed with people.

He thought with a slight smile that the Viscount outvied every other gentleman present, just as Claribel stood out amongst the younger women like an orchid in a field of buttercups.

The Duke's partners at dinner were sophisticated beauties whom he had met in London and who he learnt were staying at neighbouring houses.

"We were told," one of them said, "that the party was being given specially for you. I could hardly believe it until I arrived here. I thought you never stayed away except with your own particular friends."

"There are exceptions to every rule," the Duke replied.

"You certainly have a good excuse," the speaker went on.

She was looking at Claribel as she spoke, and added:

"Surely it is unnecessary for her to be so rich, especially when your Ward is a wealthy young man?"

"I have never met anybody yet who had enough money!" the Duke remarked cynically.

The food, if possible, was even better than the night before.

Once again the gentlemen were not allowed to linger over their port but repaired to the Ball-Room.

The Duke had no wish tonight to stay any longer than necessary.

He found himself looking forward to the moment when he could escape and see Giōna.

At the same time, he was aware that to disappear too obviously would be a mistake which might have far-reaching consequences.

He was therefore forced to dance, which was something he most disliked and usually avoided, with several of the older women present, and finally he asked Claribel if she would honour him by being his partner in a waltz.

He noticed that she accepted eagerly. She did not seem shy and was undoubtedly a good dancer.

Only when they had circled the room in silence did she say in an engagingly soft voice:

"I do hope Your Grace is enjoying yourself. Papa has tried so hard to please you, and so have I."

"I should be very ungracious if I did not appreciate your efforts," the Duke answered.

"And we appreciate you," Claribel said.

She spoke in a sweet, ingenuous way which would have deceived even a more experienced man as being completely natural.

"Lucien was afraid that you might be upset at leaving London in the middle of the Season," the Duke remarked.

"How can he be so foolish?" Claribel replied. "I love the country! It is so beautiful, and when I return home here I have time to think."

"Is that what you want to do?"

"But of course! But knowing how clever Your Grace is, I am afraid you will find I am very ignorant even after an extensive education in many subjects of interest."

It was all too glib, too contrived, the Duke thought, and it had certainly been thought out very carefully, doubtless by Sir Jarvis.

He made the appropriate reply and after the dance was finished he danced with an older woman, then took her through the open windows of the Ball-Room into the garden.

As he did so, he was well aware Sir Jarvis was watching him go, and he thought that this was the moment when he might escape if he could do it cleverly.

A large number of men who disliked dancing, as the Duke did normally, were standing about under the trees where there was a table containing drinks of every sort, which were also obtainable in the room next to the Ball-Room.

Because it was a warm night most people preferred to be out-of-doors, and as the Duke emerged with his partner on his arm he walked up to two men he knew well.

"Hello, Dawlish!" he said to the man nearest to him. "Would you be so obliging as to fetch my partner and me a glass of champagne? We have both pleased our host by dancing to his Orchestra on an overcrowded floor, and we certainly deserve some refreshment."

Lord Dawlish laughed.

"I was surprised to see you dancing, Alverstode," he said. "I thought you never took to the floor."

"Shall I say that Lady Mary tempted me?" the Duke replied. "I think you all know one another."

They did, and Lady Mary, who was very conscious of her charm, exerted it to keep the three gentlemen amused.

It was only after a little time that the Duke said:

"Excuse me for a moment. There is somebody over there to whom I must speak."

"A man or a woman?" Lady Mary questioned.

"Definitely a man, and definitely about a horse!" the Duke replied, and they all laughed.

He moved away from them and vanished into the shadows, then he was hurrying across the unlit part of the garden which led him to the cascade.

He found the steps, and because he knew how late it was he almost ran through the wood.

The stars and the moon, which was high in the Heavens, made the view that he had seen last night in the sunset even more breathtaking tonight.

But the Duke had eyes only for the fallen tree-trunk a little to his right, and it was with an inexpressible relief that he saw that Giōna was there waiting for him.

"Good-evening!" he said as he sat down beside her. "It was difficult for me to get away."

"I knew it would be, and I did not really expect you would come," she replied. "Besides, I was quite certain you were only a . . . dream."

"I promised you I am very real, and I have been thinking about you," the Duke replied.

He saw her eyes widen in the light from the moon. Her face seemed very pale, and he thought she looked thinner than she had looked the night before.

"Have you had anything to eat all day?" he asked.

She gave a little laugh.

"How can you remember things like that? As a matter of fact, everybody forgot me as they had so much to do."

The Duke took something from the tails of his evening-coat.

"I thought that might be the case," he said, "so I brought you this."

As he spoke he put down on her knee one of his fine linen hankerchiefs, in which were wrapped a number of finely cut pâté sandwiches.

During the dances he had managed to find them in one of the Sitting-Out Rooms which for the moment was empty, and had quickly transferred the whole plateful into his handkerchief.

Giōna looked at them. Then she asked:

"They are pâté?"

"Yes."

"How can you think of anything so ... wonderful? I have almost forgotten what it tastes like, except sometimes in the night I pretend I am eating it again. It would be very much more delicious than the thick slabs of cold mutton which appear to be the staple diet in the Servants' Hall."

"I thought the sandwiches would please you," the Duke said.

Giōna wrapped them up again in his handkerchief and said:

"I am not going to eat them now because I want to concentrate on every mouthful, which I cannot do if you are beside me."

"Now this is what I came to tell you," the Duke said. "I am leaving first thing on Monday morning at about eight-thirty, with the excuse that I am in a hurry to get to London."

Giōna stiffened as if she thought that after this she would never see him again, but he went on:

"And you are coming with me!"

"Y—you ... mean ... that?"

"All we have to decide is where I pick you up."

Giōna thought for a moment. Then she said:

"There is a thick belt of trees about two or three hundred yards from the Main Lodge. They are enclosed by a fence which is easy to climb."

"You will be there?"

"If you really ... mean you will ... take me with ... you."

"You know I never break my promises."

"I shall be ... able to bring ... very little with me."

"There is not need for you to bring anything," the Duke said. "Besides, it might make anyone suspicious who saw you leaving the house carrying a bundle."

"I thought that myself."

537

"Then just saunter away as if you were going for a walk, and leave me to do everything else."

Giōna clasped her hands together.

"I am . . . dreaming! I know . . . I am . . . dreaming!"

"You are awake," the Duke said firmly, "and you have to use all your intelligence to make sure that nothing stops you from reaching the trees you have described to me."

"I shall . . . never be able to . . . thank you."

"There is no time for that now. I think it would be a mistake, even though I would like to see you again, for me to come here again tomorrow evening."

Giōna nodded.

Her face was turned to his and the Duke saw that now she was looking at him with an expression of trust and something akin to adoration, which he found very touching.

"Keep out of Sir Jarvis's way tomorrow," he said, "and remember that the darkest hour is always before the dawn."

"Nor nearly as . . . dark as it . . . was," Giōna said. "Ever since we met last night there has been a . . . hope in my heart that seemed to . . . come to me from the . . . stars."

"Go on believing and thinking that until Monday morning," the Duke said. "Now I must leave you."

"Yes . . . of course."

"Your back is better?"

"Much . . . much better!" she answered, but he knew she was being brave.

He put out his hand, took hers, and raised it to his lips.

"Until Monday morning," he said. "And come hell or high water I will be waiting for you!"

She gave a little laugh as if she appreciated the expression. Then as the Duke rose to leave he asked:

"By the way, there is somebody employed at the house, or perhaps outside, who is called 'Jack.' Who is he?"

The Duke knew by the way Giōna started that his question surprised her.

"Why do you wish to know?" she asked.

"Is there any reason why you cannot tell me who he is?"

"N—no . . . I suppose . . . not."

The Duke waited and after a moment Giōna said:

"I think you must be speaking of Jack Huntsman."

"What does he do? Is he an employee of Sir Jarvis?"

"He schools the horses . . . and trains those bred on the Estate."

"Anything else?"

"I think you should . . . ask somebody else . . . about him."

"I am asking you, and it might arouse suspicion if Sir Jarvis thought I am inquisitive about any of his staff or about anybody here."

As he spoke, the Duke thought that he was taking a rather unfair advantage. At the same time, here was obviously another mystery, and the sooner he solved it the better.

Giōna was aware of the implications of what he said, and after a startled little glance at him she said:

"He . . . he gives . . . Claribel . . . riding-lessons."

"Thank you."

The Duke had learnt what he wished to know and thought it was something he might have suspected.

Giōna had risen to stand beside him and he thought in the moonlight how very slim and insubstantial she looked, and in her grey gown she appeared to be part of the shadows.

There was only the light in her eyes to reassure him that she was not just a shadow.

"Good-night, Giōna!" he said in his deep voice. "Take care of yourself until Monday. We have a long drive in front of us, and I would not have you fainting on my hands."

"I would not do that," Giōna replied, "and thank you for the sandwiches."

"I hope you will have more than sandwiches to thank me for in a few days' time."

Then he was hurrying away through the trees, and only when he was out of sight and she could no longer hear his footsteps did Giōna sit down on the trunk of the tree again.

She looked for a long time over the moonlit valley beneath her as she prayed that what the Duke had planned would come true.

Nobody rose early the following morning because the dance had not finished until dawn came up over the horizon and the stars faded in the sky.

The Duke went riding an hour later than usual, but even so he awoke at his usual time and once again was beset by the problems of Giōna, Sir Jarvis, and Lucien, who appeared every moment to be becoming more entangled with Claribel.

However, nobody was aware that he was anything but at his ease as he joined the gentlemen at breakfast.

Quite a number of them were drinking brandy instead of eating the food which was waiting on a side-table in silver entree dishes kept hot by lighted candles beneath them.

"You look disgustingly healthy, Alverstode!" one of his friends remarked as he sat down at the table.

"You should not drink so much," the Duke replied. "You know as well as I do that one pays for every glass the following morning."

"I know that!" his friend groaned. "But I find it impossible to keep awake without it."

The Duke ate an excellent breakfast, drank with it his usual two cups of coffee, then left the room to find out if the newspapers had been delivered.

The Butler in the Hall informed him that today's and yesterday's newspapers were in the Library, and the Duke found not only the papers but, to his satisfaction, that there was nobody to disturb him.

He therefore settled down to read the Parliamentary Reports and the Racing News. He had nearly finished the latter when Sir Jarvis came into the room.

"I heard you were here," he said, "and I have come to tell you that we are going down to the stables where one of my men is breaking in a new stallion, a superlative animal which I think might interest you."

The Duke knew he would indeed be most interested and followed Sir Jarvis without asking any questions.

When they reached the paddock which lay beyond the stables he heard Sir Jarvis say to the man who was waiting for them:

"Bring out Rufus, Jack, and let us see how you handle him."

The Duke had heard exactly what he had hoped for and expected, and he was more interested in the man who was handling the horse than in the horse itself.

Jack Huntsman, who was over thirty, he thought, was a good-looking, somewhat raffish man with an insolent air which would undoubtedly gain him a lot of success with women.

His physique was almost perfect, slim, broad-shouldered, and while definitely not a gentleman he was a cut above the grooms who worked in the stables.

Rufus was spirited, obstreperous, and determined to unseat the man on his back, but there was no doubt that Huntsman was a good rider and an experienced one.

However, the Duke thought he was a little more severe with the spur and the whip than was necessary for such a young animal.

They watched for about twenty minutes until Sir Jarvis, as if he thought the Duke might be bored, said:

"I have several other horses for you to see which were out to grass yesterday, but I have had them brought in for you to have a look at them."

"I have a feeling you are trying to make me jealous," the Duke said.

"On the contrary, I am still interested in the idea of a certain co-operation between us."

The Duke wondered what Sir Jarvis would say if he replied that he would rather co-operate with the devil.

Instead he merely answered enigmatically:

"I am always interested in new ideas."

Then he changed the subject by asking Sir Jarvis what horse he was entering for the races at Ascot.

To the Duke the day seemed interminable, the hours passing slowly while he was well aware that Lucien was becoming every moment more closely involved with Claribel.

They sat together, talked together, and in the afternoon they went drinking in one of Sir Jarvis's High-Perched Phaetons.

At dinner the Viscount was naturally placed on Claribel's right, and she made no effort to speak to the man on her other side.

After dinner several of the guests wandered outside onto the terrace, but the Duke settled himself at the card-table and played for high stakes until one of his opponents threw down his cards, saying as he did so:

"You are too damned lucky, Alverstode, and I am too damned sleepy. I am going to bed."

"And so am I," the Duke's partner said. "I am getting too old for late nights."

He was not the only one; the ladies definitely were not looking as

541

beautiful as they had the night before and were all ready to proceed up the stairs, most of them carrying lighted candles in gold stands.

Hibbert was waiting in the Duke's bedroom, but when he went to take off his evening-coat the Duke held up his hand.

"What I want you to do, Hibbert," he said in a low voice, "is to find out how I can reach the stables without being seen. How can I manage it?"

"Is it something I can do for Your Grace?" Hibbert asked.

"No, I want to go myself."

"Best wait a little while, Your Grace."

"I agree," the Duke said, "but not too long."

Hibbert left him to come back about ten minutes later.

There was no need for either of them to speak. The Duke merely followed Hibbert along the main corridor, where half the lights had already been extinguished, and down a narrow staircase to the ground floor.

They moved through twisting passages until they reached a door which Hibbert unbolted and unlocked to let the Duke out.

"You'll be able to find your way back, Your Grace?" he whispered.

The Duke thought that if he could find his way about Portugal and France with the hopelessly inadequate maps which the troops had been issued, he could find his way back to his bedroom at Stamford Towers.

Outside, he took his bearings and set off in the direction of the stables.

He had noticed this morning that there was a large Barn filled with hay set rather picturesquely amongst some birch trees.

It did not appear to be in use, or perhaps the hay was just in reserve for an emergency, but it struck the Duke that it would be a very romantic place for a rendezvous near the house.

He moved towards it, keeping in the shadows until he finally found a place where he could hide behind some rhododendron bushes.

Then he settled himself comfortably, aware that if he was wrong in his supposition he would have a long wait and what would prove to be a pointless waste of time.

And yet his instinct that had never failed him told him unmistakably that he was on the right track, and as usual his instinct was right.

After he had been waiting for about a quarter-of-an-hour there was a sound from the direction of the house and from another door came a figure in a dark blue velvet cloak over a white evening-gown.

Claribel, for that was who the Duke knew it was, kept close to a hedge of flowering fuchsias which was overshadowed by chestnut trees.

When she had nearly reached the Barn, the Duke was aware that somebody had come out of the darkness of it and was waiting for her.

One quick glance told him that it was Jack Huntsman, and he waited only a few more seconds to see them disappear.

Then hurriedly but silently he retraced his steps back to the house, along the passages, and up the stairs to the main corridor where his own bedroom was situated.

He did not stop there, however, but hurried on for quite a long way until he reached the room where he knew Lucien was sleeping.

Just for a moment he hesitated, wondering whether he was doing the right thing.

Disillusionment was, as the Duke knew personally, something that could be very painful and leave a scar for a long time.

And yet the alternative was worse: to be married to a woman who was promiscuous and who would swear eternal fidelity while she was still enamoured with another man.

The Duke's lips were set in a hard line as he opened the bedroom door without knocking.

~

Lucien had not felt tired when he went to bed. He had been too elated at the things Claribel had said to him.

"Think how wonderful it will be when we are married," she had said in her soft, beguiling voice. "We can give even bigger and better parties than Papa gave last night."

"I am not interested in parties," Lucien said, "only in being with you."

"We shall be together," Claribel said, "but it will be exciting to entertain and to stay with your Guardian."

"I want to show you Alverstode," Lucien said, "but what is more important to me is Frome House. It is not so big or perhaps so magnificent, but it is beautiful, and when my mother was alive everybody

543

said that the parties at Frome were more amusing than those they enjoyed anywhere else."

"Did you entertain Royalty?" Claribel asked.

"Royalty is usually rather boring because there is so much pomp and circumstance involved."

"Nevertheless, that is what I would enjoy," she said, "and you will arrange it for me, will you not?"

"You know I will do anything that you want," Lucien replied passionately. "Tell me that you love me and that no other man has ever mattered to you in the same way."

"You know that I love you," Claribel said, "but you must not be jealous."

"I am jealous!" Lucien insisted. "I hate your dancing with anybody but me. I hate the way men look at you, and if a man flirts with you when we are married I swear I will kill him!"

Claribel gave a very pretty laugh.

"Oh, dearest, there is no need for such dramatics. Once we are married, I will be your wife."

"The most beautiful, adorable, exciting wife any man ever had," Lucien said.

She had put her hand on his and he thought it would be impossible to feel so intensely without dying of the wonder of it.

When he reached his room he had pulled off his evening-coat and settled down to write a poem to Claribel.

He thought he would tell the servants to see that it was put on her breakfast-tray tomorrow morning, and he could imagine how lovely she would look as she read it.

However, he found it a little harder than he had expected, and he had written only two lines to his satisfaction when the door opened and he saw to his surprise the Duke.

He put down the quill-pen, wondering as he did so what his Guardian could have to say to him.

He was surprised when the Duke shut the door very quietly behind him and crossed the room to say in a lowered voice:

"I want you to come with me, Lucien, I have something to show you."

"At this time of the night?"

"I know it is late, but it is important."

"Of course I will do what you want," Lucien said, "but I cannot imagine . . ."

"Let us hurry," the Duke said, "and I want you to promise me that from the moment we leave this room you will not speak a word."

"But why?"

"Just give me your promise."

"Of course, if you want me to, but I would like to understand . . ."

"There is no time for explanations," the Duke said quickly. "Come with me, and whatever happens, whatever occurs, I hold you to your promise that you will say and do nothing."

The Viscount smiled.

"This is all very 'cloak and dagger'!"

All the same, he was beginning to be intrigued.

He put on his evening-coat again as he spoke, and the Duke opened the door and led the way down the corridor.

Once again he traversed the staircase and the corridors and they went out through the door he had left standing open.

Only when Lucien had followed him behind the rhododendron bushes did the Duke become aware that the moon was now high in the sky directly overhead and the Barn was as brilliantly illuminated as it would be by daylight.

The Viscount was looking about him in sheer astonishment.

He could not see why his Guardian had brought him here in the middle of the night, for no apparent reason, and he wondered if in fact the Duke had been over-imbibing at dinner.

Then he told himself that that was extremely unlikely and there must be a good reason, but what it could be he had not the slightest idea.

In the meantime, as he was obviously supposed to wait, he might as well finish his poem in his head, which would enable him to write it down as soon as he was permitted to return to his own room.

By the time he had added three more lines to those he had already composed, he was feeling rather stiff from standing so long.

Then he was suddenly aware that the Duke stiffened.

He looked at him, then followed the direction of his eyes, and froze into immobility.

Coming from the direction of the Barn, which was almost directly opposite him, two people appeared.

It was Claribel's deep blue cloak that Lucien noticed first, for it was one he had helped her into earlier in the evening when they had walked in the garden and she had said she was feeling the cold.

He had placed it lingeringly over her shoulders and she had thanked him in a way which made him long frantically to kiss her, but he realised there were too many people about.

Now he could see her talking to some man whom he did not recognise, and he was sure it was nobody from the house-party.

Claribel took a step forward and Lucien could see now to his surprise that the man was wearing riding-clothes.

Then, as he could only wonder why Claribel was there and what she was doing, she turned back to the man and put her arms round his neck.

He pulled her roughly to him. Then he was kissing her, a long passionate kiss which made the Viscount feel as if a red-hot poker were searing his forehead.

As he realised fully what was happening, he would have rushed forward, but the Duke, anticipating this action, took his wrist in a grip of iron.

As he did so, Lucien remembered that he had given his word that whatever happened he would not speak or move.

He thought afterwards that it might have been for a few minutes or a few hours that he watched the woman he loved locked in another man's arms.

Then they separated and Claribel turned and ran swiftly back along the side of the fuchsia bushes in the shadow of the chestnut trees and disappeared.

Jack Huntsman yawned before he walked not into the Barn but towards the stables.

Only when he was out of sight did the Duke relinquish his hold on his Ward's wrist and lead the way back into the house.

CHAPTER FOUR

$\mathcal{N}$EITHER THE DUKE nor the Viscount spoke until they had reached the latter's bedroom.

Then Lucien stalked in to say:

"I am leaving!"

His voice was raw and the Duke was aware how much he was suffering.

"I think that would be a mistake," he said quietly.

"If you think I am going to stay here and meet that woman again, you are much mistaken! She lied to me, she pretended, and all the time . . ."

Words failed the Viscount and he clenched his fingers together in an effort at self-control, but his voice broke on the last word.

"What would be a mistake," the Duke said, "is for them to have the slightest idea of your feelings or of what you have discovered."

"I want to confront them with it!" the Viscount muttered between gritted teeth.

"I am sure you do, and it is what I would like to do myself," the Duke said. "But you will have your revenge, that I can assure you, though not yet!"

He realised that the Viscount was hardly attending to him and after a moment he went on:

"What I suggest we do is leave with dignity, without either Sir Jarvis or his daughter having any idea of what we have discovered, and I would be obliged if you would drive my Phaeton to London."

For a moment what the Duke had said hardly percolated the Viscount's dazed mind. Then he asked in an almost incredulous tone:

"Did you say—drive your Phaeton?"

"That is what I asked you to do."

"But you never allow anybody to drive your horses!"

"On this occasion it is important that you should do so. I have sent for my D'Orsay Curricle as I have a call to make in another part of the country before I return to London."

The only thing that could have soothed the Viscount's feelings at this particular moment was the prospect of driving the Duke's outstanding team of chestnuts which was the envy of every owner of horseflesh.

It was also well known that he allowed nobody other than himself to drive either them or a number of other horses in his possession which he looked on as being particularly outstanding.

Realising he had captured his Ward's attention, the Duke went on:

"We depart at eight-thirty and Hibbert will call you at seven o'clock. We will leave our host believing that the visit has been a success, and only when you do not communicate with his daughter will he begin to worry, and so will she, as to what has occurred."

As if he thought this would certainly perturb Claribel, the Viscount's eyes sharpened and the Duke was aware that he was now thirsting for revenge.

"Let me assure you," he said, "that I have a debt almost as great as yours to settle with Sir Jarvis, and I am just waiting for details which will confound and, I hope, destroy him!"

"Do you really mean that?"

"I am not speaking lightly."

"Then tell me what you intend to do."

"All in good time," the Duke replied, "and when you do hear it you will realise, although you must find it difficult at this moment, that you have had a lucky escape."

He did not say any more.

He only opened the door, nodded to his Ward, and left him to what he knew would be the misery and despair of any young man who was in love and realises he has been betrayed.

Then when he reached his own bedroom the Duke was thinking of Giōna and hoping with a fervency that surprised him that nothing would prevent her from reaching the wood where he was to meet her the next morning.

~

Driving across country in a D'Orsay Curricle which travelled faster than any other vehicle the Duke possessed, and which was drawn by his most reliable pair of perfectly matched black stallions, he thought that everything had gone more smoothly than he had dared anticipate.

When he and Lucien had breakfasted downstairs at eight o'clock there had been nobody to keep them company, and only when they had left the Breakfast-Room and were proceeding across the Hall did Sir Jarvis come hurrying down the staircase.

"I had no idea," he exclaimed before he had reached the last step, "that you were leaving so early! I cannot imagine why I was not informed."

"I understood you were aware," the Duke answered, "that I have to reach London as early as possible. You know as well as I do that His Royal Highness dislikes being kept waiting."

There was nothing Sir Jarvis could say to this, and he turned to the Viscount to ask:

"Why must you go too, Frome? I know that Claribel was expecting you to stay for luncheon."

The Duke was aware that his Ward had stiffened as Sir Jarvis spoke to him, and, being afraid of what he might say, he interposed:

"Lucien is obliging me by driving my Phaeton," he said. "Another reason why I have to leave so early is that I have to call on my way on an elderly relative who is in ill health. It is a bore, but a duty which cannot be avoided."

"I quite understand," Sir Jarvis said in a voice which showed he did nothing of the sort.

He was in fact looking at both of his guests with an expression which told the Duke very clearly that he was perturbed at their precipitate departure.

What was more disturbing was that the Viscount had not formally asked him for his daughter's hand in marriage.

"A most enjoyable visit!" the Duke said as he moved towards the front door. "Once again, I must congratulate you both on your house and the beauties of your garden."

Sir Jarvis did not answer because he was walking behind the Duke, beside Lucien.

"Claribel will be disappointed that you are returning to London so soon," he said, "but I hope you will be able to dine with us tomorrow. We shall look forward to seeing you."

The Viscount was about to refuse, when the Duke turned his head slightly and he changed what he was about to say to mutter:

"You are very kind."

Then before Sir Jarvis could say any more he had swung himself up into the Duke's Phaeton to take up the reins with an undisguised eagerness.

The Duke just paused to mutter to his Head Groom:

"Be careful His Lordship does not spring them, Ben!"

Then he walked a few paces to his D'Orsay Curricle, and his second groom, handing over the reins, sprang up into the small seat behind.

The black stallions were fresh and hard to control, but the Duke had time to notice that Sir Jarvis, standing on the steps and watching them go, had a puzzled expression on his face and a frown between his eyes.

The Duke followed the Phaeton ahead of him until, as they passed through the large ornamental gates, he noted with satisfaction that the dusty road outside was empty and there were no houses in sight.

It was quite easy to see where the high wall of the Estate ended and the wooden fence which bordered the wood began. He drew his horses slowly to a standstill, saying to his groom as he did so:

"Put up the hood, Ben."

He thought the groom might be surprised, for it was well-known among his staff that unless it was raining torrentially or snowing His Grace preferred driving in the open.

His groom clambered down to pull up the half-hood which was skilfully designed so as to cause the least possible reduction of speed, and the Duke saw a slight figure climb lithely over the wooden fence which enclosed the trees and come running over the rough grass towards him.

He wasted no time in words but merely put out his hand to draw her into the seat beside him, then drove on, hardly giving Ben time to scramble up behind.

They proceeded for a little while in silence, the Duke well aware that

Giōna was breathless not so much from the quickness with which she had run to him as from excitement.

He glanced at her and saw that her eyes were shining and there was a faint flush on her pale cheeks.

He also realised, now that he could see her in the daylight, that she was painfully thin, and the bones of her wrists were protruding in the same manner that he had noticed amongst the children in Portugal after the French had retreated, taking all the available food with them.

She was still wearing the same grey gown that he had seen her wearing before, only now there was a small woolen shawl over her shoulders.

He thought it was sensible of her to protect herself against feeling cold during the long journey that lay ahead of them.

She wore no bonnet, and for the first time he could see the colour of her hair. It was not dark as he had expected but was the colour, he thought, which one could most nearly describe as ash, but which was very much more beautiful than the mere word suggested.

It seemed to hold both the light and the darkness in it, as if sunshine and shadow combined to make a colour he had never seen on any other woman.

It was the perfect complement to her eyes, which were the grey of a pigeon's feathers.

"You have escaped!" he said with a smile.

"I cannot . . . believe it! Am I really . . . leaving all that . . . despair and . . . misery behind?"

"I swear that nobody shall ever beat you again," the Duke said, "and the future I envisage for you will, I believe, make up for the past."

"How can I have been so . . . fortunate as to be in that one . . . special place when you came through the . . . wood to look at the . . . view?"

"Being a Greek, you must be aware that the gods look after their own!" the Duke said lightly.

She gave a little chuckle before she said:

"I am very . . . very grateful to . . . them."

After that they drove in silence, the Duke enjoying the perfection of his horses, Giōna aware that every mile took her farther away from the terror of Sir Jarvis.

Only when she saw an Inn ahead and realised that the Duke was slowing did she look at him enquiringly, and as if she had asked the question he said:

"I am quite certain you are hungry and had no breakfast before you left."

"Even if it had been there, I would have been too excited to eat it."

"I have already warned you that I dislike women who faint from exhaustion!"

"I shall be all right."

"I have no wish to take a chance on that."

It was as they drew nearer to the Inn that Giōna said:

"Supposing I am seen? We are not so far from Stamford Towers, and Sir Jarvis might make enquiries about me."

"I have thought of that," the Duke replied. "This is a very out-of-the-way, old-fashioned Inn where your uncle would never expect me to eat."

He thought that Giōna was still unconvinced, and he added:

"You will find tucked into the side of your seat my evening-cape which will cover your gown, and I am going to suggest, as you look very young and very slight, that if you let your hair down I shall mention quite casually that you are my younger sister who has just left school."

Giōna gave a little laugh of sheer amusement.

"You are . . . wonderful! You make everything so . . . exciting and exactly like a story in a novel."

As she spoke she was pulling the pins from her hair, which was arranged very simply in a large coil at the back of her neck.

As it fell over her shoulders the Duke saw that it was long and he thought that like everything else about her it was very beautiful.

It took Giōna only a moment to slip the woolen shawl from her shoulders and to clasp the Duke's black cape with its velvet collar and crimson silk lining at the base of her throat.

As they drove into the courtyard of the Inn the Duke saw the Inn-Keeper approaching and knew he was delighted at the prospect of guests who owned such superb horses.

Ben, who obviously had his Master's instructions, jumped down to say:

"This be Sir Alexander Albion, who requires a private room where he can have luncheon for himself and his sister, Miss Juliet Albion."

The Landlord scratched his head.

"Oi be honoured that the gent'man should patronise moi Inn. Oi've no private Parlour, but there be nobidy in the Dining-Room."

"Then keep it that way," Ben said, and hurried to help Giōna down from the Curricle.

While she washed her hands and tidied her hair Giōna explained to the Inn-Keeper's wife that she had lost her bonnet in the wind from the speed at which she and her brother had travelled over the open country.

"Have ye got naught to cover yer head, Miss?" the Inn-Keeper's wife asked solicitously.

"My brother would not stop to fetch my bonnet," she replied, "but he has consented to have the hood up, and I am quite all right."

"Oi might 'ave a piece o' ribbon, Miss, if that'd be any help," the Inn-Keeper's wife suggested.

"That would be very kind of you," Giōna replied.

Accordingly, when she came downstairs with her long hair neatly brushed there was a blue ribbon to keep it in place, and it was tied in a small bow on the top of her head.

There was a twinkle in the Duke's eyes as she explained how she got it, and when they were alone having luncheon he said:

"Now you really do look like a School-girl!"

"In three months' time I shall be nineteen," Giōna replied.

Before this she had exclaimed with delight when they sat down in the small Dining-Room of the Inn to be served first with slices of pâté.

"How can they have anything like this here?" she began.

Then she added quickly:

"But of course, you brought it with you."

"My valet is very solicitous for my comfort," the Duke answered. "He does not approve of the type of food which is obtainable in most country Inns."

"I am glad I am so hungry!" Giōna said with a smile.

But although the cold chicken stuffed with grapes and mushrooms was undoubtedly delicious, she could eat only a very little of it, and the Duke was aware that after the privation she had endured it would take her some time to regain a normal appetite.

The wine which Hibbert had also provided from Sir Jarvis's cellar tasted as golden as it looked, and Giōna said with a little sigh as the meal finished:

"I have lain awake at night thinking of food like this, but I thought I should never taste it again."

"I shall look forward to seeing you do better justice to it in the future," the Duke said drily.

Then, as he had expected, Giōna asked:

"Where are you . . . taking me?"

"To somebody who will look after you while I make the enquiries you wish me to make."

Giōna looked a little apprehensive.

"I . . . shall not be with . . . you?"

"Not at the moment, and I think you are intelligent enough to be aware that as you are under-age and your uncle is your Guardian, I could be accused of abducting a minor."

Giōna gave a little cry of horror and said:

"I had forgotten . . . forgive me . . . but I had forgotten there was a law to that effect in England . . . I should not have . . . come with you."

"Would you have been able to refuse my offer of help?" the Duke asked.

"B—but the punishment for . . . abduction is . . . I believe . . . transportation."

"You have not answered my question."

"If I tell you I would have refused, it would not be . . . true," Giōna said. "You are like Perseus saving me from the Sea Monster, or St. Michael and all his angels coming to my aid! But now that I am . . . free I . . . realise I must . . . leave you."

"How do you propose to do that?" the Duke enquired.

"If you give me a little . . . money . . . a very little . . . I could some-how find my way to the village where Mama lived before she ran away with Papa. My grandfather will now be dead . . . but there are people who will remember him . . . and who might find me a way of earning my own living."

The Duke, looking at her closely, was aware that she was not speaking for effect but was quite serious in her proposition.

"I have very different plans for you," he said, "and because I think you feel you are under some obligation to me . . ."

"A very big one," Giōna interposed.

"You will do what I want," the Duke finished.

"You know I will do anything . . . anything you ask of me," she promised.

The Duke knew it was in the nature of a vow.

"Very well," he said in a practical tone, "the first thing is to chose a name for you, because naturally you cannot call yourself Stamford."

"N—no . . . of course not!"

"I was going to ask you anyway," the Duke went on, "the name of your mother before she married."

"It was Hamilton."

The Duke repeated it as if he fixed it in his mind. Then he said:

"Because of your Christian name, and because you do not look entirely English, I somehow expected it to be Greek."

Giōna smiled.

"My grandmother was half-Greek. Her name was . . . Andreas."

"Then that is how you shall be called for now," the Duke said. "Giōna Andreas. I hope it pleases you."

"I am very proud of my Greek blood."

"There is a straightness to your nose," the Duke added, "which I have seen on the Caryatid maidens at the Acropolis, and particularly on statues of the Goddess Athene."

"Now you are making me so conceited that I feel I can hold my head high wherever I happen to be in the future."

"I think that is something you have done during the difficulties of the past," the Duke said. "Now I have one more question before we are on our way. Have you any idea of the year in which your mother and father were married?"

"She often said to me that I was born exactly twelve months after she ran away with my father," Giōna said, "so I am sure that she was married in August 1799."

"That makes the marriage much easier to trace than it would have been otherwise."

"Then you . . . really will . . . search for a . . . record of it?"

Giōna's voice was breathless, and the Duke said:

"I think you are almost insulting me by asking the question."

"I know you said you would . . . but I can hardly believe . . . when you are so important and obviously have so many things to occupy your mind . . . that you would really . . . concern yourself with my . . . problems."

"I thought I had convinced you that I am concerned."

"You have now, and I want to say 'thank you' but my vocabulary is very limited . . . so I can only say it from my heart . . . and I hope you understand."

"I will certainly try too."

Because there was something in Giōna's voice that was very moving, he deliberately replied casually, and as she spoke he rose to his feet.

He was used to women falling in love with him, and although he was quite certain that Giōna did not know the meaning of the word in the sense in which he knew it, the look he had thought of as one of admiration was still there.

He was uncomfortably aware that it would be an additional problem if she regarded him as anything more than a rescuer and a Sword of Justice.

That was what he intended to be, the Duke thought, the avenger of her uncle who had treated her so abominably and who should be punished as he would be prepared to punish anybody he found torturing a child or an animal.

He found it impossible to forget the weals he had seen on Giōna's back.

He was also certain that she was being truthful when she said that Sir Jarvis was prepared to weaken her hold on life by inadequate feeding and by what amounted, apart from her physical suffering, to mental persecution.

The mere fact that he had styled her a "bastard" and had defamed her mother would prey on the mind of any young girl as sensitive as Giōna who suddenly found herself orphaned and bereft of everything that was familiar.

Then, combined with Sir Jarvis's brutality was the perfidy of his daughter, and the more he thought of them both and of their behaviour, the more the Duke was determined that they should pay for their sins.

He knew he had a long way to go before he would have the satisfaction of bringing his plans to success and getting Sir Jarvis where he wanted him—on his knees.

The Duke had learnt when boxing never to underestimate his opponent and during the war to expect the unexpected.

As they drove on he was going over and over in his mind every detail of what had now become a campaign, determined to make sure he had not been careless or left anything to chance.

It was almost as if he were drawing up a battle-plan and looking for weak spots where the enemy might break through.

As the afternoon progressed the countryside changed a little, and as Giōna looked about her with interest, the Duke knew they were nearing Buckinghamshire, where the Alverstode Estate was situated.

He now knew every highway and lane, and as if the horses were aware that they were not far from home and their own comfortable stable they seemed to quicken their pace without waiting for their driver to encourage them.

Twenty minutes later the Duke said in a tone of satisfaction:

"Welcome, Giōna! We are now driving on land which has been in my family's hands for four hundred years."

"How exciting!" Giōna exclaimed. "But I thought you were not . . . taking me to your house."

"I am taking you to stay with my grandmother," the Duke answered. "She is a very redoubtable old lady who was once a great beauty, but now, because she is old and suffers from rheumatism, she is often very bored. I have the idea you will give her a new interest."

"Are you going to . . . tell her the whole . . . truth about me?"

"I shall tell her because she will enjoy it," the Duke replied, "but nobody else must know except my Ward, Lucien. You quite understand, Giōna, that nobody, and I mean nobody, must be taken into your confidence."

"I promise I will speak of it to nobody!" Giōna said. "But if I am with you grandmother I shall . . . see you sometimes?"

"I am not yet ready to disappear," the Duke replied briefly.

Once again they drove in silence.

As they drove in through a pair of finely wrought ornamental gates Giōna saw in front of them not a large but a very beautiful house built in the reign of Queen Anne, and the Duke was aware that she clasped her hands together as if she was nervous.

He thought as he glanced at her that he had never known a woman whose eyes were so revealing and showed her innermost feelings as clearly as if he were looking into a clear stream.

There was no time to say anything as he drew his horses up outside the porticoed front door and Ben jumped down to run to the horses' heads.

As he did so, two grooms came running from the stables beside the house, touching their forelocks respectfully when they saw who was in the Chariot.

The servants were slower in opening the front door, and it was the Duke who helped Giōna onto the ground, and as her fingers touched his, he was aware that she was cold and trembling.

"There is nothing to make you afraid," he said quietly as they walked up the steps to the front door.

A Butler with white hair came hurrying into the Hall.

"Your Grace!" he exclaimed. "This is a surprise, and Her Grace'll be delighted. She was complaining only yesterday that Your Grace was neglecting her."

"I am here now, Simpson, as you see," the Duke replied. "Where is Her Grace?"

"In her *Boudoir,* Your Grace. Seeing as she's been in some pain these last two days, Her Grace hasn't come downstairs."

"Then I will go up to her," the Duke said, "and I want you, Simpson, to take Miss Andreas to Mrs. Meadows so that she can tidy herself after our long drive."

"I'll do that, Your Grace."

Simpson smiled at Giōna as he said:

"If you'll come with me, Miss, but we'd best walk up the stairs after His Grace, seeing as I can't go as fast as I used to."

The Duke went ahead, aware as he walked along the landing at the top of the stairs that Giōna was talking pleasantly to the old Butler who could only climb up slowly.

The Duke knocked on the door of his grandmother's *Boudoir,* then opened it.

As he had expected, she was seated in an arm-chair in the window with her legs raised on a foot-stool and covered with an ermine rug.

On her lap was a small King Charles spaniel which first growled when the Duke opened the door, then barking with excitement bounded towards him.

The Duke bent to pat the spaniel before he walked towards his grandmother.

He noted that despite the lines of pain on her face she was looking very beautiful, and her white hair was as well arranged as if she were attending an Assembly.

She was also wearing several rows of pearls, rings on her fingers, and a bracelet which glittered in the sunshine as she held out her hands towards him.

"Valerian, is it really you? How delightful to see you!"

"It is really me, Grandmama," the Duke replied, "and forgive me for being so remiss in neglecting you, but the Regent is very demanding."

"He always was, even when he was a young man," the Dowager agreed, "but you did not let me know you were coming."

"I did not know myself until two days ago, Grandmama, and now I need your help."

The Duchess released his hand and said:

"If it is another of those tiresome orphans you wish me to employ, the answer is 'No!' The last one you persuaded me to have in the house upset Simpson with his impertinence, and the one before broke half-a-dozen of my best Sèvres tea-cups."

The Duke had heard all this before, and he was just about to reply when his grandmother went on:

"You have two, or is it three, Orphanages you support, and that is where orphans should be. Not with me!"

The Duke was well aware that it was no use explaining that after a certain age the orphans had to leave the Orphanage to make room for other children and go out to work.

But as he drew up a chair beside his grandmother, he said:

"I have with me, Grandmama, a very different orphan from those you have helped before."

"I will not have him!" the Duchess said firmly. "So before you start trying to coax me, Valerian, the answer is 'No'!"

"I am sorry about that," the Duke said, "because this orphan—who is a 'she,' by the way, and not a 'he'—will intrigue you, and I need your help not only in looking after her but in punishing and bringing to justice a man whose crimes will astound and horrify you."

"I very much doubt it," the Duchess replied.

There was silence. Then, as if her curiosity was too much for her, she asked:

"Who is this man?"

BARBARA CARTLAND

"Sir Jarvis Stamford!"

The Duchess stared at her grandson incredulously. Then she said:

"Not the father of that girl whom Lucien has been pursuing and whom everybody expects him to marry?"

The Duke laughed.

"Grandmama, you are incorrigible! There is not a rumour, a piece of gossip, or a scandal that you, living here in the country, are not aware of long before it reaches me!"

"There is not much else to amuse me now that I can hardly leave my bedroom!" the Duchess snapped.

"I am not complaining," the Duke said. "It only makes my story easier. Yes, Sir Jarvis Stamford is the father of the girl who *did* interest Lucien."

He deliberately accentuated the past tense, and the Duchess sat up in her chair.

"You mean he has finished with her? Or has she refused him? From all I hear, she would be ready to capture somebody more important than Lucien if she could find him."

"What I am going to tell you, Grandmama," the Duke said, "is the whole story from the beginning, and when you have heard it you will understand why nobody must have any idea of the truth, except yourself."

The Duke spoke in a voice which made his grandmother aware that what he had to impart was in fact very serious.

Then before he could speak the door opened and a footman came in carrying a silver tray on which there were two glasses and a wine-cooler containing a bottle of champagne.

He set the tray down on a small table, and when he would have poured out the wine the Duke rose to say:

"I will do that, Henry."

"I thanks Your Grace."

The footman would have withdrawn, but the Duke saw that on the tray there was also a plate of sandwiches.

"Ask Simpson," he said, "to see that Miss Andreas, who is with Mrs. Meadows, has tea and plenty to eat. I am sure Mrs. Goodwin is already cooking some hot scones for tea."

"I'll tell Mr. Simpson, Your Grace."

The door shut and the Duchess said:

"Now, tell me about Sir Jarvis and of course Lucien. I am not accepting this orphan of yours or providing her with hot scones until I know what this is all about."

The Duke handed his grandmother a glass of champagne.

"I know the Doctor has forbidden you any alcohol, Grandmama," he said, "but as you listen to my story you will need some sustenance."

"What you are really saying is that you hope the wine will make me mellow enough to accede to your wishes! I assure you I shall not let it cloud my common sense!"

The Duke smiled slightly, helped himself to a sandwich, and took a sip of champagne before he began.

Then he related exactly what had happened since he had condescended to visit Stamford Towers.

The Duchess did not interrupt. She merely became so interested that she forgot to drink her champagne.

She listened with her eyes on her grandson's face as he told her about the beatings Giōna had received and the moment by the stables when he and Lucien had watched from behind the rhododendron bushes as Claribel kissed her lover good-night.

Only when he had finished did the Duchess exclaim:

"I have always known you to be truthful, at least to me, Valerian, and you could not have invented a plot more incredible than anything fabricated by Sir Walter Scott."

"It sounds fantastic," the Duke agreed, "but I can assure you it is the truth and is very real to Giōna."

"What sort of girl is she?"

"Beautiful, intelligent, and with Greek blood in her veins."

The Duchess raised her eye-brows as she said:

"From what you have just told me, I guess that villain Sir Jarvis told her she was born out of wedlock so as to make sure she did not flaunt the fact that she was his niece."

"That is my explanation," the Duke agreed, "and it is all part of his plan to hide a guilty secret."

"And what is that?"

"That is what I intend to find out," the Duke replied. "He obviously paid his brother to stay abroad, the residue of which he very conveniently claimed when he died. He was also afraid that Giōna might in some way reveal whatever it is that he has been hiding for so long."

He paused before he continued slowly:

"This must be the reason why he has allowed her to meet nobody and why he wishes to dispose of her without actually having to commit murder."

"I never believed such things happened except in books!" the Duchess exclaimed.

"Well, they do!" the Duke replied. "But you will now understand, Grandmama, why I want to leave Giōna with you. I want you to turn her into the attractive young woman she should be, so that when the moment comes it will be impossible for Sir Jarvis, short of shooting her dead, to deny her existence."

"And when will that moment be?"

"When I am ready!" the Duke replied, and there was something ominous in his voice.

In an attractive bedroom, Giōna, having washed and tidied herself to the best of her ability, waited apprehensively.

An elaborate tea had been brought to her by two footmen, and while she appreciated the hot scones, the paper-thin sandwiches, and the fairy-cakes that were so light it seemed they might fly away, she found that after a few mouthfuls she was not hungry.

She was too afraid of what would happen to her when the Duke left her, as she knew he intended to do.

She found herself wondering frantically if it would not be best after all to go off on her own and hide somewhere where Sir Jarvis could not find her and she would not be an encumbrance or a danger to the Duke.

But she had not a penny-piece in her possession and she certainly had nothing she could sell.

She had been almost too astounded to protest when, after Sir Jarvis had brought her home from Italy to Stamford Towers, her clothes were taken from her.

Instead she had been provided with the ugly grey cotton gowns that were made by the seamstress in the house.

"Why should I have to dress like this?" she had asked, being able in those days to show some spirit even though she was already aware that her uncle disliked her.

"You will wear what I tell you to!" he replied sharply. "As a bastard whom your father and mother have foisted on the world, you are fortunate I do not send you to the Workhouse or make you an assistant in an Orphanage to look after the unfortunates in the same position as yourself."

"I will not have you telling such lies about my father and mother!" Giōna replied hotly. "They were married ... I know they were married! Do you imagine that Mama, who was the daughter of a Parson and believed in God, would ever have done anything so ... wicked?"

Sir Jarvis had not argued, he had merely beaten her. Only after innumerable beatings which had left her humiliated and in agonising pain had Giōna realised that there was no use trying to defend her father and mother, who were dead.

Now she thought that when the Duke had gone perhaps his grandmother would despise her and once again she would be little more than a servant in a different household.

The door opened and Giōna thought that Mrs. Meadows, who had left her alone to enjoy her tea, had come to collect the tray, but it was the Duke.

She jumped to her feet with a little cry.

"I was afraid you had ... forgotten me!"

"I am sorry if it seemed a long time," he said, "but my grandmother was very interested in all I had to tell her, and now I want you to come and meet her."

"I ... I was thinking that perhaps ..." Giōna began in a hesitating little voice.

Because the Duke knew by the expression in her eyes exactly what she was thinking, he interrupted to say:

"I told you to trust me. You also promised to do everything I wanted. I hold you to that promise, Giōna."

She raised her chin and he liked the pride which made her do so.

She had taken off his elegant evening-cape and he thought that despite the ugly grey gown she wore, with her hair falling over her shoulders she looked very lovely.

At the same time, he was aware that his grandmother would not miss the sharpness of Giōna's chin, the way her cheek-bones were too prominent, and the dark shadows under her eyes.

He held out his hand, saying as he did so with a smile that was irresistible:

"Come along. Once you know my grandmother, you will know that she is not so frightening as she may at first appear."

Giōna wished she could believe him, and he thought as they walked along the corridor that she was telling herself that nothing could be worse than what she had suffered at Stamford Towers.

The Duke opened a door and for a moment Giōna could only see the golden sunlight and smell the fragrance of flowers.

Then she was able to focus her eyes on the elderly woman with white hair.

The Duchess held out her hand.

"My grandson has been telling me about you, Giōna," she said, "and I hope you will enjoy staying here with me."

Giōna curtseyed.

Then as her fingers touched the Duchess's she knew that they gave her the same feeling of safety and security that she had felt with the Duke.

"I am ... afraid of ... being a ... nuisance to you, Ma'am," she replied in a nervous little voice.

"I think actually you are going to bring me a new excitement," the Duchess said. "I am already intrigued and at the same time very compassionate about what I have heard of you, and my grandson has given me very strict instructions about what we are to do in the next few weeks."

Giōna looked at the Duke enquiringly and he said:

"First of all, although it may not interest you, I have suggested that my grandmother and you choose the gowns which you should be wearing as your father's daughter."

He was quite certain as he spoke that no woman, young or old, could resist the idea of a whole new wardrobe of fashionable gowns, and he waited for the excitement to light Giōna's eyes and he was not disappointed.

"New ... gowns?"

"Dozens of them!" the Duchess said firmly. "And as my grandson is footing the bill, we need not spare any expense!"

The light in Giōna's eyes dimmed for a moment.

"But . . . Ma'am . . . I do not . . . think I can . . ."

"You will be able to pay me back," the Duke said quietly, "when I prove as I intend to do that all the money your father left is yours and I have made sure it is refunded to you."

For a moment Giōna was speechless.

She knew that the Duke was telling her she would receive not only her father's money but the assurance that she was legitimately born, and her voice trembled and broke as she cried:

"I know . . . now you are not . . . Perseus or St. Michael . . . but Apollo bringing . . . light and . . . healing to the world as he drives his . . . chariot across the . . . sky."

Before she could prevent them, the tears of happiness which filled her eyes ran down her cheeks.

CHAPTER FIVE

*T*HE DUKE, SITTING DOWN at his desk in the Library after breakfast, found a pile of letters awaiting him.

Some of them which were official documents and invitations had already been opened by Mr. Middleton, but those that were private and personal were always placed in a separate pile.

He saw that the top two were from ladies who were endeavouring to engage his interest but for whom at the moment he had little time.

He picked up the one beneath, and, realising it was in his grandmother's hand-writing, he opened it with an eagerness that was unusual.

For two weeks now he had had no news of what was happening at the Dower House, and he had deliberately refrained from sending a groom with a note or asking his Secretary to make enquiries on his behalf.

He told himself it was most important that there should be as little connection as possible between him and Giōna until he was ready to expose her uncle.

Although he was sure he could trust his own servants, there was always the chance that some careless remark or an inquisitive underling would start the ball of gossip rolling.

He was in fact extremely anxious that Sir Jarvis should not be suspicious that he was aware of Giōna's whereabouts.

He knew that Sir Jarvis was perturbed and bewildered by the behaviour of the Viscount.

Lucien had informed his Guardian that he had been receiving invitation after invitation to Stamford House in Grosvenor Square, and he had also had several notes from Claribel which, although he did not say so, were obviously of a passionate nature.

The Duke thought with satisfaction that, if nothing else, he and Lucien had Sir Jarvis and his disreputable daughter puzzled and perhaps more than a little apprehensive as to what had gone wrong.

Now he drew out the thick parchment paper which was engraved with the Alverstode crest, on which his grandmother had written to him in her spidery but always legible hand-writing, and read:

My dearest Grandson:

I think it is time You paid me a Visit, and I have something to show You which I am sure You will find Interesting and in fact Intriguing.

May I suggest that it might be a good Idea to bring Lucien with You? I understand he is behaving as might be Expected, which at the same time is good neither for His reputation nor for His health.

Come as soon as You can, and I shall welcome You with the deepest Delight.

I remain,
Your most affectionate
Grandmother,
Charlotte Alverstode.

The Duke smiled as he finished the letter and thought it was so typical of his grandmother that she was aware of what was happening in London and was in consequence as concerned about Lucien as he was himself.

As she had said, it was to be expected that after the shock of Claribel's perfidy he should repair his broken heart in an orgy of riotous living.

The Duke had been regaled by his friends and a number of interfering well-wishers with an almost daily account of what Lucien was doing.

There was nothing particularly reprehensible about it, except that riotous behaviour in public places, even though they were only low dance-halls and brothels, was never desirable.

He was also drinking too heavily and as usual not taking enough exercise, which resulted in his having a "Byronesque" pallor with lines of dissipation under his eyes.

It then struck the Duke that the reason his grandmother had asked him specially to bring Lucien to the Dower House was not perhaps the obvious one.

He had often heard her say in her worldly-wise manner that the "antidote for one love-affair is another," and he thought now that what she was suggesting, while being too discreet to put it on paper, was that Giōna would erase the memory of Claribel's beauty from his mind.

It occurred to the Duke that it was something he should have thought of himself.

Lucien and Giōna were the right age for each other, and what could be a better punishment for Claribel than that her despised cousin should marry the man on whom she had set her own ambitious sights?

There was a smile of satisfaction on the Duke's lips as he put down his grandmother's letter and rang the gold bell that was on his desk.

The door opened almost immediately and Mr. Middleton came into the Library.

"Send a groom to His Lordship's lodgings, Middleton," he said, "with a note asking him to accompany me to the country this afternoon. Tell His Lordship we will have a light luncheon here first, and beg him not to be late."

"I will do that, Your Grace," Mr. Middleton replied.

"Get the groom off as quickly as possible," the Duke ordered, "then we must settle down to these letters."

The letters did not take as long as he had anticipated, and the Duke had time to think further on his grandmother's idea, as he supposed, that Lucien should fall in love with Giōna.

He imagined it would not be difficult as Lucien was invariably en-amoured of any outstandingly beautiful young woman.

The Duke vaguely remembered that in the past he had appeared to have a *penchant* for fair-haired charmers, but that might just have been a coincidence.

However, as a connoisseur of beauty, he was certain that he was not mistaken in thinking that once she had put on a little weight and was well-dressed, Giōna would look sensational.

He was far too diplomatic to make any suggestions to Lucien of anything more than that he thought it important they should both visit his grandmother and talk to Giōna.

"Have you learnt anything of importance about that swine Stam-ford?" Lucien asked aggressively.

He had arrived looking as usual a "Tulip of Fashion," but one glance at him was enough to tell the Duke that he had obviously been drinking heavily the night before and had doubtless had little sleep.

He ate practically nothing of the delicious luncheon the Chef had prepared, and the Duke made no comment when instead he drank several glasses of brandy.

Then as they were finishing luncheon Mr. Middleton came hurrying into the Dining-Room.

The servants had served the coffee and withdrawn, but nevertheless, as it was unusual for him to be disturbed at meal-times, the Duke looked up in surprise as his Secretary walked quickly across the floor.

"I thought you would want to know at once, Your Grace," Mr. Middleton said, "that our enquiries in the Dover area have been suc-cessful!"

"You mean they have discovered where the marriage of James Stam-ford and Elizabeth Hamilton took place?"

"Exactly, Your Grace! Here are the papers."

Mr. Middleton held out several papers to the Duke, which he took and read, thinking as he did so how thrilled Giōna would be.

She had been right, and her odious uncle had deliberately, the Duke was sure, called her a bastard just to make her unhappy.

Her parents had been married in a small village on the outskirts of Dover on 9 August 1799, as a copy of the Church Register attested.

"Good!" he exclaimed with satisfaction. "Thank you, Middleton. This is certainly one step in the right direction."

"What else have you unearthed?" Lucien asked. "Surely by now you have ferreted out something tangible about that blaggard!"

"I must ask you, My Lord, to be patient for a little while longer," Mr. Middleton replied. "I have three of the best men obtainable in Liverpool at the present moment."

"Liverpool!" the Duke exclaimed.

"My informants tell me that the scandal which Your Grace thought you remembered took place in Liverpool."

"Why there?" Lucien enquired.

"Because, My Lord, it was connected with the slave-trade, and a great number of the slave-ships were sent out from and returned to Liverpool."

The Duke sat upright.

"Are you telling me, Middleton, that Sir Jarvis's huge fortune came from slavery?"

"That is so, Your Grace, and while his father made a fortune before him, Sir Jarvis increased it a hundred-fold!"

"I might have guessed it!" the Duke said contemptuously.

"There was nothing criminal in the traffic at the time," Mr. Middleton said respectfully, "not if it was straight and above-board."

Lucien was listening intently.

"So what he did, and what Cousin Valerian thinks he remembers," he said, as if he was working it out for himself, "was something criminal."

"That is what we have to prove," Mr. Middleton replied, "but I think My Lord, in just a few more days I will be able to put in front of His Grace a statement proving that Sir Jarvis acted in both a shameful and an illegal manner."

The Duke pushed his chair back from the table and crossed his legs.

"I want the details now, Middleton!"

"No, please, Your Grace!" Mr. Middleton pleaded. "I have no wish to raise Your Grace's hopes only to be unable at the last moment to produce any evidence."

He looked pleadingly at the Duke and went on:

"We have, as Your Grace well knows, a wily and cunning man to deal with, who will use every means fair or foul to wriggle out of any trap we set for him unless it is one made of cast-iron."

"I understand," the Duke said. "Have it your own way, Middleton.

But quite frankly I am eager to go ahead, and I find it very frustrating to be obliged to see Sir Jarvis on every Race-Course and sporting it in a number of decent Clubs."

"I hope when you have finished with him he will never again be able to show his face in any place which is patronised by gentlemen!" Lucien said vehemently.

He was speaking against Sir Jarvis, but the Duke was aware that he was hating Claribel with the violence of a man who has been betrayed.

At the same time, he thought sympathetically that he was sure Lucien was still hurt and scarred by a love that in its own way had been idealistic and therefore did not die so easily.

He rose to his feet.

"Come along, Lucien," he said, "let us go to the country. At least there the air is clean and the sun is shining."

The Viscount did not seem particularly enthusiastic at the thought of encountering such pleasures. At the same time, he obediently followed his Guardian from the Dining-Room and ten minutes later they were on their way.

The Duke was driving his chestnuts and as usual they gave him so much pleasure that for a little while he forgot the unhappy young man sitting beside him.

Then he was sure that his grandmother in her wisdom had been right to send for him.

The drive to Alverstode took a little more than two hours at the rate at which the Duke travelled.

As he swung into the drive of his grandmother's Dower House, he knew that if he had not broken his own record he had certainly been only a few seconds outside it.

The mellow red-brick Queen Anne house was very lovely in the afternoon sunshine, and the Duke, appreciating its perfect symmetry, thought he might say the same about Giōna's features, especially her straight little nose.

He drew up his horses outside the front door, and as he and Lucien stepped down from the Phaeton, a groom appeared from the stables and Simpson was standing at the top of the steps to welcome them.

"I hardly dared hope that Your Grace'd be here afore tomorrow," Simpson said.

"I hoped to surprise Her Grace," the Duke replied. "Where is she?"

The Duke thought the Butler would say that she was upstairs, but instead Simpson answered:

"In the Drawing-Room, Your Grace, and Miss Giōna is with her."

That was all the Duke wished to know, and he strode across the Hall too quickly for Simpson to keep up with him and opened the door of the Drawing-Room himself.

Dramatically he stood still for a moment in the doorway and waited for the cry of welcome he expected from his grandmother.

She was sitting in the sunlight at the open window with Giōna beside her and exclaimed:

"Oh, Valerian, I am so glad to see you!"

The Duke moved forward and as he did so Giōna ran to him.

He had a quick glimpse of eyes that were shining as if the sun had been caught in them, of hair of a strange colour arranged in a fashionable manner, and of a white gown decorated with frills and flowers.

Then her hands were holding on to his and she was saying with a lilt in her voice that sounded like the song of the birds:

"You have . . . come! I have so . . . longed to see you . . . and now . . . you are here!"

She made it sound like a paean of joy and the Duke smiled as he said:

"Can this really be Giōna, or am I being introduced to a strange young woman?"

Giōna laughed, and then as if he rebuked her for being so impetuous she dropped him a respectful curtsey.

"I am deeply honoured to meet Your Grace!" she said demurely, but her eyes were twinkling.

"Let me look at you," the Duke said.

She was not in the least shy, but threw out her arms, crying:

"Yes, please look! Your grandmother and I have been so anxious to gain your approval."

She was gowned in the height of fashion, but the Duke found it difficult to take his eyes from her face.

He could see that the sharp lines of her chin and cheek-bones had already softened, while the sparkle in her eyes and the sheen in her hair told him that proper feeding and a feeling of security and happiness were working the miracle for which he had hoped.

He did not speak, and after a moment Giōna asked anxiously:

571

"You are not . . . disappointed?"

"How could I be?" the Duke replied. "Grandmama has waved a magic wand!"

As he spoke he found that his grandmother was being greeted by Lucien, who had entered the room behind him.

"I am delighted to see you, dear boy," she said, "and now I want you to meet my guest, whom I think you have heard about but never actually seen."

"No, I have never seen her before," Lucien replied.

He held out his hand, and as Giōna curtseyed, his smile swept away much of the signs of dissipation on his face.

The Duke somewhat belatedly kissed his grandmother's cheek, saying as he did so:

"I presume you have spent a fortune!"

"Then you presume right," she replied, "and Giōna and I intend to spend a great deal more."

"Only if . . . I can . . . afford it," Giōna said in a quiet voice before the Duke could reply.

He knew there was a question behind what she said, and in reply he put his hand under her arm and drew her towards the French windows which opened onto the terrace.

"May I leave Lucien to entertain you for a few minutes, Grandmama?" he asked. "I have something of importance that I wish to tell Giōna alone."

"There is a lot I want Lucien to tell me," the Duchess replied, and she smiled at the Viscount in a manner that was still irresistible, despite her age.

"I am so sorry for all the cruel and unnecessary suffering you have been forced to endure," she said softly.

The Duke guessed as he drew Giōna away that by the time they returned Lucien would have poured out his miseries, and as it was to somebody so sympathetic and compassionate as his grandmother, it would do him a great deal of good.

His knowledge of men told him that what Lucien found even worse than the frustration of having to wait for their revenge on Sir Jarvis was that he was unable to confide in any of his usual friends.

They would undoubtedly have plied him with questions as to why he was no longer interested in Claribel and were mystified by his behaviour, which was wilder and more outrageous than it had ever been before.

And yet there was no plausible explanation he could make to them, nothing he could say to excuse his excesses.

"Grandmama will comfort him," the Duke told himself.

He drew Giōna through the French windows and down through the rose-garden to where there was an arbour covered with honeysuckle and roses.

They reached the arbour and there were comfortable silk cushions waiting for them on the seat.

The Duke sat down and turned sideways so that he could look at Giōna, thinking as he did so that she was now not only one of the loveliest young women he had ever seen but also the most unusual.

He had been half-afraid that once she was dressed fashionably, the Greek look which he admired might vanish or at least be diminished.

Instead, she looked even more Greek, and her grey eyes looking at him held the same adoration which he would have missed if it had not been there.

"What have you to . . . tell me?" she asked breathlessly.

"I have something to give you," the Duke replied.

As he spoke he handed her the papers that Mr. Middleton had given him just before he left London.

As she took them from him he thought her fingers were trembling, and as she read what the papers contained she saw the quiver of excitement and happiness which ran through her.

For some seconds it was, he knew, impossible for her to speak. Then at length, in a voice so low he could barely hear it, she said:

"It was true . . . I knew it . . . was!"

"It was a great help that you knew the exact month and year and that you thought it was in the vicinity of Dover."

She read what was written on the papers again and again, as if to reassure herself that what she had longed for was actually written down.

Then after a moment she raised her grey eyes and he felt as if the light in them was almost blinding.

"How . . . can you have . . . done this for . . . me?" she asked. "And how can I . . . thank you?"

"I knew it would make you happy."

"Far happier than I can possibly say. Although I knew it was untrue, the mere fact that Uncle Jarvis could jeer at my darling mother and disparage her made me feel as if I were being pelted with mud."

"And now you are flying away to the top of Olympus," the Duke said with a smile.

"Not away from . . . you," Giōna said quickly, "because . . . without you I would . . . feel afraid."

He knew what she was thinking, and he said quietly:

"It is only a question of a little more waiting and a little more time before your uncle will be discredited and never again will he be able to menace you."

"I . . . I cannot believe that is . . . true."

"Then trust me," the Duke said. "In the meantime, as you well know, you must stay here with my grandmother and nobody must be aware of your true identity."

"Her Grace has been so wonderfully kind to me . . . and I am very happy. At the same time, I am still afraid that I may have put . . . you in a . . . dangerous position."

"You are still thinking of me?"

"Of course," she replied. "Could I think of . . . anything else when if you had not . . . rescued me I might by this time be . . . dead?"

There was a little throb as she said the last word and he knew it was still a very real fear.

"You have to forget the past," he said, "just as Lucien has to forget what happened to him. I therefore suggest that you be kind to him. He needs your help."

"Your grandmother told me that he has been behaving in a some-what wild manner. I can understand that he has been trying to hide his suffering from other people."

"That is true," the Duke agreed. "At the same time it is not doing him any good, and, if you get the chance, I think you might try to give him a new interest."

He was aware that she looked at him enquiringly but she did not ask any more questions. Instead she said:

"Please tell me what . . . you have been . . . doing and what is the latest news from Parliament."

The Duke was surprised that she should be interested, but he told her of the Bills that were being passed through the House of Lords and the speech he intended to make about one of them.

"Is His Majesty's health really bad?" she asked when he had finished speaking.

"Very bad," the Duke replied, "and I cannot think that he will live much longer."

"Then the Regent will be King," Giōna said, "and I think that recently, because I have had to wait as he has had to do, I began to understand that nothing is more difficult than what Papa called 'possessing one's soul in patience'!"

The Duke laughed.

"Is that what you are doing?"

"I do not know about my soul," Giōna replied, "but my mind is very, very impatient, and it makes my body nervous and restless."

"Nevertheless," he smiled, "it is now very elegantly adorned, and you look very different from the little grey shadow I found sitting on a tree-trunk."

"Always in my dreams," Giōna answered, "I see you walking towards me. I know now, even if I did not . . . realise it at the time, that you were . . . enveloped in the . . . light of Apollo."

"It sounds very poetical," the Duke said lightly.

"It is, and that is why . . ."

Giōna stopped.

The Duke looked at her enquiringly. Then he asked:

"Have you been writing a poem about what happened?"

There was a faint flush on her cheeks as she answered:

"I did not mean to tell you . . . but it is a poem to . . . you. I merely tried to . . . express what I feel about . . . you in verse because it is easier than in prose."

"I am honoured," the Duke said. "When may I see it?"

"Never!"

He looked surprised and she explained:

"It is so inadequate. There are no words even in poetry to describe you, and when I have written a page I tear it up . . . ashamed that I am . . . unable to convey adequately what I am . . . feeling in . . . words."

"Perhaps it is the language that is at fault," the Duke suggested. "Try writing in Greek."

She gave a little cry and clasped her hands together.

"What a wonderful idea! It is something I shall do, then I think I will not be so embarrassed to show it to you."

"I shall be waiting to read it," the Duke said.

As he spoke he wondered if there was any other woman of his acquaintance now or in the past who could have written a poem about him in Greek.

Then he told himself that he must encourage Giōna to concentrate not on him but on Lucien.

As they walked in the garden he said:

"Now do as I tell you. Try to help Lucien. It may eventually do him good to have loved and lost, but for the moment he is finding it a very painful experience."

It was a great surprise to the Duke that his grandmother was well enough to dine downstairs with them, and later that evening he watched Giōna walk onto the terrace and a second later Lucien joined her.

They were leaning on the stone balustrade and had started to talk quietly to each other. The Duke could not hear what they said, but there was no doubt that Lucien was speaking eagerly in a voice that was very different from the sullen drawl that was all his Guardian had heard for the last fortnight.

"They make a very charming couple," the Duchess said complacently.

"They are certainly both very good-looking," the Duke replied.

"Giōna has all the stability and intelligence that a young man like Lucien needs," the Duchess went on. "She is a very sweet creature, the servants all adore her, and every dog and horse in the place will come if she calls them."

"She is certainly exceptional," the Duke agreed.

"It has made me very happy to have her here. In fact I feel better than I have felt for years."

"I have always said there is nothing wrong with you, Grandmama, except boredom."

"Well, nobody can be bored with Giōna," the Duchess said, "and even if she had not such an intriguing story which makes her like a heroine in a novelette, I should still find her adorable."

The Duke knew this was very high praise from his grandmother, who seldom liked young women, and he thought that with such attributes it would be very surprising if Lucien was not soon "off with the old love and on with the new."

He looked and found that they had left the terrace while he had talked to his grandmother and were now out of sight.

He told himself that was just what he had been hoping for, and then as he saw that the sun was sinking low in a blaze of glory he remembered that was how it had been when he had first seen Giōna, seated on the fallen trunk of a tree.

He had known then when he spoke to her that she was very different from what she appeared and even in her ugly grey gown she had been beautiful.

He glanced through the window. Soon the stars would be coming out and the last glow from the sun would have disappeared behind the trees.

Suddenly he remembered how as he had looked at Giōna the moonlight had revealed the look of adoration in her eyes.

He wondered what she and Lucien were saying to each other and if she was looking at him in the same way.

For some reason he could not understand, he suddenly felt extremely irritated.

It made him rise to his feet to walk to the table where Simpson had left a decanter of brandy and several glasses.

Without speaking the Duke poured himself out a glass of brandy, and with the glass in his hand he turned and walked across the room to stand looking out into the garden.

He supposed that by this time Giōna and Lucien would be seated in the arbour where there was the fragrance of honeysuckle and roses.

In the twilight it would be very romantic, and he wondered what Lucien was doing.

Was he frightening her by being over-impetuous? Or was he expressing his admiration too fervently?

"Dammit all!" the Duke muttered beneath his breath. "He might even try to kiss her!"

At the thought, there was a feeling rising inside him which was different from anything he had ever felt before.

He could not explain it to himself, nor did he wish to. He only knew that it was a mistake for Giōna to be alone in the garden with a man she had only just met, besides being extremely unconventional.

The Duke put down his glass of brandy untouched.

"I think, Grandmama, I will take a stroll outside," he said. "I feel it is very airless in here."

"Why, of course, dearest! I agree with you. It has been very hot today."

Without waiting for her reply, he was already walking out onto the terrace and down the steps which led to the lawn, and his footsteps seemed to ring out on the stones.

His grandmother watched him, a slightly puzzled expression in her shrewd old eyes. She had summed up a great number of men one way or another in the passing years.

Then, as if a new idea had come to her, there was a faint smile on her lips and she sat back a little more comfortably in her chair to await the return of her guests.

The Duke walked casually, as he told himself, towards the arbour but when he reached it he found it was empty.

He was surprised.

"Where the devil have they gone?" he wondered.

Giōna and Lucien had in fact walked on from the rose-garden into the herb-garden and from there towards the Maze.

When they reached it Lucien said:

"I hated that Maze when I was a small boy because it frightened me. Now I think I hate it because it is like my life: a lot of paths which end abruptly and make me realise I have wasted my time exploring them."

He spoke bitterly and Giōna said:

"If one always got exactly what one wanted at the first attempt, think how dull it would be."

"Dull?"

"Of course, and one would just give up trying."

She felt that the Viscount did not understand, and she explained:

"Suppose you always knew what horse was going to win the race? What would be the point of watching it? If you shot down every bird you aimed at, it would hardly be worthwhile going out shooting. It is the same with other things in life. I think failures only make one keener to succeed.''

"I suppose I understand what you are saying,'' Lucien said, "but it is a very different thing when one is disillusioned with—people.''

"The point is that we should not blame them but ourselves.''

The Viscount looked at her in astonishment.

"Do you believe that?''

"Of course! I believe that our instinct is one of the most precious things we possess. If we are deceived by a person's character, that is our stupidity—for we should never expect from people more than they are capable of giving.''

She paused.

"Go on,'' the Viscount prompted. "I am trying to follow you.''

"Our failures are rather like flowers which fade too quickly, so we throw them away. But there are thousands of others waiting for us to pick them. It is, if you think about it, very exciting when one has such a variety of choice.''

The Viscount stared at her. Then he laughed.

"You are extraordinary, and not in the least like any other girl I have ever met.''

Giōna smiled.

"If that is true, it must be the result of my foreign travels. The world makes one realise what exciting people there are in a dozen different nations, and the only sadness is that there is not enough time in one's life to get to know them all.''

"I believe Cousin Valerian did tell me you had lived abroad.''

"I have travelled a great deal,'' Giōna said, "and it is something you should do.''

She saw that the idea had not occurred to Lucien, and she went on:

"I cannot tell you how wonderful India is and how different from any other place in the world. It is not only the Indians themselves, who are beautiful with charming good manners, but there are so many creeds and castes that every day one learns something from them, as from the country itself.''

She looked up at the sunset.

"To me, India is crimson and gold. It is shining and mysterious, and it is a mystery that is part of one's heart and soul and always of one's mind.''

She spoke almost as if she was inspired.

Then as he looked at her the Viscount asked:

"What is stopping me from seeing for myself and perhaps feeling as you do about it?"

"If you can afford it—visit India," Giōna said. "Money is the only stumbling-block for most people."

The Viscount gave a sudden cry.

"You have solved it!" he said. "You have answered the question that has been haunting me these past two weeks."

"What question?" Giōna asked.

"What I should do with myself," he replied, "and, if I am honest, how I can—forget."

He spoke the last word in a low voice, and Giōna said quickly:

"I thought you would be feeling like that. That is why you should go away."

"Of course I should," the Viscount agreed, "but I could not think where to go, and I do not want to be alone in any other part of England."

"No, of course not!" Giōna said. "It would only make you miserable and you will keep regretting the past, which is something you must not do."

She looked towards the sunset as she said:

"A new future is waiting there for you, strange, exciting, different from anything you have ever seen or known before. But if you do not find India as wonderful as I anticipate you will, then there are many other countries which will give you new ideas and I think too new ambitions."

The Viscount drew in his breath. Then he said:

"Thank you. You have shown me the centre of the Maze, and now I know I can find my way!"

Giōna turned to smile at him, and he took her hand in his and raised it to his lips.

"Thank you," he said again as he kissed it.

As he came round the corner of a yew-hedge the Duke saw Giōna and Lucien standing at the entrance to the Maze and the graceful stance of the Viscount as he kissed Giōna's hand.

It struck him that it would be impossible for two people to look more elegant or more romantic, but their appearance gave him no pleasure.

Instead, an emotion something like anger seemed to burn through him, making him feel as if he saw them both coloured as crimson as the sunset.

Then, because he was intelligent he knew, undeniably, incredibly, and utterly unexpectedly, that what he was feeling was jealousy!

CHAPTER SIX

*T*HE DUKE SPENT a restless night trying to convince himself that what he had felt when he saw Lucien kissing Giōna's hand was not jealousy. He told himself he must have drunk too much at dinner, or else was feeling on edge at having so little news of Sir Jarvis.

Whatever it was, the idea was ridiculous! How could he at his age be concerned with a girl of eighteen?

He had already assured himself not once but a dozen times that his concern for Giōna was entirely impersonal.

His real object was to bring Sir Jarvis to justice both for his treatment of what was little more than a child and for the manner in which both he and his daughter had been prepared to deceive Lucien.

But try as he would, it was impossible for him not to find himself a dozen times a day thinking of Giōna, of her strange Grecian beauty and the expression in her eyes when she looked at him.

He tried to tell himself as he drove back to Alverstode House that whatever his feelings over Lucien had been, they were unnecessary.

Then as they moved along the narrow lanes which lay between the Dower House and Alverstode itself, Lucien remarked:

"I have decided to go to India!"

"To India?" the Duke exclaimed in surprise. "What makes you think of going there?"

"Giōna has convinced me that it would be a good idea, and I want to get away."

There was a pause of some seconds before the Duke asked:

"Is she thinking of accompanying you?"

"No, of course not! Why should you think she would do that? Besides, I want to go alone."

"Yes, of course," the Duke agreed, "and on consideration I think it would be a good idea for you to travel."

Obviously gratified at his agreement, Lucien talked eagerly of the places he would like to visit, until they reached Alverstode House.

As the Duke was anxious that nobody should guess that Giōna was staying with his grandmother, he had made it quite clear when they left London where he and Lucien would be.

He had then remarked casually to his servants after he arrived that he was dining at the Dower House.

Because news of interest on the Estate travelled as if on the wind, he was quite certain that by this time his servants and quite a number of other people would be aware that his grandmother had a visitor.

He hoped that because there were a great number of things that required his attention at his home, nobody would connect him in any possible way with Giōna.

Yet, when he was alone he found himself thinking how lovely she looked in her new gown and it was difficult for him not to appreciate the warmth and sincerity in his grandmother's voice when she spoke of her.

One thing had come out of the evening which was unexpected: Giōna was sending Lucien away and it would therefore be difficult for anybody, even somebody as skilful as the Duchess, to encourage her to be interested in him.

"I suppose it is too soon for him to think any girl attractive after Claribel," the Duke told himself ruefully.

Then once again there was that question in his mind as to why he had felt so strange when he saw Lucien kissing Giōna's hand.

Hibbert called him at his usual early hour and he went riding, knowing there was no question of Lucien rising early enough to join him.

He resisted an impulse to ride in the direction of the Dower House and instead galloped over the Park in the opposite direction.

Breakfast was waiting for him when he returned a little later than usual, and he was just finishing what had been a satisfying meal when the Butler announced:

"Mr. Middleton has arrived from London to see Your Grace."

"Mr. Middleton!" the Duke exclaimed in surprise.

Then before he could say any more Mr. Middleton walked into the Dining-Room.

"Good Heavens!" the Duke ejaculated. "What brings you here so early in the morning? Has the house burnt down, or have I been robbed of everything I possess?"

"Neither, Your Grace," Mr. Middleton replied.

He waited for the Butler to close the door and they were left alone in the Dining-Room before he said:

"I received news last night that I thought should be in your hands immediately."

"About Sir Jarvis?"

Mr. Middleton nodded.

"Sit down and tell me about it," the Duke invited. "Will you have a cup of coffee?"

"Thank you, that can wait," Mr. Middleton replied, "but this is urgent."

"I am sure it is. You must have left London before dawn!"

Mr. Middleton sat down at the table and drew some papers out of a brief-case.

"You were quite right, Your Grace," he said, "in suspecting there had been some scandal, and it is in fact very much worse than we thought."

There was a look of satisfaction on the Duke's face as he settled himself in his chair to listen.

"We already knew," Mr. Middleton went on, "that Sir Jarvis's father had made a considerable amount of money out of the slave-trade, and Sir Jarvis was in it in a very big way."

"His ships, I imagine, were based at Liverpool?" the Duke interposed.

"The majority of them," Mr. Middleton agreed, "and I hardly need add that he was one of the slave-traders with a reputation for being more ruthless and more avaricious than the others."

"That is what I might have surmised," the Duke remarked.

"However, in 1800 he overstepped himself," Mr. Middleton continued. "A cargo of slaves being carried in one of Sir Jarvis's ships from Africa was, on arrival in the Port of Savannah, barred from entering the harbour because a large number of the Negroes aboard had contracted Yellow Fever."

The Duke was aware that this would have involved the strictest quarantine since Yellow Fever was notoriously infectious.

"As it happened," Mr. Middleton went on, "Sir Jarvis was actually in Savannah at the time, waiting to receive a high price for the slaves that were to be disembarked and placed in the stockade where prospective buyers could inspect them."

The Duke nodded, knowing the procedure regarding slaves which he had read in the reports put before Parliament.

"Apparently," Mr. Middleton continued, "Sir Jarvis was furious when the ship was forced to anchor outside the port, and no amount of persuasion or bribery on his part could change the authorities' ban until the ship had received medical clearance."

Mr. Middleton paused for breath, and the Duke asked:

"Then what happened?"

"Apparently, from the reports my investigators have received, Sir Jarvis suddenly changed his whole attitude and informed everybody that the precautions were very wise and the only people he was sorry for were the Captain and crew aboard the ship."

The Duke raised his eye-brows but he did not interrupt, and Mr. Middleton went on:

"In fact, he was so sorry for them that he sent several barrels of rum aboard so that they could at least enjoy themselves while they were waiting."

Mr. Middleton's voice lowered as he remarked:

"The rum must have been very potent, for that night the ship, according to my reports, was set on fire, and nobody was awake to give the alarm."

"What you are saying," the Duke said slowly, "is that the rum was drugged!"

"That is a supposition that has not been easy to prove," Mr. Middleton said. "The ship burnt quickly and there were few survivors."

"Why was that?"

"Because in Sir Jarvis's ships all the Negroes were in chains below-decks. This was not the usual practice of the trade, except in ships where there had been riots or where the wretched creatures had tried frantically to throw themselves overboard."

"So there was no chance of their getting away?"

"None survived," Mr. Middleton said, "except two of the crew, who were badly burnt."

"It is the most monstrous thing I have ever heard!" the Duke cried.

"Now we come to the main part of our investigations, Your Grace," Mr. Middleton said. "The Shipping-Company put in a large claim to the Insurance-Writers and it was they who thought the whole thing was suspicious and raised the question of arson."

The Duke made a sound but Mr. Middleton continued:

"I have been in touch with them, and they considered they had a very good case against the Shipping-Company of which Sir Jarvis was not only the Chairman but the main Share-Holder."

"Then why did they not prosecute him?" the Duke enquired.

"They were about to do so," Mr. Middleton replied, "when they found that that particular ship was solely owned by another Director of the Company."

"Who was that?"

"Sir Jarvis's brother, James Stamford!"

The Duke started.

Now he was beginning to understand the secret which had kept Giōna's father abroad for so long.

"A warrant was actually made out for the arrest of James Stamford," Mr. Middleton was saying, "but it was found that he had gone abroad the previous year, and although the warrant is still in existence it has not been executed because he never returned to this country!"

"So that is how Sir Jarvis got himself out of trouble!" the Duke exclaimed harshly.

"The detectives I hired for this investigation," Mr. Middleton said, "found a man in Liverpool who retired many years ago from the firm, and they managed to persuade him to make a statement admitting that he had tampered with the documents regarding the ownership of the vessel."

"It was obviously not very difficult," the Duke observed, "to alter the name of 'Jarvis' into 'James.' "

585

"That is exactly what the clerk said when he was questioned," Mr. Middleton said with a smile.

"It was clever! Very clever!" the Duke murmured.

"There was quite a lot about it in the newspapers at the time," Mr. Middleton continued. "Mr. William Wilberforce asked questions in Parliament, and the Abolition of Slavery Society spoke out violently against any ship-owner chaining slaves with the result that even if the ship was in great danger there was no possibility of their freeing themselves. However, without a scapegoat the whole controversy died down."

The Duke was seeing it all so clearly, realising how extraordinarily astute Sir Jarvis had been.

His brother James had already decided to live abroad for a time until the gossip and scandal over his marriage should subside.

That Sir Jarvis was prepared to make him a very rich man if he would save him and the family name from disgrace by continuing in exile indefinitely would not have seemed such a hardship at the beginning of his marriage, when he was wildly in love and asking only to be with the woman who had captured his heart.

He could understand what Giōna had meant when she said that later her father was sometimes restless and homesick for the country of his birth and for the sports and pastimes he had always enjoyed.

What was unforgivable was that, having saved his brother from social disgrace if nothing else, Sir Jarvis had then deliberately robbed and ill-treated Giōna because he was afraid that in some way she might reveal his guilty secret.

Now there was no question that he must be brought to punishment, and that was something about which the Duke was determined.

"I suppose there would be no difficulty in proving what you have just told me?" the Duke asked.

"None at all, Your Grace," Mr. Middleton replied. "It was because I am so anxious that every detail could be substantiated and that I could produce witnesses who were not only reliable but who would be accredited in Court, that this investigation has taken longer than Your Grace hoped."

"I am now extremely grateful to you, Middleton," the Duke said, and there was no mistaking the satisfaction in his voice.

Mr. Middleton rose from the table.

"I will put these papers on Your Grace's desk," he said, "so that you can peruse them at your leisure. There is only one thing which I must admit is slightly unfortunate."

The Duke looked at his Secretary sharply.

"And what is that?" he enquired.

"It is that I am afraid," Mr. Middleton said hesitatingly, "that Sir Jarvis by now will be aware that we are making enquiries."

"How do you know?"

"The investigators were instructed to work with the greatest possible secrecy," Mr. Middleton replied, "but the behaviour of one Senior Clerk in the firm of which Sir Jarvis is still Chairman, and the fact that he disappeared the day after people had been there, makes them suspect that he had come South to notify Sir Jarvis of what was taking place."

"That is unfortunate," the Duke said, "and I presume he may now know or at least guess that I am behind the enquiries you have been making."

"I cannot completely rule out the possibility, Your Grace."

The Duke was silent.

He was thinking of Giōna and as he did so his instinct, which had always warned him of danger during the war, told him now that if Sir Jarvis was aware that it was he who was behind the enquiries, then he would also suspect who was responsible for Giōna's disappearance.

The feeling of danger was so strong, so insistent, that he told himself it was imperative that he should see Giōna immediately to warn her not only of what had occurred but that it might even be necessary to move her somewhere else.

He rose to his feet, saying as he did so:

"Thank you, Middleton! Thank you very much! Now have some breakfast after your journey, and I will see you later in the morning."

"I Thank Your Grace."

The Duke walked from the Dining-Room, and when he reached the Hall he was wondering whether to ride or to drive to the Dower House.

Then the Butler came towards him to say:

"The horses that Your Grace ordered to be brought round for Your Grace's appraisal are outside."

The Duke remembered then, which he had forgotten, that he had told his grooms when he finished riding that he wished to see a pair of bays that he had bought at Tattersall's the previous week.

"I will drive them with a High-Perch Phaeton," he had said, "and see how they work out."

Now it struck him that if he drove them to the Dower House he would be "killing two birds with one stone" and also assuaging his sense of anxiety.

Then he laughed at his fears and was sure that his feelings of danger and emergency were quite unnecessary. It was surely impossible for Sir Jarvis to guess where Giōna was hidden.

Nevertheless, there was no point in taking risks.

"I am going to the Dower House," he said to his Butler.

As he walked towards the front door Hibbert came down the stairs with a clean pair of gloves to replace those he had worn during his early-morning ride.

He had no idea why, but his instinct told him to take Hibbert with him, and without troubling to make any explanation he said:

"Come with me, Hibbert. I want you!" and walked down the steps towards the Phaeton.

Fortunately it was not Ben who was in charge of it, who would have been offended if he had been replaced by the Duke's valet, but one of the younger grooms.

The Duke swung himself into the driving-seat and picked up the reins. Hibbert would have climbed up onto the small seat behind had not the Duke ordered him sharply to sit beside him.

The bays, which had been sold as being well-trained though spirited, set off at a sharp pace.

The Duke quickly had them under control and they moved out of the courtyard, and some way along the oak-lined drive they turned along a grass track which was the quickest route to the Dower House.

Hibbert did not speak, but the Duke knew he was alert with curiosity and had a feeling in his bones that "something was up."

But the Duke still made no explanation, saying only:

"I have the idea I may need you, Hibbert, so be ready and on your guard."

"Against what or whom, Your Grace?"

"To be honest, I have no idea," the Duke replied. "But we may be in trouble."

"I hope that's true, Your Grace," Hibbert said with a grin. "A man gets soft in peacetime."

The Duke smiled.

It was what he thought himself, but he did not trouble to answer, concerning himself with his horses.

～

Giōna had not slept well because she had sensed when the Duke had said good-night that something had annoyed him.

She had no idea what it would be, but there was a harsh note in his voice, his eyes looked like steel, and she thought he had retreated into a shell which made him seem impersonal and out of reach.

"What has ... upset him? What could ... I have ... done?" she asked herself.

Although she went diligently over in her mind everything that had been said during the evening, she found no clue to the sudden change in his attitude between dinner and the time when they had said good-night.

If Lucien had not been there, she thought, she would have been brave enough to ask him if anything was wrong.

But there had really been no opportunity, and after the Duke had joined them in the garden they had immediately walked back to the house, where he had made his farewells to his grandmother.

"Shall we see you tomorrow?" the Duchess had asked.

"I have no idea," the Duke replied in a cold voice which made Giōna look at him in surprise.

"Well, Giōna and I will be waiting eagerly for your return whenever it may be," the Duchess replied. "I hoped you would have luncheon with us."

"I will think about it."

The Duke kissed his grandmother's cheek in a perfunctory fashion and walked towards the door.

He had not spoken to Giōna, but she followed him into the Hall and looked at him pleadingly as he took his tall hat from one of the servants and threw his evening-cape over his arm.

She could not help remembering how he had loaned it to her to enter the Village Inn pretending to be his sister, and she thought that if he were not in such a strange mood she would have been able to make him laugh about it.

However, he was moving to the front door while she said wistfully: "Good-night . . . Your Grace."

He did not look at her nor turn his head. He merely replied: "Good-night!" as if he were speaking from the icy reaches of the North Pole.

"Good-night, and thank you!" Lucien said.

She wondered if he would have said more, but as if he realised he was keeping his Guardian waiting he hurried after him to jump into the closed carriage.

They drove away, and Giōna, watching until the carriage was out of sight, felt as if it carried her heart with it.

It was not until several hours later in the darkness of her bedroom that she admitted to herself that she loved the Duke.

"I love him! I love him!" she whispered into her pillow, and she knew it was like looking at the moon, or because to her the Duke was Apollo—the sun.

"He saved me . . . he brought me . . . hope and gave me a new life. How could I ask for . . . anything more?" she whispered to herself.

But she knew that in fact she wanted a great deal more from him. She wanted him as a man, she wanted him to approve of her, to admire her, and most of all to love her!

She asked herself how she could be so absurd or indeed so presumptuous, and yet the answer was very obvious.

Nobody could control love, and she was aware that it was only because she was so ignorant about it that she had not known the moment she saw him that he had taken her heart from her and it was no longer her own.

"I love . . . him! I love . . . him!"

There seemed to be nothing else to say, and she tossed and turned until the stars outside faded and the first golden fingers of the dawn crept up the sky.

It was only then that she fell asleep, with the word "love" still on her lips.

Giōna awoke early and was dressed long before it was possible for her to go to the Duchess's room.

Because the Duchess had been a beauty she could not bear anybody to see her until she had powdered and rouged her face and her hair had been arranged by her lady's-maid.

Only then, with the windows open, flowers scenting her room, and looking elegant against the lace-trimmed pillows, was the Duchess prepared to see any members of her household who wished to consult her, and of course Giōna.

"It is a lovely day!" the Dowager said when Giōna reached her bedside. "I hope that my grandson when he visits us may take you driving."

"I would love that!" Giōna exclaimed. "But perhaps he has . . . more important things to do."

"I doubt it," the Duchess said firmly, "but I wish now I had suggested it to him yesterday afternoon. You have been cooped up here long enough, and it would be quite safe for you to drive round parts of the Estate where you are not likely to be seen."

Giōna gave a little sigh.

"There are so many things I want to talk about to His Grace."

There was something so wistful in the way she spoke that the Duchess said quickly:

"I am sure he will realise that and will join us for luncheon. Tell Agnes I want to get up so that I shall be ready when he comes."

The Duchess noticed the eager way in which Giōna ran across the bedroom to find her lady's-maid, and she thought there was no doubt that the child was in love with her grandson.

It was something she had hoped would not happen because she was well aware of the Duke's reputation for loving and leaving the women who pursued him.

But last night she had changed her mind.

The Duchess had had too many love-affairs of her own not to recognise the signs when a man was jealous.

She was quite certain that the reason why the Duke had walked so purposefully into the garden and had come back with a frown between his eyes, behaving in a manner which showed that he was keeping himself strictly under control, was that his feelings towards Giōna were not only those of compassion.

591

The Duchess thought that any other girl of Giōna's age would be too young for an experienced, sophisticated man of twenty-nine, but she had not been with her these past weeks without learning how intelligent she was.

What was more, travelling all over the world had given her a very different outlook from that of the girls who had seen nothing but their School-Rooms before they were pitch-forked into society.

'Giōna does not think about herself,' the Duchess thought, 'but about nations, peoples, politics, and religion, and those are the subjects which will keep a man interested eventually rather than a pretty face.'

At the same time, the Duchess was apprehensive.

Nobody knew better than she did how unpredictable her grandson could be, and who indeed could know for certain whether what he was feeling was love or merely boredom?

He had made Giōna his responsibility, but her apparent interest in a younger and very handsome man might make him decide abruptly that she no longer interested him or had any claim on him.

Then the Duchess told herself that she was sure that was not true.

"I shall just have to wait and see," she said with a little sigh as her lady's-maid came hurrying into the bedroom to help her rise and dress.

Knowing it would be some time before the Duchess appeared, Giōna walked downstairs wondering what she should do with herself.

She knew that what she really wanted, because she was so eager to see the Duke again, was to watch for the appearance of his horses in the drive.

"Please, God, let him come soon!" she prayed.

It was perhaps a very trivial thing to pray for, and yet she knew it came from her heart with an intensity she could not control.

"Come . . . soon! Come . . . soon!"

She felt as if every step she took on the stairs repeated the words, and that they flew towards him on wings and he would be aware how much she needed him.

Then just before she reached the bottom of the stairs she heard the sound of wheels and thought with a leap of her heart that her prayer was already answered and the Duke was there.

Then she saw old Simpson move very slowly on his rheumaticky feet towards the open door, and a man's voice said:

"Tell Miss Stamford Oi be wantin' to speak wi' 'er."

"Miss Stamford!" Simpson exclaimed in surprise. "There's no-one here of that name."

"Aye, there be," the man said. "Oi means the young lady as be a-stayin' 'ere."

"Miss Andreas? Is that whom you're referring to?" Simpson enquired.

"Tha's right. Tell 'er t' come to the door."

When Giōna had heard the man ask for her she had stood still and now was standing on the bottom step of the stairs and holding on to the bannister.

She thought with a sudden contraction of her heart that something was wrong.

Then it flashed into her mind that only one person would call her by her rightful name, and that was her uncle.

Wildly she thought she must hide, but as she was about to turn and run back up the stairs, Simpson looked in her direction, aware that she was there, and the man to whom he was talking saw her too.

"Tha' be 'er!" he said in a voice that seemed to ring out.

Before Giōna could move, before she could turn round and run up the stairs, he had stepped into the Hall and picked her up in his arms.

She gave a scream of terror, but before she could protest or realise what was happening, he ran down the steps with her and, lifting her up, bundled her onto the seat of a High-Perch Phaeton.

As she gave another scream of sheer fright and terror, she realised who was driving the horses and felt her voice die against her lips.

"Tie her in, Jake!" Sir Jarvis said harshly, and the man fastened a thick leather strap round her waist, which held her imprisoned to the back of the seat.

Then he stepped back and swung himself up into the seat behind as Sir Jarvis whipped up his horses and they were off.

"What . . . are you . . . doing? Where are you . . . taking me?" Giōna tried to gasp, but her voice was incoherent.

Her uncle turned his eyes from the horses he was driving to look at her, and she thought the expression on his face was the most terrifying and evil thing she had ever seen.

"I am taking you back where you belong," he said, "and I will make sure that you not only never escape again but regret having made any attempt to do so!"

"Y—you have ... no right to do this ... to me ..." Giōna tried to say.

"I have every right," Sir Jarvis replied grimly. "I am your Guardian, and you will certainly cease to talk of 'rights' by the time I have finished with you!"

There was something so ominous in the way he spoke that Giōna felt almost as if he drained away her life from her and already she was dying as she had been when the Duke had rescued her.

She wondered how her uncle could have discovered where she was, what the Duke would do when he found that she had gone, and if she would ever see him again.

She knew Sir Jarvis did not speak lightly when he told her he would make sure she would be unable to escape another time, and she knew without him putting it into words what treatment would be awaiting her at Stamford Towers.

As if he was aware of what she was thinking, he said:

"Just as you are strapped into this Phaeton beside me, so in future I will see that you are chained to the wall of your room. You will be treated like a prisoner, Giōna, and you will receive the same punishment as any felon or criminal, for that is what you are."

Giōna shut her eyes.

The way her uncle spoke made her feel that she was already enduring the whip-lashes she would undoubtedly receive later, and she only hoped that if he intended to kill her, as she was sure he did, he would do so quickly.

Then to her surprise she realised that Sir Jarvis was slowing his horses.

She opened her eyes and saw that they were in a narrow lane where the branches of the trees met overhead.

It was like a tunnel except that the sunshine was percolating through the leaves, making a pattern of gold which she would have thought beautiful if she had not been so terrified.

"Is this the right place, Jake?" Sir Jarvis asked the man who was sitting behind him.

As he spoke, another man appeared from the bushes beside the road, and as she looked at him Giōna saw that he was exceptionally burly and thick-set.

There was something about him which made her think of a prize-fighter, and she was sure that was what he was. A moment later he was joined by the man who had been sitting behind her uncle.

Giōna stared at them in terror and knew that her first supposition was right.

They were pugilists, and because neither of them was wearing a coat she could see their muscles bulging beneath the cotton shirts which they wore with handkerchiefs round their necks.

"Give me a hand with the horses," Sir Jarvis said sharply.

The man called Jake did as he was told and pulled the horses across so that the Phaeton now blocked the lane completely.

When this had been done to Sir Jarvis's satisfaction, the horses put down their heads and started to crop the grass, which to Giōna's surprise he allowed them to do.

Then he thrust his left hand, which was nearest to her, into the pocket of the riding-coat he wore.

She had been too frightened to look at him until now, and she realised that it was a tiered caped coat in which she had seen him before, but she wondered why he needed it as it was a warm day.

As his hand went into the pocket he appeared to be testing something, and with a frightened stab of her heart she was sure it was a pistol.

Then he took the reins in his left hand and drew from the other pocket of his coat a second pistol, which he looked at to see that it was cocked before he put it back in his pocket.

"What . . . are you doing? What are you . . . waiting for?" Giōna asked.

She thought her uncle would not answer her question, but he replied:

"I thought you would like, my dear niece, to see me destroy the man who has taken it upon himself, doubtless at your instigation, to menace my security."

Giōna gave a little gasp and he went on:

"This, of course, is something I cannot allow, and so as you have interfered and aroused his curiosity, you will watch him die!"

"W—what are you . . . talking about? What are you . . . saying?" Giōna asked frantically.

"You know what I am saying," Sir Jarvis said. "It will of course be

595

very unfortunate that the most noble Duke—such a handsome man!—should have been set upon by Highwaymen—such an unscrupulous lot—and left for dead on his own land.''

The way he spoke made Giōna give a scream of sheer terror.

"How can you . . . consider such a . . . thing? . . . How can you want to . . . kill anybody . . . least of all the Duke?''

"If he dies it will upset you, and that is why, you tiresome little bastard, I have brought you here to witness his death!''

"How can you . . . do such a . . . thing? And it was not . . . true what you . . . told me! Papa and Mama *were* married! I have seen the . . . record of it!''

Giōna almost shouted the words at him, and once again Sir Jarvis looked at her with an expression of such loathing that she shrank away from him as far as the strap round her waist would allow her to do.

"So the inquisitive Duke had found that out? That is another reason for me to exterminate him, just as I intend later to exterminate you!''

"You are mad!'' Giōna gasped. "But if I must die . . . please do not . . . kill him! He was . . . only being kind . . . and helpful.''

"Very kind and very helpful!'' Sir Jarvis mocked. "And anxious, I understand, to bring me to justice, which is something I have no intention of allowing.''

"Talk to him . . . beg him to . . . spare you,'' Giōna pleaded, "but . . . please do not kill him.''

"Because you are obviously besotted with the man,'' Sir Jarvis said, "I know now I was right in thinking that it would perturb you to watch his execution. And what could be more appropriate than that you should be wearing the finery that he has obviously paid for while you do so.''

His eyes travelled over her gown, then came back to her face as he said:

"You obviously wish to look your best for the Duke, but let me tell you something: Before he appears, if you scream or make any attempt to warn him, I will smash this pistol into your face so that in the future no man will look at you except in horror!''

He saw the terror in Giōna's eyes and added:

"A broken nose and no teeth are not attractive! No, Giōna, you will be silent.''

"Please ... please ..." Giōna began, wanting desperately to plead not for herself but for the Duke.

Then Jake, looking up the road ahead of him, exclaimed:

"Oi finks he be a-comin', Guv'!"

"Then do exactly as I told you," Sir Jarvis ordered.

Giōna saw the other man draw a pistol from his pocket.

Giōna held her breath.

She could hear as distinctly as Jake had the sounds of horses' hoofs in the distance, until round the corner a little way ahead of them she saw first a pair of perfectly matched horses and a second later the man who was driving them.

There was no mistaking the angle at which the Duke wore his riding-hat or the breadth of his shoulders in his tight-fitting, grey whip-cord jacket.

He must have seen them as soon as they saw him, for he began to draw in his horses. Then as they drew nearer, Giōna saw that Hibbert was sitting beside him and wondered frantically what she should do.

She knew that her uncle had not spoken idly when he had said he would smash her face with his pistol. But she told herself that that was immaterial if she could save the Duke's life.

She was sure there was not a remote possibility that while driving on his own Estate he would be carrying a pistol with him.

Having broken her nose and teeth as her uncle had threatened, he would still shoot and kill an unarmed man.

"What ... shall I do? What shall I ... do?" Giōna asked herself frantically, and could only watch with terrified eyes as the Duke came nearer and nearer.

As he finally brought his horses to a standstill he saw Sir Jarvis waiting for him and also Giōna.

"Good-morning, Your Grace!" Sir Jarvis said mockingly.

"I imagine you are waiting to speak to me," the Duke replied. "Do you intend that we shall shout at each other, or shall we alight and talk in a more civilised manner?"

"As you have somebody to hold your reins," Sir Jarvis replied, "and I do not wish to trust my niece with my cattle, I suggest you come to me."

As her uncle spoke, Giōna realised that Jake must have hidden himself, and though she wanted to cry out that the Duke must not alight, she could not for the moment see what she would gain by doing so.

The Duke handed Hibbert the reins, and as he alighted, the second prize-fighter came from behind the bushes with his pistol in his hand, pointing it at the valet.

Then, so swiftly that it made Giōna catch her breath, Jake rushed at the Duke and attempted to strike at him.

The Duke was taken by surprise, yet he avoided the blow which undoubtedly would have knocked him down, and it only brushed the sleeve of his coat while his top-hat fell from his head.

Then the two men were fighting in a manner which showed Giōna that they were both extremely proficient and experienced pugilists.

For a moment she was terrified that another blow from Jake would send the Duke spread-eagled on the ground.

She had been aware of his strength when he had carried her as if she were nothing but a doll down the steps and lifted her into the Phaeton.

She could see the huge muscles on his arms as he struck out again and again at the Duke and found to his surprise and fury that each blow was ineffective.

The Duke, after his first astonishment at being attacked, settled down to fight in the experienced manner he had been taught at "Gentleman Jackson's Boxing Academy."

While he was hampered by his coat and his opponent was not, he was aware that he was fighting for his life.

However, because he was slimmer, lighter, and certainly more agile than Jake, the Duke amazingly seemed to hit him frequently while he himself remained unscathed.

Then suddenly, so quickly that she could hardly believe it had happened, the Duke caught Jake with an upper-cut on the point of the chin. His head went back, and as he staggered the Duke hit him again and Jake fell backwards on the road and lay still.

As he did so the second prize-fighter, holding Hibbert at pistol-point, turned his head to watch what had occurred, and then the valet acted.

He brought down his hand stiff as a bar of iron on the man's neck with a blow that was certainly not in the Queensberry Rules but was the chop of death he had learnt from the Chinese on his travels.

The man fell as if pole-axed, but Giōna was only watching the Duke.

There was a smile of satisfaction on his face at having defeated his opponent, and it was then that she was aware that her uncle had drawn his pistol from his right-hand pocket.

"Well done, Your Grace!" he sneered. "But unfortunately Round Two is still to come!"

As he raised his pistol dramatically to bring his aim down on his defenceless victim, Giōna slipped her hand into the other pocket of her uncle's coat and pulled out the other pistol.

Without thinking, without even pausing, she pointed it at his heart and pulled the trigger.

With a resounding explosion the pistol kicked in her hand, and Sir Jarvis, after one moment of immobility, toppled forward and out of the Phaeton onto the road.

As he did so his finger must have tightened on the trigger of his pistol, for it went off, and the second explosion frightened the Duke's horses so that they reared up.

Hibbert desperately tried to keep them under control, but they moved the Phaeton backwards and forwards and in doing so upset Sir Jarvis's horses, which until now had been quietly cropping the grass.

There was a mêlée of horses and wheels, before the Duke sprang into the seat vacated by Sir Jarvis and, taking up the reins, tried to control the terrified animals.

They were bucking and shuffling against each other and only when the two teams had been separated and quieted did Giōna give a cry and put out her hands towards the Duke.

"It is all right," he said soothingly as he put his arm around her.

"I ... I ... killed him!" she murmured. "I killed him ... as he intended to ... kill you!"

"I realised that."

Then as he tried to pull her closer he saw that she was strapped to the back of the seat.

He did not say anything, but undid the buckle with one hand before he asked quietly:

"You are all right?"

Giōna rested her head against his shoulder, and with an effort she managed to say:

"I am ... all right."

"Try not to faint now," the Duke said. "I have rather a lot to do!"

It seemed such an odd thing to say that for a moment she forgot about herself as he jumped down from the Phaeton to say to Hibbert:

"What are we to do with this lot?"

Hibbert grinned and his eyes were shining.

"They won't be doing nothing, Your Grace."

He looked down at the ground as he spoke, and the Duke realised that in the confusion after the pistol-shots, the wheels of the Phaeton had passed not only over Sir Jarvis, who was doubtless dead anyway from the shot which Giōna had fired at him, but also over Jake.

The Duke looked at the bodies for a moment, then he said:

"The only people who would be accountable for this mess would be footpads."

"That's just what I was a-thinking myself, Your Grace."

The Duke looked at the man who had been holding up Hibbert and had been felled with the pistol still in his hand.

He then picked up the pistol which had fallen with Sir Jarvis and placed it in Jake's hand.

Then, as if Hibbert realised what was expected of him, he tied the reins in a knot and climbed down.

As they had been together for so long in the war, he knew that his Master would dislike what was obviously the next task in order to leave a misleading but convincing picture to be discovered.

It was therefore the Duke who held the bridle of one of his own horses and one of Sir Jarvis's while Hibbert emptied Sir Jarvis's pockets, took his watch from his waistcoat, a signet-ring from his little finger, and a pearl pin from his cravat.

He then looked at the Duke for orders.

"Stick them in a rabbit-hole in the wood," the latter said.

Hibbert disappeared amongst the trees and the Duke stood watching him go while Giōna was watching him.

It seemed almost a miracle that he had survived, and although she told herself she ought to feel guilty of having murdered a man, all she could do was to thank God fervently in her heart that the Duke was safe.

"Thank ... You! Thank ... You!" she whispered, and her prayer sounded like music that might come from the birds in the trees.

Hibbert came back and the Duke said:

"The sooner we get out of here the better! Somebody will shortly be coming this way."

"I was thinking that myself, Your Grace."

"Then let us waste no more time."

The Duke released the bridle of the horse which had belonged to Sir Jarvis and, going to the side of the Phaeton, held out his arms.

For a moment Giōna thought she was still too frightened to move.

Then because she knew it would be like touching Heaven to be close to him, she moved towards him and he lifted her from the Phaeton and carried her across to his own.

He set her gently down next to the driving-seat, and as Hibbert jumped up behind, he turned his bays with an expertise that only a Corinthian could achieve.

Then they were moving swiftly away from the three dead men lying in the roadway.

They went only a short distance up the road before the Duke drove into a field, and by driving to the other side of the trees brought them back again onto the road which led to the Dower House.

It was only then that he spoke for the first time, aware that Giōna was sitting limply beside him, too exhausted for the moment to be able to think of anything except that he was safe and she no longer need be afraid.

"You are all right?" he asked again.

"You are . . . safe!"

"Thanks to you," he said quietly. "But I will talk to you about that later. Now it is very important that you should do exactly as I tell you."

She looked up at him with wide eyes and he went on:

"Nobody must be aware that either you or I were present at that regrettable and dramatic event that has just taken place."

He drove his horses slowly as he went on:

"In a short time we shall be informed that footpads—and there are quite a number of different types in this neighbourhood—have held up a gentleman who was on his way to call on me at Alverstode House and robbed and killed him."

He paused before he continued slowly:

"It will seem a somewhat complicated crime, because obviously a third man must have got away with the spoils, having quarrelled with his confederates."

Giōna drew in her breath.

"Uncle . . . Jarvis," she said with a tremble in her voice, "intended that you should appear to have been . . . killed by . . . Highwaymen."

"But I am alive, Giōna," the Duke said. "Now you do understand that there must be no question of your knowing anything of what occurred?"

She nodded.

"I know you are intelligent enough to act a part of which is going to be difficult for you, but it will save both you and me from a lot of very uncomfortable questioning."

As he spoke, the Duke thought that nothing could be worse than if Giōna was suspected even of being present when her uncle had died, let alone of being instrumental in killing him.

"I am relying on you," he said, "and because I believe you are clever, I am asking you to save us both by a piece of acting which would be greatly applauded if you were on the boards."

"I will . . . try."

"I know you will," the Duke said with a smile. "What I want you to do is to walk home from here and say that your uncle only took you with him a short distance because he wished to speak to you alone."

"That man you . . . knocked down . . . picked me up from the . . . bottom of the stairs and . . . carried me out to the . . . Phaeton."

"Who saw it happen?" the Duke asked sharply:

"Only Simpson."

"Tell him it was a joke, the sort of thing your uncle thought funny. You must be convincing."

He took her hand and kissed it.

"I will see you later today," he said. "Remember, everything depends on your appearing as if nothing untoward had happened."

He brought the horses to a standstill and Giōna saw that the lodge-gate was only about twenty yards ahead.

"You are . . . safe," she said in a very low voice, as if she was confirming it to herself rather than to him.

"And so are you, for the rest of your life," the Duke replied quietly.

Their eyes met and it was difficult to look away.

Then Giōna climbed down from the Phaeton and started to walk along the road to the gate.

She was aware as she did so that the Duke was turning his horses once more and driving back along the road.

But as she walked on Giōna was conscious of those words that repeated themselves again and again in the beat of her heart:

"He is . . . safe! He is . . . safe!"

CHAPTER SEVEN

"*I* THINK I WILL GO UPSTAIRS and rest," the Duchess said as she and Giōna walked from the Dining-Room.

"I think you . . . would be . . . wise . . . Ma'am."

Giōna spoke in a hesitating voice which made the Duchess look at her sharply.

"A rest would doubtless do you good," she said. "You are looking as pale as when you first came here."

"I think . . . it is the . . . heat," Giōna answered quickly. "I will go into the . . . garden and get some . . . fresh air."

"Yes, do that," the Duchess agreed. "Perhaps my grandson will be here at tea-time to tell us what has delayed him."

Giōna did not say anything, and when the Duchess had walked slowly up the stairs she turned and went onto the terrace.

She had taxed her self-control almost to breaking point in playing the part the Duke had demanded of her.

When she had got back to the Dower House, Simpson was hovering in the Hall in an agitated state.

"What happened to you, Miss Giōna?" he asked. "Why were you carried off in that extraordinary way? I were a-wondering what to do about it."

With a superhuman effort, Giōna managed a light laugh.

"It was just a joke on the part of my uncle," she said. "He meant to surprise me, and succeeded. When we had gone a short way he told me I could walk back. It is the sort of trick he thinks is funny."

The anxiety in Simpson's old eyes cleared.

"So that's what it was all about, Miss!" he exclaimed. "I was a-fearing all sorts of strange things might have happened to you, and were just about to send out the grooms to search for you!"

"There is nothing stranger than that I have got my slippers dusty," Giōna replied. "I will go upstairs and change them."

She went up to her bedroom and to her relief there was nobody there, the housemaids having finished tidying it.

She sat down in a chair and for a moment the room seemed to swim round her and a darkness came up from the floor.

Then she told herself that the Duke trusted her, that it was far too soon to collapse, and that she must act her part so skilfully that, as he intended, nobody would have the slightest suspicion of what had happened.

But as the morning progressed she could only think that she should be more ashamed of having killed a man, even though in doing so she had saved the Duke.

But was he safe from scandal and from the gossip which would inevitably involve him if by some mischance anybody learnt what had really happened?

She was well aware what a story the chatterers in the Social World would make of the fact that the Duke had fought Sir Jarvis and that his daughter wished to marry Lucien, who had not proposed.

And worst of all, she, Sir Jarvis's niece, had somehow become entangled with the Duke of Alverstode.

What would be thought, what would be said, and what the newspapers would print whirled round in Giōna's mind until she knew that the only thing which could dispel the feeling that she might go insane with anxiety was to see the Duke.

She began to count the hours until there was a chance of his appearing.

She had to calculate how long it would be before somebody found the three dead men lying in the road, and if—which was likely—it was one of the Duke's employees, he would report it first to the Duke's house before there was any question of telling the Magistrates.

Even so, Giōna was certain that the Duke would somehow keep free from all the consternation and speculation and would come to luncheon.

She found herself listening for the wheels of his Phaeton drawing up outside the front door, and it was only with the greatest difficulty that she did not run to look out the windows every five minutes to see if there was any sign of his horses coming down the drive.

When at last there was the sound of hoofs on the gravel, it was only a groom carrying a note to the Duchess.

The Duchess, who by this time was downstairs, read it and handed it to Giōna.

For a moment the Duke's strong, upright writing seemed to swim in front of her eyes, then she read:

Forgive me, Grandmama, if I cannot have Luncheon with You as I had hoped, but I am detained by some tiresome Business. However, I hope I may be with You sometime during the Afternoon.

I remain,
Your Affectionate and respectful
Grandson,
Valerian.

" 'Some tiresome business,' " Giōna repeated beneath her breath, and prayed that he was not making too light of something which was very serious.

Now as she walked amongst the roses, thinking of the Duke, a sudden thought made her feel as if she had been struck a heavy blow.

If in fact no serious difficulties arose from Sir Jarvis's death, not only would the Duke be safe but so would she! In which case there would be no need for him to protect her any further.

She had been so terrified of her uncle and he had menaced her for so long that it was only now that she was gradually realising that because he was dead, she was a free person and could go anywhere she liked.

If this had happened to her when she was at Stamford Towers she knew she would have felt like a caged bird who could suddenly fly up into the sky. But now she knew that in becoming free she would lose the Duke.

He had taken care of her and helped her to escape and brought

605

her here to safety only because he had felt sorry for her! And she was aware, without his telling her, that he loathed cruelty of any sort.

She was sure that she meant nothing to him as a woman and that only his sense of justice and his compassion had impelled him to save her from degradation and death.

Now he would no longer be interested!

Instead of feeling happy about her future, she could only see the loneliness and emptiness of it.

She would have money, for the Duke would see to it that what her father had left would be restored to her. Then he would return to his friends, his sports, and the responsibilities of his distinguished position, while she would be left with nothing but an aching heart.

I love him! she thought. *But what could my love mean to him when any of the famous beauties who surround the Regent can be his for the asking?*

She had heard of his successes from the Duchess, who liked to talk of the scandals of the *Beau Monde* and without really meaning to had said many things that enlightened Giōna as to her grandson's attractions.

Her comments on what appeared in the Social Columns of *The Times* and *The Morning Post* often brought strange stabs of pain, although Giōna had not at first realised why she was distressed.

"I see that Lady Mary Crewson was in attendance at Buckingham Palace this week," the Duchess had remarked yesterday. "I always found her a tiresome woman, but she is very beautiful. I suppose I can understand what Valerian saw in her, although his interest did not last long."

The Engagement Columns always evoked revealing remarks.

"So the Duke of Northumberland's daughter is engaged at last!" the Dowager had exclaimed one morning. "I thought she was still wearing the willow for Valerian. She would have made him a very suitable wife, but he would not look at her!"

Women and more women! Giōna was sure they were all as beautiful as the sunrise, or as the moonlight flooding the valley when she and the Duke had sat together on the fallen tree.

Without realising where she was going, Giōna found her way to the arbour and sat down on the seat.

She tried to steel herself against what she was sure the Duke would say to her when finally he arrived.

She wondered why he was taking so long.

Perhaps the Chief Constable suspected that the scene they had set to suggest a quarrel amongst footpads was not genuine. If he suspected the Duke of having killed her uncle, then she would have to clear him by telling the truth.

She was certain that the Duke initially would try to take the blame, but that was something she could not allow him to do.

Under an interrogation the whole sordid story would be revealed, the tale of her uncle's cruelty would strip her naked to the public gaze, and she would never again be able to hold up her head.

If, on the other hand, everything worked out as the Duke had planned, then he would say good-bye, perhaps suggesting that she could stay a little longer with his grandmother.

But she could hardly remain an uninvited guest forever, and in fact from today she must start planning her own future.

Perhaps she would rent a house in London and could pay some respectable elderly woman or a widow to chaperone her. Or perhaps it would be better to leave England and return to a life of travelling restlessly to any part of the world that was not at war.

She would be alone, completely alone, and she knew that in the future no man would ever attract her, for having given her love once, it was no longer hers to give again.

She wanted to cry at the misery of her own thoughts. Then she told herself that if the Duke found her in tears he would despise her for not being able to carry out his orders more competently.

Already his grandmother suspected that something was wrong because she was so pale, and perhaps Simpson had not really believed the story she had told him.

Because she was disturbed and upset, everything seemed ominous and frightening as the difficulties, the problems, and the questions closed in upon her.

She suddenly felt almost as if she must scream aloud, when she looked up and the Duke was there!

He had approached without her hearing him, and now he stood just outside the arbour, though for one moment she thought he was just a figment of her imagination.

Her heart seemed to stop beating before she sprang to her feet and with a cry ran towards him.

"What has . . . happened? Why have . . . you been so . . . long? Is . . . anything . . . wrong?"

The questions seemed to tumble incoherently from her lips and she could not control them.

Without thinking, without even meaning to do so, Giōna held on to him almost as if he might escape and leave her without replying.

"Everything is all right," the Duke said soothingly. "I am sorry if I have been a long time in coming to you, but it was unavoidable."

The calmness of his voice made Giōna look up at him searchingly, and her eyes seemed to fill the whole of her small face as she asked:

"They . . . believed it? They . . . accepted that it was . . . footpads who . . . killed Uncle Jarvis?"

The way she spoke was so unsteady that the Duke put his arm round her as if to support her.

"The Military are already searching for the murderer, although they admit that without any idea of what he may look like, they have little hope of capturing him."

He smiled slightly as he spoke. Then he said very quietly:

"There is no need for you to worry any more. You saved my life, Giōna."

He felt her tremble as if she remembered the moment when she had thought he must die and it was still too vivid to be anything but an agonising terror.

"Forget it," he added, "and let me thank you instead, because I am in fact very grateful indeed for being here with you."

There was a note in his voice that made her look at him wonderingly, but without the fear that had been there before.

The Duke gently pulled her a little closer. Then he said:

"I have been wondering as I came here how I could express my happiness at being alive, and this is the way I wish to do it."

As he spoke his lips came down on hers.

Just for a moment Giōna could hardly believe it was happening, then as the Duke took possession of her mouth she knew that this was what she had longed for!

This was the only way it was possible to express the love that had made her yearn for him and pray for him all through the darkness of her misery and despair.

Now she felt as if her whole body came pulsatingly alive and there was no longer darkness but a light that enveloped them both yet came from their hearts.

The Duke's kiss was at first very gentle, as if he was afraid to frighten her.

Then as he felt the softness of her lips and the quiver that went through her at his touch, he pulled her closer still and his mouth became more insistent, more demanding.

He knew as he felt her respond that the feeling he had awakened in her and felt in himself was different from anything he had known before, but he could not explain it in words.

He knew only that everything about Giōna was different from all the other women who had attracted and intrigued him but inevitably sooner or later had bored him.

What he felt for her was not only physical, although he certainly wanted her as a woman, but she also aroused something entirely spiritual in him.

It was a secret ideal which he had always been aware of and which lay at the back of his thinking, but which he had never shared with anybody else.

Now as he felt the same adoration on her lips that he had seen in her eyes, he knew that because she believed in him he would strive to live up to her idea that he was Apollo bringing light and healing to the world.

It flashed through his mind that there was a great deal they could do together to prevent other monsters like Sir Jarvis from perpetrating cruelty on those who were too weak to defend themselves.

Although the slave-trade had been abolished by an Act of Parliament twelve years ago, there was still slavery in many other walks of life, which, although it might have a different name, still meant the strong exploiting and degrading the weak.

609

Then as he raised his head Giōna murmured:

"I love . . . you!"

As the Duke heard the irrepressible note of rapture in her voice and saw by the expression in her eyes what she felt for him, he knew he was the most fortunate man in the world.

"I love you too, my precious!" he replied. "And nobody shall ever frighten or ill-treat you again."

Her face was transformed with happiness, then as she gave an inarticulate little murmur, he said:

"I will look after you, and now there is nothing to prevent us from being married as soon as possible."

"M—married?"

It was difficult to articulate the word.

"There is nobody to whom we must apply for permission," the Duke said, "and the only Guardian you will have in the future, my lovely one, will be your husband, who will be me!"

"Are you . . . are you . . . really asking me to . . . marry you?" Giōna whispered.

"It is not really a question," the Duke replied, "for I will not allow you to say 'No.' I want you, my darling, and it is difficult to tell you how much."

"I love you until you . . . fill the whole world . . . and the sky . . . and there is . . . nothing else but you!" Giōna said. "But you ought to . . . marry somebody very . . . much more . . . important."

"I intend to marry you," the Duke said firmly, "and the person who will approve of my choice and who matters to me more than any of my other relatives is my grandmother."

"You are . . . sure? Quite sure of that?" Giōna asked.

"Very sure," the Duke smiled, "but it is really of no consequence what Grandmama or anybody else thinks. I love you, and that is the only thing that matters to me."

"And to . . . me!" Giōna cried. "But are you certain, really certain in your heart that you . . . want me for . . . ever?"

"For ever and ever as I have never wanted anybody else," the Duke confirmed. "Oh, my darling, do you not realise how sweet and beautiful you are?"

She turned her face up to his and he looked down at her with an expression in his eyes that made Giōna's heart turn over in her breast.

It was the look she had longed to see, and now she knew that, unbelievable though it might seem, the Duke loved her as she loved him.

She had a feeling that what they were saying to each other had been ordained long before they had met or had even been born.

He would say it was fate or the gods that had brought them together, but she knew she had been right in thinking that like Apollo he had brought light into the darkness and misery of her world when there had been nothing but pain and the expectation of dying.

As if he knew what she was thinking, the Duke drew her closer to him and said:

"Never again, and this is a vow, my dearest heart, will I allow you to be unhappy or afraid. Never again will you suffer or feel alone and without love."

"How can you say such wonderful things to me?" Giōna asked.

"They are easy to say," the Duke answered, "because you are the most wonderful thing that has ever happened to me."

"That is what I should be saying to you," Giōna said passionately. "You came to . . . me when I was . . . in despair, and now I want to . . . kneel at your feet and pour out my love as a . . . thank-offering."

The Duke gave a little laugh as he answered:

"I will not have you kneeling at my feet so long as I can hold you in my arms, my beautiful one. But I want you to pour out your love because it is the most precious thing I have ever known, and I need it and want it."

He did not wait for her answer but was kissing her again with possessive, demanding kisses that seemed to Giōna to hold the fire of the sun.

She felt an echoing flame within herself, and as the Duke drew her closer and closer still, she thought that the wonder and glory of it seemed to leap in a shaft of crimson towards the sky.

It was so wonderful, so ecstatic, that when finally his kiss ended she turned to look up at him wonderingly, as if she stared at the glory of the Divine.

At the same time she was aware that the Duke's heart was beating violently, as hers was, and they were both a little breathless.

"I want you!" he said, and his voice was deep. "I want you, my darling, in a thousand ways, but only when you are my wife will I be able to show you how much you really matter to me."

He touched her cheek with his fingers, running them along the line of her chin, then down the side of her soft neck.

It gave Giōna a sensation she had never known before and made her breath come quickly between her lips.

"You make me . . . feel . . . very strange," she whispered.

"What is it like?" the Duke asked.

"Like . . . like . . . a shaft of . . . sunshine."

The Duke smiled.

"My darling, you are so sweet and unspoilt!"

"Are . . . you laughing at me . . . because I am . . . ignorant?"

"Only adoring you because your innocence is what I never thought to find, but it also excites me!"

"I . . . excite . . . you?"

"More than I dare tell you at this moment."

He felt her draw in her breath and he said:

"I will ask you again—how soon will you marry me?"

"Now! This . . . second!" Giōna cried.

He laughed gently.

"That is what I want you to say, and so let us go and talk to Grandmama, for it will cure her rheumatism and make her twenty years younger if we are married here in her house and she can make all the arrangements."

"I am sure she will do that . . . if only she will . . . agree that I am . . . good enough for you."

"I think she had the idea that you might marry Lucien."

"Lucien?" Giōna exclaimed in astonishment. "But how ridiculous! He is only a boy."

"I am rather afraid that you may think I am too old for you."

"I think that you are perfect . . . the most wonderful man that ever existed, and when one is in love . . . I do not think that . . . age matters one way or the other."

"That is true," the Duke agreed, "and when we are together,

my darling love, we are the same age because we think the same and feel the same, and in the future, because of our love, we will grow more and more like each other.''

''That is true . . . I am sure it is true!'' Giōna cried. ''But will my love be . . . enough?''

She looked away from him before she said in a low voice:

''You do realise that I am very . . . ignorant about all the things that interest you in . . . England because I have never . . . lived in this country? I shall make mistakes . . . and perhaps you will be . . . ashamed of me.''

The Duke smiled and pulled her close to him again.

''You are insulting me by telling me I am very insular,'' he said. ''But I think we both agree that in our minds and our imaginations we can encircle the world, in which case what does it matter what happens in London if we are touching the peaks of the Himalayas or sailing over the Red Sea?''

Giōna laughed and he thought it was the prettiest sound he had ever heard.

''Only . . . you would say . . . something like . . . that.''

''Actually, I am rather surprised at myself,'' the Duke admitted. ''I am not as a rule given to poetic fantasy!''

She looked up at him and he knew what she was thinking by the expression in her eyes.

''You are right,'' he said softly, ''it is love that has changed me, love for you, my precious little goddess with the Greek nose, love which makes me feel entirely different from any way I have felt before. I shall never again be surprised at anything I say, think, or do.''

''That is . . . how I love you,'' Giōna murmured, ''only . . . please . . . because I want to be with you . . . and you to teach me . . . let us be married very . . . very quickly.''

''That is one thing about which we are in complete agreement!'' the Duke said firmly.

He put his arm round her shoulders as they walked together back to the house, then as if he could not help himself he drew her almost roughly against him and once again he was kissing her.

Now his lips were demanding and fiercely, insistently possessive, as if his need of her spirit or her soul made him attempt to draw it from her lips and make it his.

The fire in him awakened a fire within Giōna, and she felt as if they were both being consumed by their love until it carried them into the sky.

They were one with the stars under which they had once sat and talked, one with the sun, crimson and gold, which moved round the world and whose light was never extinguished.

Shining, dazzling, brilliant and compelling, it was part of God.

A shaft of it joined Giōna with the Duke to bind them together for eternity.

About the Author

BARBARA CARTLAND, the world's best known and bestselling author of romantic fiction, is also an historian, playwright, lecturer, political speaker and television personality. She has now written over six hundred and twenty books and has the distinction of holding *The Guinness Book of Records* title of the world's bestselling author, having sold over six hundred and fifty million copies of her books all over the world.

Barbara Cartland is a Dame of Grace of St. John of Jerusalem; Chairman of the St. John Council in Hertfordshire; one of the first women in one thousand years ever to be admitted to the Chapter General; President of the Hertfordshire Branch of the Royal College of Midwives; President and Founder in 1964 of the National Association for Health; and invested by her Majesty the Queen as a Dame of the Order of the British Empire in 1991.

Dame Barbara lives in England at Camfield Place, Hatfield, Hertfordshire.